D1477324

The Sunset Dream

The Sunset Dream

Catherine Gavin

HODDER AND STOUGHTON
LONDON SYDNEY AUCKLAND TORONTO

British Library Cataloguing in Publication Data

Gavin, Catherine
  The sunset dream
  I. Title
  823'.914[F]   PR6013.A83

  ISBN 0 340 25590 0

Again to my husband
JOHN ASHCRAFT
At our home in San Francisco

CONTENTS

MAPS

BOOK ONE

THE CONQUERORS

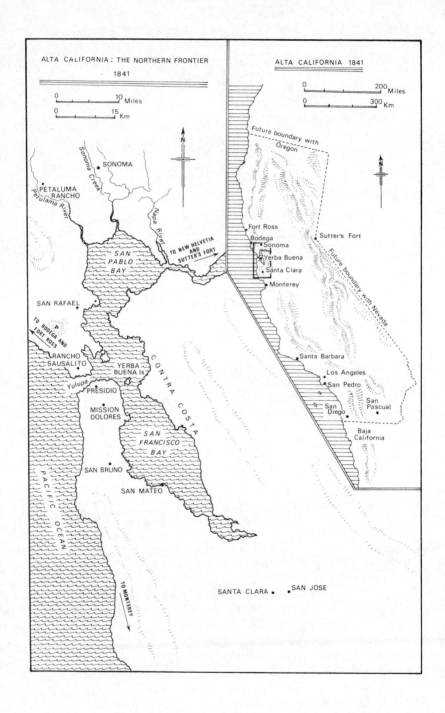

ALTA CALIFORNIA: THE NORTHERN FRONTIER
1841

0   10 Miles
0   15 Km

N

SONOMA

Sonoma Creek

PETALUMA
RANCHO

Petaluma River

Napa River

SAN
PABLO
BAY

TO NEW HELVETIA
AND
SUTTER'S FORT

SAN RAFAEL

TO BODEGA AND
FORT ROSS

RANCHO
SAUSALITO

Yulupa

YERBA
BUENA Is.

CONTRA COSTA

PRESIDIO

MISSION
DOLORES

SAN
FRANCISCO
BAY

PACIFIC OCEAN

SAN BRUNO

SAN MATEO

TO MONTEREY

SANTA CLARA •   • SAN JOSE

ALTA CALIFORNIA 1841

0   200 Miles
0   300 Km

Future boundary with
Oregon

N

Fort Ross
Bodega
Sonoma
Yerba Buena
Santa Clara
Monterey

Sutter's Fort

Future boundary with Nevada

Santa Barbara

Los Angeles
San Pedro

San
Diego

San
Pascual

Baja
California

Part One

The Russians

I

The Russians had been a threat to California for many years.

Don Santiago Estrada told his sons that when the Russian explorers and fur traders crossed the Bering Sea from Siberia into Alaska, the King of Spain ordered his viceroy in Mexico to colonise California as a barrier to their progress. That was a matter of history, and Don Santiago was proud that both his grandfathers had been officers in the first expeditionary force from the City of Mexico into Alta California.

The barrier was not entirely effective. After the creation of the Russian-American Fur Company in 1799, the Russians came out of their Alaskan base at Sitka, embarked on the Pacific Ocean, and built a strong place which came to be called Fort Ross on the northern coast of California.

Hunters of the seal and the sea otter, they began farming at Fort Ross to feed their fishermen and trappers in the barren lands of Alaska. Next they moved quietly south to the fertile valleys running inland from Bodega Bay, where they built a little harbour which they called Port Romanzov. From there, defying all international embargoes, they moved into the Farallones Islands thirty miles from the mouth of San Francisco Bay. Don Santiago, one of the first Spanish colonists to take up a land grant on the northern frontier near the Mission of San Francisco Solano, predicted that the Russian invaders would some day attack the Californian capital at Monterey.

After New Spain became the Republic of Mexico, few of the

younger Californios took much interest in their own Territory, far less in the politics of the Czar. Don Santiago's elder son, Luis, pleasant and easy-going, never troubled to argue with his father. The younger boy, Felipe, had his own point of view. As a novice fruit rancher near Bodega Bay he had made friends with the Russian settlers, and said they were no aggressors, but hardworking, peaceable farmers. Riding home to the Rancho Estrada on the last Tuesday of April 1841, Luis thought his brother might be right. Certainly the Russians he had found stranded at the Sonoma Creek landing could hardly be called a threat to anyone.

Of course he had offered help and hospitality to the three Russian gentlefolk and their boat's crew of sullen sailors sheltering in his own sheds at the *embarcadero*. They looked so bedraggled compared with the brilliant company of Californios he had left the day before.

Don Luis Estrada was in high spirits. When his father died in the previous September he was barely twenty-five, harassed by the responsibilities of a rancho of twelve thousand acres and the problems of a grieving mother, a wilfully innovative brother and a flighty little sister. He left home only twice in six months, to sail across San Pablo Bay and through the Boca del Puerto to the little pueblo of Yerba Buena, to consult the Boston agents who bought his hides and tallow. But after Easter Luis had gone further afield, crossing San Francisco Bay to the Contra Costa country, where he was invited to a wedding in the Peralta family at the Rancho San Antonio. In a week-long fiesta of music, dancing and outdoor sports he had flirted with pretty girls and won horse races against young caballeros like himself. The shadows of the winter had ceased to oppress Luis Estrada.

It was the season which the Indians called the Time of New Grass, and the fresh green was spreading across Sonoma valley like the wild oats on the mountain slopes. From the dirt road beside the creek, which when the Estradas arrived nine years earlier had been a trail which only their friendly Indian guides could follow, he saw living green on the scrub oak and chaparral, and on the pastures where eight thousand head of cattle were grazing, each one marked with the Estrada brand. Twelve *caponeras* of twenty-five horses, and eight *manadas* of brood mares, never stabled, roamed among the cattle. The irrigation channels dug by his father sparkled in the sun.

When Luis checked his horse at a clearing in the woods, the preserve only a few years earlier of antelope and elk, it was to look down another new road running through cleared land to the Mission of San Francisco Solano. Around the mission, now secularised by order of the Mexican government, lay the first houses built in Sonoma, which had given its name to valley, creek and mountain. Luis had sent a messenger to Sonoma only half an hour before. It was too much to expect the man to be on his way back already, and the road was empty.

Touching spurs to his mount, he galloped past Agua Caliente, named by his father for the hot springs used by the Indians for their sweat baths. Fifty Indian families, the men all his own field hands, lived in the *ranchería* at Agua Caliente. Their huts were hidden from the road by a thick screen of evergreen oak and madrone, but Luis could smell cooking, and knew the squaws had already begun to prepare the evening meal. In a few minutes he came within sight of his own home, four-square in its four-foot thick adobe walls. The yard gates were opened at the watchman's shout, and two Mexican *vaqueros* came running out to take Don Luis's horse. They threw the reins, at his order, over the hitching rack in front of the long rail fence, which was the fourth side of a large square courtyard with a well in the centre.

The yard was the hub of the rancho, and of the work constantly going on in the dairy, the brewery, the implement repair shops and the weaving shed. The blacksmiths in their outdoor smithy, the men at the tallow try pots, the *mozos* drawing water from the well were all dressed in blue cotton trousers and loose shirts, with beaded headbands over their shoulder-length black hair. They raised their hands in a grave greeting to their returning master.

The buildings on the three remaining sides were thatched with tule reeds, the roof extended into eaves protecting the narrow patio which ran all round the single-storey ranch house. In front of the family and guest rooms, opposite the gate, the redwood posts supporting the eaves were wreathed with trellised grape vines and pink Castilian roses, already covered with buds. It was from this greenery that Luis's little sister came running to greet him, and pulled him by one hand across the yard to their waiting mother.

Doña Maria del Pilar de la Guerra y Estrada was as imposing as her name. She was a small woman, in middle age too heavy for her height, but she moved round her domain so briskly and with so much authority that her children and her servants still believed in her youthful power to command. Her maid Rita, a discreet person of thirty-five, stood behind her in the shadow of the eaves. Rita dropped a curtsy as Luis stooped to kiss his mother's hand and then her cheek.

"Dear boy," said Doña Maria, "we're so glad to have you back. Was it a happy wedding?"

"Wonderful! The Peraltas were magnificent hosts –"

"And who was La Favorita?" the girl interrupted. She was a pretty girl, with black hair and green eyes, the true *ojos verdes* of Castile, and the thought crossed her brother's mind that she would be more attractive still when her mother allowed her to dress like the charmers of the Peralta marriage. He was tired of seeing his womenfolk in mourning.

"The bride was La Favorita," he said. "What else do you expect at a wedding?"

"Yes, of course, but next to the bride?" the girl insisted, and her mother said with a smile, "The beautiful Maddalena Yorba."

"No," said Luis, "it wasn't Doña Maddalena. It was her little sister, Isabel."

"You see?" cried the girl. "Other people's sisters are allowed to go to weddings, and dance, and enjoy themselves –"

"Hush, child," said her mother. "Luis will tell us all about it when he's had food and wine, and got rid of the dust." Her son, who had given his vicuña hat, imported from Peru, to an Indian houseboy, was shaking out his travelling poncho, fringed with silver, which was dusty indeed. A second Indian servant knelt to unfasten his heavily rowelled silver spurs.

"Leave my spurs alone," Luis said to the boy. "I'm riding back along the creek. We have some unexpected guests," he explained to his mother. "I want you to make them very welcome."

"Guests?" she said, and looked at her daughter with a smile. "I thought you wouldn't come back alone. So you brought Don Carlos Rivera home with you?"

"Carlos had to go home with his cousin from Santa Clara," said Luis. "I've a letter for you in my trunk, mother, and a gift for his betrothed from her devoted lover."

"So devoted that he rode away in the wrong direction," said the girl.

"It was a matter of business which couldn't be put off. Ah, thank you, Rita!" He smiled at the woman, who had gone indoors as soon as she heard Luis say he was going to ride again. She had brought him a glass of wine on a small salver, and a bright serape to wear instead of the heavy poncho. Luis drank quickly, and told his mother that their unexpected visitors were none other than the Russian Commandant of Fort Ross, Alexander Rotschev, with his wife, the Princess Helen, and her cousin, Prince Peter Gagarin.

"*Russians!*" "Where did they come from?" "What are they doing here?" "How did you meet them and where are they now?"

Luis folded the red and green serape across his shoulders and laughed at the storm of questions. "They don't speak Spanish very well, but as far as I can make out the Rotschevs went to Yerba Buena to meet their cousin, back from a voyage to the Sandwich Islands on behalf of the Fur Company. They left the pueblo before dawn this morning, planning to visit General Vallejo on their way back to Fort Ross. The party expected Vallejo's overseer, Ortega, to meet them at the Sonoma landing with horses, after they'd crossed San Pablo Bay. Ortega didn't show up, and they'd been waiting several hours before I arrived myself."

"Ortega is quite unreliable," pronounced Doña Maria, "but General Vallejo had a riding accident on Saturday. He was probably in no state to remember the Russians. What amazes me is that he invited them in the first place. But then he's always running after foreigners."

"What amazes me is that they didn't start walking," said the girl. "They could have been at Sonoma in less than an hour."

"They didn't know where they were, Puss," said Luis. "Is

General Vallejo badly hurt?"

"He broke his ankle, according to the *capataz* when he came back from Sonoma yesterday," said Doña Maria. "I suppose we ought to send a messenger to enquire."

"I sent Bernardo, to tell him the Russians were coming to us," said Luis. "Pedro went back for men and horses, and they're going to put the baggage on the ox cart. It won't be long before our guests arrive."

"Gracious heaven, we've no time to lose!" cried Doña Maria. "Wait!" She caught at her son's arm. "What about the sailors who rowed them across the bay?"

"They're men from the *Volga*, impatient to get back to their ship. I told Pedro to see that they got food and drink."

"Very well then, Luis. Hurry now." The Indian servants, seeing their master running towards his horse and scenting some imminent happening, began drifting across the yard towards Doña Maria, who promptly began to give her orders.

"Rita, take two of the maids, and make sure the guest rooms are comfortable. The great chamber for the princess and her husband, and one of the bachelor rooms for the other gentleman. Put warming pans in the beds. Rosalie, see that Benito sets the dinner table nicely. Take my keys, and look out three bottles of the wine Father Quijas enjoyed on Easter Sunday. The burgundy."

"Father Quijas enjoys everything that comes out of a bottle," said the girl under her breath, but she hurried into the *sala* with old Benito, one of the servants the Estradas had brought with them when they journeyed north from Monterey, and who, like the woman Rita, was a *mestizo*, of half Spanish and half Indian blood. Benito was beginning to be past his work, but today he went at it with a will, helping his young mistress to unfold a cloth of the finest damask and giving a final buff to the silver. She set out the crystal goblets, and ran to the patio to see if she could find enough roses in bloom to fill a bowl for the centre of the table. They could both hear a hum of activity from the kitchen, where Doña Maria was giving her orders to the cook, and the slap of mocassined feet on adobe bricks which meant that the maids were running up and down the patio at Rita's direction. The girl, who was only eighteen, felt as if the Rancho Estrada were coming alive again after the long sad winter. She was singing as she hurried to her own room to plunge her hands and face in a basin of cold water. She had just time to look in her mirror and draw a comb through her loose black hair, before she heard the sound of approaching horses.

It was part of the lavish hospitality of the Californios to send twice as many horses as were needed for the use of their guests. The vaquero, Pedro, having been impressed by the foreigners, and told by Don Luis to fetch mounts from the caponera reserved for the family, had thought fit to bring twelve animals for two men and a lady; with the three mounted vaqueros who had followed Luis from the rancho, the cavalcade was impressive as it crossed the apron of turf between the road and the yard gate. Doña Maria and her daughter, coming up to the fence as the new arrivals began to dismount, saw at a glance that the mettlesome Estrada palominos were almost too much for the Russians. The lady had been so defeated by the broad loop of silk attached to her side saddle as a stirrup that Luis had improvised a leading rein, and was quick to lift her down when they halted at the gate. When he relieved her of her heavy, hooded cloak the Russian princess was seen to have a slender figure, a sweet face, and golden hair lank and damp from the salt air of the marshes.

Her husband and her cousin swung out of the heavy Spanish saddles thankfully, and bared their heads to the ladies. They were both tall men, much taller than Luis Estrada, although he was above medium height, and the younger man was as fair as the princess. They bowed low as Doña Maria swept her curtsy, and Luis introduced them formally: Princess Helen Rotschev, the Commandant of Fort Ross, and Prince Peter Gagarin. He added,

"This is my sister, Maria del Rosario; we call her Rosalie."

"*Está es su casa, señores.*" Doña Maria spoke the stately Spanish words of welcome. "This is your house."

"You overpower us with your kindness, Señora Doña Maria," said Alexander Rotschev, equally formal. But Rosalie, in her impulsive way, took his wife's cold hand in hers, and said, "Do come indoors, Princess! You must be half frozen!"

Five minutes later the Russian lady was unwinding the

scarves and shawls worn during the long chilly wait by the creek, and exclaiming with delight at the comfort of Doña Maria's 'great chamber'. It was not very large, but it was heated by a small brazier of burning wood, and two silver ewers filled with steaming water stood in silver basins on a washstand with a marble top. A mahogany fourposter, with a canopy and curtains of blue brocade, stood in the centre of the carpeted floor. The white satin counterpane, embroidered with the family crest of the Estradas, was already turned back to reveal snowy linen pillows with goffered hems.

Doña Maria beamed with pleasure at her guests' admiration. As for every Spanish mistress of a house, her chief pride lay in a beautiful guest bed and bedding. She beckoned to Rita, who was waiting in the doorway with a laden tray in her hands.

"Some hot chocolate will warm you both," she said. "Now, is there anything else that I can get you? Your baggage will be here very soon, and you must have a good rest before we dine."

"I feel rested already," said Princess Helen charmingly. But when she was alone with her husband she hardly tasted the chocolate, preferring to warm her hands on the cup while she looked anxiously at Rotschev.

"Something went wrong, didn't it?" she said.

"My poor darling, I'm sorry you've had such a weary day!" he countered quickly. "It's all that wretched man Vallejo's fault, I'm sure."

"But Don Luis told us, on the way here, that General Vallejo had had a riding accident, and may be in great pain. And I still don't know what you mean to say to the general. You haven't even told Peter about his proposal."

"I haven't had a chance."

"Peter came ashore before noon yesterday."

"And we were either at the Presidio, or at Vioget's tavern, with never less than twenty people round us, for the rest of the day."

"We were in that horrible place by the marshes, with the skulls and bones of slaughtered animals piled up beside us," said the princess with a shudder, "for hours before Don Luis came to our rescue."

"How could I discuss such a delicate matter in the presence of the boat's crew?"

"You could have spoken in English, or in French."

"All right then, my dear, if you want the truth, I thought if Peter found out too soon what was in the wind, he was quite capable of ordering the sailors to take him back to the *Volga*, and sailing for Sitka tomorrow morning."

"Oh Alex, he wouldn't do that! He's planning a hunting trip along the Columbia river next month. And he did say he was looking forward to the fiesta we're planning in his honour."

"I don't think Peter's as fond of parties as you are, my love. And in his present mood he might do anything."

"What d'you mean by that?"

"His mission to Honolulu was a failure, that's obvious. And as long as the Fort Ross deal isn't completed, he might try to make *me* out a failure when he sees the governor at Sitka. Then I'd get another black mark at St. Petersburg."

Princess Helen drank the last of her chocolate, and picking up a towel from the washstand began to dry her hair. Hers had been a great romance, ending in an elopement in defiance of her family; it had taken her ten years to understand that her charming husband – a poet, a musician, a true cosmopolite – was also an inefficient administrator and the victim of imaginary persecutions wherever their official exile took them both. She sighed, and said,

"I don't think Peter would try to make you out a failure, he has too good a heart."

"And your own heart's tender where Peter Gagarin's concerned, isn't it? To hear you talking about the dear old days at Petrovskoi is like eavesdropping on a pair of childhood sweethearts –"

"Are you forgetting that he was the only one of all my family who took my side when you and I fell in love?"

"Peter was a romantic boy of eighteen ten years ago. Now he's an Inspector of the almighty Russian-American Fur Company, and I don't think he'd let anyone stand in his way to the top. But I'll talk to him, if these good people give us ten minutes of privacy tonight – Come in!"

It was Rita who tapped at the door, Rita the picture of discretion in her black dress, her braids of dark hair and her downcast eyes. Two of the houseboys were in the patio behind her.

"Your honours' baggage has arrived," she said. "May I be allowed to help the princess to unpack? La Señora says dinner will be ready very soon."

Nothing happened very soon in a Spanish household, and the stars were out before Doña Maria was satisfied with her dinner arrangements and went to find her daughter. There were three cooks at the rancho, one an old woman (capable, but too stringy and toothless to be tempting) who cooked for the Mexican vaqueros in their bunk house, and one a fat jolly creature who prepared food for the Indian servants in the outdoor kitchen where the oven stood near the plaster, brick-lined kilns and the querns for pounding maize and corn. The younger woman who cooked for the family and their guests worked indoors in a kitchen with a tiled range and ovens. She had been trained by Doña Maria, and had the help of two kitchen maids and a *tortillera*, who over her own little brazier would prepare the tortillas served instead of bread throughout the meal.

Doña Maria, in stiff black silk with a Spanish comb of carved amber in her greying hair, looked disapproving when she found her daughter in a white cambric wrapper, dressed for the evening only by having put on white silk stockings and heelless black satin slippers.

"Rosalie! Not ready yet! What in the world have you been doing?"

"Waiting for you, mother. Rita said you were going to bring me the present from Don Carlos."

"Well? Why should that delay your dressing?"

"Because Rita said she had been helping the Russian lady to put on a beautiful blue dress, in the very height of fashion. And she wears her hair in ringlets, too, she was shaping them round a little stick. So I wondered – couldn't I wear one of *my* new dresses, just for tonight?"

"Now Rosalie. The Princess Helen is a married lady and can wear anything she likes. Your new clothes are to be kept until Don Carlos comes to claim his bride. Let him be the first to admire your finery; and surely, my dear, you don't want to wear colours in a house of mourning?"

No, of course not. She was so quenched, when she turned to her mirror and saw the straight black hair and the green eyes, that the mother relented so far as to say, "Wear the pretty lace *camisa* Luis brought you from the French ship, with your black silk *rebozo*. And Rosalie, I think you might wear this – the gift from your future husband."

Doña Maria took her hand from behind her back, as if she were playing a game with a child, and held out a leather jewel case, which Rosalie took with a cry of pleasure. Her face fell when she saw the contents. Don Carlos's gift was a pair of gold earrings, very long, with filagree danglers, and hooks which looked too thick for Rosalie's small pierced ears.

"He might at least have had them cleaned," she said.

"A man doesn't bother about such things, dear. Don Carlos told Luis they belonged to his mother."

"They belonged to his horse, I should think."

"Really, child! Wear them or put them away, but get dressed and come to the sala! I don't want the dinner to be spoiled."

Rosalie Estrada took her mother at her word. She put the earrings away by flinging them to the back of a drawer, and she looked at the handsome gold bracelet which had been Carlos Rivera's betrothal gift a year before. The bracelet followed the earrings into the drawer. Then Rosalie fastened her black silk skirt over her white petticoat and put on the new white lace camisa. It was cut low, and she folded her black rebozo modestly across her breast, in one deft movement knotting up her hair and pinning the knot with a small tortoiseshell comb. She was ready to face the blue dress and the golden curls.

2

Considering that the Russians were strangers to their hosts, the talk was very animated when Rosalie entered the sala. She found that within the last ten minutes a letter had been received from General Vallejo, explaining with every flourish of Spanish courtesy that the Russians had been waited for at the landing on the Petaluma river near his great new rancho. They had simply misunderstood the directions when they travelled to the embarcadero on Sonoma Creek. Rotschev, embarrassed and apologetic, took all the blame on himself, and Rosalie saw scorn in the brilliant blue eyes of Prince Peter Gagarin, but Doña Maria tactfully said it was a happy misunderstanding which gave her the pleasure of their company. In arranging for the gentlemen to pay a call of regrets and kind enquiries on General Vallejo next morning, the ice was broken before they took their places at the table.

The sala of the Rancho Estrada was a pleasant, lived-in room, arranged according to the taste of the rancho's late master. The dining table was on the left, near a door which he had caused to be cut in the wall of the kitchen, so that contrary to the general practice hot dishes were served hot. In the middle a circle of chairs surrounded a mahogany table holding a chessboard, with chessmen in a sandalwood box, a tambour embroidery frame and a portfolio of watercolour sketches of Monterey. At the other end of the room was a tall secretary with half-filled bookshelves above it, and a flat writing desk holding an inkstand and writing materials set between a celestial and a terrestrial globe.

On the walls were two religious pictures in the style of El Greco, and a portrait in oils which the Russians took to be an Estrada ancestor, but which was in fact a primitive representation, showing a stiff Spanish face above a stiff Spanish military collar, of the 'Good Viceroy', Don Antonio Bucareli, who had encouraged the forebears of the young Estradas to set out on the long road to Alta California. Behind the dining table two guitars, one adorned with ribbons, hung from carved elk horns on the wall. The room was lighted by wax candles in girandoles made of Mexican silver from the Taxco mines, and round Rosalie's bowl of Castilian roses candelabra of sterling silver held candles of spermaceti wax.

The Russian lady was not dressed in the height of fashion, of which neither Rosalie nor Rita had any idea, because the Paris fashion was for tucks and frills and enormous balloon sleeves, and Princess Helen was too completely a woman of the world to wear such styles at the back of beyond. Her dress was very simple, made of smoky blue cashmere, but Rosalie realised, as she dropped her curtsy to the company, that the elaborate clothes they had been sewing for her wedding would be antiquated before they were ever worn.

The dinner, served by Benito and two Indian maids, was a welcome change from the usual Californio cuisine, which leaned heavily on tamales, refried beans and chili peppers. After a soup made with spring vegetables Luis carved two roast chickens, served with new potatoes and a salad of tender lettuce, which caused Princess Helen to exclaim that his garden produce was far ahead of the spring crop at Fort Ross.

"We're quite a distance further south, Princess," said Luis.

"Rosalie must get some of the credit," said her mother. "She supervises the gardeners and sees to it that they keep the cooks well supplied."

"Are you interested in gardening, Doña Elena?" asked Rosalie shyly. "I'll show you our kitchen garden tomorrow morning, if you like."

"Please, and when you come to Fort Ross I'll show you my flowers. Do you grow flowers too?"

"A few, but only the roses are in bloom as yet."

In the warmth of the sala the green sepals of the Castilian roses were curling back and the pink petals beginning to unfurl. Their delicate scent mingled with the aroma of the noble burgundy which Benito, on his master's orders, was pouring with a generous hand. Luis raised his glass and toasted his Russian guests, while his mother looked at him with mingled jealousy and pride. She had not often seen him in his father's seat at the head of the table, for when they were alone her children sat respectfully on each side of her place at the foot, but she realised that the young man in the high carved Spanish chair was a brilliant figure. The two Russians in their black dress coats and white neckcloths, his sister in black and white, even the princess in her blue gown, were so many foils to the young caballero. He wore a waistcoat and trousers of crimson velvet, the waistcoat open over a white frilled shirt embroidered with a design in colours, the trousers split on the outer seams and laced as high as the knee, over white silk stockings, with gilt cord. His black hair shone, and his side whiskers, like the thin line of black moustache, had been carefully trimmed. The wine had brought a slight flush to his clear olive skin. "So like his father!" thought Doña Maria. "So different from poor Felipe!"

Then, as if she had been disloyal to her younger son, she told her guests that the compote of apples and pears, offered with cream cheeses from her own dairy, were the fruits of Felipe's orchards on Salmon Creek, where he had also planted olives, figs and peaches brought from the derelict Mission gardens. The Rotschevs praised his enterprise: they had heard from their own farmers of the activities of Don Felipe Estrada. It was Peter who said across the table:

"Have you visited your brother's farm at Bodega, Doña Rosalie?"

She said, "No, never." And then, with a blush for her own boldness, "But please, will you tell us about the Sandwich Islands?"

Prince Peter had drunk discreetly, but just enough to take the sharp edge off his defeat at Honolulu. On his first important mission as an Inspector, he had utterly failed to convince the native ruler, King Kamehama III, of the desirability of trading only with the Russian-American Fur Company. Everywhere he went in the Sandwich Islands he found that the British factors of the powerful Hudson's Bay Company had been before him. Finally, at a farewell banquet, King Kamehama had told his Russian guest in public that he 'wished to work more closely with Queen Victoria'.

He was ready to take up Rosalie's challenge. In his halting Spanish, with a Russian idiom here and a native word from the Islands there, Peter Gagarin took his revenge on 'the dusky monarch', as he called him, by describing the absurdities of the island life. He was a good story-teller, and he made them see the court at Honolulu, the luaus of roast pig and pineapple, and the fat princesses reclining on their lanais while their attendants waved palm-leaf fans above their heads. The most corpulent of the ladies, he declared, bore a shocking resemblance to one of the pigs, with cowries and seashells round her neck instead of the animal's sacrificial garland of orchids and tropical fruits. It was lightly and amusingly told, and everybody laughed; only his cousin Helen, who knew him so well,

detected the savage sarcasm beneath the comedy. She remembered what her husband had said about Peter's ruthlessness,
and was glad to change the subject when Doña Maria rose
from the table.

"May we not have a little music?" she begged, with a glance
at the guitars, and Rosalie, delighted, lifted the instruments off
the wall. Taking the beribboned guitar for herself, she waited
until Luis had pulled out chairs for the others round the centre
table and, with one foot on a stool, struck a chord on his own
guitar, followed by an octave of rippling notes in which she
joined, like the echo of their gaiety. The rancho day began so
early that as a general rule the family retired at eight o'clock.
Now it was after nine, and they were having what Rosalie
Estrada had enjoyed so seldom, a *valecito casaro*, 'a little home
party', which might easily last for another hour! The brother
and sister began to sing.

They sang the songs their parents had taught them, learned
in childhood from their own parents, so completely had the
tiny Spanish society of California reproduced its own image
during nearly seventy pastoral years. These were not the songs
of New Spain, but of Old Castile: the love songs and the
ballads which the young caballeros had sung beneath the
barred windows of their sweethearts in Monterey, and before
that in the City of Mexico and in Madrid. Princess Helen,
remembering the romance which had led her into exile, was
touched by the tender and rueful tunes. Her husband, the only
real musician present, thought the songs delightful, but that
Luis's high Spanish tenor was too thin to accord completely
with his sister's warm contralto. Peter Gagarin followed
neither the words nor the music, but watched the sweep of
Rosalie's small hand over the strings, and the provocative tilt
of Rosalie's dark head. He wondered if there had ever been a
more seductive fashion than the Californian, the black skirt
short enough to reveal slim, white-stockinged ankles, and the
modest fringed rebozo which failed to conceal the lines of the
young breast beneath the white lace camisa. He had admired
the traditional costume when the *Volga* put in at San Pedro,
Santa Barbara and Monterey, on the return voyage from
Honolulu: none of the pretty, chattering Spanish girls who
wore it at the dances and *meriendas* he attended had touched his

cold heart like Rosalie Estrada in her lonely home.

It was nearer ten o'clock than nine when Luis and Rosalie bowed to each other across their guitars and swept their closing chords. The party broke up then, for the travellers admitted to being tired, and when Luis followed his guests into the patio the Indian living quarters were in darkness. In the starlight they could see two watchmen on duty, patrolling steadily along the fence. Nearer at hand, two servants were also on duty, one of them a houseboy squatting on his hunkers with a lighted lantern by his side. Rita, with a shawl drawn tightly round her, was leaning against one of the rose-covered posts with a lantern for Rosalie. Luis himself showed the Rotschevs to the 'great chamber', and the houseboy, with his lantern bobbing, led Prince Peter to his narrow room.

Rita had an extra shawl, and wrapped it round her young mistress, for the April night was sharp. She had lighted the candles, put a warming pan in Rosalie's bed, and was ready with nightdress and hairbrush for a long session of brushing and confidences. The mestiza had been a girl of seventeen when the newborn Rosalie was put into her arms, and through all the years which followed the child had had no secret of mind or body from the trusted servant. Always, when there were guests at the rancho, Rosalie had been bubbling over with excitement, eager to talk over every detail of the entertainment with her maid. She was excited tonight, for Rita felt her trembling when she put the shawl around her. But she stopped with her hand on the latch of her bedroom and whispered, "Go to bed now, Rita. I'm much too tired to talk."

Peter Gagarin stretched and yawned as he hung up his coat. Four weeks in a cramped berth aboard the *Volga*, followed by a night on a flea-ridden couch in Yerba Buena, made him appreciate the feather mattress and the white sheets and pillows of the rancho, and he was half asleep as he wound his watch and started to undress. He was in a small room with white-washed walls and a woven rug on the wooden floor. There was a crucifix above the bed, beside which was a broad shelf covered with coarse cotton lace, holding two lighted candles in silver sticks and a woven Indian basket filled with coins. Luis had explained when he showed Peter to his room that he followed his father's custom of bestowing on every guest food and shelter, a horse and money in his purse. He added that he doubted if the coins were legal tender, and letting the money trickle through his fingers Peter Gagarin doubted it too. There were French *louis d'or*, Maria Theresa *thalers* and Portuguese *moidores* mixed with Spanish doubloons, museum pieces now but touching as a gesture of goodwill. Prince Peter had been a guest in the palaces of St. Petersburg – along the Moika Quay, where his house was standing empty except for the servants – where princes filled malachite bowls with uncut rubies, sapphires, diamonds, among which their friends might choose a jewel at will. That ostentation had never touched him like this basket of money, so freely offered with the Californio's other gifts: a bed for a guest, a meal, and a horse to ride away.

★   ★   ★

When Luis returned to the sala he found his mother thriftily snuffing out the candles in the girandoles.

"Ah, there you are, my dear," she said. "Rita said you wanted to talk to me."

"If you're not too tired."

"I'm never too tired for a talk with you, Luis," she said, and sat down at the foot of the dining table, from which the cloth had been drawn. The candles still burned in the candelabra, and the scent of the roses was very strong. "I've been thinking we neglected you tonight."

"How so?"

"Rosalie and I were looking forward to all your news of the wedding. Instead of which we heard about the Sandwich Islands and the trials of life at Fort Ross."

"We'll have plenty of time to talk about the Peralta wedding when our Russian guests have gone. Didn't you enjoy this evening, just a little?"

"I was thinking how much your dear father would have enjoyed it all."

Luis nodded sympathetically. He turned to a side table, on which Benito had placed clean glasses and a decanter of port, and poured himself half a glassful. He heard his mother's soft voice behind him:

"Tell me about Maddalena Yorba, Luis."

"There's nothing to tell." He drew a leather stool up to his mother's chair and sat down. "Doña Maddalena is very pretty, very well-bred, and very dull. I was content to admire her from afar."

"What a pity," said his mother with feeling. "Her grandfather is one of the richest landowners between Monterey and the pueblo of Los Angeles. It's the match your father wished for you."

"He wouldn't have wanted me to marry a boring wife, I'm sure. I told you, her sister Isabel was voted La Favorita at the wedding – witty little monkey that she was."

"Well then, if *she* pleases you –"

"Mother, Isabel Yorba isn't yet fourteen."

"Oh!" said Doña Maria, checked. "Thirteen, that is too young. Still, your father and I were betrothed when I was only fifteen. In two or three years this girl would be just the right age for Felipe."

"Felipe will never do anything so conventional as court an heiress. He'll bring us home a foreigner one of these days. A Russian farm girl from Bodega, or a Kanaka from the Sandwich Islands. No, no, I was only joking," said Luis as his mother gave a gasp of horror. "Never mind about Felipe and me. What I want to talk to you about is Rosalie's wedding. You had time, before dinner, to read Carlos Rivera's letter?"

"Since you made such a point of it, I did."

"Did you show it to Rosalie?"

"She didn't even ask to see it."

"Good."

"I take it you know the contents?"

"He told me he was going to ask you to advance the date of their wedding from September to June. Was there more?"

"He said that but for the lamented death of Rosalie's father, they would have been man and wife six months ago."

"I'm glad they're not," said Luis Estrada. "I don't think Carlos Rivera is the man for Rosalie."

"But he's her promised husband, Luis! Their fathers made the match two years ago –"

"A match made by two dead men," said Luis sombrely. "Must it be binding on a living man and a girl?"

"Is there any reason why it shouldn't be? Did you hear any

28

gossip in the Contra Costa country? Do people say Carlos leads an immoral life?''

Luis checked a smile. The opportunities for sexual promiscuity, which was what his mother meant by immorality, were so few and far between in their flowering wilderness that for the young caballeros early marriage and the begetting of large families were the only outlets for their normal appetites. He thought it very likely that Carlos Rivera, living alone since his parents died, had made free with some of the Indian girls at his rancho; he thought it improbable that the man had been driven to the few wretched drabs who hung around Yerba Buena Cove and the Presidio.

"Gossip doesn't enter into it," he said. "What worries me is what I saw with my own eyes. Carlos Rivera is an inveterate gambler. Last week at the fiesta he was plunging from one bet to another, on the fall of the cards or the races we rode, on any game of skill or chance, and he lost more often than he won. He went home with his cousin to Santa Clara to try to borrow money, and this precious letter asking you to hold the wedding in June is the first step to getting his hands on Rosalie's fortune.''

"Rosalie's fortune will be well safeguarded," said his mother calmly. "Her settlement was properly drawn, and witnessed by the *alcalde* of Yerba Buena. Are you annoyed because you weren't consulted in the matter?''

"Considering that a written marriage contract is something new, among our people, yes, I do think I might have been consulted. I never even saw the document. Where is it now?''

"In your father's deed-box, of course. Inside the secretary.''

"May I have the key?''

"At this hour of the night?''

"As good a time as any.''

Doña Maria reluctantly detached from its ring the smallest of all the keys in the bunch which hung at her waist, and gave it to her son. He had already opened the flap of the secretary and lifted out a heavy mahogany box, bound with brass, which he carried to the table.

He only had to lift the lid of the iron receptacle which made the deed-box heavy to see the solid gold coins which his father had set aside towards Rosalie's dowry. Several parchments lay on top of the lid, the first being the grant from the Governor of California which gave Don Santiago his title to the land in the valley. Attached to it was the *diseño*, a sketch which showed the boundaries of the future rancho. Luis remembered his father showing it to his old friend Father Fortuni, the priest of San Francisco Solano, on the day of their arrival. Father Fortuni had been the official witness when Don Santiago threw earth to the four points of the compass to indicate his possession of the grant, and afterwards he had blessed them all.

"Many young men gamble at cards and give it up when they have the responsibility of a wife and family," said Doña Maria. "What are you looking at? Can't you find the contract?"

"Here it is. Signed by my father and old Rivera, and witnessed by Don Francisco Haro. He's not the alcalde now."

"Does that matter?"

"I don't suppose so." Luis read on in silence. The financial provisions of the marriage contract were quite clear. Maria del Rosario brought her dowry to the marriage without conditions, while resigning all claim to a share in the Rancho Estrada, and Carlos Antonio made over the ownership of his own rancho at his death to his wife and to her legitimate heirs for ever. Under the Spanish law of community property the profits from the rancho, or *bienes gananciales*, would be shared between the husband and wife during their lifetime.

Luis Estrada was not learned in the law, for all he ever had of schooling ended when he left Monterey at the age of sixteen, but one of the clauses in the contract struck him as peculiar. He would have expected the Rivera rancho to go to his sister and her children, whereas the residuary legatees were merely defined as her legitimate heirs.

"Are you satisfied?" asked his mother.

"No, not really. I still don't know what made my father choose Carlos Rivera for Rosalie's husband."

"Because his great-grandfather led the expedition from New Spain which founded the Mission of Santa Clara. The Riveras have as many quarterings of nobility as the Estradas, and your papa wanted his girl to marry one of the aristocracy, and not a Mexican upstart like the Vallejos. Just as he hoped you would marry Maddalena Yorba –"

"Never mind the Yorbas. As this document stands" (he returned it to the deed-box) "Carlos gets Rosalie's dowry unconditionally, and the Rancho Rivera, which is her portion, may be gambled away within the next two years." Luis replaced the box in the secretary, and slipped the little key into his vest pocket. "I'll take care of this," he said, "I want to look over the contract with Felipe. And if I were you I'd be in no hurry to answer Carlos's letter. He'll be at Santa Clara for at least a week. When you do write, tell him June is impossible for the wedding, but ask him to pay us an early visit here. I want Rosalie to have a chance to know him better."

Doña Maria wanted to say "You're being intolerably high-handed!" but instinct told her Luis was no longer to be domineered over. She said she would have a serious talk with Rosalie when the Russian guests had gone. Luis told her it mustn't be too serious. "Rosalie needs a little less lecturing and a little more freedom. I wish you had let me take her to the Peralta wedding."

"I wasn't equal to the journey by ox cart and boat, and since her betrothed husband was to be present she would have had to be chaperoned by a lady of her own family."

"Maybe that was the custom in Monterey when you were a girl, mamma. But this is Sonoma, Eighteen Forty-one! Vallejo's sisters, and the young Carrillos, have a lot more fun than Rosalie. Give her a chance to enjoy herself, mother! Surely you want her to be happy?"

She was happy at that moment, smiling in her sleep at a pleasant dream. In his room, not far from Rosalie's, Peter Gagarin slept without dreaming, motionless in his narrow bed. Neither of them could know that a few casual words, spoken in all kindness by her brother, had sealed their fate and their destruction.

3

Don Mariano Guadalupe Vallejo, General Commanding the Northern Frontier, was in an irritable mood on Wednesday morning. His broken ankle was so painful that he was beginning to wonder if the Indian bonesetter had done his job well. He was fretting that without his supervision his wife, Doña Francisca Benicia – always preoccupied by their many children – and his overseer, Ortega, would make some mistake in directing the construction work in progress on his great rancho near the Petaluma river. He was annoyed because his brother Salvador, abetted by his secretary, Victor Prudon, was objecting to his plan of being taken home to the rancho in an ox cart or a litter instead of staying at his military headquarters, the Casa Grande at Sonoma. He moved restlessly on the long rattan couch to which he had hobbled from his bedroom supported by the two men.

"Shall I get you another pillow, *hermano?*" asked Don Salvador. "You really should have stayed in bed."

"Thank you, but I'm very well as I am. If Luis Estrada brings the Russians here as early as his letter promised I'll be in bed at the rancho long before it's dark."

The Autocrat of Sonoma, as his antagonists called him, was in his early thirties and looked ten years older, not because of dissipation or his present pain. Very little active soldiering had been required of him since he took the Northern Command in 1835, for the Coast Indians were not as aggressive as the Indians of the Plains, and whatever hostility had been aroused by the coming of the Spanish had been put down by Vallejo in a few minor campaigns. The Russians, whom it was his special mission to repel, had made no further advances into Alta California. He had put on weight from sheer good living, and out of uniform the belly bulge controlled by his military sash was all too obvious. Vallejo's face was pale and plump, his black hair beginning to recede. He was the son of a sergeant in the Mexican army, which he had joined himself at the age of fifteen, but on this particular day he was wearing the clothes favoured by those of the Spanish aristocrats, the *gente de razón*, who were still faithful to the past. Beneath grey satin knee breeches one plump leg was sheathed in a white silk stocking, the other encased in a plaster made of mud and aromatic herbs, put on wet and allowed to dry. His white silk shirt was open at the neck beneath a full-skirted dressing-gown of purple brocade.

"I see the Russians coming now," said Salvador, who was standing by the narrow window.

"Are you sure?"

"Luis Estrada is riding in with two strangers, who else can it be?"

"Very well," said the general, "the captain has his orders, and Victor, you must do the honours at the gate." The secretary bowed and left the room.

"They're in no hurry," grumbled Don Salvador, looking out. "They've halted, and they're looking around them as if they owned the place. Luis Estrada should have changed his coat before paying a formal call on you. He wants to show the Russians he's a working ranchero, I suppose."

"He *is* a working ranchero, more so than you are, *compañero*. And I'm not exactly formally dressed myself."

"Are you planning to say anything to Rotschev about his stupidity in going to the wrong place yesterday?"

"Call a man a fool when I intend to do business with him? You'll never learn, Salvador! All it took was patience and forbearance to bring about what the government desired. The Russians are leaving: this summer, next winter, next spring, it doesn't matter. California will be rid of them without a shot fired in anger . . . What are they doing now?"

They were looking about them, as Don Salvador had said. Luis, with a *reata* looped at his saddle, wore the fringed waistcoat of dressed hide and the dusty sombrero of a man who had been riding the range with his foreman at first light. He had halted his vaqueros (three cowboys always at his horse's hoofs) and his guests at the western limit of the plaza, and was explaining the landmarks to the Russians. There, two storeys high, with a watch tower above it, was the Casa Grande, and next to that the barracks. Beyond the plaza to the east was what had been the Mission of San Francisco Solano, with its cross and bell and tiny chapel, opposite which an inn for travellers was being built. There were other houses round the plaza, and Luis explained that the Mexican government gave ten acres of fertile land and ten head of livestock to each new settler. "So far there's been no rush to take up the smallholdings," he said. "My father tried to set an example by building what he liked to call his town house." He pointed out a two-roomed adobe on the south side of the square.

"Is it occupied?" asked Rotschev.

"It has to be occupied, by order. An old Spanish major-domo of ours named Guzman lives there with his Indian wife."

There were so few signs of life in the big dusty plaza, hacked out so short a time before from the redwoods and the chaparral, that for a moment it appeared to Peter Gagarin like a stage-set waiting for the players. He had travelled across the Russian Empire from the Gulf of Finland to the Sea of Japan, changing post horses at some of the loneliest *isbas* of Siberia, without coming across a township which could be compared to this northern outpost of the Mexican Republic. He saw it as a 'Potemkin village', one of those, all façade and no back, which the lover of Catherine the Great had caused to be built to flatter her with a false assurance of her prosperity when she went on her imperial journeys. Here the few buildings had backs as well as fronts, were built of solid, sunbaked adobe bricks, were inhabited, and yet the impression of theatricality remained, to be confirmed in the next instant by a rush of men in uniform from the little barracks. There was the blast of a trumpet, the salute of a single ball from a brass cannon which nearly burst with the effort, and in response to one man's frantic tugging the colours of Mexico rose to the top of the flagstaff on the watch tower. A young captain brought a dozen men to attention at the gate of the Casa Grande.

Riding forward, the Russians raised their tall beaver hats in salute to the flag, and Luis touched the brim of his sombrero. The Mexican flag meant very little to him. Not that he lamented the passing of the Spanish dominion, or opposed the principles of the revolution which had taken place when he was an infant. He was merely indifferent. For the young Californios of the frontier even the territorial capital at Monterey seemed far away, and given over to the intrigues of successive governors. For them Mexico was *la otra banda*, the other shore, and a shore so distant that the City of Mexico was forty-eight days' ride from Monterey. Luis only grinned when Peter Gagarin whispered, "Is this a guard of honour for the commandant of Fort Ross?"

"No," he said, "it's the whole garrison," and followed Victor Prudon and the Russians up an outside staircase into the reception room of the Casa Grande.

After the strong sunshine in the plaza, the big sala struck Peter as dark and sparsely furnished. There were a few Mexican stools with hide seats, and two rattan chairs with fan-shaped backs which like the general's couch with its foot rest had come from the Sandwich Islands. In these chairs the two Russians were received like guests at a royal levee. Vallejo, when the presentations were made, received their expressions of sympathy with charming deprecation. "I was trying to be young again," he said. "Hoping to impress my vaqueros with my skill at the reata. I deserved to take a toss!" He showed more concern for the misunderstanding of the day before, and hoped the princess was none the worse for her long cold wait by the water. "But I knew you were all in the best of hands," he said, "with my admired old friend Doña Maria and her lovely daughter, La Favorita of Sonoma. All's well that ends well, and we can still have our talk at Petaluma, Don Alessandro. I hope you'll all be equal to another ride, this one of only fourteen miles?"

"Of course, General, of course," said Alexander Rotschev. "We have a far longer ride ahead of us before we reach Fort Ross." Peter Gagarin caught the obsequious tone, and frowned. The commandant of Fort Ross is cringing before this tub of lard, he thought. There was something in the portly, supine form of Vallejo which reminded him of King Kamehama III, lolling in his chair of state at Honolulu and announcing his devotion to Queen Victoria, while the young Inspector of the Russian-American Fur Company sat at his feet in such another fan-shaped chair. He was glad to break off the recollection and stand up to greet a newcomer, whom Vallejo introduced as 'my brother-in-law, Señor Jacob Leese'.

Mr. Leese was tall and clean-shaven, and with his sandy hair and high cheekbones was unmistakably an American. Some years before he had sailed round Cape Horn to become one of the first Yankee traders in Yerba Buena, when there were only a few shacks and tent dwellings round the cove. Now he was a Mexican citizen, the husband of one of Vallejo's sisters, and the holder of a grant recently made by the general's nephew, Governor Juan Alvarado, of eight thousand valuable acres at the bay. He also owned one of the new houses at Sonoma, from which he had walked across the plaza to greet the Russians.

His arrival changed General Vallejo's semi-official reception into a social occasion. The secretary, Monsieur Prudon, presented the captain of the garrison, eager for compliments on the smartness of his men, and the master of works at the new inn opposite the old Mission. With the two Mexicans came an Irishman called Thomas Murphy, who assisted Vallejo in the administration of his own vast properties and his charge of the National Rancho at Suscol. When they were all assembled Indian servants offered wine. General Vallejo was no vintner, but having taken over the vines of the derelict Mission he had produced a beverage which had nothing in common with Luis Estrada's burgundy but the name of wine. It was crude enough to dry the mouth and blacken the tongue, and after one sip Peter Gagarin put down his glass unostentatiously and joined Jacob Leese where he stood near the window.

"Señor," he said to the American, "would it be considered impolite if we were to speak English?"

"I guess not," drawled Leese. "The general can speak a pretty lively brand of English himself when he has a mind. French too."

They both glanced at Vallejo. Under cover of the rising hum of conversation Alexander Rotschev had drawn his chair closer to the couch and was speaking in low tones.

"You were good enough to call on us two days ago in Yerba Buena," said Peter in English.

"I was sorry to miss you," said Leese. "Guess I turned up too late at Vioget's tavern. I didn't want to disturb the lady by an early call, but when I got there I was told you'd all gone to lunch at the Presidio."

"Captain Prado sent horses and an escort, and was most insistent on entertaining us. He and his officers were very hospitable."

"Ah! Captain Prado's luncheon parties are apt to be prolonged. I had to leave for Sonoma before you returned to the pueblo. But now, sir, I hope Mrs. Rotschev – with you all – will still pay her visit to the Petaluma rancho? I know the ladies are longing to make her acquaintance."

Peter bowed. "I hope it can be arranged," he said. "But while I have this opportunity, Mr. Leese, may I ask you a direct question? Is it true, as I was told at the Presidio, that you're renting some of your premises at Yerba Buena to the Hudson's Bay Company?"

"Yes sir, that's perfectly true, though premises is a mighty grand word for those sheds of mine along the waterfront. They'll have to be fixed up before the Company's factor moves in, and that won't be before September. William Rae, his name is, and the lease is signed already. Mr. Rae wants everything shipshape before Sir George Simpson's visit of inspection at the end of the year."

"I heard of Sir George in the Sandwich Islands. He appears to be a great traveller."

"You might have heard of him in Alaska," said Mr. Leese in his dry way. "He's the man who won the contract for the Hudson's Bay Company to supply food to your people at Sitka when the Bodega produce wasn't plentiful enough."

"So I have been told," said Peter Gagarin. "I take it the Company doesn't propose to sell food at its new trading post in the land of plenty, Alta California?"

"Guess not," said Jacob Leese. "I heard tell of manufactured goods from England, from Manchester I reckon, to be freighted down from Fort Vancouver or the Oregon country."

"The Company is very active, sir. I found they had been beforehand with us at Honolulu."

"Yes, I daresay; you Russians stick to the fur trade, you see, and the British ain't afraid to branch out in all directions. But the Company's not all-powerful," said Leese, studying the Russian's handsome, sullen face. "They're not likely to be in the running when Fort Ross comes on to the market."

"Comes on to the market!" Peter echoed. "That's impossible."

"You mean you don't know Fort Ross is up for sale?"

In his astonishment Mr. Leese raised his voice, and General Vallejo broke off his low-toned conversation with Rotschev to ask what they were talking about.

"Mr. Gagarin appears to be unaware of the Fort Ross negotiations, General."

Vallejo looked from the younger Russian's angry face to Rotschev's startled one, and smiled. "You've been too long at sea, Prince Peter," he said, "or you lingered too long in the Sandwich Islands if you haven't heard that Fort Ross has become an encumbrance to your countrymen. Don Alessandro hasn't told you about the decision to abandon it?"

"He has not." The words were snapped out viciously, and Rotschev muttered that nothing had been settled yet. There had been offers to purchase – more than one; he was waiting for instructions from the Governor of Alaska.

"Fort Ross is not for sale." Peter's response was immediate and automatic, and Vallejo's sly malice was rewarded as he studied the set of the young man's jaw and Rotschev's pallor.

"I'm amazed that the commandant of Fort Ross hasn't confided his intentions to you, Prince Peter," he said, and Rotschev, still in a low tone, said they had not yet had any opportunity for a private talk.

"I see no need for an exchange of confidences," said Peter contemptuously. "Fort Ross does not belong to the commandant, to offer for sale or to surrender. He holds it in trust for a higher power."

"I understand that orders for the sale of the Fort and the farms at Bodega were issued by the Governor of Alaska, sir," said Jacob Leese. "A matter of six weeks ago."

"Indeed?" said Peter coldly. "Then, as General Vallejo says, I've been too long at sea. But perhaps the general himself has been too long confined to this little Mexican village to know that the Governor of Russian Alaska is only a naval officer, and answerable to the Department of Commerce. You may take it on my authority that the Russian-American Fur Company will not give up any of its possessions in California, unless by order of the Czar."

4

On the first of May, so early that the morning star was still shining, Rosalie Estrada was riding beside Prince Peter on the way to the fiesta to be held in his honour at Fort Ross.

How this had come about she scarcely knew. She thought it was because of Princess Helen's diplomacy in broaching the subject at luncheon after Luis and the two Russians returned from their call on General Vallejo. It had been a very lively luncheon, for Luis invited Jacob Leese and his handsome wife to ride back with them to the Rancho Estrada. They were accompanied by Mrs. Leese's sister Encarnacion, the wife of Captain Cooper, an Englishman who commanded the *California*, a cruiser which was the Mexican government's only vessel in Californian waters. The two sisters of General Vallejo were enthusiastic about a fiesta at Fort Ross, and it seemed to be taken for granted that Luis and Rosalie, with their brother Felipe at Bodega, would be of the party. It was as if the Autocrat of Sonoma, stretched out on his couch and wrapped in his robe of imperial purple, were able to influence events at a distance, for it was certainly her secret jealousy of the Vallejos which caused Doña Maria to give her grudging consent to Rosalie's presence at the fiesta.

The girl, hearing Princess Helen's repeated assurances that she would make Rosalie's well-being her chief care at Fort Ross, was ready to adore the Russian lady as the one responsible for her unexpected treat. She knew nothing of Luis's plea for more freedom for his sister, any more than she knew of the embarrassing scene at the Casa Grande. But because of that scene Luis tried a new manoeuvre, more subtle than Princess Helen's desire to have youth and beauty at her fiesta. He thought Vallejo had badgered Peter Gagarin, as he in his teens had often been badgered by the general, and he was determined to protect the young Russian from more of the same treatment, whether in Sonoma or at the Petaluma rancho. The strain between Peter and Rotschev was all too obvious. "I'll separate them!" decided Luis. "They can settle their differences with pistols if they like, but not in my house or on my land."

Before luncheon was over it was agreed that the Russian party would break up. The Rotschevs would go on with the Leeses and Mrs. Cooper to stay with the Vallejos at Petaluma, while Peter shared Luis's outdoor life until they all met on Saturday for the ride to Fort Ross. Doña Maria protested, since like all Californios she expected any visit to last at least a week, and privately she thought Peter Gagarin, arrogant and cold, a poor exchange for his charming cousin Helen. But he pleased her, on the first evening of their diminished party, by playing chess with her, and playing so well that she declared she hadn't enjoyed a game so much since her husband died.

Doña Maria was even better pleased with the young prince during the next two days, when he entered so whole-heartedly into Luis's interests that they both came home too tired for guitar music or sitting up late. On the first day they took part in one of the rodeos regularly held on the rancho to cull out the Estradas' cattle from other stray beasts in the free-ranging valley. The Estrada brand was conspicuous. It was an ox-yoke drawn vertically, to represent a primitive letter E, and the two young men rode with thirty vaqueros to round up the ox-yoke branded cattle. Peter rode so well that Luis began to plan an expedition to lasso the wild horses, of which there were thousands beyond the Mayacamas mountains, descendants of the first horses brought by the Spanish to California.

Peter laughed and declined. "I learned horsemanship when I was a boy in the Corps des Pages," he said. "You were born to the saddle." He was not at ease with the heavy Spanish stirrups cut out of a block of solid wood, and the leather *tapaderas* which protected the rider's legs from brush. But he was a better shot than Luis, as he proved next day when they went to shoot wild duck in the tule reeds of the marshes. They were eager to describe their day's sport at the dinner table, while the ladies listened indulgently.

Peter Gagarin had the Russian gift for languages, and made great progress in Spanish during his days with Luis. He answered all Doña Maria's questions on his bachelor home in St. Petersburg and the family estate at Petrovskoi, which belonged to his cousin Ivan. His widowed mother lived with his married sister in Moscow. Rosalie asked no questions, and the prince had so little to say to her that her mother became meditative, and watched them both closely on the evening of the second day. She said nothing, however, and even gave the girl permission to take some of her trousseau dresses to Fort Ross. Rosalie had asked once about the letter Luis had brought from Don Carlos to her mother, and being told it was only an apology for his absence had shrugged and changed the subject.

The dresses had gone ahead in the ox-drawn baggage cart, and Rosalie set out behind her brother with the two Indian labourers who knew every blade of grass between the rancho and the Petaluma river. She was revelling in the sunny morning as they trotted north in the opposite direction to Sonoma and the creek landing when Peter Gagarin, riding alongside, asked her how far the dirt road ran.

"Not very far. It ends in the scrub a few miles from here, and then we cross the creek by a ford."

"Was it meant to go anywhere?"

"Oh yes. When the Carrillos built the Rancho Cabeza de Santa Rosa this road was going to link it to the Sonoma Mission, but that came to nothing."

"Is there a pueblo at Santa Rosa?"

"Not yet." The gaiety drained out of Rosalie's face. "I don't know if there will ever be a settlement at Santa Rosa," she said, "and I don't care. That hateful place cost my father his life."

"Doña Rosalie! You mean there was an accident?"

"Not an accident. Santa Rosa was another of General Vallejo's clever deals with his nephew the governor. Not content with his own fifty thousand acres, he got eight thousand more in the name of his mother-in-law, Doña Maria Carrillo. Her eldest sons took on hundreds of Mission Indians, neophytes as they were called, who'd been homeless since the missions were secularised. That was four years ago, and the next year, 1838, there was a smallpox epidemic at Santa Rosa. The Carrillos didn't seem able to do much about it. The poor Indians crowded into their *temescales*, because they thought sweat baths were a cure for anything, and of course that only spread the infection. It was my father who went among them when the smallpox was at its height and vaccinated the survivors."

"Your father was a doctor?"

"No, but an Englishman called Richardson vaccinated us all when we were at Yerba Buena on our way north, and he taught my father how to do it."

"Did your father die in the smallpox epidemic?" asked the man gently.

"No, it was the Indians who died by the hundred. The smallpox was their gift from civilisation, my father said. But he had a low fever for a long time after he came home, and my mother thought his heart was affected. He died quite suddenly last September."

The Russian murmured a few words of sympathy. He was beginning to think there was more to Rosalie Estrada than charming looks and a pretty singing voice. He had been attracted to her at first sight, but having heard her mother's frequent references to the coming wedding he had been circumspect while at the rancho. In his world the seduction of a married woman was a commonplace, while a girl on the eve of marriage was to be respected. Above those physical conventions of his class and time was Peter Gagarin's increasing need to know the mind of Rosalie.

They crossed the ford and rode in single file round the flank of Sonoma Mountain until they came on an expanse of grass and wild oats starred with the crinkling yellow buds of the poppy. Then Luis and Rosalie broke into a gallop, with Rita the maid, mounted on a tall pony, trying to keep up with them, and Peter two lengths behind them all. How those Californios rode! He admired the girl with one foot in a stirrup made from a broad length of silk, so perfectly balanced on the palomino mare, and wondered how Helen had endured the long ride north from the Vallejo rancho.

The Indian calendar had changed from the Time of New Grass to the Time of Rivers in Spate, and the Petaluma river was running strongly at the ford. Jacob Leese, with a young man beside him, was on the further bank, waving his sombrero to encourage them. "We beat you to the rendezvous, and Don Felipe's here!" he shouted as the riders plunged across with the horses up to their knees in river water. Peter Gagarin bowed from the saddle to the Estradas' brother.

Felipe Estrada, at twenty-one, was neither as charming nor

as handsome as his elder brother. He was short and thickset, with a broad solemn face, and in his earth-coloured velvet suit and plain homespun shirt he was not, like Luis, a bird of bright plumage. It was he who led the way to the place where the ladies were waiting. "It's really too early to stop for lunch," he said, "but it's too far out of the way to go to my rancho or the Russian settlement. I told Señor Leese we ought to picnic at the Cords'."

The place chosen for their halt was a cabin among the redwoods, where a few fields had been cleared for cultivation and a corral made for cows and calves. It was a homestead recently built on land leased by General Vallejo to a young American named Robert Cord, a fur trapper who had crossed the Sierra Nevada with the bride he brought back from a visit to St. Louis. They had done all they could to make their guests comfortable, bringing out chairs for the ladies and Indian blankets to lay against their saddles for the men sitting on the grass. It was quite an encampment when the vaqueros and Indian guides were included. They had to be fed before the valuable palominos were taken back to the rancho, General Vallejo's men having brought fresh horses for the journey through the forest. There was food to spare for everyone, for the saddlebags had been stuffed with eatables and wine in leather bottles, while the Cords contributed sourdough bread and fresh sweet butter, with coffee from a huge tin pot. It was a new taste to Rosalie, and she sampled it much as she sampled Mr. and Mrs. Cord. They were a new breed of Americans to her, quite different from Mr. Leese and his business friends from Yerba Buena, and they talked to the visitors in a lively, independent manner which surprised her. Mr. Leese had to do a good deal of translating, although Robert Cord talked the *lingua franca* of the mountain men, a mixture of French, Spanish and Indian dialects. He was tall, with a fine head on broad shoulders, and long red hair. His wife was almost as tall as he was, and wore her black hair in a plait.

After lunch she asked the ladies to come indoors to use the primitive sanitary arrangements in a lean-to. She explained that the one-room cabin had been built by her husband from redwood logs he had felled and planed. It had only the bare necessities of furniture, but a cheerful fire was burning on the hearth, and on one side of the adobe chimney hung a long rifle, on the other a little shelf of books. Mrs. Cord pointed them out with pride to Princess Helen, the only one who spoke English. "I carried them on my back when we crossed the mountains," she said. "I was a schoolmistress back in St. Louis when Cord came courting, and I don't aim to forget all my book learning."

"I have some novels by Sir Walter Scott at Fort Ross," said the princess. "I'll send them down to you by the next messenger to the settlements."

"They'll be worth their weight in gold to me, ma'am."

It was time to mount the horses from the Vallejo rancho. The Cords stood waving as the party moved off, Robert Cord with his free hand round his wife's shoulders. They were a striking couple, Cord in his fringed buckskin jacket and deerskin leggings and his wife in a blue merino dress with a fresh white apron, and her eyes glowing at the thought of the promised books.

"How happy they are," said Rosalie, looking back.

"They're the kind we want," said Jacob Leese, who was riding beside her. "I hope Cord's going to settle down now. Trouble with a man like him is, once a hunter always a hunter. He was a trapper on the other side of the Sierra Nevada for half a dozen years, alone in the mountains except for the annual rendezvous where they all meet to trade their furs, and drink and – er – dance with the squaws. The wonder is that an educated woman would marry him when he went back to the States, but Mrs. Cord seems game for anything. Leona Faxon, her name was, and I'm told the Faxon family's very well thought of in St. Louis."

"Is he any good as a farmer?" asked Peter, from Rosalie's other side.

"He's taken to it pretty well, but you mark my words, sooner or later he'll light out again, looking for the pot of gold at the rainbow's end."

"He doesn't sound like a good investment for General Vallejo," said Rosalie.

"Bless your heart, he *is* a good investment. He's as good as a wilderness scout to my brother-in-law. Up in this neck of the woods he keeps an eye on the Indians –"

"On the Russians too?" asked Peter, and Leese smiled.

Rosalie cut in quickly. "I think Señora Cord was very brave to cross the mountains with her husband."

"No braver than you and your mother were, when you first came to the northern frontier."

"That wasn't the same thing at all," she said. "We were a whole family, with our cowboys and servants, and Spanish troops not so far away at the Presidio, and of course dear Father Fortuni at the Mission. And we had no mountains to cross."

"But you'd no roof above your head any more than the Cords did when you first arrived."

"That's true, and even the adobe bricks had to be made for the rancho first. Do you know what a *palizada* is, Prince Peter? It's a shelter made of hides, stretched round redwood posts for walls, with a hide roof on top, and that's where we lived when we first came to the valley. Don't look sorry for me! I had a wonderful time. I was only nine, too little to be useful, and I played with the Indian children, in and out of the creek, the whole day long."

"You're going to see something real different from a pali-zada when we get to Fort Ross," said Leese. Peter said nothing, but bent sideways and took Rosalie's gloved hand from the rein. He slipped the gauntlet back, and with a whisper of "*Maravillosa!*" put his lips where the pulse beat in her wrist.

Luis Estrada, riding behind them, saw the kiss and dismissed it as a Spanish gesture of flirtation, a tribute to La Favorita of Sonoma. He was flirting himself with Doña Encarnacion Cooper, an old flame, but her repartee grew forced as they went deeper and deeper into the heart of the redwood forest. It was a long ride through an empty land as the trail led through the redwoods to the broad river which the Indians called Shabaikai, the Snake, and the Russians had named the Slavianka. It was a more formidable barrier than the Petaluma, running high between the tall trees, with driftwood appearing from time to time on its turbulent surface, and churning over the sandbar as the Slavianka met the waters of the Pacific where roiling waves struck the jagged rocks at the river's mouth. The sun was setting, and on the opposite shore the travellers saw soldiers from Fort Ross, who had come to meet them with fresh mounts, and a carriage drawn by three horses in a troika.

"Now, darling, you'll be able to drive home in something like comfort," Rotschev told his wife, who had been complaining for an hour that they ought to have come north, as they had gone south, by ship. One of their guides started to cross the ford, and they could see that even near the bank the water was up to his horse's belly. Princess Helen gasped, and gave her reins to Luis Estrada, who helped her to cross the river. She, and all the women, had dripping skirts when they landed, and the princess lamented that there was not room for all four ladies in the little carriage.

"I can easily ride the rest of the way," said Rosalie.

"Fourteen miles?"

"We'll probably catch up with you before you get very far."

It was a brave boast but a silly one, for as they tackled the first steep ascent Rosalie realised that there would be no overtaking on the way to Fort Ross. She watched the open carriage disappear as the horses in the troika picked up speed. It was the first time she had ever seen a passenger vehicle other than the ox cart in which her mother travelled to Sonoma, on the rare occasions when mass was said in the Mission church. The sound of the harness bells grew fainter in the dusk.

"Do people drive troika all the time in Russia?" she asked Prince Peter, once again riding by her side.

"All the year round," he told her solemnly. "In winter the horses are harnessed to sleighs lined with furs and mounted on iron runners to cross the snow."

"How lovely!" she said. "I've never even seen snow."

There was another and steeper ascent after the first one, and as darkness began to fall Rosalie rode on in a trance of fatigue. She tried to picture a Russian landscape, like a flowery California meadow turned to white, where she drove with Peter Gagarin to the ringing of sleigh bells and the purr of iron runners over the snow. She roused herself from the fantasy more than once to encourage Rita, slumped wearily in the saddle of a rawboned mare. At last the darkness yielded to the flare of torches, held by soldiers to show them the turning from the cliff track and the way into a sheltered valley. After half a mile they saw more lights in front of a stockade of redwood, twelve feet high, above which rose the cupola and belfry of a Russian chapel. They saw the Russian flag with the double eagle of the Czars and the St. Michael emblem of the Russian-American Fur Company. "Welcome to Fort Ross!" said Rotschev, as he helped Rosalie to dismount. But Peter Gagarin said "Welcome to Russia!"

★　★　★

Next morning, as a bugle shrilled outside the barracks, Peter came out of the bath house at Fort Ross. It stood with several other buildings on the flat land south of the valley road, and so was outside the walls, but he could well imagine the scene inside. The Russian soldiers, better drilled than General Vallejo's little army, would be doubling across the square to fall in, and Commandant Rotschev, in the military uniform which did not suit him, would be preparing to take the salute and read the orders of the day. Peter smiled grimly. He walked round the eight-sided south blockhouse, and halted on the cliff to look out over the Pacific.

He was dressed in a belted Russian blouse of emerald-green silk and black trousers tucked inside soft black leather boots. Having enjoyed a steam bath, and the shock of several pails of cold water flung over him by an orderly, Peter felt invigorated enough to solve whatever problems lay ahead. Beneath the place where he stood, at the foot of a steep path – little more than a gulley – which led from the fort to the shore, there was, and had been since the Russians came, a ranchería of Miwok Indians. They were a gentle, friendly tribe, some of whom were employed at the fort, and had always been on good terms with its inhabitants. They worked in the tannery and other manufactories established at shore level, and at the yards where five ocean-going ships had been built in the early days of Fort Ross. On this Sunday morning there were only two Russian vessels to be seen: the schooner *Young Julia*, lying at the wharf on the north side of the cove, while anchored in the roadstead, too big to come alongside, was the *Elena* corvette of five hundred tons. Peter had been given much useful information by her commander, Captain Sagoskin, when they met the night before.

Behind him were the fortress and the flag, impressive witnesses to the far-reaching power of Russia. Fort Ross was magnificently situated, with the ground rising on the landward side into a wooded region cleared for the development of farms. The redwood stockade was pierced with embrasures for carronades, and the two blockhouses, or bastions, two storeys high, were each armed with six cannon taken from the French during the war of 1812. Other pieces of heavy artillery defended the sally-ports outside which the sentries paced, and as Peter had been told, there was a large supply of arms and ammunition on the ground floor of the 'old' Commandant's House, in which he had spent the night.

He had been invited to join Alexander in the 'new' house as soon as the parade was over, but Peter lingered in the bright morning, pacing up and down on the turf which smelt of thyme. He was rehearsing what he meant to say to Rotschev. The very sight of Fort Ross, impregnable by land and sea, the symbol of Russian power in California, had affirmed his resolution that 'they' must not be permitted to sell it to the highest bidder. Rotschev might have been surprised to know that by 'they' his wife's cousin did not mean himself or Governor Etolin at Sitka, but other and more powerful men in faraway St. Petersburg. The Charter of the Russian-American Fur Company had been granted by the Czar Paul I in 1799, confirmed by his son Alexander I in 1819, and renewed by Nicholas I in 1839 for a period of twenty years. Was it credible that less than two years later all the Company's possessions in California should be put up for sale? Peter knew that Baron Wrangell, the Imperial Commissar, had been rebuffed in Mexico when he attempted to gain free entry for the Company's ships to all the ports of California. The negotiations had broken down because the Mexicans had refused to treat with a commercial company, and Czar Nicholas I had refused to enter into a transaction with a government of revolutionaries. But the intention, in Peter's mind, was perfectly clear. California ought to pass under Russian influence, and 'they', the intriguers in St. Petersburg whom he intended to expose, were swayed by jealousy of the Russian-American Fur Company, which they called an empire within the Russian Empire.

The parade had been dismissed, and the troops were at their

morning meal in the barracks when Peter Gagarin walked across the great square to the 'new' Commandant's House. It was a one-storey wooden building, and the small rooms had to be used for several purposes. In Rotschev's study Peter found him at breakfast with his three little children and their governess. Princess Helen, wearing a pale-blue satin wrapper, looked rested and content. She smiled as Peter kissed her hand.

"How nice you look in your Russian clothes!" she said.

"And how energetic you are," Peter countered. "I should have thought you deserved a long rest this morning, Helen."

"It's the Spanish ladies who are resting in their rooms," she laughed. "*I* have a family to look after! Say good morning to your cousin, children." At a look from their French governess the little Rotschevs stood up to bow and say in chorus, "Good morning, Peter Alexeivich!" He had tried to make friends with them on the night before, but they were still shy of this tall kinsman with the cold blue eyes.

"Give Prince Peter some tea, mademoiselle," said Helen to the Frenchwoman, who presided at the samovar. "And Peter dear, I owe you an apology. You ought to be under our own roof, but you see we only have two spare bedrooms, and I felt one should be given to Mrs. Cooper and Doña Rosalie. Mr. and Mrs. Leese have the other."

"Of course," said Peter amiably. "The Estrada brothers and I are very comfortable in your old house, and we sat up late last night, smoking and talking with some of the officers. I was glad to meet Captain Sagoskin again."

"He said he knew you at Sitka last winter. You're not eating anything."

"Sagoskin and I had an early breakfast in the officers' mess before he went back on board the *Elena*." Peter crumbled the bread on his plate and smiled at Rotschev. "You didn't tell me you visited the Farallones when you sailed south with him in the *Elena*. I hadn't realised the islands were to be included in the great sell-out."

"I think the children have finished, mademoiselle," said Rotschev, clearing his throat. "Will you take them to the schoolroom, please?"

"Oh papa, no lessons this morning!" "You promised!" "We want to stay with mamma!" The princess silenced the babble of protest and hugged them all. "Do as papa says, darlings," she said. "Mamma will come to you very soon." She looked apprehensively at the two men when they were left alone.

"The Farallones have no value, Peter Alexeivich," said Rotschev. "Last week I found nothing but a miserable group of hunters there. A few Russian soldiers and thirty Kodiak natives from Alaska, whose only achievement in fifteen years has been the almost total extermination of the seals in those waters. There has been no attempt to establish a real settlement on the Farallones, nor will there ever be: the islands are not worth holding on to."

"But you said nothing about it when you met me at Yerba Buena. You allowed me to hear your plans from an American stranger."

"Yes, well, I'm sorry you had to hear about the sale of Fort Ross in such a public manner."

"Forty-eight hours after my arrival," Peter reminded him.

"I'd hoped to have a talk with Vallejo first, and hear what he had to propose before I put the whole design before you."

"Yes, I gather the general means to make his own bid. Waste of time, Alexander; the fact is that Fort Ross must not be put up for sale."

"I was afraid you would raise some objections –"

"And you were afraid that if you told me your wretched story while I was still within reach of the *Volga* I would have gone on to Sitka without delay."

Rotschev gave his wife a look which said "I told you so." But it was to Peter that he said, "When you arrive at Sitka Governor Etolin will tell you that it was by his orders that I opened negotiations in California."

"Etolin's orders! Since when does a naval hydrographer issue orders on behalf of the Company? I know the men in St. Petersburg who are out to ruin the directors if they can. I intend to see them broken, and if you go down with them, that's your affair."

"Peter darling –"

Rotschev interrupted his wife. "Let him speak," he said. "But before you continue your tirade, Peter Alexeivich, I must remind you that you've been out of touch with St.

Petersburg for the better part of a year. The directors of the Company themselves decided that the fur trade with California had become unprofitable, and that all the Californian establishments should be abandoned."

"While I intend they should be held and increased until the whole of California is ours."

"Peter, what do you mean?" gasped Princess Helen.

"I mean that after Russian Alaska, the Empire should extend its rule over Russian California," he said. "The Company must go far beyond the trapping of a few thousand seals and otters. We have a fleet, a force of soldiers, and a thriving town for our base at Sitka. We have a strong body of Russian colonists in Alaska, and a serf population of Aleuts and Tlingits. But so far we have only toeholds on the American mainland. Here, and at Bodega, and another, twenty times more important – which you, Alexander, say has no value – in the Farallones islands, which guard the entrance to San Francisco Bay. For God's sake, man! They're only thirty miles seaward from la Boca del Puerto, which in turn is guarded by some old cannon as useful as that toy of Vallejo's in the plaza of Sonoma. And by *eight* Mexican soldiers under the dashing command of Captain Prado, that swaggering sot we met at the Presidio. The Territory of Alta California is defended by eight men at the Presidio and thirteen at Sonoma – in all, less than a quarter of the force you paraded here this morning."

"The garrison of Fort Ross is intended for defence and not for attack," said its commandant.

"Defence against whom? The Indians, who like us better than their Spanish conquerors? Defence against the Mexicans? Mrs. Cooper says her husband's cruiser is unarmed. Against the *California*, we can muster six corvettes and six brigs of the Company's fleet alone, and we can call on two, or perhaps three frigates of the Russian Navy. If such a force were to appear off the Farallones, and call on the Mexicans to surrender, in half a day Captain Prado and his ruffians would invite us to take possession of the Bay of San Francisco."

"And we should have committed an act of war," said Rotschev, "do you think the Great Powers will accept that without protest?"

"What can the Powers do? Write indignant Notes to their

ambassadors in St. Petersburg? Austria and Prussia will bow to the *fait accompli*. Britain and France, the arch intriguers, are trying to take possession of California before we do. You know very well how long and hard the Hudson's Bay Company has worked to gain possession of the Oregon country for Britain and drive the Russian fur traders out of the Pacific. As for the French – I met one of their spies at San Pedro, not ten days ago. A young man called Duflot de Mofras, sent from Paris to their embassy in Mexico, to plot for the transformation of California into the New France they lost in Canada. Do you want to see the greatest prize in the Far West pass under the Tricolore? California is ready and willing to be raped by the first comer – and it must be Russia."

"So you'd commit our country to a war in the Pacific?" said Rotschev. "I'll have nothing to do with it."

"I never supposed you would," said Peter contemptuously, and Helen intervened at last.

"Alexander's right," she said. "A war in the Pacific – it's impossible! What makes you think the Czar would agree to it? If Nikolai Alexandrovich ever went to war, it would be to realise the Byzantine dream of all the Romanovs – to win back Constantinople from the Turks, and with it the command of the Black Sea. Do you seriously think you could persuade him to care about Yerba Buena and Monterey?"

"No," said Peter, "but his son and heir could. And I have the ear of the Czarevich."

"Who is probably thinking of nothing this spring but his marriage to Princess Marie of Hesse."

"Oh, you women," said Prince Peter Gagarin, with sovereign indulgence, "all you can think about is a royal wedding. The Czarevich will be a sober married man by the time I reach St. Petersburg. Even travelling post after I reach Okhotsk I can't be there before October."

"You told us you meant to attend the fur fair at Kiatka in October."

"On the Chinese border? For the sake of Russian California I'll give up the fur fair," Peter told Princess Helen, and turned to Rotschev. "Alexander! Your delaying tactics didn't work. Even if I'd gone straight to Sitka from Yerba Buena in the *Volga*, I'd been held up there for nearly a whole month. As it is,

Sagoskin will pick me up here when the corvette comes back from San Pedro, and I'll sail in the frigate *Neva* from Sitka to Okhotsk at the end of May."

5

It was not a good beginning for a fiesta. The raised voices could be heard all through the little house, and Rotschev was quiet and glum when he met his guests. Peter and Helen, with their long training at the court of the Czar, were experts in dissembling, and were all smiles and polite attention as the newcomers were shown the sights of Fort Ross. Jacob Leese's keen eyes went from one Russian to another. "Ructions!" he said to himself, "they had a proper row this morning. Let's hope it doesn't end in a shoot-out before we get away." In his roving life Leese had seen a good deal of gunplay, and gunplay between Russians was no concern of his. He was at Fort Ross, not only to see and memorise all he could to tell his brother-in-law. General Vallejo had been impressed in spite of himself by Peter Gagarin's rigid opposition to the sale of the Russian properties. Feverish and in pain after the jolting journey by ox cart to his rancho, Vallejo had made his health the excuse for avoiding a conclusive talk with Alexander Rotschev, and the making of a formal offer. But he was eager to have Leese's assessment of the current capital value and military dispositions of Fort Ross.

The Spanish guests, from all Leese could hear, were impressed by what they saw as they strolled round the wide square with the well, as usual, in the centre.

"What a huge place it is," Rosalie was saying.

"Bigger than the Petaluma rancho," said Felipe.

"Pooh! General Vallejo's rancho, indeed! Luis, isn't Fort Ross even bigger than Yerba Buena?"

"Twice as big." At that time there were about twenty houses, along with the Boston agents' stores, at the village of the Good Herb. There were fifty inside and around the stockade of the Russian fort. That smart child put her finger on it, thought Leese. The proper comparison to make is with the pueblo by the bay, as I know, and I've played my hunch for all it's worth that it's at the bay, and not in this memorial to the last century, that the money will be made in the future.

Rotschev evoked the past when he told Rosalie that the place was given its name at a ceremony of dedication in 1812, when '*Rus*', a poetical name for Russia, was drawn by lot from a number of names placed at the base of an image of Christ. It was the American trappers who occasionally came to the fort who had turned the name into 'Ross'.

"My father used to talk of the Presidio Ruso, or the Fuerte de los Ruses, when we first came to the frontier," she said. "Is the image in the chapel?"

"There's a famous ikon in the chapel," said Peter, who was following them, "let me show it to you, Doña Rosalie." She looked in perplexity round the tiny chapel with its wooden walls, on one of which hung the five hundred years old ikon sent by the Czar Paul I with the original founding party of Fort Ross. There was no ikonostasis, but a wooden lectern held a copy of the Scriptures.

"It's Sunday," she said. "Will there be a service here today?"

"There's no priest of the Orthodox church nearer than Sitka, I'm afraid. Alexander reads prayers to his family before breakfast."

"I thought I heard you praying before I left my room," she said innocently. "You were shouting."

"Yes, well, that was another kind of service."

"I believe you're just as godless as we are at Sonoma."

"You've the Mission chapel there, I saw it."

"Yes, the first little chapel Father Altimira built. We're not quite in outer darkness – yet."

It was dark in the Russian church, but the sun was dazzling in the square. Peter suggested they look at 'Helen's garden house' before they joined the others, who had drifted out to the thyme-scented cliff. "I haven't seen it myself yet," he confessed, "but it should be pretty. She's had all sorts of flowers sent out from Petersburg."

It was a small conservatory with glass walls and doors, heated by wood-burning braziers, where magnolias and camellias were trained against redwood posts to make their branches meet in an arch of pink and white under the glass roof. Succulent green plants cascaded from shelves fixed to the walls, while arum lilies and roses of many colours were blooming in low stands on each side of a narrow central passage. "How beautiful!" said Rosalie. "But when I remember showing Princess Helen our kitchen garden, and boasting about my lettuces, I wonder what she can think of me?"

"She thinks you're a lovely girl, and so do I." Then, taking both her hands, Peter said gently, "This place suits you."

Rosalie was out of mourning at last, dressed in white muslin with the skirt scalloped in rose red, and a little silk rebozo of silk in shades of red and pink and cream. Her colour was rising in the scented warmth.

"You're going to be married in September?" Peter asked.

"Perhaps."

"Only perhaps? I thought it was a settled thing."

"My mother thinks it is."

"You mean you aren't sure?"

"Sure about a man I've seen twice in my whole life? Please don't talk about it! Everybody talks about it! I meant to forget all that while I was here!"

"Forgive me," Peter said. "I only wanted to know if you were going to be happy."

"Happy! How can I tell?" Rosalie wrenched her hands away, and hurried out of the garden house to join the others.

They were all enthusiastic about a scheme proposed by Captain Sagoskin, for which Princess Helen blessed him in her heart. A picnic, or merienda, was an indispensable part of every country fiesta, but could hardly be organised by a lady who had returned to her home only the night before, and Captain Sagoskin's plan was that they should all picnic aboard the *Elena*, being rowed out to the corvette in her dinghy and the two rowing boats kept tied up to the wharf. It was such a novelty for the Californios to be sea-borne that there was much talk and laughter as they all embarked. Princess Helen, not depending on the provender in the corvette's galley, sent a relay of soldiers down the cliff path with baskets of food and wine for all aboard, and after two glasses of wine a sailor produced his balalaika and sang to them.

The Miwok Indians put off from the cove in their dugouts, made from fallen trees or driftwood logs, to circle the *Elena*. Unusually for a Californian tribe they were good fishermen, and had a catch of Pacific salmon ready for the cooks at Fort Ross to prepare that night. They had long conquered their fear of the white men in the great boats, and shared the interest with the party gathered on the top of the cliff when the *Elena* sailed on the evening tide. With her white sails set she moved over the sunset waters of the Pacific like a fairy ship, the ladies said, and they protested when Jacob Leese, in his prosaic way, said she was only going to San Pedro to pick up a cargo of wheat from the southern valleys.

"You took your hat off. You let your face get brown," said Rita, as she helped her young mistress to dress for dinner.

"So did I, Rita," said young Mrs. Cooper. "It hasn't done me any harm."

"Doña Rosalie has a delicate complexion, señora," said Rita, with a look which said, "and you're as brown as I am, hat or no hat." The Mexican lady laughed good-naturedly. She had been out of humour the night before, when she found the half-breed intended to sleep on a pallet at the foot of the big bed she was to share with Rosalie, but Rita made herself so useful, and was helping them both to dress so deftly, that she was glad to have the woman's help. Rosalie wore a white dress and a white rebozo, at her mother's behest: her long sash was pale green. Tied in front, with the fringed ends falling to the hem of her skirt, it looked like one of the exotic fronds of greenery in the garden house.

Dinner was almost as much of a picnic as the luncheon aboard the corvette, for Princess Helen had chosen to have it served on small tables crowded into her husband's study. They ate the salmon caught by the Indians, encased in a flaky pastry and called *koulibiak*, accompanied by a yellow wine from Russia, and a *pashka* dripping with whipped cream and candied fruits. When the meal was over it was clear that the study had been used so as to leave free the largest room in the Commandant's House, which Rosalie thought of as the sala. But the sala at the Rancho Estrada was never like this one, with its Persian carpets and chandelier of blue and white glass, the crystal chains and drops glittering in the light of forty candles.

It was a family heirloom, Princess Helen told the fascinated girl, and had come from St. Petersburg.

She saw the walls lined with books, the portraits of ladies with powdered hair and low-cut gowns, of gentlemen in perukes or steel breastplates under shoulder sashes, and to her delight a piano, the first ever seen in Alta California. When Helen swept her hand along the keys she struck an answering chord in Rosalie's heart. "I know you love music," Helen said, "we shall have some fine singing tonight. Here come Major Cherbatov and his friends."

"But they're not the singers," said Peter, as the young major who was the effective commander of Fort Ross made his bow. He and two other officers, with their wives, had been invited to swell the audience and share the cordials and liqueurs which were handed round. The four best soldier-singers in the garrison had been ordered to appear with their balalaikas.

The first day of Princess Helen's fiesta ended in music, and all the morning of the second was spent in preparing for the merienda. The chosen picnic place was only five miles away, but the provisions had to be taken there by ox cart, the drivers starting early. Then three little friends of the Rotschev children, with their two pretty older sisters, had to be brought from the home farm and installed with Princess Helen and the governess in two more carretas, lined with hides and shaded by white cotton awnings. Rosalie and the Vallejo sisters preferred to ride, followed by the men on horseback, and were gaily spreading the white tablecloths and setting out the picnic fare before the jolting carretas came into sight. The commandant of Fort Ross had brought two armed Russian troopers, for what purpose was not clear unless – mused Jacob Leese – they were intended to resist a British invasion from the Oregon country, or an uprising by the gentle Miwoks. Mr. Leese was not a poetical man, but several times during the long happy afternoon he thought it was 'mighty pretty to see the folks enjoying themselves'. He, as usual, wore a black frock coat and a light sombrero, but the other men were almost as brightly clad as the ladies. The uniforms, the serapes and the parasols were like a parterre of summer flowers. He wondered how many more meriendas would be held in this sheltered place high above the Pacific surge. The Russians were on their way out, that was for sure, and Leese knew better than most that for the Californios, too, the pastoral days were drawing to a close. It was hard to realise, listening to the songs and the laughter, that he was witnessing the end of a society.

They feasted on roast turkey, chicken and tamales, with sweetmeats and wine, and *refrescos* for the children, who were sent off as soon as the late luncheon was over to gather wildflowers for the ladies to make into nosegays. It was the pretty custom for each lady to give her posy to the caballero of her choice, and this was managed tactfully enough. There were only three unmarried girls, and the French governess, who could hardly be counted as a girl, was applauded when she gave her flowers to Felipe Estrada, who looked like being odd man out. Luis kissed Mrs. Cooper's hand when she handed him his nosegay, and she appeared to feel no regrets that her husband was at sea. The Russian girls honoured the officers, giggling at their compliments. The prettiest bouquet was the one made by Rosalie Estrada, a golden nosegay of buttercups, yellow poppies and yellow lupins, and no one was surprised when she beckoned to Prince Peter to receive her favour. The surprise was that he neither bowed nor kissed her hand, as the other men had done. He went down on his knees before her and kissed the proffered flowers instead, raising his eyes to hers with a look her brothers long remembered.

That brought the nosegay ceremony to a close, as Princess Helen, rising rather hastily and shaking out her pale-green skirts, said it was time for mademoiselle and the children to start on the long slow journey home. The two armed sentries, who had eaten and drunk in abundance, were to ride on each side of the ox cart.

The ladies began to fold the tablecloths and pack the hampers while the men strolled in the pine wood, where the trees cast longer shadows as the first light of a flaming sunset began to appear above the ocean. When they came back, the wine glasses were filled again, and Alexander Rotschev proposed a toast to "Doña Rosalie, La Favorita of Fort Ross!"

She swept them a curtsy worthy of an actress, or a young princess at the court of the Czar. Rosalie had been conscious of her power all through the day, and was now in a mood which her mother would have checked immediately, when her real sweetness was overlaid by vanity and an inordinate love of admiration. She knew she was called La Favorita of Sonoma, but she saw no merit in being the favourite of a little pueblo on the northern frontier. To be La Favorita of Monterey, as she might have been but for her father's quixotic decision to join his friend Father Fortuni in caring for the dispossessed Indians – that would have been something. But to be La Favorita of Fort Ross, with a prince at her feet and her brothers to witness her triumph, was the breath of life to Rosalie Estrada.

"Now let's sit down for a little while and tell stories," said Princess Helen, trying to keep control of her merienda. In the last hour of any picnic tales were told by men and women who had to make their own amusements: old legends of Castile and the Mexico of the Viceroys, and new romances of Alta California. The elder Vallejo sister brought the Russians into the legendary days by reviving the greatest romance of all, the doomed love of Concepcion Argüello and Nikolai Rezanov.

All the Russians had heard of Count Rezanov, who visited California in 1806 on a mission from the Czar, fell in love with the pretty daughter of the Presidio's commandant, and died on his homeward journey across Siberia before they could be married. All the Californios had been brought up on it, had wept over it, had sung doleful ballads about 'Concha' or 'Conchitita' and her tragic story. Rosalie in her early teens had sighed over the Spanish girl waiting in vain beside the empty bay. She was amazed to hear Peter say,

"I met Doña Concepcion at Santa Barbara, on my way back from the Islands."

They all spoke together then. "What?" "Is she still alive?" "What does she look like now?" "I thought she died years ago!"

Peter smiled his cold smile. "I agree that it would have been more romantic if the poor girl had died of a broken heart, but in fact she's very much alive."

"How did you come to meet her, Prince Peter?" asked Mrs. Cooper.

"When the *Volga* put in to Santa Barbara, the alcalde was good enough to give a little reception for the officers and myself, and Doña Concepcion was among the guests. She seemed a very pleasant lady, as far as I was able to talk to her, and she's obviously held in great respect. The alcalde says she does a great deal of good among the poor."

"It's amazing." Mrs. Leese said what they all felt. In the vast Territory of California, where the tiny communities were so isolated, it was as if the Argüello family had been swallowed up in the passage of nearly forty years. "Is she still beautiful?"

"Well," Peter hesitated. "She must be nearly sixty, I suppose. And then she was dressed as a nun –"

"She belongs to a lay order, the Third Order of St. Francis, Prince."

"That I didn't know, but she was dressed as nuns are in Russia, with a long dark robe, and a what-d'you-call-it on her head."

La Favorita of Fort Ross had kept quiet long enough. She was dismayed by the portrait of the tragic 'Concha' as an elderly religious, to be shown off at his receptions by a provincial mayor. Rosalie captured her audience again by saying, too loudly:

"I never thought she was so very romantic, after all. Count Rezanov was a widower with a young family, and old enough to be her father."

There was a guilty laugh, and Jacob Leese, in an attempt to be humorous, said Doña Rosalie obviously didn't believe in second marriages.

"If they were so very much in love, why didn't they elope?" persisted Rosalie, and now all eyes turned to the Rotschevs, whose elopement of ten years back was well known to the Californios. Princess Helen, with her accustomed tact, said how sad it was to think of that poor girl waiting for her lover, and not knowing until many years had passed that he had not deserted her. "He died of a fall, didn't he, Peter?"

"A fall or a fever, there are conflicting stories. But I know he was buried at Krasnoyarsk, I saw his grave."

It cast a chill upon the company. Luis Estrada, to bring the scene to an end, got to his feet and said, "Poor Argüellos, I'd forgotten they went to live at Santa Barbara, but of course it was long before our time. Don Luis, Concepcion's brother, was Rosalie's godfather, and he died young. He was our one and only California-born Governor, señor comandante, were you aware of that?" He knew he could trust Rotschev to change the subject. The Argüello Governorship, in the interim between Spanish rule and Mexican rule, was too delicate a topic to be discussed in the presence of General Vallejo's brother-in-law and his two sisters. Luis wanted them all to start moving now, back to Fort Ross, on to the end of the day. But Rosalie in her sharp change of mood continued recklessly:

"I'm sorry for Concepcion Argüello, but she brought it on herself. She allowed Count Rezanov to go away alone, and to do what, please? To get the Czar's permission, to get the King of Spain's permission, maybe even to ask the Pope's permission for two Christians of different churches to get married! If she had really loved her Nikolai she would have eloped with him to Siberia, and then his life would have been saved."

6

"So what d'you think of dancing, Russian style, Felipe?" said Luis Estrada as they rode south from Fort Ross.

Felipe laughed. "I haven't been to many balls," he said, "but last night's dance in the armoury, if that's what they call it, was less like a *baile* than a waterfront *fandango*."

"Those polkas and mazurkas were something new, but the girls thought they were marvellous, and no wonder, when there were three men for every girl. Rosalie had to split her dances all evening."

"I was proud of little Rosalie last night." Felipe turned in his saddle to look for his sister. She was within sight but not within earshot, riding with Rita and two of the vaquero escort across the flowering meadows which led down to Salmon Creek. "And she behaved herself at the *baile*. I don't know what mother would have thought of the way she and Gagarin were acting at the picnic."

Luis laughed. "Flirtation is part of a merienda – always has been and always will be."

"You think that's all it was?"

"Good God, what else could it be? You should have been at

the Peralta wedding if you wanted to see a real flirtation, multiplied by twenty."

"I hope you're right," said Felipe. "But I think Carlos Rivera has stayed away too long."

"We may have him among us sooner than you think." It was as good a time as any, with the women riding so far in the rear, for Luis to tell his brother about Rivera's proposal to advance the date of the wedding, and the terms of the marriage settlement.

Felipe whistled. "What are you going to do?"

"It's obvious that by September I'll have to find the money somehow, even if it means mortgaging all next year's hides to the Boston agents."

"You still think of hides as California bank notes, don't you, Luis?"

"What else?"

"There could be other sources of revenue."

"Such as apples and apricots?"

"I didn't mean that." They rode on without speaking while Felipe considered his sister's marriage settlement. "Except for the clause about the heirs, it sounds like a badly drawn document," he said at last. "Old Haro must have been in his second childhood by that time, and of course our dear papa was a spoiled priest at heart. He never had any idea of business."

"Business?"

"There is such a word, as you'd know if you could see past hides and tallow. I'm thinking of going into business on my own account before too long."

"I thought you were in business, if you mean buying and selling. Aren't your orchards really doing well?"

"They are, and this will be a great fruit country some day, but what I didn't know when I was nineteen, and pestered my poor father to set me up on Salmon Creek, was that the finest produce in the world has got to find a market. Here my best customers are the Russian farmers and the whaler captains, but apart from them there's no market at Bodega Bay. As long as our wonderful government on *la otra banda* will only allow foreign ships to stay forty-eight hours in port, I've precious little hope of selling or transporting soft fruit in good condition. I'm thinking of going into business with Robert Cord."

"The Americano?"

"Americano's only a word like business, and often means the same thing. We've been talking about setting up a sawmill here on Salmon Creek."

"You haven't given your fruit rancho much of a trial. You and Cord the trapper will make a restless pair."

"That's the way they are, the Americanos. Or else they wouldn't be here. Roberto Cord is one of the new breed, the real pioneers. The mountain men found their way across the Sierras, and now they're bringing their wives with them. They won't have to woo the Spanish ladies, as Leese and the others did, to get a land grant from the governor and a place in our society. They don't give a damn for our society, they want to be their own men."

"I've always thought of Leese as one of us," said Luis. "He embraced the Catholic faith and became a Mexican citizen when he married into the Vallejo family."

"That's what all the Americanos did who came here in the Boston ships. You know what they say among themselves? 'A man leaves his conscience at Cape Horn' – does that say much for the sincerity of their Catholic faith?"

"California can absorb them all," said Luis confidently. "Even the Russians, if they choose to stay."

"Señor Nikolai, the Fur Company's agent at Bodega Bay, says they're going, and he's a better-informed man than our host of the last few days. Personally I'm sorry, I've got on well with the farmers, but the Russians were only an incident, not an invasion as my poor father used to think. It's the men from the States you have to worry about, hermano, for they're the ones who'll challenge a way of life you seem to cherish." He turned again in the saddle. "Why are those women dawdling? Let's ride, Luis! I told Pepita to have a meal ready for us, and it's past midday already."

Don Santiago Estrada had not wasted much time or labour on the ranch house he had built on his younger son's fruit farm. As far as it was possible for any building of adobe brick to look temporary and skimped, so was Felipe's home, with which, however, the owner appeared to be quite satisfied. His housekeeper, old Pepita, came out curtsying and showed them into the one-storey house with the tule roof, of which only the entrance was closed with a wooden door. Serapes closed off the spaces to right and left of the main room, which had an earth floor and a long rough table set with tin dishes and cutlery and with four tin candlesticks holding tallow candles. Behind the table an adobe bench was built into the wall, and four leather stools were drawn up on the other side. By these signs Luis guessed that Don Felipe Estrada was in the habit of eating with his labourers.

Beyond the draped serapes there were two bedrooms, each provided with two frame beds strung with rawhide thongs and covered with Indian blankets. At one side of the yard Pepita and her husband occupied a room attached to the outdoor kitchen, while on the other was the bunkhouse for the Mexican workers. It was a drab setting for youth and beauty, but Rosalie seemed delighted with it all. She and Rita took one of the bleak bedrooms – Luis was to share the other with Felipe – removed their riding clothes, and in plain cotton dresses sat down to eat the overspiced, overcooked food prepared by Pepita. Rita demurred at eating with her masters, and was told by Felipe not to be a fool. After all, they had known Rita Sanchez all their lives.

It was not a meal to linger over, and soon they were exploring the orchards, while Felipe discussed some of his problems with his brother. If the little house was depressing, the fruit trees were in their springtime glory, and Rosalie walked under the pink and white blossoms with the exalted feeling of being one with the spring. She heard very little of what her brothers were saying. She was listening to the voice of Peter Gagarin, as she had heard it after the ball in the moonlit courtyard at Fort Ross. "Rosalie, may I come to you at Don Felipe's rancho? I must see you alone . . . dearest."

Dearest . . . dearest . . . it was the word which summed up all the enchantment which had possessed Rosalie Estrada since the day she set out on horseback for Fort Ross and entered what to her was a world of luxury. In her dreams that night she relived the dance in the 'old' Commandant's House, where the Russian weapons and ammunition were discreetly hidden behind draperies and coloured screens, the picnic where she was acclaimed as La Favorita and Peter Gagarin fell to his knees at her feet, the pianoforte music which filled the room where the Petersburg chandelier flashed in its prisms of silver and blue. Next morning, Luis contrived to take her aside and ask her if she wouldn't rather leave with him that day and ride with him to the Carrillo rancho at Santa Rosa, where he meant to break his journey on the way home. She answered quickly:

"Oh no, because that would hurt poor Felipe's feelings! And mamma meant me to stay here with Rita, and see what we can do to make the place more comfortable. You know it was one of the reasons she allowed me to go with you to Fort Ross."

Yes, he knew that was true. He said Felipe would bring her home in ten days, or a couple of weeks, and she was to be a good girl, keep Rita with her all the time, and not wander away from the fruit ranch unless Felipe went with her. It was the usual admonition, at which Rosalie had been apt to sulk in the past; but now she listened with such smiling assent that Luis rode away with a vague sense of dissatisfaction. Still, as he told himself (making for Robert Cord's cabin, where he meant to rest his horse) Felipe's adobe dwelling was less isolated than the Rancho Estrada was even now, with the Russian farms at no great distance, and the little settlement at Bodega Bay only six miles away.

When he had gone Rosalie tackled the domestic problems of the adobe with a zeal which made Rita smile. Chests which stood in the corners of the sala, and had probably been used for seats, were opened to reveal glass and china, bed and table linen sent from the Rancho Estrada and never unpacked until now. The tinware was banished from the table, and after being scoured by the resentful Pepita with river sand until it shone, was arranged on the pine dresser which had previously held such items as Felipe's guitar with a broken string, several pairs of gauntlet gloves and tarnished spurs, and even a branding iron with the Estrada 'E' in the form of an ox-yoke. While Rosalie worked in the sala, Rita took stock of Felipe's body linen, and set Pepita to a thorough washing of shirts which badly needed mending. When the shirts were spread on the orchard grass and sprinkled with rain water to hasten the process of bleaching, Rita followed her young mistress to the banks of Salmon Creek, from which Felipe's irrigation chan-nels led, and where Rosalie was gathering the pink farewell-to-spring flowers growing in profusion beneath the cottonwoods. When Rosalie looked up and smiled the mestiza dropped down beside the kneeling girl.

"Is that another nosegay for the prince?" she asked.

"He told me he would come tomorrow."

"Oh Rosalie, *querida*, is that wise?"

"It's what he wants."

"Surely he knows you're pledged to marry another man?"

"He doesn't think it matters. And neither do I."

"You'll break your mother's heart."

But Rosalie only laughed, and ran back to the house with her hands full of flowers. He was coming tomorrow! She felt like an actress in one of the Spanish plays her father had read with her, waiting for the three knocks, and the rising of the curtain on the lighted stage.

Peter Gagarin came to the fruit ranch next morning, as he had promised, riding to Salmon Creek from the Russian farm where he had spent the night with the farmer, Klebnikov, by his side. There was no doubt in his mind that he was doing the right thing, nor did the thought that his courtship of Rosalie might be an abuse of the Estrada hospitality ever occur to him. Satisfied that his intentions were honourable, his only problem, once his declaration was made, was how to get the girl he meant to marry out of California and into Russian Alaska. From there, to his self-confident mind, the path to St. Petersburg was clear.

His cousin Helen had guessed where he was going when he left Fort Ross only a few hours after the guests at the fiesta, on what he called a tour of inspection of the Russian farms. She had accused him of making a fool of a little country girl entrusted to Princess Helen's care, and when he told her that he loved Rosalie Estrada, whose mother was justly proud of their Castilian blood, Helen had retorted that he had merely been attracted to the first pretty face he saw after his long voyage to the Sandwich Islands. There was just enough truth in this to make it rankle, for Peter had indeed spent months of self-imposed celibacy, having been too proud to take any of the Kanaka girls who would have willingly shared his bed at Honolulu. But his growing passion for Rosalie was not merely physical. Her mind attracted him as much as her elusive beauty, and he was fascinated by her experiences as a child of the frontier. "She'll be a sensation in St. Petersburg," he thought, and his smile startled farmer Klebnikov, who was telling him a gloomy story of coyote thefts.

Felipe Estrada, riding home from an outlying orchard, saw the two Russians approaching, and reined in his horse in surprise. "So he came after her!" was his first thought, and he wished ardently for the support of his brother Luis. But the laws of Californio hospitality prevailed: he greeted his guests cordially, with "*Está es su casa, señores!*" and only allowed himself to add, "You're a long way from Fort Ross, Prince Peter!"

"I have to visit all our farms, and the Kuskov settlement, señor," Peter explained, "and I hope to find that Doña Rosalie is none the worse of her long ride south." She looked all the better for it, as with glowing cheeks she appeared at the farmhouse door to add her greeting to Felipe's, and "She knew he was coming!" was her brother's conclusion as he saw that she was wearing a high Spanish comb, with a pink rose in the black hair sleeked over her left ear. But she carried off the situation better than he did, with a quiet welcome to both the guests, and a graceful presiding over what, but for Rita's intervention, would have been a disastrous midday meal. The rammed-earth floor of his living room, and the shabby serapes which took the place of doors for the first time seemed inadequate to Felipe Estrada, but the savoury eggs and fruit flan produced by Rita (Pepita's contribution was burned tortillas) added up to a respectable meal, and the Estrada wine was always good. As they ate and drank, Peter Gagarin talked, in a far more forthcoming way than at Fort Ross, of his return journey to St. Petersburg. In about ten days' time, he said, he hoped to sail to Sitka in the corvette *Elena*, and if the *Neva* left Sitka on the appointed date, the twenty-fifth of May, there should be no difficulty about ice in the Bering Sea. They would make the port of Okhotsk in six weeks' time.

"Six *weeks!*" said Rosalie. "Why, it didn't take us that long to come north from Monterey, did it, Felipe?"

"Just about," said her brother. "The carretas took a long time on the way."

"And when you reach Ok – Okhotsk, what then?"

"From Okhotsk it's an eight weeks' journey to Krasnoyarsk, where Rezanov is buried." Peter said it deliberately, to remind the girl of what the name of Rezanov and his unhappy love had made her say at the merienda, and he saw by her lowered eyes that Rosalie had taken his meaning. He went on relentlessly, she had to know what – if she chose – would lie before her in the journey across Siberia. "From Krasnoyarsk, with any luck, it's only six weeks to St. Petersburg. I shall be home on the Moika Quay before snow flies."

"In October." Rosalie had been counting on her fingers. "Five months from now."

"It's a hard way to travel for anyone, man or woman," said Klebnikov. "My wife was exhausted when we arrived at Sitka. And New Archangel wasn't the place then they say it is now."

"The largest civilised community for two thousand miles," said Peter. "With schools, hospitals, churches, and a very gracious lady in the person of the Governor's wife, Madame Etolin . . ."

"It all sounds very grand," said Rosalie, rising. "Now Felipe must show you what wonders *he* has worked. Wouldn't you like to see the orchards?"

Farmer Klebnikov reverted to the theme of coyotes, and the damage they were doing to his hen-runs, as soon as they were out of doors. Prince Peter, offering his arm to Rosalie, followed him smiling. The Russian farmer was engrossing the Spanish ranchero, and the faint pressure of Rosalie's hand on his own arm told him that she had understood his careful explanation of the long journey which lay ahead. But she said nothing until he gently guided her over one of the irrigation channels, and then she said "When do you leave?"

"I ought to be back at Fort Ross by the end of next week."

"A week soon goes."

"A week could be for ever, if you wish it, Rosalie."

She stopped beneath one of the blossoming trees, and looked up at him. Her lips were trembling.

"Dearest! You told me in the garden house that you hardly knew that man they want you to marry – I don't even know his name –"

"Carlos Rivera."

"Rivera – that you'd seen him only twice, and you don't want to marry him. Tell me, for I must know, could you love me?"

"I think I could. But we mustn't talk about it now –"

"Where can we meet alone, tomorrow?"

★   ★   ★

The trail along the coast, southward from the ford of the Slavianka, was bleak and windswept, often shrouded in fog, but at the point where it met the dirt road which the Russians had made from Bodega Bay to their farms it ran through a noble stand of redwoods, less than a mile from Felipe's home. It was not too difficult for Rosalie to slip away next day after the heavy midday meal, when Felipe took off his boots and threw himself on his bed for the siesta now required by all the workers as the increasing heat of May enveloped the inland valleys. When she reached the redwood grove Peter was already there, with his horse tethered to a tree. He took her in his arms without a word and stooped to kiss her: in the passion of that first kiss she realised with a shock that his hands and cheeks were icy cold. Only his mouth was warm.

"But you're frozen!" she whispered. Peter laughed and drew her closer to him until she felt with her whole body his own body's warmth. "There was a heavy fog at Port Romanzov," he told her, and when she looked bewildered, corrected the name to 'Bodega Bay'.

She drew away from him then, as if the Russian name which none of the Spanish used had pointed up the barrier between them, but Peter Gagarin gave her no time to think. He led her to a fallen tree over which wild vines were climbing, spread his coat on the mossy trunk, and made her sit down with his arms around her, caressing her with hands and voice, and telling her how he had loved her at first sight and dared to hope that she loved him too. Rosalie hardly knew what she said to him. It was the first time a man had kissed her on the lips, had released a torrent of new sensations in her body, new emotions in her heart, and she was afraid of herself rather than of him. She was pliant in his arms but not acquiescent, nor would she stay in the redwood clearing longer than half an hour. She would be missed, she said; she would come again tomorrow, but she must go now. Shaken himself, Peter let her go. The words "I love you" were all they needed for a pledge.

Next day he asked her to marry him. She said "Yes!" without coyness and without hesitation. She had counted the cost of what she was about to do, and was ready to face the consequences of her mother's and her brothers' anger. For Carlos Rivera's feelings she had no consideration whatever. She was not his wife, and as Father Quijas came so seldom from San Rafael to Sonoma, their betrothal had not even been blessed by a priest. A broken engagement was not unknown, even among the Spanish aristocracy, and (putting her arms trustingly round Peter's neck) Rosalie was sure he could persuade the Estradas to accept him as her future husband.

What did she mean by 'future', he wanted to know.

That before too long, after he had ridden back with her to the Rancho Estrada, and told her mother and Luis that they loved each other, everything would somehow be arranged, and then they could be married. Thus Rosalie, trying to make her fairy tale come true.

He told her it was impossible. "God knows," he said, "I want to claim you before all the world. I want to take all the responsibility, to convince your family that you will be cherished for the rest of your life – I'd cross swords with Rivera if he wanted satisfaction on the nice point of honour – but, my beautiful darling, there simply is not time. I *must* leave for Sitka as soon as the corvette returns; I *must* cross the Bering Sea before the end of June; I *must* be in St. Petersburg before the middle of October. The future of California depends on it."

"The future of *California*?" She was clever and sharp, he had known that by the way she spoke of Vallejo and the Carrillos at Santa Rosa, but her cleverness was bounded by her own little world, for even her concept of California stopped at the northern frontier. And she had been influenced by the cult of *mañana*, never more powerful than in the splendid pastoral years of the Territory in which she had been born, where there was no sense of urgency, still less of alarm. She had no eyes to see the writing on the wall.

Peter Gagarin saw that he had gone too far. He was clever enough to give her a very simple explanation, without any reference to French and British ambitions in the Pacific, but praising the work of the early Spanish colonists, so worthily carried on by young men like her brothers. "You know better than I do, darling," he flattered her, "that since California came under Mexican rule, things have not been the same. So much land left undeveloped, so many petty rules cramping the merchant ships, so many people dependent on the favour of a Mexican Governor, or an autocrat like your friend Vallejo." All that would be changed, he said, if the Russian presence were stronger in California. And the change could be achieved without delay if the Czar Nicholas Alexandrovich could be persuaded to recognise the Republican government of Mexico. Which so far he had refused to do.

"And you intend to persuade him, Peter?"

"I'm going to try." And seeing her still doubtful, he said, "It means that mine will be the most important mission to St. Petersburg since Rezanov left the Presidio nearly forty years ago."

"How you harp on Rezanov!" she said. "Have you forgotten what happened to Concepcion Argüello?"

"But it wouldn't happen to you, my love!" He turned her downcast face to his, and kissed her. "Don't you remember what you said at the merienda, that Concepcion should have followed her lover to Siberia and beyond? I don't ask you to follow me, darling, I ask you to come with me, so that there will be no parting –"

"No parting!" she whispered. "But Concepcion and Rezanov – they're in songs and ballads, they're a romance! You and I are real –"

"Very real." He tightened his clasp. "Rosalie, you must trust me. Sail with me to Sitka, it isn't a long voyage; and there Madame Etolin will look after you, and the priest will marry us, and we'll drive troika across Russia to my palace in St. Petersburg."

"Will Father Veniaminov marry us?"

"Father Veniaminov!" said Peter in surprise. "What do you know about him?"

"He came to the rancho once when I was small. I hardly remember him, but my father and mother liked him very much. You know he came all the way from Alaska to visit the

Missions in Alta California? He brought gifts from his church to our Mission at Sonoma. Is he at Sitka still?"

"He's on his way back to Alaska, darling, he went to Petersburg to be made a bishop. You mean you'd like him, an Orthodox priest, to marry us?"

"I think it would be marvellous."

Peter Gagarin gave silent thanks, as he kissed her, for an unexpected boon. He knew well enough that to arrive in St. Petersburg with a Catholic wife could put an end to any hope of an audience of the Czar and perhaps even to the favour of the Czarevich. The Heir's betrothed, a Lutheran princess, had embraced the Orthodox faith after much instruction and ceremonial; Princess Peter Gagarina would arrive in the city on the Neva as an Orthodox bride. He blessed the saintly Ivan Veniaminov, and whatever trumpery gifts he had bestowed on the Mission of San Francisco Solano.

He wisely said no more of their marriage plans on that day. Arrogant and self-willed though he was, Peter Gagarin had enough imagination to realise that the thought of an elope-ment, and a tremendous journey far from her home and kindred, might have its terrors for a young girl. He kept fear at bay by caresses, by praise of Rosalie's beauty and her courage, and begged her to think of him and his impatience to return to her, during the next few days.

"But where are you going?" she asked in dismay.

"I must ride to the other farms, darling. To the Kuskov settlement first, and then to the Heiden farm nearer the Slavianka river. I'll try to get back to Port – to Bodega Bay on Tuesday night, and next day we'll be together again."

"Won't you come to Felipe's house and see me there?"

"I don't think I could act a part in front of Felipe, dear. Could you?"

No, she could not. Even to return from that clandestine meeting in the wood, strolling up from the path beside the creek and pretending to be interested in the fig trees, swinging her hat and humming a tune, was acting a part almost too difficult for Rosalie Estrada. She resented Rita's sidelong glances, she read a hidden meaning into Felipe's quiet remark that in the middle of the next week they ought to ride to Sonoma. "Luis wants me to look over your marriage settlement," he said in his heavy-handed way. "Our bride is going to be a very important person." With the classic plea of a headache Rosalie went early to bed.

She changed her mind again and again in the days that followed. What Peter had said about the extension of Russian power in California had impressed a girl who had no sense of nationality, and was learning to admire all things Russian. When she tried to visualise her life in Russia she saw a stately palace on the Moika Quay, full of blue glass chandeliers, pianofortes and lackeys bowing to a young princess.

But in the meadows with Rita, who was glad now to be able to account for every minute of her young mistress's day, she stripped the golden poppies of their petals to tell her fortune. She would, she would not leave everything which had made her life for eighteen years and go off with a stranger. She might, she might not, renounce the dreams not three weeks old, and return dutifully to the Rancho Estrada and marriage with a man who was also a stranger to her. He loves me, he loves me not: she convinced herself on the second day that he did not love her, that his visit to the outlying farms was a subterfuge, that he would sail alone from Fort Ross to Sitka and leave her for ever. She was frantic with love and fear when Wednesday came, and in the redwood clearing she flung herself into the Russian's arms.

Peter Gagarin had not meant, until the last moment, to take her virginity. With a mind which had always ruled his body, a mind divided between his dream of a Russian California and his passion for the Californio girl, he might have been able to control the desire swollen by a few days of absence. But the mind yielded, the control snapped, when Peter felt her absolute surrender, licked from her cheeks the tears of joy which greeted his return. In that secret place beneath the redwoods, on the soft carpet of moss and spring flowers, it was the most natural thing in the world to make Rosalie his own.

In the triumph of his conquest, in his love and gratitude, Peter was for setting her on his horse and walking by his side until they reached the fruit farm, where they would tell Felipe of their marriage plans. It was Rosalie herself (smoothing her dishevelled dress and pinning up her hair) who begged him to let her go home alone. They would *see*, she whispered, they would *know*; Felipe might challenge him to a duel, would certainly send for Luis, or take her straightaway to Sonoma. No, no, the first idea was the right one: the ship to Sitka, the wedding there, the letters begging for forgiveness and understanding. He might go to the edge of the wood with her, but no further; and then – there was tomorrow.

Rita saw and Rita refused to know. The mestiza saw the bruised mouth, the heavy eyes, she watched the body's languour, the voluptuous movements as Rosalie prepared for bed that night, but she refused to admit to herself what these things might mean. Apart from the first afternoon, when she had really been asleep at the hour of the siesta, Rita had been aware of Rosalie's absences, but after long years of subservience to the Estradas she had no way to put her awareness into words. Rita was betrayed, in this crisis, by her double heritage of the Spanish procrastination, the mañana, which she had from her father, and the fatalism she had inherited from her Indian mother. It was not her place to stir up a hornet's nest of suspicion. Especially as the Russian prince was soon to leave California.

Felipe neither saw nor knew. Astute as he was in reading the signs of the times where the American adventurers were concerned, he had no experience of the duplicity of lovers, never having been in love himself. He saw that Rosalie was moody, sometimes laughing hysterically and sometimes sitting at her sewing in a dreaming silence, but he supposed such moods were natural in a girl soon to be married. The attraction between Rosalie and the Russian was too obvious to be ignored, but Luis had dismissed it as a mere flirtation, and in such matters Felipe was willing to defer to Luis.

It was now the middle of May, and very warm. Peter Gagarin wore his brilliant Russian blouses with thin cord breeches and a light sombrero as he rode the triangle between the Klebnikov farm, the harbour he still liked to call Port Romanzov, and the wood where he met Rosalie every afternoon. In the vast empty sunlit land he came and went unobserved to the trysts with his lover, the meetings when desire fed on desire and their consummated love rose every day to a new peak of perfection. There were only three such trysts, after all, for on Saturday he told her that he must ride north to the Czernik farm on the coast, change horses and ride on to Fort Ross. The corvette *Elena* was due there on Sunday.

"Then, only two more days, my darling, and Captain Sagoskin's ship will be back at Bodega Bay, and you and I will set sail for Sitka!"

"Oh Peter!" Rosalie was pale, and there were tiny beads of perspiration round her nostrils and beneath her eyes. "If only we could leave now from Bodega!"

Leaving her alone was the weak point of the plan, and Peter whispered that if he had only known then what he knew now he would never have allowed Sagoskin to sail from Fort Ross without arranging for the *Elena* to put into Bodega on her way north. "But Sagoskin's a good fellow," he assured her. "You said you liked him, when we had lunch aboard the *Elena*. He'll be delighted to do me a favour, I know; and this way we can go straight to Sitka, don't you see?"

Yes, she did see. "But what about Felipe, Peter? How am I to reach the harbour without his knowing?"

"Don't worry about Don Felipe, I'll take care he's out of the way. Six miles to Bodega, darling, and that's all! Bring your woman with you, if you like. You ought to have a maid on the journey, oughtn't you?"

"Rita? She's my mother's maid, not mine. I can't imagine her ever deserting La Señora."

"Try her and see. You'll want to leave a letter for your brother, won't you?"

"I must." Rosalie's green eyes were full of tears, and her sob was her last protest against the fate she had chosen. "Oh Peter! Shall I never see them again – my mother and my brothers?"

He lifted her off her feet then, and swung her to the level of his great height as he boasted, "Of course you will! I'll bring you back in triumph – when I'm the Governor of Russian California!"

It was not empty bravado, as he found later in the day at the farm on the coast road. Czernik, the owner, was an educated and influential man who had held high office in the Russian-American Fur Company, and who had hoped to extend the Company's influence, synonymous in his mind with the Imperial interest, by increasing his farming possessions in Alta California. He had heard rumours of the impending sale, and was as much opposed to it as Peter himself. Peter's plan of a direct appeal to the Czar had his enthusiastic approval, and the two men sat discussing ways and means until the fading of the sunlight on the floor of the business room caused Czernik to get up and look out of the window.

"There's a fog rolling in," he announced. "I wish, Your Highness, that you'd stay here overnight, and ride on to Fort Ross in the morning."

"I might miss my passage to Sitka if I did that. Don't insist, my friend! I know you mean to be kind, but as we've just agreed, this is a matter of life and death."

"Drink a stirrup cup then. A glass of vodka, to keep the fog out of your throat."

They drank to 'Russian California' and the household assembled in the yard to see Prince Peter start. They brought up what was called the best horse in the stable, an ugly skewbald with a tendency to move sideways rather than forward. A groom buckled on Peter's saddle-bags, with his clothing and the reports punctiliously written, just as he had brought them from the Klebnikov farm. He remembered with pleasure the instructions left with Klebnikov, before he took the coast road, about a message to be sent to Felipe Estrada on Tuesday.

There was still sunshine in the farmyard when he waved goodbye. He refused the offer of company, saying the road ran clear to the Slavianka, where the ford was marked, and clearer still once he crossed the dark river. For Peter thought of the next few hours as a chance to be alone, the last before he faced the Rotschevs and their reproaches, a chance to think of the girl who had given him all her love, and of all they would be to one another on the long journey to St. Petersburg.

The skewbald gelding, dancing sideways, took Peter's thoughts off Rosalie, and the fingers of fog stealing in from the ocean made him turn up the collar of his riding coat. The wind was rising, too, and he was chilled to the bone when he dismounted on the cliffs before the descent towards the river to tighten the girths. If this is the best horse in Czernik's stable, he thought, I'm glad he didn't lend me the worst, and his stablemen deserve to be flogged. The poor brute was saddle-sore, and had been jibbing at the heavy Spanish saddle and the weight of the saddlebags. Peter sacrificed a shirt to make pads between the leather and the abraded hide. There was no habitation between the cliff top and the home farm at Fort Ross where he could go to change horses or seek shelter from the fog, now wrapping horse and man in a blanket of grey, but he remembered having seen a ranchería of Miwok Indians on the low ground north of the Slavianka. The Indios were skilled with animals, and could let him have ointment and cloths for the skewbald. Otherwise he and his mount might not see Fort Ross that night.

Coming from the Petaluma river two weeks ago, the track had been clear to the Slavianka. Coming from the cliffs he found himself in heavily wooded country, where the road he had followed was lost in brush and chaparral. The skewbald neighed and stumbled, neighed and tossed its head, so that Peter tightened his grip on the reins and cursed. The blazes on the trees, which Czernik had told him would mark the approach to the ford, were invisible in the shrouding fog. He came out at a foot's pace to cleared ground, checked his horse and listened.

He was on the bank of the Slavianka. He heard the roar of the river in spate, and the ebb and surge of the waters on the unseen sandbar. Even the further shore was hidden, for the river was wide; all he could see was the nearer water, and here and there a driftwood log, or a tree-trunk, borne on to the ocean.

The fog lifted for a moment. He could see the fringe of jagged rocks beyond the bar, and was confident that he had reached the ford. He remembered that the women had ridden across it with no more damage than wet skirts. He remembered Rosalie looking back at him and smiling, with her little foot in that silken stirrup, and he urged the skewbald down the bank and into the water.

Immediately it covered him up to the thighs. He knew that his mount had lost its footing, and was swimming; he lay along its neck and urged it on. The surface of the river shone with a lurid glow, as if the sunset light were trying to pierce the fog, and in that glow he saw a log borne down upon them. He leaned sideways and tried to thrust it aside. But the weight of the timber and the force of the water were too much for him.

His horse was struck on the head, kicked wildly and went down, while Peter, jolted from the saddle, was hit on the temple by the heavy wooden stirrup.

Dazed and stunned as he was, he clung to the leather tapadera with all his might. He and the skewbald were being carried down the river irresistibly, while the roar of the ocean came nearer, and he knew the horse had ceased to swim. It was kicking out, whinnying and choking, and Peter began to choke too as the water rose above his head. He made one last effort to get back in the saddle, but his grasp had weakened, and the horse's hoof was stronger. When the iron shoe crashed on his eyes and nostrils Peter ceased to struggle. Maimed horse and lifeless rider drifted out to the Pacific.

7

The rains in the hills which turned the Slavianka into a torrent brought a freshet of water down the Salmon Creek before daylight in Sunday, and all that day Felipe kept an anxious eye on his irrigation sluices. By Monday he was satisfied that his orchards would not be flooded, and that he could trust his capataz to oversee the spring work for a week. He told Rosalie and Rita to be ready to ride to Sonoma the next day. But on Monday evening the plan had to be changed. A messenger arrived from the Klebnikov farm, begging Don Felipe Estrada to ride there on Tuesday morning to give the farmer his advice. An assessment for land tax, which he didn't understand and didn't mean to pay, had arrived from the Sub-Prefecture.

"Tell Señor Klebnikov I'll be with him before midday," said Felipe, nothing loath to put a spoke however small in the wheel of the Territorial government at Monterey. "Rosalie, we'll have to postpone the ride home for another day. You don't mind, do you?"

"I'm quite happy here," she assured him, and turned away to hide her pleasure in the knowledge that Peter had kept his word. Felipe was 'taken care of' as far as Tuesday went, although there was a moment of alarm when he was ready to start, and suddenly proposed that Rosalie should ride over to the Russian farm with him. "Come on, it's only five miles," he said. "They'll make you very welcome, and it'll be a change for you."

"Honestly, Felipe, Rita and I have a lot of sorting out to do, of our own clothes and yours. And we have a long ride ahead of us tomorrow."

"That's true." But the young man was rather pleased when his sister got on horseback just as she was, in her cotton skirt and camisa, and rode a couple of miles with him on his way to the Russian farm. He thought how pretty she looked as she waved him goodbye, with her black hair falling about her face and her skin glowing from the summer sun, before she started back at a gallop.

Rita, gossiping in the outdoor kitchen with Pepita, heard the flying hoofs and an order called to the stable vaquero. After a little while she went to look for Rosalie. The girl was sitting at the table in the sala, sealing a letter with wax; she blew out the tallow candle as the maid came in.

"Put on your heavy skirt, Rita," she said sharply. "You and I are going for a ride."

"We're going to the Russian farm, after all?"

"We're going to Bodega Bay."

"Rosalie!"

"I'll explain as we go along."

In a matter of minutes, while Rita expostulated, Rosalie was dressed in her own riding clothes, with a silk scarf knotted tightly round her head. She picked up a wallet which she had packed earlier in the morning, and thrust it into one of the saddle-bags the vaquero brought. With one foot on his hand she sprang to the saddle; Rita got up more stiffly from the mounting block.

"I must come too, señorita," said the man.

"You stay where you are."

"Rosalie, your brother –"

"Don't shout, Rita. D'you want the whole rancho to hear what I have to tell you?"

She rode fast towards the redwood grove where she had

kept her trysts with Peter, and there Rosalie drew rein and waited for Rita to come up beside her. The pace had left the mestiza breathless, but still she was the first to speak.

"I know what you have to tell me. You're going to meet the Russian prince."

"Better than that," said Rosalie, "I'm going away with him."

"Going to Fort Ross?"

"Going home with him to Russia."

In Rita's concept of time and space, Rosalie might have said she was going to the moon. She knew Monterey and Sonoma, and the empty valleys stretching between, but for all anyone had ever told her Russia might have lain on the far side of the Sierra Nevada. When she learned that Prince Peter was coming to Bodega by ship, and would take her nursling across the ocean, she burst into tears, and begged the girl to think of her home – her brothers – her poor mother. "Remember the little twin girls who came between Luis and Felipe, and died of fever when they were three years old," she said. "Must La Señora lose her last beloved daughter too?"

"How can I remember my poor little sisters when I never even knew them?" Rosalie retorted. "And I'm not going to die. I'm going to have a marvellous life, and Prince Peter has promised to bring me back some day. Rita, if you don't stop howling I'll leave you at the roadside."

She was quite capable of doing so, for Rita was no horse-woman, but they had entered the fog belt now, and the horses had to be allowed to pick their way along the dirt road until they came out on the cliff above Bodega Bay. The fog blew in from the ocean in ribbons and tendrils, twisting and shifting round the two women as they paused on the cliff top to see what lay below. There was not much of a settlement at Bodega. Two or three wooden dwellings and a watch tower were built on the slopes above the harbour, and nearer the wharf were storehouses, one of which flew the Russian-American Fur Company's flag. Rosalie's face fell. She had been so certain, from what Peter had told her, that the *Elena* would be in harbour, and he himself either watching from the deck or pacing the shingle impatiently. It was a shock to see that there was only one ship in harbour, a whaler flying the Stars and Stripes.

"He isn't here!" said Rita thankfully. "Rosalie, come home! Come home before Don Felipe has time to miss you!"

"I left a letter to tell him where I had gone. We'll ride down to the harbour, Rita; the *Elena* is late, that's all."

There were only a few white men lounging and smoking by the harbour wall, sailors, if Rosalie had known it, from the American whaler she had not been able to identify, and there were a few Indians squatting on the shingle and looking as if they regretted the bargain struck when they sold Bodega to the Russians for three blankets, three pairs of trousers, three hoes, two axes and some beads. Instinctively Rosalie kept away from them all, and dismounted by the storehouses, where there was a hitching rack to which she and Rita tied the horses. There, she made her only appeal to the mestiza.

"I'm going on a very long journey, Rita. Prince Peter says he'll gladly take you with us if you're prepared to come."

"I can't leave my mistress, Rosalie. If *you* leave her, La Señora will need me more than ever. But don't do it, querida, don't go away! Don't trust yourself to a man who hasn't even kept his promise to meet you here!"

Rosalie flushed angrily. "The corvette is late, I tell you, and the Russian agent will know why." She turned to the wooden building over which the flag of the Fur Company was flying. Before she reached it the door was flung open, and a girl of about her own age appeared on the step.

"Now is that clear, Mr. Nikolai?" she said over her shoulder. "Skipper Putnam wants the water casks filled by three o'clock, and he'll send up for the provisions before then. Better put some of your own hands to nailing up the casks –"

Of this exhortation, spoken in a high, self-confident voice with a decided 'down-East' twang, Rosalie Estrada understood perhaps one word in two. She was listening to the *lingua franca* of the American whalers which made the Alaska run between April and October, a mixture of English, Spanish, Russian and Aleut which sounded coarse on the lips of the crews of the 'hell-ships', as the whalers were called in the Far North, and coarser still from a girl. This girl wore a dark-brown dress with white muslin at the neck and wrists, and a pale-blue bonnet bought in a New England village from which locks of straight sandy hair escaped. She looked at Rosalie with interest and pleasure.

"Hallo!" she said. "Do you speak English? *Habla Usted español?* I'm Content Putnam, and that's my father's ship, the *Washington.*"

"It is a pleasure, señorita," said Rosalie. "Is it possible to speak to Señor Nikolai?"

"Hey there, Mr. Nikolai!" shouted Miss Putnam, "Come out from behind your desk and make your bow. You've got a visitor." The Russian agent was already at the open door.

"At your service, madam –"

"I am Rosalie Estrada, Señor Nikolai. I think you know my brother Felipe –"

"Very well indeed. Did Don Felipe escort you here this morning?"

"He was sent for by Señor Klebnikov. I rode over with my maid, because I – I am expecting a messenger, a message, by the corvette *Elena.* Captain Sagoskin has – has the matter in hand." The stammered words broke off at the surprise in the Russian agent's face.

"The *Elena* was due to leave Fort Ross today for Sitka," he said.

"That's right," said Content Putnam, "we spoke Captain Sagoskin on Friday morning, off Point Reyes." There was curiosity now, as well as interest, in her sharp little face. Her eyes were grey, with sandy lashes.

"I think Captain Sagoskin expected to call here before sailing north," said Rosalie.

Nikolai looked from one young lady to the other, and then at the half-breed servant, standing tense and frightened in the background. "I think there must be some mistake," he said. "Doña Rosalie, will you do me the honour of visiting my home while we wait for your messenger? My wife will be happy to offer you some refreshments – and Miss Putnam too, of course! See, my house is no distance away –"

They looked where he pointed at the wooden houses with the gingerbread ornamentation on the hillside. At that moment a flag was raised in signal from the watch tower and a voice called out "Sail ho!"

The harbour of Bodega was almost landlocked, being protected from the Pacific by a curved peninsula and from the bay by a narrow half-moon of land. It was not until the vessel signalled entered harbour by a narrow strait to the south that the Russian agent lowered his spy-glass. "It's not the corvette," he said. "It's the schooner, the *Young Julia*. And the flag –" he stopped in response to Content Putnam's sudden clutch at his wrist. The skipper's daughter knew, as Rosalie Estrada did not, the significance of the Russian-American Fur Company's flag, which the schooner was flying at half mast.

"I'm afraid there may be some bad news, young ladies," said Nikolai. "Please wait here while I go and find out. I wish there were some way to make you comfortable!" There was only one comfortable chair, his own, which his clerk pulled out from behind the desk, one wooden chair for business callers, and the clerk's high stool. The young man followed his master, while the two girls and Rita remained standing, gazing out of the one small window as the schooner rounded the point and glided slowly to her mooring place.

"There's my father!" said Content, handing Rosalie the spy-glass. "There, on the deck of the *Washington*. He's hailing the *Young Julia*." The short and sturdy figure of the Yankee skipper was armed with a speaking trumpet; in the office nothing distinct could be heard. Men were shouting; that was all they knew.

"Oh, what can have happened?" fretted Rosalie. "Why can't we go down and find out? That ship came from Fort Ross, didn't she?"

"Yes, she did." Content put a hand on her arm. "But let's wait here till Mr. Nikolai comes back."

"Why?"

"Because I'm afraid there may be bad news of your – messenger."

"Oh *no!*"

Content turned to the mestiza, who was pressed against the door and wringing her hands, and said in her atrocious Spanish, "Don't just stand there whimpering! Can't you see your young lady's feeling faint? Go and get her some water in that glass – there, just under your nose! There's a spring on the hill beneath the watch tower. Hurry!"

When they were alone she put her arm round Rosalie's shoulders. "Look, my dear!" she said urgently, "whatever the matter is, don't give in. Don't let those foreigners see you cry!" Rosalie, bewildered by the word *estranejeros*, was on the verge of tears. "Why doesn't that damned Russki come back?"

The agent was making his way up from the harbour, with the shingle slipping beneath his feet. He had shaken off the captain of the little schooner, who was telling his story as best he could to Skipper Putnam, and he was not aware that Rita, with an empty glass in her hand, was clambering up the rocky road to where she had seen two horsemen silhouetted for a moment against the enveloping fog on the cliffs. He opened the door of his own office very quietly.

"Señor!" said Rosalie Estrada instantly, "has anything happened to Captain Sagoskin?"

He had suspected it was Sagoskin she had come to meet, now he was sure.

"No, no, my dear young lady, put your mind at rest," he said. "The schooner was ordered here by the commandant of Fort Ross, to bring me some terrible news. His cousin, his wife's cousin rather, Prince Peter Gagarin, has been the victim of a tragic accident. He is dead."

"It isn't true."

"Alas, it is true, Doña Rosalie. He was drowned in the Slavianka river probably three nights ago; the Indians found his body, horribly mutilated, cast up against the rocks on Sunday morning."

The crowded room tilted round Rosalie. She fell back against the tall wooden desk, struck her head, became aware that she was saved from crashing to the ground by a young arm, laid her cheek against a girl's shoulder, and fell fathoms deep into darkness.

Out on the hill, Rita was scrambling towards the horsemen. She was sure of their identity now. One was Don Felipe, whom she supposed to be at the Russian farm, and the other was Pedro, one of the Mexican vaqueros from the Rancho Estrada. Felipe flung himself off his horse at the sight of her.

"Have they gone?" was all he said, and at the look on his face Rita shrank away. "She is here – she is safe," she said. "I think – the man has left her."

Felipe seized her upper arm and flung her to the ground.
"You treacherous bitch, you connived at this!" he said. There
was blood on Rita's brown hand where the glass had broken.

"It's false, Don Felipe! I begged her not to go!"

"Where is she?"

"With another Russian, and a foreign woman. There."

"Get on your horse. Pedro, ride back with Rita to my
rancho and wait for me."

Pedro had to help the woman to mount. She sucked the
blood from her hand and spat it out, and the Mexican saw the
hate in the black Indian eyes.

"For God's sake, what's going on?" he asked, and she
seemed to become aware that he was there.

"You tell me, Pedro. Is anything wrong at the rancho? Is my
mistress ill?"

"La Señora and Don Luis had a quarrel last night, the
houseboys said. I was roused at midnight and ordered to carry
a letter to Don Felipe. I met him on the way, and that's all I
know. Where's Doña Rosalie?"

Rosalie was sitting up in the big chair. She was aware of
Content holding brandy to her lips and of the Russian agent
fanning her with a sheet of office paper. She heard Felipe's
voice mingling with the other voices above her head. Dead,
the voices said. Drowned, an accident in the fog. Dead, tragic,
he was our guest last week, we were his guests two weeks ago.
Dead, and what a loss to Russia. My wife will be grieved, my
mother will be distressed, my father will be sorry because he is
dead.

"He can't be dead!" she said violently, and Felipe took her
hands. "Rosalie, pull yourself together," he begged. "You've
had a bad shock, so have we all. I want you to come home with
me now and rest –"

"I can't rest until the ship comes in," she said. "I promised
to wait for the *Elena.*"

Felipe straightened up. "My sister is not herself," he said.
"The best thing I can do is take her home quickly."

"If she's fit to ride," said Content Putnam.

"Señorita –"

"This young lady is Captain Putnam's daughter, Don
Felipe. I think you know her father," said the Russian.

Felipe bowed. "I have the honour," he said. "May I ask both of you, as a great personal favour, to say nothing of my sister's . . . distress, outside this office?"

"You have my word for that," said Nikolai.

"The *Washington* will be in the whaling grounds off Alaska for the whole summer," said Content. "D'you think I'm likely to start gossiping with the Eskimos?"

"You're sailing with your father?"

"He promised I should sail with him when I was seventeen. Now I am."

In that quick exchange of sentences they had looked at each other with understanding, and then Felipe, with a nod, turned back to his sister. "Are you ready?" he asked. She was trying, as Nikolai held the door open, to retie the knot in her headscarf, which Content had loosened.

A group of men, including the crew of the *Young Julia*, stood near the office as if unwilling to intrude. The agent gave one of them a sharp order to bring up Don Felipe's horses.

"I'd like to go with you, Señor Estrada," said Content Putnam. "Your sister needs help."

"She'll be well taken care of. And some day I hope to thank you, señorita." The look of recognition passed again between them, and Content released her hold on Rosalie. "Can you mount?" she said.

"I'll put her up," said Felipe, and in a different tone to his sister, "Don't make a bigger fool of yourself than you have already!" She shuddered, and let him lift her to the saddle. They rode away together through the fog.

Some time later, when they were back at the fruit rancho and Rosalie's frozen silence had changed to weeping, Rita came out of the shabby bedroom to say she had given the girl a drink to make her sleep.

"A drugged drink?"

"A drink made from herbs," she answered evasively. "The sleep may be very heavy. She will not be fit for a long ride tomorrow."

"See that she's fit by Thursday, then. We're needed at Sonoma. And now get back to her."

The sun was shining and there was silence in the yard. Felipe felt alone and helpless. He walked to the little brazier where

Pepita made tortillas and saw fire in the wood ashes. He took from his vest the foolish letter Rosalie had left behind and flung it on the embers. "I'm going with Peter to Sitka to be married . . ." the words leaped out at him as the flames caught. He had no need to read Luis's letter again, for he knew the words by heart:

"This evening my mother told me she had written to Carlos Rivera to say the marriage could take place in June. Warn Rosalie before you start for home."

Rosalie kept her bed next day, weeping and refusing food, and by evening Felipe was scared and angry enough to tell her that she must make an effort next morning to start back to Sonoma, because Carlos Rivera would soon be coming to claim his promised bride. For his sake, and for all their sakes, she must tell no one of her reckless plan of eloping with a stranger. "I shall tell Luis," he concluded, "but mother must never know."

"We loved each other, Felipe. We were going to be married at Sitka."

"You little fool, he would have abandoned you at Sitka," said her brother harshly. "You must have been meeting him without my knowledge before things came to this. No man respects a girl who meets him secretly –"

"We loved each other." The feeble repetition annoyed Felipe so much that he said "You'd better hear what Luis has to say," and began to read the letter aloud:

Mother waited several days after I got home before she told me that she sent old Guzman with a message to Rivera while we were all away. She knew I would be angry because it was contrary to my wishes and advice. She said she decided to hurry on the marriage for Rosalie's own protection. She had obviously been attracted to the Russian prince, and next month there might be a flirtation with a Mexican officer, the month after with an American from a Boston ship. A girl of Rosalie's temperament was better off in her husband's care –

"Oh, stop!"

"That's what your own mother thinks of you," said Felipe

brutally. "A girl who can't be trusted. By God, you've proved that, haven't you? If mother had been wise she would never have allowed you to go off with the Russians but kept you at home, and that's where you're going tomorrow. I can't wait to get you out of my care and out of my house."

★   ★   ★

"Gracious, child! If this is how you look after a holiday, you'd have done much better to stay at home!"

"I'll be all right tomorrow, mother."

"You came too far in one day. Why didn't you stay the night with the Vallejos at Petaluma?"

"They invited us, mother, when we changed horses there. But we were both anxious to get home," said Felipe.

He had brought Rosalie home by all the back trails he knew, with Pedro and Rita following through the deep woods, and they were exhausted.

"Felipe, bed is the place for you too," said his mother.

"I'll have a glass of wine with Luis first."

By the next morning the brothers had entered into a conspiracy of silence, which gradually extended in mystery and confusion to the whole population of the Rancho Estrada. Pedro had been so effectively silenced that the men in the bunk house knew nothing of what had gone on at Bodega, while Rita would not for a world have disturbed the complacency of La Señora. In a few days Luis and Felipe left for Yerba Buena, to arrange the financing of the second portion of Rosalie's dowry with the American agent Nathan Spear, and there they were joined at the tavern by Don Carlos Rivera, supported by his cousin from Santa Clara. The young man made a clean breast of his gambling debts and promised, for cash down, to abstain from high play in future: the cousin, Don Jaime Rivera, pocketed most of the cash against the IOUs he held. It was an unsatisfactory meeting, but it ended with the Riveras returning to the rancho with the Estradas, where Don Carlos "at long last!" he said, "kissed the hands and feet of his beautiful betrothed."

It was only a figure of speech, a Spanish flourish, for Rosalie gave him her cheek to kiss and thanked him for the gift of his mother's earrings, which she was wearing. This time his gift was a splendid one, a rope of matched pearls from Loreto, where the Yaqui Indians had been pearl divers long before the Spanish came. She promised to wear the necklace on their wedding day.

Don Carlos was twenty-six, a year older than Luis but looking younger because he was not as tall, and slightly built, with curling black hair like a boy's. He appeared to advantage in a suit of olive-green velvet, the slashed trousers laced with silver thread. He was garrulous, and so was his cousin, a fine-looking man of forty; they both talked incessantly at the ceremonial dinner presided over by Doña Maria, and Felipe in his cynical way thought they were excited because the money question was as good as settled. It had a bearing on the wedding date, for the Boston agents refused to complete their deal with Luis before the delivery of that season's hides, and Doña Maria herself had begun to realise that June was too soon for the celebration of her only daughter's marriage. The first week in July was agreed upon for a fiesta which would last at least three days.

When the cousins had ridden away next morning, with many compliments and much showing off of horsemanship and waving of sombreros, Luis drew Rosalie into the sala while their mother was busy elsewhere, and said,

"Do you really think you can be happy with this man?"

"Does it matter?"

"It matters a great deal."

"Then what if I say no?"

"Then . . . you might pay a visit to our kinfolk in Monterey, while I do my best to wind up the whole business. But you seemed to accept the idea of a wedding in July: were you sincere?"

"July or January, what does it matter to me now? As long as the payment of my dowry is settled to suit you it can be next week for all I care."

"The marriage settlements were arranged by my father, not by me."

"So was the marriage! Papa chose Don Carlos not for himself but for his ancestors who were grandees of Spain. I wonder what he would have said to a Russian prince whose family was older than the Czar's."

Staring at her proud and bitter face Luis could only say, "I'm sorry, Rosalie, so very sorry, that you should have had this great unhappiness. I wish Prince Peter had lived, but as for marrying him – it would never have done, my dear, and in time you'll see that, and come to forget him. Only, if you want to break it off with Rivera, tell me now."

"Thank you, Luis, I know you mean to be kind. But why didn't you break it off, as you call it, when mother told you she had sent for Don Carlos?"

"Because I didn't know then how far things had gone between you and Prince Peter."

"How *far*?"

"I mean that you were actually planning an elopement."

"Luis, do you realise that only two weeks ago Peter was with me? That we were talking about our wedding at Sitka and our journey to St. Petersburg? And now all you can say is that some day I'll forget him. Don't ask me to forget. Don't ask me ever to forgive the people who murdered him."

"Rosalie! He wasn't murdered! He drowned – it was an accident –"

"Ah, that's what they want you to think," she answered cunningly. "That's what Señor Nikolai told me, of course he was on their side. The Rotschevs planned it all. The Rotschevs and that man Czernik, who said he was the last man to see Peter alive. He was killed at the Czernik farm only a few hours after he left me."

"He was drowned in the Slavianka. The Indians who found his body testified to that."

"They were paid to testify. Peter was killed at the farm, shot and stabbed, *mutilated*, that's what Nikolai said, so that he could never reach the Czar and stop their wicked plot. So that he could never be the Governor of Russian California."

8

The distance between the ranchos was so great, and the Russian community so isolated, that weeks passed before the news of Peter Gagarin's death reached Sonoma. It was eventually carried to General Vallejo by his tenant Robert Cord, the mountain man turned farmer and secret agent, and by that time the Autocrat of Sonoma was more interested in a live Frenchman than a dead Russian. This was Monsieur Duflot de Mofras, whom Peter had met in San Pedro, and who was now journeying through the Territory in search of material for a travel book. He had met everyone of consequence in Monterey and Yerba Buena, where he had amused the American traders by standing on the shore, waving his arms and shouting about the 'potential' of the vast empty bay. He played the part of the picturesque and exuberant Frenchman to perfection.

General Vallejo had a shrewd idea that the travel diary, or whatever Duflot claimed to be writing, was in reality a detailed account of Alta California, political, geographical and ethnic, to be completed when the young man returned to the French Embassy in Mexico, and then presented to the government at Paris as the guide for a French take-over of the Territory. He was convinced of this when Monsieur Duflot paid his respects to the General Commanding the Northern Frontier at Sonoma in early June. Under the comic exaggerations, the assumed naïveté of the French tourist, Duflot had a cold and calculating brain. Vallejo was amused by him, and gave a dinner in his honour at the Casa Grande. The guests were all men, among them Luis Estrada, who enjoyed himself for the first time since the ill-fated fiesta at Fort Ross. He was beginning to hope that his sister was forgetting Fort Ross. She seemed much calmer and more like her old self.

Rosalie had not forgotten, and never would, but at eighteen she was too young to show the ravages of shock and despair as an older woman would have done. Her face was still a pretty child's face, and in the mornings which followed the long nights of weeping her eyes were as clear and green as the long Pacific rollers which broke on the strand at Bodega Bay. It was not apparent to her mother and brother that Rosalie's gaze was no longer candid but the dissembling look she had learned from Peter.

Rita recognised it, but Rita alone of the household knew about the nights when not even the thickness of the adobe walls could muffle the sound of Rosalie's sobs. Crouching in the patio, she scratched at the girl's door a score of times, begging admission which was always refused. By day Rosalie accepted the maid's services as before, submitted to being dressed and undressed, helped to bathe and to wash her hair, but the nights were hers alone, to weep for Peter, to indulge her hatred of those she thought of as his murderers. Some day, she vowed, she would bring them to justice – when she was a married woman and the mistress of a rancho she would go to Monterey and kneel to Governor Alvarado, demanding vengeance for the man who, as the Russian Governor of California, had planned to sit in Alvarado's place.

In a totally perverse way, she was beginning to tolerate the idea of her marriage. It was no longer an outrage to think of sharing Carlos Rivera's bed, for that bed would be in another place, a different home, where she could never picture the tall form of her first lover. At the Rancho Estrada everything spoke of Peter. Here they had lived for a few days under the same roof, here his blue eyes had met hers across the dinner table, here he had listened to her singing, from that gate they had ridden away together to the fiesta at Fort Ross. The sight of the palomino she had ridden that day, like the sight of her beribboned guitar on the wall, was a wound to the heart of Rosalie Estrada.

In June Don Carlos made another appearance at the Rancho Estrada. He had hired a longboat from Don Antonio Richardson, the English holder of the Sausalito grant, and with his own men at the oars had crossed the bays to the landing stage on the Sonoma Creek. This time he came empty-handed, for Doña Maria, a traditionalist in most respects, had never favoured the old custom of a bridegroom's providing most of his bride's trousseau. She thought it was indelicate for a young man to go aboard one of the French merchantmen which visited the bay from time to time to finger the transparent lawns and silks of nightdresses and petticoats, compare the prices, and then with a knowing smile to present his purchases to his bride. So the vaqueros had only to carry down to the embarcadero the boxes and bales containing Rosalie's belongings and household linen, which had been ready for more than half a year. Don Carlos did his chattering best to make himself agreeable. In spite of his noble descent and the Spanish grant by which he held his rancho he was a townsman at heart and an inveterate gossip. Some of his descriptions of his own relatives who would attend the wedding were malicious and entertaining, and made Rosalie laugh.

The guests were the great problem. Feeding them through a three-day fiesta would be easy, but where were they to sleep? If every possible work room were emptied of tools and implements and arranged as a bedroom, only half the expected company could be accommodated at the rancho. Doña Maria was disappointed that Don Mariano Estrada, the head of her husband's family, was too old to face the journey from Monterey, but she would not hear of curtailing the guest list for the first wedding at the Rancho Estrada. The difficulty was resolved by that prolific and unobtrusive lady, Doña Francisca Benicia Vallejo, who offered the hospitality of the Casa Grande at Sonoma to the bridegroom and his entourage.

"Now Vallejo will try to run the whole fiesta," said Luis. "He'll probably suggest taking the place of Rosalie's godfather, since poor Luis Argüello is dead."

"I'm not afraid of that," said Rosalie, "I have two brothers to protect me."

She swept him a little ironical curtsy, which made her mother frown. "You may thank God you have your brothers, child," she said. "General Vallejo will not presume to take your father's place, even though we have to rely on him for so much – this gracious hospitality, and bringing Father Quijas here to perform the marriage ceremony. It would never have done for an Estrada to be married by one of those Mexican missionary priests from Zacatecas."

The priest, who enjoyed good living, was suffering from a digestive complaint, and it was not until three days before the wedding that Father Quijas reappeared, riding from San Rafael on one of Vallejo's horses, with Vallejo's troopers as his bodyguard. He spent the night at the Casa Grande, and early next morning rang the bell of the little church to call his flock to prayer. Some of the former neophytes among the dispossessed Indians had been sitting on the step, wrapped in blankets, since before dawn.

Father Quijas listened in the confessional to many Indian and Mexican voices through two long days at Sonoma. It was near the end of the second day when he heard a woman's voice speak in the purest Castilian. He knew at once that his penitent was Rosalie Estrada. The confession she had to make was one he had heard many times before, but on the lips of the girl whose marriage vows he was to hear next day it was a special sorrow for a priest who was worldly-wise as well as pious. Before he gave Rosalie absolution he laid a heavy penance of prayer upon her, and bade her go on pilgrimage to the shrine of the Virgin of Guadalupe in the Contra Costa country.

Rosalie rode home at a furious pace, so that Pedro and Bernardo, the two vaqueros ordered to escort her, had to ride hard to keep up with their young lady. Her heart was in a turmoil of rebellion. Whatever comfort she had expected from her confessor had been eclipsed by a sense of degradation in having to make an Act of Contrition for the sin of loving Peter Gagarin. She felt herself still to be so completely his that if there had been any place in which she could have taken refuge in the whole of Alta California she would have set out for that place that night. But there was nowhere: who would take her in? Could she travel the one hundred and fifty miles to Monterey and throw herself on the mercy of her Estrada kin? Could she even ride fourteen miles to the Petaluma river and beg shelter from Doña Francisca Vallejo, with a baby in her arms and four or five children clinging to her skirts? The thought of the river made her think of the Cord cabin in the redwoods, and she had a sudden fancy that the two Americans might stand her friends. But flight would mean a scandal, and a public scandal was what she had been trying to avoid for more than two months past. Felipe was already at the rancho, and he was quite clever enough to guess where she had gone. She urged her horse ahead of the vaqueros. There was no escape for Rosalie Estrada. The guests were gathering for her wedding, and Don Jaime Rivera, Carlos's most distinguished relative, was already established with his wife in the 'great chamber' once occupied by Princess Helen and her husband. She saw lights in several of the guest rooms as she dismounted at the gate, and walked across the yard which had been swept and raked and made ready for her wedding ball. The thought of it brought the first access of shame, the first realisation that she was about to do a great wrong to Carlos Rivera. Only courage carried her into the patio, and when she reached her bedroom door she fainted.

When she came back to her senses her camisa was open at the neck, her skirt unfastened, and Rita was holding a wet cloth to her brow.

"My hair!" she said weakly. "It's soaking!"

"Don't try to sit up yet. What happened to you?"

"I rode home too fast, that's all."

"*You?*"

"Have they gone in to dinner yet?"

"No, but La Señora was asking for you."

"She knew where I was going." Rosalie put her feet to the ground; the dizziness had gone. "Quick, Rita, help me to dress. I can't keep the Riveras waiting."

Rita was deft and speedy. The pale-green satin bodice and skirt were on, with the matching sash, the heavy gold bracelet and the antique earrings. Rosalie pinched her cheeks to bring the colour back.

"What if you have a child?" said Rita from the shadows.

"If I have —" Rosalie paused for a heart-beat, and laughed an artificial laugh. "Aren't you anticipating? I'm sure Don Carlos will expect an heir some day, but let's not plan for the christening before we hold the wedding!"

"I don't mean his child. I mean the Russian's child."

"That's quite impossible."

"Is it? Rosalie, it's eight weeks since we came back from Bodega —"

"I won't listen to you."

"You had better listen. Because I may be the only person who can help you now."

"What sort of help could *you* give me?"

The mestiza came close to Rosalie and whispered a few words in her ear. The girl pushed her away in horror.

"Never!" she gasped. "It's a mortal sin!"

"It's your life that counts, querida. But there's still time, there's just time, for something else."

"What do you mean, you crazy woman?"

"I can help you make Don Carlos think the child is his."

★   ★   ★

95

At the beginning of July, when the Indian calendar marked the Time of Heat, the green hills which sheltered the Sonoma valley had turned to golden brown. The early mornings were still cool, and on Rosalie's wedding day the Indian cooks and kitchen maids were at work soon after dawn, completing the preparations for the marriage feast. Everybody but the bride was in a fever of activity. Rosalie was very quiet. She submitted to being dressed by her mother alone, in the white satin skirt and bodice, the white silk rebozo and the pearls from Loreto. Her hair had been lightly curled into the conventional locks on each cheek, and then in a knot, secured with the tall ivory comb, a family heirloom, over which was draped the white lace mantilla her mother had worn as a bride.

"You look beautiful, Rosalie," said Doña Maria emotionally. "Your father would have been proud of you today. Now don't start crying and spoil your dress!" But Rosalie's eyes were dry. It was her mother who wiped away the tears as she walked with her daughter to the gate. All the guests who had slept at the rancho were already mounted, all the friendly faces smiling and all the friendly voices saying "Beautiful!" as Felipe Estrada came forward and took his sister's hand.

It was the custom for a Spanish bride to ride to church on the same horse as her godfather, the lady in front and the gentleman behind her on the pillion of fine leather, half-moon shaped and lined with sheepskin. General Vallejo had had the tact not to offer himself as surrogate godfather for the dead Luis Argüello, and Rosalie had asked Felipe to carry her to church. "You deserve it," was her enigmatic explanation, and he had not dared to ask her what she meant. It was safer to tell her she looked lovely, as he lifted her to the saddle, and slid her foot in the white satin slipper into the stirrup, which that day was made of white satin too.

He and she were mounted on Felipe's favourite horse, a red roan, and as they took the road to Sonoma he was reminded, much against his will, of their ride back to the fruit rancho from Bodega Bay after she heard the news of Prince Peter's death. He wondered if Rosalie were thinking of that day too, when he felt the deep sigh which shook her body as they approached the pueblo and saw the crowd of guests assembled in the plaza. But she said nothing, and even her greeting to the bridegroom was drowned in the noise of the solitary cannon, fired, by Vallejo's orders, at the moment of the bride's arrival.

Don Carlos rode out to meet them, with Luis Estrada by his side, bowing low over his saddle as he kissed Rosalie's hand. He was smiling and self-confident in a suit of indigo velvet with a sash of salmon pink and spurs inlaid with gold, as handsome a bridegroom as Rosalie was a beautiful bride. The wedding chimes were rung on the bell which had been given to the old Mission by the friendly Russian priest, and the Mexican soldiers formed a guard of honour as Carlos led Rosalie into the tiny chapel. It was so small that only relatives of the happy couple could be admitted, no exception being made even for General Vallejo and his wife, while all the others, in their brilliant garments, waited in the sunny plaza with what appeared to be the entire population of Sonoma.

The chapel of San Francisco Solano was dark, with the daylight coming in through narrow windows. The walls were painted with primitive Stations of the Cross. Rosalie's father was buried beneath the flagstones in front of the sanctuary, one step from the altar rail where she knelt with Carlos as Father Quijas celebrated their wedding mass. As the gold silk sash of wedlock was wound round both their necks, she knew that in the sight of God and man she was bound to him for ever.

When the newly married pair came out of the chapel hand in hand, there was such a surge forward by many of the guests to embrace them, such a hasty mounting of their horses by the others, that a cloud of dust rose from the plaza, and the Mexican troopers had to clear a space for one of the Rivera vaqueros to lead forward the beautiful white mare which was the bridegroom's traditional gift to the bride. The reins were made of white leather, and rosettes of white satin had been arranged to hold bunches of real white roses to the harness. The pillion on which Carlos took his place behind Rosalie was white too, and heavily stitched with a pattern of gold thread. Their friends fell in behind them, but as the singing and cheering began, punctuated by rifle shots fired by the excitable young men, some of the livelier spirits rode out ahead of the bridal couple, or jostled for place to ride alongside. To Rosalie, stunned by the marriage vows and the mass which followed, it seemed as if the man riding so easily on the pillion never stopped talking, calling back to the friends who shouted their congratulations, even – once or twice – joining in the singing, until they reached the gate of the Rancho Estrada, where Doña Maria was tremulously waiting to greet them. Apart from the compliments when they first met in the plaza, and the exchange of vows, he had hardly spoken to his bride at all. But when he lifted her down, and in the moment of time before he led her to her mother, Carlos Rivera held her in his arms, pressed close to his body, and said in a voice unlike his own:

"Will you try to love me, Rosalie?"

When Doña Maria gave them both her blessing, and welcomed Carlos as a son, the whole cavalcade of guests was upon them, kissing, praising, wishing them well; the vaqueros were leading away the horses, and old Benito and his helpers were offering the first glasses of wine. The Indian labourers, on holiday, had brought their wives and children from the ranchería to see their young lady in her bridal dress, and were given great baskets of food and sweetmeats to hold their fiesta in their own way. Four of the vaqueros, headed by Pedro, strummed their guitars as the guests slowly found their places at the long trestle tables in the yard, made by the rancho's workmen and covered with fine linen strewn with flowers.

It was the custom for the bride to be seated between her fathers temporal and spiritual, and Luis, of course, deputised for his dead father. Rosalie was glad to have Father Quijas on her other side, with his thick body interposed between herself and the man who had so strangely asked her to try to love him. It was also the custom for the priest who performed the marriage ceremony to preside at the feast, and in this role Father Quijas always excelled. Today, before he proposed the toast of the happy couple, he made graceful allusion to their parents, pioneers of the northern frontier, and worthy descendants of those who left Europe to bring Christianity and civilisation to New Spain. This was well received by the guests who sat at the flower-strewn tables, the Noes, Bernals, Miramontes, Haros, with the Castros and the Peraltas from the Contra Costa, all representatives of the Spanish presence in Alta California. They laughed and applauded the padre's quips and jokes. It was hard for Rosalie to smile and play with her fan when she remembered his solemn tones of yesterday in the confessional, and the penance which he had laid on the young woman whose virtues he was now extolling to the skies.

General Vallejo proposed the health of Doña Maria, their gracious hostess, and slipping naturally into the role of master of ceremonies, called for music and song from the guitarists. More wine was poured, and soon the whole company was filled with the spirit of fiesta. Don Carlos, addressing his bride for the first time, asked her if she was ready for the wedding dance.

She tried to smile. "I think some of the guests would rather have a siesta."

"No one would want to sleep who could watch you dance," he said gallantly, and rising with a signal to the musicians he held out his hand to Rosalie.

The guests got up too and gathered in a circle to watch the wedding dance, while the servants began to clear the tables. The young men and girls were waiting for this moment, which meant that dancing among themselves could soon begin.

Don Carlos Rivera was an excellent dancer. Slight and supple, he was at his best in the dance which symbolises a man's courtship, as he advances and retires, turns and twirls round his almost passive lady. His dark eyes were fixed on Rosalie as she performed her graceful side steps to the music of the guitars. The dance ended to the "Olés" of the spectators, and a shower of money fell round the feet of the bridal pair.

It was another established custom, only meant to stand for good wishes for a prosperous married life, but the chink of the silver dollars roused Rosalie from the state of shock in which she had existed since Rita made her realise that she might have a child. One of the Mexican coins struck her satin skirt and left a little speck of dust. It reminded her that her marriage was a financial transaction, a contract from which – as had been explained to her – both sides stood to benefit; and in her revulsion she came very near stooping to the dust and gathering up a handful of money to fling in the faces of her friends. She let the dollars lie, of course, they would be picked up and distributed among the servants; and she curtsied and smiled prettily at the company as her mother came and took her hand.

"Rosalie, you must rest now. Come into the house, and you

can dance to your heart's content when the ball begins."

Only the older ladies had a real siesta. There was too much excitement in the air for sleep, and the younger girls preferred chattering under the cottonwoods by the creek to sitting in the hot sala with their elders. The men passed the time in shooting at a target, some using rifles, and Don Carlos proving to be the best pistol shot. Luis thought he was handling himself very well, certainly better than the Peralta bridegroom of April, who had shown temper at the continued banter among the young men taking full advantage of the convention that the newly married couple should have no opportunity of being alone until the third night after the wedding. Carlos's self-confidence and talent for light chatter made him impervious to the teasing, and the only time he resisted was when the wedding ball began at sunset, and a handsome young de la Guerra claimed a kinsman's right to the first waltz with Rosalie.

Carlos was clever enough to ignore the impudent young-ster, and with a calm "Come, Rosalie!" led her out to the sound of the guitars. It was the first time she had danced with a man's arms around her since the last night at Fort Ross, when she waltzed with Peter Gagarin. With her hand on her hus-band's slight shoulder, with his eager face so close to her own (for he was very little taller than she was) Rosalie was faint with desire for Peter, for his great height above her, his strong hand in hers, and the silence which had enclosed them in a world of their own and turned the waltz into an act of love.

Carlos was as garrulous in the dance as on the way back from Sonoma, although Rosalie had no idea what he said, and when the waltz was over he surrendered her, with a light kiss on her hand, to General Vallejo, resplendent in his uniform, who claimed his official right to lead out La Favorita of Sonoma for the next dance in the baile. The sunset faded and the lovely warmth of the valley brought out the scent of flowers as the dew began to fall, when the torches were lighted a new group of guitarists replaced the first, and the dance went on. It was broken for an hour by a sumptuous supper, at which the wine flowed freely. Don Carlos was on his feet for the last waltz, long after the guests staying at the Casa Grande had made their way back to Sonoma, and he was no more fuddled than a bridegroom had a right to be when his new brothers-in-law took him off to Felipe's room. Rosalie, exhausted, slept in her mother's bed.

After a late start, the second day was like the first. There was dancing before noon and horse-racing after the midday meal, when some of the older men played cards in the sala. Luis, watching shrewdly, saw that Carlos refused every invitation to play, nor did he bet on the fall of the cards or the speed of the horses. "It may work out all right," thought Luis. "He'll pull himself together, if she's kind to him, and he'll take her mind off that damned Russian." He began to hope, as he watched his sister waltzing that night with her husband, that she was already starting to be kind to him.

On the third and last afternoon of the fiesta they held the *cascarón* ball. The cascarónes were blown hens' eggs filled with scent or scented scraps of gilt paper, which the women had been preparing for weeks, and the dancers tried to keep their supplies hidden until the right moment came for breaking them over the heads of their friends. The older spectators, clapping hands in time to the music of galops and quadrilles, were adroit in trapping the young dancers, and the Commandant of the Northern Frontier scored several tactical successes over the youthful caballeros. By sunset the courtyard had a flooring of gilt paper, and Luis Estrada seemed to walk down a golden path as he went to his sister and whispered,

"The horses are at the gate, Rosalie, and Carlos says it's time to go."

"Already?"

"It'll soon be dark, and you've a very early start tomorrow."

Drenched in scent, and with a powder of gilt on her white dress, Rosalie had been lost in simple enjoyment of the mischief and fun of the cascarón ball. The words 'it'll soon be dark' fell on her heart like a knell. But she was able to smile as the kissing and blessing began, to bid goodbye to the friends who crowded after her to the gate, but no further: it was Luis alone who walked across the turf with his sister. As he had done in church, he put her hand into her husband's hand, and stooped to kiss her.

"God bless you, Rosalie," he said. "Carlos, take care of her."

He turned and signalled to the musicians. They struck up a waltz, for the young guests meant to dance until midnight, and the four Rivera vaqueros who would row the bridal couple across San Pablo Bay next morning fell into place behind Carlos and Rosalie. The little party rode into the stillness of the darkening woods.

Carlos was the first to break the silence.

"Tell me about the house we're going to," he said easily. "Is it near the Casa Grande?"

"It's nearer Señor Leese's house, but nothing like as big as his. It's just a little adobe, which my father built to have a stake in the pueblo. A man called Guzman, an old steward of ours from the Monterey days, lives there with his Indian wife."

"Will they be there tonight?"

"The Guzmans? They'll be sleeping at the Leese house, like Rita."

"Too bad the Leeses missed the wedding. But he seemed to think his Fourth of July celebrations more important than our marriage!"

Carlos laughed, and Rosalie tried to echo his laughter. In fact she had been thankful when the Leeses and the Coopers left Sonoma to attend the American fiesta at Yerba Buena. She wanted no reminders of that other fiesta at Fort Ross.

"You really think we ought to start as early as five o'clock tomorrow?" she said.

"We must, if we want to get home before it's dark." Carlos reached across and touched her hand. "Rosalie, I hope you won't be disappointed in your new home. Seeing the way you live at the Rancho Estrada made me realise that things have gone downhill at my house since my mother died. You'll have a lot to do to get it back in proper order."

"I'll do my best." She was quite sincere in saying that. All she could do now was try to make the best of her ill-starred marriage.

"It's too bad Rita isn't coming with you. She strikes me as a capable woman," said Carlos.

"My mother couldn't spare her. But I'm sure she'll have everything in readiness for us tonight."

Rita had been in Sonoma since the day before. Banishing the Guzmans to the Leese house, she had cleaned and polished, spread white sheets from the rancho, hung fresh white curtains, and set a dozen candles ready to be lit. The Estrada town house, as Don Santiago had jokingly called it, was indeed a small adobe, of only two rooms and a lean-to, but besides the barred windows on the plaza there were larger windows at the back, overlooking nearly an acre of well-tended garden. These Rita had opened wide, and the little house was filled with the fresh wild odours of the valley night. She was at the door, ready with her curtsy, when she heard the riders coming down the plaza.

"Your honours must be very tired," she said in her submissive way. "There is fruit and wine to refresh you, or anything else you care to choose."

Carlos laughed. "I hope you don't mean food, Rita, after three such days of feasting! I'll drink a glass of wine while you look after your young lady."

"I want to take a bath and wash my hair," said Rosalie, when the two women were in the bedroom. "I reek of scent, it's horrible."

"I've hot water and sponges ready to bathe you. But your hair must wait, it takes too long to dry. Come, let me take your dress off first. How that gilt paper sticks!"

The gilt was still in Rosalie's hair when the refreshing sponge bath was completed, and she was in a white nightdress and wrapper of French silk. But the high Spanish comb had been removed, and the black hair was falling loose when Rita said,

"Start brushing it out yourself, querida. I must fetch something I've prepared for you."

The girl sat on a low stool beside the great bed which almost filled the room. She heard her husband talking – was it to another man? and then say,

"What have you there, Rita?"

"A herbal drink for Doña Rosalie, señor, it will do her good. May I pour you some more wine?"

She heard the clink of bottle and glass, and was on her feet when Rita came in with a covered cup on a salver.

"Who's that with Don Carlos?"

"Only one of his vaqueros," Rita soothed her. "He brought a valise for his master from the Casa Grande. Now drink this, and let me brush your hair."

She took the cover off the cup, and one more scent, of pungent herbs, mingled with the cloying perfume of the cascarónes on Rosalie's discarded garments.

"I heard you tell him it would do me good," said Rosalie, trembling. "How do I know it won't do me harm?"

"Haven't I cared for you from the very day you were born, my darling? How could you think I would ever do you harm?"

"Then swear to me this drink is innocent."

"I swear it on the Cross."

The girl took the cup and drank the hot sweet liquid to the dregs. Then Rita made her sit down, and began to brush her hair with rhythmic strokes, listening to the sound of the vaquero leaving, the shutting of the door, and the change in Rosalie's breathing from shallow to deep and slow as the powerful aphrodisiac began to work. She slipped to her knees at the girl's side and kissed her hand.

"I'll come back and make chocolate for you both at half past four," she said. "And I will come to you whenever you need me, whenever you send for me, remember that! And now, go to your husband. Go quickly, and show him you are ready to take his love."

She slid away like a darker shadow in that room of shadows, and was gone. Sonoma lay asleep beneath the rising moon. And warmth was rising in Rosalie's moist body: a physical hunger and a spiritual recklessness both due to the Indian potion. She seemed to have grown too big for the little room, too inflamed to act the virgin bride, timidly waiting for her bridegroom to approach her. "Go to your husband!" Rita had said. She flung the door between the two rooms open. Carlos Rivera had a double-barrelled pistol in his hand.

In that moment of shock, when her first thought was "He knows it all! He means to kill me!" and her second was "Let him fire! Let him end it now!" the look of dismay on her husband's face, as he threw the weapon into the open valise with a chink of metal on metal and closed the lid, was so ludicrous that Rosalie found strength to whisper:

"Do you always travel armed, Don Carlos?"

"Rosalie! Darling!" He seized her in his arms. "Did I frighten you? I wouldn't scare you for the world! . . . It isn't loaded. I told Roberto to bring it to me in the morning, but the damned fool packed it with my clothes . . . There's nothing to be afraid of, sweetheart. Don't tremble so!"

"I'm not afraid of – of firearms. But is the road so danger-ous?"

"Not with me to take care of you. I promised Luis –"

The broken words gave way to kisses. His lips and hands began to explore her body. And Rosalie let him carry her to the white bed, first wondering at his strength and then welcoming it, forgetting in a flood of contrived passion how it had been with Peter, on the flowers, beneath the redwoods; abominably consenting to the ultimate excesses of her bridegroom's lust.

9

The home to which Don Carlos Rivera brought his bride on a cold and windy summer evening resembled the Rancho Est-rada only in its adobe walls and roofs of tule. It was in good repair, but in the flickering light of the torches carried by the soldiers who escorted them from a welcoming supper at the Presidio it looked as if cracks might appear at any moment in bricks not softened by vines or Castilian roses. The courtyard was closed, not by a fence, but by a wall built of the whitened skulls and bones of cattle. This was a common custom in Alta California, but one which Rosalie's father had never followed. She tried not to shudder as she curtsied to the commandant of the Presidio and thanked him for his hospitality.

"You must excuse us now, Captain Prado," said Carlos. "Doña Rosalie is tired after her long journey."

"I shall do myself the honour of riding out very soon and enquiring for your health, Señora Doña Rosalie," said the gallant captain, and led his entire army of eight troopers back to their tumbledown barracks. Carlos was straining his eyes to distinguish, between the torchlight and the cloudy moonlight, the dim shapes of his servants in the yard. "Where the devil have they all gone?" Rosalie heard him mutter. "Roberto, go and find Luisa," he flung at the vaquero who had come with them from Sonoma.

"Is anything the matter?" said Rosalie. "I think Captain Prado expected to be asked to take wine with us."

"We'd have had him on our hands till daybreak," said Carlos irritably. "The only thing the matter is that half of my damned Indians appear to have gone off to a fiesta at the Mission. Ah, there you are, Luisa," as an elderly Mexican woman came up with a curtsy. "Take your lady to her room and see that she has everything she needs."

Carlos handed his wife into a little sala, with a bedroom beyond it, both lit by tallow candles. Rosalie had a fleeting impression of white walls hung with cheap coloured prints of saints and angels, and of a big mahogany desk where Carlos flung down the pistol in its holster which he had worn all day. Roberto came hard on his heels with the valise of the night before, and through the half-open door Rosalie saw her husband remove something from it and lock it in one of the desk drawers. She heard the chink of coins, and remembering the clink of metal on metal when he threw the pistol into the valise she realised that it had contained more than a change of clothing. "The gun wasn't meant to protect me!" she thought painfully, "it was to protect my dowry!" Then Luisa closed the connecting door and began to help her new mistress to undress.

"All right, Luisa, I'll do that." Carlos came in and sent the maid away. Through the long day of travel he had been in a fever of impatience for the hour when he could hold his bride in his arms again, and now he was frantic to renew the ardours of their wedding night. His long fingers deftly undid the ribbons, slipped down the silk, and his lips were moist upon her neck as he stammered out his love and admiration. The candles were extinguished, the passionate silence fell.

Not half an hour had passed when the bride rose from the bed decked with a white satin spread embroidered in silver with the arms of the Riveras and the Estradas – her mother's own work – and declared that she would rather spend the night in a leather chair against the wall than among sheets and blankets infested by an army of fleas.

The bridegroom did not feel obliged to do the same. There always had been fleas at the Rancho Rivera (as he explained to his lady, and was told to "Be quiet!" for his pains), everybody knew that *las pulgas* were the curse of Alta California, and there was nothing to be done about it. Rosalie must lie down again and try to get some sleep. He slept himself, in frustration and fatigue, and awoke to the sound of voices in the sala.

Rosalie was not talking loudly, but incisively. She said, "As soon as Don Carlos has had his chocolate, you and the other women are to take that feather mattress off the bed and burn it, the blankets too. The sheets must be soaked in lye and washed."

"It will ruin the linen," said Luisa, as insolently as she dared. "Those are the best sheets, that came in the señora's boxes from Sonoma."

"Yes, well, you should have known better than to put clean sheets on a dirty bed. Now show me the other rooms and let me see if I can find a clean bedstead, at least."

Carlos was out of bed and pulling on his clothes before the women had left the sala. He had half a mind to go after Rosalie and make her come back to share his chocolate and let him coax her into a better mood. But an Indian boy, obviously aware that he was under new management, appeared with a tray, and behind the boy with the chocolate came his capataz, with an account of all the work needing to be done on the rancho, where the slaughtering ought to be begun without delay. Carlos contented himself with walking across the yard while his horse was being brought up, and confronting Rosalie where, with the now tearful Luisa, she was grimly shooing half a dozen hens from one of the rooms kept for guests.

"Don't try to do it all in one day, querida," he said, with a flick of his riding whip to his sombrero.

"There's a great deal to be done," was her rejoinder.

"Don't say I didn't warn you," said Carlos, and rode out of the yard with his grinning vaqueros behind him.

In a certain sense one pattern of their marriage was set that day. The brilliant fiesta was over, and so was the fever of their wedding night: if Carlos Rivera had indulged in any dreams of idle days and passionate nights with his lovely bride they went up in the smoke of the bonfire which consumed bedding, draperies, floor covers and fleas. For nearly a week fire and water cleansed the Rancho Rivera. The missing servants reappeared by twos and threes and were put to work, and plenty of coarse food was set on the table when Carlos rode in from the range. By nightfall he was too tired to talk, or to object to the penitential leather pallets on which the new bedding from Sonoma was spread.

If Carlos Rivera had wanted to show his bride that he could work as hard as she could (and he was half amused and half affronted by her attack on his slovenly home) the season was favourable, for the *matanza*, the slaughtering, was soon in full swing. This took place in corrals close to the Rancho Rivera. Rosalie's father had held his matanzas beside the embarcadero on Sonoma Creek – where Princess Helen had found animal skulls and bones in plenty when she landed there in April – but at Rosalie's new home the whole process took place within sight and earshot. The bellowing animals died a bloody death, and the hides were stripped off and staked out to dry before they were carried down to the longboats of the waiting American ships and taken to be cured in the southern ports. Much of the meat was kept for cooking and drying, the rest left to the buzzards, while the tallow, in two qualities called *manteca* and *sebo*, was tried in the great pots in the yard. In those July days the smell from the try pots, the charred wood and the mess of blood and manure often nauseated Rosalie as much as the unappetising midday meal of beefsteaks, beef tongue, red peppers, beans and garlic all set on the table in one pottery dish. Only the trade winds, which blew in from the ocean punctually at noon, and the wet clouds which often covered the twin peaks which the Spanish had called *Los Pechos de la Choca*, 'the breasts of the Indian maiden' helped her to endure the matanza days.

Carlos was too indolent by nature to keep up his activity in the corrals for long. After about ten days he told the capataz to take charge and Rosalie to put on a riding habit: "You haven't been off the place since we came home," he said. "Leave whatever you're doing to Luisa, and come for a gallop with me."

"Where shall we go?"

"Wherever you like."

"My father took me to the Mission once. I'd love to go there again."

"How long is it since you went there with your father? Nine years? Ten? You'll find it changed, and not for the better."

"But Father Mercado from Santa Clara comes to say mass there?"

"It's a long ride from Santa Clara. He comes from time to time."

"It's only a mile from the rancho, Carlos," she said when she was in the saddle, and two vaqueros moved up behind them. "Do we need a bodyguard?"

"The road isn't always safe and I always go armed. It's better to be careful."

It was exhilarating to be on horseback again, and galloping, but Rosalie's spirits fell when they reached the Mission of San Francisco de Asís. In the years since the secularisation all the buildings where in the great days of Christian witness four thousand neophytes had been baptised, housed, fed and taught useful trades, had fallen into ruin. Doors, windows and roofs had all been carried off. The graveyard beside the church was choked with weeds and bushes, and its collapsing walls had been shored up, rancho style, with the skulls and bones of slaughtered animals. A few Indians, shivering in the wind, were huddled on the steps of the church.

The first settlers had selected a site for the Franciscan Mission on the banks of a rivulet which flowed down from Los Pechos towards the bay, and which, since they found it on the feast day of Our Lady of Sorrows, they named the *arroyo de los Dolores*. A shallow lake, dried up for many years, was similarly called the Laguna de los Dolores, and as time went by the Mission itself came to be called the Mission Dolores, a place of sorrows and acquainted with grief.

"This is horrible," said Rosalie, when they had dismounted. "Was there nobody to take care of it, as General Vallejo did at Sonoma?"

"Don Francisco Guerrero, the alcalde, is supposed to be the steward."

"Then I don't think much of his stewardship."

"My rascally servants come here from time to time to clear

the rubble. It's a good excuse to drink and dance as well, and that's where they were, celebrating our wedding, the night I brought you home."

"But look at the churchyard! My godfather is buried here –" She began to tug at the creepers covering the tombstone of Don Luis Argüello.

"My father knew him well," said Carlos. "Did you know his sister was baptised here in the Mission Dolores?"

"My godfather's sister? Concepcion Argüello?"

"Yes, the famous Concha. Surely you've heard the story of Conchita and her Russian lover?"

"Everyone has heard that story." Rosalie caught at her husband's arm. She remembered the merienda at Fort Ross, and her scoffing words about the romance of Rezanov and Concepcion Argüello. Carlos kissed her little hand as they entered the church.

It was larger than the Mission at Sonoma but only a few yards broad, with roof timbers of redwood and a ceiling which the Indian neophytes had painted with their own vegetable dyes. It looked so desolate that it was hard to believe mass was still said there. The holy-water stoup was empty, and there was no sense of a Presence in the chapel. Carlos threw a few coins to the Indians squatting beneath the columns in front of the door when they came out.

"At least the altar is beautiful," said Rosalie, on horseback.

"It came from the City of Mexico."

"But there's dust on it. The Mexican government should be ashamed."

Carlos shrugged. Like all Californios, he expected nothing from the authorities of *la otra banda*. But when they were back at the rancho he said to Rosalie in the sala, as he unstrapped his pistol holster:

"Rosalie, I know your father was a deeply religious man. Your mother told me Don Santiago did as much as Vallejo to save the Mission church at Sonoma. I don't want you to start thinking you can save the Mission Dolores. We shall only go there with the other rancheros when Father Mercado comes to hear confessions and say mass, and I forbid you ever to go there without me."

"You forbid me! Why?"

"The Mission isn't a safe place nowadays."

"Surely you weren't afraid of a few poor sick Indians, whom my father would have taken home to feed and heal?"

"No, I wasn't afraid of them. But sometimes there are drunken cholos, or desperate white men, even deserters from the American ships, skulking about in the ruins beside the church. Guerrero arrested a gang of Mexican cattle rustlers there only two months ago. They were bandits from Sonora, they'd come a long way."

"Bandits, Carlos?"

"Yes, that's why I carry a gun on the range, and keep firearms in the house." He opened his desk drawer, and showed her a brace of flintlock pistols, with beautifully chased butts, in a velvet case. "Those were my father's duelling pistols," he said.

"Did he fight many duels?" she asked with a faint touch of mockery in her voice.

"He was out on one affair of honour, to my knowledge . . . Be careful, dear, that's loaded!" For Rosalie had slipped his own double-barrelled pistol from its holster, lying on the desk, and was examining it.

"Don't worry, I know how to handle firearms." She handed it back to him. "My father taught me to shoot at a target when I was fourteen."

"You never told me that before! Was it for sport or self-defence?"

She dropped her gaze. "For self-defence, I suppose."

"So even Don Santiago, the friend of the Indians, believed in taking sensible precautions on his rancho."

"The Indian risings were over before we reached the frontier. And my father told me never to forget how the Indians came to greet us as friends, with flowers and gifts –"

"Which you repaid many times over," said Carlos. "We're being too serious, my dear. Don't you think we ought to begin enjoying ourselves? Now we've put our house in order and been to church again, isn't it time for a fiesta?"

So their friends and neighbours thought. The hardest of the summer work was over for the cattlemen, and only those who were raising wheat had the labours of the harvest ahead. On the pastoral ranchos which covered the seven hills above the bay the slaughtering season was the climax of the year. As soon as it ended the guitars were brought out, the dance went on, and it was time to break in on the bridal seclusion of the young Riveras.

There were some fine days at the beginning of August, and Rosalie, riding to the hospitable ranchos on her beautiful white mare, began to see beauty in the unfamiliar countryside. In the wind and cold of July she had missed her happy smiling valley protected by the golden hills, and thought the blown sand from the ocean beach a poor exchange for the flowery meadows of Sonoma. Now when she looked across the bay she was calmed, in the confusion of a new fear, by the sight of Picacho Prieto, the dark peak called by the Indians Tamalpais, on which the sombre colours changed from green to mauve to umber between sunrise and sunset. From all the ranchos where Carlos and Rosalie were made welcome it was possible to see Mount Tamalpais.

The first invitation, and the one Rosalie was most eager to accept, came from the Castros in the Contra Costa country, who had been among the wedding guests. As she rode from home on the first part of the journey to their great rancho, that paradise of gardens, orchards and grape arbours set in the rolling wheat lands, she thought what an easy penance Father Quijas had imposed on an erring member of the *gente de razón*. She only had to be taken in a boat across the narrow strip of water which the Indians called Yulupa, the Sunset Strait, and the Spanish named La Boca del Puerto, and then escorted on horseback to the home of the Castros to enjoy a day of luxury. In the course of the day she asked to visit the tiny chapel which the Castros had built for their Indians, and there ended her 'pilgrimage' by kneeling before the altar-piece, a painting of the miraculous cape on which the brown-skinned Virgin appeared to a poor Indian, which hung in the Shrine of Guadalupe in the City of Mexico. She said prayers of contrition on her knees before the altar, and repeated them when she was home again. A crude copy of the painting hung in the sala of the Rancho Rivera, as in so many humbler homes, and Rosalie carried it to the bedroom and set a stool before it to serve as a *prie-Dieu*. But she often told her beads at the open window, looking at the Indian holy place of Tamalpais.

Don Francisco Guerrero, the alcalde or mayor of Yerba Buena, and his pretty young black-eyed wife entertained the Riveras at that favourite form of merienda, a strawberry feast. As the Indians had shown the first Spanish settlers, the sand-hills were covered in summer with the delicious fruit, and when the Guerreros' great woven baskets of berries were emptied there was of course an open-air supper and a dance. There was dancing again at the rancho of the Miramonte family near the Presidio, where the women made a little laughing mystery about making the bride drink the water of the Polin spring, and the outdoor sports included firing at a target. No lady could beat Mrs. Jacob Leese, whose husband had taught her to be a dead shot with a rifle, but Doña Rosalie Rivera shot well enough to prove that she could handle a pistol. Carlos applauded. The fiestas had revived his taste, never long dormant, for company and entertainment, and he began going regularly to the Presidio or the tavern for cards and wine. He complained that Luis was 'taking the devil of a time' to complete the terms of the marriage settlement, and she had to remind him that Luis was to visit them in September to transact the final business.

Carlos drank a good deal at Vioget's, but only showed it by an excessive courtesy to Rosalie. On one occasion, when he had dined at the Presidio and matched glass for glass with Captain Prado, he was quarrelsome when he came home and accused Rosalie of being cold to him – 'cheating him of love', was the expression he used. She took no trouble to coax him into a better mood. Since the first night in Sonoma she had been completely indifferent to his caresses. She only submitted to him to make quite sure he would think himself the father of Peter Gagarin's child. She thought he had been paid for his name and protection in the cold cash of her dowry.

The loose camisas she wore about the house, and the draped rebozos she wore out of doors hid the very slight alteration in her figure, and neither Carlos nor the young caballeros who came to visit him saw any difference in Doña Rosalie. On the morning when Luis was expected she put on one of her trousseau dresses, and knotted the sash as tightly round her waist as possible before running out at the sound of horses' hoofs. It was a disappointment, which showed in her face, when Felipe rode into the courtyard with Carlos.

"Rosalie, how well you look!" her brother said heartily, as he swung off his horse. "I wish I could have brought Luis with me. He sent his love –"

"But what's the matter?" she said. "We were both counting on seeing him –" She saw from Carlos's satisfied look that Felipe had been given the means to complete the marriage contract.

"He thought he'd better stay at home," said Felipe. "Mother hasn't been too well. Now, now, there's nothing to worry about, but Luis thought she shouldn't be left alone. So I came instead, and spent the night at San Rafael with Señor Murphy –"

She remembered to say "*Está es su casa, mi hermano,*" and led him indoors, quite aware of Felipe's appraising glances at the furniture and silver in the sala, pleased with the order she had created, and glad that she could offer her brother a guest room no longer in use as a hen-roost. Carlos, she could see, was anxious to set out for Yerba Buena and Nathan Spear's office as soon as the traveller had had something to eat and drink, and though she impulsively said "Take me with you!" she was not surprised to be told by both men that she mustn't bother her head about business, but get ready for the Independence fiesta in the morning.

Felipe Estrada was pleased with what he saw at the rancho, and better pleased with his brother-in-law's good sense as the settlement was completed. With Luis's written authority, Felipe confirmed the transfer to Carlos of the proper number of hides from that year's matanza, and – with the receipt in his hand, discharging all obligations by the Estradas to Carlos Rivera – sat by while Carlos, still on paper, bartered at least half the value of the hides for farm implements, seeds, food-stuffs for man and beast, and new household furnishings. It was a prudent outlay, and Felipe could only approve when Carlos ended by buying a polished pink coral necklace for Rosalie.

She was wearing it next morning when they set out for Yerba Buena. It was the sixteenth of September, the day when Mexico became independent not long before Rosalie was born, and although the two young men were not sympathetic to *la otra banda*, they admired Jacob Leese's impartiality in celebrating the independence both of the land of his birth and the country of his adoption. Felipe had even gone so far as to wear the Mexican colours, sporting a green suit with a red sash, gold lacings in his slashed trousers, a gold-handled knife in his boot and his father's golden spurs. "Why, Felipe, how fine you are!" exclaimed his sister. "You're grand enough to be going courting!" She was amazed to see him flush, but he only said in his gruff way, "I can't compete with Carlos," for Carlos, in red with a darker red serape, was a vivid foil to Rosalie in white. The three riders were brilliant against the scrub as they rode, up one long hill and down another, to the pueblo of Yerba Buena.

From the hilltop they saw it all, the Pacific, the narrow strait and the bay steel-blue in the sunshine, with the wooded islets lying on its breast. They saw the hills on the Contra Costa and the high purple crests of Tamalpais, and they saw, riding at anchor in Yerba Buena Cove, two American ships dressed overall with bunting in honour of the day. Captain Cooper had brought the government ship, *California*, into the harbour to join in the celebrations, and she too was decked with the flag and the colours of Mexico. From far down the slope they heard the sound of music and firecrackers.

Every year it was the custom to say nothing could be better than Jacob Leese's Fourth of July fiesta, and every year it was agreed that his Mexican Independence Day party surpassed it. Each time, as Yerba Buena grew, the fiesta was bigger and brighter, with more guitar players, more piñatas full of toys for the children to break, more dishes of chicken *mole*. There were more sports and games which seemed to spread further and further outside the pueblo, from El Rincón to Leese's Punta de la Loma Alta, the hill from which there was a splendid view of the bay. But the pueblo itself was what amazed Rosalie. Far from consisting of a shabby tavern and a few trading shacks, it now boasted a regular street, the Calle de la Fundación, and on this street, where Richardson's solitary tent had been pitched six years earlier, Richardson's town house stood next to Jacob Leese's, with Nathan Spear's, handsomer than both of them, not far away. Thirty families now lived in the pueblo, and twenty more had gathered from the ranchos; it was a company of nearly two hundred people who were thronging the rooms and strolling in the gardens of the American traders and the Englishman who had turned Mexican and Catholic like all the others. The factor of the Hudson's Bay Company had just been installed in his new warehouse.

Rosalie was persuaded by Mrs. Leese to sit down and drink a cup of chocolate. There was to be a banquet in the afternoon, she said, and dancing later, but those men – with a resigned sigh – wouldn't be kept from their horrid bull-and-bear baiting, and probably cock fighting too. But Mr. Leese wouldn't let it go on too long, and at least the fights were on the far side of the plaza. Rosalie insisted on seeing the plaza? Such energy, in this heat! It was already established in Yerba Buena that September was a hot month. In fact, a stiff westerly had begun to blow at midday, and the fruit trees in the gardens of the Calle de la Fundación were bending in the blast. Rosalie tied the pink ribbons of her wide straw hat more firmly as they crossed the plaza, where a girl in a pale-blue dress was struggling with her own. Rosalie exchanged smiles with the stranger, and recognised Content Putnam.

She had never expected to see the American girl again, the girl who had waited with her in a Russian office at Bodega Bay, while a Russian schooner crept round the headland with her flag at half mast. Here was the girl who witnessed her collapse when she heard of Peter's death and tried to comfort her: this girl knew one of the deepest secrets of her heart! There was no expression on her plain little face, weathered by months at sea, as Mrs. Leese, who seemed to know her well, introduced Miss Content Putnam to "our bride, Doña Rosalie Rivera y Estrada".

Miss Putnam curtsied to the young married lady and Rosalie forced herself to smile. Mrs. Leese said "Where is your papa, señorita? I didn't know the *Washington* had entered port."

"She's lying over at Whalers' Harbour, and pa doesn't reckon to get away for a couple of hours yet. I got tired waiting and came over in the longboat."

"Without a chaperone, you naughty girl!"

Content grinned. "I didn't have a chaperone among the Eskimos," she said. "And here comes Mr. Felipe Estrada, guess he'll walk me around the square and show me all the sights."

"Shall we walk with them?" said Rosalie uncertainly, amazed at the sight of Felipe offering his arm to the American girl and taking her away to have refreshments.

"No more walking for you in this heat. You'd much better come back and rest on the sofa until dinnertime."

There was an overflow of the festivities into the Richardson and Spear houses, but Rosalie, still 'our bride', dined in the Leese sala at Mr. Leese's right hand. With his duties as host, and the need to propose toasts to the Republic of Mexico and to the Governor and General Vallejo in their absence, it was some time before he could devote himself to the guest of honour, and then he said confidentially to Rosalie:

"I haven't seen you to talk to since we were all together at Fort Ross. I reckon you were as sorry as I was to hear about Prince Peter's tragic death."

She knew better now than to call it murder. She said, "I felt very sorry for Princess Helen. She was so fond of her cousin."

"Terrible thing," said Mr. Leese. "Mind you, he was a fool to try to ride the ford alone. But that was how he struck me, a headstrong fellow in spite of all his brains. I remember how mad he got, the first time I saw him in Sonoma, when he heard Fort Ross was up for sale."

"That wasn't true," said Rosalie.

"Oh, but it was, Doña Rosalie. Hasn't your husband told you that the new purchaser completed the deal just the other day?"

"My husband isn't interested in Russian affairs." She forced herself to ask, "Who is the purchaser, señor? General Vallejo?"

"No, it's not my brother-in-law. He did make an offer, but one of his rivals got ahead of him. Did you ever meet Captain Johan Sutter?"

"I've heard my brothers speak of him. But he lives far away; up the Sacramento river – leagues and leagues away from Fort Ross . . ."

"Time and distance don't mean much to Sutter, since he arrived from Switzerland. Governor Alvarado gave him a huge land grant, which he called New Helvetia, and there he lives at Sutter's Fort in tremendous style. He's bought Fort

Ross, with the Kuskov and Bodega settlements and all the farms thrown in, for thirty thousand dollars. The Russians will be leaving California before the end of the year."

Rosalie was too stunned to say more. She knew Leese was telling the truth, but all she could realise was that Peter, if he had lived, would have reached St. Petersburg too late to prevent the Russian withdrawal from California. Although she had never fully grasped the length of the journey she had hoped to share as his wife, had never been able to find on her father's ancient terrestrial globe the relation of Alaska to California or of Russia to Alaska, she was sure of one thing: that Peter meant to be in St. Petersburg in October. And this was the sixteenth of September. She clenched her hands in her lap and felt that she might faint.

Mrs. Leese saved the situation by giving the sign to the ladies to leave the table. The sala had been curtained, and lit by candles, but outside it was a golden September afternoon, and the children were waiting in the garden, ready for boisterous fun. Some of the young fathers came out and set them to foot races; they declined to start pony races, because the ball was soon to begin. Carlos escorted Rosalie along the Calle de la Fundacíon to Nathan Spear's house, where dancing had already started in the largest sala of the pueblo, and the first sight that met their eyes was the grave and secretive Felipe, in his brilliant green and red, waltzing with a little figure in blue cotton, with sandy hair in a prim snood.

"Who is his partner?" Carlos whispered, and Rosalie told him it was an American girl, a sea-captain's daughter, from the *Washington* lying off Sausalito Point.

"She's no beauty, but she dances well."

"Would you like to dance with her?"

"Leave her to Felipe. I want to dance with my wife."

Sooner or later, Rosalie thought, they would meet and talk. But she knew one thing about Content Putnam: she would be as well able to keep a secret as any Estrada of them all.

The Americanos and the Californios danced in the salas of the Calle de la Fundación as the dancing spread from one garden to another, the vaqueros danced in the plaza with the girls who appeared from nowhere when there was a fiesta, and the sailors held a noisy fandango inside the tavern. Rosalie

danced first with Carlos, then with Mr. Leese and some of the
young caballeros who had been at her wedding, and while she
changed partners she was aware that Felipe was still dancing
with the little American in the blue dress. After a long set of
quadrilles Captain Prado brought her a glass of wine, while
Carlos stood talking with his last partner, Doña Josefa Guerrero, in the shelter of a grape arbour. Rosalie sat still and let one
of the Castro boys fan her; she was surprised when Carlos
came up and said,

"Haven't you danced enough for one day, my love? Here
are all the Noes going home, we'll have company with them if
we leave now. Where's Felipe?"

It was not like Carlos to be among the first to leave a fiesta,
but Rosalie was very willing to go home. She wanted to be
silent, to lie in the dark and think of the destruction of Peter's
great purpose, and of the Russians giving up all they had won
in California. Felipe, unexpectedly, refused to leave the ball. It
would be impolite to their hosts, he said, if they all left early,
and besides he wanted to talk to Captain Putnam, who had not
yet come ashore. They were not to worry about him. He had
an invitation to spend a day or two at the Rancho Sausalito . . .

"So convenient for Whalers' Harbour," murmured Carlos,
as they waited for the horses. "What would you say if he
presented us with a Yankee sister-in-law?"

Rosalie shuddered. "What would my mother say! You're
not serious, Carlos?"

"No, but I think Felipe may be."

"But he hardly knows that girl!"

"He says the *Washington* arrived in Bodega Bay ten days
ago. They left the whaling grounds earlier than usual and Don
Felipe Estrada, with his friend Señor Cord, was entertained on
board several times. A lot can happen in ten days, my dear!"

The Noe family joined them then, and all the riders set off to
climb the hill beside Jacob Leese's house. The sun had long
since set, but the light lingered over the Pacific in streaks of
cinnabar and vermilion, under the violet flecks of cirrus cloud
which promised another windy day tomorrow, and Rosalie in
her utter dejection longed for her darkened room and her soft
clean pillow to hide her weariness and her despair.

The Sunset Dream

Even though it was the day of a great Mexican fiesta, the house servants now stood in too much awe of La Señora to run off to join the pathetic survivors of the olden days in the ruins of the Mission Dolores. They were all waiting in the yard, holding torches, ready to take their master's spurs and serape, and their mistress's riding cloak. Luisa was hovering in the sala, waiting for orders: she was sharply told by Carlos to leave them alone.

"Rosalie," he said, drawing her close to him, "when I was dancing with Doña Josefa she put an idea into my head which would be very wonderful – if it were true."

"I saw you dancing with Doña Josefa," said Rosalie wearily. "What did she have to say?"

"She told me I had done well to take you to the Miramonte rancho. Because she could guess you had been drinking from the Polin spring."

"I don't understand."

"Nor did I, at first. Then I remembered the story my mother and her sisters used to tell, about the Polin spring which existed on that ground long before the Spanish came. The Indians told the first Miramonte that the Polin spring would bring a baby spirit to every girl who drank from it."

"It's a pretty legend, Carlos."

"Rosalie, are you with child?"

With her face buried on his shoulder she whispered "Yes."

"Rosalie! My darling! Look at me!" He forced her to raise her head and began to kiss her passionately. "Is it really true? Why didn't you tell me sooner?"

"Because I wanted to be sure. And," she added in a flash of inspiration, "I hoped my mother would be able to come to me."

"My poor sweet! She shall come to you later on, I promise you. Next spring, Rosalie? It'll be in April, won't it?"

"Yes, in April." She hardly realised that the moment of revelation had come and he believed it all.

"I knew it and I thank God for it," he was saying solemnly. "That wonderful night in Sonoma – I knew it would mean a child. You gave yourself to me so utterly –" He was kissing her hair, her hands, her lips, and what he was murmuring Rosalie hardly understood. He had never relaxed his hold on

her, and she felt as if only his arms kept her from slipping to the
ground. Then he said,

"If only my father and mother were alive! They'd be so
proud! So happy to know that you and I would give a new son
to the Riveras."

10

The Russians were leaving California. The rumour which
began to circulate at the fiesta of Mexican Independence was
soon confirmed as a fact, and among the American traders
there was some wagging of heads and laughter at the way
Captain Sutter had outsmarted General Vallejo. Reports from
Monterey said that the general had overreached himself in
July, when he made an offer to buy not only Fort Ross but the
land on which it stood; whereupon Governor Alvarado, no
longer on the best of terms with his overbearing uncle,
declared that the land had never belonged to the Russians and
must revert to the government of Mexico.

The founder of New Helvetia, coming along two months
later, had cleverly made his offer of thirty thousand dollars for
the buildings only of Fort Ross, this to include the Kuskov
settlement and the farms as well as the installations at the
harbour of Bodega. The farms being built of wood could be
dismantled and hauled overland to be added to Sutter's Fort on
the left bank of the Sacramento river, and it was rumoured that
Robert Cord and Felipe Estrada had already proffered a tender
for the haulage contract. Two of the Russians whom Peter
Gagarin had known, Klebnikov and Nikolai the port superintendent, would remain at Bodega Bay for a final settlement of
all matters outstanding after the Russians, headed by Alexander Rotschev and his princess, had left for Alaska. This was
expected to take place in December.

It was years since the easy-going Californios had thought of
the Russian settlers as a menace. That dread had belonged to an
earlier generation, when the building of Fort Ross had alarmed
men like Santiago Estrada: now, in the golden sunset of the
pastoral years, there seemed to be no enemy in sight, either

beyond the Sierras or beyond the seas. Even Sutter's ambition seemed to be satisfied with the purchase of Fort Ross. He had thirty white men inside Sutter's Fort, working as loggers, blacksmiths and carpenters, and his energies were turning towards a future city on the Sacramento.

For several weeks passed before all these rumours were collated and discussed by the patrons of Vioget's tavern, and brought home piecemeal by Carlos Rivera. All Felipe was able to contribute, on his return from Whaler's Harbour, was an account, most unwillingly delivered, of his haulage plan; impenetrable as ever, the young man preferred to talk about the coming child, whose advent Carlos announced to him within minutes of his arrival. He congratulated both Rosalie and Carlos warmly, and prepared to ride home satisfied that the troubles of the month of May were forgotten.

"I think Rosalie would like to see her mother," said Carlos when the two young men were alone. "Is there no hope of Doña Maria's paying us a visit?"

"Absolutely none. Don't tell Rosalie, but mother seems to be suffering from a heart complaint, like my father. She's up and about every day, but the journey from Sonoma would be too much for her."

"Have you thought of calling in a doctor? There's a clever American doctor at Los Medanos, in the Contra Costa country."

"John Marsh? I've heard of him. But I don't think my mother would take kindly to an Americano. She dabbles among the medicines my father used on the Indios, not that they did him any good himself. Whatever you do, don't alarm Rosalie about her. She'll be happy to hear about the baby."

"So will my cousins at Santa Clara."

Carlos, in his excitement, would have liked the whole of Alta California to hear about the new Rivera, and Rosalie had to beg him to say nothing for the present. A letter to Don Jaime Rivera and his wife, she conceded, must be written, but as for the neighbours, she implored, let them wait to see the evidence with their own eyes. She didn't want to discuss it –

"Doña Josefa Guerrero guessed it right away."

And so did Mrs. Leese, thought Rosalie. She said, "It was

only a guess, Carlos. I don't want to talk about our – our hopes to those strange ladies."

"I'm sure they only want to be your friends." Carlos was vaguely dissatisfied. There were few reticences beyond those prescribed by modesty among the rancheros. Their attitude to life was entirely realistic: a wedding was naturally followed by the birth of a child within a year, and families and friends joined in the rejoicings. That Rosalie wanted to make a secret of it was beyond his understanding. However, as she said, their neighbours would soon see the evidence with their own eyes.

The *Washington*, they heard, had sailed for the southern whaling grounds, and Felipe's courtship, if it had ever begun, was at a standstill. Father Mercado came from Santa Clara to say mass at the Mission Dolores, and one week later a murderer awaiting transportation and trial at Monterey escaped to the ruins of that same Mission, where he was shot dead by a posse of Captain Prado's men. Life had returned to normal on the shores of the great bay.

Rosalie Rivera was ailing. Her pregnancy, so prosperous during the weeks of concealment, had not gone well since the Mexican Independence Day. Either she had caught some infection at the pueblo, where many inhabitants had come down with a low fever declared in aching throats and limbs, or she was binding herself too tightly with the lengths of homespun linen which kept her figure slim, but she was beset by headaches and digestive upsets. She fought these by wild bursts of energy, when her maids flew in all directions with pails and brooms, followed by spells of lassitude and torpid sleep. Carlos was anxiously kind to her. She never fully realised, then or ever, that there was no vice in her young husband. He was a child of pastoral California, a pampered caballero, who had the makings of a good man in him. If their marriage had taken place as their fathers planned, Rosalie might have been petulant and capricious for a time, as became La Favorita of Sonoma, and yielding by degrees to own herself a happy wife and mother. But the Russians had come to the Rancho Estrada, and Rosalie, bereaved and guilty, was still living in the Russian dream.

Carlos began to be vexed, as time went by, that she refused

to go visiting, or even to receive their friends, on the grounds that she ought not to ride horseback, or was simply not presentable. He told her she was beautiful, that she couldn't live in seclusion until April, and he did succeed in arranging a luncheon for a score of people at the rancho on Christmas Day. Next day he was able to persuade her to take a gentle ride with him to the limits of his property, following the bed of the dry arroyo which had once fed the Laguna de los Dolores, and it was then, when the horses were walking the trail round one of the twin peaks, that Carlos and Rosalie saw a ship on the ocean, flying the Russian flag.

"Here comes the party from Fort Ross," said Carlos.

"I wonder what brings them to the bay," said Rosalie, with foreboding. "I should have thought they would make straight for Sitka."

"They have to pick up the contingent from the Farallones. I'll ride down to the Presidio later and get the news."

He was never loth to visit the Presidio, and usually stayed there late, but Carlos came home to dinner, laughing over a Russian scandal. Rotschev had embarked the Russians from Bodega and Kuskov, and also from the islands outside the bay, but he had another reason for ordering the *Constantine* to anchor in Whalers' Harbour: they had lost a lady. One of the young wives from Fort Ross had decamped with a Spanish officer (not known at the Presidio and said to be from Monterey) her husband, a youthful lieutenant, had sworn to find the guilty pair and avenge his honour.

"What it is to have a faithless wife," said Carlos lightly. "He'll never find them."

"You think not?"

"They're half way to Sutter's Fort by this time, he keeps open house for runaways."

"Or else they're on the high seas, bound for Monterey."

"Not they. Rotschev has his spies at Bodega Bay, none of his people would dare embark from there. And they haven't been seen at Whalers' Harbour or Yerba Buena."

"Did you happen to hear the woman's name?"

"Now who could remember their outlandish names?" said Carlos. "Rosalie, if they're not to sail at once, should we send an invitation to the Rotschevs? To return the hospitality they gave you at Fort Ross?"

"Princess Helen is a wretched sailor. She wouldn't want to cross the strait from Sausalito."

"She'll have rougher seas to cross before she's back in Russia."

So far as was known, the former commandant of Fort Ross and his lady did not leave Whalers' Harbour for the next few days. The Russian brig took on water and supplies for the journey to Alaska, while the runaways were sought in vain. The patrons of Vioget's tavern soon had a new interest in the arrival of Sir George Simpson, the Governor-in-Chief of the Hudson's Bay Company, in the company's barque *Cowlitz*, to inspect the new trading post at Yerba Buena.

Sir George was accompanied, not altogether to his own pleasure, by Monsieur Duflot de Mofras, that indefatigable traveller and diarist, whose notes on Alta California were now complete, and who planned to leave for the City of Mexico on the last day of the year.

There were two American ships, the *Alert* and the *Bolivar*, in Yerba Buena Cove, along with the British barque *Index*, and with so many visitors in the little port Captain Prado was delighted to order a banquet at the Presidio. Much wine was drunk, and the host had a violent quarrel with the alcalde, in which swords were drawn a full inch from their scabbards, to the quiet amusement of the foreign guests.

Carlos Rivera was sure they were laughing at the fiery Mexicans as they made their way back to their ships. After a certain point in the evening he had drunk much less than the other men, and was sober enough to kick awake the two guards sound asleep among the skulls and whitened bones outside his rancho. Sober enough to protect the candle flame with one hand when he entered the room where Rosalie lay asleep, and draw his fingers aside slowly enough for the yellow light to fall by degrees on her pale face. There was the mark of tears on the cheek turned towards him, and a lock of black hair lay between her swollen breasts. Carlos struck out the candle flame with his hand. He wrapped his serape closer round his shoulders, and as Rosalie had done the night he brought her home, he sank down in a leather chair to pass the few hours that remained till daybreak.

He left the house before Luisa brought Rosalie's chocolate, and she passed the morning sewing in the sala. She had made very few preparations for the coming child: all now depended on the acceptance of an unexpected and premature birth in February. But the next day was New Year's Eve, which seemed to bring the birth of the child so near that her hands had to be busy, and she only laid the little robe aside when the servants came in to prepare for the midday meal. Carlos came home wet through, for it was the height of the rainy season, and he changed his clothes before sitting down to eat. He had not shaved, and the black stubble lay grimy on his olive skin.

He ate and drank only a little before sending the maids from the room.

"Rosalie," he said, "do you remember that story I told you about the Spanish officer who ran away with the Russian girl?"

"Yes, of course I do. Have they found them?"

"Not a trace of them. But last night I heard an even more dramatic story – about a Russian officer and a Spanish girl."

"Indeed!" she said coldly. "Would it amuse me?"

"Oh, I should think it might. I had it from that amusing rattle, Monsieur Duflot de Mofras, who thought it a suitable tale for a large audience of men."

"Go on."

"It seems that when he was at Fort Ross this summer he was talking one night with the skipper of a vessel called the *Young Julia*. Do you know the name?"

"A Russian supply schooner, I believe."

"You are well informed. This man had the melancholy duty, only last May, of carrying to the Russian establishment at Bodega the news of Prince Peter Gagarin's death by drowning in the Slavianka. Which of course I heard mentioned when I was at Sonoma."

"Well?"

"It seems a beautiful young Spanish lady was at Bodega Bay to keep a tryst with the unfortunate man. She was seen by the *Julia*'s crew in a state of great distress, and was removed from the scene by her brother."

"How did her brother come into it?"

"Apparently he had ridden after the lovesick lady."

"Very romantic." She had her breathing and her muscles under control and her eyes never wavered from his own.

"Have you any idea who the girl could have been?"

"Had Monsieur Duflot?"

"He named no names. But as you were with Felipe at Bodega about that time, I thought you might have heard of her."

Rosalie got up from the table – reared up, was how Carlos thought of it, for she seemed to be taller than her actual height – and said, "I think you had better order the horses, Carlos. I see I have been very remiss – very inconsiderate. I ought to have gone to the Princess Helen as soon as the *Constantine* arrived, and offered her my deepest sympathy on her cousin's death. We must do so now. We must ride to the cove and hire a boat, and then cross to Sausalito and call upon the princess. Perhaps she can throw some light on Monsieur Duflot and his fairy tale."

"Don't be a fool, Rosalie. It's blowing a gale, and raining in torrents; you'd get your death in an open boat."

"It's simpler, isn't it, to tease a woman in a warm room? Did your drunken cronies at the Presidio dare to insinuate that Felipe Estrada was the brother, and I was the girl?"

Carlos had risen to face her. In his doubt and vexation of spirit he was forced to admire her. "Nobody –" he began, but she caught the word from his lips.

"Nobody dared? So much the better for that man and his fables. Now understand me, Carlos; if you won't face the strait in a storm, or the princess in her sorrow, then you had better go to Sonoma and tell your tale to my brothers. But in that case take your father's duelling pistols with you, because you'll need them."

He seized her hand and raised it to his lips. "By God, Rosalie!" he said, "I admire your courage. I hope to heaven it's justified."

★   ★   ★

She faced him down on New Year's Eve, but when February came in with the feast of the Purification of the Virgin, Carlos sat alone in the sala, with a bottle of wine and a glass in front of him, and the flames of Candlemas burning in front of the cheap pictures of the saints. He had said his prayers over and over again when Rosalie fell into what the women called her premature labour, and he was well aware that all his Christian servants were praying to their old Indian gods as her cries of pain rang through the rancho. All was silent now except for her moaning, and the muttering of the women beside her bed. He knew that twins had been born, a boy and a girl, who though premature would live, but Carlos had not seen them yet. He knew that Luisa, who was in charge, was angry because he had refused to send to the rancho of Lake Merced when Rosalie's labour began: the wife of the ranchero, Don José Galindo, was said to be skilled in cases of difficult childbirth.

"The Laguna Merced is too far away," he said. "It would be hours before the señora could get here. I thought old Rafaela was a competent midwife!"

"For the Indian women, perhaps," said Luisa. "They give birth with ease, but your lady is in great distress, señor, and may need more help than Rafaela can give her."

"Then get back to your mistress, woman!" Don José Galindo was the grandson of Juan Bautista de Anza, who had led the great expedition to the bay in 1776; there was no family more respected, or better connected than his. Carlos had no intention of letting any of the Galindos know what was going on at the Rancho Rivera on this windy Candlemas Day.

Rafaela's daughter Juana, a buxom Indian squaw with a child of her own at the breast, came to help her mother at the end, and the babies were alive and mewling like two kittens. Carlos could hear them in the next room. Luisa came back to him at last, and told him Doña Rosalie was in a high fever and verging on delirium.

"Let me see her now." Juana and Rafaela were holding her hands as she tossed from side to side in the great bed. Rosalie's face was an ugly red and there was sweat on her brow. She greeted Carlos, when he stroked her cheek, with a babble of indistinguishable words.

"To think there's no priest nearer than Santa Clara!" wept Luisa. "Ought not Roberto to go for Father Mercado?"

"Better to fetch the American doctor," said Carlos grimly. He saw that the women had lighted half a dozen candles beneath Rosalie's picture of the Virgin of Guadalupe, and for good measure had attached some dried-up Indian charms to the headboard of the bed. "Where are the children?"

Somehow he had expected them to be lying on their mother's breast. She was too restless for that, and Juana, proudly producing a rush basket, laid the tiny occupants along Carlos's arms.

He stood staring down at them in the light from the candles. They were very small, but well formed, with their minute finger-nails complete and a fuzz of golden down on each little head. Their features were alike and clearly marked with a look that was not Spanish, and when the boy opened his drowsy lids –

"His eyes are blue," said Carlos.

"All babies' eyes are blue," Luisa said, and took them from his lax arms.

"I'll sit up in the sala," said the man. "Come to me at midnight, and I'll decide what should be done."

When he left the bedroom Rafaela was trying to get the new mother to swallow a cooling draught. Carlos, too, poured himself some wine. Blue eyes – yes, he had heard of that milky, indeterminate blue of the newborn which darkened to the brown of the Spanish inheritance, or changed to green, like Rosalie's Castilian eyes. But not the sapphire glint of that boy's! The three women intent on their charge, and not daring to raise their heads, heard the crash as Carlos threw his wine glass into a corner of the room.

★　　★　　★

John Marsh, one of the first settlers to arrive in California from the United States, had earned a BA degree from Harvard in 1823. He chose to consider it as an MD when he reached Alta California thirteen years later, and nobody objected. 'Doctor' Marsh was a good physician according to his lights, and a better cattleman. Under a Mexican grant he held the Rancho Los Medanos on the Contra Costa, and increased his herds by charging one head of cattle for every mile he travelled to a patient's sickbed. He reckoned, as he dismounted in the yard of the Rancho Rivera, that his trip had already been very profitable.

Over a week had passed since the twins were born, for Dr. Marsh was not at home when the messenger arrived from Carlos, and the young man came out to meet him with an anxious face. Doña Rosalie was very weak, he said, and unable to nurse her little girl.

"Your vaqueros said you lost the boy, too bad," said Dr. Marsh.

"Yes, we lost him."

"Better luck next time" – cheerfully. "Now let me have a look at the lady."

There was a young Indian woman in the bedroom with Luisa, and Dr. Marsh sent them both out while he examined his patient. She had had a pretty sharp go of the milk fever, he told her, but the febrifuge he had brought would do her good. She mustn't take any more of their Indian potions, he would tell the women so. And this was the baby! Fine, fine, a nice little girl. Who was suckling her? That Indian woman?

"Yes, Mariquita," said Rosalie feebly. "There was another wet-nurse, called Juana. I don't know where she went."

"Did Juana deliver you?"

"No, it was her mother, old Rafaela," said Rosalie, "but she's gone away too. And oh, señor, my boy!"

"There, there, don't cry," said Dr. Marsh. "You'll have half a dozen of them yet. How long did the poor mite live?"

"I don't know."

"You don't know?"

"I was ill, you see. I can't remember. Carlos came and told me he was dead."

"You mustn't get so excited, Doña Rosalie." Dr. Marsh was startled when the girl raised herself in bed and seized his frilled shirt front.

"Señor doctor, will you do something for me? Will you go to my home, the Rancho Estrada at Sonoma, and tell my brother Luis how you found me? Tell him my little son is dead. I meant to call him Luis, say, but he died unbaptised, an innocent child cast into limbo, and I'll never get well unless they forgive me and let Rita come to me –"

"You must be calm, dear lady. Who is Rita?"

"She used to be my nurse, and she knows all about it. She told me it would be all right, there in that hot room at Sonoma where she made me drink the love drink . . . Promise me you'll take my message, señor, but don't tell my husband . . ." Her voice trailed off, and Dr. Marsh, laying down her wrist in which the blue veins were throbbing, said,

"I promise, señora, if *you* promise to be good and go to sleep now. Remember you have a little daughter left you, and a husband to get well for, too." He took the baby from its cradle and waited for Rosalie to hold out her arms. It was a beautiful child, with blue eyes and a fluff of golden hair beneath its embroidered cap – to the doctor's eyes, quite obviously an infant which had come to term. No resemblance to the mother, and none to Don Carlos Rivera. Dr. Marsh had lived long enough among the Californios to be surprised at nothing.

He had to make a detour to see a patient at San Rafael (counting off the miles by water as by land), so that it took him several days to reach Sonoma, where he told a story carefully edited for the sake of Rosalie's ailing mother, and parried the questions of Luis Estrada. The young ranchero agreed that Rita, escorted by the cowboy Bernardo, should start next day for Yerba Buena.

"Won't you come with me yourself, Don Luis?" Rita ventured to say. "I'm afraid for my young lady, alone with that man –" He stopped her with a look.

"I'll follow you as soon as I can," he promised. "It's better Felipe and I ride together, and he'll be here in a day or two." Rita, anxious and fearful, set out alone with the vaquero.

It was after dark when they arrived, and a pert young Mexican woman who said her name was Mariquita told Rita that her master and mistress had retired for the night and could not be disturbed. But Carlos heard the voices in the yard, and came out of the guest room which he had occupied since the birth of the twins to explain Rita's presence to his servants.

"You must forgive a chilly welcome," he said. "Doña Rosalie chose to make a little mystery out of asking Dr. Marsh to fetch you. She only told me tonight that you were expected."

"Señor, how is she?"

"Better, I think. She was out of bed for a couple of hours

yesterday, and for longer this afternoon. But you mustn't pay too much attention to everything she says, Rita. She's very fanciful. You'll find her illness has changed her a good deal."

She thought Don Carlos had changed too. In a baggy jacket and trousers, dun-coloured in the feeble light from the house, he looked ten years older than the brilliant caballero of the Sonoma wedding.

"And the little baby, señor?"

'They say she isn't thriving," said Carlos with indifference. "Mariquita, look after Rita and then take her to your mistress. Roberto," to his own vaquero, "make sure this man gets food and wine and a bed in the weaving shed, there's no room in the bunk house. I'll see you in the morning, Rita."

She watched the vaquero take Bernardo to a door on the other side of the yard, and she watched Don Carlos shut himself into the guest room. She knew she must be refreshed and calm when she went to Rosalie, and calm she was when in the shadowy room where a baby was crying she held the unhappy young mother in her arms.

"Oh Rita, Rita, why didn't you come to me before?"

"How could I, querida? Felipe came home saying a baby was expected in April, so I thought all was well and it was I who had been mistaken –"

"Look at her."

Rita lifted the little creature from its cradle and tried to hush its wailing. She saw the blue eyes under the heavy lids, the fluff of gold hair, and something in the baby face which made her think of Peter Gagarin.

"Oh, my poor darling, I see, indeed I see!" she whispered. "Does he know?"

"I'm sure he knows. He heard about that awful day at Bodega Bay, and he went across to Sausalito and talked to the captain of the *Young Julia* before the Russians left for Alaska. He knows about me and Peter."

"But he accepts the child as his own?"

"He says he'll take her to be christened when Father Mercado next comes to the Mission."

"Have you chosen her name?"

"Maria de los Dolores. Isn't it right for her?"

Mary of the Sorrows, the saddest name of all. Rita sighed as she laid the fretful baby in its mother's arms, and Rosalie said, "She isn't well, is she? I don't think Mariquita's milk agrees with her."

"Mariquita? Is that young slut your wet-nurse?"

"Yes, she is, since Juana went away." And to Rita's anxious questions, Rosalie repeated the story of the two Indian women who had nursed her and disappeared, followed since Dr. Marsh's visit by Luisa, the Mexican housekeeper, who left on the pretext that she was needed at Santa Clara.

"But where did the Indians go, dear? Back to the ranchería?"

"There's no ranchería here," said Rosalie. "The Indian workers come and go, it's not like home . . . And I don't think he wants anybody here who could tell about the boy."

That was all she would say, and Rita, chafing her cold hands and feet, felt the icy touch of fear on her own neck. She fed more wood into the brazier, and lulled the mother and child to sleep. She lay down at the foot of the bed for a while, and just before four o'clock slipped into the yard and made her way to the weaving shed.

Rita had decided in the sleepless hours that Bernardo must ride back to Sonoma and tell Luis Estrada he must come at once to his sister. The intuition of her Indian heritage told her that there was danger in the air of the Rancho Rivera. All a mestiza servant, having no authority, could hope to do was protect Rosalie and her infant until a more powerful guardian arrived to take them away for what could diplomatically be called a long convalescence. She was startled to find that the door of the weaving shed was open and creaking in the wind.

"Bernardo! Bernardo!" she whispered. There was no reply.

She crept inside the strange room, hardly daring to move or let go the handle of the door. Then the shutter of a dark lantern clicked open, and silhouetted behind it Rita saw Carlos Rivera, sitting on the folded Indian blankets of an empty bed.

"Have I spoiled your rendezvous with Bernardo?" said the voice behind the lantern.

"My *rendezvous*, señor?"

"It's perhaps too grand a word to describe what happens when a maid sneaks out to a cowboy's bed."

"We don't do such things at the Rancho Estrada."

"You're fortunate. We're not so particular at the Rancho Rivera."

"What have you done with him?" The beam of lantern light swung round the scene: the looms with their fabrics, the storage chests, the single chair, the absence of any sign of Bernardo's occupancy.

"I sent him off half an hour ago, with one of my own men who had to go to the Rancho Sausalito. Your fellow will have an early start on his journey home. Now state *your* business, woman."

"I wanted to give him a message to Doña Maria, to reassure her about my young lady's health. I didn't expect to find *you* in a servant's room, señor."

"Well, are you satisfied that there's been no foul play? I told my capataz to meet me here with the horses, we have a rodeo today. Now get back to Doña Rosalie. You came here to nurse her, not to interfere in my affairs."

It was true enough about the capataz. Followed by a boy leading the horses, the man passed Rita with a gruff greeting as she went back across the yard. Her sense of danger was not lessened by the departure of Bernardo towards Sausalito at the unlikely hour of half past three. Yet as she went indoors she had an impression of sorrow as well as danger. The young man sitting alone in an empty room, drained of energy, was as wretched as the girl who had learned to fear him.

Rita would have been happier, as the day of the rodeo passed, if she had known that fifty miles away Luis Estrada had come to the same conclusion as herself. Another and more probing talk with Dr. Marsh had persuaded him that his sister should be in his care. Felipe, who had ridden in from Salmon Creek, was inclined to agree with him, although –

"Can't we wait until the day after tomorrow, Luis?" he asked. "I ought to see Vallejo. He's making difficulties about transporting the Russian buildings across the Carrillo land at Santa Rosa –"

"To the devil with the Russians and the Carrillos too," said Luis, for once roused to action. "We ride tomorrow, and let Vallejo wait. He's only being obstructive because his offer to buy Fort Ross was rejected while Sutter won."

It was true that a farewell gift from the Russians to General

Vallejo, consisting of a dressing case fitted with toilet articles and a table service of monogrammed silver, fit for a commander in the field, had hardly consoled the recipient for the loss of Fort Ross to Captain Sutter. Felipe shrugged his shoulders, and proposed that they ride to the bay by San Rafael and Sausalito. "Señor Murphy will give us a bed tomorrow night," he said, "and Don Antonio's people will ferry us across. But remember, when we see Carlos Rivera, you'll have to do the talking."

About the time when her brothers were discussing their journey, Rosalie had her first outing. Warmly wrapped, she strolled in the yard when the sun was at its height, and then sat in the sala for an hour. Rita, waiting on her, and giving little Dolores a preparation made from cow's milk in a silver spoon, was struck again by the silence of the rancho. The men, of course, were working at the rodeo corrals, but the only guard at the gate was a feeble old Mexican, and Mariquita was the only woman Rita saw all day. It was a great contrast to the busy, populated world of the Rancho Estrada.

Don Carlos made a brief appearance after Rosalie was back in bed. He stood leaning against the door jamb, apparently very tired, and said he was not fit to appear in a lady's bedroom. She was feeling better? that was good. She had been out of doors? very good, but she mustn't overdo it. And when Rosalie, with an attempt at her old manner, said she meant to have luncheon in the sala next day, he bowed too low, and said alas! he had been invited to the Presidio, and would ride on to Yerba Buena. On the following day, he hoped to see Doña Rosalie resume the place of honour at his table.

Under the sting of the sarcasm, Rosalie passed a restless night. Next day she was fully dressed by the time he set out for the Presidio, and gave him a curtsy, as grand as his own bow, when he rode away. Then she turned to Rita, and said, "They'll play faro at the tavern until it grows dark, and maybe later. You and I have time to ride to the Mission Dolores."

"Ride! You're not fit to ride anywhere!"

"Oh yes, I am. It's only a mile away, and *I must go*. I can't wait any longer —"

"But querida, there's no priest at the Mission to hear your

confession. You'll have to wait until the padre comes from Santa Clara –"

"I can't wait longer to see my baby's grave."

It was said with the wild look which had terrified Rita on the first night, and there was the damp of fever in the moist hands which clutched her own. But Rita could not, had never been able to, resist; she went submissively to the corral and told one of the men to saddle the white mare for her mistress and another beast for herself. Mariquita, with the baby girl in her arms, stood watching in amazement as they rode out between the barricade of skulls and whitened bones.

There were other watchers, too, as they set off at a walk, for the vaqueros were lounging round the bunk house, and Rita heard a shout. "Roberto!" said Rosalie between set teeth. "He'll go to the Presidio to fetch Carlos home. Rita, ride!" In spite of her promise to keep to a gentle walk she urged the mare to a gallop, and very soon they were at the Mission Dolores.

There was the usual group of bedraggled Indians on the crumbling steps. There was the gravestone of Don Luis Argüello, which Rosalie herself had cleared of lichen and creepers, and there were other memorials which looked as if centuries instead of years had passed over them. But nowhere in the tiny cemetery, where the few stones leaned tipsily against each other, could be found the newly cut turfs which covered a baby's grave.

"It isn't here!" Rosalie was almost beyond speech by the time they had stumbled up and down between the berry vines covered with new buds and tearing their skirts, not once but half a dozen times. "Oh, where is he? What have they done with him?"

"Is there a burying ground back at the rancho?" Rita clutched at a straw. "The parents of Don Carlos –"

"Are buried at Santa Clara. Rita, speak to *them*!" She indicated the wretched Indians, and Rita, who hardly knew their dialect, learned from one old man, once a neophyte of the Franciscans, that there had been no burial in the graveyard of the Mission Dolores for many, many moons.

"Rosalie, what did Don Carlos tell you? Did he actually say the child was buried here?"

"I can't remember. He said the boy was dead, that's all I know. Rita, he killed him!"

At the wild shriek Rita crossed herself, and cried out "My God! No!" But Rosalie was on horseback already, and galloping down the dirt road to the Rancho Rivera.

The peon on guard scrambled to his feet as she pulled the white mare to a halt. "Did Roberto ride to the Presidio?" she flung at him. The man, gaping, could only say, "He rode, he rode, señora, I know not where!"

"There isn't much time, Rita, we have to hurry." Rosalie ran into the sala, snatched up the baby and told the terrified Mariquita to go to the kitchen and wait till she was sent for.

"Rosalie, I beg you, do nothing rash. Ask your husband calmly to tell you everything. He must be able to explain –"

"Explain murder?" Rosalie pulled open one of the drawers of the desk and took out a velvet bag. Over her gloved hands poured the creamy waterfall of the pearls of Loreto.

"Rita, take my child. Take the pearls I wore at my wedding, and use them to find safety for Dolores. Otherwise Carlos will kill her too."

"Oh, my God, what are we going to do?" cried Rita. "Rosalie, listen. When we came in to Yerba Buena Cove yesterday I saw a Russian ship at anchor. The men told me she was bound for Monterey. If we ride across country with the baby we can go aboard and they will take us all to safety –"

"And then? Shall I throw myself on the mercy of my kinsman Don Mariano Estrada? Will he give his protection to a runaway wife and her lover's child?"

"If he refuses I know where to find shelter. I have a sister in Monterey, married to an Englishman –"

"Too late," said Rosalie. "I hear the horses on the road. Take Dolores. Hide in the bedroom. Don't be afraid."

The baby was whimpering, out of sight in the bedroom, and Rosalie heard men's voices in the yard. She stripped off her gloves and the silk scarf she had twisted round her head. Then she opened the second drawer and took out the double-barrelled pistol Carlos had carried to their wedding at Sonoma. She slipped off the safety catch, wrapped the weapon in the scarf and laid it on the desk.

"You rode to the Mission, señora," said Carlos from the doorway.

"As your spy Roberto told you."

"As my servant informed me, according to his duty. You went to the Mission alone, or as good as alone, against my express orders; why?"

"I went to look for my son's grave."

"Oh," said Carlos Rivera, and came farther into the sala. "You went to look, and you found nothing?"

"Because you killed him, and left his body to the coyotes –"

"Be silent, you madwoman," said Carlos. "The brat's alive."

"*Alive*? Then where is he? My baby! What have you done with him? Answer me!"

"He's with the right kind of people to bring up a wayside bastard. You didn't think I would allow the name of Rivera to be given to your Russian lover's spawn?"

Rosalie gasped. She clutched at the desk, and felt the silken scarf beneath her hand.

"Do you remember what you told Luisa, the first morning after I brought you home?" he went on relentlessly. "I heard what you said: 'You can't put clean sheets on a dirty bed.' But that was just what you made me do, you lying devil – put my clean sheets on your dishonoured body."

She levelled the pistol and shot him through the scarf, point-blank, between the eyes, and as Carlos fell, Peter Gagarin's lover put the smoking weapon against her heart and pulled the trigger.

Part Two

The Americans

I I

Her name was Dolly. So said her foster father, Henry Winter, who had a fancy for pet names and diminutives. His own nickname had been Chips when he was a carpenter in the British merchant navy, and it stuck to him in the ships of the Pacific coastal trade and later on the beach at Monterey. His mestiza wife had been baptised Maria del Carmen, but she was 'Carrie' to Chips, and as for the child whom a desperate woman brought to them from the Russian ship lying off Monterey, he declared that 'Dolores' was too big a mouthful for a midget.

So she was Dolly always, and *la muñequita*, the little doll, or Goldie for her golden hair, and sometimes even Princess, a fanciful name which her Aunt Carrie discouraged.

Before he took the orphan child under his protection Chips Winter had been considered little better than an odd-job man by the Spanish and Mexican inhabitants of Monterey. The elderly English carpenter with his bag of tools on his shoulder was not an impressive figure in the town for seventy years the capital of Alta California, with a population of one thousand, four times the size of Yerba Buena. But Chips was taken up by the leading American citizen of Monterey, Thomas Oliver Larkin, who kept him in steady work on the reconstruction of the only Customs House on the Californian coast, and on the redwood interiors of the handsome two-storey house he was building for his own family. He allowed the Winters to live rent free in a one-room adobe dwelling built on to the Larkin home, with a door on the Calle Principal and a back door on the Larkin garden.

When Dolly Winter told the story of her life, in several different versions and several different cities of the world, she sometimes said that she could remember that pretty garden, with the fountain and the flowers, and a little girl called Adelaida, the daughter of the house, who was Dolly's first playmate. But this may have been a confused recollection of other gardens and other children, because before Dolly was two years old the Winters moved into a much larger adobe on the slope between the Castillo and the Customs House. It seemed as if their adopted child had brought good fortune with her.

When this was hinted to Chips he was able to retort that his increasing prosperity came from better-paid work. An Englishman named Jack Swan, who as a sea cook had been one of his shipmates in the old *Soledad*, settled in Monterey and employed Chips in the building of a combined apartment house and saloon which was like nothing ever seen in Alta California. The four apartments were two-room units divided by partitions which could be rolled up, while the bar had a big back fireplace much appreciated by the customers on foggy nights. It was well patronised by the liberty men from the American frigates which put in to Monterey, and by the Englishmen on shore leave from Admiral Seymour's squadron, which seemed to the observers in Monterey to be constantly in the offing. The seamen liked Monterey, a pretty town straggling along a crescent-shaped bay, where the houses had red tiled roofs and adobe walls plastered and covered with whitewash, and life was as animated as befitted the seat of territorial government and of the *junta departamental*.

However high the arguments raged in the wineshops about the fall of Governor Micheltorena and the threats of his successor, Governor Pio Pico, to remove the capital to the remote Pueblo de Nuestra Señora la Reina de Los Angeles, Monterey, in the last pastoral years of California, was a happy place for children. They ran barefoot through the streets from the Royal Chapel to the Noble Harbour, splashing in the bay where the Indians netted the sardines which threw themselves on the beach in shoals. They watched the foreign sailors coming ashore in their longboats and the soldiers drilling at the Castillo, and begged for sweets from the American shop-keepers. From the time she was able to toddle Dolly Winter followed the children. When she was four she could sing their songs and dance with them on the beach with a crown of flowers on her head. In her shabby dress she was distinguishable from the others only by her fairer skin and the wealth of golden hair which Aunt Carrie brushed as religiously as Rita had brushed the black hair of Rosalie Estrada.

She never felt the lack of a father and mother. They had been English aristocrats, Chips told her, who died of fever on the Old Spanish Trail, and he made sure that Dolly could speak English at the same time as she began to chatter in Spanish. She felt quite secure in the care of Uncle Chips and Aunt Carrie. Jack Swan was another uncle to pet and spoil her, and she liked to sit on his knee when the saloon-keeper came to drink a noggin of rum with his old shipmate.

Other Americanos – so-called whether of American or English origin – occasionally came to see Chips Winter. Then Dolly was made to curtsy and be silent, while Aunt Carrie, a submissive woman far more Indian than Spanish in her mixed heritage, kept flicking invisible dust off the chairs and tables. The talk then was of the future of California, and the ambition of the new President of the United States, James K. Polk, to extend American rule to the shores of the Pacific. This was far above Dolly's head, but in her small feminine heart she was aware that these visitors were men of power. Certainly the financial power of Monterey was in their hands, for most of the showy caballeros galloping into town from their ranchos owed money to the American traders. The latter, with that passion for work which made the Californios laugh, had supplementary activities. Josiah Merritt had a law practice, and recorded the transactions of financial entrepreneurs like Thomas O. Larkin, who in 1844 had been appointed the first United States Consul to California. William Hartnell kept a school as well as the office where he had given the young Mariano Vallejo instruction in business methods before the future general joined the Mexican Army. Larkin, Hartnell,

David Spence, Hugh McCullough – Dolly, who had a musical ear, liked their harsh names less than the liquid Spanish of de la Torre, Gutierrez, or Don Mariano Estrada, who had once been the Commandant of Monterey. Even better than the Spanish names she liked the sound of John Charles Fremont, which began to be mentioned often as the Christmas of 1845 drew near. When Dolly asked Chips Winter who Fremont might be, he answered with a dry laugh, "They call him the King of the Rocky Mountains!"

Charmed by the romantic title, Dolly played at being the Queen of the Rocky Mountains for a whole day, with a shawl tied round her waist for a train, and then she forgot Fremont in the excitement of Christmas Eve, when Chips took her to the Royal Chapel. Not to worship, for the old man was a sturdy agnostic who had weaned Maria del Carmen from her Catholic faith, but to see the annual presentation of the nativity play. Called *Los Pastores*, the story of the shepherds at Bethlehem was repeated in the homes of the rich during the Christmas season, but never to better advantage than in the gaunt old church built by the Spanish as part of their colonising mission, with a makeshift stage in front of the high altar as a throne for the Virgin and the Child. The Royal Chapel was brilliant with candles and echoed with the shepherds' songs. For an impressionable child like Dolly Winter it was a riot of music and colour. She was envious of the young woman, clumsy and touching in her earnestness, who played the Virgin, terrified of the Evil One in his dress of crimson flame, awestruck by the Angel Gabriel with his widespread purple wings; but most of all amazed to see, among the littlest shepherds singing hosannas, some of her own playmates.

"Uncle Chips," she whispered, "why can't I be a shepherd with a long gown and a silk wand?"

"Shepherdess, Goldie. Only little boys can be shepherds."

"But two of them are girls! You know Pilar and Paquita Soto –"

"They're both older than you are."

"Pilar's only six! Can I be a shepherd next year, when I'm five?"

"We'll see." He put his arm round her. "Why, darling,

you're trembling! You mustn't get so excited, it's only a play."

But the excitement lasted until Dolly was in bed in the dark, making the first speculative effort of her life as she tried to imagine what it would be like to stand on a candlelit stage in a great dark place, to wear a white robe and feel what she had instinctively felt in the Royal Chapel – the crowd's emotion responding to the emotion of the players.

Monterey itself began to resemble a lighted stage in the days after the New Year, as certain well-rehearsed actors prepared to speak their lines in a new production, and the name of John Charles Fremont was heard as often in Jack Swan's bar as in the homes of the Americanos. The man Chips Winter called the King of the Rocky Mountains was in more prosaic terms an American officer, formerly a lieutenant in the Corps of Topographical Engineers, who had furthered his career by exploring and surveying the passes of the Rockies and the routes over the Sierras in two arduous expeditions. He was now on his third such journey in the West, and was reported to be on his way to Sutter's Fort at New Helvetia, which had become the staging point for all the immigrants moving in to California from the United States.

Every Californio who took the trouble to think was aware that the appointment of Larkin as the American Consul in California proved the growing desire of Washington to annex California, a Mexican possession, to the United States. He was President Polk's appointee and undercover man, bent on using the influential men of the Territory to bring about the annexation by peaceful means. Fremont was the son-in-law of Senator Thomas Benton, a leading believer that the Union could only fulfil its manifest destiny by moving westwards to the Pacific. Every Californio who appreciated a quiet life hoped that his land would not share the blood-boltered fate of Texas, detached from Mexico and admitted to the Union after ten years of strife.

The men under Fremont's command were alleged to have come on a peaceful mission with a scientific purpose, but the mere presence of American troops in the Territory was as vexatious to the Californios as had been the establishment of the Russians at Fort Ross.

Fremont was heard of at Yerba Buena, which he left after a short stay to head south to Monterey – a far cry, his critics said, from the Rocky Mountains, and a terrain where his talents as pathmarker and topographer were certainly not required. Spanish surveyors and Spanish soldiers, with Indian labour, had long since made the main roads and were making more. But the Montereños turned out to see the American troops arrive, and thought they marched well all things considered, for their uniforms and equipment had suffered severely on their arduous trek across the mountains. They brought an auxiliary force of Americans from Sutter's Fort, who also were shabby and emaciated, and seemed to have little idea of discipline. The usual formalities were carried out with courtesy at the Presidio and the Castillo, and food and water were supplied to the Americans as soon as they pitched camp.

Mr. Larkin, as American Consul, of course offered his hospitality to John C. Fremont, and next day the two men lunched alone together at the house on the Calle Principal which Dolly Winter was later to claim among her earliest memories. Mr. Larkin had been anxious about his meeting with Fremont, and grew more anxious as the meal went on. There was a quality of theatricality about the engineer which jarred on him. It expressed itself even in Fremont's attire. His shirt and trousers were army blue, but the flannel shirt was open at the neck and over it he wore a deerskin hunting tunic. He wore mocassins instead of army boots. Larkin wondered what impression this calculated effect of being half army officer and half wilderness scout would make on the Californios.

"I'd like to tell you about some of the men you'll be meeting later this afternoon," he said when cigars were lit, "and then you must tell me what you think of them. I know President Polk wants an independent report, from an observer like yourself, of the situation here."

"I'm not worried about the *military* situation," said Fremont with emphasis. "From what I've already seen Monterey can easily be captured by land or sea."

"I wasn't speaking in terms of attack or surrender," said Larkin with a frown. "The situation I want you to assess is a human one. In all my correspondence with President Polk I've

stressed the need for friendly negotiations with the Californios. I'd like to know who you, as a fresh observer, think will
be willing to support California's entrance to the Union, and
who will be against it."

"They may not have much choice in the matter," said
Fremont. "Since the Mexican government rejected President
Polk's offer to purchase all California, his attitude has har-
dened considerably. I doubt if an appeal for 'friendly negotiations' would weigh with him now."

"But his Cabinet, sir! The Secretary of War wrote to me as
lately as October, saying the Californios would be received as
brothers within the Union. I've repeated this again and again
to my Spanish friends –"

"I'm prepared to bet," said Fremont, "that Mr. Polk, as
Commander-in-Chief, will overrule the Secretary if he de-
cides that California can only be won as a prize of war."

"I'm very sorry to hear you say so."

"What is Governor Pico's attitude?" asked Fremont.

"Ambiguous, to say the least of it. I'm sorry he won't be
here today. He rode south last month to attend the great Yorba
wedding at San Gabriel, and went on to visit his brother in Los
Angeles. But Doña Isabel Yorba's bridegroom will be with us,
for the happy couple stopped on their way to Sonoma to visit
his kinsman, Don Mariano Estrada. He gave a splendid fiesta
for them last week at the Rancho Buena Vista."

"Is the bridegroom's name also Estrada?"

"Luis Estrada."

"Then I heard about the marriage from his brother Felipe,
whom I met at Yerba Buena. I thought it strange he hadn't
accompanied Don Luis to his wedding, but I was told the
brothers weren't on good terms. Is it true they disagreed over
the division of their sister's estate?"

"I never heard the rights of it," said the cautious Larkin.
"There was some sort of scandal, I believe, but it was hushed
up very quickly. A little brandy?"

He had no intention of enlarging on the tragedy at the
Rancho Rivera to a man who had had his own share of family
scandal. John Charles Fremont, born in Georgia, was the
bastard son of a French *emigré* and an unhappily married
woman, and his birth had been an outrage to the lady's family

and her husband's which had resounded through the South. He said, "Felipe Estrada married an American girl, old Skipper Putnam's daughter. Did you get the impression that he's favourable to our cause?"

"Oh, certainly; that energetic little lady has brought him round. Do you imply that Don Luis's collaboration is not so sure?"

"Not sure at all," said Larkin. "He's a man of only thirty – about your own age, sir – but he's one of the old Spanish nobility, and as reactionary as his kinsman, Don Mariano. I've an agent on the frontier, a man called Robert Cord, who knows both the Estradas well, and he describes Don Luis as a man who thinks himself above politics, but who might be a dangerously able leader in the event, which God forbid, of war."

"I heard of Robert Cord at Sutter's Fort as an agent of General Vallejo. Now it seems he's on our side. What about Vallejo's loyalty?"

"He's absolutely loyal to Mexico, but I've heard him say, time and again, that he hopes for a voluntary association between California and the United States."

"You know him well, then?" said Fremont.

"We're connected by marriage, sir. My half-brother, Captain Cooper of the *California*, married Vallejo's sister Encarnacion. I believe the general would be glad to meet you, if your journey north should take you near either of his homes."

"I'm obliged to you, Mr. Larkin," said Fremont. "I think I can plan on a visit to Sonoma before midsummer. And now I believe your guests are arriving . . ."

Luis Estrada was the last of the invited guests to appear in Mr. Larkin's handsome sala, and Larkin caught his look of surprise at Fremont's informal dress. Luis himself was dressed as befitted a bridegroom. He had lost his romantic good looks in the hard years following the tragedy of Rosalie, and with his harsher features and gold-laced coat looked more like one of the Spanish officers of 1776 than the light-hearted ranchero who had danced at the Peralta wedding. But he had met his bride at the Peralta wedding when she was still a child, and pretty, witty Isabel Yorba had returned his love and kept faith with him against the opposition of all her relatives. The patriarch of the family, Don Tomas Yorba, immensely rich and powerful in the south, had thundered from his Rancho Santa Ana that he would never give his granddaughter to an Estrada, "to bear a name tainted with the crimes of murder and suicide". But the lovers had persisted, and when Isabel was eighteen Don Tomas himself, with a shrug of the shoulders, had given her in marriage at the altar of San Gabriel. Her husband, in the four ecstatic weeks of their slow journey to Sonoma, was happier than he had been since the tragedy of Rosalie.

"Don Mariano presents his compliments, señores," he said with a bow to Larkin and Fremont, who were standing side by side. "He regrets very much that he can not do so in person."

"He isn't ill, I hope?" asked Mr. Larkin.

"He was quite well when we all left Buena Vista this morning," said Luis. "I think the ride into town was too much for him. He had an attack of faintness at the luncheon table, and I persuaded him to remain at the Casa Estrada."

"Quite right, Don Luis, pray give him our heartiest good wishes," Thomas Larkin said. "And," he thought, "the old fox is no more faint than I am: he wanted to dodge the meeting. Whichever way the cat jumps, he'll be able to say he never met Fremont." It was an old man's device, and the younger Californios present were exercising their own form of deviousness by overwhelming Fremont with compliments on his remarkable achievements – "opening up the Territory, giving us hope for improved communications with our neighbours" and so on, without ever allowing the conversation to turn to politics. The purpose of Mr. Larkin's reception was frustrated, but he admired the Spanish grace of the performance. So did Luis Estrada. There had been few guests at the rancho since Rosalie's tragedy and the death of his mother, and Luis had seldom been in a gathering of important men. Now, standing next to General Castro in the group surrounding Fremont, head and shoulders above the slim little American with the blue eyes and olive skin who so obviously wished to impress the Californios, he remembered a similar occasion when Vallejo was the host, and another foreigner, Prince Peter Gagarin, had defended his country's interests with pride. For the first time since the tragedy he thought of Peter as an honest man and a Russian patriot rather than as the villain who had ruined his sister's life. "God knows," he thought, "we might have been as well off with the Russians as with the Yankedos, if we had to choose."

Through the buzz of talk he approached Fremont with the question every man in the room wanted to ask.

"You're a long way from your camp in the Rockies, señor," he said. "What route do you intend to follow when you leave Monterey?"

"Towards Oregon," said Fremont readily. "My government, as you may know, is in dispute with the British over the line of latitude to be fixed as the international boundary. New maps and surveys of the area must be provided."

"Ah yes!" "Of course!" "Most interesting!" Few of Larkin's guests knew the difference between latitude and longitude, but all were delighted to think that a quarrel with the British could distract American belligerence from themselves. Oregon was agreeably far away, and Luis wished Fremont luck in his arduous journey.

"And you, Don Luis?" said Fremont. "Do you intend to stay long in Monterey?"

"We leave the day after tomorrow, if Don Mariano feels up to a long ride. He has set his heart on accompanying us to the rancho of one òf his sons, twenty miles away."

"I hope our paths may cross again some day."

"I too, señor." Luis turned to Larkin and explained that he must leave. "Doña Isabel asked me not to stay too long," he said. "She was alarmed by Don Mariano's fainting fit at luncheon."

"And Don Luis is impatient to return to his beautiful bride," said General Castro slyly, and in a flurry of laughter and good wishes Luis was able to make his escape. The distance from the Larkin house to the Casa Estrada was so short that even a man who rode everywhere thought riding home was out of the question, and he set off on foot along the Calle Principal.

He had enjoyed every day of his visit to Monterey, whether at the Rancho Buena Vista or in the town house full of memories of his boyhood, and a special pleasure had been showing Isabel the scenes and places he remembered from those days. The town had grown since he was a child, but remained essentially the same, with only a few people in the streets at dusk, and the riding lights appearing on the few ships lying in the Noble Harbour under the tattered banners of the sunset. It was so quiet that Luis could hear the waves breaking on the distant beach.

But now his sense of enjoyment was gone. The personality of Fremont had so jarred upon him, the man's very presence was so disquieting, that Luis forgot to recall the felicity, so soon to be his again, of holding Isabel in his arms in what had been his parents' bridal bed. He felt isolated in the little world of Alta California, cut off from the great events moving behind the mountains. It would be many weeks before he, and others like him, could know that on the same day of the reception for Fremont, President Polk had ordered General Zachary Taylor to prepare to cross the River Nueces, occupy the left bank of the Rio Grande del Norte, and bring his guns to bear on the Mexican town of Matamoros.

What Luis Estrada and Mr. Larkin's other guests learned all too soon was that Fremont, instead of riding north to Oregon, had led his men south into the Salinas valley, and there, on the pretext that General Castro was harassing American settlers, had raised the American flag on Gavilan Peak.

★   ★   ★

Luis Estrada entered Vioget's tavern at Yerba Buena on a fine May afternoon, just as his brother and sister-in-law were finishing their midday meal.

He stood unobserved by the doorway, watching them. They were talking eagerly – they always had plenty to say to one another – and Content was marking each point of her argument, whatever it was, by counting on her fingers. She looked singularly unattractive to Luis, with her sandy hair twisted into a knot and her brown dress covered by a black calico overall with patch pockets on the skirt and a special pocket on the bib to hold her pen case. Felipe, like his brother, looked older than his years, his shoulders rounded by desk work, and as the senior partner in the thriving firm of Estrada and Putnam he wore a business suit cut in the American style.

Then they looked round, and saw Luis, and were cordial. Was Isabel with him? No, what a pity! He would stay the night, of course? They would see about a room for him at once, or rather as soon as he had had something to eat and drink. The stew was unappetising, but Luis was hungry, and the wine at least was good. He ate quickly, while Content plied him with questions about Isabel and all her projects for the summer. They had been guests at the rancho at Easter, and Content had been impressed by the bride's grasp of all a woman's duties as the wife of a great ranchero.

"And what brings you to Yerba Buena, brother?" Felipe enquired. "A visit to the agents? Spear and Hinckly are both around, I saw them at the wharf this morning."

"Business of another sort, Felipe. I've had a letter from Don Mariano at Monterey, which I want to discuss with you – if you can spare the time."

It was the sort of gibe Luis had taken to making after Felipe became a businessman, and he regretted it. But his brother said "Certainly!" and Content, getting up and brushing crumbs from the calico overall, said briskly "Let's all go to our room, then."

Luis had hoped to talk to his brother alone, but Content had a finger in every pie, and besides there was nowhere for the girl to go unless she remained alone in Vioget's crowded bar and dining room. The Estradas occupied one room in the tavern. Isabel had been horrified at their living arrangements when she met her new relations towards the end of her wedding journey, and even Luis felt diffident at sitting in the bedroom of a young married couple, although it was much more of an office than a bedroom. There was a wardrobe, and a bed pushed out of the way against a wall to make room for a big work table piled with daybooks and ledgers, where Content kept the books of Estrada and Putnam. She had never enjoyed housekeeping, and they ate all their meals in the dining room.

It was Content's lack of femininity and her ability (much greater than his own) to cope with the prosaic details of business which jarred on Luis. Discussing her, as he often did, with Isabel, he would admit that she seemed to suit Felipe, and that at least they had had the decency to postpone their marriage until after his mother's death. It had been another, if a minor, Estrada scandal, that the two had been married almost in secret by a missionary priest, in the private chapel built for the Indians on the Castro estate in the Contra Costa, the bride refusing to be received into the Catholic church or to promise that their children should be brought up in the faith. They had been married over two years now, and there was no sign of any offspring. Luis smiled to himself as he followed the scrawny figure of his sister-in-law into the shabby room.

"When did you get Don Mariano's letter?" Felipe began.

"About a week ago. I couldn't leave the ranch sooner. Here, read it for yourself."

My dear Luis [the old man's letter began]
I write to tell you about an extraordinary meeting of the *junta departamental* which I recently attended here. The subject was the war between the United States and Mexico which seems to be inevitable since General Taylor crossed the Rio Grande at the end of March. In the event of war, the future of California will be in jeopardy, and the junta discussed the alternatives open to the Territory. General Castro, who is the hero of the hour since he drove the adventurer, Fremont, out of the Salinas valley, said "better monarchy than anarchy", and cast his vote for an association with Britain or France. General Vallejo, voting for 'democracy', said California should unite with the Americans, whom he called 'our brothers'.

"They're not *my* brothers," Luis interrupted Felipe's reading aloud. The reader glanced at Content and went on with the letter in silence. It was an impassioned plea to Luis to return to Monterey and take his rightful part in the councils which should ensure California's fidelity to its old Spanish past.

"You're not taking this seriously?" he said as he folded the letter and gave it back to Luis.

"Very seriously indeed."

"And you want my opinion of it?"

"I do."

"Then my advice is, forget it. Let them squabble in Monterey, as they've been squabbling for years, and look after your wife and your rancho; California will never be involved in President Polk's war with Mexico."

"You and I are citizens of the Republic of Mexico," said Luis.

"It's the first time I've ever heard you say so. You used to sneer at *la otra banda* –"

"There comes a time when a man must stand on his country. And the danger of war is present as long as Fremont is in the Territory."

"You're thinking of his escapade at Gavilan Peak? That was a piece of impertinence, if you like, but Castro taught him manners, and now he's far away in Oregon. Luis be sensible –"

"I'm leaving for Monterey tomorrow morning."

"And you're not taking Isabel?" said Content.

"For a very good reason," Luis smiled. "She's expecting a child in December."

"Oh, Luis!" cried Content, clapping her hands and starting out of her chair, "what a lovely Christmas gift!"

It was the first spontaneous and womanly thing Luis had ever heard her say, and he kissed her cheek and patted her thin shoulder.

"Congratulations, brother," said Felipe. "But is this the wisest time to be leaving Isabel alone?"

"Her sister, Doña Maddalena Martinez, is coming to be with her."

"Doña Maddalena lives in Los Angeles," said Content. "It will be a long while before she can reach Sonoma. How would it be if I went to the rancho and kept Isabel company until her sister arrives?"

"That's exceedingly kind of you, Content," said Luis, touched. "I – in fact, I was going to ask if Felipe could visit the place once or twice while I'm gone. I've every confidence in my capataz, but the vaqueros need keeping up to the mark, and so –"

"I'll take Content to Sonoma myself in a day or two, as soon as her father gets back from Bodega," said Felipe. "With Captain Putnam and Robert Cord to look after the business, I can easily be away for a few days."

"Is Cord in the pueblo? I never knew any man move as fast from place to place as he does."

"And carrying the latest news, at that," said Felipe, rising.

"You might walk along to the workshop with me now, and have a word with him. He must have been expecting me for the past half hour."

Luis bit back the words, "I'm sorry to have wasted your valuable time!" It occurred to him that his brother might be as anxious for a private talk as he was. He took up his sombrero, flung his bright serape round his shoulders, and followed Felipe out to the little harbour called Yerba Buena Cove.

Several Americans were chatting by the tavern door, and one of them stepped forward to speak to Felipe in English. Luis, with a slight bow, walked on, and stood waiting by the fence of the outdoor corral. He could see that by contrast with the static beauty of Monterey Yerba Buena was an expanding and even a bustling place. There had been an influx of American immigrants by sea, as well as a proportion of the first stragglers across the Sierra Nevada, and there were many new trading ventures. Estrada and Putnam, 'Builders, Shippers and Contractors' had a workshop near the first rudimentary wharf where the timber (planed at the sawmill on Salmon Creek managed by Robert Cord, and transported to Yerba Buena by Captain Putnam, retired from whaling) was carpentered into the frames of houses such as the Russians had put up, and as easy to take down. Luis thought of them as shacks.

Contrary to the rumours which reached Fremont, the Estradas had not quarrelled over the disposition of Rosalie's estate. Since her girl child had disappeared, with Rita, off the face of the earth, her two brothers were her legal heirs. The alcalde, Don Francisco Guerrero, agreed, and Don Jaime Rivera, arriving with his own copy of the marriage settlement, could make no counterclaim. With the alcalde as witness to the new document, Luis then transferred his half share of the Rancho Rivera to his brother Felipe, in return for Felipe's cession of an equal acreage of the land at Sonoma, where he now retained only his fruit farm, the redwood stands, and the sawmill next to which the Cords had built themselves a house. There had been no dispute about any of it, and yet there was a breach between the brothers, caused by the manner of Rosalie's death and Felipe's refusal to engage in more than a token search for Rosalie's daughter.

Because of this chill, Luis had never asked Felipe why he allowed four thousand acres of range land to lie empty of horses and cattle. At the time of the settlement the cattle had been sold on the hoof to the Boston agents in the hide and tallow trade, the horses bought by other rancheros, and the proceeds divided, with the contents of the house, between the heirs. Afterwards – and Luis silently gave him credit for this – Felipe ordered the adobe house and all its dependencies to be destroyed, saying he never wanted to set foot in the accursed place again. Soon the chaparral and the scrub oaks began to spread over the tumbled bricks, and the Rancho Rivera, lost and forgotten, disappeared into the general name of 'The Mission'.

"Sorry," said Felipe, coming up to him at the fence. "That fellow wanted to know when Cord was expected back from Sutter's Fort. I said he would be at the workshop this after-noon."

"*Was* he at Sutter's Fort? I thought you meant he was coming down from Salmon Creek."

"He was on a hunting trip up the Sacramento."

"Queer way to run a sawmill."

Felipe looked round and saw no one within earshot. "Luis," he said, "I didn't want to challenge you in front of Content. But will you tell me what in the name of God you hope to achieve by this crackbrained journey to Monterey?"

"In the first place, I can demand an interview with the man who wasn't mentioned in Don Mariano's letter – our worthy Governor, Pio Pico. I can ask him to keep California clear of all foreign entanglements, and respect the Territorial tie with Mexico. And according to how Pico answers, I can offer my sword to José Castro. I can redeem the honour of the Estrada name."

"And the 'fidelity to the old Spanish past' that poor old Don Mariano was rambling on about? That letter of his could have been written in 1776."

"When our forefathers came north to civilise and Christia-nise this country."

"Of course!" said Felipe. "The Christian mission. That was the argument I heard my father use again and again, when I was a boy of twelve or thirteen, and he was trying to persuade my mother to leave her home and friends and settle among the Indians on the frontier."

"I honour him for it." The brothers walked on in silence until Felipe stopped and said,

"Yerba Buena is flourishing, don't you think?"

"It seems so."

"Many people think the bay must be one of the biggest natural harbours in the world, and that some day there will be a great city where this little village stands –"

"Well?"

"Luis, your cattle are marked with the ox-yoke E, the brand my father devised when he built the rancho. I've never been interested in cattle. I want to put the Estrada brand on the future city." And as Luis stared at him uncomprehendingly, he went on, "Stay here and help us! Don't go south after some romantic dream which could end in your own death! If I can work with the Americans, why can't you?"

"We're going to war with the Americans," said Luis coldly. "And I won't let you over-persuade me a second time."

"I? When did I ever 'over-persuade' you?"

"When you made me believe it was useless to continue the search for Rosalie's child."

"For God's sake!" said Felipe, "are you at that again? Don't you remember that the alcalde and the troops from the Presidio searched the countryside for ten miles around, even across in the Contra Costa; that there wasn't an Indian ranchería they didn't enter, besides going back to the ruins of the Mission Dolores again and again? If the child still lives, she's with one of the Indian tribes in the mountains, and there's nothing more we or the Riveras can do about it."

"She may be growing up an Indian squaw, while we divide her inheritance."

"I doubt if an illegitimate child could have inherited the Rancho Rivera," said Felipe.

"She was our own flesh and blood!"

"She was Peter Gagarin's bastard," Felipe said, and led the way downhill.

"Even so," said Luis at his shoulder, "it's because of that lost child, and because of Rosalie, that I'm going to Monterey to declare for California."

"*What?* Where's the connection?"

"Because I was weak and indolent, I betrayed my sister. I could have stopped her marriage, and I did not. I could have gone to her along with Rita, instead of waiting for you so that there would be two of us to tackle Carlos. I left her to die alone – to kill alone, and I have that to remember for the rest of my life. I've also got to remember that it was I who brought Peter Gagarin into our house. But there'll be no more betrayals, Felipe, I promise you!"

"Luis," Felipe interrupted, "will you wait for a day or two? Wait until we hear what Vallejo has to say? He must be on his way back to Sonoma by now. You ought to make sure of seeing Pico, if that's what you want; and Pico may be in Los Angeles. Wait –"

"Wait for Robert Cord, and the news he gathered on the Sacramento," said Luis. "Here comes your hunter now."

The American coming with long strides to meet them gave no sign that he was disturbed because his country was threatening war with Mexico. He shook the Californio warmly by the hand, enquired for Doña Isabel, and answered Luis's own kindly enquiries for Mrs. Cord and the boy. He said "the boy", because he could never remember their firstborn's outlandish name. Princess Helen had not forgotten her promise to send some novels by Sir Walter Scott to the cabin in the redwoods, and the Cord baby had been given the name of Ivanhoe.

Robert Cord at thirty-six was an impressive figure. He still wore the frontiersman's fringed doeskin jacket with a red neckerchief and deerskin leggings, clothing which suited the long rifle in his hand. He had not been hunting animals, but travelling by boat down the Sacramento from New Helvetia.

"What's new at Sutter's Fort?" Felipe asked.

"Plenty," said Cord laconically. "An immigrant party arrived while I was there. They plan on homesteading, at least the womenfolk do. The men are hot to go to war."

"War's coming, then?"

"Sure is. The Mexicans tipped their hand in April, when they chased Taylor back across the Rio Grande. They killed American citizens on American soil, so I reckon Mister Polk has got his war all right. He's drafted a war message to

Congress, and forty thousand men have volunteered from Texas and the Mississippi states. They say transports are setting out for Vera Cruz."

"I told you so, Luis," said Felipe. "The war will be fought on the Rio Grande, and from Vera Cruz north to Mexico City. There'll be no fighting in California."

"What news of Fremont?" said Luis urgently. "Did he go to Oregon after Castro defeated him at Gavilan Peak?"

"Not he," said Cord. "I saw him three days ago at Pete Lassen's rancho on the upper waters of the Sacramento, well within the Territory of California. One of his men told me they were waiting for an American officer called Gillespie, carrying orders from Washington, who was due to meet them on the Klamath Lake. My guess is that Fremont hopes his orders will be to take California, and by force if necessary."

12

Doña Isabel Estrada, nineteen years old on the first of May, had a great deal of natural dignity as well as her fair share of Spanish pride. She was proud of her descent from members of the first band of colonists to enter California from New Spain, and she was proud of her husband's determined courtship in the face of many objections from the Yorbas. What she felt when that husband, within half a year of their marriage and in the third month of her first pregnancy, left her to go on a journey with an unpredictable ending she revealed to nobody – not even to his brother, when Felipe and Content, accompanied by Robert Cord, arrived one summer evening at the Rancho Estrada.

Isabel was not as classically beautiful as her sister Maddalena, whom Luis's mother had first thought of as a bride for her son, but she had brown hair which curled of itself and large brown eyes, and she looked very pretty indeed as she hurried across the yard to greet her unexpected guests. She welcomed Content's arrival to keep her company, only asking how

Felipe would get on without her, and concealing her amusement when the older girl replied,

"My father's there, you know, and we've hired a young clerk from the Hudson's Bay Company to work on the books in the evenings."

The letter from Luis which Felipe delivered she left unopened on the desk in the sala until she had shown all her guests to their rooms. It had disappeared when they all met in the sala for an excellent evening meal, a welcome change from the Vioget tavern cooking, and was not referred to until the following morning, when Isabel intercepted Felipe as he came back from the bunk house, where he had talked to the capataz and the other vaqueros.

"Felipe," she said, as abruptly as his wife might have done, "I didn't want to talk politics in front of Content and Señor Cord, who must have a different point of view from ours; but I'm disturbed by Luis's letter. When he left home it was only to go to Monterey to talk to Governor Pico. Now he says that under the threat of an American invasion he is prepared to enlist under General Castro. Is that what he told you?"

"It is, and I did my best to talk him out of it. I reminded him that there are no American troops nearer than New Mexico, nor American warships nearer than San Diego. There's no reason why Polk's war should spread into California –"

"Luis is suspicious of that man Fremont."

"Fremont isn't in command of an army, Isabel dear."

"Luis says an armed rabble is more dangerous than an army. And Fremont can enlist an armed rabble if he heads for Sutter's Fort."

He wondered what sort of armed rabble General Castro was likely to command. He only said, "If Luis is thinking of fighting Fremont he's heading in the wrong direction. Are you worried, Isabel?"

"Not about Luis!" she said proudly. "I'm – sorry – that his new decision means he may be away from home much longer than we thought. But I know he's right to want to defend California, and I'm sure my brothers and my cousins will feel the same way."

"I was thinking about yourself when I asked if you were worried."

She looked about her: at the gracious adobe dwelling, where the pink Castilian roses were twining again round the red-wood pillars, and beyond at the rich pastures beneath the gold-brown hills; her husband's property, some day to be the inheritance of their child, and she said,

"No, I'm not worried. Any more than my grandmother was, or my great-grandmother, when they first came to Indian country. And please don't mind about leaving Content with me. We're only three miles from Sonoma, and the protection of General Vallejo."

With that Felipe had to be satisfied. He returned almost at once to the bay, where word had been received from a trading vessel that a ship was on the high seas carrying a group of Mormon immigrants to Yerba Buena, for Felipe meant to make a profit on the housing of the Mormons. Robert Cord left at the same time, to go back to the sawmill on Salmon Creek, and the two girls were left alone with a houseful of servants to look after them.

Content was to occupy the room which had been Felipe's, and Isabel, going to ask if she could help with the unpacking of the boxes brought from the great bedroom, was startled to find her sister-in-law taking from a leather case two handsome duelling pistols with chased silver butts and filagreed barrels. She had found an old gun belt of Felipe's hanging from a hook in the whitewashed wall, and was stowing the pistols into the holsters.

"Guns, Content?" she managed to say. "Where did you get them?"

"Felipe made me take them. He said he knew there were no firearms in the house, and he thought we ought to be protected."

"Are they loaded?"

"Of course."

"They look like antiques," said Isabel, examining the pistols from a distance. "How did Felipe come to own them?"

"They belonged to his father," lied Content. In fact they had belonged to Rosalie's father-in-law, but as Content well knew, Rosalie's name was never to be mentioned at the Rancho Estrada. She put the gun belt back on its hook, told

159

Isabel she ought to be in the fresh air, and proposed a turn round the garden.

As the days went by Isabel began to realise that her American sister-in-law was genuinely kind and genuinely honest. She did not harp on Isabel's condition, as her sister Maddalena was sure to do when she arrived; indeed she fought shy of baby talk, and declined, because she disliked sewing, to add even one garment to the layette already in preparation. But she was deeply interested in the productivity of the rancho and the sale of hides and tallow, and she taught Isabel how to draw up a profit and loss account, a financial flight quite beyond the average ranchero.

General Vallejo and his wife came to see them, while Don Salvador, now occupying his own house in Sonoma, brought his wife, also a Carrillo (for the Vallejo brothers had married sisters) to visit the two girls a few days later, and life went smoothly on as the June days grew warmer and the labourers busier in the fields. Only one disquieting piece of news reached Sonoma, and was carried to the rancho by the vaqueros: that an armed band of Americanos, presumed to be from Sutter's Fort, had attacked a Mexican officer of cavalry on the Sacramento river, and had made off with all the horses of his troop. It was not clear if this was an act of brigandage or of war. The aggressors were not in army uniform, and could be classified as common horse thieves. In a day or two Sonoma relapsed into its sunny and peaceful silence.

In the very early morning of the fourteenth of June, when all in the barracks and the pueblo were still asleep, another armed rabble, mounted on stolen horses, burst into the plaza at Sonoma. Some of the Americans were from the eastern States, and were educated men, inflamed for the time being with some wild notions of patriotism, and they were the leaders of a band wearing the fringed tunics of the frontiersmen and waving their sombreros as they whooped their way across the plaza. The leaders demanded instant admittance to the Casa Grande. General Vallejo, roused from sleep, received them with his usual courtesy, and on being informed that they intended to proclaim the Republic of California, sent for his brother Salvador and offered them wine. Wine was sent out to their followers, dismounting and tethering their horses before they stood to arms, with rifles at the ready against their non-existent foes. Inside the Casa Grande the Vallejos were said to be negotiating with the invaders, most of whom were drunk by the time the negotiations ended. General Vallejo, his brother Salvador, his secretary and Mr. Leese were put on horseback and taken away by a posse to imprisonment at Sutter's Fort. They left to shouts of "Hang the Greasers! Throw the Greasers into jail!" It was the first time the Autocrat of Sonoma had ever been called a Greaser, that ugly epithet from the days when Mexican labourers loaded greasy hides on to the Boston ships. The shouts changed to laughter and cheering as William Ide, a schoolteacher from Vermont, solemnly proclaimed the Republic of California.

The residents of Sonoma took heart. The Vallejo ladies were under house arrest, but apparently there was to be no bloodshed. The few American settlers joined in the cheering, and even helped to make a flag for the new republic. On a yard and a half of white cotton cloth a lone star, for Texas, and a grizzly bear were painted with pokeberry juice, with a broad strip cut from a red flannel shirt along the bottom. To a critical eye the bear strongly resembled a hog, but nobody dared to criticise as the Mexican flag was lowered and the Bear Flag raised in its place. The day was followed by a night of revelry, and the riff-raff of the Bear Flaggers, including Indians, Mexican cholos and desperadoes from the mountains embarked upon a long carouse.

The Blue Wing Inn, which Vallejo had built some time earlier, was drunk dry before morning, as was the Mexican *posada*. The leaders of the 'republic' were not sorry when the spirits and wine ran out. They had tolerated the licence which followed their bloodless victory, and now they wanted to get on with drawing up a constitution and rules which would enable them to hand over a smoothly running pueblo of Sonoma, the key to the northern frontier, to Fremont when he came among them in a few days' time. But not daring to push their authority too far with the rascals among their men, they turned a blind eye on the stragglers who set off among the farms round Sonoma, looking for drink and mischief.

It was not until sunset on the day the Bear Flag was raised that news from Sonoma reached the two girls at the Rancho

Estrada. It was carried by Jaime, a vaquero, who at Isabel's orders had ridden in with his saddle-bags full of good things for the Indian widow of old Guzman, now living alone in the little 'town house' on the plaza. From that observation point Jaime had seen the celebrations, while from the widow and her friends he had received a fairly straightforward account of the departure into captivity of the two Vallejos. Some of Jaime's fellow cowboys followed him to the patio, standing at a respectful distance while he told his story to his young mistress. Isabel grew pale as she listened, but she was as calm as ever when she said,

"Thank you, Jaime. Close the gates and post four sentries, all armed, and tell the capataz to come to me first thing in the morning. Then we shall see what is to be done."

The men bowed and retreated, while Content whispered, "What are your sentries armed with, Isabel? Flintlocks of the Spanish Conquest?"

"There are shotguns in the bunk house, Luis said." And then, with sudden tears, "Oh Luis, why did you go away?"

Why indeed, thought Content grimly, as she led the sobbing girl into the sala and made her sit down. "Isabel," she said, "do you think you could ride as far as the Rancho Petaluma?"

"Whatever for? You heard what the man said – the general is a prisoner and his wife's under house arrest. There's no one at his rancho who could help us."

"There are six hundred field hands and vaqueros on the place. I should think they could take care of a handful of renegade Americans."

"Americans!" Isabel caught at the word. "Content, you're an American. If they come our way you can talk to them in their own language. You can persuade them to leave us in peace. Why should they want to injure two harmless women? We have our own servants to protect us . . . And Luis trusts me to look after his possessions . . ."

She talked on in disjointed sentences, while Content tried to soothe her, all the while thinking this was the same romantic nonsense as Luis was probably spouting at Monterey. Just as well he isn't here, or my Felipe either. If they'd been in Sonoma this morning, they'd have been taken off to Sutter's

Fort like the Vallejos, with their hands tied behind their backs. 'Why should they want to harm two women?' said the little fool. Content had seen American seamen brawling on the docks of a dozen ports: she had no faith in the chivalry of the breed.

There was no disturbance during the night, and at five o'clock the capataz presented himself before La Señora, sombrero in hand, to enquire if the work was to go forward as usual. It was the day for the weekly rodeo, when the mavericks or strayed cattle were culled from those bearing the ox-yoke E of the Estrada brand.

"Yes, Don Luis would wish it," said Isabel calmly. "But don't go more than five miles from the house, and be prepared to come back if I should send for you."

"At the Señora's orders," said the man, and Isabel went indoors to join Content at the breakfast chocolate. She had braced herself to go on as usual, and the two girls went from weaving shed to kitchen to dairy, as the sun grew hot in the sky, and the sweet scents of June rose up from the valley pastures.

It was about ten o'clock when the sentries at the gate raised a shout at the arrival of a half-grown boy from the Indian ranchería. He was out of breath, for he had run all the way through the woods from the place where the road to Sonoma crossed the road to the embarcadero. He had been hunting squirrels, and had seen a great band of Americanos, all drunk, shouting and singing, and some of them were heading towards the Rancho Estrada.

"Well done, boy," said the young Señora. "All you women" (for the Indian cooks and maids were crowding round her) "go up the path by the creek to Agua Caliente and stay there. The houseboys too. Rinaldo," to one of the sentries, "ride and fetch the capataz and the vaqueros. Content, where are you going?"

Content was already in her own room, buckling on the belt with the pistol holsters. Even pulled to the tightest notch, it was too big for her, and the weight of the pistols dragged it down almost to her knees. Isabel gasped a protest when she ran back into the deserted yard.

"I'm not taking any chances," Content said roughly.

"We're not going to stay here and get ourselves killed. Listen to that!" The sound of raucous singing was clearly audible now. "We've got to hide. But we can watch from the cottonwoods and see what happens."

Dragging Isabel by the hand, she raced her down through the vegetable garden to the Sonoma Creek, where the cottonwoods bent shivering above the water, and there was room in two thick clumps for the girls to shelter. Content, from her place among the trees, could see that Isabel was holding on to a stout branch, and seemed to be on the verge of fainting.

The Indian boy had exaggerated the size of the band of marauders. They were led by two Americanos, Patrick Sweeny and Terence Murphy by name, the others being two Mexican cholos and two Indians of the sort now being encouraged to rise against their one-time masters. With their rifle butts they clubbed down the sentries as they fumbled with their unaccustomed weapons, and jumped their horses over the gate into the yard.

From the cottonwoods the two trembling girls could hear what they were singing:

> The minstrel boy to the war is gone
> In the ranks of death you'll find him

and then a shout of "Anybody home? Come out and pour us wine, ye spalpeens!"

They staggered as they dismounted, but they stumbled inside the rancho, and ranged from room to room, shouting for "Drink for the Bear Flaggers! Wine for the founders of the California Republic!" while the two Indians, dragging out the white satin spread from the great bedroom, began filling it with loot of all sorts, table silver, candlesticks, ornaments and even kitchen utensils. The Mexicans followed Murphy and Sweeny into the sala. There they found wine, which they drank from the bottle, but so little of it that Sweeny in disgust threw his bottle at the painting of Bucareli, the Good Viceroy. The stiff Spanish face above the stiff Spanish collar was defiled by a trickle of red which looked like blood. Then they attacked the secretary, bursting open the mahogany lid with rifle butts, and smashing the lock of the strongbox, pawing through the

papers in search of money. Like the wine, the Mexican dollars
were in short supply, and when they had filled their pockets
and kicked the papers around the floor, they decided to teach
the inhospitable Greasers a lesson by holding a little housewarming. To get brooms from the kitchen and hold them to
the fire in the brick ovens was the work of a moment. The
Mexicans threw short, and singed the redwood pillars, but
Sweeny and Murphy threw in long, practised curves, and
soon the tule roof was blazing in two places, with the flames
leaping higher among the reeds.

"They're not far away, Pat, the ovens were hot!" Murphy
had the wits to say, and at that moment Sweeny's eye was
caught by a flutter of pink ribbon on the little gate which led to
the vegetable garden. It was Isabel's sash, which had caught on
the woodwork of the gate in her flight.

"There's women here, Terence my boy!" screeched the
leader. "Sure and ye're right they're not far away! Come and
have a cuddle with the little dears –"

But the quick ears of the Indians had caught the drumming
of hoofs on the dry ground. "Riders!" one of them cried.
"Men are coming!" and the Mexicans said "*Vamonos!*"

"Come back, Pat! Don't be a fool! Ride for Sonoma!"
shouted Murphy. But his friend, blind with drink and resentment against a gracious way of life which he had obscurely
understood inside the sala, was already lurching down the
slope towards the creek. As his confederates mounted and
raced to jump the fence, he saw Isabel in her white dress
clinging to the trees.

Content he did not see, because Content in her brown calico
was better hidden, and she took the pistols from their holsters
and held one in each hand. The man had a rifle, but he threw it
aside as he seized Isabel, and the two of them struggled on the
edge of the creek, Isabel screaming, and her assailant fumbling
at her bodice and the fastening of her skirt. Whatever vile
words he was saying Content did not hear. There was a
roaring in her ears, the pounding of the terrible fear that when
she fired she would hit Isabel, and then her brain cleared to an
icy coolness, and with the pistol in her left hand she fired a
warning shot which missed Isabel's attacker by a yard. It was
enough to make him drop the fainting girl and face Content.

She steadied her right hand and fired. She aimed at his heart but hit him in the stomach, not much above the groin, and as Sweeny sank slowly to his knees the blood from the great artery pumped his life away into the grass.

Content replaced her pistols with the methodical care of extreme shock, and stumbled to where Isabel lay. She stooped for a handful of creek water and threw it in her face. "Come on," she said, "Don't look at him, He won't do any more harm. Can't you hear the voices? The vaqueros are here."

"I – can't," gasped Isabel. "He – hurt me, when he threw me down."

"You've got to try," said Content, "the rancho's on fire."

Somehow she got Isabel to her feet, passed an arm round her waist and urged her back towards the house. Isabel was a dead weight, but they reached the top of the garden, where Content's hoarse cries brought some of the vaqueros rushing to their aid. The capataz himself carried his young mistress to the shelter of the weaving room and laid her down on a pile of blankets. There was no water to moisten her lips or bathe her forehead, for all the water from the well was being passed along a chain of men organised by Pedro in an attempt to save the two wings of the ranch house. The sala and the bedrooms were blazing, for the fire had spread from the reeds to the rafters, and burning wood was dropping on the floors. The papers which the Bear Flaggers had scattered on the floor of the sala – the land grant, the diseño, the baptismal certificates, even Rosalie's marriage contract – had all caught fire, and were blowing through the open door like separate tiny flames.

"Can you leave La Señora, Doña Contenta?" said the sweating capataz at the door of the weaving room. "There are more Americanos coming down the road."

Content had been kneeling on the floor, chafing Isabel's icy hands, "Darling," she said, as Isabel's fingers tightened on her own, "let me go for just a few minutes, I'll be right back. I'll try to get you brandy – or something," she added desperately. Was there to be another raid on the rancho? The ammunition for her pistols was in one of the blazing rooms, and the vaqueros were armed only with their knives. On an impulse she unstrapped the encumbering gun belt and thrust it deep into one of the chests of yarn which stood between the looms in the weaving room. Then she went out to face the new hazard, and the band of a dozen men who were hitching their horses beyond the fence, well out of reach of the fire.

Although they wore the deerskin tunics of the Bear Flaggers, she saw at once that they were no desperadoes. Two of them, with their rifles unslung, were mounting guard on the half-sobered Murphy and the two Mexicans: the Indian raiders, having stuffed as much silver as possible into their tunics, had melted into the woods along the track which led to Santa Rosa, and were never seen again. One, the obvious leader, shouted orders to help the fire-fighters, and when he saw the slight figure of a woman, with a smudged face and a dress smeared with earth and grass stains, he came towards her with his sombrero in his hand.

"Do you speak English, madam?"

"I'm an American citizen. My name's Content Estrada."

"Mine is Macdonald; your servant, madam. Are you the wife of the ranchero, Don Luis Estrada?"

"His sister-in-law. Don Luis is in Monterey, but his wife is here. She was attacked and savaged by one of your men, less than an hour ago."

"My God!" said Macdonald. He looked at the house, where the flames were beginning to die down. Some of the vaqueros, seeing that there was to be no fight, had climbed up the charred redwood pillars to cut the undamaged reeds away from the burning tule. "My God!" he said again, "this is a bad business. Three of the farmers near the pueblo rode in to tell us they had been robbed and terrorised this morning. A fellow called Murphy, whom we intercepted on the road, admits having been here, but says they were led astray by Patrick Sweeny, who stayed behind."

"He stayed all right," said Content. "You'll find his dead body down by the creek."

"Sweeny's *dead*? How did he die?"

"I shot him."

"*You* shot him?"

"He was going to rape my sister-in-law. What would you have done?"

"You were carrying a gun? Where is it now?"

"I threw it into the creek," said Content.

The young Bear Flagger was utterly confounded. How the law stood in such an affair was beyond him. The fragments of Scots Law which he had retained from one year at Edinburgh University seemed to have no bearing on the case of the infant Republic of California versus Content Estrada.

"Come and see my sister-in-law, Doña Isabel," the girl said. "Then I think you'll understand. Especially when I tell you she is expecting a child."

Macdonald followed her into the weaving room. Isabel, in her torn clothing, lay on the pile of blankets with closed eyes.

"Yes," said Macdonald, "I see. Will you remain with the lady, Mrs. Estrada? I must see that the fire is out before I talk to you again."

It was nearly an hour before he came back. In that time the shouts of the fire-fighters had dwindled, the dreadful crackling of wood and reeds came to a stop, and Isabel moved and talked normally. She was sitting up when Macdonald came back, unbarred the door and motioned Content out into the yard.

She faced him in the implement shed, and there he said abruptly:

"Sweeny's body has been found and will be taken to our headquarters. Is your sister-in-law able to ride with you when I take you in?"

"Take me in where?"

"To Sonoma. Mrs. Estrada, you have confessed to the murder of Patrick Sweeny. It is my painful duty to place you under arrest until you can be brought to trial."

"When you Bear Flaggers have set up a judiciary, I suppose," said Content contemptuously. "Where do you propose to imprison me – in the *calabozo* with all the drunks from your last night's celebrations?"

"No, madam. You will be placed under house arrest with the Vallejo ladies."

"We have a house of our own in the plaza. Take us there if you must, but remember what I told you before, I'm an American citizen. I don't admit the authority of the Bear Flag horse thieves and cattle rustlers. The law in Sonoma is in the hands of the alcalde. You must allow me to defend myself, and I'll send to the alcalde and ask him to file charges against your men for robbery, arson and attempted rape."

He thought she was a spitfire and a shrew, but he rather admired her spirit, and Sweeny was no loss: he was the worst type of 'Pike County blackguard', in the cant American phrase for a footloose wanderer. He agreed to let her call one of the vaqueros ("Pedro, there, will do") to go into the maids' rooms and find some garments for his mistress and herself. All their own belongings were destroyed by fire. And on the pretext of giving Pedro, the best rider among the vaqueros, some idea of what to look for, Content was able to whisper to him:

"As soon as we've gone, tell the capataz to give you Don Luis's best horse, and then *ride!* Ride to the sawmill on Salmon Creek and tell Señor Cord what has happened. Say we need him at Sonoma –" She had no time for more, for the Bear Flagger was moving in their direction, but Pedro nodded, and she trusted him.

As soon as Neil Macdonald was sure that the fire was out and would not start again he ordered the return to Sonoma. The three marauders were under armed escort, and each of the two girls had a man behind her on a pillion. Content was no horsewoman at the best of times, and was limp from shock and exhaustion, while Isabel lay supine against the broad chest of an American. As he rode at the rear of his sorry cavalcade Macdonald had time to wonder if he had done right in arresting the sister-in-law of a powerful ranchero, one of those whom the official American policy was to conciliate. He knew that John C. Fremont belonged to the war party rather than the conciliation party, and although Fremont had kept out of the way while Sonoma was captured, he would soon arrive to savour his triumph. It might be possible to convince Fremont that he, Macdonald, had acted correctly at the Rancho Estrada. His immediate worry was how he could best tell his story to respected leaders like William Ide and Robert Semple.

It seemed as if the whole of Sonoma was in the plaza, staring and muttering, when he rode in with the two girls. He escorted them to the little adobe town house, made sure they had provisions and posted two sentries at the door. Isabel and Content passed from the nightmare into the gentle hands of old Guzman's widow, who insisted that La Señora should be put to bed at once in the room where Rosalie and Carlos Rivera had spent their wedding night. She brought her a drink to make her drowsy, and hoped that sleep and rest would stave off what she feared. But the inexorable process of waste and pain had been set in motion. Long before Robert Cord rode hell-for-leather into Sonoma, and with only the old Indian woman and the inexperienced Content to help her, Isabel Estrada lost her baby, and the ruin of the day was complete.

13

The alcalde of Sonoma was a man named Berryessa. His old father and two younger Californios, the Haro twins, encountered Fremont and his men near San Rafael and were shot dead, on the grounds (said Kit Carson, Fremont's wilderness scout) that "Fremont said he had no time for prisoners." Their killing was a reprisal for the murder of two Bear Flaggers named Cowie and Fowler in revenge for several attacks on the ranchos near Sonoma. The 'Republic of California' had made a bad beginning, and there was an undercurrent of resentment when Fremont reached Sonoma on the twenty-fifth of June. He was there for the celebration of the Fourth of July, following a short excursion to San Francisco Bay, where he made the theatrical gesture of spiking the obsolete cannon of the Castillo of San Joaquin. For two weeks the army engineer was the Autocrat of Sonoma, while Vallejo and his friends lay behind bars at Sutter's Fort, listening to the catcalls of "Greasers!" from American immigrants preparing to fight the inhabitants of the golden land to which they had come to make their fortunes.

Before news of the trouble on the frontier could reach Monterey, Luis Estrada had left for the south. As Felipe had predicted, Governor Pio Pico was not in the territorial capital but in Los Angeles, and after spending a few days with his old kinsman at the Casa Estrada Luis was impatient to follow him. While he was Don Mariano's guest he several times encountered an Englishman doing joinery work on the premises, and noticed vaguely that the man brought a little English girl called

Dolly to play with the children of the Mexican servants. But the Winters, like all the foreign residents of Monterey, were on the periphery of Luis's vision. The only people he really saw were men like General José Castro and his friends, who swore as day after uncertain day dragged past that they would never allow California to fall like a ripe fruit into the hands of the Americanos.

This was exactly what happened while Luis was at San Gabriel with his wife's brothers, young men as eager as he was to ride on to Los Angeles. President Polk's war had been endorsed by Congress, and on the seventh of July the US frigate *Savannah* of the Pacific Squadron put in to the port of Monterey. Commodore Sloat took possession of the town in the name of the United States and raised the American flag. On the next day Captain Montgomery of the US sloop of war *Portsmouth* went ashore at Yerba Buena and raised the Stars and Stripes in the plaza to the cheers of the American traders and agents, most of whom had taken Mexican citizenship in earlier days. The alcalde, Don Francisco Guerrero, was dismissed, and a Spanish-speaking naval officer, Lieutenant Washington Bartlett, was appointed in his place. Captain Montgomery then despatched another American flag to Sonoma. The Bear Flag was pulled down, the Stars and Stripes run up, and the one-month Republic of California came to an inglorious end. Captain Fremont, not for the last time in his mercurial career, had to revert to a subaltern rank, and at Commodore Sloat's orders marched his bully-boys off to Monterey.

The American annexation of Monterey should have been a moment of supreme satisfaction to Consul Larkin. Instead it was tinged with regret. So many young Californios had disappeared from the town, so many families failed to share in the fiestas for the officers of the Pacific Squadron or the fandangos for their sailors that it was easy to estimate how support for Castro had increased. General Castro had joined forces with General Andrés Pico, the governor's brother, at Santa Barbara, and they had mobilised a force of light cavalry ready to strike at the Americanos in any direction. They were living off the country, so that the food supplies to Monterey grew less as the American military requisitioning increased, and soon there was hunger in the town, which bred resentment. The free association, the brotherly tie which the consul had desired were non-existent.

As at Yerba Buena, the Mexican alcalde had been deposed by the naval commander, and the appointment of the Reverend Walter Colton in his stead was one of the few immediate benefits of the American occupation. Colton was a naval chaplain, a gentle, humane man whose administration of justice was tempered with humour, and was better received than the prosy sermons he preached to the tiny Protestant community. Jack Swan deserted his tavern to listen to Mr. Colton preach, and so did Henry Winter, the agnostic, at a service with little Dolly for the first time since Christmas Eve. The child fidgeted through the long discourse. With her inborn sense of the theatre, she knew that the man in the white surplice had not the gift of controlling his audience, and at last she whispered,

"It's not the same, Uncle Chips!"

"What's not the same?"

"The same as The Shepherds, and the Devil, and the Angel Gabriel –"

"S-sh!" – as Jack Swan, on Dolly's other side, held back his laughter.

When the minister greeted them after the service Chips was half afraid of a rebuke for inattentive Dolly. But he only stroked her golden hair and said, "Is this your little grand-daughter?"

"My little niece, sir."

"And you are –"

"Henry Winter, to serve your reverence."

"Ah yes, the carpenter! Mr. Larkin has told me about you. The house they've offered me needs a few repairs to make it comfortable; could you step round and see me tomorrow morning?"

The good man might have said "the house they've requisitioned for me", because all houses standing empty, as their owners discreetly retired to their ranchos in the country, were being snapped up by the military government which quickly followed the raising of the Stars and Stripes. Dolly, as usual, insisted on accompanying her foster-father to his new job, and although ordered to stay with the servants appeared in the parlour in search of sweets. Mr. Colton, whose wife had remained in Philadelphia to await the birth of their first baby, was tender-hearted to all children, and he thought Dolly Winter bewitching. He was a busy man, but he found time to teach her simple rhymes and watch her dance, sometimes for a flower or a candy, sometimes for no reward at all; daily and unconsciously teaching her the lesson that beauty and charm are powerful weapons in the conquest of a man.

South of Monterey the American forces, regular and irregular, stumbled about in search of Castro or Pico and their men. For a while there was no clash of armies, only an occasional collision, and the first success of the Californios was at Los Angeles, where Captain Archibald Gillespie, USA (he who brought the Washington despatch to Fremont in May) had occupied the pueblo. The Angeleños elected a Mexican officer called José Maria Flores to be their leader, and in August the dashing Captain Gillespie of the 80th Dragoons had to fight, was defeated, and forced to withdraw from Los Angeles with the honours of war.

It was in the time after this victory, when the American forces were regrouping under Commodore Stockton of the Pacific Squadron, with Fremont under his command, that Luis Estrada, in the Flores camp, received the first news of what had taken place at the Rancho Estrada. The exploits of the Bear Flaggers were already known, and had inflamed the courage of the Californios, but of how far they affected himself Luis was still ignorant. He had to read between the lines of Content's letter, written in terse if ungrammatical Spanish, and obviously not the first:

Since I last wrote [the letter began] we have all gone back to the rancho, where Mr. Cord lost no time in having the new roof put on. We have had no answer to our letters to you, and Isabel is pining for news, but she is much stronger, and I think is beginning to get over her disappointment. Mrs. Cord, bringing Ivanhoe, rode down from the mill with Pedro, and she has been a great help to us all. With Doña Maddalena here I feel now I can leave Isabel, and Felipe is coming to take me back to Yerba Buena on Sunday. Please come home soon.

Yours, etc . . .

Content had thought it wiser to say nothing, in any of the letters, of her defence of Isabel against the Bear Flaggers, or the mixture of threats and cajolery Robert Cord had used to set herself free. She thought she had said quite enough to be going on with, and so did Luis, as he sat in a woodland camp where the first chill of September could already be felt. A new roof – that probably meant arson, and Isabel's disappointment undoubtedly meant that there would be no baby at Christmas time. Poor darling! He would write at once, for there was a courier riding north that night, though whether the man got through the American lines was another matter. But that silly "come home soon" was irritating. Did his Yankee sister-in-law think a soldier could desert at will, as soon as he had bad news from home, and why hadn't Felipe written himself? Luis half guessed at the reason: the prudent Felipe would not risk a letter written to a *guerrillero*, and signed with his own name, falling into the hands of the new American authorities, on whose goodwill so much depended.

The courier carrying letters for the northern frontier was lucky to start his journey only a couple of hours before the Americans attacked Flores's men in their bivouac at the Sepulveda rancho. Once again the attack turned into an inconclusive skirmish in which the Californios melted into the hills and were able to regroup themselves for another trial of strength with Captain Gillespie. That unlucky officer, evicted from Los Angeles, had marched his men to the port of San Pedro and joined a force led by Captain Mervin of the USS *Savannah*. Thus reinforced, the Americans marched back fifteen miles, to be attacked at daybreak by Californios armed with a four-pounder gun. A superb cavalry charge, supported by the four-pounder, put the Americans to flight through a countryside from which the enemies had driven off all the horses: there were by this time some fourteen hundred Californios under arms.

President Polk's war had bogged down on the very terrain where he had counted on an easy victory. Things were no better in Mexico, for after crossing the Rio Grande General Zachary Taylor had won one victory in the State of Nuevo Leon and then no more. The President had begun to incline to General Winfield Scott's theory that Mexico could only be conquered by a landing at Vera Cruz and a march upcountry to the capital. The Navy declared itself equal to the long voyage and the landing; but what about the longer voyage round Cape Horn to be undertaken by the New York regiment which had volunteered to fight in California? The American residents in Monterey, seeing their town fast becoming a military garrison, began to think of moving to less troubled parts of the Territory.

Thomas Larkin was among those who decided to send his wife and family out of the danger zone. Yerba Buena and all the shores of the great bay were well protected by Captain Montgomery and the new alcalde, and a big demonstration of loyalty to Commodore Stockton, the new Governor of California and Commander-in-Chief, was planned for early October. Mrs. Larkin was very willing to be present, and improved on her husband's idea by suggesting that little Dolly Winter be taken north with the party. She had been susceptible to Dolly's charm even longer than the Reverend Walter Colton, if only for the sake of the baby friendship between Dolly and her own little daughter, Adelaida.

But Chips and his Carrie shook their heads when they heard that Mrs. Larkin intended to make a stop on the way to the bay with Don Jaime Rivera and his family at Santa Clara, and then go visiting in the Contra Costa country.

"Dolly's too much of a madcap to go gadding from house to house that way," said Chips. "Too excitable. Ain't that so, Carrie?"

"I should never have a moment's peace if she were away from home," said his wife.

"Then you come too, Carmen!" said Mrs. Larkin. "You'd be a great help to us!"

"I cannot leave Enrique, señora." Maria del Carmen spoke with such decision that Mrs. Larkin let the matter drop, and contented herself with leaving a basket of good things for the hungry little household. Dolly, who had been sent out of doors when the discussion began, went back to the Calle Principal with Mrs. Larkin for a garden game with Adelaida.

"You'll have to let her go some day, Carrie," said Chips when the visitor had gone. "You'll never keep that one cooped up in Monterey."

"She isn't five years old yet, Enrique. And to let her go to the Riveras!"

"If all your sister said was true there's no danger they would recognise her," said Chips drily. "Any more than Don Luis recognised her when he saw her at the Casa Estrada. The Russian left his stamp *there*, poor devil!"

"If they got their hands on her they would kill her as they killed her brother."

Chips Winter shrugged. He knew there was nothing to be done with Carrie in her Indian mood. He contented himself with saying, "Luis Estrada's in a fair way to be killed himself, if the campaign drags on," and went quietly off to Jack Swan's tavern, where there was a roaring fire and no sign of the poverty creeping over Monterey. There was even a newspaper, an innovation of Mr. Colton's, edited and published by Robert Semple, one of the Bear Flaggers who had yielded to Robert Cord's persuasions to take no action against Content Estrada.

A copy of the *Californian*, as the paper was called, reached Luis Estrada when he was camped near one of the Yorba ranchos, and informed him of the great fiesta given in Yerba Buena on the fifth of October in honour of Commodore Robert Stockton. It was not solely a Yankee festival, for all the foreign consuls were present, with officers from the French and Russian Navies – the latter represented by a brig from Sitka, a name which made Rosalie's brother bite his lip. There were programmes printed on blue silk, there were banners, there was of course a band leading the procession from Portsmouth Square, as the little plaza was now called, to the waterfront. And behold! who should be in the procession but the former Commandant of the Northern Frontier, Don Mariano Guadalupe Vallejo, recently a prisoner in Sutter's Fort, and now smiling, applauding the American conquerors, and willing to collaborate with them in their administration of what had been the Mexican Territory of California!

There were some who said this showed a truly Christian spirit of forgiveness on Vallejo's part, since at Petaluma his rancho, crops and cattle had been despoiled by the rabble commanded from the rear by John C. Fremont. But Luis Estrada called it black treachery on Vallejo's part, and longed more than ever for a victory in battle which should show the American invaders that the Californios were ready to die for their country.

Their chance came early in December, but before that an event took place which shook the confidence of the Americans in Monterey. Informed of the ill-health of the family he had sent north to safety, Consul Thomas Larkin left the town to ride to Yerba Buena, even though he knew there was a large concentration of what he called the enemy in the Salinas valley. On the night of November 14, which he was spending in the house of his friend Don Joaquin Gomez, Larkin was snatched from his shelter by 'the enemy', and remained a hostage on Californio hands for the next two months. His capture was a loss of face for the Americans, and an encouragement to those in the north who had been quiet enough under the powerful hands of Montgomery and Stockton. The Spanish-speaking alcalde of Yerba Buena was kidnapped a few weeks later, and with Lieutenant Washington Bartlett as a hostage the disgrace to the United States Navy was considerable.

Although Fremont's followers were now dignified by the name of the California Battalion, the resistants in the south had had few contacts with regular soldiers, apart from Gillespie's men driven out of Los Angeles, but General Pico's scouts were soon able to report that a force of the United States Army was advancing into California. These men were under the command of General Stephen Kearny, who had scored more successes in New Mexico than had General Taylor on the Mexican side of the Rio Grande. Success may have made Kearny overconfident, or perhaps, as was later claimed, he had taken bad advice from Kit Carson, the ubiquitous wilderness scout, but when he started from Santa Fé he was leading fewer than one hundred and fifty men to the recapture of Los Angeles. His plan was to join forces with the Marines from the warships at San Diego, and also with Captain Gillespie and his men. They were to meet south-east of Los Angeles, at a point where the road from Santa Fé crossed the hilly approach to San Diego, but without taking into account the existence, at the intended rendezvous, of a hamlet called San Pascual. The inhabitants had evacuated their little pueblo, now in the hands of General Andrés Pico and a force of Californios which was smaller than Kearny's, but consisted of superb horsemen mounted on fresh horses.

Their weapons were in a sense medieval, for they were armed only with the long lances which in the happy pastoral days they had used for sports and competitions at fiestas. Luis Estrada, honing his lance to a lethal edge, wondered if it would come to hand to hand fighting, using the knives they all carried in their boots. He was not afraid, being borne up on a great surge of emotion which blotted out all thoughts except the thought of vengeance on the Americanos, and when Kearny's men appeared, trotting through the defile, he was in the van of the attack with Castro and Pico. The Americans had hardly time to unsling their rifles when the horsemen were upon them, their lances held horizontally in a tremendous charge. It was all over in a matter of minutes. Eighteen American soldiers fell dead, as many more lay wounded on the field as the Californios, without a single casualty, wheeled, re-formed, and galloped back to the shelter of a neighbouring rancho. There, over a bottle of wine, the leaders held a council of war.

"To our next victory, señores!" cried Luis Estrada. He was drinking his measure of wine from a leather water flask, battered and scratched in the campaign, and in his leather jerkin and torn leggings he too was battered out of all resemblance to the bridegroom in gold lace and velvet whom Castro had met at the beginning of the year. The Mexican general exchanged a glance of pity with General Pico.

"We may not be so lucky at the next encounter," Pico said.

"Why not?"

"Because today we were able to split the American forces. Next time, if our scouts are right, the Marine reinforcements will be here from San Diego. And they will bring up the naval guns."

"I drink to victory by Christmas!" said Luis obstinately. "And to our comrades who won the day at San Pascual. May their name live for ever!"

"Amen to that," said José Castro. "But remember, my dear Luis – for ever is a very long time."

There was no victory by Christmas. There was, at Monterey, steady drenching rain, increasing distress among the poor, and a total absence of news – even of the victory of San Pascual – which made the candlelit nave of the Royal San Carlos Chapel the brightest place in town. The nativity play was presented there as usual on Christmas Eve, with one small golden-headed girl as the littlest shepherdess, and again at Mr. Colton's house on the twenty-sixth. It was Mr. Colton's intervention which had secured Dolly Winter her coveted part in *Los Pastores*, and desperately worried as he was, anxious about Mr. Larkin's safety, and inclined to be irritated with his invited guests for the levity which made them rejoice in a fiesta, any fiesta, at such a time, he was still able to admire the seriousness which the child brought to her part.

It had become a tradition among the nativity players that after the first performance in the church, which was devout and solemn, some of the actors should broaden their readings when they performed in private houses. Mr. Colton, as a clergyman, was annoyed with the men playing the Hermit, the Hunter and the Evil One, as they introduced slapstick comedy into the scene where they threw dice. The melodies of the violin and guitars which the players brought with them were more secular than holy. The Angel Gabriel forgot his lines, the Hermit used his lash too freely and sent the Virgin Mary into an unseemly fit of giggles. The children caught the infection, and giggled too; only Dolly kept her gravity. She sang sweetly, she moved gracefully in the simple dances, and right to the end of the performance remained completely inside the part of one of the shepherdesses in *Los Pastores*. She was the only one of the players to be sincerely congratulated by Mr. Colton. He took her small hand and led her back to the Winters, sitting consumed by pride and embarrassment at the back of the room, and then he stooped and kissed her.

"Well done, little Dolly," said the Reverend Walter Colton, "you're a born actress."

She always remembered those words, and quoted them in the years of her dubious celebrity in Paris, when she was asked to describe her first appearance on any stage. The nativity play and the kind clergyman were in fact all she did remember of the rainy winter months preceding her fifth birthday. Certainly she recalled nothing of the American Conquest, which was completed not long after that wet St. Stephen's Day. General Pico's pessimistic prediction came true on the seventh of January, 1847, when at the Battle of San Gabriel General Kearny, with Commodore Stockton and a combined American force of 600 men routed an equal number of Californios by the use of heavy artillery. Luis Estrada received a head wound, serious enough to immobilise him at the Yorba rancho of Santa Ana for two weeks before he was able to start for Sonoma with his brothers-in-law as escort. In that he was fortunate, for he was spared the duty of attending General Andrés Pico when he signed the Capitulation of Cahuenga on January 13, the American officer receiving the surrender being none other than the inspiration of the Bear Flaggers, John C. Fremont.

Before Luis reached home one landmark of his young manhood had changed its name. The hostages were released and Consul Larkin went back with his family to Monterey. Lieutenant Washington Bartlett, the kidnapped alcalde of Yerba Buena, made a more enduring contribution to American history. He issued a proclamation that since the name of Yerba Buena was 'unknown beyond the immediate district', in order 'to avoid confusion and mistakes in public documents' the pueblo was thenceforth to be known by a new name:

SAN FRANCISCO

BOOK TWO

SEEING THE ELEPHANT

I

The girl who made her stage début in *Los Pastores* at barely five was not much more than eighteen when she arrived in San Francisco. In a fit-up theatre in San José on the previous evening she had played Julie, the ingénue, to Katharine Catt's Jeanne the Outcast in *The Lyons Mail*, and in a few days' time she would begin a six months' engagement with the Catt Company in the city where good acting was rated only less important than gold.

At the Jack Swan Dramatic Adobe in Monterey, where she began her career as a balladist, or singer between the acts of a play, Dolly Winter was noted for a chilly beauty, a taunting, teasing manner, and the capacity when she had the right partner for a sudden passionate surrender which delighted audiences unused to subtlety. She was very cool, very much her stage self, when a servant ushered her into the bedroom she was to occupy in the Catts' house on Telegraph Hill, but when the door was closed she kicked off her shoes, picked up her skirts and danced a silent dance of triumph. Her hair shook loose beneath her feathered bonnet, and Chips Winter, dead three months before, would have recognised his Goldie.

It was not a grand room, for the Catts had not made a fortune in their wanderings from a showboat on the Mississippi through the mining camps of California's Gold Rush days to a tour of New South Wales, but the house was on Calhoun Street, a centre for the actors who for ten years had provided entertainment for the insatiable San Franciscans. Her window looked over the bay crowded with ships, including a little ferry-boat setting out to San Antonio Creek, where a new settlement was growing on what had been the Peralta rancho. She saw teeming wharves and muddy streets full of theatres, restaurants and shops which to another eighteen-year-old might have spelled romance, and to Dolly Winter meant future riches.

Brought up in a little town from which the importance of a capital had passed away, Chips Winter's foster-daughter hardly knew how fortunate she was to be beginning her life in San Francisco in the late summer of 1860, not long after bars of silver had been carried through the streets as proof of a great new strike at the Comstock Lode in the Sierra Nevada. The city had survived and grown with the immense influx of immigrants by land and sea which followed the discovery of gold at Sutter's Mill in the January of 1848. They came by sea round Cape Horn, they crossed the Isthmus of Panama, they travelled by covered wagon across the plains and climbed the mountains: by whatever route they came to California in search of gold they called themselves the Argonauts, like the Greek heroes who sought the Golden Fleece. The city survived murder, robbery and violence as ex-convicts from Australia clashed with the Vigilantes; survived the fires of the 1850s which burned the town to the ground six times over; survived financial panic and civic corruption. When she joined the Catt Company at Monterey Katharine Catt's husband Tom had sometimes teased Dolly Winter with her indifference to the affairs of her country, now divided on the issue of slavery. She teased him back by saying that she had lived through too much history before she was ten years old.

"Why, Mr. Tom," she would say with mock earnestness, "I was *living* here when General Kearny arrested John C. Fremont for insubordination and marched him back to Washington to be court-martialled. I saw Colton Hall being built for the Constitutional Convention, and I cheered with the other kids when California became a State of the Union. I watched all those crazy men setting out for the gold diggings, and I believe my Uncle Chips would have gone along with them if Aunt Carrie hadn't been sick with the complaint that killed her."

"He might have come back a rich man, Dolly."

"Or ruined, like so many of them. There are more ways of getting rich than by labouring with a pick and a shovel."

"What do you mean to do – marry a millionaire?"

"Maybe."

Though there were no millionaires on Telegraph Hill, once Jacob Leese's Rancho Punta de la Loma Alta, it meant, for Dolly, an advance into respectable Bohemia, where the house-holders had nothing in common with the Hill's Gold Rush population of Chilean whores and Greasers from the Mexican State of Sonora. The Chileñas, if they still existed, were shacked up with the vagrant population of Happy Valley, outclassed by the seductive French prostitutes who, with their *macquereaux*, had arrived to make their own sort of killing in the days of sudden riches. The summits of Telegraph Hill and Russian Hill were still covered with chaparral and rough herbage, the grazing place of wild goats, but Russian Hill was being laid out in streets along the lower slopes, and no one could explain how it came by its peculiar name. Some said Russian sailors, drowned in the wreck of a vessel from Bodega Bay, were buried there, but nobody knew for sure. All traces of the Russians had disappeared from California, except for the name of the Russian River, once called the Slavianka, in which Prince Peter Gagarin had lost his life.

Prince Peter's daughter, bored by history and living for the present, had read the theatre columns to some purpose from the time she could read newspapers at all. At first she identified with the child actresses so dear to the sentimental miners, come down from the diggings to blow in their gold in the melodeons round Portsmouth Square: with Anna Maria Quin, who at the age of six played Hamlet in Tom Maguire's Metropolitan Theatre on Montgomery Street; with Sue Robinson, 'the Fairy Star of the Gold Coast'; with the Worrell Sisters, known as 'The Juvenile Graces', and with La Petite Clorinda. It was the golden age of *les petites*, but as Dolly grew older, and more road companies played Jack Swan's theatre, her interest turned to boys, especially the talented Booths. Junius Booth, junior, was too old to be her hero, but Edwin was the rage of San Francisco, and his appearances in the mining country were so inflammatory that he was known as 'the Fiery Star'. They had a younger brother called John Wilkes, whom the critics castigated, and who lit a bonfire of his own later on.

From the impassioned style of the city's dramatic critics and theatre columnists, Dolly Winter learned that to every star in the making there came a moment called 'the big chance', and if the aspiring star were a woman the chance had to be seized without hesitation. The arrival of the Catt Company in Monterey was her own chance, and she took it, although with no illusions. Her powerful sense of the stage, strengthened by years as balladist, understudy and odd-job girl at the Jack Swan theatre told her at once that the Catts, Tom and Kitty, were second-raters; that Kitty was too old to play Cordelia and Tom to play Hamlet, and that although Mrs. Katharine Catt was described as an actress-manager, she was not in the same class as the women who dominated the San Francisco stage in the decade following the discovery of gold. Dolly followed the career of a gifted newcomer from Madame Vestris's company in New York, Laura Keene in *A Midsummer Night's Dream*. Miss Keene returned to New York to open her own theatre, but her beauty (horribly maligned in newspaper woodcuts) and her popularity inspired young Dolly Winter to change her name, already shortened from Dolores, into Laura.

Miss Laura Winter, soon to be the toast of San Francisco! The girl leaning out of her little window above the bay sighed blissfully as she looked across the water at the narrow strait by which the great ships entered. Years before, at the time of his flamboyant and useless gesture in spiking the ancient cannon of El Castillo, John C. Fremont had been inspired to rename the strait known to the Indians as Yulupa, the Sunset Strait, and to the Spanish as *la boca del puerto*. With the Golden Horn of Constantinople in his mind, and the treasures of the Orient in view, he decreed that the strait should be known in future as the Golden Gate. Laura Winter, who knew little about the Orient and cared less, thought the name was a good omen for herself – a young girl knocking at the Golden Gate of fortune.

"If ye please, miss," said the little Irish maid-of-all-work, bursting into Laura's room without the formality of a knock, "the mistress says will you come down to the parlour and meet Mrs. Judah!"

"Mrs. Judah! Good heavens, I haven't even changed my dress! Tell them I'll be downstairs in ten minutes –" and Laura turned to the wooden washstand and began pouring cold water from the jug into the china basin. A summons to meet Mrs. Judah was a royal command, for among the older women of the San Francisco stage no one was more important than the actress who for thirty years had played in support of every tragedy queen in America. She was a tragic figure in her own right. As a young player she had been popular in New

Orleans, before leaving the South with her husband and two children to act in Havana. On the way the ship was wrecked and most of the passengers, including Mr. Judah, were drowned. Mrs. Judah and the children, lashed to a spar, floated and struggled for four days before they were rescued, and by then the children were dead; they had died of starvation before their mother's eyes. It was some time before Mrs. Judah was able to act again, and from her first appearance at the Boston Museum she only played the parts for which her appearance now fitted her, those of prematurely aged and suffering women.

Not everybody knew that her sufferings had been assuaged by a happy second marriage, and that in private life she was Mrs. John Torrence. To the San Francisco audiences she had delighted since early Gold Rush days she was eternally Mrs. Judah, tragic widow and bereaved mother, designed by nature to play Volumnia to Edwin Booth's Coriolanus, or Emilia to Catherine Sinclair's Desdemona.

The years had so much developed Mrs. Judah's stage presence that she now seemed larger than life, and certainly too overwhelming for Kitty Catt's stuffy little parlour. The windows were shut because the summer wind was blowing, and clouds of sand from the dunes were spiralling along Calhoun Street; Mrs. Judah found it necessary to fan herself, with the gestures of Clytemnestra, as she interrogated Mrs. Catt on her latest protégée.

"I must say you've a good heart, Kitty," she observed. "If she's as pretty as you say she is, is it quite wise to have her under the same roof as Tommy?"

"It's only for a few weeks," Kitty explained. "Mrs. Wilson says she'll have a vacancy in the boarding-house at the end of the month. I promised Laura's uncle to look after her until she found her feet in San Francisco. Besides, she isn't Tommy's type. He likes the little roly-poly ones, confound him."

"Tall, is she?"

"Five foot nine, but she says she's stopped growing."

Mrs. Judah sniffed. "Those girls will say anything. Can she act?"

"She's good in certain parts, or she will be when she's had some speech training. She moves well. She's got a good singing voice, soprano. I'd like to know what you think of her, Marietta. There's something very taking about her, and also something I can't quite place. I want to be sure she'll please a San Francisco audience."

"You mean you wonder how she'll please Maguire," said Mrs. Judah shrewdly. "How do you mean you can't place her? Didn't I hear there was some mysterious story about her birth?"

"Chips Winter stuck to it that her father was an English lord, who died with his wife on the Old Spanish Trail."

"I'm surprised they didn't say he was a prince. The number of bogus royalties we've had here since '49 would fill a book."

"She doesn't claim to be a Ladyship. She only wants to be billed as Laura Winter, instead of Dolores –"

"She's smart, at that. Dolores is too Spanish, too Mission-bells, too weepy. But fancy her setting up as another Laura Keene! I could tell your young lady a thing or two about Red Laura, from her start as a London barmaid –"

"Now, Marietta, you know you never were in London."

"I was in New York when she was the talk of the Vestris company . . . Is this the child?"

It would have been unthinkable for Mrs. Judah, the queen of tragedy, to rise to greet the girl who had quietly entered the room, but she was immediately aware of a presence, as yet undeveloped, which might one day equal her own. She held out her hand, well pleased, as Laura greeted her with a respectful curtsy.

"So you're Miss Winter," she said. "Kitty, you told me she was pretty. You didn't say she was a beauty! You'll have to call a lights rehearsal for tomorrow, to make sure she's properly lit right from the start."

"Gas lighting!" said Laura. "We only had candles at the Jack Swan theatre."

"Ah, I was forgetting you're a real trouper," said Mrs. Judah flatteringly. "Come sit by me and tell me how it all began."

Molly, the Irish maid, created a diversion at this point by stumbling in with a tray holding three glasses of bitter lemonade, and soon Laura, on the sofa, was deep in the story of how when the American military occupation began, the officers of

'Stevenson's Regiment', the New York volunteers stationed in Monterey, had insisted on getting up private theatricals in Jack Swan's saloon.

"The partitions he built, or rather my uncle built, between the little apartments could be rolled up," she explained, "and when a stage was set up at one end it was like a real theatre. The first show they put on was called *Putnam, or The Iron Son of '76*. Of course I didn't see it then, I was too little, but I remember Lieutenant Derby, who played the lead in all the army shows. They said he was marvellous as Major Putnam –"

"I thought the horse was the star part in *The Iron Son*," said Mrs. Judah.

Laura laughed delightfully. "Don't I know it! I understudied the Goddess of Liberty when I was twelve, and one night I actually got to play, when the poor old Goddess (that was Madge Mayhew, Miss Kitty) was too drunk to stand; I really thought I was somebody that night. But when the hero came on, riding Black Vulture, I was completely upstaged. I dried up and miscued him, it was awful! Imagine being upstaged by a horse!"

She had inherited Peter Gagarin's gift of racy narrative, and the old tragedy queen, studying the vivid blue eyes in the expressive face, the energy of the slim young body in the plain blue cotton dress, thought, "I hope she can act as well as she talks, poor child! But she uses her hands too much, they always do . . ." She gave a little nod of approval to Kitty, who came in on cue:

"Laura, Mrs. Judah has brought us all an invitation from Mr. Maguire to attend a benefit performance tonight. Would you like to be in the audience for a change? Or are you too tired, after the trip from San José?"

"Tired?" All the scorn of eighteen was in Laura's eager voice, and Kitty Catt checked a sigh. She was forty, and having once been a plump girl suited to her husband's taste, she was now a portly matron like most of San Francisco's theatrical ladies, whose appetite for massive meals had given them massive figures. She would have welcomed an evening in her own home, but Tom Maguire owned the theatre he had let for six months to the Catt Company, and an invitation from him was not to be turned down. "Whose benefit is it, and who's going to play?" asked Laura, looking from one face to the other.

"It's for an old English actor called Wilfred Park," said Mrs. Judah. "He was playing the mining camps when you were a mere child: you probably never heard of him. But now he's tired and sick, so Tom Maguire enlisted some of his old friends to get up a benefit show for him – it's a bunch of old stagers you're going to hear tonight, my dear! But you'll like to see the Bella Union –"

"The Bella Union!" said Laura. "I thought it was a gambling – a saloon!"

"You're accustomed to that," said Kitty Catt drily. "What was Jack Swan's theatre but a glorified saloon?"

"Oh yes, of course . . . I'm sorry, I didn't mean . . . I somehow thought it would be in Mr. Maguire's new theatre, where we're opening on Monday?"

"Poor old Wilfred asked for the Bella Union. He used to top the bangers there in the Gold Rush days. And now little Lotta Crabtree tops the bill tonight. Well, that's the way it goes! Mrs. Crabtree said 'Over my dead body!' but Maguire persuaded her to give in for Wilfred's sake, and she simply said that if one vulgar word were spoken in front of dear little Lotta, she would march the child out of the Bella Union immediately."

"She's hardly a child at thirteen, with Lola Montez for a teacher," said Kitty. "I'm surprised Tom Maguire asked them. I thought he was at outs with the Crabtrees since Lotta's father shot him in Portsmouth Square for criticising his darling daughter –"

"It was only a flesh wound," said Mrs. Judah calmly. "And it was three years ago. Lotta's come a long way since then, and Maguire knows how much she's worth. She's the rising star of San Francisco, you may be sure of that!"

Laura was aware of a new feeling, not yet identifiable as jealousy. She was clever enough to say how much she looked forward to seeing Lotta Crabtree.

Mrs. Judah got stiffly to her feet. "I must be going," she said, "Kitty, try to get a rest this afternoon, you look exhausted. And make sure Tom escorts you to the show tonight."

"Tom'll be there," said his wife. "He's in a very chastened and virtuous mood today."

"Doesn't sound like Tom!"

"He's finally realised he's too old to play the juvenile lead in *Our American Cousin*. So Leyburn plays the Cousin, and Tommy plays Lord Dundreary."

"You're opening in the *Cousin*?"

"Yes, a week from Monday."

"And what will your part be, my dear?" asked Mrs. Judah, turning graciously to Laura. "Augusta? Or Mary Meredith?"

"I'm understudying Miss Kitty as Florence Trenchard," said the girl.

"She has to get accustomed to a bigger theatre than Jack Swan's," said Kitty. "Tom and I thought an understudy was the way to start."

"She won't be an understudy for long," said Mrs. Judah, and Laura Winter coloured at the compliment. Mrs. Judah ended her visit on a practical note. "Come backstage when the show's over, and we'll have a glass of wine," she said to both of them. "And remember there'll be a tremendous crush, so *don't wear hoops*."

Preparing her modest finery for the benefit performance, Laura was inclined to regret her crinoline. Without hoops, she thought her white silk dress looked home-made, as indeed it was, for Aunt Carrie and her schoolmistress had made Laura an excellent needlewoman, and she had sewed the dress herself. But she had a pelisse in shades of green and blue to lay about her shoulders, and she had dressed her hair in the way the Empress of the French had made fashionable, turned back from her brow and brushed into one shining golden curl upon her shoulder. Also she was wearing her necklace, shorter by several pearls since the day when Carlos Rivera had brought it as a bridal gift to Rosalie Estrada.

"Shall I wear my pearls?" she had asked Kitty Catt, one of the few people who had seen them.

"Yes, do, dear," said Kitty. "I think Maguire will be impressed."

She was wearing them as she asked the question, for having no strongbox or lockfast place Laura had worn the necklace under her bodice since the day Chips Winter put it into her hands. The pearls of Loreto, warmed by flesh, were brighter than they had been when they were wrapped in a red silk neckerchief inside the sea chest which came with Henry Winter round Cape Horn, and the old man, dying quietly of pneumonia, had smiled when Laura first put them on.

"I knew they would become you, Dolly, and they've kept you all these years. I sold them one by one, as your poor mother wanted; they've paid for your food and clothes, and Doña Ilaria's school, and shelter for us three . . . you don't blame me for it, darling?" said the old man.

"They couldn't buy the love and care you gave me," said the girl with a sob, and there were tears on the cheek she laid against his own. "But how do you know what my mother's wishes were?"

"She told Aunt Carrie's sister, when she took you from your mother's arms beside the Old Spanish Trail."

"Do you know my parents' name?" It was a question which had crossed her mind, occasionally, through the years.

"Can't say I ever heard it," said Chips uneasily. "Your father was dead and the poor lady was dying when Margarita met up with them."

"Then how did she know they were aristocrats?"

"The wagon master must have told her."

"But not their name?"

The sick man raised himself on his elbow. "I've told you all I know," he said feebly. "Goldie, what are you bothering about? Your folks are gone, and you're alive . . . you'll be a famous actress some day . . . make it on your own . . . so proud of you . . ." He was muttering incoherently when Jack Swan came in, full of concern for his old shipmate, and told Dolly he would sit with Chips a while. It was the last real talk she ever had with her foster-father, but the last words he said two days later, as she knelt by his bed with his calloused hands in hers, were "Don't pry, Princess! Let it alone! Let it alone!" Jack Swan thought he was wandering, but the girl knew better; as she closed Chips Winter's eyes she thought his warning not to disturb the secret of her parentage was more ominous than any mere evasion.

The thought, "Who were they? Who am I?" crossed her mind again as she fastened the pearls of Loreto round her neck,

and she put it resolutely aside. At least she knew the answer to
the second question. She was Laura Winter, actress, and she
was on her way to the conquest of San Francisco.

2

Fourteen years after Captain Montgomery raised the Stars and
Stripes in the old plaza, the plaza itself – now Portsmouth
Square – was still the hub of San Francisco. Streets had been
laid out, land reclaimed from the bay by using ships abandoned in the Gold Rush as a foundation, and after each
disastrous fire had consumed the wooden stores and counting
houses, newer and more important buildings of brick, stone
and marble had risen in their place. But the City Hall, the Post
Office, the very necessary fire houses, all radiated from Portsmouth Square, and the brothels, gambling hells and eateries
surrounding a space where deals were made and rivals exchanged pistol shots were dominated by the place of entertainment best loved by the Forty-Niners – the Bella Union.

It was a vibrant mixture of bar room, card room and
vaudeville theatre, the patrons of the theatre being obliged to
enter it through the bar. "Exactly like Uncle Jack's!" Laura
exulted silently, as she made her way behind Kitty through the
crush – she had not missed Kitty's critical reference to the
'Dramatic Adobe' of Monterey. And exactly like Jack Swan
the patron of the night's entertainment was standing at the
door of the auditorium to greet his patrons, but without old
Jack's urbanity. Thomas Maguire, almost illiterate when he
abandoned cab-driving in New York to join the Gold Rush,
was a thrusting, aggressive individual, whom more men than
Lotta Crabtree's father had wanted to take a shot at, but he
was, and remained for forty years, one of the greatest forces in
the San Francisco theatre.

"Well, Kitty me love, you're looking blooming," was how
he greeted Mrs. Catt. "And is this the new ingénue you picked
up in Monterey?" He looked Laura up and down with a greasy

familiarity which was tinged with respect when the ingénue swept him a disdainful curtsy.

"Well-grown young lady, upon me word," said Maguire. "Bit on the tall side, eh Kitty? You'll have to match her with a tall juvenile; I doubt if young Leyburn's up to her height . . . D'you speak French, me dear?"

"I'm just a girl from the country," said Laura. "Spanish is my other language," and Maguire grimaced.

"If ye could have parley-vooed a bit we could have billed you as the latest attraction from Paris," he said. "The Frenchies all go over well in San Francisco. Well, we'll see what we can do, and meantime you ladies ought to take your seats. Tommy me boy, it's still ten minutes to curtain up. There's time for you and me to have a glass at the bar."

Tom Catt accepted with alacrity. He had been sulky about old Park's benefit, having meant to spend his first evening back in town in a prowl among the hack-parlours and groggeries of the Long Wharf, but a drink and a confidential chat with the great Maguire added up to a valuable start to their six months' appearance in one of his theatres. He squired his wife and Laura to excellent seats in the middle of the hall, and departed just as the orchestra made its appearance and began tuning up.

Laura looked around her eagerly. She had been impressed by the façade of the Bella Union when they arrived. With a new coat of white paint it stood out among the gambling hells of Portsmouth Square because of its cleanliness, and the imposing row of columns which divided its second-storey windows. The inside was tawdry, and the faded velvet and brocades seemed impregnated for ever with the smells of cooking fat, whisky and cigars, fighting with the rank patchouli and frangipani of the women's scents. The house was full, for anything sentimental appealed to the San Franciscans, and the old trouper's farewell benefit attracted young as well as old. Especially when the most talented young comedienne in California led the second half of the bill.

The first half of the programme had been put together as a blend of nostalgia and humour, and was opened by a veteran favourite in the person of 'Doc' Robinson. The worthy doctor, so-called because he had at one time kept a druggist's shop in Portsmouth Square, had arrived broke in San Francisco with the other gold seekers of 1849, and earned his first dollars selling guillemots' eggs from the Farallones, where the Russians no longer possessed a fur-hunting colony. But the Doc, or 'Yankee' Robinson as he was sometimes called, had a turn for the stage, both as playwright and as manager, and at his little 'Dramatic Museum' had scored a hit with his own first play, Seeing the Elephant.

To 'see the elephant', which in old American slang meant to reach a summit of achievement, had taken on a sinister meaning among the miners of the Gold Rush days. To fail to strike pay dirt, to lose his shirt at cards, to get rolled by the Mexican bar girls, all entitled a man to say he had seen the elephant, and in spite of the forty million dollars in gold dust and nuggets taken out of the mines in one year only, 1849, by the end of the decade there were many more who had 'seen the elephant' than could say they had "struck it rich". The black humour had never failed to please the San Franciscans, and eleven years after his first stage hit Doc Robinson, at Wilfred Park's benefit, still received a thunderous ovation for his song:

> Oh, California, that's the place for me!
> Where they dig the gold and sleep in mud,
> And the elephant do see,
>
> Then I'm off to California,
> The elephant to see,
> For he always, with a charming grace,
> Invites you up to tea

Laura had never heard the song before, and even as she tapped out the rhythm with the toe of her slipper, she was surprised at the vivid audience reaction, the almost childish enthusiasm – as surprised as she was at Kitty Catt, wiping tears of enjoyment from her cheeks.

"Good old Doc!" said Kitty. "You'll meet him on Sunday, Laura. He and his wife are our neighbours on Calhoun Street, and they keep open house every Sunday for professionals."

"I'll enjoy that," said Laura politely. More than that silly song, she thought, for comedy was not her line, and she was better pleased by the turns which followed. She applauded actors too grand to have appeared at Jack Swan's Dramatic Adobe, and actresses like Sarah Kirby Stark in the death scene from *The Fate of a Coquette*, another version of *Camille*, and the great Catherine Sinclair as Portia in the trial scene from *The Merchant of Venice*. Mrs. Judah was awesome as a sleep-walking Lady Macbeth, and Mr. Park, the object of the benefit, recited 'To be or not to be!' in the manner learned when he understudied Edmund Kean as Hamlet at Drury Lane, about the time of the Battle of Waterloo. The old man was trembling and in tears when he finished, and Maguire, at the back of the hall, nodded approval as the first half of the bill ended with a few rousing songs from Harry Leyburn, the juvenile lead of the Catt Company.

Leyburn might not have been tall enough to play acceptably opposite Laura Winter, but he had a fine baritone voice, and often appeared as a balladist, seeing nothing ridiculous when playing Hamlet to Kitty Catt's robust Ophelia in appearing between the acts to sing 'A'e Fond Kiss' by Robert Burns. He flattered Doc Robinson by ending his turn with a number written and sung by the doctor in the early days of his Dramatic Museum, called 'The Used-up Man'.

O! I ha'nt got no home, nor nothing else, I s'pose,
Misfortune seems to follow me around where'er I goes,
I come to California with a heart both stout and bold,
And I've been up to th' diggings, there to get some
lumps of gold.
    But I'm a used-up man, a perfect used-up man,
    And if I ever get home again, I'll stay there if I can

It got an even bigger hand than 'Seeing the Elephant' and the curtain was rung down after a burst of cheering which again surprised Laura Winter. She had never known such a frenetic audience, feasting on its own enthusiasm, and she had a premonition that any San Francisco audience would be diffi-cult to command. She found her mouth was dry with nervous excitement, and was glad when Tom Catt, like most of the men in the audience, went out to the bar in the interval and, having slaked his own thirst, brought back glasses of wine for the ladies in his charge. The drink and the noisy conversations conducted from row to row completed the informality of the old 'Belly Union' hall, while newcomers admitted at half price, and standing against the walls, added to the mounting excitement of the audience.

At the height of the noise a lady dressed in black caused a momentary silence by taking a reserved place in the middle of the front row. Then someone whispered, "Mrs. Crabtree! Now Lotta's here!" and the name "Lotta! Lotta!" was repeated to the sound of subdued clapping.

"That's Lotta Crabtree's mother," Kitty informed her new ingénue. "She's usually in the wings when the kid's on stage. It isn't often she watches from the front."

"Let's hope her little angel doesn't hear any naughty words backstage," said Tom with a grin, and Kitty snapped, "There's nothing she can't have heard already," as the orchestra burst into a lively polka.

The curtain went up on an empty stage. Empty only for a moment, because Lotta Crabtree, who disliked being found posed in a classic attitude, centre stage, came on to the polka tune in an outburst of dancing energy. She was small for her thirteen years, piquant rather than pretty, with a mop of red hair and dark eyes, and she wore a childish white dress and white dancing slippers. Her mother, who made all her costumes, decided that at the benefit there would be none of the quick changes for which Lotta was famous. A sailor's cap, a sunbonnet, a plaid or any article which could be proffered from the wings would be enough to sustain the impersonations which had contributed to the little star's success. As it was impossible to black-up on stage, Lotta had regretfully dropped 'Topsy' from her routine. She had been a famous Topsy in an early stage version of *Uncle Tom's Cabin*.

Lotta Crabtree had been on the stage since she was eight, and only superb health and energy had carried her through as hard an apprenticeship as any child player ever knew. She came of solid Lancashire stock on both sides, her parents having emigrated from England to New York, where she was born, but the Lancashire virtues were more evident in the mother than in the father, whose drawing a gun on Tom

Maguire was one of the few positive actions in a depressingly negative life. Mr. Crabtree, who brought his family to San Francisco four years after the Gold Rush began, was one of those who had 'seen the elephant', and his wife Mary Ann one of the many who became the breadwinner by opening a boarding-house. This was up-state, in Grass Valley, a mining camp which had become a prosperous little town, and in Grass Valley there began an extraordinary stage friendship.

Shortly before the arrival of the Crabtrees, the population of Grass Valley had been enriched by the arrival of an Irish adventuress, born Eliza Gilbert, and her third husband, a newspaperman named Patrick Hull. Mrs. Hull, who was an actress, was obviously writing her own scenario for Love in a Cottage, but as she had been accustomed to a bigger stage than Grass Valley the marriage was doomed to failure from the start. For Mrs. Hull was better known as Lola Montez, the mistress of King Ludwig I of Bavaria. She had been evicted from his country by the Jesuits, gone back to the stage, and made herself notorious in San Francisco by interpolating an erotic Spider Dance of her own choreography into a perform-ance of *Charlotte Corday*. The Bavarian king had created her Countess of Lansfeld in the days when she was the power behind the throne, and it was as the Countess of Lansfeld (Patrick Hull having disappeared from the scene) that she relieved the tedium of Grass Valley by befriending a redhaired imp called Lotta Crabtree.

The Spider Dance was beyond the powers of a child of eight, but Lola Montez taught Lotta some dance steps and stage tricks which the child picked up like a clever monkey, before she wearied of the simple life and went off to act in Australia. Lotta went on dancing: at Rabbit Creek, at Rough and Ready, up and down the valleys, along the mountain circuit, into Petaluma and Sonoma, in the travelling company of a manager called Matt Taylor. She danced on bar room tables, on ramshackle stages, in the shabby Gaieties Theatre on the waterfront of San Francisco, in the Mexican State of Sonora – travelling by boat, by stage coach, by mule wagon, sometimes sleeping exhausted in her mother's arms as a one-horse cart jolted them to the next one-night stand, but always alert and smiling when she faced the rough men who adored her in the camps along the Feather, the San Joaquin and the Sacramento. They threw their tributes at her feet. Mountain flowers, gold nuggets, silver dollars, the trumpery trinkets which the pedlars carried, all averred that Lotta Crabtree was –

"The Queen of the Rocky Mountains, that's what the fellows call her," whispered Kitty Catt. "She's good, though," she added grudgingly.

"Very good." Laura had never seen a performance like it. This chit of thirteen, five years her junior, had her audience in complete control. They laughed at her jokes, they were ready to weep at her sad songs, during the whole hour in which she held the stage. She showed them acrobatic dancing, turning cartwheels from one side of the stage to the other, gave an imitation of Elisa Biscaccianti, 'The American Thrush', singing 'The Last Rose of Summer', and even a take-off of Doc Robinson and his 'Seeing the Elephant'. She used back-up singers only twice. A quartet of men in blackface joined her in 'Ole Bull and Old Dan Tucker', a skit on the Norwegian violinist then popular in the United States, and they played their banjos when Lotta led them in the rousing chorus:

> Loud de banjo talked away
> And beat Ole Bull from de Norway,
> We'll take the shine from Paganini,
> We're de boys from ole Virginny

In her last number Lotta was joined by her rivals, the Worrell Sisters, otherwise 'The Juvenile Graces'. Sophie Worrell was only twelve, but like her sisters Irene and La Petite Jennie, she was swarthy and stout, unlike the fairy-tale figure in white who danced ahead of them in the 'walkaround' or cakewalk which ended most variety shows. 'Miss Lotta the Unapproachable' was the Graces' kindest name for their most formidable competition, but they were seasoned players, and smiled bewitchingly as she led them forward to take a bow. The last bow, of course, was Mr. Park's, and as Lotta led him down to the flickering gas footlights she laid her cheek against his trembling hand in a childish gesture of affection which brought down the house and the curtain.

"I wonder how often her mother rehearsed her in that one," commented Kitty Catt as they made their slow way backstage.

"It was cute though," said her husband. "If Maguire cared to put on *The Old Curiosity Shop*, Park and Lotta'd be good as the Grandfather and Little Nell."

"She'd be better as the Marchioness," said Laura, and Tom Catt looked up at her slyly. "Claws out, eh?" he said. "I'm glad you've read your Dickens, kiddy. And you've got an idea there. I might try it myself sometime."

The dressing-room at the Bella Union was cramped and on that night crowded. Mrs. Judah, still in the night robe of Lady Macbeth, was holding court in a mere cubicle, behind a table laden with bottles of wine and glasses, and the substantial supper which Tom Maguire had provided for the players in the benefit. Mr. Park was there with his old wife, long ago retired from the stage, and Doc Robinson with his, who gave Laura a hearty invitation to visit them on Sunday, and so many other notabilities that the new ingénue took her place in the background, on a bench with the Juvenile Graces, eating a few more pounds on to their substantial frames. With their mouths full, they told Laura that the star of the show would not join in the jolly supper.

"Far too grand for the likes of us."

"Her mamma thinks we're a bad influence."

"Just imagine, Lotta might even speak to a *boy*."

"Here they come now," said Sophie Worrell warningly. Through the door set wide open to admit the tainted air of the Bella Union to the airless room, Laura saw the little star, pale where the make-up had been creamed off her face, with a shawl over her red curls, and a warm cloak held round her shoulders by her mother. They heard her say "Good night!" to someone in the wings, and then the great roar from the crowd in the bar and the loungers in the square outside.

"Lotta! Lotta! Bravo, Lotta! Hurrah!"

Laura found that Mrs. Judah had left her seat at the table and taken La Petite Jennie's place at her side.

"Are you hoping they'll cheer you like that some day?" she asked.

"I could never do what she did tonight," said Laura honestly.

"No, I don't see *you* dancing a hoe-down or an Irish jig. But you have your own style, child, and if you work as hard as Lotta works, you'll get your cheers. Only you've got to have what she was born with –"

"What she was born with, madam?"

"Heart," said Mrs. Judah.

"The audience loved her."

"Because she loves them. When she goes on stage she opens her whole heart to them, and the love spills over. Don't waste your love on anything but your audience, my dear, when your turn comes."

It might have been Aunt Carrie talking. So thought Laura, half resentfully, as she undressed in her little bedroom at the Catts'. Only it had been man's love, not stage love, that Maria del Carmen dreaded for her foster-daughter, and the child had learned her lesson so well that at eighteen she was as un-approachable as – what was it Kitty Catt had called young Lotta – 'the Queen of the Rocky Mountains'. Blowing out her candle she realised why the nickname had seemed familiar. "Why, that's what I used to call myself, when I wanted to play in *Los Pastores*," she reflected. "The Queen, because Uncle Chips told me there was a man they called the King . . . I remember now . . . it was Fremont." She thought resolutely about those old times until sleep obliterated the new times in which she was by no means so sure as she had been in the morning that she could conquer San Francisco. She fell asleep wondering what had befallen that other amateur Thespian, John Charles Fremont.

3

One who had followed Fremont's career with obsessional hatred was Luis Estrada. Sometimes his wife thought that the wound he received in the last battle for California, with its long aftermath of blinding headaches, had clouded his judg-ment, because "everybody else," she would say pathetically, "seems to think Fremont was so generous at Cahuenga, telling our people to keep their weapons and go home quietly." To Luis this 'generosity' was intolerable condescension, and he gloated over every detail of Fremont's court-martial for insubordination to General Stephen Kearny. It was tactless of Isabel to keep pointing out with what good grace General Vallejo, who had lost so much more than the Estradas, had accepted the fact of the American Conquest.

"If he wants to collaborate with the Occupying Power, that's his affair; you won't find me attending their military balls and parties," Luis would growl, to which Isabel, who seemed to have lost her touch with him, would retort that at least the Vallejos and their friends in Sonoma were having more fun than the Estradas, stuck on a derelict rancho miles away . . .

"If it's derelict, whose fault is that? I'll never understand why you allowed the vaqueros to leave the rancho when the Bear Flaggers were running amok. There were enough of our men to have beaten off a few drunks before it came to robbery and arson –"

"I sent them out because you wanted the work to go on as usual. Everything would have been all right if only you'd been here yourself. But no, you had to go off and fight a war you couldn't win –"

"The Americans haven't captured Mexico City yet."

Mrs. Robert Cord, who was a good deal at the Rancho Estrada before and after Luis came home, thought some of the bickering was due to the deep disappointment both Luis and Isabel felt in the loss of their first child. She also – but then Leona Cord was an insatiable novel-reader, inventing fictional situations for everyday life – thought Isabel's sister, Doña Maddalena Martinez, had increased Isabel's bitterness by constantly harping on Luis's 'cruelty' in leaving his young wife alone in a post of danger while he was serving a lost cause. Leona, who enjoyed military balls and parties after her years of seclusion in the redwood forests, tacitly agreed that the pueblo of Sonoma was a far more amusing place than the Rancho Estrada. It was the headquarters of the Army of Occupation, with General Persifer Smith in command, and with a detachment of Stevenson's Regiment present there was of course an outbreak of amateur theatricals. Vallejo made over an old

warehouse to the military, for the inevitable presentations of
The Iron Son of '76, *Box and Cox*, *The Lady of Lyons*, and
suchlike, and repaid their hospitality with entertainments in
his old lavish style. Still an advocate of 'foreign' marriages, he
organised a splendid wedding when his sixteen-year-old
daughter Epifania married Captain J. B. Frisbie, USA, and
another when her sister Adelaida married the captain's doctor
brother.

Luis Estrada refused invitations to all such gaieties. He
would sometimes stand looking at his father's secretary,
which had come from Spain two hundred years before it was
smashed open by the Bear Flaggers, and which no carpenter in
Sonoma was skilled enough to repair to perfection. The tule
roof of the rancho had been replaced without difficulty, but
the dark wood of the secretary was now seamed with cracks
where the inlets had been clumsily done, and Luis thought it
looked like his own life, cracked and held together with
makeshift joins. He thought less, in the beginning, of the
papers which the secretary once contained. That came later.
The four years of military government before California
became the thirty-first State of the Union seemed, to the
rancheros and the people of the pueblos, like a paradise
compared to what came after.

President Polk's victory over Mexico, which had taken
longer to win than he anticipated, was marked in February
1848 with the Treaty of Guadalupe Hidalgo, which added
Texas, New Mexico and California to the United States.
Among its many provisions was one which declared that the
Spanish and Mexican land grants made to all title-holders
would be respected. This assurance meant nothing to the vast
army of immigrants following the Gold Rush, who squatted
indiscriminately in the fertile valleys, and within three years of
the Treaty the Land Laws of 1851 brought immediate confusion and years of litigation to Luis Estrada and scores of others
like himself. Luis was in a worse position than most, for all the
papers relating to the Rancho Estrada had been burned by the
Bear Flaggers, and only his brother was now alive to support
his affidavit that the land had been properly granted by the
Mexican Governor to his father.

"I remember it perfectly," said Felipe, summoned to Sonoma for a conference with his brother. "I remember father pulling up the grass, breaking branches and throwing stones to indicate ownership, with Father Fortuni as his witness. The good padre's dead, and I would be considered a prejudiced witness: do you think that bunch of Yankee land sharks will listen to what I remember about stone-throwing when I was a thirteen-year-old boy?"

"Then what do you advise me to do, hermano?"

"Do what I've done, sell what you can and get your price before you're cited to appear before the Land Commissioners."

These were three in number, all Americans, no Spanish representation being permitted. What Felipe had sold was his property on the Salmon Creek, including the sawmill, for immigrants from New England had seen the potential of the land along the Slavianka, now called the Russian River, and a native of Vermont named Jenner had established himself at the very spot where the Miwok Indians found the drowned body of Peter Gagarin.

Before he was called before the Land Commissioners Luis was able to sell Agua Caliente, where his father had lodged his Indians in their own ranchería, to an American officer who had fought in the Mexican War, and rejoiced in the name of 'Fighting Joe' Hooker. Then began the long struggle to prove his right to the land without a single document to support his claim, the long arguments with lawyers in a language he barely understood, the lawyers' fees which drained the purse of a man who had painfully learned that hides were no longer 'California bank notes', and the endless delays of litigation. Luis had his private vexations too. His most trusted vaqueros left him to join in the search for gold. The capataz, as steady as Old Time, was the first to go, then Pedro and Bernardo, who had shared his boyhood, and others who could ill be spared. His wife suffered a second early miscarriage soon after his return, and in the following year brought to term a still-born son. It was not until 1850 that Isabel gave birth to a living child, whom her parents called Maria de las Mercedes, in gratitude for the mercies at last accorded them.

The Land Commissioners' judgment, handed down after interminable delays, was that Mr. Luis Estrada had a right to one thousand acres surrounding his ranch house, while what remained (minus the sale to Hooker) would be rated as public land, to be put up for auction in one thousand acre lots and used for agricultural development only. Whereupon Mr. Estrada, not deigning to rub shoulders with what he called small-holders, improved his little adobe in Sonoma, building two extra rooms on the ground floor, and four more, reached by a wooden staircase, on a new floor above, with a row of dwellings for his servants at the foot of a much developed garden. The change to a new home made Isabel Estrada very happy. Sonoma had become a sociable place, where one could meet officers with names like Sheridan, Sherman, Ulysses S. Grant, along with Captain Farragut from the new Navy Yard at Mare Island, and drink tea instead of chocolate with the gaunt American women who had crossed plains and mountains to reach the golden goal of California.

Isabel's sociabilities were not shared by her husband. He was glad that she was happy, and that their little Maria was lively and healthy, playing in her sheltered garden, but he rode the three miles to the old rancho every day of his life. He was his own capataz now, overlooking the remaining stock and supervising the cultivation of the remaining fields. His daily presence among the labourers, and the rifle he carried at his saddle along with his reata, had a good deal to do with keeping his land clear of the squatters who overran the valleys, but it was difficult to keep the buildings in good repair. Little by little the adobe crumbled, and the rancho on the northern frontier became as derelict as others, further south, which had suffered in the war with Fremont.

That was how Luis now saw the Californian Resistance. He followed the vagaries of Fremont's career with compulsive interest. He jeered when Fremont, elected a US Senator from California, took his seat in the Senate only twenty days before Congress adjourned, and failed to be returned at the next election. Seventeen working days in the Senate out of a total of twenty! There was a legislator for you! But Fremont, in one of the upsurges of his career, bought the Mariposa rancho ("when better men were being turned out of theirs," said Luis) and found gold there in enormous quantities. John C. Fremont, however, was no businessman. Encumbered by debts and lawsuits, he had to give up the operatic style of Mariposa, where two Delaware Indians rode before his carriage in Spanish costume, and depart for Europe. There his lady was presented to Queen Victoria, and the pair hobnobbed with the future Emperor Napoleon III. Even Isabel Estrada sighed when she read accounts of the toilettes worn by Jessie Fremont at the Court of St. James and the Palace of the Elysée. But Luis's chance came again when Fremont won the Republican nomination for the presidential election of 1856. In California no one was more active than Luis in campaigning against the man once known as the King of the Rocky Mountains. He surpassed himself as an orator in raking up the old scandals of 1846: the Berryessa murders, the depredations of the Bear Flaggers, the long intrigues by Fremont to keep himself in the background and let others do the fighting. James Buchanan, a Democrat, was elected President.

"You ought to go into politics yourself, Luis," urged Felipe, who had been impressed by a speech his brother made in San Francisco.

"I can't afford it," said Luis. "Don't you know I'm a ruined man?"

"Vallejo's losses were far greater than yours, and he keeps his name before the public."

"Because he likes flattery. And Isabel has suffered enough already; I won't degrade her to the position of an assemblyman's wife in Sacramento."

Sacramento, a new town near Sutter's Fort, was the fifth choice as the capital of California. Monterey had been the nominal capital at the time of the Constitutional Convention, then for two years it was San José, known as 'the legislature of a thousand drinks'. General Vallejo's vanity caused him to sink more money than he could afford into the creation of two new towns, Vallejo named for himself and Benicia for his wife, each of which in turn was the state capital, until in 1854 the thriving town of Sacramento was the final choice.

"Isabel likes company," said Felipe. "She might enjoy spending part of the year in Sacramento."

"With the Yankee land sharks? I think not."

"Well," persisted Felipe, "if Robert Cord can be a State Senator, I should think you might. I remember the days when

Leona had to write his letters for him –"

"Cord had a highly educated wife behind him, pushing him on."

"So had your friend Fremont. Remember his election slogan, 'Fremont and Jessie!' as if the lady were to share in the Presidency?"

"Probably one of the reasons why he lost," said Luis with satisfaction. "But if it comes to what the Yankees call 'gumption', I don't know any woman who has more than your own wife, Felipe."

The new San Francisco, born on the day in February 1849 when the SS *California* entered the bay with the first contingent of gold seekers, agreed that Mrs. Philip Estrada (for Spanish Felipe quickly became English Philip or even American Phil) had gumption to an uncommon degree. She was neither lovely nor lovable, and those who said she had a brain like a man's did not mean to be complimentary. But she had one merit greatly esteemed at the time: she was virtuous, and the sentimentality of the Gold Rush era was as much centred on virtuous women as it was on little children. Before 1849 was over more than seven hundred ships were cleared through the port of New York alone for San Francisco. Twenty-four thousand men, nearly all under forty, and five hundred women landed at the port by the Golden Gate, where only a thousand people had lived before: saloons, gambling hells and brothels sprang up by the score, and a woman who could live among the rabble and keep her virtue was indeed prized above rubies. The men who did business with Estrada and Putnam would never have dreamed of uttering an improper word to the little lady who often met them alone in the firm's small office in Montgomery Street when her husband was out showing prospective clients the building lots he had carved out of what had been the Rivera rancho. Since old Skipper Putnam died (with a proviso, given the insanitary nature of the first graveyards in the town, that he be buried at sea) and Robert Cord proved that he still had a wandering foot by joining in the Gold Rush, Philip Estrada had exchanged the building trade for buying land for a song and selling it for a fortune. He was considered to be a sharp operator, with a wife who was sharper still.

If Content was respected in the office, she was equally respected in the paths of the growing town. Not one of the rowdies, not one of the Sydney Ducks, as the Australian roughs were called, but raised his hat to the determined little woman making her way along the busy wharves or down the muddy ravines which passed for streets, usually flourishing a baggy umbrella like one of the lances of San Pascual. Everybody knew that Mrs. Estrada had been there before time began. She had carried her own drinking water, price fifty cents a bucket, in the days when fresh water came from a cistern at Sausalito and was ferried across the bay in casks aboard the *Water Nixie*. She had given first aid to the injured when fire swept the city, and lived in a tent when hotel fires twice made the Estradas homeless. She was one of the six charter members when the first Presbyterian church was founded in 1849, and thereafter one of the loudest if least tuneful singers of hymns when its Church Tent was inaugurated.

The other godly matrons of the church admitted Mrs. Estrada's merits, but said she "put herself forward" and surely, with her many occupations, must neglect her children. For the Estradas had two little girls, Faith born in 1848 and Hope in 1849, who so far from being neglected, and left too much to hotel servants, were healthy, happy little things without a trace of the Estrada beauty. They were typical New Englanders, with fair hair and grey eyes like their mother, and when she led them to church on Sundays, with the air of one launching a personal attack on the Pope of Rome, some wag was sure to mutter, "There go Phil Estrada's three blessings – Faith, Hope and Discontent!"

While their neighbours were settling down in homes of their own, the Estradas moved from one hotel to another, telling the inquisitive that in hotels they would stay until they could move into the finest house in town. They did so in 1854, after ten years of marriage, and one year after they had opened a handsome office suite in the new Montgomery Block. Their home, equipped with the new gas lighting, was in South Park, built in the English style by an English architect called George Gordon round a private flower garden to which only residents had the keys. There was no housewarming, but some months after the Estradas moved to South Park they gave a splendid

christening party for their long-awaited son and heir. He was
baptised by the Reverend Albert Williams of the First Presbyterian Church, and Philip's rearguard action, insisting that
the boy be given his grandfather's name of Santiago, was soon
defeated by a general inclination to call the baby Jim.

When the party was over, and the happy parents alone in
their room, Philip remarked that some of his Spanish friends
from the old days had commented on the baby's resemblance
to his uncle.

"Nonsense, he looks just like you," said Content, unhook-
ing her corset with a gasp of relief. "You all three have dark
hair and dark eyes – why should that make our baby look like
poor Luis?"

"I see it myself," said the father. "He'll be a better-looking
man than I ever was – Luis over again."

"If he's as good a man as you are, and as big a success, that's
all I want," said Content, and Philip, touched by the unusual
compliment, took her affectionately in his arms.

"I guess I haven't done too badly," he said, in the American
idiom which sounded odd on Spanish lips.

"You've done what you set out to do," she whispered.
"You always said you'd put the Estrada brand on this city, and
you surely have."

It was as near as Content ever came to what she dismissed as
'sweet talk', and her softer mood continued through the first
happy years of Jimmy Estrada's life. She gave up going to the
office, and keeping her church and the new Mechanics' Institute as her only outside interests, devoted herself to her home
and family. Every fine afternoon she played with her little girls
and boy in the privileged garden, and rain or shine they were
all at the door to welcome Philip on his return. Life was
tranquil and happy, with all the old tragedies fading into the
past, until the day in November 1860 when Robert Cord
arrived from Sacramento.

There was nothing remarkable about the morning. Philip
Estrada was in Montgomery Street, writing letters for the next
day's mail steamer eastbound via Panama, when he heard a
familiar voice in the outer office. He reached the door of his
private room almost as a clerk opened it to announce "Senator
Cord and Mr. Ivanhoe, sir."

"Robert! Welcome back to San Francisco!" In the Salmon Creek days they would have greeted each other with a Spanish *abrazo*. Now a warm handshake sufficed, and Philip patted the arm of the tall lad behind his father.

"Ivan, how you've grown! How old are you now – sixteen?"

"Going on eighteen, Mr. Estrada," said the boy.

"Just turned seventeen," amended his father. Robert Cord was still a striking figure, wearing a snuff-coloured frock coat and a wide-brimmed hat, and with no grey in the long red hair brushed behind his ears. His tall son, wearing the round jacket of a schoolboy, too short in the sleeves, had inherited his father's well-cut features with his mother's brown hair and eyes. Ivanhoe Cord, who detested his name, was politely silent in the presence of his elders, but he was not shy. He looked round the handsome office with the assessing look of a grown man.

"What brings you to the city, Senator?" asked Philip when his guests were seated. "No trouble in our honourable legislature?"

"None at all. Just a little business, a good excuse for a jaunt to the bay."

"And when did you get here?"

"This morning early. We've been strolling around, seeing the sights while Leona had a rest. She never sleeps well on the boat."

"Why didn't you let us know you were coming? There's always room for any or all of the Cords at South Park, you know that."

"Thanks, Phil, but this was a last-minute decision," said Cord, with an uneasy glance at his son. "We're at the International Hotel on Jackson for a couple of days. This fellow's got a school term to finish, you understand . . ."

"I hear you led your class last year, Ivan," said Philip kindly, and the boy bowed.

"He's got a good brain, when he cares to use it," said the senator. "Well, never mind that . . . When do we get to see you and Content? Will you join us at the theatre tonight, and for supper afterwards?"

"The theatre?"

"Content doesn't disapprove of play-acting, does she?"

"Not if it's Shakespeare."

"This time it's Scott. You know how Leona is about Walter Scott?"

"Guess we all know that!" They laughed. Mrs. Cord had called her elder daughter Rowena, the younger Jeanie Deans, and not until their youngest child was born had his father put his foot down and insisted on the family names of Robert Faxon Cord.

"The Catts are playing in *The Heart of Midlothian*, and Leona as good as ordered me to get a box at Maguire's theatre. Will you come?"

"I'd be delighted, and Content would be too, but unfortunately she's not at home. She's gone to Sonoma for a few days. My sister-in-law hasn't been too well – poor Isabel – and she sets great store by Content's nursing, although heaven knows it's of the rough and ready sort."

"I know Content's style," said Robert Cord. "Well, that's too bad. Leona will be sorry to miss her, but you'll come on to supper, won't you? Tom and Kitty Catt are old friends; I've asked them to have a bite with us after the show."

"Fine with me."

"Good, then that's settled." Robert Cord looked at his son. "How about you getting back and seeing if mother's ready to go out? (She wants to go to Toomey and O'Keefe's to shop for glass and china," he explained to Philip.) "Tell her I'm going to have a chat with Mr. Estrada, and I'll be back at the hotel by one."

"Yes, sir." The boy rose immediately. "Goodbye, Mr. Estrada. I'll look forward to seeing you tonight."

Very adult, very self-assured! "He's growing up to be a fine young man," said Philip, when the door closed on Ivan Cord.

"He's growing up too damn fast for me," growled the senator, as Philip took a cut-crystal decanter from a redwood cabinet and poured two glasses of whisky. "He's the reason why we made the trip to town, confound him."

"I thought there was something," said Philip discreetly. "Want to tell me about it? Any chance that I can help?"

"Not a hope in hell. But here's the thing –" Robert Cord was only too glad to unburden himself. They had come to San

Francisco, he said, at his wife's urging: she wanted to enrol young Ivan, at the New Year, in the Reverend Henry Durant's private school for boys, with a view to special tutoring in Greek as a qualification for entrance to Yale.

"I know nothing about their eastern colleges," said Philip, "but why Yale?"

"Dr. Durant's a graduate of Yale. And Leona wants Ivan to go to Yale, take a degree in Law and pass his bar exams."

"Well, what's wrong with that? Don't you approve?"

"I approve all right. I hoped he'd come straight into the business with me, but a sound law training always comes in handy . . . Phil, it's the damned kid himself who doesn't approve, as you call it. Just seventeen, and he has other views."

"Such as?'

"He thinks of nothing but the silver strike in Nevada. Figures that if I'd grub-stake him to a claim at the Comstock Lode, he'd be a Silver King before he's twenty."

"Or dead of a rock fall or a gunshot wound."

"Exactly, that's what I told him. I said the Comstock was a place for grown men, not schoolboys. I told him what a rough time I had working a claim at Hangtown in '48, when I was twice the age he is now, and he came back at me with, 'But dad, you made a fortune?'"

"So you did."

"Hardly a fortune, but I didn't see the elephant, and I found the way to get rich wasn't by placer mining. Hangtown was rough going, even for me, and I'd grown to my full strength, which Ivan hasn't. Leona's scared out of her mind he'll run away from home."

"At seventeen. Robert, how old were you when you ran away to the fur trappers?"

"Fourteen," said Cord reluctantly. "But I lit out from a rotting cabin and a brute of a stepfather."

"I know." Everybody knew; the cabin in Kentucky and the stepfather had been in the preamble to every election speech made by Senator Cord.

"Ivan has a fine home and a chance at the education I never had. Why would he want to set out with a rifle and a blanket to dig tunnels and work in the dark, or get scalped by Piutes on the warpath?"

"To show he's as good a man as you are, maybe. Looks like we'll have to think about making way for the younger generation, Robert!"

"It's all very fine for you, your boy's only six," grumbled the senator. "Phil, do you know if Jim Fair's in town, or Jim Flood? I know them better than I know John Mackay. The Silver Kings, as they're called now."

"No, why?"

"I thought if I could have a word with Flood, he might keep an eye on the kid in Virginia City, if the worst comes to the worst. My God, it's not three years since Flood and O'Brien were keeping a saloon at Washington and Sansome, and now they're two of the Silver Kings, the richest men in California."

"Before you tackle Fair or Flood," said Philip, "what are you going to do about Dr. Durant?"

"Leona and I are taking Ivan for an interview tomorrow morning, ten o'clock, and the young cub has promised to be on his best behaviour. 'I'll give the doctor a fair chance, father,' he said. I didn't like the way he said it."

★   ★   ★

Another ambitious youngster, who was giving the stage a fair chance, was Miss Laura Winter. After a few months with the Catt Company she was sensible enough to admit to herself that the early discipline of Jack Swan's Dramatic Adobe had been invaluable in teaching her to take the rough with the smooth, for she had neither set San Francisco on fire nor dislodged Lotta Crabtree from her throne as the Queen of the Rocky Mountains. After the Park benefit Lotta had revived one of her dramatic successes, as Gertrude in *A Loan of a Lover*, and had since appeared in vaudeville at several of the city's leading playhouses. Laura had been working hard to little praise at Maguire's new theatre. She learned that a vocal projection which had been right for an audience of two hundred at Monterey was inadequate for two thousand in San Francisco, and had intensive coaching from Tom Catt in a naturalistic way of reading lines which showed Tom to be far ahead of his time. She understudied Miss Kitty, and Lizzie

Warden the soubrette, and when her name appeared on the programme the critics were less than enthusiastic. She was described as 'an adequate Nerissa' in *The Merchant of Venice*, and – ambiguously – 'a pathetic Perdita' in *The Winter's Tale*.

Laura shook down into the Catt Company all the quicker for going to live in Mrs. Wilson's theatrical boarding-house. It was on Clay Street between Dupont and Kearny (and if she had known it, close to the spot where Jacob Leese's house had stood when Dupont was the Calle de la Fundación) very near the heart of theatre-land, and well within the charmed three miles of gas lighting which made the city brilliant by night. Mrs. Wilson was a former actress who ran a clean and comfortable house, but was not particular about the hours her lodgers kept or the friends they entertained in their rooms. She liked to see young folks enjoying themselves, she said, and beamed when the girls had gentlemen callers who took them for buggy rides or picnics. Many a clandestine letter passed from Mrs. Wilson's apron pocket into some girl's eager hand, and many a young man slipped a dollar into that same pocket when he left the boarding-house in the small hours of the morning. Under the surface of propriety it was a slipshod, dissolute atmosphere, and one in which Laura Winter throve like a hothouse plant.

She made great friends with Lizzie Warden. The soubrette of the Catt Company did not fear her rivalry; they were too different to be type-cast as heroines, and Harry Leyburn the juvenile lead, who was Lizzie Warden's lover, had been astute enough to nickname Laura The Giraffe. The two girls went about in a crowd of spirited young people, riding on the ocean beach, picnicking in the dunes where trade winds blew sand into the food, and sometimes when the theatres closed for the night going on to the melodeons, where the charge for admission was twenty-five cents, and even down the wharves to the 'one-bit' houses or the dance halls where the Negro owners admitted black and white alike.

Laura was not vexed at having no part in *The Heart of Midlothian*. Kitty Catt of course was playing the Scottish heroine, Jeanie Deans, and Lizzie was better equipped to play the flighty Effie than Laura would ever be. She was glad to be spared an appearance as an extra, among the crowd tersely designated on the programme as 'Scotch Peasants', and to be back at her old occupation of balladist, singing a song which had nothing whatever to do with the play. Into a Scottish tragedy with a happy ending the Catts had inserted a lyric which was sweeping the country, from *The Bohemian Girl* by Balfe.

Laura was dressed in blue tarlatan and made up before the principals, and peering through the peep-hole in the curtain while the audience was filling up the seats. Maguire's theatres had grown more ornate with the years, and this one had a domed ceiling, tinted amber, from which bronze gaseliers hung over balconies ornamented in red and gold. The occupants of the stalls were very well dressed, and she saw a distinguished-looking group moving in to the OP box in the Grand Tier. Three men, and a majestic lady in dark-red velvet – that much she saw before the stage manager ordered her into the wings as the musicians began tuning up.

"Are you comfortable, Leona?" Senator Cord asked his wife in dark-red velvet, and she adjusted her spreading crinoline with a smile. "Ask Phil if *he*'s comfortable," she said. "There doesn't seem to be too much room for his chair."

There was not indeed a great deal of room for four adults, all of them elaborately attired. The men wore black dress coats and white ties, and so did the boy Ivan, who looked twenty rather than seventeen in the formal clothes which Philip thought must be required for receptions at Sacramento. They all wore white gloves, and Philip thought, with an inward smile, of Robert Cord's calloused hands swinging his partner at the fandangos he frequented when he came down from Salmon Creek to let off steam. They were growing old along with San Francisco, except that San Francisco was for ever young.

If the Catt Company's presentation of *The Heart of Midlothian* was not an entire success it was Tom Catt's fault. He had decided that the play would be improved by a few laughs, and casting himself as David Deans, the father of Jeanie and Effie, he played that stern Scots Covenanter as a comic character, with a kilt, a Highland bonnet and a crooked walking stick. Playing opposite her real-life lover, Harry Leyburn, as Staunton, Lizzie Warden as Effie was tender and convincing, but she had not weight enough for the court room scene, which was carried magnificently by Kitty Catt as Jeanie Deans. Skilful make-up took fifteen years off her age, and with a plaid wrapped over her kirtle she looked no more substantial than a healthy country girl had a right to be. Leona Cord whispered to Philip, "She's splendid! I wish our own little Jeanie Deans could see her now!"

Philip Estrada was not enjoying the play. As far as he could follow the argument (and thanks to Tom Catt's mutilation of Scott's novel the court room scene was difficult to follow) Effie Deans was about to be condemned to death not so much for child murder, since her child's existence was still possible, as for concealment of her pregnancy. It revived old recollections of a wretched time Philip had done his best to forget, and of Rosalie, as loving and appealing as Effie Deans. Effie standing at the bar of justice to hear her sentence, with her dark hair shading her face, became confused in his mind with Rosalie as he had found her heartbroken at Bodega Bay. When the Doomster appeared, 'a tall haggard figure, arrayed in a fantastic garment of black and grey', the theatre was absolutely still, the audience hushed. The actors in the court room seemed turned to stone. The Doomster named the date and time when Effie Deans was to be 'conveyed to the common place of execution, and there hanged by the neck upon a gibbet. "And this," said the Doomster, aggravating his harsh voice, "I pronounce for *doom*."'

The curtain fell. The audience, purged of pity and terror, was slow to applaud. A collective sigh, like the breath of a sated animal, preceded the first handclaps which became a storm of clapping. In the OP box of the Grand Tier, Robert Cord was the first to rise. He handed his wife into the little anteroom behind the box, where wine and glasses stood on a table. He was also the first to speak when the glasses had been filled and emptied. "My God! I needed that!" he said, and the others nodded. But Ivan, who had been studying his programme, exclaimed that there was a balladist next. "Let's go back to our seats, mother!" he said. "We don't want to miss anything, do we?"

Among Tom Maguire's novelties was the use of an extra drop curtain for ballads and between-acts specialities, painted with the San Francisco idea of a European scene. The Rialto, the Leaning Tower of Pisa and St. Paul's Cathedral had all pleased the public, and in his new theatre Maguire, well aware of the fondness of San Franciscans for all things French, had ordered his artist to paint a Paris scene. The man had chosen the Arc de Triomphe, bathed in a golden light, with a diminishing perspective of tall grey houses disappearing in a golden mist. Against this majestic background a young girl was seated in a gilt chair, holding a guitar. She wore a crinoline dress of pale-blue tarlatan, the loops of the skirt caught up with pink silk roses, and ribbons of the same colour hung from her guitar. Another silk rose was clasped into her golden hair. Philip heard young Ivan whisper "What a stunner!" as the balladist began to sing the song from *The Bohemian Girl.*

When other lips and other hearts their tales of love shall tell,
In language whose excess imparts the power they feel so well,
There may, perhaps, in such a scene some recollection be
Of days that have as happy been, and you'll remember,
You'll remember me

That evocation of remembrance, following on his equation of Effie Deans with Rosalie, struck a responsive chord in Philip's heart. The singer herself did not make him at once think of his dead sister, rare though it now was to see a girl playing a ribboned guitar: it was the tinkle of pianos which echoed through the mansions of South Park. But in the space of a breath the balladist brought another recollection. As she raised her head at the end of the verse he saw a feminine and lovely facsimile of the face of Peter Gagarin.

"Oh God!" Philip had no idea if he spoke aloud, or groaned, or sighed. He only knew that without a word of apology he had taken up the mother-of-pearl opera glasses which lay on the red velvet ledge in front of Leona and focussed them on the girl with the guitar. Her fair hair, her blue eyes, her striking profile leapt close to him, and were unmistakable. There, in a woman's shape, was the tall young Russian he had first seen at the Petaluma crossing, then at Fort Ross, then when he followed Rosalie to the place of their love and their tragedy. He heard Leona saying in Spanish, "Are you all right, Felipe?"

"Perfectly all right." It wasn't true, there had been a gap in his brain as if the shock of recognition had been too much for him, and he had missed the beginning of the second verse.

'Miss Laura Winter'. He could read the name on the programme when he laid down the opera glasses. How had she come by that name, and where? She had her father's face, but not her mother's voice: Miss Winter's was a soprano, soaring into the upper register, and equal to the grace notes and the cadenza of the song:

> When hollow hearts shall wear a mask 'twill break
> your own to see;
> In such a moment I but ask that you'll remember me,
> That you'll remember, you'll remember me

4

Effie Deans, saved from the gallows by the courage of her sister, was reunited with her lover, and their lost child was found alive. Tom and Kitty Catt took their bows, standing in front of the whole company including the balladist, and the curtain rose and fell five times before the applause came to an end. Lizzie Warden, with Laura by her side, was chattering excitedly in front of her make-up mirror, with Lady Staunton's feathers still in her hair, when Kitty Catt slipped between them.

"You lucky girls!" she murmured, too quietly for the other women in the dressing room to hear, "I've just had a message from Senator Cord. He asks 'the two lovely young ladies, Effie and the singer' to join us all at supper. He's sending a carriage to bring us to his hotel in half an hour."

"But Harry and I were –" Lizzie Warden began, and Kitty said decidedly, "Never mind Harry and you for one night, and do as the senator wishes. He could be a big help when we play Sacramento. Now hurry up and change."

"Miss Kitty – I've nothing to wear," said Laura.

"Wear your costume then, I don't mind for this once, but take that flower out of your hair and get off every speck of make-up. I don't want to look as if I'm taking a couple of melodeon girls to the International Hotel!"

"Why is Mr. Cord important?" asked Laura, wrapping a towel round her shoulders and reaching for the cold cream when Kitty had hurried away.

"Well, you heard her, he's a State Senator, and some people think that's important, but better still, he's very rich."

"Is he indeed," said Laura. "How did he make his money? Was he a Forty-Niner?"

"No, he was here before the Gold Rush and had a head start. Now he's a big contractor in Sacramento – roads and buildings, that sort of thing. Harry would know," said Miss Warden, still exasperated at missing a celebration with her lover. But she was a good enough actress to be all smiles as she and Laura followed the Catts into the dining room of the International Hotel and curtsied gracefully to Mrs. Robert Cord.

Leona's life had taught her something about acting too. She had smiled acquiescence when her husband had proposed inviting 'those sweet little girls' to supper, and she had even used the formula 'papa knows best' to quell Ivan, who was muttering that *two* such stunners ought to be shown off at Delmonico's or the Poodle Dog instead of the dowdy old International. But the hotel guests were not too antiquated to rustle with interest and admiration when the actors came in, and their table, bright with hothouse flowers, soon became the centre of attention. For Ivan the Comstock Lode seemed far away.

Laura at once recognised the group from the OP box. She identified the boy, who looked far too pleased with himself, and the older man with the thick body and the heavy Spanish face, who was Mr. Estrada. Mrs. Cord she dismissed as the typical Californian matron, stout and greying but imposing in her crimson crinoline: the senator, as well as being *very rich*, was the handsomest man in the room. She was seated between the boy Ivanhoe and Mr. Estrada, and looked with approval at the specially written menu.

In a time of over-laden tables it was pleasantly restrained, offering fresh oysters from the holding beds in the bay, a choice of game dishes, and fresh fruit as well as the inevitable ice cream. Champagne was served in fluted glasses, and Ivan Cord, elated by the first sip, set himself to monopolise the pretty girl in the blue crinoline, while his father divided his attentions between Kitty Catt and the attractive Lizzie. Leona and Philip Estrada discussed the play. Philip remembered very little of what had happened on the stage after the song 'Then You'll Remember Me'. From time to time, as the waiters moved between them with the food and wine, he stole a glance at the singer. Seated beside her he tried to persuade himself that he had only imagined her resemblance to Peter Gagarin. She was just a pretty fair girl with a dazzling complexion, innocent even of the pearl powder which Kitty and Lizzie had discreetly used, with a soft voice which had English inflections. Then she turned with a smile to include him in the conversation. He saw the blue eyes and the high Slavic cheekbones: he saw the face of his sister's Russian lover.

It might have been a glance from his mother which caused young Ivan to address himself to his game pie and let Mr. Estrada talk to Miss Winter, but Philip had to speak now, and muttered a banal compliment on her delightful singing. Did she take acting parts as well? Yes, she had a small part next week in Lytton's *The Rightful Heir*, and Mr. Catt was coaching her for a really big part in *Twelfth Night*. By William Shakespeare.

"Are you excited about that?"

"Oh very, it's marvellous to get a leading part so soon. I've only been with the company for three months."

"Did you join Mr. and Mrs. Catt in San Francisco?"

"No, in Monterey, after they played the Jack Swan theatre."

"Do your parents live in Monterey?"

"I have no parents, Mr. Estrada," said Rosalie's daughter. "I was brought up by two dear good people who lived in Monterey, after my father and mother died on the Old Spanish Trail. They were English aristocrats . . ."

Then it all came out, the story she was to tell so often and so well: the fever which struck down the travellers from Santa Fé, the devoted woman, Margarita Sanchez, who brought their baby to her childless sister, the happy childhood, the Dramatic Adobe, until Philip, overwhelmed, asked if she knew where Margarita Sanchez was living now.

"I never even saw her, that I can remember," said Laura. "If she's still alive she may be in Los Angeles. I've an idea that she married there, but I don't really know. My foster-parents lost touch with her, somehow – and after all, it was a long time ago."

She was right there. It was nearly twenty years ago, the tragedy that began at Fort Ross: this girl's whole lifetime. Philip said, "Did you go to school at Monterey?"

"Certainly I went to school! I went to Doña Ilaria Buelna's private school for girls, on the mesa just outside the Presidio walls, for nine years!"

"I remember when her father, Don Antonio, opened that school on the mesa."

Laura raised her eyebrows. She said in Spanish, "Are you a Montereño, Señor Estrada?"

"I was born there."

"Related to the family of Don Mariano Estrada?"

"He was my father's cousin."

"How interesting. My uncle often worked for him."

"Did you learn to speak English at Doña Ilaria's school?"

"Oh, no, at home. My Uncle Chips – Uncle Henry Winter – *was* an Englishman, like my own father. Doña Ilaria taught us just enough French to recite 'Maître corbeau sur un arbre perché' – that sort of thing."

"But no Russian?"

He didn't know what possessed him to say such a foolish thing. The girl looked at him coldly for the first time, as if she resented his questions, and saying sharply "Why Russian?" turned back to Ivan Cord. He was aware that Leona had been listening compassionately.

Robert Cord had apparently been engrossed in what Kitty was saying about their coming visit to Sacramento (for whatever Tom Catt might do, his wife never lost sight of their business interests) but he still had the keen eyesight and acute hearing of his solitary days as a trapper in the Rockies, when quick eyes and ears could mean survival. He had listened to everything Laura Winter said about herself, and Philip had interrogated her so well that there was only one more question Mr. Cord needed to ask his beautiful guest.

When the party was over, and he laid her pelisse round her shoulders, he asked Laura where she lived.

The Cords went to their rooms as soon as the actors left. The schoolboy lounged off to bed, and his father, smoking a last cigar in the sitting room of their suite, heard Leona chatting with the chambermaid who had come to help her off with her voluminous evening dress and garnet parure. Presently she appeared in a flannel nightdress and a cashmere wrapper as ample as her crinoline, sat down on a capacious sofa, and after a few remarks about the coming interview with Dr. Durant, said hesitantly:

"Robert, that girl, Miss Winter –"

"What about her?" He wondered what was coming next.

"Did she remind you of anybody?"

"*Remind* me? Who should she remind me of?"

"Do you remember the Russians who came to our first little cabin by the Petaluma?"

"My dear girl, there were Russians coming and going all the time, between the Bodega settlements and Fort Ross."

"This man came with the governor of Fort Ross and Princess Helen. He was a prince himself, with the same name as hers had been: Gagarin. They came with the Estrada boys and Doña Rosalie, on their way to a fiesta at the fort."

"I remember now. Tall fellow, very fair?"

"The Winter girl looks exactly like him. And you remember the scandal at the Rivera rancho, less than a year later?"

"I know the prince was drowned in the Slavianka, long before the Rivera wedding." Cord ground out his cigar. "You don't seriously think *he* was the cause of the scandal? And that this little actress girl is his daughter?"

"And Rosalie Estrada's."

"Oh, for God's sake. Leona, you read too many novels."

"You think I'm romancing, do you?"

"It wouldn't be the first time." He stood up and stretched lazily. "Come on, dear, let's go to bed; it's late." But Leona, with her grey plaits hanging limply on her heavy breast, sat stolidly still on the over-stuffed cushions. "Philip Estrada thinks so too," she said.

"Phil does? How'd you know? Did he *say* anything when you and he were talking at the end?"

"No, he didn't say anything. I just know."

Her husband stared at her. A wife in a thousand; she'd fought half his battles for him, and she had those intuitions, which were mostly right. He took her hand, and pulled her to her feet. "Then don't you say anything to him," he ordered. "It's only your fancy, there's nothing in it. I'll have a word with the girl, if you like, find out more about her background, but don't put ideas into Phil's head. We've got enough problems without raking up an old scandal from before the Conquest, and maybe spoiling a young girl's life, for all I know. So keep quiet, Leona, d'you hear me?" He shook her thickening wrist for emphasis.

"I'll keep quiet," said Leona Cord. "We don't need a scandal in an election year."

★   ★   ★

Philip Estrada needed no one to put ideas into his head. The ideas were all there, changing and feverish, and he was glad to see no more of the Cords during their brief visit to San Francisco. That it had been successful he knew from a note in Leona's pointed handwriting, delivered by messenger and saying that Dr. Durant had thought so well of Ivanhoe's attainments that he believed with two terms of coaching at the college, especially in Greek, the boy should pass his Yale entrance easily. Ivanhoe himself ('thank heaven!' interpolated his mother) now seemed eager to begin his studies in San Francisco at the New Year.

Never gregarious, Philip withdrew into himself during the days when he waited for Content's return. He resisted the impulse to watch Laura Winter once again, because the idea of seeing her act in a play with the all too appropriate title of *The Rightful Heir* was hateful: he would have to convince Content of the educational value in a performance of *Twelfth Night*. The words of Laura's song came back to him at any hour of the business day. "When hollow hearts shall wear a mask 'twill break your own to see/In such a moment I but ask that you'll remember me" . . . on that girl's lips the words were a

223

reproach to him. But it was not Laura he remembered. It was the young Rosalie.

He had been harsh in his judgment of his sister at the time of her disaster. Now, if her guilty love had produced such a beautiful creature as Laura Winter, he no longer dared to blame her. He was himself the father of daughters, growing up in a city where violence and lawlessness were always close beneath the surface gentility, and where they might as easily succumb to temptation as Rosalie had succumbed with the first handsome stranger who came her way. Faith and Hope were now twelve and eleven, old enough to show that they had their shares of the Estrada self-will and the Putnam aggressiveness. They were busy little girls, active at work and play, but quite different in looks and disposition. Faith was like her father, thickset and heavy featured, and she had some musical talent, walking twice a week to her piano lessons with a lady teacher, escorted by Mary Donovan, the under-housemaid. Content said she was altogether too fond of the servants' company, running off to Biddy the Irish cook and 'spoiling her dinner' with too many snacks and sweetmeats. Hope was ambitious: she wanted to lead her classes and be invited to all the children's parties in South Park, and from being a plain infant she was turning into a rather pretty girl. Jimmy at six was learning the three Rs from his mother, and with every year looked more like what his uncle Luis once had been.

What Luis was now his brother heard when Content came back from Sonoma, laden with presents for the children sewed or devised by their little cousin Maria, and able to give a fair account of Isabel's health.

"You did her good, Content," said her husband fondly, when the little girls and Jimmy had been shooed off to bed. "You bucked her up, as Robert Cord would say."

"She needs bucking up," said Content. "She's like Luis, she lives too much in the past."

They were sitting in the room pretentiously called the library, which boasted a yard-long shelf of calf-bound 'classics', seldom opened by anyone but Faith. There was a ferocious oil painting of Skipper Putnam above the marble fireplace, and near it on the wall hung the duelling pistols which

Content had used to such purpose against the marauding Bear Flagger so many years before. They were of course unloaded. San Francisco was a city where pistols were still carried as a matter of course. The editorial offices of the many newspapers often rang with revolver shots, sometimes fired by the editors, sometimes by contributors. Duels were fought, citizens' arrests were made by force of arms, and the ladies of the night carried little pearl-handled pistols for protection in their dangerous trade. But Philip Estrada abhorred violence and the antique weapons were a symbol of the past he preferred to forget.

"What was the real trouble this time?" he asked. "It's usually after a disagreement with Luis that Isabel takes to her bed."

"You're right, but this time it was a problem, not a disagreement." Content paused, to give emphasis to her next words. "Count Haraszthy wants to buy the Rancho Estrada – what's left of it."

"Good God, Content? The whole place? To set it out in vines?"

"Exactly. He's done so well with the land he bought from Vallejo, when the general first brought him to Sonoma, that he wants to expand his vineyards. And of course the land alongside the creek is ideal – well watered and sunny, and protected by the hills. Count Haraszthy says he'll give a good price for it."

"Luis wouldn't know a good price from a bad one. It's taken him fourteen years to adapt to cereal farming instead of cattle breeding; he knows nothing about wine-making, nothing at all. Does he *want* to sell?"

"He's so strapped for money, he's willing to consider it. It's Isabel who wants to hold on to everything they have left, so as to have a dowry for Maria when she marries."

"A dowry – when they need food and clothing first? I'd better go up to Sonoma myself and talk it over with the pair of them."

"Yes, but there's no immediate hurry. Count Haraszthy's planning a trip to Europe, at the state's expense, to bring back vine cuttings from several countries to his vineyards at Buena Vista. That's when he'll need more land. But if Luis doesn't make up his mind to sell, some of the other farmers in the valley might get in ahead of him."

"Yes, I quite see that. And is he . . . behaving himself?"

"I only saw him the worse for drink one night, when he got into a card game at the El Dorado. And that's what Isabel's afraid of – if he sells off all the land, and has nothing left to do, then it'll be more and more El Dorado, more and more Blue Wing Inn, more and more Battle of San Pascual – well, you know the story."

"Poor old Luis." They went upstairs to bed, with Philip's arm round his wife. He looked down at her fondly in the light of the big gaselier on the landing. She was only four years younger than Leona Cord, but she hadn't let herself go like that massive lady. Not a thread of grey in her hair, not an inch on the narrow waist which he could almost span with his two hands! For half an hour, in the renewed pleasure of possessing her, in the familiar creature comfort, Philip Estrada forgot his brother and his sister, and slept soundly for the first of many nights.

But next day he remembered his purpose, and introduced it craftily at the family dinner table, at which Jim did not as yet appear. A visit to the play – how did that appeal to them? A play by Shakespeare, he said hastily, to dispel the doubt in Content's eyes, and of course the little girls' shrieks of joy did the rest. Faith wanted to know the story of *Twelfth Night*, which no one present could tell her, and Hope at once requested a new sash for her best party dress. When the chorus of "Oh mamma, please!" had died down Content said indulgently, "Very well. Papa says you were good obedient girls while I was gone, and if he thinks you deserve a treat, you shall have it. But don't make too much of it to Jimmy, because he really is too young for an evening at the theatre. Shall we go on the opening night, papa?"

"The second might be better," said Philip. "Let them get settled into their parts." What he wanted was to read the newspaper reviews, and even the actors' names. Laura Winter had only said Tom Catt was coaching her for a part, and as a newcomer she might have been dropped from the final cast. If she had been, Philip was superstitious enough to think it would be a warning to let the whole matter of her identity slide into oblivion. Let his be the hollow heart to wear a mask, 'Twould break her own to see . . . However, the leading paper carried not only her name, but began its review with the words:

"The revelation of the evening was Miss Laura Winter as Viola."

Tom Catt's version of *Twelfth Night* was no easier to follow than his version of Scott. He had kept in the Clown's songs, thus avoiding the use of a balladist, but he had cut out Sir Andrew and Sir Toby as too challenging to his own rôle as Malvolio. Apart from his overplaying the performance was controlled. Kitty, as Olivia, did not shine, but Lizzie Warden was a sprightly Maria and Leyburn a handsome Orsino. Laura was obviously nervous in her opening scene as the girl Viola, and her voice shook as she began:

"What country, friends, is this?"

"Illyria, lady."

"And what should I do in Illyria? My brother he is in Elysium."

For Philip Estrada the shock of those first words was as painful as when the tragedy of Effie Deans, betrayed maiden and bereaved mother, began to unfold upon that very stage. Now he was to watch the drama of a girl who had lost her brother, Sebastian, her identical twin; and he remembered something buried under layers of deliberate forgetfulness. Rosalie had borne not one child, but two. As well as the girl whom Rita had kidnapped? saved from death? (he was still not sure which) there was a boy who died at birth, and was buried God knew where.

He glanced along the front row of the Grand Tier. He had not taken a box, as making them too conspicuous, and the two girls were seated between Content and himself. He sensed their perplexity, which was shared by the audience, not quite sure what to make of this unconventional Viola. Her appearance in boy's clothes, masquerading as the page Cesario, was usually good for a laugh from the more volatile section of any San Francisco audience, and the little Estrada girls giggled dutifully, while beyond them her husband could hear Content's disapproving hiss of "Tights!" But Laura as Viola rose above her audience. She spoke her lines as Tom Catt taught her, as naturally and thoughtfully as if the familiar words were coming to her lips for the first time. She did not, like the great ladies who had played the part before her – the Mariettas, Catherines, Laura Keenes – take two paces down to the flickering gas of the footlights and boom out the famous speeches to the back of the gallery. " 'Tis beauty truly blent, whose red and white, Nature's own sweet and cunning hand laid on," was spoken only to Olivia. But they heard her at the back of the gallery – Tom Catt had seen to that – and an audience which could have prompted her through every word listened enchanted to:

Make me a willow cabin at your gate
And call upon my soul within the house

spoken, not with love, but with the chill detachment of Laura's untouched youth.

Philip Estrada was aware of the enchantment, the subjugation of the audience, but he responded less to the speeches than to Laura's physical presence. As Cesario she wore a dark-blue doublet and tights of the same colour, which made her legs seem very long, and her golden hair, worn loose as the girl Viola, was swathed closely round her head beneath a dark blue cap with a long scarlet feather. The resemblance to Peter Gagarin was more striking than ever, and Philip listened (holding little Faith's hand, which she had slipped into his) to lines which seemed to have a special meaning, as when Olivia said,

"You might do much. What is your parentage?" and Cesario replied,

"Above my fortunes, yet my state is well. I am a gentleman."

"*Above my fortunes, yet my state is well!*" Philip silently repeated the lines along with Olivia. Was it his duty to restore the fortunes of the beautiful creature moving with long-legged grace across the stage? And how to set about it? He saw the boy-heroine reunited with her lost twin brother, become a girl again and find love in the arms of Orsino, Duke of Illyria. The audience roared its approval of the happy ending. Tom Catt led out his wife to take a bow and Leyburn led out Lizzie instead of Laura Winter. The generous Catts had decided it should be Laura's night, and the final ovation was reserved for

her, alone on the stage. A bouquet was handed up to her across
the footlights, a bouquet of the pink Castilian roses now raised
in greenhouses, and though it was the first stage bouquet she
had ever received Laura kept in character and acknowledged it
with a smile and a stiff boy's bow. Then the whole company
took the final curtain call, and the play was over.

Mary Donovan, the Estradas' under-housemaid, was waiting up in the South Park mansion to take their cloaks and
shepherd the little girls to bed.

"Thank you, Mary," said Content. "Those children are
asleep on their feet, and so am I."

"I hope you enjoyed yourself, ma'am," said the young
woman. "Come away upstairs, Miss Hope, you can tell me all
about the play in the morning."

"Stay a minute, Content," said Philip, as his wife set her
foot on the bottom stair. "There's something I want to say to
you."

"Can't it wait until tomorrow?" she said with a yawn. "It's
really very late. And I want to look in on Jimmy –"

"Master Jim's asleep, isn't he, Mary?" said Philip impatiently.

"Sound asleep, sir, bless his heart."

"Content –"

"All right, I'm coming," she said, and followed him into the
library. Faith, from the upper landing, called down to know if
Mary could hear her say her prayers.

"Of course; now be quiet, and don't wake Jim."

Philip held the library door open for his wife. A bright fire
was burning in the polished steel grate, and she went straight
up to it, resting her bronze kid slipper on the fender.

"Are you cold?" said Philip.

"It was too hot in the theatre, and then chilly in the
carriage."

"I thought so too." Philip poured himself a glass of brandy
from a decanter on the console table.

"Is that to keep out the cold?" asked Content. "Or to brace
yourself for whatever you have to say?"

He detested the sarcastic note, but he knew how well she
could always read him, and fumbled for the words.

"There's nothing wrong at the office, is there?" she said.

"Everything's fine at the office. It's – that girl – the girl who played Viola –"

"Yes?"

He told her he had reason to believe that she was the daughter of his sister Rosalie and Peter Gagarin.

Content wasn't the woman to go into hysterics. She kept her face averted, looking at the flames, and said in her flattest down-East voice, "What reason?"

"Her very strong resemblance to Prince Peter."

"I have to take your word for that. Remember I never saw the man! I only saw your sister twice, and Peter Gagarin never. Anything else?"

He was starting his story when the maid came in to say Miss Hope was asking if she could have some hot milk.

"Little monkey!" said her mother, "she's playing up her visit to the theatre for all it's worth. Just this once then, Mary, she can have her hot drink and pretend she's a famous actress – and, Mary –" as the Irish girl curtsied, "you can bring me a glass of hot milk too."

Content saw by her husband's scowl that he resented the interruption. So much the better; it would give her time to think, and put him off his ridiculous story . . . But the story came pouring out, as Laura Winter had innocently told it at the party: the orphan taken by Margarita Sanchez to the kind foster-parents at Monterey, the English aristocrats dying on the Old Spanish Trail. She interrupted it to say in her most literal way:

"The Trail ran from Santa Fé to Mexico, that's a far cry from Yerba Buena. It passed near Los Angeles, I grant you, but what would Margarita Sanchez be doing there? You think she was Rosalie's maid Rita, I suppose?"

"Who else?"

"You and Luis looked for her for twenty miles around the bay, and she had only a day's start of you, as near as you could ever figure out."

"According to the vaqueros, when we ran them to earth at the Presidio."

At the recollection of the deserted Rancho Rivera, and what the brothers had found there, Philip Estrada flung himself down in an armchair and covered his eyes with his hand.

"You can't go on the strength of a resemblance," said the level voice. "There are plenty of tall fair girls in San Francisco who hadn't Russian fathers! So what do you propose to do about it? Go to Los Angeles and look for Margarita Sanchez, if she's still alive?"

"Why shouldn't she be?"

"The others are all dead."

The door opened again, and Mary entered with a silver salver holding a glass of hot milk. "I put a little nutmeg on the top, ma'am," she volunteered. "I've noticed you like it that way."

"Thank you, Mary," said Philip Estrada harshly. "We shan't need you any more tonight." He took up the decanter. "Brandy'll do you more good than nutmeg, Content," he said, and poured a measure into the milk. "You're shivering."

Content's voice and hand were steady, but she had not been able to control one long shiver, and she wrapped more closely around her the handsome Indian cashmere shawl which she had allowed to fall from her shoulders as she sank into an armchair. He laid his hand on her neck. "Try not to distress yourself, my dear," he said.

"I'm distressed for you, Philip. It's horrible to see you under a delusion – a fancy which is only another shadow of the past –"

"A fancy, as you call it, which can easily be proved a fact."

"By what means? By making investigations at Monterey?"

"By meeting Miss Winter again, and finding out more about her childhood than I could ten days ago."

Content smiled for the first time. "Quite," she said, "I can see you were handicapped at the Cords' supper party. It was Robert's idea, I suppose, to invite her to the hotel?"

"Yes. But wouldn't it be possible to ask her to come here? Would *you* meet her, Content?"

"Talk to her by all means – in her dressing room at the theatre, at a restaurant, wherever suits you best. But I think Mrs. Catt should be her chaperone – in the lamented absence of Mrs. Cord."

"You don't think I'm serious, do you?"

"I think you're very serious. But I think you might be about to do a great wrong to this girl, as well as to all the rest of us, by raising hopes of a name and an inheritance to which she has no right."

"No right?"

"If you could prove twenty times over that she is poor Rosalie's daughter, that doesn't mean she has any right to the estate you and Luis shared. Because that was left to your sister's legitimate heirs. And you are banking on her resemblance to your sister's lover."

"I can't forget that I'm a rich man because I shared in that estate."

"The Rivera land gave you a start," she acknowledged. "The rest of your fortune came from my father – and from me."

"You mean from the money your father lent me when we were first married, and which I paid back?"

"I mean the money for the water lots the alcalde put up for sale for fifteen dollars each in '47. You paid that back and sold the lots for ten thousand dollars each in the Gold Rush days. I said to my father, 'Phil had the best of that bargain!' And all he said was, 'Sharp fellow, Phil! Never mind, my dear; it's all for you and for your children!' That's the man *he* was! And I worked side by side with you for ten years, to make sure of our children's fortune – I'm not about to see it squandered on an interloper, who hasn't even made a claim on us; nor will she, if you hold your tongue!"

"I doubt if Luis will be impressed by the Putnam sacrifices."

"If you bring Luis into this, you'll destroy Isabel," said Content. She got up, and in her barbaric shawl she was a strangely menacing figure. "You'll put the Estrada brand on this city in a way you never meant. Even eighteen years ago you and Luis couldn't hush up the story. Even with Don Francisco Guerrero, poor man, to help you quash an inquest, there wasn't one of your precious *gente de razón* who didn't know what happened at the Rancho Rivera. And now think of the scandal sheets! The yellow press! San Francisco will ring with it – the wicked uncles and the missing heiress – discovered on the boards of Maguire's new theatre!"

She dominated him, of course; she always did. When he muttered, "Oh God, Content, I don't know what to do!" she knew that she had won. Falling to her knees beside his chair, she chafed his cold hands in hers and begged him to be reasonable, to let the dead past bury its dead. "If she were poor, or ill, or homeless, I would say we should try to help her," she urged in the softest tones at her command, "but Laura Winter isn't any of those things. She's young and beautiful. She has talent, as we saw tonight. She may be at the beginning of a great career on the stage. Why should you spoil it all for her by trying to prove that she is what in fact she may not be?"

"Is that how you see it, Content?" he said doubtfully. "How would you feel if it were one of our own girls, left friendless, and having to earn her living on the stage?"

"I don't think Miss Winter will be friendless long."

"What do you mean?"

Content sat back on her heels, heedless of her half-empty glass and the spilt milk on the white fur rug. "You hardly took your eyes off the stage tonight," she said, "Didn't you see someone you knew in the audience?"

"For all I know a score of our friends could have been there."

"One in particular."

"Who?"

"Robert Cord."

"Cord? I thought he went back with Leona and the kid to Sacramento."

"He was in the front row of the stalls, clapping fit to split his gloves. I bet you a dollar that great bunch of roses came from him."

Philip was speechless.

"I bet you *five* dollars," said Content relentlessly, "that while we're here beating our breasts over the poor little orphan girl, she's in some smart restaurant celebrating her first stage triumph with Senator Cord."

5

If Content Estrada had been able to place her bets, she would have won them both. When the lights were extinguished in the South Park mansion, Laura Winter was enjoying a *poussin Véronique* and a glass of champagne at the Poodle Dog. The bouquet of pink roses was in a silver-plated wine cooler beside her chair, placed there by order of Senator Cord, who had sent her the flowers, and who was now presiding over a charming little supper party of four people.

His invitations to Miss Winter and Miss Warden had been delivered to their boarding-house in the afternoon, and to Mr. Harry Leyburn at the theatre before curtain-up. As Lizzie said, there was plenty of time for Laura to run to Verdier's 'City of Paris' store on Clay Street for some extra bit of finery to wear at supper, to liven up that old black dress; to which Laura had replied enigmatically, "He must take me as I am." Her appearance in the fashionable restaurant was less sensational than her entry, in her stage dress, at the International Hotel, and at the Poodle Dog (which began life in the Gold Rush days as the *Poulet d'Or*) she had to face the competition of the best dressed and bejewelled women of the city. But Laura was serenely aware that her plain black dress with its single hoop, its high neck and elbow sleeves, showed her skin and hair to the best advantage, and round her neck she wore the pearls of Loreto.

The former frontiersman was an accomplished host. He did not bore his guests by reminiscing, as older men so often did, about the great shows he had seen at the Jenny Lind Theatre in the days of gold, nor did he anticipate the nation's troubled future by political talk. He knew his guests would rather talk about themselves than Abraham Lincoln any day, and by repeating the time-honoured formula "You were wonderful in your big scene where . . ." he made all the actors happy. The only time he talked about himself was when Laura asked him, with lowered lashes, what had brought him back to San Francisco so soon. He replied that he was looking for a house to rent. "I saw a place on Stockton Street today which may be suitable," he said. "Mrs. Cord thinks our boy should have a home to come to while he's in college, and our girls are beginning to clamour for 'accomplishments', whatever that may mean . . . Miss Warden, you look tired. Another glass of champagne?"

"We all ought to be going," said Laura. "What time is it?"

"A quarter to one," said Leyburn.

"But surely you haven't an early start. You don't play a matinée?"

"No, but we've a green-room call at three."

"Then I mustn't keep you." Mr. Cord signalled to the waiter and paid the bill. They were almost the first to leave the supper room. San Francisco was tireless in the pursuit of pleasure, and in the private rooms upstairs in the Poodle Dog men and women were pursuing the pleasures of bought love. Outside they were in the vicious heart of the town. The curtains were drawn over the windows of the most expensive brothels, the lights were bright in the saloons and gambling hells, while the prostitutes of Dupont Street, where they stood, prowled on their beats between the light and the dark.

"We haven't far to go," said Laura, as Lizzie took her lover's arm and they started off down Clay Street.

"You oughtn't to be living here at all." Robert Cord slipped his hand under Laura's thin wrap as they crossed Dupont, and cupped her arm between the frill of her sleeve and the top of her glove.

"Will you drive with me tomorrow, if it's fine?" he said.

"If you think it's wise."

"When may I call for you?"

"Not before noon."

It was all so quick, and their voices had been so completely drowned by the many noises of the street, that Harry and Lizzie had no idea of what had been said as they turned at Mrs. Wilson's door to thank their host. Harry Leyburn walked back with Senator Cord to his hotel, and the senator, once alone among items of bedroom furniture which looked like so many coffins, lit a final cigar with the increasing certainty that he was about to make a spectacular fool of himself.

By next morning his mood had completely changed, as he

set off down Clay Street in a rig hired from a livery stable, with two high-stepping greys between the shafts and Laura Winter sitting by his side. It was a cold day, and she was wrapped in a woollen cloak, with two of his pink roses tucked over her left ear under the little fur cap she wore.

"Flowers in your hair," he said, "I like that. It's what the Spanish girls used to wear."

"But my parents were English, you know."

"Yes, you told us. Where would you like to go?"

"Anywhere!" It was the eagerness, the sheer abandonment to gaiety, which Robert Cord enjoyed. She made him feel careless of all considerations of prudence and responsibility, only proud to be seen with her as they drove through the financial district and turned west. "I thought we might have gone out to the Presidio," he said, "but you'd be blown to pieces on the sand dunes, and it's foggy too. Let's go along the Mission road and see if it's milder there."

It was milder in the warm belt of the Mission district, at least among the streets lined with the mean houses built by Philip Estrada for the men who had seen the elephant and returned defeated from the gold diggings of '49. Cord told Laura that he had cut and planed some of the lumber in those houses, in the days when he had a part share in a sawmill on Salmon Creek.

"And then you struck it rich yourself – on the Columa, wasn't it?"

"At Hangtown, back in '48. It's quite respectable now, and they call it Placerville," said Cord.

"Do you never feel you'd like to follow the new strike at Virginia City?"

"The Comstock Lode? No, and for two good reasons. First, I don't understand that kind of mining, and very few people do; and second, mining for gold or silver is a young man's game."

"You're not old!" The blue eyes, which met Cord's grey eyes so candidly, saw no sign of aging in the keen face which still belonged more to the mountains than to the plush-hung rooms of Sacramento politics. In the high rig, behind the spirited greys, they might have been any young man and any girl, with their lives before them, out for a spin on the Mission road.

The track along which Rosalie and Carlos Rivera had ridden to so many fiestas after their wedding had been a made road for some time, and the three-mile drive to the Mission Dolores was a favourite Sunday outing for the 'bloods' of the town. The Mission itself was more tumbledown than ever, the gravestones askew in the ground and thickly covered with vines and chaparral, but part of the outbuildings had been converted into a tavern called the Mansion House, famous for milk punch. The turf over which Rosalie had stumbled in her agonised search for her son's grave was used for horse-racing or, upon occasion, for fighting with fists or pistols. On this foggy Wednesday morning there were only a few horses tied to the tavern's hitching rack, but there were the usual loungers round the ruined buildings – men more Spanish or Mexican in appearance than the wretched Indians of the bygone time.

"Shall we go in and sample the milk punch?" said Robert Cord.

Laura looked distastefully at the dingy tavern. "What makes you think I'd ever want to be seen in a place like that?" she said.

"No, you're right, it doesn't look very inviting. There's the Lake House, that we passed back a ways: shall we see what they can give us by way of a lunch?"

Laura laughed. "I never eat luncheon," she said. "Mrs. Wilson sets a great table at breakfast, and I ate – what time is it? just over an hour ago."

"D'you mean you'll have nothing between now and supper?"

"Lizzie and I have something light before the show . . . What does this man want?"

One of the loungers had exerted himself so far as to leave the Mission wall, settle his ragged serape, and, with a leer, ask in Spanish if *el señor* wanted to have his team looked after. The senator flung him a coin for his only answer, and turned the horses' heads in the direction of San Francisco. "I'm sorry," he said, "this is no place to bring a lady. The real reason I thought of stopping is that I've a present for you. Now I'll have to produce it at the roadside, in what seems to be turning into a sandstorm. Maybe I can find a sheltered spot."

He found one where a clump of manzanita and toyon bushes had not yet been uprooted by the builders' picks and shovels. It was not far from where the gate of the Rancho Rivera had once been, and when Laura looked to the north, beyond the Golden Gate, she could see the slopes of Mount Tamalpais streaked with the bars of wintry sunshine which had pierced the fog.

Robert Cord halted the greys and wound the reins round the carriage whip in its metal socket. "Take off your gloves, Laura," he said.

She obeyed. What kind of a present could it be for which hands must be bared? But he had only wanted to kiss those cold hands, first the slim fingers and then the palms, before he cupped them over a little leather case embossed with the name of Shreve and Company, and told her to open it.

What was inside, on a bed of dark-blue velvet, was a wafer-thin gold watch, the size of a half dollar. It was meant to be attached to the bodice of a lady's dress by a pin concealed behind a gold true-lover's knot. It had a gold face and Roman numerals: the second hand made two complete sweeps before Laura spoke.

"It's perfectly lovely, Senator Cord –"

"Robert."

"Robert. But you know I can't possibly accept it."

"Why not? You never seem to know the time of day; I thought it would be just the thing for you."

"I mean I can't accept such a costly gift from you. How could I ever wear it? How could I explain it to Lizzie – or to Mrs. Catt?"

"How do you explain the pearl necklace you wore last night?"

"I always wear my necklace. I'm wearing it today." She opened the collar of her cloak, and he saw the gleam of pearls.

"You didn't wear it on stage, when you were singing –"

"I had it tucked away." She made the faintest movement of her hand, and instantly the man thought of her naked breast, and the pearls lying hidden beneath white folds of lawn and lace. "It belonged to my mother," she said, and hid her face on his shoulder.

"Laura! Darling! Forgive me, I should have known!" He held her close to him. "Please take the little watch and wear it. Please!"

She raised her head. "I can't possibly, Robert. I can't take such a valuable gift from a man I – hardly know. But believe me, I do want to thank you." Her parted lips were very near his own.

There had been times in his young manhood in the Rockies when Robert Cord would come upon a spring of fresh water, and alone in the wilderness would fling himself full length to drink from it. In Laura's mouth he quenched his thirst again, and drank from the fountain of eternal youth. It was not until many hours later, when he was on the night boat to Sacramento, that he thought if the little gold watch had been set in diamonds she might have been willing to accept it.

★   ★   ★

A green-room call, in the language of the Catt repertory, meant an informal reading of parts with an eye to future castings, held in the already shabby green room of Maguire's new theatre. The great success of *Twelfth Night* had inspired Tom Catt to hold over the production for a second week, after which he proposed to put on a medley of 'Scenes from Shakespeare' in which every member of his company would have a speaking or singing part. But since he believed Laura Winter's personal success as Viola was due not so much to talent as to the appeal of long legs in well-fitting tights, he wanted to hear her read Rosalind's part in *As You Like It*, when she would again appear in male costume. The principal 'Scene from Shakespeare' would of course be 'Give Me the Daggers', always a favourite on tour, in which he and Kitty played Macbeth and Lady Macbeth.

He had not mentioned *As You Like It* in the green-room call, which was primarily for readings from *Romeo and Juliet* to decide whether Laura or Lizzie Warden should play Juliet in the company's next big production. Mrs. Catt had reluctantly decided, on the sage advice of Mrs. Judah, to abandon Juliet for ever, and play the Nurse.

"You got away with it as Jeanie Deans," said Mrs. Judah, "but you can't make them believe in you as a fourteen-year-old girl any more, my dear."

"I know it," sighed Kitty, "and the next step down will be to play Emilia."

"Are you going to put on *Othello*?" said her friend in

surprise. "Who'll you cast as Desdemona, if not yourself?"

"Laura, maybe?"

Mrs. Judah shook her head. "She comes on too strong for Desdemona. I can picture her strangling Othello, but not him strangling her. If Tom had the nerve to cast a Negro as Othello, it might work."

"Leyburn's all right, blacked-up."

"I still say he's not tall enough for Laura Winter."

Mr. Harry Leyburn, perfectly satisfied with his own appearance and with the fact that he had played Romeo to acclamations nearly one hundred times, prepared for the green-room session by drinking steam beer and enjoying the free lunch at a celebrated saloon on Sansome Street in the company of his friend Jack Dashwood, who alternated the parts of Tybalt and Mercutio.

"I bet you're hoping Lizzie gets to play Juliet," said Jack as they discussed the reading.

"Sure, I'd like it for her sake, but if it's Lizzie *or* The Giraffe it's all the same to me. The Giraffe's damn good in her scenes with me this week – and it'd be great to stand beneath that balcony and not have to spout my lines to fat old Kitty mooning down at me."

"Rather you than me. Come on, let's cut along and get it over with."

They walked so fast in the cold afternoon that they were in the theatre a good ten minutes before Laura came in with Lizzie Warden and an actress called Clara Luckett, who in her late twenties played everything from Lady Capulet to Jessica in the same amiable monotone.

"There you are, Laura," said Tom Catt. "Harry tells me you've made a conquest of Senator Cord."

"I'm very much obliged to Mr. Leyburn," said Laura coldly, stripping off her gloves. There was something in her blue glance at Harry, and in her voice, which made Tom believe for a moment in that cock-and-bull story of her aristocratic birth.

"I only said what a fine supper we had last night," said Harry.

"Come off your high horse, Countess, and sit down," said Tom Catt. "I want you two girls to read a scene from *As You*

Like It first." He threw two tattered 'sides', stitched into brown paper covers, across the stained wood table.

Laura, tired and excited, did not read well. She had been studying the part of Juliet, and Rosalind, read sight unseen, took her by surprise. A grunt of "Passable!" was all Mr. Catt awarded to Rosalind and Celia.

In the balcony scene Lizzie read Juliet first, and her past experience, combined with her genuine emotion at playing to her lover as Romeo, gave depth to her performance. Laura fared less well. Jack Dashwood was the Romeo, and forced the pace, so that her speeches came too quickly and sounded staccato even in her own ears. Tom Catt said roundly that she would have to work hard on the part. "Juliet was a girl in love at first sight," he said. "You're too businesslike. You read 'Parting is such sweet sorrow' as if you were running to catch the boat to Sacramento."

"Or the honourable senator," suggested Jack Dashwood. Laura started up in a fury. "For shame, Mr. Dashwood," she cried. "How dare you make a mock of me?"

"If the cap fits, wear it," said Jack coolly. He thought it was fun to see The Giraffe in a rage.

"That's enough," said Tom Catt. "We'll break now. It's half past four, and you all need a rest before curtain-up. Miss Winter, will you stay behind for a minute, please?"

She had mastered her temper before the others left the room, but Laura's cheeks were still red as she looked for her cloak and slung it round her shoulders. Tom Catt patted her hand.

"Calming down," he said, "that's right. What got into you, Laura? You're generally such a good sport. I thought you could put up with a little horsing around in the green room."

"I don't like to be made fun of."

Tom sighed. "Well now," he said, "I wonder if you were wise to accept Senator Cord's invitation to the Poodle Dog last night, even with Lizzie to keep you company."

"Why shouldn't I? Miss Kitty herself said the senator could do us all a great deal of good in Sacramento."

"You watch out that he doesn't do you a sight of harm in San Francisco."

"What do you mean, Mr. Catt?"

"Listen, my dear girl. I've known Robert Cord since we first came to California, more than ten years ago. He's one of the powers behind the power in this state. He's one of the money men behind the new railroad project. He's in line to be the next US Senator from California, and that without buying a single vote. He's also fifty years of age. On all counts he's just too big a property for a kid of eighteen to handle."

Tom Catt saw anger in her eyes, but Laura was too clever to snub him. She said "I'm very grateful to you, sir", dropped him her pretty curtsy, and a few hours later gave a first-rate performance as Viola.

Discussing the incident with his wife, Tom thought he had nipped any silly romantic notions in the bud. Robert Cord was not known to have affairs, and was hardly likely to break out at this important moment in his career. Moreover when the Shakespeare season ended in February the Catt Company would be going on tour. The new mining towns of the Comstock Lode were crying out for entertainment, and Lotta Crabtree had cut short her presentation of *A Loan of a Lover* to depart for Downieville and Virginia City. It was a risky business to take her party over the mountains by stage coach in the dead of winter, but where the little Queen of the Rockies led other troupers were bound to follow.

What the Catts did not anticipate was Robert Cord's speedy return from Sacramento, still in search of that mythical rented house, and in another two weeks, almost on the eve of Christmas, he was there again to applaud Lizzie Warren in the part of Juliet. Laura seemed quite philosophical at reappearing as a balladist, singing 'The Last Rose of Summer' in the middle of the Shakespeare play. That night she wore Robert Cord's Christmas gift to supper at Delmonico's. Insisting that her woollen cloak was too thin for the season, he made her accept a black broadcloth cape, not ornamented with the fussy bugle beads and passementerie which were the height of fashion, but lined with beaver skins which he had chosen with the hand of a connoisseur. She wore it constantly for the next two months, while she walked through the pattern Robert Cord had set at the start. Every ten days, or thereabouts, he spent two nights on the river-boat and one day in San Francisco, taking Laura for a drive at noon and to supper with a group of friends after the show. Once or twice he persuaded her to lunch alone with him in the dining room of the Occidental Hotel or the Lick House, but he never repeated the mistake of asking her to enter a disreputable place like the Mansion House Tavern. Neither did he offer her a present as modest as the little gold watch.

"When's your birthday, Laura?" he asked one day.

"I don't know for sure but Aunt Carmen said I was born on Candlemas Day. The second of February."

"That's not very far away." And on Laura's nineteenth birthday he brought her a little velvet case from J. W. Tucker, the city's leading jeweller, which contained a diamond brooch. She absolutely refused to take it. But she thanked him with one of the rare, impassioned kisses which were the refreshment of his life.

Sometimes he wondered where the whole thing was going to end. He had never been a loose-living man, and although he had sometimes picked up a girl at a fandango and gone back to her room with her when he was alone in the young exuberant San Francisco of the Gold Rush days, he regarded the episode of no more importance than the furtrappers' annual rendezvous with the squaws. Nor had there been any such episodes for a dozen years. And now, at fifty, to be seized with this passion for a girl more than thirty years his junior! He wanted Laura Winter as he had never wanted any woman, and he meant to have her: the only question was – how?

Before the Shakespeare season came to an end he was beginning to run short of convincing reasons for going to San Francisco, and welcomed the opportunity afforded by a letter from Dr. Durant. The schoolmaster regretted to inform him that Ivanhoe's work had fallen off since his promising beginning. His attitude to his teachers and classmates was surly and indifferent. "I'll have to go up to the city and give that boy a talking-to," said Cord. "I wonder what's got into him?"

"Wouldn't it do if I wrote to Ivanhoe?" said Leona. "It's not a good time for you to be away from Sacramento."

Cord knew she was quite right. His firm had won important contracts for the building of the new Capitol, where the foundation stone was to be laid with full Masonic honours in May. His voice was needed in the Legislature, now debating the consequences to California of Jefferson Davis's election as

President of the newly formed Confederate States of America and his call for one hundred thousand army volunteers. California was not a slave state, but how would California react to the imminent threat of war?

"Oh, I think it's better I go up to town, my dear," he answered her. "I want to see Dr. Durant personally, and tell him it's not like the boy to be impertinent."

Dr. Durant, seen face to face, said it was not a matter of impertinence. The boy was too apathetic to be cheeky: he was sullen and withdrawn to a degree. But Ivan, summoned from his classroom to be lectured by his father, was not at all withdrawn. He was highly articulate in saying he hated the curriculum and the teachers and wanted to go home to Sacramento.

"Mr. Thorburn tutored me at home last holidays. I bet I could learn more from him in a week than I can from old Durant in two."

"Dr. Durant says you aren't even trying to learn. What's the matter, Ivan? You aren't still hankering to make your fortune on the Comstock, are you?"

"At least I'd be my own master there."

"You've got to stick it out here until the end of the semester. You mustn't let your mother down."

"Did you come to San Francisco just to tell me that? Or to spend another evening at the theatre?"

"What the devil do you mean, boy?"

"I mean you're a nice one to talk about letting my mother down, when you're making a fool of yourself with that actress! All the fellows here are laughing about it, and laughing at me, too! I can't stand it any longer! You're the talk of the town, you and Laura Winter! My mother ought to throw you out of the house –"

"Hold your tongue," said Robert Cord. The boy was sobbing with rage. He waited, mastering his own temper, and then said coldly, "If you were a man I would knock you down for that. I don't thrash snivelling brats. What you need is army discipline, and I'll make sure the school sergeant gives you punishment drill. Now go back to the other children and ask Dr. Durant to come speak to me."

He was soothed by supper with Laura at the Maison Dorée.

She exerted herself to be charming, and was rewarded when half-way through the meal Robert Cord suddenly told her that he "couldn't go on like this". It wasn't good enough, these occasional meetings, always in public, never fulfilled. "I'm in love with you, Laura," he said. "What are we going to do about it?"

"That's up to you, isn't it?"

"I suppose it is. I'm not coming back to the city, darling, until I can get things straightened out at home and make the right plans for our happiness. When does your tour begin?"

"Not till the end of March. We open the second part of the tour in Sacramento, with *Our American Cousin*. Like the night you and I met first."

"So we'll meet again in Sacramento, and decide on our future. We *must* have a future, you and I!"

She gave him so cool a kiss when they parted that he went back to his hotel in a fever of frustrated desire, which might have been assuaged if Robert Cord had known that Laura returned his passion. For a time she had merely been fascinated by what Tom Catt let fall about Cord's position as the power behind the power, the man with a future in the United States Senate. She was as ambitious for herself as Peter Gagarin had been when he aspired to be the Russian Governor of California, and her ambition to succeed as an actress had been overtaken by the wish to be the power behind Senator Cord. She pictured herself as his wife, a leader of Washington society, the Dolly Madison of the Eighteen-Sixties.

Now Laura's own body was betraying her. Cord's virility had broken down her resolution to yield nothing, because she had never met a man like him. The simpering Spanish boys of Monterey, bemoaning their families' lost grandeur and marrying Laura's friends as soon as the girls were out of Doña Ilaria's exclusive school, had never attracted her, any more than the loose-living Leyburns and Dashwoods of the San Francisco stage. But Robert Cord's powerful arms around her, his hard mouth on her own, excited Laura into longing for a complete surrender to a lust more powerful than ambition. When they met in Sacramento and their future took shape, she would wait no longer before yielding to his love.

Abraham Lincoln was inaugurated as the sixteenth President of the United States on March 4, 1861. On the same day the flag of the Confederacy, the Stars and Bars, was unfurled at Montgomery, Alabama, where the seven original Southern states had declared their secession from the Union. Leona Cord waited until the next day before she spoke more seriously to her husband than she had done since he came back from the city with a carefully edited account of his talk with Ivanhoe.

She began by asking him how California would 'go' in the event of war.

"It's hard to tell. Feeling seems to be pretty evenly divided between the North and the South."

"I'm afraid there are very difficult times ahead . . . I hope you mean to do your duty, Robert."

"I'm well over military age, my dear."

"Your duty doesn't lie in the army, and you know it. I haven't told you about a visit I had from Mr. Mark Hopkins while you were away. He seemed very vexed that you missed a railroad board meeting when you went to San Francisco."

"I sent a messenger with an apology."

"Of course, but there was something personal they wanted to discuss with you. Something that would take you to Washington, in a very special position of trust and confidence."

"You're talking like one of your novelists, Leona." He glanced at her fireside table, as usual piled high with books. "What sort of position do they mean?"

"I'll leave that for them to tell you." Leona Cord put *Framley Parsonage*, which she had been pretending to read, on top of the pile, and crossing to her husband's chair laid her hand on his shoulder.

"You and I have come a long way, Robert, since we set out from St. Louis twenty-two years ago," she said. "I want to see you go a long way further. Maybe to the very top. Don't let yourself be turned aside for a fancy."

★   ★   ★

The Catt Company, each with his own fears and ambitions, was preparing for its spring tour. Tom Catt was busy with his stage manager, Mr. Robson, discussing the logistics of trans-porting painted flats, battens and curtains for the bare little stages of the north across two bodies of water and miles of rough roads along with his actors and their baggage. Kitty directed most of the rehearsals in an empty warehouse near the wharves. On the advice of Tom Maguire she took *The Octoroon* out of the repertory. It was an old favourite in the mining camps, but a story of slavery in the South was sure to cause friction as the war fever began to mount.

There was no need to fear heckling or rowdyism in the first part of the tour. Of the four places they were to visit, San Rafael and Sonoma had grown up round the old Franciscan Missions, while Santa Rosa (which Rosalie Estrada had doubted would ever become a settlement) and Petaluma were thriving towns created by the need to provide food for San Francisco. Enterprising hunters were early on the scene to shoot game birds and venison for the market, and the Ameri-can settlers who had 'seen the elephant', or had not troubled to look for him, cultivated the rich valleys. The days had gone when General Vallejo's great rancho with its six hundred servants and labourers dominated the Petaluma river. It was the farmers and merchants, making the best use of the navig-able stream, who were the masters now. There had been a theatre at Petaluma, beginning modestly in an upstairs room, for half a dozen years, and the Catts were sure of good audiences there.

At San Rafael, where they opened, the company got a better reception than they deserved, for the players were under-rehearsed in Dion Boucicault's *The Colleen Bawn*. It was a very recent hit in New York, and although pirated copies had been 'rushed' to San Francisco there had hardly been time to learn the lines and stage directions. But there were Irish immigrants in the audience, and the play's theme of the murder of an Irish girl by a British officer was so popular that the curtain fell to rousing Hibernian cheers. Encouraged, the actors played with more confidence in Petaluma, with Laura Winter as Moya in *The Colleen Bawn* and Lady Gay Spanker in *London Assurance*. They were all in high spirits when they moved on to Santa Rosa at a pace very little faster than the speed of the Estradas and their Russian guests when they rode those trails on the way to Fort Ross. The Wells Fargo stage coaches were drawn by four horses, but heavily laden with passengers and baggage, and at their easy pace there was time to enjoy the flowering of the California spring.

If the human pace was slow across a land still isolated behind the Sierras, the news travelled with the speed of the telegraph and the newspapers printed it, so that even a company of strolling players, as Tom Catt called them when in romantic mood, was aware of the drift to war which followed Secession. The government of the Confederacy had begun to seize federal forts and navy yards in the seceding states, so far without any opposition. When the players were about to leave Santa Rosa there was a rumour of resistance at Fort Sumter in Charleston, South Carolina – a rumour of which there was no confirmation at first light on the fifteenth of April, when Tom Catt hired a rig and a driver to take himself and Robson, the stage manager, from Santa Rosa to Sonoma. He thought it courteous, as well as sensible, to pay a morning call on Don Mariano Vallejo, once the military commander and now the mayor of Sonoma, whose interest in the drama had been sturdy since the days of Stevenson's Regiment.

"I hear his brother Salvador's in town," Tom said to his wife as he dressed hastily, "and the Leeses are at their rancho too. If they all bring their families along that's as good as thirty seats, maybe more, sold out for every performance. With the vineyard people it'll be standing room only. Goodbye, Kit; see you in the afternoon."

"Be sure you book us into the El Dorado."

"Robson's done that already."

And when the horse-drawn wagons hired in Santa Rosa rolled into the plaza of Sonoma in the golden April afternoon, Mr. Robson was indeed standing outside the El Dorado Hotel, looking even more anxious and harried than usual. Without any greeting he said to Mrs. Catt, "The boss wants to see you right away, ma'am. And the whole company in the theatre in about an hour from now."

"Oh my God, Robby, not a rehearsal call!" protested Leyburn. "*Not* with curtain-up at eight o'clock!"

"I don't know what he wants, I'm sure," said the stage manager. "He'll tell you himself. Now you'll have to get unpacked, and settled in – there's plenty of room in this town, four hotels, so you can spread yourselves around."

Laura, like Lizzie and Clara Luckett, was given a little room in the Blue Wing Inn, almost exactly opposite the old Mission church where Rosalie's tragic wedding had taken place twenty years before. Sonoma had changed a good deal in that time. General Vallejo's Casa Grande was standing empty while the Mexican barracks was used for storage. The old adobes still stood – notably the Estrada 'town house' on the south side of the plaza, but the new houses and shops were built of stone and wood along streets which had been laid out in all four quarters, with pleasant little gardens and shade trees which took away the dusty look of the old pueblo. Vallejo had built a new home for his large family less than a mile beyond the town. As its mayor and a State Senator, he was still one of the leading citizens of California.

"This is the prettiest place we've played yet, but it's not any livelier than Monterey," said Laura as the three girls walked round the plaza to reach the theatre. The Bear Flag days, the Gold Rush days were far behind Sonoma now, and there was a sunny, sleepy, scented atmosphere in the grassy streets. There were not many people about, and the girls from San Francisco were conspicuous in their pretty dresses and thin slippers. So thought a sturdy child of ten, walking hand in hand with a lady in a worn black silk dress, and a straw bonnet with a black ribbon.

"Mamma," said the little girl, Maria de las Mercedes Estrada, "who are those ladies, do you know?"

"They're strangers," said Isabel Estrada, "I think they might be actresses from the touring company Countess Haraszthy was just telling us about."

"They've got lovely clothes" – wistfully. "Mamma, can't we go to see them act? The Haraszthy girls are going tomorrow night."

"Papa wouldn't like it, dear."

"Why not?"

"You'll understand when you're grown up."

And even then, thought Isabel, as she led her daughter towards the little Estrada adobe, now their only home, will she ever understand that her father refuses to enter the playhouse because Vallejo, whom he still calls a collaborator and a traitor, put it at the disposal of the Occupying Power? Oh, my poor Luis, how much your obsession makes you miss!

The three girls hardly gave the mother and the child a glance as they hurried on to the theatre. It was as depressing as most country fit-ups, with a stage of splintered planks only half furnished, by Robson and the usual local help, for the first act of *London Assurance*, and left empty for the entry of Mr. Catt. When he came on it was obvious to his company that he was about to play Shakespeare, not Dion Boucicault: it was King Henry V who strode across the unlighted boards, and his delivery was the one he used for the speech before Agincourt.

"Ladies and gentlemen," he began, "I think you all know that I left Santa Rosa before you in order to pay my respects to Don – to Mr. Mariano Vallejo. I arrived at his elegant place of residence just in time to accept, with our worthy Robson, his generous invitation to an early breakfast, consumed before his urgent departure towards the capital of our golden state. Yes! Senator Vallejo has gone to Sacramento, attended by his brother and Mr. Jacob Leese. We shall miss their genial presence as we 'strut and fret our hour upon the stage'."

It was almost impossible for the actor-manager to talk simply. But, mopping his brow with a red handkerchief, he blurted out, "The war's begun."

They were so much accustomed to express their feelings by mime that most of them gesticulated and were silent, waiting for the next orotund speech. Only Leyburn had the nerve to break the stage wait with the query, "At Fort Sumter, sir?"

"Yes, Harry. Yes, my friends," boomed the deep voice from the stage. "That is the overriding circumstance which has taken the senator back to his legislative duties." He paused for effect. "Two days ago the Confederates at Charleston called on Major Anderson, commanding the fort, to surrender. When he refused to do so the shore batteries, in the very early morning of the twelfth, opened fire on Fort Sumter. They fired on the flag of the United States."

"My God!" said someone at the back of the hall.

"According to the telegraphed reports," Tom Catt went on, "the hoped-for relief force failed to arrive in time. Major Anderson returned the Confederate fire through the thirteenth, until his ammunition was exhausted. Yesterday, the fourteenth of April, 1861 – a day which will live in infamy – he and his gallant garrison left Fort Sumter with drums beating and colours flying, and our nation was condemned . . . to all . . . the horrors . . . of a fratricidal struggle."

There were no gestures or exclamations now. Only Jack Dashwood said in a stage whisper, " 'Cry God for Harry, England and Saint George!' "

6

They fired on the flag. That was the first, the total and the final condemnation of the Confederacy's act of war at Fort Sumter. To all the supporters of the North it was equivalent to an act of treason, and there was an immediate response to President Lincoln's call for seventy-five thousand volunteers to join the United States army. The call was debated in the California state legislature, and also, informally, noisily and sometimes violently in the streets of San Francisco.

The old Spanish families had lost their lands, money and prestige since the Conquest, largely thanks to the depredations of the Land Board, but those of them who could still make their voices heard in their communities – like Luis Estrada in Sonoma – were sincere in their support of the South. Their pastoral heritage, and their paternalistic employment of the Indians, gave them an affinity with the Southern planters and their retinues of Negro slaves. The Yankees who had come round the Horn, or across the plains, or who had braved the early horrors of the Isthmus of Panama route, felt a similar empathy with the Northerners who shared their Puritan ethic and devotion to hard work. When the two cultures clashed the spirit of 1846 was revived, and arguments were started which could sometimes be settled only by the Colt or the Bowie knife. The Catt Company came back to find a city decked with flags and banners, where the prostitutes were doing a roaring trade and all the saloons were crammed.

Their week at Sonoma had not been unsuccessful, thanks to the support of the farmers and the vineyard workers, and the war news came in slowly enough to be cushioned by a couple of days' delay. The actors themselves lived too completely in a world of illusion to be greatly moved by events taking place three thousand miles away, fast as these events followed on the surrender of Fort Sumter. On April 17 Virginia seceded from the Union, and was followed into the Confederacy by three more Southern states. On the same day Jefferson Davis invited shipping in Southern ports to attack Northern merchantmen under Letters of Marque, and two days after that President Lincoln ordered a naval blockade of all the ports of the seceded states. The actors returned to San Francisco at the end of the week to learn that the important US Navy Yard at Norfolk, Virginia, had been captured by the Confederacy.

The men of the Catt Company took it all very calmly. The most bellicose was Harry Leyburn, who had voted against Lincoln, and was now the only actor ready to answer the President's call to arms. This involved him in emotional scenes with his mistress, and her two friends sat up late with the weeping Lizzie in the Blue Wing Inn while the young men drank too much of the excellent Buena Vista wine in the El Dorado. Laura Winter felt detached from the whole thing. Everybody said the North would win – twenty-three states ranged against the South's eleven, holding all the industrial power and war potential – and like most young women at the beginning of a war certain to be over by Christmas she was euphoric about the outcome. Her only concern was how the war would affect herself, and she saw no further than her arrival in Sacramento.

She knew the Catts were deeply concerned about their own prospects. In a sense they were thankful that their show-boating days were over, since the Mississippi basin might become one of the main theatres of war, but in those days they had made many dear friends in New Orleans and along the river, and were not unsympathetic to the cause of the South. Tom was attracted to a foreign land where there was peace; Laura was disturbed at being asked casually one day how she would like to see Australia. As far as the early summer touring went, Tom Catt had finally decided not to visit Virginia City or Mount Davidson, or any of the mushroom towns springing up in the area of the silver lode. Nothing but booze and fighting in the tent cities! He wouldn't risk his players or his props among the 'Washoe widows' as the lone miners called themselves; he certainly wasn't going to run the risk of highway robbery.

"Lotta Crabtree made a fortune there, her mother says, and they're safely back in town," said Kitty.

"Lotta's in a class by herself, and good luck to her," said Tom. "Sacramento, Rough and Ready, Grass Valley and Nevada City, and maybe Downieville will do us fine."

"It doesn't give us very much time to make up our minds about New South Wales."

"I won't be sorry to see Sydney Heads again," said Tom. "We've always played to big houses in Australia."

"Yes, but I'd hoped we were settled in our own home in San Francisco. And the war isn't going to come to California."

"That's what they said in '46."

The stage costumes were cleaned and mended and packed in the big baskets, and the stage props were crated and loaded on to the Sunday boat for Sacramento. The company trooped aboard, at first not sorry that Tom Catt's desire to economise on the price of cabins was giving them a chance to travel through the delta lands and see the river scenery by daylight, but it was a windy day and the novelty soon palled. There was a new stern-wheeler under construction called *Chrysopolis*, City of Gold, which next year would do the one hundred and twenty-five mile trip to Sacramento in under six hours, but the present passengers had to resign themselves to a far longer voyage. A gargantuan midday dinner took up two hours of the time. Laura sat at one of the long tables in the dining saloon along with the Catts and Lizzie Warren, who complained of a sick headache and could touch nothing but a cup of tea.

"Better lie down in the ladies' parlour, dear," said Kitty. "Laura, are you game for a turn round the deck? I'm dying for a breath of fresh air."

Some of the men went out for a smoke on deck, but most of the women passengers preferred to take coffee in the main lounge, where there were red plush upholstered armchairs, marble-topped tables, long gilt mirrors, potted palms, and all the accessories which turned a river steamer into a floating hotel.

"Are you looking forward to Sacramento, dear?" asked Kitty, when they were out on the chilly deck.

"It'll be interesting to see the state capital."

"Yes." Kitty stopped beside the rail. "Laura, I've had a letter from Mrs. Robert Cord."

"Indeed."

"She said they were looking forward to *Our American Cousin* tomorrow night."

"It's one of your great parts, Miss Kitty."

"They're giving a big reception in their own house on Tuesday evening, with the governor and his wife as the guests of honour. Tom and I are invited. And Mrs. Cord asked me to bring 'the two charming young ladies' – that's what she said – 'who came to supper at the International Hotel.' "

"How very kind."

Katharine Catt bit her lip. Would nothing shake the composure of the minx? Laura stood there all polite attention, wrapped in that magnificent cape, and if her lovely colour was a little higher than usual it could be due to the wind blowing through the cattail reeds on shore. "Do you think you should accept the invitation?" she asked bluntly.

"Why not? It will be nice to see Mr. and Mrs. Cord at home, and meet the rest of the family," Laura said.

"As long as you don't expect the senator to pay you the same attentions he did in San Francisco."

"You mean the theatre bouquets?"

"I mean the little suppers in the smart restaurants –"

"Lizzie and Harry were invited too."

"I know they were, and that's why I said nothing. We like our young actresses to be seen in public, and I don't suppose there was any harm in it, but Laura, you're too young to go on making yourself conspicuous with a man old enough to be your father."

"Perhaps you'll allow me to be the judge of that."

The hauteur of the retort made Kitty blink. Before she could find words to check the insolence she heard her own name spoken, and turned to see a man taking off his hat.

"Miss Kitty, by all that's fortunate," he said. "I needn't ask how you are, because you're looking splendid. What brings you up the river today – business or pleasure?" He had an attractive Southern accent.

"You don't have to ask that," said Kitty. "Like you, we only travel on business. Not as profitably as you do, perhaps." She caught his look of interest at Laura. "Miss Winter, may I introduce Mr. Jerome Lasalle? Miss Winter is a new member of our company, Jerry. She's been appearing in our Shakespeare season in San Francisco."

Mr. Lasalle bowed. He was a man in his late twenties, of above average height and slender build. His black hair was worn long, and he sported a moustache and imperial in the style made popular by the Emperor of the French. Laura noted that he was extremely well dressed, with shepherd's plaid trousers and a black frock coat, while the tall hat he held in his hand was of well-ironed silk. He wore a white ruffled shirt and a narrow black tie. A gold signet ring with a crest, worn on the little finger of his left hand, was his only visible adornment.

"I'm happy to meet you, Miss Winter," he said, "I'm a former member of the Catt Company myself."

That accounted for the theatrical look, then. His style was so like that of the gamblers who haunted Portsmouth Square that Laura had decided he was one of them, working the riverboats.

"What parts did you play, sir?" she said demurely, "juvenile leads?"

"I was the call-boy on the *Natchez* showboat, wasn't I, Miss Kitty?"

"Don't be so modest, Jerry, it doesn't suit you. You were playing Oberon to my Titania when your uncle came aboard with Father Cassidy at Memphis, and bundled you back to your Jesuit college."

"They were trying to make a seminarian of me," Lasalle explained to Laura. "It didn't take. And you, Miss Winter? Don't tell me, let me guess . . . You play Celia – no, Rosalind; and Viola of course. Miranda?"

"Lady Gay Spanker," said Laura with a laugh.

"You've been reading the San Francisco papers, Jerry," said Kitty Catt.

"No, on my honour, I've been away since midsummer. I only got back last week."

"I thought you were missing from your usual haunts. South of the border, were you?"

"For a while. And you, Kitty? After Sacramento, where? I may be able to carry a spear for you, if you're short of walking gentlemen."

"Has your claim on the Comstock petered out so soon?"

"No, it's doing well, according to my partner. Did you know I had an English mining engineer for a partner, called Watson? I'm on my way to meet him in Nevada City."

"Then our paths may cross again. Nevada City! What memories that place must have for you!"

There was a shrewish note in Kitty's pleasant voice, but there was cordiality in Tom Catt's exclamation of "Fellows, look who's here!" as he approached with some men of the company and shook Jerry Lasalle by both hands. Kitty said, "Laura and I must go and look after Lizzie. Don't stay in the cold too long, Tom, remember your voice."

They found Lizzie Warren in the ladies' parlour, lying on a sofa with her eyes closed, but with a frown between them which showed she was not asleep. Laura took a fresh handkerchief from her bag, soaked it with eau de cologne and laid it on her friend's forehead.

Lizzie looked up. "Oh, darling, how good that feels!"

"Can't you sleep, Lizzie?" Kitty asked.

"I took two grains of chloral. Maybe it wasn't enough."

"Don't take any more, dear. Remember you've got to play tomorrow."

"I thought you went on deck," said Lizzie vaguely.

"We did. And guess who we met," said Kitty. "Your old flame Jerry Lasalle."

"He was never a flame of mine!" said Lizzie with more animation. "I played Peaseblossom to your Titania, Kitty, when he was Oberon, and that's all! Wasn't he run out of Virginia City last spring, after a gunfight when they found five aces in the deck?"

"Something like that," said Kitty, rising. "Now don't talk any more, but try to sleep. I'll see you get some tea before we land at Sacramento." She crooked a finger at the coloured maid and gave her fifty cents to bring a blanket for the sick girl. Then she and Laura went back to the saloon where a small band was playing, and tea was being served.

"No sign of Tom," said Mrs. Catt crossly. "I hope he hasn't got into a card game with that rascal Lasalle."

"Is he a rascal?" said Laura. "I thought he was rather attractive."

"Girls always do. If ever a kid who started out with everything made a mess of his life —"

"Where does he come from, Miss Kitty?"

"New Orleans. His family was old French and ultra Catholic, and so was his wife. Jerry ran away from the Jesuits, as you heard him say, and after he married, too young I grant you, he ran away from his wife too. Of course with their religion there could be no divorce, and Jerry came West to try his luck in California."

"In the gold fields?"

"At the gaming tables. He got mixed up with that notorious woman they called Madame Moustache, and the pair of them ran a gambling saloon in Nevada City until the citizens turned respectable and threw her out. Oh, I couldn't tell you the scrapes that man's been in —"

"But now he has a claim on the Comstock?"

"Yes, he had a real bit of luck there, but of course, being Jerry, he had to spoil it all. Oh, thank heavens, here comes Tommy now!"

"I'll go and see what Clara's up to," said Laura. She made her escape, glad that Kitty's resentment of Jerry Lasalle had taken her mind off Robert Cord. She would see him tomorrow night! And Laura's daydream lasted through a voyage which became increasingly wearisome, though punctuated by an enormous supper, until sodden with food and drink the passengers disembarked at Sacramento.

There was a crowd on the levee to greet them, and the Union flag was flying from many of the buildings on a waterfront smaller, but as colourful and even noisier than the Embarcadero at San Francisco. The Catt actors, pushing their way through the Sunday-night tipplers and carney barkers, were glad to reach the lobby of the St. Charles Hotel, an obstacle course of spittoons and expectorations which had missed the spittoons, and lost no time in going to their rooms. In the light of morning the whole place looked better, as Sacramento revealed itself to be something more than a rough-and-tumble waterfront. It was a thriving, bustling town of many streets, not all of them built up, running from the works on the new Capitol site, surrounded by what would one day be the Capitol Mall and already was a handsome residential quarter, to the business district by the river. It also represented what most people had already forgotten, the second decisive check in the career of the Swiss adventurer, Captain Johan Sutter.

The American Conquest, which he had supported in every way, had been Sutter's first check. Two years before gold was discovered on his land (though without making him rich) the Americans had frustrated his dream of seeing Sutter's Fort and the New Helvetia rancho becoming the site of the capital of California, to be called Sutterville. Their planners, with the connivance of his own son, had moved the townsite from where the adobe walls of Sutter's Fort were beginning to crumble, down to the confluence of the Sacramento and American rivers, and gave it the territorial name of Sacramento. Captain Sutter's unlucky purchase of Fort Ross, for which he had never paid the full price to the Russians, had involved him in such tedious litigation with the Land Commissioners that the Swiss pioneer was as completely ruined as the former General Vallejo, whom he had once held in prison, as Luis Estrada, as the Yorbas and the Peraltas and all the Spanish dons whose prosperity had ended with the pastoral years. As for the Russians, they were hardly ever spoken of in the state they had hoped to dominate. They still held Alaska, but a purchase of that bleak land by the United States was already being rumoured.

Sacramento had no time to look back on the Russians in its eagerness to look forward to the future. The Pony Express had its western terminal there, its riders covering the two thousand-odd miles to St. Joseph, Missouri, in the fabulous time of ten days. The Wells Fargo coaches drove to all points of the state from Sacramento, including ghost camps of the Gold Rush with names like Whiskeytown, Deadwood and Poker Flat. Sacramento boasted several theatres, the first of which, the Eagle on Front Street, was also the first theatre to be built for that purpose in California. The Eagle had lasted for less than four months, closing its doors on January 4, 1850, having been built too near the flooding river. When water lapped round the ankles of the audience it was an inconvenience felt even by the drama-mad citizens; when the water rose to the feet of the actors on the low stage it was time to call a halt.

"They say," observed Harry Leyburn, as he strolled with his friends past the collapsing Eagle, "that an actress from New Zealand, a Mrs. Ray, was actually submerged when the river rose."

"Submerged? D'you mean she *drowned*?" said Laura fearfully.

"I suppose you could be submerged without drowning," said Harry, who liked to tease The Giraffe.

"Don't mind him, darling," said Lizzie. "We'll be safe enough at the Forrest."

Lizzie was in excellent form that morning, much to Laura's relief. Kitty Catt had said, the night before, that if Lizzie continued to be indisposed Laura would have to take over her part of Mary Meredith in *Our American Cousin* instead of appearing as the balladist, and she had set her heart on singing in the middle of the play. She wanted Robert Cord to see her as he had seen her first, in her blue crinoline with the pink silk roses, and hear her singing 'Then You'll Remember Me', which now must have a special meaning for them both.

She was so eager to go on stage with her guitar that Lizzie Warren, coming off, had only time to whisper, "Good luck! The Cords are in front," before Laura took her place on the velvet stool they used on tour. The Forrest Theatre was only partly darkened for the ballad, and Laura was well accustomed to looking out over the audience. She saw Jerome Lasalle at once, standing beside the stalls exit and conspicuous in an evening cape with a white satin lining. The handsome tawny head of Robert Cord was nowhere to be seen, but as she began the second verse Laura saw his wife in the stalls, accompanied only by her scowling schoolboy son.

It was long before Laura slept that night. For the first time she doubted her power over Robert Cord. In the weeks of their separation, had he ceased to care for her? Decided that a clean break was better than an uncertain future? Then why the invitation issued by his wife? Next morning's paper reminded her that a man in authority might have more than love on his mind in time of war.

'California's Contribution to the War Effort,' ran the headlines.

'Important Mission entrusted to Senator Cord.'

The lengthy column which followed was typical of American journalism, a mish-mash of leaks from the legislature, unconfirmed rumours and editorial speculation, while what Senator Cord had been asked to do or when he was going to do it remained a mystery. Laura had to work through a rehearsal of *London Assurance* and then the performance of *Our American Cousin* before a cab took the Catts, Lizzie and herself on the long drive uptown to the Cord mansion on L Street.

Built only four years earlier, it was revealed by moonlight brighter than the municipal gaslamps as an imposing residence of three storeys, the second with a balcony above the front door, and the third with a mansard roof and dormer windows. The stucco front had been painted brown, ornamented with Greek designs in terracotta, and the door, opened by a man-servant, was reached by a double and a single flight of stone steps. Tom Catt whistled audibly as he followed the ladies into an entrance hall planned for receptions, with drawing rooms on the left-hand side and a dining room on the right, all with archways instead of doors and rich Turkey carpets on the parquet floors. If that cool observer Jacob Leese had been there he might have thought it was a long way back from L Street to the cabin on the Petaluma river.

The hall was lighted by a gaselier of twelve lamps, their glass shades tinted red, purple and amber, the colours falling on a mahogany table which held a silver punch bowl presided over by Ivanhoe Cord. His mother was receiving her guests with her elder daughter by her side. Rowena Cord was only fifteen, and wore a schoolgirl's white book-muslin with short puffed sleeves, but she was already very pretty, a reminder of what Leona Faxon once had been. Leona herself was resplendent in a dress of moiré antique, dark blue in colour, with a necklace and bracelets of cameos set in gold.

"My dear Mrs. Cord, what a splendid gathering," cried Kitty Catt. There were over a hundred people moving through the rooms, and in the further drawing room there was dancing to a small orchestra.

"This has turned into a celebration, and we wanted our friends to share it with us," said Leona. "Miss Winter, how d'you do? I enjoyed your song last night, even though I'd heard it before . . . The senator will be here in a moment. He's in his study with the governor and Mr. Mark Hopkins. There's so much to discuss, so much to plan, before he leaves."

"Where's he going?" asked Tom Catt.

"Didn't you read about it in this morning's paper?"

"I read something I couldn't make head nor tail of," said honest Tom. "Seemed like the senator was going to win the war single-handed —"

"Oh Tom, you are a tease!" laughed Leona. "Of course, the great news wasn't confirmed when the paper went to press. But the official telegram arrived from Washington this afternoon. President Lincoln has invited the governor and my husband to join his Finance Advisory Committee!"

"Congratulations!" "Well done, Robert Cord!" "Another honour for the Golden State!" "Guess Old Abe knows he can't win without California gold!" Laura hardly knew who spoke, for some late arrivals had joined their group, but she was aware that Leona Cord was looking at her searchingly, and with a cold smile she said, "It will be an immense journey for the senator."

"Only seventeen days to St. Joseph, Missouri, by the Overland Stage," said Mrs. Cord. "My husband and I crossed the Sierra Nevada on foot, when we first came West."

"Is Mark Hopkins going to Washington too?" asked Tom Catt, and Laura silently blessed him for the intervention.

"No, just the governor and Robert," said Mrs. Cord. "Rowena" (turning to her daughter) "why don't you take Miss Winter to meet some of the young folks, and see if you can find a partner for her? Don't you like to dance, Miss Winter?"

"Am I too old to be this lady's partner, ma'am?" said a new voice, "Miss Laura, may I have the honour of the waltz?"

Laura had no idea of what the band was playing, whether waltz or polka or galop. She only knew that Jerry Lasalle was bowing before her, and that his black-sleeved arm offered her an escape from the kaleidoscope of words and faces encircling her. She said, "I shall be happy, sir," and was half-way down the hall with him when the music stopped.

"Too bad," said Lasalle, "but I claim you for the next dance, whatever it is. And now we have an interlude for conversation. Come into the dining room and let me find you something to eat."

The waiters (among whom Laura recognised two from the St. Charles Hotel) were moving round the dining room with laden salvers. Laura took a morsel of cake, a sip of wine, and smiled at her deliverer.

"That's better," said he, "you've been looking startled ever since you saw me."

"Not startled. Surprised to see you here."

"No place for a black sheep, eh? I'm sure the fair Kitty has spared you none of the details of my murky past! But the governor is a good friend of mine, and I'm here as one of his – entourage, I suppose you'd call it. Except, of course, when state secrets are being discussed." He indicated a pair of sliding doors in the back wall of the dining room. "The nobs are there in the senator's study, discussing the plan they mean to present to President Lincoln."

"Mr. Lasalle," said Laura, "what *is* the Finance Advisory Committee?" She was annoyed when he laughed.

"Nothing you need bother your pretty head about," he said. "Let's talk about you instead. You're looking wonderful tonight!"

The words were some compensation for what Laura Winter felt to be the falsity of her position in the Cord home. She knew she looked her best in her simple black evening dress, now embellished by a long golden wrap bought in San Francisco, folded round her shoulders and lying like a banner beneath her golden hair. Jerry Lasalle touched the fringe with the tip of one white-gloved finger.

"This is beautiful," he said. "Where did you find it?"

"In a funny little shop in Leidesdorff Alley. The man said it was Old Russian work."

"I'm no judge, but it makes you look like a princess."

"Flatterer!" said Laura, as the band struck up a waltz. "Our dance!" said Jerry, and stopped as the sliding doors opened, and the three men he had called the nobs joined the company.

The Governor of California and Mark Hopkins were both bearded men, pompous and self-important. Robert Cord, their host, still looked young by comparison, and he flushed like a young man when he saw Laura.

"Miss Winter, this is an unexpected pleasure," he said.

"I was happy to accept Mrs. Cord's invitation, sir," she said coldly, though her heart was beating fast. Robert Cord bowed low, and with eyes for no one else begged for the favour of a word with Miss Winter in his study. Jerry Lasalle held back the sliding door to let her pass.

If Laura in her confusion had been able to analyse it, she would have seen that Robert Cord's sanctum was much more a business room than a study. The work table with its bundles of neatly tied papers held merely the overflow from his downtown office, and though the fire was bright there were no armchairs with well-placed reading lamps to suggest evening hours of browsing through new books and periodicals. It was merely an annexe to the spacious reception rooms, but it did contain bookcases far better filled with books than the Philip Estradas' library at South Park. Nor had these books been bought by the yard, but with discrimination and affection, over the years by Leona Cord. If Laura, standing pensive by the fireside, had known where to look she would have seen in the shadows a little shelf holding the books Leona had carried across the Rockies in a bag slung over her shoulder, and beneath it another with a row of the precious Scott novels which Princess Helen had sent her from Fort Ross. Above the books hung a framed charcoal drawing, made by some nameless immigrant with a turn for sketching, of the young pioneer with a woodsman's axe on his shoulder in the days when Cord was felling redwoods to build his first cabin by the Petaluma.

The politician whom that young pioneer had become knew only too well that attack was the surest form of defence, and so almost his first words to her were, "My darling, why are you going to leave me?"

"I? Leave *you*?"

"When I heard your news, I said to myself, 'She means to put an end to our meetings. She knows that what would make me so happy is quite impossible. And I have no right to spoil her life –' "

"*What* news? What are you talking about, Mr. Cord?"

"Your decision to go to Australia with the Catts."

"I haven't decided any such thing! *They* may have, for all I know; there have been hints, suggestions if you like, but nothing definite, and if there were, I wouldn't go! *You* are the one invited to go to Washington –"

"I didn't accept that invitation until I was told you were going to New South Wales."

"Who told you?"

"My wife had it from Mrs. Catt."

They stared at each other and understood that they had been manipulated: that a foolish, if not a guilty, fancy had been drowned in the tide of war. Laura said, "Which do you think the more important – that a young, unknown actress should go to New South Wales, or that a man like you should go to Washington?"

Cord said painfully, "The nation is at war, my darling. And the President thinks I can be of some use to him."

Until now he had not dared to touch her. He had put his hand out to take hers when Laura said, "Of course you're right, and you must go. I'm in the wrong; I was a fool to come here tonight and allow myself to be humiliated. I should have known when you weren't at the theatre yesterday that whatever we had in San Francisco couldn't go on, mustn't go on . . . but I wanted so much to see you again –"

It was with an actress's gesture that she turned towards him, the gesture Tom Catt taught her when he rehearsed her as Cordelia, with her hands spread open in surrender and the golden scarf dropping low. "So young, and so untender?" asks King Lear, and Cordelia answers in the soft voice Laura had just employed:

"So young, my lord, and true."

Robert Cord's self-control broke. He seized her in his arms and felt her young body, in an abandon never known before, mould itself to his as he stammered that he loved her, would never let her go, would protect her always, and when she in her passion wound her slim arms round him he kissed her mouth, her throat, and the pearls at her neck –

Then the sliding doors were flung wide open, and Ivanhoe Cord, crying "You bastard! Bringing your mistress here – insulting my mother in her own house –!" struck at his father with a boy's strength and a man's anger.

Laura recoiled as Cord turned in fury on his son. He seized the boy's shoulders and thrust him towards the open door. "Go to your room, Ivan!" he said. "I'll deal with you later. Governor, I apologise for this impudent cub" – for the Governor of California was in the front line of the spectators who had pressed forward from the dining room to enjoy a family scandal. One of them actually brushed past Robert Cord and came into the study.

"This way," said Jerry Lasalle, drawing Laura's arm through his own, "it's high time we had our dance." He opened a side door and led her into the room where the band was playing and couples were waltzing in ignorance of the ugly little scene which had ended with Ivanhoe Cord's rush up the staircase at the far end of the house.

"Damn fool boy," said Lasalle amiably, "they shouldn't have put him in charge of the Roman punch. I noticed he was drinking two for every one he poured for the guests . . . You all right?"

"Perfectly."

He nodded and said no more. He was a beautiful dancer, better than any of the young actors, but Laura was too tense to yield to the rhythm of the waltz. Instead of listening to the music she was listening to the hum of voices. She was watching the faces which, now that she and her partner were going round the parquet floor (with the carpet up and highly polished) for the third time, seemed all to be turned in their direction. And Jerry Lasalle watched the burning colour rise in her pale face.

"It's after midnight," he said as casually as he had claimed his dance. "Would you like me to take you back to your hotel?"

"I don't want to run away . . ."

"Take the advice of an old hand," said Jerry, "there are times when it's just as well to beat a tactical retreat."

"As you did when you went to Mexico?"

"Exactly." A twisted smile gave life and humour to Lasalle's conventional good looks. "I'm glad you haven't lost the power of repartee."

She ignored this. "I can't go back to the St. Charles without the Catts."

"Here's some more good advice: leave a message and forget the Catts. Tom doesn't count, and Kitty can be left to simmer till tomorrow morning. By that time some new sensation'll have blown up. Bless you, when I was her call-boy on the *Natchez* we took fist fights and gunplay in our stride; a little episode like tonight's wouldn't have mattered at all."

He had been guiding her through the dance nearer and nearer to the front door, where only the manservant was still in attendance, and he asked Laura where she had left her cloak.

"I've no cloak, just this scarf."

"Just that gold thing! What women will do for vanity! But it isn't cold tonight . . ." It was balmy when they reached the street. The mild air was scented with garden flowers and the freshly turned earth and new grass plots round the foundations of the Capitol. There was a long row of private carriages and hacks outside the Cord mansion, and Jerry Lasalle persuaded with a five dollar bill the cabby who had been hired by one Senator Sproat, to drive "this lady and myself" to the St. Charles Hotel instead – and "go round by K Street" he added as the door was closed.

"I want to show you something," he said to Laura, "but never mind that now. I haven't had a chance, yet, to tell you how much I enjoyed your singing on Monday night."

"Thank you."

"You really have a charming voice. Doesn't Tom Catt think it might be well worth training?"

"It's my speaking voice Tom's trying to train right now."

"That's a pity, because Tom's a ranter."

"On stage, but it isn't how he's been teaching me."

"A bit of rant doesn't come amiss among the miners. Which reminds me, I'm leaving tomorrow for Grass Valley. What are you playing there?"

"Alida in *The Poor of San Francisco.*"

Lasalle could see by the light of the infrequent street lamps that the burning blush had faded from Laura's face. She chatted quite naturally on the familiar topics of the theatre until they neared the waterfront, when the driver was told to stop at 52 K Street. "Senator Sproat can wait ten minutes longer, it won't do him any harm," said the silken Southern voice. "Now, Miss Laura, here's what I want you to look at."

K Street, in the 50s block, was made up of small stores and business houses two or three storeys high. Across the front of number 52 a sign bore two words, Cord Construction. Number 54 had once been a hardware store owned by Collis P. Huntington and Mark Hopkins. They had joined forces with Leland Stanford, a grocer, and Charles Crocker, a dry goods merchant, and in the upper office of number 54 the Big Four, as they were already called, had established the headquarters of the great railroad they had organised. The offices were still lighted at midnight, and men in their shirt sleeves, with papers in their hands, moved to and fro across the windows.

"I want to tell you the facts of life about the Finance Advisory Committee," Jerry began, "or rather, why two elderly gentlemen like the governor and Cord are going to sweat out seventeen days on the Overland Stage to St. Joe (and God knows how many after that) to make their services available to Mr. Lincoln. The President knows California is too far away to send a substantial body of recruits to the Union army. He'll be happy to take money instead. Our heroes will be equally happy to make the money available – for a consideration."

He stopped, and said, "You're supposed to ask, what consideration."

"I'm out of my depth."

"You won't drown. Look at that lighted office. That's the powerhouse in this town. That's where the plans are being made for what will some day be a great transcontinental railroad. Mr. Lincoln's support for the project is the price he'll be asked to pay for California gold."

He had lowered his voice when they stopped outside the office where the plans for the Central Pacific Railroad were being made, and equally mindful of the cab-driver on the roof Laura herself was whispering. She said, "Tom Catt told me

months ago that Mr. Cord was one of the money men behind
the railroad project."

"I don't know about the money, but he's certainly the
undercover man, and that's why Mark Hopkins, who *is* a
financier, was at tonight's meeting. Hopkins was a grocer in
Hangtown when Cord was prospecting there in '48, and
they've stuck together ever since."

"Why are you telling me all this, Mr. Lasalle?"

"Because I want you to understand that Robert Cord's a
gambler. I'm one myself and I know the signs. Oh, I don't
mean he plays cards. He gambles in futures, as they do on
'Change, and chiefly in his own. My hunch is that he has
presidential ambitions. We have a backwoodsman president
now; Cord thinks we might just as well have a frontiersman
president in '64 or '68, and this trip to Washington is the way
to higher things. Now the cards are on the table, Miss Laura:
d'you still want to stay in the game?"

"I should like to go back to the St. Charles now."

Lasalle dismissed the driver at the door of the hotel. He
would walk back to his own place, he said, and took Laura's
cold hand for a moment to say goodnight. "Forgive me if I've
been brutal," he said. "Now let me give you my last piece of
advice. Don't talk to any of the company tonight. Lock your
door, and if Kitty Catt comes knocking at it, don't open up.
Things'll look quite different in the morning, you'll find out."

"You've been very kind, Mr. Lasalle."

"Jerry."

"Jerry, then. Goodnight."

The 'place' frequented by Jerry Lasalle since his early days in
California was the Old What Cheer House, on the south-east
corner of Front and K. Popular at any hour of the night, it was
unusually crowded for one o'clock in the morning, and Jerry
learned that there had been some delay in the departure of the
night boat to San Francisco. The barmen were working 'all
out' according to the man who served him, to satisfy the
passengers killing time before they left. The noise in the
downstairs area was deafening. Jerry swallowed a brandy, lit a
cigar and strolled down to the waterfront. As he listened to the
stern-wheeler's bell ringing, and saw the passengers humping
their portmanteaux and valises down to the quay he thought

about the scene in Robert Cord's study, the fool kid's outburst, and the frustrated, maddened look on the old goat's
face. From the vantage point of Jerry's twenty-eight years, the
senator was of course an old goat, if not worse, and the
discovery that the impeccable Cord, the archetypal pioneer
and frontiersman, had a weakness for the young and the
vulnerable, was merely comic – if it didn't turn out to be
tragic for the girl. He thought she would be all right. He was
sure, after his talk with her, that the fool kid had been lying or
crazy when he screamed out that she was his father's mistress.
There was a cool innocence about Laura Winter which made
her, at the worst, a foolish virgin.

He had succeeded in persuading himself that the humiliating
scene which would be discussed in every parlour in Sacramento on the morrow would do the Catts nothing but good at
the box office, since everybody and his brother would want to
have a look at the great man's light o' love, when he saw a
belated passenger running towards the gangway, and in the
light from the ship's portholes recognised the cause of all the
trouble, the fool kid Cord.

"Hallo, Ivanhoe," he said, stepping forward. "Leaving
town?"

"Who the devil are you?" said the boy truculently. He had
changed out of his evening clothes, and wore a light overcoat
but no hat. His only luggage was a gaudy carpet-bag.

"I'm Jerome Lasalle. I was one of your father's guests
tonight."

"Lasalle. I guess you're the gambling man."

"Good guess," said Jerry. "Trying a little gamble of your
own, are you? I heard you were interested in taking a chance
on the Comstock."

"What if I am?"

"You're going in the wrong direction, that's what. Or is it
too much to hope you're going back to school in San Francisco?"

Ivanhoe, with an oath, said it was none of Lasalle's business.
He must have run half the way down L Street, for he was out
of breath and sweating; he was also not far from tears. Lasalle,
unperturbed, said he was smart to keep away from the Comstock mines. "The miners don't like fresh kids," he said.

"Cussing and carrying on like you're doing, you'd be liable to get your head blown off your shoulders in Virginia City."

"Could happen anyway," said the boy. The last bell rang on board the night boat, and a voice shouted "All a-aboard!" "I don't know what the hell it's got to do with you," said Ivan Cord, "but if you see my – my father" – his voice broke on a sob – "tell him I'm off to fight for the Union."

7

Jerry Lasalle's prediction that some new sensation would have blown up by morning was proved correct. By noon the prime topic in the Sacramento bars was not that Senator Cord had been caught embracing an actress (the nature of the embrace being exaggerated with each telling) but that his son had run away from home.

Not trusting his own temper, Cord decided to 'let the whelp stew in his own juice' overnight, and waited until seven next morning before he went to Ivan's room. His first thought when he saw the scattered clothes and the open chest of drawers was that Ivan had run off to the silver mines. He wasted time in enquiries at the offices of Wells Fargo and the Overland Stage before picking up the boy's trail on the waterfront, and by then the night boat had berthed in San Francisco. Ivan had half an hour to transfer to a Pacific Mail Steamship Company's boat for Panama, which had cleared the Golden Gate before his father despatched an urgent telegram to Philip Estrada at his office in the city.

"I knew he wasn't at our house, and I didn't think he'd be at Dr. Durant's, but I sent a clerk out to the college, just in case," said Philip, telling Content the story in the evening. "I went down to the Sacramento wharf myself, and I soon had news of him. He'd been talking freely on the trip downriver about going off to the war, and the Pacific Mail agent told me about selling him a ticket to Panama. When he gets across the Isthmus to Chagres the wretched boy can easily find transportation to New Orleans."

"And then what?" said Content. "What does a Union recruit do in a Confederate city?"

"I don't know, but he'll fall on his feet as his father always did. There's a lot of old Robert in young Ivan; that's why they haven't been getting on together."

"Poor Leona."

"Yes, write her a letter of sympathy, won't you? I telegraphed to Cord immediately, of course."

"So at least he knows where the brat is. Could he have him brought back from Panama?"

"My guess is that he'll take the patriotic line, and make some political capital out of it for himself."

Philip Estrada knew his man. Next morning's papers, while giving more details of the important rôle Senator Cord was going to play in Washington, praised the patriotism and adventurous spirit of his son. ' "If I were eighteen again, I'd do what he has done," said our frontiersman Solon, whose early adventures in the Rockies are famous,' gushed the leading paper of Sacramento, which in a well-known editorial ploy ran a 'blind' story in the adjoining column headed 'Applause at the Forrest Theatre/For Miss Laura Winter/Charming Songstress of "California Gold".'

It was Tom Catt who gave Laura permission to change the ballad she was to sing that night. Kitty professed herself too angry to speak to the girl, although the real cause of her anger was Laura's escapade with Jerome Lasalle, against whom she had expressly been warned.

"Why is she so mean about Jerry Lasalle?" wondered Laura. "He's smart and funny, and he was very nice to me –"

"She was rather sweet on him herself in the *Natchez* days," said Lizzie Warden.

"But she must be ten years older than he is –"

"Age doesn't always matter, does it, darling?" said Lizzie, who was in a waspish mood herself these days, and Laura went off to talk to Tom.

"Sure, sing 'California Gold' if you like, it'll be a change," said Tom abstractedly. "It's one of Lotta Crabtree's big successes. You'll have to change your style a bit."

"Yes, I know." With Jerry Lasalle's careless words ringing in her ears about the price the railroad's undercover man would ask Abraham Lincoln to pay for California gold, Laura began by altering her appearance. She exchanged the ingénue's blue tarlatan for a white crinoline from Wardrobe, cut very low, and with her own golden scarf round her bare arms and shoulders. She dressed her hair into the old-fashioned 'Blenheim spaniel' ringlets and put gilt powder on her eyelids instead of blue. With rouge and lip salve she looked older and harder as she struck a chord on her guitar and looked out over an audience in which, for the first time since they played Sacramento, there was standing room only.

Tom Catt had been as quick as Jerry Lasalle to estimate the box-office draw which 'Cord's ladylove' would be in the town. The day before, she had only been a beautiful girl with a measure of talent: now she was what appealed far more to Americans – a notoriety. And she was giving them good value for their money as she dashed into 'California Gold' with a spirit she had never shown before.

Womanlike, Laura had resented her humiliation at Mrs. Cord's hands far more than Robert's folly. "I enjoyed your song last night, even though I'd heard it before," the woman had said, before telling her schoolgirl daughter to 'see if she could find a partner' for Laura Winter. Run away and play with the little ones! It was like dismissing a naughty child! And Laura, at her make-up mirror, said to herself, "I know plenty of other songs, and I'll find my own partners, ma'am! I've been a sentimental fool and I know it, but never again. Never again as long as I live."

> She shall have golden ringlets
> And golden bonnets too,
> Little golden garters
> And pretty golden shoes.
> And if she should get married
> And put to bed, heigho!
> Her kiddies shall be solid gold
> In California, O!

sang Laura, with a toss of her head, a shake of her curls, and a touch of her tongue to her upper lip which stressed the innuendo. And went on:

So in a trice take my advice
And do not fail to go
Unto the land of glittering gold,
In California, O!

It was not an invitation but a challenge to her audience, and they took it up after the next verse, shouting in unison:

And we are told there's lots of gold
For all who choose to go
On board a ship and take a trip
To California, O!

She went off to a storm of applause, having effectively spoiled Kitty Catt's next entrance, and causing that lady to whisper, "Kindly remember we're playing the Forrest, not a Long Wharf melodeon!" as they passed each other in the wings.

"What's she trying to do, out-Lotta Lotta?" Tom Catt wondered more than once, as the opening of *London Assurance* found Laura giving a new reading of 'Lady Gay Spanker', harsh, abrasive and so fast that it was difficult to keep up with her, and with such a disregard of the text that even the amiable Leyburn was moved to complain of being miscued. But they played to packed houses, in an atmosphere of mounting excitement and war fever, and the Catts, counting the takings, almost regretted having to leave Sacramento. In the busy streets of the town there was at least safety, and Tom was troubled by rumours of a nest of bandits in the valleys, who had stripped another road company of everything but the clothes they stood up in, somewhere in the vicinity of Rough and Ready.

The Catts were booked to play a split week, three nights in Rough and Ready and three in Grass Valley, where the dynamic career of Lotta Crabtree had begun. Of the two communities, Rough and Ready was by far the more primitive, with a record of violence which included the murder of Big Jim Cameron, the owner of the Catalina mine, and the immediate lynching of an innocent man. Founded by a group of Mexican War veterans, who named it for their general,

Zachary Taylor – 'Old Rough and Ready' – the community
had actually seceded from the Union in 1850, though for a
matter of months only, as a protest against a miners' tax, and
this led to some humorous quips about the greater Secession
over which the nation was now at war. It was a picturesque
mining village, where the miners still wore red shirts and the
one hotel had a shop selling food and clothing as well as a bar
room hung with red calico on the street level. The Catt players
were fairly well received, but they were in Lotta Crabtree
country now, and their performances of *The Poor of San
Francisco* seemed to impress the rough-and-readies less than
the fact that the tiny Lotta had first danced in public there on
the anvil of Fibb's Smithy when she was the pupil of Lola
Montez.

"Treat this as a rehearsal for Grass Valley, kids," advised
Tom Catt. "We'll get a real discriminating audience there, and
at Nevada City too. Not but what they're decent fellows here.
A dozen of them are going to ride along with the stage on
Thursday morning, to be a bodyguard in case anything goes
wrong."

"What do they say about the bandits, Mr. Tom?" asked
Lizzie Warren, who was looking pinched and nervous.

"The miners had a posse out last week, after the last
incident, but they couldn't run the Mexicans to earth. Probably they're holed up in the Sierra by this time, so we'll be all
right."

"All Mexicans, are they?" asked Jack Dashwood.

"So I'm told," said Tom Catt. "And I don't know as I blame
them," he remarked to his wife later on. "Some of those
Mexican boys saw their fathers stripped of everything by the
Land Board, and their home ranchos overrun by squatters. It's
no wonder they try to take it out of the Americanos when they
can."

"Don't be a fool, Tom," said Kitty Catt. "Better not let the
miners hear you taking up for a bunch of thieves and cattle
rustlers. They might try sending a posse after *us*."

It was quite a short distance to Grass Valley from Rough and
Ready, down the old lode trail leading from what had been
John C. Fremont's Mariposa mine, but long enough to make
the actors feel that they were coming into an entirely different

country. They were as yet hardly in the foothills of the Sierra Nevada, and Grass Valley lived up to its name in being a place of lush green meadows and tall pines, with houses built of stone and brick with spacious wooden verandahs. It looked prosperous and it was. Grass Valley was the aristocrat of the northern mines, where the first and greatest quartz deposits of California had been discovered, and where the simple operations of panning and rocking for gold along the streams had been replaced by stamp mills and subterranean workings. The itinerant miners, ever moving onward in search of a lucky strike, had been replaced by skilled workmen, many of them Mexican and others Cornish, who made their homes where their employment was. There were bar rooms and gambling saloons in Grass Valley, but there were also respectable hotels, churches and handsome dwellings, making the town a bastion of respectability compared with the new wild frontier of the Comstock Lode.

Of its unregenerate past, Grass Valley kept only the memory of Lola Montez, who had been a king's mistress and a scandalous dancer, and who now, at the end of her short life, was devoting herself to the rescue of the fallen women of New York. Even the memory of the town's most notorious resident was sweetened by her affection for its dearest: Grass Valley was where Lotta Crabtree's career began in what was then the Alta Saloon and was now the Alta Theatre. She had been cheered to the echo in the Alta only a few weeks before the arrival of the Catts.

The play they presented in Grass Valley was *The Poor of San Francisco*, adapted from *The Poor of New York*, which Dion Boucicault had written during the gold panic of 1857. The theme was the greed of gold, and although the stages of the northern mines were not equipped to provide many of the sensational effects of the original, Mr. Robson and his stage hands produced enough charcoal fumes in the fire scene to set the audience coughing, and the shower of gold which fell upon the grand finale was much admired. The miners were caught and held by the first words, "Gold prices are rocketing!" They cheered the hero's outburst that "those who are obliged to conceal their poverty under the false mask of content are the most miserable of the Poor of San Francisco" and identified

with the weakling who failed to find gold in Australia. "Guess
he'd seen the elephant, poor devil!" was an audible remark
from one member of the audience, which was loudly cheered.

But the most violent reactions were provoked by the villain
of the piece, Gideon Bloodgood, and his villainess daughter,
Alida. Bloodgood was a stock character whom the miners
loved to hate, a swindling banker, and the part was played up
to the hilt by Tom Catt. Laura Winter played Alida, and for
the first time had the experience of being booed on stage. The
robust audience hated Alida from her first appearance in
crinoline and parasol outside 'Bloodgood's Bank in Montgomery Street'.

> Bloodgood: Alida, my dear child, what brings you to this
>   part of the city?
> Alida: I want two hundred dollars.
> Bloodgood: My dearest child, I gave you five hundred
>   dollars last week.
> Alida: Pooh! What's five hundred? You made ten thousand
>   in Michigan Southern last week.
> Bloodgood: But –
> Alida: Come, don't stand fooling about it, go in and get the
>   money. (Loudly) I must have it!

That was when the hissing started. The boos came when
father and daughter were unmasked and foiled (two verbs dear
to sensation drama) and Tom had to console Laura after the
curtain fell. "It wasn't you they were hissing, dearie, it was the
character. Just tone it down a bit tomorrow." But on Friday
Laura was shriller and harsher than before, and on Saturday
night, at the last performance, she was not only hissed when
she stepped forward to take her bow, but above the whistles
and catcalls there was a shout which she liked even less:

"We – want – Lotta! We *want Lotta Crabtree!*"

Laura was the first actress out of the dressing room that
night, with the make-up hardly creamed off her face, and a
warm shawl hastily wrapped round her street dress. She
pushed through the loungers on the sidewalk before they
could recognise her, and only halted when she heard the voice,
and felt the restraining hand, of Jerome Lasalle.

"Jerry! What are you doing here?"

"I paid my money to see the show, like the rest of your admirers," said that mocking voice, "and I've been waiting to congratulate you."

"I hope you were edified by what you saw – and heard."

"Very. Don't walk so fast! Nobody's going to eat you."

They were well along Mill Street by now, away from the theatre crowd, and by the light from the windows Laura saw that her companion was no longer the dandy of Sacramento. He wore a red open-necked shirt with a coloured scarf under a dark frieze jacket, with trousers of the same material tucked into boots with spurs and fancy stitches. "Are *you* dressed for the stage?" she asked, "or have you gone back to mining?"

"Not exactly. I've been staying with the mine manager, out at the Empire; the whole crowd came in to town to see the show tonight."

"How are you going to get back?"

"I left my horse at the livery stable. Now tell me, how have you been?"

"Very well, thank you."

"Not unhappy any more?"

"I was never unhappy at all."

Jerry smiled. "I'm glad to hear you say that," he said. "You put on a good show tonight in a thankless part. And a better show still when those yokels were cheering Lotta Crabtree instead of you . . . Where are you going?"

"Clara and I are rooming in a little boarding-house down here."

'Here' was a pleasant side street of clapboard houses and flower gardens, out of sight of the vertical shafts and stamp mills of the mines.

"Are you going to get a rest tomorrow, or do you go posting on to Nevada City?" asked the man.

"It's so near, we're going at different times. Some tomorrow with Mr. Robson, the Catts early Monday morning, and the rest of us by the Wells Fargo coach at ten."

"I guessed right, then. I booked a seat on that coach, just in case."

"Oh! Of course, you're going to meet your partner there."

"I met him here, soon after I left Sacramento. Our business

is settled, all but a few signatures, which won't take long."

"Then why —"

"Because I want to be near you, that's why. You need someone to look after you."

"Thank you, Mr. Lasalle, I can look after myself." But she smiled alluringly as she said it, and stopped by the white picket gate of the little guest-house, acting the awkward pleasure of a country girl being escorted home by an equally awkward swain. Then, with a swift change of mood, and a lowered voice, she asked mischievously, "Jerry, who was Madame Moustache?"

"Oh, you've heard of her, have you? Kitty doesn't miss much! Her real name was Eleanor Dumont – French of course, and in spite of her downy upper lip she was a fascinating woman. I think you would have liked her, Laura."

"But what did she *do*?"

"She ran the best blackjack saloon in Nevada City five or six years ago. After I joined her she started a baccarat game, and I ran that."

"You were her partner?"

"I was, until the pickings got too thin, and the virtuous ladies from New England came west to join their husbands. They soon got some of the livelier spots closed down."

"But not the theatres?"

"The theatres *burned* down, as they all do sooner or later, but the Metropolitan on Main Street, where you'll be playing, is a good new house. Better get all that gilt paper out of your hair before you make your entrance."

"Don't be ridiculous, of course I shall! It came from that awful 'shower of gold' in the finale, and takes for ever to brush out."

The tiny clippings of gilt paper, less noticeable on Laura's golden head than on Rosalie Estrada's black locks, at least did not reek of scent like the gilt from the cascarónes which clung to Rosalie's hair on her fatal wedding night. As part of the restful Sunday, hard brushing and a foaming shampoo removed the last traces of Alida Bloodgood and the Alta stage from Laura's outward appearance, and she was as fresh as the morning when she joined her fellow passengers at the Wells Fargo depot in Grass Valley on Monday the thirteenth of May.

The distance to Nevada City was so short that more than one stage line covered the distance every day, and the Catts, with other members of their company, left from the Exchange Hotel on the Cleveland and Roys coach. The Wells Fargo coach could accommodate eight inside and five on the roof, and on this trip the roof was so laden with the actors' baggage that it was lucky only two more inside passengers were there to join the congenial group of Harry Leyburn and Lizzie, Jack Dashwood and Clara, and Jerry Lasalle who had strolled up to join Laura with an admiring bow. The morning was so warm that she had no wrap over her striped dress of apple-green and white, and the coach was so crowded that she held her wide-brimmed straw hat with its apple-green ribbon on her lap.

The crowding was due to the elderly couple who introduced themselves, in thick German accents, as Mr. and Mrs. Hummel, storekeepers in Nevada City and returning from a visit to their married daughter in Grass Valley. The Hummels were fat, and it was fortunate that the young actresses were slender, for Mrs. Hummel wore hoops beneath her ample petticoats and held a wicker hamper of provender which obviously included cheese. She objected, on account of the dust, when Jack Dashwood tried to open the window.

The road was not dusty, because it had rained in the night. It wound upwards between tall trees from the canyon through which flowed the water called Wolf Creek, long ago exploited by the first placer miners. The tableland at the top of the hill was known as the Ridge, and beyond it a pass which the Indians had used as a game trail for centuries led down again to Deer Creek, on the banks of which Nevada City had taken its wayward shape.

The driver, a bow-legged man called Jed, pulled up his four horses on the summit of the Ridge and climbed down from his seat.

"You folks like to get out and stretch your legs?" he said, opening the door. "Them boys from Gold Flat're late again. Dang me iffen I ever knew them to be on time."

"Still keeping your Monday rendezvous with the Flatters, Jed?" said Jerry, stepping out first to give his hand to the ladies.

"Why, Jerry Lasalle!" said the driver coolly. "Didn't reckernise you in them fancy duds. Guess you've riz in the world these days. Now, ma'am, ye don't want to hold on to that mighty hamper —"

"Wouldn't anybody like a little snack?" said Mrs. Hummel, beaming. There was a huge cooked sausage among her supplies, with freshly baked bread and a box of *lebkuchen* as well as the odoriferous cheese, and half a dozen bottles of home-brewed beer, one of which Jed accepted promptly. His mate on the driver's bench, riding shotgun, refused a drink and remained seated with his weapon across his knees.

"What goes on at Gold Flat?" said Laura. She and Jerry had moved away from the Hummels and their hamper to enjoy the scented breeze from a poplar grove.

"Just what you might expect, only it's not mining, it's gold refining," the man explained. "They send two men up with the week's product every Monday morning, and one of them travels into town on the coach to bank it at Wells Fargo."

"Why don't they drive straight into town themselves?"

"They can't, because there's no direct road, only an Indian trail along Deer Creek. Also they probably think there's more protection, sitting between the driver and the guard."

Laura nodded. She knew the driver was armed as well as the man with the shotgun, and that under the seat they shared was the red Wells Fargo coffer which carried gold from one bank to another. It was the 'treasure box' which caused the coaches to be held up so often by lawless men on dark and lonely roads unlike this flowery tableland between two singing creeks.

"Is that the Sierra?" she exclaimed, as their stroll brought them out of the poplars to the place where the side road to Gold Flat met the highway, and they had a clear view across the foothills to the mighty peaks of the Sierra Nevada on the horizon, capped with snow. "How beautiful!" she said, to Jerry's nod.

"It's grand when you see it for the first time, from California," he acknowledged. "I wonder what it looked like to the Yankees, when they saw that barrier between them and the gold."

"*My husband and I crossed the Sierra Nevada on foot, when we first came west.*" Leona Cord's words, her almost contemptuous dismissal of a flighty girl, came back to Laura with the burning memory of humiliation. I *will not* think of them, she silently vowed. "And some day I'll go east myself, further than Washington, maybe further than New York. To Europe, anywhere away from here –"

"Hark to the bells," said Jerry Lasalle. "The Gold Flat boys are coming. We'd better get back to the coach."

"They seem to be having a picnic," said Laura. The women were sitting among the flowers and grasses, the two actors munching apples from Mrs. Hummel's hamper, while Jed and Mr. Hummel were deep in talk, leaning against the coach. Only the guard remained watchful, and when the two lead horses tossed their heads and rang the bells on their own collars in response to those other bells coming nearer and nearer, he spat out his quid of chewing tobacco and said,

"Better git aboard, folks, the Gold Flat boys are here, and we're behind time a'ready."

"Soon make up the time, Sam," said the driver, knocking out his pipe as a covered wagonette, drawn by two horses, appeared at the edge of the poplar grove.

"Hold it!" said the guard. "That's the wagon from the Flat all right, but who's the Greaser holdin' the reins? Here, you!" he shouted, "don't come no further till I see yore passengers!"

The Greaser, or Mexican, obeyed him instantly. At ten yards' distance he reined his horses to a halt. One man jumped down from inside the wagon; another, on horseback, spurred from behind the shelter of the canvas hood. He took off his sombrero with a flourish, and bowed to the startled company.

"Señores! El Chico at your service!"

"Chico!" The guard raised his rifle and fired. The bullet missed the Mexican driver and tore through the canvas. The horseman, with a smile, shot him dead.

"I fired in self-defence," he said. "Don't go for your gun, you fool," he said to Jed, who was clambering over the wheel to grope for his rifle on the treasure box. "The shooting's over; no one will be hurt unless he wants to be. Stop screaming, ladies; I don't make war on women. Pedro, Miguel, get their guns."

Only Harry Leyburn and Jerome Lasalle were wearing pistol holsters. They unbuckled their gun belts and threw them on the ground as the two armed Mexicans approached and ran their hands over the young men's bodies in search of knives, but Dashwood and Mr. Hummel were also searched for firearms before the elderly German was allowed to kneel beside his wife, who was in a state of collapse on the grass. While the search was going on the man who called himself El Chico sat motionless in his saddle with his pistol in his hand. Alone among the three robbers his face was covered to the eyes with a yellow bandanna. When he dismounted and walked towards his victims they could see that his eyes were piercingly blue.

"Now then," he said – his English was hesitant but colloquial, his accent Spanish – "whom have we here? Two old folks, harmless; six who are young and handsome. You're not miners, by the look of you –"

"We're actors, you bastard," said Harry Leyburn, "you won't get any loot from us."

"We're not petty thieves, to steal your rings and watches, señores. And the young ladies, are they actresses?"

Lizzie Warden, who had fainted when the guard was killed, had recovered consciousness, and was supported by Clara Luckett. Laura was bending over them both. Now she turned to face El Chico, who took her hand and made her stand erect.

"Señorita," he said, "You are beautiful. *Muy linda!* What's your name?"

"Laura Winter."

"Where do you come from?"

"Like my friends, from San Francisco."

"Spanish or *Gringa?*"

"English."

The bandit, Pedro, muttered something, and El Chico nodded. "You're right, *amigo*," he said in Spanish. "Let's get on with the job. The box goes into the wagon, and you drive back to camp. Be careful how you lift it down."

The body of the dead guard was sprawled over the Wells Fargo treasure box. When they lifted the box down, the corpse fell on the other side of the coach and from there to the ground. At the sound of the thud Mrs. Hummel gave a choking cry and sank backwards in her husband's arms. El Chico himself pulled down Jed's rifle and threw it into the covered wagonette along with the pistols on the grass.

"Now," he said genially, when his men had driven away, "we shall all be more comfortable. I could do various things to make sure you won't ride or drive to Nevada City and raise a hue and cry. I could shoot all the coach horses and ride away on my own mount. I could set fire to the coach. Or I could take one of your ladies on my saddle as a hostage – you, *señorita actriz*, Miss Laura *linda*. Would you like to get to know me better?"

"No," said Laura with dry lips.

"It might be worth your while."

"Leave her alone," said Harry Leyburn.

"You're not acting now, señor. Save your heroics for the stage."

They had been too stunned, men and women alike, too shocked by the guard's death, to consider the man who had them in his power. The voice, with its Spanish inflections, was youthful and pleasant: his movements were young and supple, and they all knew 'El Chico' meant 'the kid'. He was not a kid in height, being taller than the tallest man there, and his brilliant eyes were cruel. He was enjoying their apparent helplessness.

"I've an objection to shooting good horseflesh," he said, "and I've no ropes to tie you up with. So, since I've got what I came for, I only want to spend a little time with you while my men drive home. Amuse me! Sing, act, dance! Do what you're paid to do. You, my impudent friend" (to Leyburn) "have you a flute? A violin?"

"I don't play any instrument. I can sing."

"Then sing a waltz tune, *amigo*, and Laura *linda* shall dance with me."

"I won't."

"Oh Laura, do!" That was the anguished voice of Clara, who was clinging to Jack Dashwood's arm while Lizzie was supported by her lover. The sarcastic devil inside Laura sneered that even if the two actors had the nerve to rush an armed man they were hampered by the terrified women. Jerry Lasalle was smiling his mocking smile, as if he knew that her refusal to dance was automatic, that in spite of herself she was drawn by those compelling blue eyes and that beguiling voice with its Spanish accent. El Chico swept off his sombrero, and she saw that his hair, worn long, was as golden as her own.

She let him draw her to the flat turf not two yards from where the dead man lay. It was like an evil dream, the stage-set of a fantasy beneath the blue sky and the tall trees, where the other characters in the drama were as motionless as the dead guard. The bandit put his right arm round her, with the pistol pressed to the small of her back.

"Sing, *hombre!*"

And Harry Leyburn sang, while Jerry folded his arms and listened, smiling still at the young man's choice of a song. It was the first waltz tune to come into Harry's head, the tune the American soldiers sang as they marched into Mexico to win California for the United States:

> Green grows the laurel, all sparkling with dew,
> I'm lonely, my darling, since parting with you,
> But by the next meeting I hope to prove true,
> And change the green laurel for the red, white and blue!

Green grows, green grows . . . it was the lilt from which the Mexicans had fashioned the word *gringo*, and Laura, feeling the armed hand tighten on her waist, wondered if the bandit thought he was being mocked and would retaliate. But he gave no other sign of understanding, and the waltz went on while the blue eyes searched her face and trees and sky became a blur to Laura. He released her at last and stood back with a bow. He whipped off the yellow kerchief to reveal a young face which was the mirror image of her own.

"Who – who are you?"

The answer to her question was a scream of pain. Jerry Lasalle had taken advantage of the bandit's one unguarded movement to slide a little pistol from the sleeve of his black coat and put a bullet through El Chico's knee.

8

For a community which prided itself on its devotion to law and order, Nevada City reacted with violence and passion to the news of the outrage at the Ridge. It might have been 1849 again, when the mining camp at the confluence of Gold Run and Deer Creek was called the Dry Diggings, or sometimes Caldwell's Upper Store, and murder was punishable by lynch law, when Jed the stage-coach driver rode hell-for-leather into the solid town of 1861. Then the sheriff and his posse took off for the scene of the crime at a racing pace; the fire bell was rung to assemble not only a crowd of volunteers on horseback but a number of citizens who had been drinking in the bar of the National Hotel and had conveyances from buckboards to carryalls stabled in the barns outside. Some of the posse, at the sheriff's order, rode down the cut to Gold Flat to look for the men intercepted by the bandits, but there was still an imposing array of lawmen and vehicles to surround the place where the stage coach stood near the poplar trees.

There Jerry Lasalle was very much in charge. He had shed his protective skin of indolence and mockery and was hard, quick, competent; his first act, when El Chico fell to his bullet, was to disarm the man, empty the chamber of the pistol he had pressed to Laura's back, and use the weapon twisted into the yellow bandanna as a tourniquet to stop the flow of blood. He helped Jack Dashwood to take one of the leaders of the coach out of its harness, and ordered the young actor to ride bareback to Grass Valley with the news that two Mexican criminals were headed that way with gold from the Flat and the Wells Fargo treasure box. Mr. Dashwood was not very willing to oblige.

"What if those two Greasers are ambushed somewhere down the road, waiting to jump out at me?"

"Take one of the rifles."

"Fire a rifle from horseback? I never did such a thing in my life."

"No, and you never danced with a bandit either, it took a

woman to do that," said Jerry savagely, looking to where Laura knelt on the turf beside the unconscious man. "Get on with you, Dashwood! Those cholos had half an hour's start, they may have gone to earth already. Hurry, man!"

El Chico came round about ten minutes before the posse arrived from Nevada City, by whom he was lifted, not gently, into a covered wagonette very like the one he had stolen from the Gold Flat men. His own horse which Jed had ridden was backed into the shafts in place of the missing leader, and Jed started downhill with four of his original passengers. Mr. and Mrs. Hummel were put into a light carriage, and Laura, in a buckboard, was escorted by several excited men. She saw the dead guard's body taken up as she was driven away.

Jerry Lasalle seemed to reach town before her, for when she alighted at the National Hotel, where the Catts and half their company were screaming questions from the verandah, he was waiting for her in the office of the Wells Fargo agent, which like the famous bar room with its long bar of Honduras mahogany where the thirsty customers were now standing three deep, was in the lobby of the hotel. The agent received her with courtesy and offered her a glass of brandy or a cordial.

"Nothing, thank you," Laura said.

"But you've just had a terrible experience. You need a stimulant."

"Then a cup of coffee, if you please. Black and very strong."

It was brought at once by an excited maid, whose eyes roved from Laura's dishevelled hair to the stains of blood and grass on her pretty striped dress. Jerry poured himself what was obviously a second drink from the brandy decanter.

"Miss Winter," said the Wells Fargo man, "I don't want to impose upon you, but if you would have the goodness to answer one or two questions it would spare you an appearance in court this afternoon."

"In court?" she said, aghast. "Why?"

"The ruffian must be brought to justice immediately. The court has been convened –"

"Is it legal?" Laura gasped.

"Perfectly legal," said Jerry. "There are four deaths to be accounted for –"

"*Four?*"

"The bodies of the two Gold Flat men were found some distance down the trail," said the agent.

"And Mrs. Hummel died on the way back to town," said Jerry. "Heart failure, from the shock."

"Oh my God," said Laura. "That poor old lady too!"

"Public feeling is running very high," said the agent. "The crime rate in Nevada County is rising every month. In the first half of April there were fourteen attacks on Wells Fargo coaches alone, five of them by this villain who calls himself El Chico. Now, Miss Winter, our driver – Jed Struthers – says the bandit talked to you more than to any of his victims, and in Spanish, which you appeared to understand."

"I was brought up in a Spanish-speaking town," said Laura. "Monterey. So of course I understood him. He only asked me where I came from – my name – that sort of thing."

"He didn't tell you *his* name?"

"Just El Chico."

"How old would you say he was?"

"I don't know. Twenty, perhaps."

"He said nothing personal while you were dancing with him?"

"Nothing at all."

"So in fact you can give us no information about him, or his gang?"

"No."

"And that's it," said Jerry decisively. "Miss Winter had a gun in her back when she danced with him, and if it hadn't been for her I might never have got in my shot. Laura, I'm going to take you back to Kitty now – and you, sir, I think you should thank the lady for her courage, on behalf of the Wells Fargo Company."

The agent was effusive in his compliments. But when he moved to open his office door Laura said she would like to have a moment alone with Mr. Lasalle.

"Well?" he said.

"Jerry, they aren't really going to try that boy this afternoon?"

"They are."

"And you'll be in court?"

"With the other men, yes."

"But will he be fit to be there? Fit to plead?"

"Do you want him to plead?"

"For his life – yes."

"Why?"

"Because," she said desperately, "Jerry, he looks so like me!"

"Just a coincidence . . ."

"So you saw it too! Jerry, try to speak to him, wherever he is. In prison? Try to find out his name and where he comes from –"

"That's what they all want to know. My dear, you've had enough. Come to Kitty, freshen up, and get some rest. Remember, you've got to play tonight – to a full house, I should think – unless your understudy plays instead. Do you really feel up to it?"

"Why not?" she said, dry-lipped. "That's what Tom Catt keeps telling us. 'The show must go on!' "

It was Tom Catt who was waiting for them in the lobby, not Kitty, because Kitty was occupied with Lizzie Warren, who had been much affected by Mrs. Hummel's death. Tom, sympathetic and quiet, hurried her through the staring crowd and up a flight of stairs to the room she was to share with Clara. "Best room in the house," he told her. "You'll be comfortable, so lie down, dearie, and try to sleep. Shouldn't wonder if Clara was asleep already."

It was a much grander room than innkeepers usually allotted to strolling players, but then Clara Luckett and Laura Winter were more than actresses in Nevada City: they were the heroines of the hold-up. The bedroom was spacious, with two windows reaching to the floor and opening on a balcony which ran across the whole width of the hotel. It had an Axminster carpet, a long horsehair sofa, and enough chairs and occasional tables to trip over. There was a lithograph of President Lincoln above the marble chimneypiece. There was a high mahogany bed, which looked narrow for two sleepers, and sprawled across it, under a sheet and a single blanket, the placid Clara lay in a profound sleep. Laura smiled, and went into the dressing room through a door beside the bed, where she poured washing water as quietly as possible. When she came out, tying the sash of her thin wrapper, she opened the french window wider and stood looking out at the mountain town. She could see lilacs blooming in the dooryards of family houses built in the New England style, a row of shops with their shutters up, and a church spire half hidden among trees. It was a peaceful townscape, from which all the dust and din of their arrival seemed to have died away, and in the silence Laura arranged a horsehair cushion on the sofa and lay down. In spite of the hard couch and the cup of coffee, strong and black, she yielded to fatigue of mind and body and fell asleep.

Nevada City was wrapped in the peace of a May afternoon for one reason only, that every able-bodied male in town was in the courthouse, or if unable to gain admittance then standing beside the jail at the corner of Court and Main. The proceedings were summary, but as Jerry Lasalle had promised, perfectly legal: the court was duly constituted, the jury empanelled, and a young lawyer who had just hung out his shingle appeared for the defence of El Chico. The witnesses were reasonably sober and highly articulate, several admiring references being made to the marksmanship of Mr. Jerome Lasalle. "Good to hev ye back, Jerry!" someone shouted, and there was a burst of slightly mocking laughter as if his name was not fragrant in Nevada City. The accused lay on a litter in front of the jury box. He had bruised his face when he fell, and it had been cleaned and dressed with a flat linen pad which covered his features almost as completely as the yellow bandanna. Jerry Lasalle, watching, thanked God El Chico was so disfigured that when Laura went on stage that night nobody in the audience would be able to say "That girl's the double of the boy we hanged!"

El Chico's record of highway robbery was enough to earn him the death penalty on its own, but that day's toll of murder brought the prosecutor's demand for instant execution. There was little the young lawyer could say on behalf of his client but that he was an orphan boy, early led astray by bad companions. It was the conventional defence, and completely useless: the three men murdered that day had been well liked in the community, and the Hummels much respected. The verdict was Guilty on all counts, and the prisoner was to be hanged by the neck until he was dead.

There was no longer a gallows in the respectable town, and

the excited men had no intention of wasting time in erecting one. There was a quicker way to the supreme punishment, and the only mercy shown El Chico was to cover him with a horse blanket, for his trousers had been cut away when his knee was roughly bandaged. The sheriff insisted on sending for a priest, somewhat against the will of the jury, who were shouting, "Git on with it! Hang the bastard!" and the priest came as they were carrying El Chico out of the courthouse and down the hill to Deer Creek.

The little brawling river, where some of the older men present had panned for gold, flowed through a gulch where alders grew and wild cherry trees shook their white blossoms over the water. Good Father Griffin walked alongside the litter, urging El Chico to make an Act of Contrition. The blue eyes of the condemned man stared at him disdainfully: the Irish priest, who had named his little church of St. Canice after a cathedral in faraway Kilkenny, seemed to make no impression on the sinner.

The bridge over Deer Creek at the foot of Main Street, built in 1851, had been reinforced to take the great ten-horse freighters coming and going between Nevada City and the Comstock Lode. There was one such freighter at each end of the bridge when the crowd arrived, and the teamsters, eager "to see the fun" as one of them put it, jumped down and joined the men scrambling along the banks of Deer Creek to get the best view possible. In the middle of the bridge a gibbet was improvised from cross beams and rope spars, and El Chico was hauled into a sitting position on his bloodstained pallet. Then, with an oath which silenced the priest's prayer, he spoke for the first time – spoke the words in English which would appear in next day's newspaper under the heading 'Dying Declaration of the Dancing Bandit'. The noose was put round his neck and his body cast from the bridge to hang bandaged and bloody, writhing and jerking in the hideous simulacrum of love until life was choked out, and only a bundle of rags hung twirling above the leaping water and the avid faces of the mob.

The yell of triumph from the gulch was heard all over town. Nevada City, like San Francisco, was built on seven hills, and on those hills planted with maple brought from the east in covered wagons, which would blaze red and golden in the fall, stood the solid brick or clapboard houses of the residents who represented solid capital, the men who had made their fortunes by quartz or hydraulic mining, requiring skilled labour and steady application. They were the new mining society, city fathers, school-board members, regular churchgoers. They had all been at the trial of El Chico and the hanging at Deer Creek. Their wives, whispering to each other above the neat white picket fences, said they were thankful that the district had been rid of a dangerous bandit, in whose proximity no virtuous woman could feel safe. They went indoors to make preparations for the suppers which might be belated. There was nothing like a good hanging for stimulating thirst and sexual appetite. It was the unvirtuous women, the prostitutes in their cribs behind the National Alley, next to the horse barns, who reaped the golden harvest of that day's work.

★　　★　　★

Among the few men in town who did not attend the hanging of El Chico, nor take part in the priapic celebrations which followed were Mr. James J. Ott of the Assay Office and Mr. Thomas Catt, actor-manager. Mr. Ott, a Swiss immigrant and first cousin of Johan Sutter, was too busy and too important to waste time on a sordid spectacle. He was the man who two years earlier had proved by assay that ore from across the Sierra Nevada had a fabulous silver content, and as a result of his judgment the stampede to the Comstock Lode began. He stood at his office door for a few moments, watching with satisfaction as the great freighters began to roll away from Deer Creek, up Broad Street and across the pass, with the bells jingling on the leaders' harness, and with that evidence of business as usual he returned to his scientific pursuits. Mr. Catt, who would have had no objection to watching a real-life melodrama, was obliged to confine himself to the Metropolitan Theatre, helping Mr. Robson and the stage hands to create such various British stage sets as St. James's Palace and Ulverstone Sands on Morecambe Bay.

"Some day they'll play melodrama in front of curtains or scrim, and all the better for it," said Tom, struggling with the shabby painted flat intended to represent royal splendour, but

Robson thought the innovation would not come in his lifetime. It was stifling inside the theatre, and they prevailed on
the doorkeeper to open all the windows until the performance
began. "Otherwise they'll roast," said Tom. "I never knew
anything like a hanging to bring out the crowd. And to think
of the Girl who Danced with the Bandit playing lead! It'll be
word of mouth publicity tonight, of course, but just you wait
till they read tomorrow's paper!"

He said as much to his wife before they left their room at the
National Hotel to go to the theatre.

"That young fellow from the paper came round," he said.
"I made sure Miss Laura gets a great puff tomorrow."

"Of course you did," said Kitty, "but Tom, that girl
worries me. There seems to be trouble wherever she goes. All
that gossip in San Francisco, then that scandal on the night of
the Cords' party. And now mixed up with the Dancing Bandit
and rescued by Jerry Lasalle –"

"She's box office, my dear."

"She's trouble."

"At least she's not in the same kind of trouble Lizzie's in,"
said Tom with a chuckle.

"Give her time," said Kitty, and then with a change of tone,
"thank heaven Lizzie isn't playing lead tonight. She's not fit to
go on, even as Juanita. I've told Daisy she must play instead."

"Daisy'll be delighted." Miss Daisy Delisle, *née* Pigg, was a
seasoned trouper of forty with a little-girl voice and manner-
isms who understudied all the women and was the stop-gap in
every crisis of the company.

"Now all we need is Winter throwing the usual tantrum
about wearing a black wig," said Kitty, by which practical
remark her husband understood that she had not been over-
whelmed by the events of the day.

The play that evening, *Two Loves and a Life*, was a tale of the
Jacobite rising of 1745. A young Jacobite rebel, Sir Gervase
Rokewode (Leyburn, in powder) condemned to death for
treason, was loved by two women: Anne (Clara, in her own
fair hair) and Ruth (Laura, in the conventional black wig of the
villainess). Ruth was the girl who had the courage, while Anne
collapsed, to beard the Duke of Cumberland in St. James's
Palace and demand a pardon for the man she loved.

Ruth's villainy (and here Laura heard the hisses again) lay in withholding the pardon when she learned that Sir Gervase, in the Tower of London, had married Anne an hour before his execution. Begged by the priest who married them to show mercy, she replied superbly:

"No one has had mercy on me, and I have blood in my veins – Spanish blood. I can love, and I can hate!"

But when she saw the man she loved at the foot of the gallows, Ruth relented, and called out *"A pardon! In the King's own hand!"* Sir Gervase, with the noose round his neck, was saved and embraced first his saviour, then his wife, then the women kissed each other – all in such a frenzy that after the curtain fell Harry Leyburn was heard to mutter, in something less than Sir Gervase's elegant diction, that 'The Giraffe and Clara like to pulled him apart.' Leyburn, concerned with his own problems, had not played well that evening and he knew it, but the usually lymphatic Clara had risen above herself to match Laura's power, and both girls had caught fire from the emotion of the audience. Whatever Nevada City may have known or cared about the Jacobite Rebellion, the sight of the gallows (a piece of hasty carpentering which Harry had been forbidden to so much as touch) and the dangling noose was so powerful a reminder of what had taken place that day at Deer Creek that the whole house was stirred to the same sexual response as had followed the actual hanging of a living man. Jerry Lasalle, watching and listening, gave Tom Catt marks for showmanship and a talent for improvisation. He had seen *Two Loves and a Life* acted by Mrs. Sinclair's company, and he knew that the execution scene should be played with a headsman, a painted axe and a wooden block. He decided, as he waited for Laura and Clara outside the theatre, not to mention the timely substitution.

The two girls came out together, pale and tired, and seemed glad of his escort back to the National Hotel. The bar was crowded, and the drinking had spread to a residents' parlour next to the bedroom where Clara and Laura were to sleep. The trio stood in the street below, looking up at the lighted windows.

"Confound it," said Jerry, "I wanted to make sure you two got some supper, but not in that rabble –"

"I couldn't eat a thing," said Laura.

"Drink, then? You've got your shawls, you won't catch cold on the balcony, will you? Wait there five minutes, and let me see what I can rustle up."

There were ironwork seats, painted white, on the balcony just outside their own windows. "Jerry Lasalle really has a kind heart," said Clara.

"A heart of gold. Do you suppose this noise is going to keep up all night?"

"The drunks will pass out eventually," said Clara. "The freight wagons never stop."

"I hate the sound of the bells." Both girls remembered that cheerful tinkle of the harness bells coming up from Gold Flat which heralded robbery and murder.

"Didn't take long, did I?" said Jerry Lasalle, pushing his way through the french windows of the parlour. He was followed by the grinning stable boy he had pressed into service, who carried a tin tray with a bottle of champagne and three glasses.

"Champagne?" said Laura. "I didn't know we had anything to celebrate."

"I was thinking of a toast," said Jerry, expertly filling the glasses and proffering the tray. "To two young ladies who tore a passion to tatters tonight, as well as I've ever seen it done. Miss Clara, you surpassed yourself. Miss Laura, I drink to your future."

At least he had pleased them and made them laugh. And because he knew that actors would talk about their parts if twenty bandits were swinging from the bridge above Deer Creek, he began the necessary process of unwinding with a few comments and questions about the performance until he saw Clara yawn and Laura loosen the golden hair flattened by the coarse black wig. It fell in tendrils on her shoulders.

"You look about fifteen with your hair down," he said.

"I feel about fifty," said Laura, and Clara got to her feet.

"They seem to be quieter next door," she said, "and I'm so tired I must lie down. Thank you, Jerry! Laura, don't you want to stay and keep him company for a bit?"

Clara Luckett had not missed the tenderness in Jerry's voice.

It was time for the two of them to be alone, and with a brief goodnight she slipped through the french window at their backs and drew the heavy brocade curtains. As she took off her shawl in the stifling bedroom she heard Laura say,

"Are you going to tell me what I want to know?"

"About El Chico?"

"About all of it. Have the Mexicans been captured?"

"They were taken this evening, about the time the play began, in a hideout in French Ravine."

"Will they be brought back here?"

"The sheriff of Grass Valley will deal with them," said Jerry. "And all the gold has been recovered."

"Wells Fargo will be pleased. And you – you didn't get a chance to talk to – that boy, before he died?"

"Not a chance. And my dear girl, you must try to forget the whole rotten story. He was a criminal, and a damnably clumsy one at that; he didn't even search his victims properly, or he would have found my second gun in my sleeve."

"Was that where you used to keep the fifth ace?"

"Laura!"

"I'm sorry! I'm really sorry, I shouldn't have said that. You may have saved all our lives when you shot him, but – I'm so unhappy, Jerry!"

When she began to weep he moved to sit beside her and put his arm round her shoulders. The lamps in the parlour had been put out, for it was after midnight, and the starlight was only challenged by the lanterns on the ore freighters, which never stopped their steady rumble towards the pass. The man and the girl on the balcony could hardly see each other except as a blur of black and white.

"Don't be unhappy, darling!" He felt her move a little closer, and tightened his clasp. "Listen, El Chico did talk before he died. I wrote it down, as best I could, and I didn't mean to show it to you tonight, but it'll be in the newspaper tomorrow, so –"

"Oh, let me see it! Light the candle, and let me read what he said!"

There was a candle in a tin candlestick on the table which held the tray, and as soon as it was lighted a cloud of moths, like the ghosts of summer nights, began to circle round the flame while Laura Winter read the Dying Declaration of the Dancing Bandit.

I am called El Chico in the Spanish tongue and [incomprehensible] in the dialect of the Wintun Indians. They kidnapped me from my cradle and brought me up in their village in the woods of Mount Tamalpais. When I was still a child they sold me as a horseboy to a band of men from Sonora, defrauded of their rights by the Americanos, who led me into a life of crime. The priest asks me if I repent. What repentance means I know not, for I was never taught the Christian faith, but I ask forgiveness of all men, and leave this life, as I entered it, unwillingly.

Laura blew out the candle and they sat in the warm darkness without speaking, until Laura said, "Did you ever see a play called *Twelfth Night?*"

"I've read it."

"I played Viola last fall in San Francisco. You know, she loses her twin brother, Sebastian –"

"Well?"

"I think that boy was my Sebastian. And I think he knew it too."

There was so much sympathy between the gambler and this girl that he neither denied it nor made fun of her, but said gently, "I'd have to know a lot more about you than I do, before I could believe that that was possible."

He thought, as he listened to the story of her English parents and her childhood in Monterey, that it was entirely possible. He had seen the mirror-resemblance, not only of eyes and hair, but of features, for Peter Gagarin had left his own imprint on the faces of his twin children. He also knew that in California, ever since the Spanish days, nothing was too melodramatic to be improbable. The missing heir, the hidden will, the bastard claimant, the murder done for a poke of gold dust, were clichés of the western scene. He was able to calm Laura by the practical suggestion that between a boy brought up on Mount Tamalpais and a girl rescued on the Old Spanish Trail there could be no possible connection: the mere facts of geography were against it. And he made her finish the champagne, which now was warm.

"I only wish I could have done something for him!" she whispered after the last freight wagon went up the hill.

"Are you a Catholic, Laura?"

"No. Are you?"

"I'm a failed seminarian, but I think I could persuade the priest of St. Canice to say some masses for his soul, if that would comfort you a little."

"I would like that, Jerry. You're very kind to think of it."

"And now I'm going to be kinder still, and tell you to try to get some sleep. Tomorrow's a new day, Laura; we'll talk about it all again tomorrow – if you still want to."

He raised her gently to her feet and held her in his arms.

"Tell me just one thing, because I have to know. When you said just now 'I'm so unhappy' was it only because of today, or because you're still in love with Cord?"

"I never was in love with Robert Cord," she said. "I don't believe I know the meaning of love."

"Then," said Jerry Lasalle, and kissed her, "I want to be the one to teach you."

9

On the same thirteenth of May which witnessed the highway robbery on the Ridge, the war in which both sides were still merely jockeying for position took a new and dramatic turn. On that day the British government formally acknowledged the Confederate States of America as a belligerent, which was an oblique way of stating that the Confederacy was a power equal in diplomatic status to the Union. Great was the rejoicing in Richmond, Virginia, now the official Confederate capital. President Jefferson Davis and his cabinet firmly believed that Britain, sooner rather than later, would enter the war on the side of the South.

Such news, carried by telegraph, relegated the drama of the

Dancing Bandit to second place in the collective mind of Nevada City. Whatever the outcome, the news was an immediate relief to Jerome Lasalle. "Don't brood over it. Try to forget about it," was his constant advice to Laura, and if she had to listen to ill-informed opinion about the British intentions, that was much better for her than the endless questions about what the local paper had taken to calling 'the Dance of Death'. He tried to shield her from the inquisitive as much as possible by taking her to lunch every day at the New York Hotel, further up Broad Street from the National and the Catt Company table, and seeing to it that she ate some at least of the set meal. "You're quite slim enough, my dear," he said, "you mustn't get too thin!" Her stage dresses had already been taken in two inches at the waist.

Jerry himself had a room at Madame Falcon's Paris House, where he had lodged in the days when he was Madame Moustache's full-time manager and part-time lover. "It's a dump," he told Laura, "but I like the old girl, and she was good to me when I came here broke." Jerry spent most of his time at the National Hotel, and in the early evening, when she left for the theatre Laura could see him, if she glanced inside the bar, playing cards at one of the green baize tables with a cigar between his lips. Presumably he played all evening, for the theatre was sold out for the whole week, but he was always at the stage door when the show was over, ready to escort her back to the hotel. There was no repetition of the balcony scene and no more kisses, except the brush of his moustache over the back of her hand when he said goodnight, for Lasalle had no intention of rushing his fences. During the whole week of *Two Loves and a Life* he made no more mention of lessons in love, but established himself as a friend devoted to the service of a girl whose unhappiness was icily hidden from the rest of the world. He let her see, without a word spoken, that he understood the crisis of identity through which she was passing.

Father Griffin, with plans for a new and larger church of St. Canice already in preparation, was delighted to accept Jerry's generous offering for masses to be said for the soul of the sinner known only as El Chico. Jerry delicately let Laura know that this had been done, and was ready when she asked him the question she had not dared to ask when they talked on the starlit balcony. Where was the bandit buried? For some days she tortured herself by imagining a shameful grave, with a stake through the villain's heart, at one of those crossroads where the harness bells of the ore freighters rang and their wheels endlessly turned on the passes to the Comstock Lode. Then she asked outright, and Jerry Lasalle told her that he had himself intervened after the hanging to prevent a burial in the paupers' field behind the jail, already overcrowded by too many victims of the gun and the hangman's rope. He had persuaded the sheriff to let the boy be buried in a little glade beneath the pines not far from the singing waters of Deer Creek, with nothing to mark the place but the freshly turned turf. "It's yore shout, Jerry," said the sheriff. "Yore the one brought him to justice, and it don't make no difference to us. But I never figgered you had a tender heart."

This was not repeated to Laura, who was comforted by Jerry's explanation:

"He was a wild one, darling. A forest grave was right for him."

She was resilient enough to give better performances as 'Ruth' towards the end of the week, and already dependent enough on Jerry to be dismayed when he told her on Saturday night that he was leaving for San Francisco next day, while the company went on to Downieville.

"I'll see you in the city, ten days from now," he said reassuringly. "We'll have fun there, won't we, Laura?"

"I'll look forward to that. But I'm rather dreading Downieville. I wonder what'll go wrong there?"

"There'll be some new sensation at Downieville, never you fear."

There was, of course; but it happened to be one of the oldest sensations in the world. The explanation of Lizzie's sick headaches and fainting fits was a simple one, which Kitty Catt had guessed at when the soubrette collapsed after the robbery on the Ridge, and on the night the troupe reached Downieville Miss Lizzie Warren, with an odd mixture of shame, pride and bravado, confessed to Clara and Laura that she was two months pregnant, and that she and her lover would be married as soon as they returned to San Francisco.

The girls kissed and petted her, while the men – for the

whole company soon heard the news – were divided between slapping Leyburn's back and commiserating with him for 'getting caught'. Being genuinely in love with Lizzie, Harry Leyburn was optimistic about the future, not least because, as he said, "this puts an end to that damfool idea of another tour in Australia."

That was where the shoe pinched for Tom and Katharine Catt. Harry and Lizzie were in some ways the mainstay of their company, and it was perhaps surprising that Harry, with his fine singing voice and stage presence, had stayed with them so long. Eighteen months earlier they had been as popular in Sydney as in San Francisco, and if Lizzie had to retire from the stage for a time there was no doubt that Tom Maguire could find a place for Harry in any of his theatres in the city. It might not be so easy for other members of the company.

"Those girls!" raged Kitty Catt in private. "You never know where you are with them. I should've thought Lizzie Warren was far too smart to get into trouble, and now look at her!"

"It's happened before, my dear, and will again," suggested Tom. "And Harry's crazy about her. You can't say it'll be a shotgun wedding."

"That's all very well, but where are we going to get a replacement for her, if we do go to Australia?"

"Delisle?"

"Oh, don't be funny, Tom."

"Winter?"

"Winter a soubrette? We hired her as an ingénue and she's been acting like a rattlesnake ever since we began the tour. All she knows is how to turn the folks against her: give her another six months in San Francisco, and with those hoity-toity airs of hers she'll be the best hated actress in the city."

"You've really got your knife into her, Kits," said Tom. "We'd better let her go, if that's how you feel." He knew his wife was going through a trying time, even physically as well as on the stage, and she showed it by an increasing jealousy of young girls. There would be no difficulty about ending Laura Winter's engagement, for her contract had only a matter of days to run, but being Tom he proposed a compromise, to include disbanding the company for six months and reforming it for a tour in Australia. If she agreed to go to Australia, Kitty should have the whole summer to rest in their own home on Telegraph Hill and get thoroughly fit to face the Christmas heat in Sydney. Tom reckoned that an idle summer would give his wife time to accept that when they opened in Sydney she would be playing matronly parts instead of Juliet and Ophelia.

They thrashed out all the possibilities so thoroughly that it was easy for Kitty to have a private talk with Laura in one of the makeshift dressing rooms while Robson and his helpers were striking stage at Downieville on the twenty-fifth of May. It was Saturday night, and they were all glad the tour was over.

"Laura dear," said Kitty, apparently intent on removing grease paint from her face, "when you came to us in August it was on a six months' contract, wasn't it?"

"Yes, it was."

"Which we renewed for three months at the end of February?"

"Yes, ma'am," said Laura, seeing what was coming.

"Well, dear, I'm sorry to say we can't see our way to another renewal, at least not at present. We don't intend to book ourselves in to any theatre in San Francisco until the fall of '62, when we come back from Australia."

"You're going ahead with that plan, then?"

"We are; with an entirely new repertoire, and new players. Now, if you're interested, I suggest you get in touch with us again about September and find out if we have any parts to offer within your range – which I'm afraid turned out to be rather a limited one."

At which outrageous statement Laura smiled.

"In the meantime," said Kitty, disconcerted as always by the girl's coolness, "your salary will be paid up to the thirty-first, of course, and I thought you might like to have a word with Mrs. Judah. She's taken an interest in you from the start, and she'll very likely find some summer work for you. How does that suit you?"

"Very well indeed, I thank you, ma'am," said Laura. She rose and curtsied, with the effect of dismissing Mrs. Catt and all her works and ways.

★　　★　　★

From the earliest days of the American Conquest, the in-comers from the Southern states had been the cream of the nascent society of San Francisco. William Gwin, the US Senator who had put Fremont out of action in his brief membership of the Senate, was a Southerner, and he and his family were still leaders of what was now Society with a capital S. Their friends the Tebbittses, the Tevises, the War-rens and others were considered the arbiters of fashion and good form. Jerome Lasalle had carried letters of introduction to some of them when he first came to California, but he was not made welcome and eventually dropped. It was only after he struck it rich on the Comstock that he was eligible to be received in the drawing rooms of South Park and Rincon Hill.

"They say he took $100,000 out of his claim at Virginia City," said the gossips, "and sold his half share in it to his partner, Leonard Watson, for another $50,000 after he came back from Mexico."

"Yes, how about that trip to Mexico? I hear he made Virginia City too hot to hold him last year."

"That *was* last year, my dear, and just the other day he captured a notorious Mexican bandit –"

"I never said he was a coward. I do say he behaved very badly to poor Clarisse Cavelier. She lives with her parents, an absolute recluse, my sister writes."

"Poor Clarisse; but she should have been a nun. Her parents forced the marriage because of the Lasalle fortune –"

"Cotton brokers; yes, the Lasalles were rich. But with $150,000 Jerome Lasalle has picked up a respectable fortune of his own. He left cards on us last Tuesday; I think I shall invite him to our next soirée."

His readmission to the Southern society of San Francisco was part of a long-term plan Lasalle was forming for the future of Laura Winter. He could hardly believe in his own luck when he called on her at Mrs. Wilson's boarding-house on the day after her return from Downieville and learned that she was, as the actors said, 'at liberty'. She didn't blurt out the news, nor appear in any way concerned, and when he asked her bluntly, "What are you going to do now?" she answered "Nothing, until after Harry and Lizzie get married. Clara and I are going to be the bridesmaids; and I've got to go out now, Jerry, and see about our hats at the 'City of Paris'."

"Leyburn and Lizzie, eh? I suppose it's going to be a white wedding?"

"Well, not exactly; they're being married by a justice of the peace. Come back on Friday afternoon, if you can, and I'll tell you all about it."

If it hadn't been a white wedding it had been very much a theatre wedding, she told him when Friday came, and Jerry presented himself with a bouquet of roses and a box of candy like a young man going courting for the first time. Tom Maguire had been one of the witnesses at the ceremony and Mrs. Judah had been the other, while Lotta Crabtree had actually graced the party which followed – "heavily chaperoned by her mamma, of course", commented Laura. There had been dancing and champagne: Lizzie looked perfectly lovely, and she and Harry were just as happy as two kids.

"So all's well that ends well," said Jerry, and Laura's smile faded.

"Ah, but it's not the end," she said. "It's the beginning. They've rented a wretched little house down in the Mission – some jerrybuilder put it up about twenty years ago, and it's practically falling to pieces, for the chimney doesn't draw and the window frames don't fit, and there Lizzie will have to sit, waiting for her baby and waiting for Harry to come home at night, and pinching the pennies to buy food and baby clothes. What a fool she's been!"

"I hear Leyburn's joining Mrs. Judah's company."

"Yes, and she's the original penny-pincher when it comes to salaries." Laura hesitated. "I had a word with her myself after the wedding. Kitty Catt suggested it, and I thought why not? She was supposed to be interested in me. But her interest didn't run as far as offering me a decent job. 'You made a mistake going into melodrama, young lady,' she said. 'Come to me and I'll give you a thorough training in Shakespeare and Old Comedy, and we'll make an actress of you yet.' Old Comedy indeed! 'No thank you, ma'am,' I said. 'I don't fancy touring the valleys in *The School for Scandal*, playing Lady Teazle's maid.'"

"Sarah Siddons played the English provinces for seven years

before she became a star in London," suggested Jerry. "Have you anything else in mind for the summer, before you go back to the Catts in September?"

"I'm not going to New South Wales with them," she said obstinately. "Playing to convicts, what an honour!"

"You're living in the past, darling. It isn't a penal settlement now. And there are gold mines in Australia too, you know. Somewhere between Bendigo and Ballarat, you might meet another millionaire."

"Don't be horrible, Jerry." She sprang up and went to the window, looking out between the dingy curtains at Clay Street, where the summer wind was blowing clouds of sand. Jerry followed her and took her in his arms.

"Forgive me, darling," he said, "I wasn't making fun of you. It's not a crime to want to be rich. And you do, don't you?"

"I *mean* to be rich," she said, "but I can't be if I start playing Lady Teazle's maid, or half kill myself touring in Australia. I can afford to pay my own way, for a while at least, until I find something better to do."

"How?"

She moved with unconscious seduction in his arms and pulled from the high neck of her plain cotton dress the incongruous beauty of the pearls of Loreto. Jerry ran his fingers along the necklace, warm from her skin, and kissed her throat. "I saw you wear them first that night at the Cords'," he said. "I didn't think they were beads. But I didn't know you wore them all the time."

"My foster-father sold a good many of them to pay for my keep and schooling," she said in a voice subdued by his kisses on her neck. "I can sell a few more, if I have to. They belonged to my mother."

"Darling!" He kissed her, and told her she was a wonderful girl and a great beauty – "Lizzie Warren was brave when she asked you to be her bridesmaid. How did she like being outshone on her own wedding day?"

"Nobody outshone Lizzie, she was far too happy." He had made her smile, at least, and he kept his advantage, caressing her and drawing her closer still to his body, so that Laura felt as never before the burgeoning of a man's passion, and the thrill of young arms around her and a young cheek pressed against her own. When he went away he left her pliant and unsatisfied, and Jerry Lasalle, as he walked aimlessly towards the wharves, was nearer being in love than he had ever been in his life. He swore at himself for his mean plan of getting her away from the theatre crowd and insinuating her into what San Francisco called society. There was an antique Colonel Lee, who claimed to be a distant relative of the general in command of the Confederate army, who with his old wife was just silly enough to sponsor (for they loved a title) the Honourable Laura Winter, daughter of the late Viscount and Viscountess Winter of London, England. He had been mean enough to think a South Park drawing room might be a proving ground for Laura, a final test for her as a partner in his master plan. What an egregious fool! He thought of the real test, that dance of death in the foothills of the Sierra, and cursed himself.

She had promised to drive with him next morning, and Laura hid herself from the sporting inmates of Mrs. Wilson's boarding-house to spend the evening in her room. She had not been quite candid when she told Jerry that she could live off the sale of her pearls if need be. There was another possibility, contained in an ill-written letter received the day before.

Dere Dolly, [the letter ran]
    I see by the paper that the Catts are not acepting bookings for this summer (maybe nobody wants them, ha ha!) so I figure you will be at a loose end for a bit. How would you like to come back to Monterey and give the boys a treat with some of your new songs at the Dramatic Adobe? We would all give a big hand to our San Francisco Star, so what do you say, Dolly? Write soon about this to your afectionate old uncle,
                                            Jack Swan

She remembered the little crowded theatre with the wooden benches and the smell of candle grease from the footlights mingling with the reek of liquor and tobacco from the bar. She thought of walking again on the beach at Monterey and standing inside the door of the church where she had played in *Los Pastores*. All put behind her, all impossible to repeat –

except for the insidious temptation to see Jack Swan again, the man who had been her foster-father's closest friend and confidant. Would he know more than Uncle Chips had told her about the circumstances of her coming to Monterey? Would he know if there had been another child, a boy, who had fallen into other hands and a far less fortunate life? Was the boy now lying in a forest grave really the Sebastian to her Viola? Had he thought so himself when he saw her by the stage coach, before he whisked off the bandanna which hid the face so like her own?

By the time she went to bed Laura persuaded herself that, following the best traditions of melodrama, she and El Chico were the children of some unfortunate girl 'seduced and abandoned' by her English lover, who without a Harry Leyburn to shoulder his responsibilities had allowed her babies to be taken from her; and she almost decided to go to Monterey and ask questions of Jack Swan. When she woke up her mood had veered to accept Jerry Lasalle's *laissez-faire* optimism, expressed in such platitudes as Let sleeping dogs lie, and Why stir up a hornet's nest? What if the mother who had given away her infants were alive, married, unwilling to be reminded of the past? Laura still thought that only two people were responsible for her life and fate: she was incapable of imagining the tormented figure of Carlos Rivera, who had given Rosalie's son to the two Indian nurses with a handful of silver dollars and ordered them to return to their tribe with the child.

To dear old Jack Swan I was Dolly Winter, she told herself. So be it. But some day I'll have a name of my own and a home all my own, and *I will be rich.*

Jerry arrived at nine, driving a gig with a pair of high-steppers between the shafts, a dashing equipage which made heads turn as they drove out of the city and along the Point Lobos road. For once it was a warm morning, and the wind had not yet risen to bend the few twisted pines on the cliffs above the Pacific. They were going to the end of the carriage road, to a point above the rocks where the seals congregated, no longer menaced by the Russian hunters from the Farallones, and where a year or two back a modest restaurant had opened its doors. At first it was unimaginatively called the Seal

Rocks Inn, and its new name, the Cliff House, was hardly more inspired, but there was stabling both for hired rigs and for the saddle horses which riders rented by the hour on the ocean beach.

Laura strolled to the railed-off edge of the cliff while Jerry talked to the stableman. Although the sun was shining, the blue sky was not reflected in the waves of the Pacific: high, curling, uniformly grey, they fretted the edge of a long expanse of grey sands, empty except for the horseback riders. The seals were barking and the gulls, circling overhead, replied with the sad cries which were said to be the voices of drowned sailormen. She was glad when Jerry gave her his arm and led her inside the little tavern.

A surprising number of people had been tempted by the sunshine to brave the Point Lobos road and the flying sand. There was a pleasant smell of cooking, and if the walls and benches were wooden, the table linen was fresh and the glasses sparkling. A man in a long white apron showed them to a table near an open window through which they could hear the breakers underneath the cliff.

"They're famous for their breakfasts," Jerry said. "Would you like fish or eggs, or both?"

"Just coffee and a roll, please."

The waiter took their order, and when he had gone Jerry whispered "Look who's here!" with a sidelong glance at a corner table where an older lady was drinking coffee and a younger one finishing scrambled eggs and a glass of milk. As if aware of Jerry's gaze, the girl turned and looked at them. Laura recognised the red curls and the vivid face of Lotta Crabtree.

The little actress smiled and bowed, and after a word with her mother crossed the room to Jerry's table, followed by the murmur of interest and admiration which was Lotta's tribute wherever she went. She was dressed in a black riding habit, the long skirt caught up in a loop, with a white cravat and a black velvet jockey cap; she carried a neat crop and leather gloves.

Jerry rose and bowed as he was introduced to Miss Crabtree and her mother, who had followed her, and the fourteen-year-old star said eagerly:

"Miss Winter, how nice to see you! We met at the Leyburn wedding, if you remember?"

"Of course I remember," said Laura, rising out of respect for Mrs. Crabtree. She stood sentinel behind her daughter, rolling up a long piece of crochet lace.

"Please don't think it very forward of me," said Lotta, "but I did hear at the wedding that you were going to be at liberty. If you've nothing better in view, I wonder if you'd care to join my company?"

"Your company, Miss Crabtree? I thought you were going out on tour."

"Oh no, I shan't tour again until the fall. I'm opening in *The Soldier's Bride* at the Gilbert Theatre in the third week in June."

"Then aren't you in rehearsal already?"

"Yes, but if you would join us as the balladist you wouldn't need many rehearsals, and you're such a beautiful singer you'd be a big draw."

"Won't you sit down and join us, ladies?" Jerry put in suavely. "Madam, may I offer you some coffee?"

"My daughter has a riding engagement," said Mrs. Crabtree, in the voice of Lancashire commonsense.

"When did you ever hear me sing?" asked Laura.

"I was at the back of the house one night when you were singing 'Then You'll Remember Me'," said Lotta. "You were great! Do think it over, Miss Winter. I'd be so pleased to have you with me."

"Have you an agent?" asked Mrs. Crabtree.

"A theatrical agent? No, I haven't."

"Lotta's agent is Jake Wallace," said her mother. "Everybody in the profession knows where to find *him*. So if you like the idea, just you have a word with Jake. Now dearie" (to Lotta) "better be off with you. Don't keep Maudie hanging about in the wind."

When the girl had gone with a smiling goodbye Mrs. Crabtree moved to another table with a view, whipped out her crochet hook and started on her fancywork again. Jerry knew that Laura was furious, that she was vain enough to resent the very thought of singing sentimental ballads while Lotta Crabtree starred in *The Soldier's Bride*, and he admired the self-control which kept a smile on her face while she sipped her cooling coffee and asked him stilted questions about his future plans.

"We'll talk about that later," he said. "You're not listening."

She was watching the riders on the sands far below, where Lotta Crabtree's red hair made her easily distinguishable. She was riding with a girl who instead of the conventional white cravat was wearing a scarf of vivid green which streamed out in the wind behind her. They galloped a long way down the sands, turned, and came back within sight of the restaurant.

"Ah!" said Laura, setting down her cup. "Now I know who Maudie is, and I imagine you do too."

"I recognise her," said Jerry carelessly.

"Maud Delorme, star of the Long Tom Melodeon! Mrs. Crabtree isn't too particular about her daughter's friends."

"It's none of our business," said Jerry. "Laura, I thought you wanted to hear about *my* plans."

"I'm sorry, Jerry, of course I do."

"I'm thinking of going to Paris pretty soon," said Jerry casually, and now Laura's attention was riveted.

"To *Paris!*"

"Maybe."

"You mean you haven't made up your mind?"

"Well, you see, it depends on a good many things. I'm going to a men's luncheon party at Colonel Lee's today, and that may help me to decide. You can help me too, Laura. Will you have dinner with me tonight?"

"Where?"

"At the Poodle Dog."

"I always enjoy the Poodle Dog."

"I mean in a private room at the Poodle Dog. Do you enjoy that too?"

"I've never tried it."

"You will tonight."

★   ★   ★

It was the custom for ladies who enjoyed *tête-à-tête* suppers in the private rooms of San Francisco's French restaurants to go veiled to their assignations. Laura Winter wore a black mantilla, a relic of fiesta days in Monterey. Dressing her hair high, she draped the mantilla over a Spanish comb and drew it forward, so that it was in essence a veiled lady whose white crinoline Jerome Lasalle helped to manoeuvre out of a closed cab at the discreet side entrance of the Poodle Dog.

A silent manservant led them up two flights of carpeted stairs. They met nobody on the way, but an elderly waiter with a napkin over his arm was at the open door of the room Jerry had reserved, and held it wide for them to pass.

"I hope monsieur will find everything to his liking," he said in French, and Jerry in the same language told him to open the champagne and then serve the supper he had ordered. Places were laid for two at a small table, where four lighted candles stood round a bowl of roses. There were more roses in the empty grate and more candles on the marble chimneypiece. The scent of the flowers did not quite dominate a faint odour of stale perfume, which seemed to come from behind the looped brocade curtains which divided the room in two.

"I didn't know you spoke French, but of course I should have done," said Laura when they were alone.

"Creole French, I'm afraid. I don't know if it'll go over well in Paris."

"Tell me about Paris," she said urgently. She had been thinking about it all day. Laura had lived long enough in San Francisco, where everything French was admired and copied, to know that the capital of the Second Empire, where Napoleon III and the beautiful Eugénie reigned at the Tuileries, was the most desirable place on earth, and Jerry's hints on the long dusty road back from the Seal Rocks had been enough to set her as wild to go to Paris as her mother had been to go to St. Petersburg. It was the solution to all her problems: the check to her career on the stage, the rumours which followed her from Sacramento, the 'insolence', as she thought of it, of Lotta Crabtree's proposal that she should warble ballads in the *entr'actes* of *The Soldier's Bride*.

"Paris can wait," said Jerry. "I want you to look at yourself first." The marble chimneypiece was set in an entire mirrored wall, stretching from floor to ceiling, which gave back the reflection of Jerry in evening black and white, with his long black hair brushed behind his ears and his black moustache and imperial carefully trimmed, and of Laura in her white crinoline and black mantilla, with her golden scarf drooping from her naked arms.

"You're lovelier than ever tonight," the man said, and kissed her bare shoulder. "The mantilla suits you. No, don't take it off!" – as she instinctively raised her hands to the high comb – "it looks wonderful on your hair. Don't you think we make a handsome couple?"

"We're not a couple."

"But we could be partners. Let's drink to us!" He handed her one of the glasses the waiter had filled, and Laura smiled as she tilted it towards him in a tiny salute.

"Is it cold enough?" said Jerry critically.

"The champagne is, but the room's very warm. Where shall I put my scarf?" There was no other item of furniture to be seen but a sideboard, which held more flowers, lighted candles and service plates.

"Let me put it away for you." Jerry drew aside one of the brocade curtains. Behind it was what appeared to be a day bed, spread with a velvet cover which could be folded back in one movement to reveal the sheets and pillows underneath. He laid the golden scarf on the cover and took Laura's trembling hand in his.

"There's a mirror in the ceiling," she said in a small voice. Faced with the essential fitting of a *cabinet particulier*, much of her assurance had left her.

"The French have some remarkable ideas," said Jerry, as a knock fell on the door. He pulled back one of the chairs at the table. "Sit down, darling; here comes supper."

He watched her while two waiters poured champagne, put a second bottle in the cooler, and disposed plates and dishes on the white linen tablecloth and the sideboard. The lobster aspic, the chicken mousse, the dessert were all cold, so that when the waiters left they could serve themselves. He thought how well the mantilla became her, not only because her white skin was so seductive, seen through the thin black lace, but because the graceful folds falling from the Spanish comb seemed subtly to alter her features, as if another personality were beginning to shine through the familiar beauty. She sipped her champagne and smiled, but he saw the blush and the quick intake of breath which came as the waiters bowed themselves out and shut the door with the snap of an outside lock.

"Have they *locked* the door?" she said.

"Only for the privacy of the guests. It means no one will disturb us unless he's sent for, and of course the door can be locked from the inside as well. Don't look so alarmed, it's not a prison! Laura darling, if you want to leave immediately after supper, or even if you want to leave *now*, you only have to pull that bell-rope – there, by the chimneypiece – and the door will be opened for you within five minutes."

"What do they do if there's a fire?"

"There have been one or two fires since the Poodle Dog was opened, and I never heard of any – accidents."

They laughed together, and ate some of the delicious food, but they soon gave up the pretence of eating, and Laura reminded him that he had promised to tell her about Paris.

"Yes, well, it's rather a long story, and I didn't really make up my mind about Paris till this afternoon," he said. "It's been a day for decisions – yours, mine, ours."

"What did *I* decide?" she said lightly. "Are you a fortune-teller, Jerry?"

"You decided that you didn't want to join Miss Lotta Crabtree's company in any capacity whatever. Am I right?"

"That, of course; but I also decided that if I weren't very careful I might find myself applying for Maud Delorme's job at the Long Tom when she joins the Crabtree entourage."

"*You* appear on stage at a melodeon?"

"If I have to. And then, on the way down, at a two-bit house, or even a one-bit house on Meigg's Wharf . . . It's happened to other girls, why not to me?"

Jerry said nothing by way of protest or encouragement. "That's the way it sometimes goes," he said, "for pretty girls who don't know when to cut their losses."

"Is that what you've done, Jerry? Was that the decision you made today – to cut your losses and clear out?"

"Not exactly," he said, "because I'm on a winning streak at present, and I'd like to keep it that way. No, mine was a purely personal decision, and I'm afraid of boring you, because it has to do with the war. You never read the war news, do you?"

"What's there to read?" said Laura. "Just the communiqué – isn't that what they call it? – 'All quiet along the Potomac'. It's same every day."

"Well, it won't be all quiet for much longer. There are

twenty-five thousand Union troops cooling their heels in Washington, all sure they're ready for action, and action they'll certainly see as soon as General Winfield Scott can lay his hands on a reliable map of Virginia. Meantime some of them have been getting up to mischief. That was what all the talk was about at luncheon today."

"At Colonel Lee's?"

"Yes. It was a men's lunch, as I told you, no ladies present, and nine out of the ten men there were over sixty. Now Colonel Lee *was* a soldier. He was on Scott's staff in Mexico, and distinguished himself at the storming of Chapultepec. None of the others ever fired a shot in anger. But if talk would do it, Abraham Lincoln would be lying dead in the White House this very minute; I never heard such a set of fire-eaters in my life."

"And they wanted you to be a fire-eater too?"

"It was implied, but all I had to do was listen. I've told you about Colonel Lee: how proud he is of being related to General Robert E. Lee, the commander of the Confederate States army. Well, a few days ago some of those restless fellows in Washington crossed the Potomac and set fire to General Lee's mansion at Arlington, which came to him through his family's connection with George Washington. The place wasn't burned down, but wrecked and looted, and General Beauregard – the man who made Anderson surrender at Fort Sumter – is yelling bloody murder and revenge. When the Northern heroes get their maps and their wits together and march on Richmond, I wager they'll get a warm welcome south of the Potomac."

"Does that mean the South will win the war?"

"Certainly not, the South will lose. They've got the spirit but they haven't got the matériel, and they certainly aren't going to get the British. That's why I decided, after listening to all that hot air from the old men at Colonel Lee's, to get the hell out of the Disunited States and go to Paris."

"Did you tell them that?"

"Not likely! They took it for granted that a man of twenty-eight would be going back to New Orleans to enlist – New Orleans, which is blockaded by Admiral Farragut and a Northern flotilla at this moment!"

"And your family is there?"

"Father's in his office, supporting the cotton embargo when he ought to be selling wherever he can find a market, and mother and the girls are at our house in the country, I imagine. I don't owe my family anything, Laura. If my parents had sent me to the Virginia Military Institute and made a soldier of me, maybe I'd be one of Lee's subalterns today, but they sent me to the Jesuits and made me a failed seminarian instead. Next, after a couple of years in father's counting house, they persuaded me into marriage at twenty, with a poor nervous girl of seventeen, and that made her worse than a widow and me a failed husband. I'm sick of failure, Laura. The Confederates will fail, because failure is in their bones, and I refuse to die for Jeff Davis and the South's dead truth."

The suppressed passion, the anger in all he said was so unlike the mocking, cynical Jerry Lasalle she knew that Laura sat in silence while he filled their glasses and took a mouthful of champagne. Then he said,

"I was a soldier of a sort, not so very long ago. In hand to hand combat, when it was a choice between kill or be killed. When the Comstock bonanza was discovered, the Piute Indians showed fight because they didn't want the white man tearing up their hunting grounds and sacred places. Just like Lee's mansion at Arlington. And they weren't using bows and arrows, they'd got rifles from somewhere, and they could ride rings around us on their ponies. So we formed a company of militia, called ourselves the Nevada Rifles, which sounded pretty good, and went after them. Once we had the whip hand it turned into a massacre. Those poor red devils died to the last man rather than surrender, and we killed them to justify our claims to the silver and the gold. I made up my mind when it was over that I would never fight again for a cause I didn't believe in. And I don't believe in slavery any more than I believe in King Cotton or States' Rights. A plague on both your houses, say I – there's your Shakespeare for you, Laura – and my decision is to go to Paris."

He set down his empty glass, reached across the disordered table and took her hand.

"Now for *our* decision, darling. Will you come with me?"

She gave a long shaking sigh – was it of triumph? and her

blue eyes seemed to grow larger as his fingers closed on hers.

"Under your protection, do you mean?" she said.

"As the saying goes." He left his chair and knelt by her side. "Darling, with all my heart I wish it could be otherwise. If I could offer you marriage it would be the great joy and honour of my life –"

"That's so easy for a married man to say."

"How can I convince you that I love you?" He pulled her into his arms as he rose, so that they stood enlaced while he drew off Spanish comb and Spanish mantilla and covered her hair, her face, her shoulders with his kisses.

She freed a hand, and he thought she was going to pull the bell-rope. But she only pushed him away from her, gently but convincingly, and said,

"You told me we could be partners. How? Do you expect me to cross the plains by the Overland Stage, or risk the passage round Cape Horn? And if we do reach Paris, how shall we live when we get there?"

"That's a lot of questions, Laura. First, we'll travel in comparative comfort on a Pacific Mail Line steamer, and cross the Isthmus of Panama to take ship for France."

"But that's the worst way of all! We might die of fever in the Panama swamps, or be robbed of everything in that port of hell called Chagres –"

"You really ought to read the papers, Laura," the man said patiently. "People don't cross the Isthmus by muleback and canoe any longer. Not since the Panama railroad was opened six years ago. And there's an American port at Aspinwall, where there are decent hotels if we have to wait for a ship to Le Havre or Marseilles."

"Well –"

"When we reach Paris I mean to rent a comfortable house, well furnished, in a fashionable quarter, where we can entertain our friends –"

"Have you many friends in Paris?"

"I have some excellent introductions to Southern gentlemen who had the sense to get out as soon as Lincoln was elected President. Gentlemen who're known to enjoy a quiet game of cards after a good dinner, presided over by a beautiful young lady."

"Card games like baccarat? Or poker?"

"I've always preferred baccarat."

"Yes, I know. Just tell me – which of the two of us is going to be Madame Moustache?"

"Laura!"

"Because isn't that the partnership you're offering me – as the *entraîneuse* in a high-class gambling house?"

"You didn't learn that word in your refined school at Monterey."

"*Entraîneuse?* The stage enlarged my vocabulary, perhaps."

"It has an ugly meaning, which will never apply to you. All I ask of our partnership is that you should be the mistress of my house and a charming hostess to our guests. You'll have a personal maid as well as the house servants, your own carriage, and clothes from the Paris dressmakers. You won't be on the losing end of our arrangement."

"What would my name be?"

"The same as mine, of course. Madame Lasalle."

Her head drooped as she said "It still wouldn't be my own."

Jerry took advantage of her moment of weakness. He took her in his arms again and said, "Darling, I know it's a big thing to ask of you: to cross the ocean and make a new life quite different from the life you know. But won't you trust me enough to work out all the practical details of how we'll travel, where we'll live, what we'll do? Won't you believe me when I say I love you, and I'll try to make you happy? Don't you realise that we're two of a kind, Laura? We both love adventure, we're not afraid to take risks –"

"I'll take one risk," she interrupted him. "I'll try your plan for a year, a year to the day after we arrive in Paris. And if it doesn't work out, then we'll be free to part. No conditions, no vows of eternal fidelity; only freedom."

"You're a brave woman, Laura. But, my God, you're cold when you strike a bargain!"

"I thought you were going to give me lessons in love," she said. "Why don't you lock the door?"

The half hour which followed the locking of the door on the inside was not an easy one for Jerome Lasalle. To be accepted as a lover on a year's probation was a blow to his pride, and his ardour was considerably cooled by the revelation of a nature as calculating as his own. Like many gamblers he was not a womaniser, and although his liaison with Madame Moustache had considerably increased his stock of carnal knowledge it was not such as he was prepared to use in his first possession of a virgin. Indeed his only encounter with virginity had been on his wedding night with Clarisse Cavelier, which the bride had spent between prayers and tears. At least there had been a dressing room in their suite at the New Orleans hotel where that fumbling, frustrated night was passed: in the narrow confines of a San Francisco *cabinet particulier* he had to watch the object of his desire struggling with her staylaces and writhing out of the complicated underpinning of her crinoline. Laura kept her face turned away from him, but she neither wept nor prayed when he took her to bed at last. If she had spoken he felt she might have asked coldly "What have I got to lose?"

What she needed to lose was her total inexperience, which turned the first contact of their naked bodies into a series of awkward collisions between nose and chin, knee and muscled thigh, but she was so beautiful in the candlelight which gave her skin a glow as golden as her hair, that Jerry forgot their infelicities in the simple desire to possess her, and he had been calmed enough by all that went before to go very slowly towards his goal. To part her lips with his own was the first small victory, then to feel her long limbs relax against his limbs, then – though she never answered his words of love with words – he heard murmurs and sighs which betrayed her rising passion, so that the conquest, when it came, was easier, more prolonged and more completely shared than Jerry Lasalle had dared to hope. She slept in his arms at last, and the lovely face on his shoulder wore the mask of satisfied desire.

Laura was the first to wake next morning. The candles had burned to their sockets and the summer dawn was stroking the window panes. She raised herself on her elbow and looked at her lover: secret face, broad shoulders, black hair curling on his naked breast. And what she said to herself was what an older generation of San Franciscans said when they were beaten by fate in their search for gold:

"Well! I've seen the elephant!"

BOOK THREE

THE ESTRADA BRAND

Part One

The War of the *Rosalie*

I

Like all wars expected to end by Christmas, the American Civil War dragged on for years, and long afterwards Maria de las Mercedes Estrada confessed to a sympathetic listener that these had been the pleasantest and most harmonious years of her early life. Luis Estrada's daughter was a chubby eleven year old when the war began in 1861 and a plump adolescent of fifteen when it ended with the defeat of the South in 1865, quite intelligent enough to see that her family was an anachronism even in the sleepy world of Sonoma.

It was not that they were poor. Luis still owned his thousand acres, and on the advice of his brother Philip had prospered by raising draught horses for the San Francisco market. The spread of horse-drawn street-car transport, and the demand for heavy animals to pull the drays conveying imported merchandise from the wharves to the stores and factories of the fast-growing city had greatly increased that market, and although cattle no longer roamed his pastures Luis felt happier and more at home with animal husbandry than with raising crops. He enlarged the little adobe house in the plaza by building outdoor kitchen premises and servants' quarters in the style of the old rancho, and adding one long living room, with a verandah overlooking the garden, across the back of the house. There was additional stabling too, including space for the pony carriage Luis bought for his wife to drive. He never made a horsewoman of his daughter, who sat her mount, he scolded, like a sack of potatoes, but she soon became a proficient whip, and drove the pony carriage better than her mother.

Maria de las Mercedes, Maria for short, was a jolly, affectionate girl, so practical and energetic as to remind her father of his own mother, Doña Maria del Pilar, in the heyday of the Rancho Estrada. The adobe in the plaza was hardly on the same scale as the rancho, but Maria was running it efficiently before she was sixteen. She kept the three house servants up to their work, and was not above taking lessons from the cook, while under her directions a gardener and his boy, working on two fertile acres, kept the kitchen well supplied with fruit and vegetables. Luis was proud of his girl, and got over his disappointment at having no son to carry on the name when he saw what happened to the sons of the men who fought with him in the California Resistance.

The young men of the next generation were emotionally crippled by the American Conquest. Some of them reacted with violence to the loss of their ancestral lands, whether to squatters or by decision of the Land Commissioners, and took to the same life of highway robbery as El Chico. Others were idle and apathetic. If they earned a living it was not in the way of their fathers, like the son of General Castro, the fat and amiable owner of a bar in Santa Barbara. Some of the defeated left California for *la otra banda*, and found in republican Mexico a different country from that of the Good Viceroys of old folks' tales. By the time of the Intervention, when French bayonets for a time upheld the uneasy throne of the puppet Emperor Maximilian, the Californios had had enough of fighting, and began drifting back across the border to idle their days away in the insignificant pueblo called Los Angeles.

The poison of the American Conquest took a different form as it worked in Luis Estrada. It completely altered his sense of proportion. While the Civil War raged on, and great masses of men hurled themselves against each other, he could never see that the armoured battlefields of the tremendous names, from First Bull Run through Antietam, Gettysburg, and the surrender of Richmond were more important than the Californios' charge with lances at the Battle of San Pascual. He never wavered in his obsessional hatred of the man who had taken the Californios' surrender at Cahuenga, and who had long ago forgotten his existence.

He continued to follow the career of General John C. Fremont, whose ups and downs resembled a fever patient's temperature chart. A 'down' very satisfactory to Luis had been Fremont's defeat in the presidential election of 1856, but on the outbreak of the Civil War there he was on an 'up' again. In July 1861 Fremont was given command of the Department of the West, which included Illinois and all the states between the Mississippi and the Rockies. His own tactlessness and greed of power soon brought about his downfall. Embroiled with the powerful Blair family, one of whom was close to Mr. Lincoln, Fremont went so far as to issue his own Emancipation Order, giving freedom to all the slaves of the 'rebels', on August 30, 1861. He did not trouble to consult the President, whose official Emancipation Proclamation was not issued until September 1862. Fremont's initiative caused anger in Washington, and 'General Jessie', as his wife was now called, travelled to the capital to plead for the President's indulgence. The net result was that Abraham Lincoln relieved John C. Fremont of his command on November 2, at the end of his 'Hundred Days' of misused ambition.

The delight of her father at this turn of events made Maria's home a happier place, and Isabel Estrada, with improved health and spirits, used his new affability to obtain some concessions about their way of life. "It's no good pretending," she told him, "that we can bring back what you think of as the lost Utopia by dwelling on the past. You and I know what we had, and what we lost, but Maria doesn't, and the child must have friends of her own age and some kind of schooling. If you want her to have playmates, who else is there but the Vallejos?"

The time was past when the name of General Vallejo drew from Luis a snarl of "Collaborator!" He had to admit that Don Mariano, who had lost, materially, more than anyone, never ceased to be the patriarch of the Lost Utopia. He had built himself a Victorian Gothic villa about a mile outside Sonoma, given it the name of Lachryma Montis, and constructed a stately approach through an avenue lined with poplars and later with eucalyptus. There he installed his wife, their enormous family, and three hundred indoor and out-door servants, devoting himself to public works as state senator and mayor of Sonoma, and to private entertaining on a lavish scale. Luis was disgusted to hear that he called the two daughters born after the Conquest 'the Little Yankees', but he acknowledged that the older members of Vallejo's family had not sunk under the old defeat. His eldest son, Platon, gradu-ated at the head of his class at Columbia, the first Spanish-speaking Californian MD, and served in the medical corps of the Union army.

Maria Estrada went to school with 'the Little Yankees' and other small Catholic girls at the classes which Vallejo orga-nised for an all too brief period. There Maria learned at least to read, write and speak English, and in her meetings with other children she first understood that her home, where nothing was heard but Spanish, was a feudal survival having little to do with the daily life of what was now a cosmopolitan village. 'Village' Sonoma still was, for contrary to all expectations it was Santa Rosa, the former fiefdom of the Carrillos, which had forged ahead as a thriving country town, while Petaluma, always a great food supplier of San Francisco, was already claiming to be the 'Egg and Chicken capital of California'. The Americans who arrived in Sonoma after the Conquest had nothing in common with the rascally Bear Flaggers. They were decent, hardworking shopkeepers and small farmers. The First Methodist church and the Presbyterian College bore witness to their religious convictions. There were Italian vintners in the valley now, with their native workmen, and Colonel Haraszthy, the father of the California wine industry, had brought Hungarians and Swiss to Buena Vista vineyards. One of the happiest days of Maria's childhood was the day when she was a flower girl at the double wedding of two of Vallejo's daughters to Arpad and Attila, two of Haraszthy's sons. It was a day of wine and roses, in which the old Californio culture mingled with the Italian, the Hungarian and the now native-born American.

Three years passed cheerfully enough until misfortune once again fell on Luis Estrada. The great drought of 1864 ruined his pastures and the condition of his big horses, all of which, contrary to modern custom, bore the Estrada brand of the ox-yoke shaped like an E. He began again to talk desperately of selling off his land to the vintners. No doubt Philip would have come to the rescue, as he had done before, but a new quarrel, fanned by Content, upset the Estrada family.

There had been few meetings between the brothers in the years immediately before the Civil War. The occupation of horse-breeder did not give Luis many opportunities to visit the city, and the journey to Sonoma, which still took as long as ever by boat and road, was beginning to be too much for Philip. He had started to suffer from the heart complaint which afflicted both his parents, and his doctor had advised him to rest as much as possible. Deprived of exercise he grew very stout, and in his early forties looked fifteen years older. Not so Luis. Though the dashing caballero with bright sash and serape had gone for ever, Luis's youthful good looks had matured, not vanished, and the women of Sonoma still looked up admiringly at the erect figure on horseback which came and went twice daily to the corrals at the old rancho. Luis now wore a baggy 'sack suit' of the style favoured by Americans, but the trouser ends were tucked into boots of ornamented leather worn with the old silver spurs, and his sombrero had the stiff Spanish brim and the cords knotted under his chin. If the loungers in the plaza tipped their hats to Don Mariano Vallejo as he drove himself into town in his smart phaeton, with a footman in livery standing at the back, it was to Don Luis Estrada on his palomino that the women dropped their curtsies.

The friendship between the sisters-in-law continued, and twice or three times a year Isabel took her little girl to stay for a couple of nights with Aunt Content and Uncle Philip and visit the fabulous shops of San Francisco. These were magic occasions for Maria, and her brimming affection went out to all the family at South Park. She 'adored' baby Jimmy, four years her junior, she 'loved' gentle Cousin Faith, so musical and bookish, and she confessed to her mamma that she was 'scared stiff' of Cousin Hope, who was so smart and pretty and condescending to the little country cousin. She thought the mansion in South Park a palace, and when she heard that it had to be given up, she thought her relatives would be heartbroken.

Actually no one was heartbroken, although Philip Estrada lamented having to spend $12,000 for the choice building site on Pine Street at the corner of Jones. The English elegance of South Park was doomed from the moment that Second, its service street for shops and tradesmen, was swept away in the great commercial expansion of the city. Rincon Hill, once a Spanish grant, belonged to the past, and San Francisco continued its onward march up other hills. The most fashionable hill, on which the Estradas were going to live, was not quite cleared for building and sometimes called Fern Hill from the vegetation and chaparral at its summit, which would only yield to the machete. But Pine and its cross streets, with Polk at a lower level to provide shops and services, was "a very good address", as Hope Estrada said, and Hope at fifteen was the arbiter of taste in her family.

Ostentation was in fashion, and the Estrada house was ostentatious from the cupola with four windows on the roof to the cellars, laundry and furnace rooms in the basement. Built of clapboard painted grey on a stone foundation, it had eight bedrooms and four bathrooms for the family and their guests and four bedrooms and one bathroom (a tremendous innovation) for the servants. There was a playroom for Jimmy and his friends, and the two young ladies had their own sitting room. On the ground floor was a dining room, a library and a double drawing room "big enough to dance twenty couples", said Hope.

If a dance were contemplated much furniture and many art objects would have to be removed first, for the Estrada house was crammed with all the cabinets, occasional tables, Oriental pottery and jars of bulrushes which money and American-Victorian bad taste could buy.

The architect had let his fancy run riot on the exterior, which included bay windows ornamented with scrolls of fretwork painted white. He had skimped on the garden space, reached by a french window in the library and also by the kitchen door, and the drying green was cut in two by a path leading to the service entry on Jones Street. A few ferns and shrubs completed the garden, and Content placed a standing order for flowers with the Chinese gardeners trading from door to door in the city.

It was Content's boast that through the whole trying period of seeing the new house built and moving in from the old, she never failed to work for her church and civic charities. In this her elder daughter was a great help, for Faith while shy and awkward in society had a deep concern for the sick poor. It was in the course of sick visiting that she contracted a bad case of measles which, as her sister Hope said crossly, spoiled the plans for a housewarming party, and left Faith, who had outgrown her strength, a weak and listless convalescent. The doctor prescribed country air. The uncle and aunt at Sonoma were delighted to offer their hospitality.

When she came back after three weeks at the adobe in the plaza she had got back her colour and her appetite, and was enthusiastic about the kindness she had received from everybody. At first she only sat in the garden with Aunt Isabel, then Maria took her driving in the pony carriage, and as soon as she was strong enough she went riding with Uncle Luis. What fun it was, riding in the valley, and how much nicer than the riding school in San Francisco, going round and round the tanbark and jumping nothing higher than the three-foot bar! Her father smiled as he listened. "I'm glad you went out to the old rancho," he said, "and you won't meet many horsemen like your Uncle Luis."

But Content, who during Faith's illness had been more concerned with the girl's body than her soul, had been a prey to doubts during the visit to Sonoma, and now asked abruptly:

"Did your uncle and aunt take you to the Catholic church while you were staying with them?"

"Yes, mamma; we all went to mass at the Mission on both the Sundays I was there."

"*Mass!*" said Content deeply. "There's a Protestant church in Sonoma, you should have gone there by yourself."

"How could I, mamma? I was their house guest; it would have been too rude to go off on my own. Besides" (with a blush of defiance) "I was glad to go. I thought it was very – interesting."

She had been going to say "very beautiful", but was warned in time by her mother's glare. Then her father intervened.

"I'm glad Luis took you to the Mission of San Francisco Solano, Faith," he said in his quiet way. "It played a big part in our young lives. Our father and mother are buried there, beneath the stones in front of the altar."

"I know, Uncle Luis showed me," said Faith, "and one day Aunt Isabel and I went to put flowers on the grave of their poor little boy who died, in the new mountain cemetery near General Vallejo's house."

"A cheerful holiday, I must say," sniffed Content, and Hope, who had more social tact than her sister, cut in with "You were going to tell us about the picnic the Vallejo girls gave. Was it fun?"

So the touchy subject was averted for that time, but only a month later Content, paying a call on California Street, encountered her daughter Faith, accompanied by the maid who was supposed to be escorting her from a music lesson, coming out of the Catholic church which in that new city was already known as Old St. Mary's. The storm broke at home, and flying the banner of 'No Popery!' Content accused her daughter of crimes ranging from underhandedness and duplicity to simony, Mariolatry and a belief in transubstantiation. Most of this passed above the criminal's head, but poor Faith, badgered to confess that Luis and Isabel had attempted to pervert her Protestant faith, blurted out that one day when they were driving Cousin Maria had told her a beautiful story about a saintly nun, known in the world as Concepcion Arguëllo, who gave her whole life to good works among the poor. It was to light a candle to the 'blessed memory' of this nun, in religion Sister Maria Dominga, that Faith had gone with Mary Donovan – not for the first time – to Old St. Mary's. Had she discussed these visits in the servants' hall, with Biddy the cook and the other servants? Yes, she had. Whereupon, with one exclamation of "Irish trash!" Content dismissed her entire staff and replaced them at a day's notice by Chinese domestics.

"Let's hope they won't convert us all to Buddhism," was Jimmy's joke when he came home from school. His mother forgave it because he was Jimmy, who could do no wrong, but she fired off a letter to Sonoma, accusing Maria of corrupting her cousin, and she greeted her husband when he came home with a dramatic appeal: "Talk to your daughter! Deliver her from the seductions of the Scarlet Woman!"

"I'll talk to her when she's fit to talk to me," said Philip. "Hope says she's cried herself sick." She had; it was two hours before Faith was composed enough to sit quietly beside her father on the big sofa in the library and tell him what she had learned of the life of Alta California's tragic heroine, Doña Concepcion Arguëllo. As might have been expected little Maria had stressed the romantic side of the story. Concha's love for the Russian, Rezanov, and his death while speeding home to St. Petersburg to ask the Czar's leave to marry her were what had thrilled the child, while to Faith, older and more inclined to religious thought, it was the fifty years of loneliness and work for others, ending with Concha's reception into the first community of nuns to be established in California, which made the powerful appeal.

"Yes, darling, hers was a sad life and a sainted one," said Philip gently, "and you're right to give thanks, when you pray, for all she was able to accomplish here on earth below. But you were wrong to do what mamma disapproves of, and keep your visits to St. Mary's a secret. You must tell her you're sorry for having offended her. But you can tell her, too, that papa understands."

The girl hugged him speechlessly but seemed to shake her head. Philip Estrada said, "Be brave and tell her now."

"Papa, do you think Concepcion Arguëllo – Sister Maria Dominga – should be canonised as a saint?"

"Oh, wait, my dear, that's going too far. I said she led a sainted life, a deeply religious life, but she was very human, Faith. Her religion was her compensation for the loss of her lover." She looked at him uncomprehendingly, and her father said, "Rezanov and Concha are two of the old ghosts of Spanish California, and when Maria de las Mercedes told you their story they lived again."

After she left him Philip Estrada sat alone in the dusk of his handsome room, thinking of two other ghosts whose story he had done his best to bury in oblivion, and remembering the picnic at Fort Ross when the story of Rezanov and Concha had been repeated to his sister Rosalie and her own Russian lover. He wondered if Concepcion Arguëllo's fifty years' imprisonment in heartbreak had really been preferable to Rosalie's terrible release.

★ ★ ★

The end of the Civil War in 1865, with General Lee's surrender at Appomattox on April 12, was followed two days later – on Good Friday – by the assassination of President Abraham Lincoln. The president was shot in a Washington theatre, but the play was that San Francisco standby, *Our American Cousin*, and the assassin had been well known in San Francisco as a young actor, John Wilkes Booth.

When the news reached the city on the Pacific, a night of rioting broke out which recalled the worst excesses of the Sydney Ducks, the Hounds and the Vigilantes. Drunken quarrels ended in broken bottles and broken heads, gunplay followed brutal beatings, and the jails could hardly hold all those on charges ranging from breach of the peace to man-slaughter. All the theatres were closed and draped in purple or black, the only decently quiet spots in a city where the long-simmering antagonism between North and South had erupted in a final burst of anger.

What effect the death of Mr. Lincoln had upon the upward career of Robert Cord was never known. He had beaten the long-established Gwin in the 1861 election for US Senator, and in co-operation with the Governor of California, Leland Stanford, had lobbied industriously for the Central Pacific Railroad, now under construction. He was known to be close to Lincoln, and was tipped in the Capitol for a minor place in the first post-war cabinet, but that situation changed when the vice-president, Andrew Johnson, succeeded Mr. Lincoln and Robert Cord settled for a second term of office in the Senate.

Whether, as Jerry Lasalle once asserted, he had presidential ambitions, also remained an enigma. He was not really equip-ped to cope with the problems of Reconstruction, and with the same patience as he had shown when he was an undercover man for Vallejo among the Indians and the Russian settlers, he began to work out a long-term plan to become Governor of California himself.

When her husband was first elected to the US Senate, Leona Cord rented their house in Sacramento to an ambitious young assemblyman, and started life all over again in Washington, DC. She was the natural means of reconciling Cord with his runaway son Ivanhoe, for the young man, joining the US Navy at New Orleans, was with Farragut's squadron when the admiral forced the boom on the Mississippi and laid siege to Vicksburg. There young Cord was wounded, severely enough to be hospitalised in Washington. After an affecting reunion at the sailor's bedside (well publicised in the California press), the boy was honourably discharged from the Navy and placed by his father in a government office which could lead eventually to a posting abroad. Mr. Ivan Cord was thought well of by his new masters, and was still in a lowly enough position to be unaffected by the chaos in Washington which followed the shooting of Abraham Lincoln.

With the governorship of California in view, Robert Cord decided to spend more time in the state during his second term of office as its US Senator than he had done in his first. He began by renting a compact furnished house on Stockton Street in San Francisco, and announced that he and his family would live there when the Senate was not actually in session. Then, without waiting for Leona to arrive with the young people, Mr. Cord set out with a party of influential business-men for Alaska.

"Come with us, Phil," he urged his old friend, making one of his first calls at the offices of Estrada and Putnam. "It'll be a historic occasion, and a great opportunity for looking over a new field for development."

" 'Fraid it's out of the question, Robert," Philip sighed. He looked enviously at his friend. Cord was fifty-seven now, eight years older than himself, and as he sat straddled across a chair, braced and taut as ever, he made Philip feel weak and flabby. He was eager for the new adventure of attending the formal ceremony of the handing over of Alaska to the United States. The Russians had had enough; the day of the Russian-American Fur Company was over, and the Czar had no need of a distant and costly possession. Not without accusations in Washington of Russian gold passing beneath the negotiating table, Alaska had been purchased by Mr. Seward, Secretary of State, for the modest sum of $7 million in March 1867, and in October the formal transfer of power would take place.

"Why out of the question? Aren't you well? You don't look too good," said the senator, noting the other man's grey pallor.

"It's the old trouble with my heart. Content would worry

herself sick if I took off on a trip to Alaska, and she's had plenty
to worry her lately."

"Something wrong?"

"I don't know if you could call it wrong. Faith was received
into the Catholic church last week."

Cord whistled. "That would be a knock for Content."

"It was."

"But not for you?"

"I said I couldn't be sorry the child had decided to return to
the faith of her fathers."

He had said a great deal more than that. He had said to his
wife, "Let me remind you that you and I were married in the
Church, twenty-three years ago. Let me remind you that for
all that time I've deferred to your prejudices, given in to your
wishes about the children's christenings, and listened to the
ranting of your Presbyterian pastors, but I'm damned if I'm
going to let you make Faith miserable because she has the
courage of her own convictions. I'll stand by her at her
baptism in Old St. Mary's, and I'll attend mass with her
whenever she asks me to; and I'll thank you, madam, to add
something that's lacking in this fine house of yours, and I
mean peace and tranquillity."

He sighed, remembering the scene, and Robert Cord said
kindly, "Never mind, Phil, I can see the trip to Alaska's out.
I'll tell you all about it when I come back."

"You're a busy man, Robert. I wonder why you've taken it
into your head to go on this picnic to Sitka? The papers have
been full of it for days."

"I got a pressing invitation to join the party, simply because
I'm one of the old hands who remember the Russian days in
Alta California. As you do too, of course."

"I remember." He remembered again, and vividly, when
Robert Cord came back bronzed from the sea voyage which
ended just before the autumn storms began, and described the
last hours of Russian America. Sitka had been "an eye-
opener", he said. Much more of a town than he'd expected,
with a hospital, schools, shops and everything, but all run
down as if St. Petersburg had been cutting off supplies for a
year or two. All but the Orthodox cathedral of St. Michael,
which Cord had visited out of curiosity, and which was

dazzling with gold leaf and the Russian paintings they called ikons on the walls. Then the ceremony had been unexpectedly moving when Matusov, the last Russian Governor of Alaska, stood to attention as his country's flag was hauled down, and the Stars and Stripes hoisted in its place.

"They looked a bedraggled little crowd, the Russkies," said Cord, "and they'd be smart to get out fast. I didn't like the look of the new military governor. He's a tough Yankee officer who went through the whole Civil War hampered with the name of Jefferson Davis, like the Confederate president, and I fancy he means to take it out on the Alaskans."

"What did your business friends think of the commercial possibilities?"

"Nix. No fertility and no natural resources, apart from furs and fishing. No wonder they're calling Alaska 'Seward's Folly'. Well, I don't suppose we'll hear of the Russkies again."

Cord had little more to say of Sitka. Apart from the Orthodox cathedral it seemed to have made no impression upon him. And yet Philip Estrada would have liked to hear more of the place for which his sister meant to set sail with her lover. He remembered her weeping, "We were to have been married at Sitka!" and his harsh, intolerant boy's voice jeering, "You fool, he would have abandoned you at Sitka!" He knew better now. He knew that if Peter Gagarin had lived, they would have been married in front of the gold ikonostasis in St. Michael's Cathedral. Ghosts of Spanish California, he had called those other lovers. Oh, poor ghosts, how tirelessly they walked!

But after the possession of Alaska dropped out of the news from sheer lack of public interest in the remote and barren acquisition, Philip and his family were glad the Cords had come back to San Francisco. Leona's company, always welcome, seemed to take Content's mind off her objections to Faith's conversion, among which 'going to church with the servants' was the least offensive. The house on Pine Street grew lively again. Faxon Cord, now fifteen, struck up a friendship with Jim Estrada, who was one year younger. Faxon had his father's red hair without his father's grace. He was a short, stocky boy with a heavy jaw.

The girls of the two families were less congenial. Rowena

and Jeanie Deans Cord (who boxed their brother Faxon's ears when he called them 'Weenie and Jeanie') were slightly older and a great deal more sophisticated than the two Estradas. They were tall, handsome girls with black hair and fine complexions, who had been spoiled in Washington and could talk of nothing but military balls and the *corps diplomatique*. Faith thought them worldly; Hope resented their challenge to her own position as an acknowledged belle.

"I don't think they're so very beautiful, mamma," she complained. "So tall! With long necks like geese! And so *bosomy*! They'll be as fat as their mother one of these days."

"They're not as smart as you are, dearie. Don't you fret," said Content. She had always admired Hope's 'smartness', the 'down-East' quality inherited from the Putnams, which in the first place had turned a plain child into a really pretty girl. Though she still had to pad her satin bodices with lawn handkerchiefs, Hope had worked successfully on her skin and hair. She had learned the delicate use of rouge, and camomile rinses had turned her sandy locks to pale gold, while her stubby little hands were always perfectly groomed and gloved. Content, who had never cared a fig for her own looks, admitted it was hard for a petite charmer like her daughter to be eclipsed by the great strapping Amazons from Stockton Street.

But Hope Estrada had been smart enough to take advantage of her expensive schooling. Having no talent for sketching and singing, the usual accomplishments of young ladies of leisure, she had concentrated on languages, and could chatter amusingly in French and German. She endeared herself to Mrs. Cord by introducing her to Balzac in translation, for Leona, since her husband's foolish infatuation with Laura Winter, had retreated more and more into the world of books, and found her happiness in the pages of Dickens and Thackeray. This was only one instance of Hope's social ability. While the Cord girls flirted with the young officers from the Presidio, Hope flattered older people by talking to them about their own interests, and became as good a listener as she was a talker. She had all her mother's driving energy, but was 'smart' enough to see that Content's domineering had undermined her marriage, and was determined not to repeat the pattern in her own life. In short, she was just the wife Ivanhoe Cord was looking for, when he came to San Francisco to pay a farewell visit to his family.

Ivan Cord at twenty-five was a great improvement on the angry boy of eighteen who had run off to enlist in Farragut's squadron. A war hero, handsome and successful, he had been appointed an attaché on the staff of Mr. Elihu B. Washburne, who was shortly to take up his duties as the United States Minister Plenipotentiary to the Court of the Emperor Napoleon III. Although his sisters complained that 'that pert little Hope' had set her cap at Ivan from the moment he appeared in San Francisco, the truth was that he saw in her a girl who would help to advance his career at any court in Europe, and within a month they were engaged. Hope, smiling up at 'Weenie and Jeanie', talked of the Court of the Tuileries and her intention to complete her trousseau in Paris. She was sure that the long reign of the crinoline was nearly over. But after feverish consultations with her dressmaker she wore hoops on her wedding day, and in a great bell of white lace and tulle was married to Ivan Cord under the even bigger bell of white roses which decorators installed in the drawing room of the Pine Street house. Described by the press as 'brilliant' and 'ultra-fashionable' it was an occasion for which the house might have been built, and the ultimate touch of 1868 chic was the departure of the bride and groom by train for Calistoga.

A honeymoon, as distinct from a bride's wedding journey to her new home, was something of an innovation. Calistoga, with its natural springs of mineral water, was another novelty, a resort developed for health and pleasure at the terminal of the Napa Valley Railroad. It was not an exciting journey for a couple whose ultimate destination was Paris, but the bridegroom's mother, following them in imagination, would have been comforted if she had seen the eagerness with which Hope took off her bridal bonnet and flung herself into her husband's arms as soon as the private car which Ivan had secured left the San Francisco station. Leona Cord, in the middle of reading *East Lynne*, would have liked to look on at a betrothal more romantic, tragic and chivalrous than Ivan and Hope's, which seemed to revolve round marriage settlements and wedding garments. But as the little train made its slow

way through the acres of vineyards in the Napa valley whatever had been practical in Ivan Cord's courtship gave way to
passion, and at each whistle stop the heady scent of the grapes
and foliage of the vintage season teased the senses of the two
who had never dared to be lovers before they were made man
and wife.

The letters which began to arrive from Europe were a clear
proof that the young Cords were happy. There was of course a
good deal about ceremonial, beginning with the presentation
of Minister Washburne's letters of credence at the Tuileries,
and Jimmy and Faxon thought there was a great deal too much
about fashion. But Hope was an excellent correspondent, if
given to showing off her French, and there was something in
her letters to please everybody. The schoolboys were thrilled
at her account of Ivan's part in an imperial boar hunt at
Compiègne, and Faith glowed at her description of the rose
windows in the cathedral of Notre Dame. Content heard all
about the furnished apartment in the rue du Bac and the
shortcomings of French *bonnes* and *femmes de chambre*, and
Philip noted the acute little remarks on politics which began to
appear in the girlish letters. There were pressures on the
Emperor to abandon his dictatorship and accept a liberal
Constitution, wrote Hope. The question of the Spanish succession was going to be troublesome. Plans were already being
made for the Empress to lead the naval procession at the
opening of the Suez Canal, constructed by her kinsman Ferdi-
nand de Lesseps, which from November onwards would
shorten the road to India. Did papa think all this pomp was
another case of bread and circuses?

"I do," said papa, when this particular letter was read aloud.
"The French Emperor is riding for a fall, in my opinion. But
the child is getting a grasp of affairs, I'm glad to see. She'll be a
great help to her husband in his career. Just as you were to me,
Content," he added as an afterthought, and his wife smiled
queerly. She was not a sensitive woman, but she knew that
their marriage was not what it had been before she had
overborne his wish to investigate the childhood of Laura
Winter. She turned the conversation to the Suez Canal, aware
that to a San Franciscan that waterway, or any highway or
railway for that matter, was of small importance compared

with the great transcontinental railroad which would be completed when the Union Pacific and the Central Pacific tracks
were joined in Utah. Senator Cord had promised Jimmy
Estrada and his own boy, Faxon, that they should witness the
driving of what was already called The Last Spike.

It was only two weeks before the ceremony, fixed for May
10, that Mrs. Philip Estrada stopped in the reading aloud of a
letter from Hope at the family breakfast table. It was the usual
heavily underlined epistle, telling of a garden party at the
Château de St. Cloud, given for the younger members of the
corps diplomatique.

We drove out with Amy and Ned Mortimer. I've told
you about them; he's one of the attachés on Lord Lyons's
staff at the British Embassy, and *great fun*. It was very
warm for April, so we all strolled in the lovely gardens
and had *refreshments* in tents among the flowers. The
Emperor and Empress came out, but not to *faire cercle*, it
was all *quite informal*, and the Empress certainly didn't
look her best. I began to feel quite funny myself –

Here Content stopped, and ran her eye down the page.

"The rest of it's all about fashion," she said. "I sometimes
feel Hope thinks she's writing for the *Gazette Rose*. Jim, you'll
be late for school. Faith, please go to the kitchen and make sure
Ho Chung understands about the vegetable order. Philip,
another cup of coffee?"

"Why have you made the dining room a desert, my dear?"
asked Philip when they were alone. "What was in Hope's
letter unsuitable for juvenile ears? Is it the baby news we've
been hoping for?"

"No baby news," said Content. "Here. You'd better read it
for yourself."

"I left my spectacles upstairs," said Philip, and handed back
the letter. "Tell me what she says."

I began to feel quite funny myself. [Content started
again] Do you remember taking Faith and me, when we
were little girls, to a performance of *Twelfth Night* at
Maguire's new theatre? There was a lovely girl who

played Viola, and disappeared from San Francisco *under mysterious circumstances*, they used to whisper about her at school. Well, dear mamma, there she was, *as large as life*, walking with the Emperor and the Empress and seemingly *au mieux* with them both! She wore a dress of violet taffeta with an apron front and ruchings at the back, with her hair swept up under a tiny hat and veil to match, and the *smartest satin boots*! She didn't cast a glance *at the likes of us*, but unfurled her lace parasol as she walked, and Ned Mortimer said, "Good old Marie-Laure de Marolles, true to the Bonaparte violets!" which made Amy laugh.

I said, "How do you mean, Marie-Laure de Marolles? Her name was Laura Winter when she was on the stage in San Francisco; I've seen her act." And Ned said, "She was Madame Lasalle when she came to Paris first, with a river-boat gambler from New Orleans, and they did so well with their high-class card game in the Rue du Cirque that first they met the Emperor's bastard brother, the Duc de Morny, and then it was an easy step to the Emperor himself. He created her Comtesse de Marolles by letters patent and set her up in a house of her own in the rue de l'Elysée, and – well, she's a damned good-looker, that's all I can say!" So Ivan said, "And quite enough too, let's change the subject, Ned!" But I asked, I simply *could not help it*, "What became of the gambler?" and Mr. Mortimer laughed and said, "He was lost in the shuffle."

"Is that all?" said Philip Estrada. He had not moved during the recital, but sat with his chin on his locked hands, staring at the tablecloth.

"Isn't it enough?" It would have been enough if Content had folded up the letter and gone about her housekeeping, but as she had never in her life known where to draw the line she was goaded by her husband's silence into the taunt:

"Fine goings on! The Duc de Morny! The mistress of the Emperor of the French! I told you there was no need to waste any sympathy on that little adventuress –"

"She ought to have been the Princess Gagarin," said Philip, and rising, he left the room.

⋆   ⋆   ⋆

There was a postscript to this letter, but it was not written for twenty months, and not by Hope Cord. Ivan Cord had been promoted to Third Secretary and posted to Vienna, where he and Hope were happily awaiting the birth of their first child when the agony of France began. The Emperor had ridden to his fall, and the Prussians had defeated the French in a bloody war when news came to California of the gambler who had been lost in the shuffle because the stakes he played for were too high. Philip Estrada read the paragraph in the San Francisco *Chronicle*, but he read it at the office and said nothing about it at home.

Word has been received here [said the *Chronicle*] of the death in a sortie from the besieged city of Paris of Mr. Jerome Lasalle, a popular figure in the early days of Nevada City. Mr. Archibald Forbes, the British war correspondent, writes in the London *Daily News*: "Captain Lasalle, who joined the Army of the Republic after the revolution of September 4, was known as a brave man and a gallant fighter. He fell in the battle of December 21, which raged from dawn to dusk on the Plain of Avron after a French sortie to recapture the village of Le Bourget, and was one of nearly a thousand men found frozen to death next day. His friends will regret that he did not live to see the liberation of Paris, on which his heart was set."

Mr. Lasalle is survived by his wife, the former Clarisse Cavelier of New Orleans.

Jerry Lasalle, who had believed in no cause, not even the South's dead truth, had found his cause at last, and died for it.

2

The year 1871 had hardly begun when Philip Estrada read Jerome Lasalle's obituary, and he supposed it was a sign of growing old that the next five years seemed to pass like so many weeks. Suddenly it was 1876 and the Centennial was upon them: not only the centenary of the Declaration of Independence but – far more important to San Franciscans – the hundred years' anniversary of the coming of the Spanish and the building of the Presidio and the Mission of San Francisco de Asís, now called the Mission Dolores.

It was also exactly thirty years since the American Conquest. Thirty years since the pueblo of Yerba Buena turned into San Francisco, and every one of the scant three decades had seen an immense leap into the future. The Gold Rush, the Silver Bonanza, the transcontinental railroad were landmarks in the great changes, social and physical, and Philip Estrada recognised that his old dream of putting the Estrada brand on the city had come true only for a very short time. The men who put their marks on the city of the Sixties and Seventies were the Silver Kings, as the four Irishmen were called who made their fortunes on the Comstock, and the Big Four, from the eastern seaboard via Sacramento, who were the bosses of the Central Pacific Railroad. All these men were known nationally and internationally: one who had made his mark further than the city was the Honourable Robert Cord, now in his second term as Governor of California.

The age of opulence had succeeded to the age of ostentation, and with the invention of the cable car, climbing the heights by mechanical means, even Fern Hill was conquered. The trees and chaparral were cleared away and the palaces of the great men were built, so that Fern became Nabob, or Snob, or finally plain Nob Hill, its main artery being California Street.

"How furious Hope would be," said Jim Estrada, when the great mansions were going up on the block above their house, "if she knew we might have gone on to California when we stopped on Pine!"

"Much Hope cares," sniffed his mother. "She's never come back to see us once in all those years!"

"It's a hell of a trip from Vienna with two little kids, ma."

"At least Ivan might have come home when his own mother was dying. Leona had her two girls with her; mine are so far away."

"Faith loves to have you visit her at Benicia, you know that."

"Benicia's further away than Vienna, as far as I'm concerned."

"Come on, ma, you know she's very happy where she is."

The years had brought to the families now united by marriage some sorrows and some happiness. Faith's vocation, and her reception into the Dominican sisterhood of Santa Catalina de Siena, had been a bitter pill for Content to swallow. But Faith was a happy novice and a happier nun, and as St. Catherine's was not an enclosed convent, but included a girls' boarding school, Faith as Sister Cecilia was happiest of all as a teacher of music. "And I'm sure," said her mother, "if all she wanted to do was teach snivelling brats the piano, she could have done that at home without all this hullabaloo."

Beyond the walls of St. Catherine's, where Concepcion Arguëllo lay buried, there was marrying and giving in marriage. Weenie and Jeanie Cord continued their flirtatious careers to the altar, Rowena marrying an impecunious young captain from the Presidio and moving with him and their children up the ladder of promotion and from one army post to another. Jeanie Deans married a young Alsatian doctor who left Strasbourg after the Franco-Prussian War and started a practice in Sacramento. Isaac Scherer was clever and amiable, and in the private belief that it would bring in the Jewish vote Governor Cord encouraged the marriage. It turned out well for the young couple and for himself, because after his wife's death the Scherers came to live in the governor's official residence and were a help in every way. Leona Cord was only fifty-three when she died of a neglected cold which turned into bronchitis and then bronchial pneumonia, and her death hit her husband hard. He sat by her bed and held her hand, seeing beyond the grey head on the pillow to the black hair of the girl who had trudged beside him through the passes of the Rockies with her book bag on her shoulder. The books were there as they had always been, piled high on her bedside table to the annoyance of the nurses, and sometimes Leona asked to be read to, and then complained that they all read so badly. The printed word, not the human voice, had always been the story medium for Leona, and as her mind began to wander she thought her grieving daughters were the book friends who had enriched her life, and called them Beatrix Esmond and

Maggie Tulliver. The night nurse was deeply religious and read to her from the New Testament. When death came to Leona in her sleep, the good woman thought her cheek was pillowed on the Bible. It turned out to be a battered copy of *David Copperfield*.

So life and death brought them to the Centennial, and although some of the older generation felt they had little to celebrate, Jim Estrada meant to turn the occasion into what his Uncle Luis still called a fiesta. Jim was now twenty-two, not as like Luis as he had been: less Spanish but more 'down-East' in a mixture which made him a very attractive young man. He was not tall, but taller than his father, with dark hair and grey eyes, run after by girls and well-liked by men, the life and soul of all the parties and riding picnics. He was very persuasive. He had healed the breach between his parents and the family at Sonoma and even got his mother to attend her elder daughter's Clothing. The only drawback was, his father said, he was no damned good at business.

He had begun well enough. Jim Estrada finished school with credit, like his friend Faxon Cord, and Dr. Durant had assured both their fathers that they were equipped to enter any eastern college, or better still, the university for which he had just received the charter. The Peralta rancho, where Luis Estrada first saw his future wife, was now the towns of Oakland, Berkeley and Alameda, and Dr. Durant, with his partner the Rev. S. H. Willey, had proved such an effective teacher that he became the first president of the University of California at Oakland with the prospect of moving to a larger campus at Berkeley if the student body increased in numbers. Jim and Faxon declared they had all the schooling they needed and were eager to get to work. Faxon predictably found a job in the Central Pacific office in San Francisco, and Philip Estrada, who had been afraid that the Cord influence would lead Jim, too, into railroading, was delighted when the boy said he couldn't wait to get started at Estrada and Putnam. He took Jim to Montgomery Street with pride and gave him a desk in the counting house. It was only a month before Mr. Banks, the elderly chief cashier, told him privately, "I hate to say this, Mr. Estrada, but Mr. James lacks application."

That was the thing in a nutshell. When the boy worked he

worked quickly and well, but when he was sent on errands he loitered round the Exchange or the wharves until he forgot what he was sent out to do, and if an answer were required, came back with the wrong one. He returned late from lunch and left too early in the evening. The other juniors were beginning to protest.

"Remember it's all new to him, Mr. Banks," said Philip. "If there's no improvement in another month, I'll talk to him."

At the end of the month 'Mr. James' told his father he thought the counting house was a beastly bore; old Banks was always hunting him about his 3s and his 5s, his 7s and his 9s, and he hadn't been taught double entry at Dr. Durant's school.

"Your mother taught me double entry when I was a young ranchero fresh from Salmon Creek. Would you like her to do a refresher course with you?"

Jim shuddered exaggeratedly. "No thanks! I bet ma would be as tough about ruling lines as old Banks is."

"Ruling *lines*?"

"Yes. He wants a double line ruled at the bottom of each statement – now wait a minute – the lower line has to be *thicker* than the top line, and exactly one quarter of an inch wider on each side. As if it made any difference to selling real estate!"

"Now *you* wait a minute, Santiago. All these details are important to your training. You have to learn to be faithful over a few things before you can be ruler over many things –"

"Yes, I know, the parable of the talents. I've heard that read, or preached from, every few weeks since I was old enough to go to church."

"It's a favourite Presbyterian theme, and I happen to agree with it. When I was starting out in business –"

"Excuse me, pa," interrupted Jimmy, "there's something I've always wanted to ask you. How *did* you get your start in business? Why didn't you carry on ranching with Uncle Luis?"

Philip said, "Lucky for you and your sisters that I didn't. Else I'd have been robbed by the Land Commissioners too." It gave him time to think, to concoct a reply other than the true one, which would have been, "I got my start through a marriage settlement made thirty years ago, and two violent deaths.''

"Poor old Uncle Luis hasn't had much luck. You haven't answered my question, pa.''

"No. Well, I got my start through your grandfather Putnam, who had some money saved up, and we started this firm in partnership. Now tell me your objections to it.''

That night when they were alone he said to his wife: "I had a long talk with Jim today, about his work.''

"You did? I thought he was very quiet at dinner. Nothing's the matter, is it?''

"He hasn't been overworking, certainly. But I think I made a mistake when I put him into the counting house straight from school.''

"He's known since he was twelve that he'd be going into the business –''

"That's just it. The whole thing has been too much of a foregone conclusion, and now he's started in it, buying and selling real estate seems a pedestrian occupation to our James. He wants to take a year off and see the world.''

"At eighteen?'' gasped Content.

"As good an age as any. Now try not to worry too much, my dear – he wants to go to sea.''

"Like my father!''

"Well, hardly like your father. Captain Putnam was a master mariner who rounded Cape Horn half a dozen times, with yourself aboard once, and knew the whaling grounds like the back of his hand. Jimmy doesn't mean to start out before the mast –''

"I should hope not!''

"– One of his new friends has offered him a job as assistant purser on the Pacific Mail run to Hong Kong.''

There was almost as much 'hullabaloo' in Pine Street about Jimmy's departure for the Far East as there had been about Faith's conversion, but Content, having wept and raged in private, put a good face on it in public, praised her son's initiative, and said, which was true, that many a young man had sailed through the Golden Gate to make his fortune in the Orient. Jimmy departed with enthusiasm. He made one voyage to Hong Kong, where a day's shore leave convinced him that all prospects of trade with California were being stifled by the British, and one to Hawaii, as the Sandwich Islands were now called. He told Faxon Cord that there seemed to be possibilities in sugar in Hawaii, and Faxon, a far less amiable but more aggressive young man, said he might go out and have a look-see himself; but Jimmy had had enough of seafaring, and returned to the comfort of his father's house and his father's firm. Philip had the good sense to employ him as an outside man 'down the Peninsula', where housing developments were springing up round Palo Alto, Menlo Park and Belmont. There the new millionaires were building country homes in every style of European architecture from the Norman keep to the Palladian villa, with one or two *châteaux* on the Loire thrown in. Jimmy talked glibly to the customers, but at home he began to speak bitterly of the uneven distribution of wealth and the life that men like Ralston, Flood and Sharon lived compared with the deckhands of the steamship lines.

"My dear fellow," said his father wearily, "it's a long time since *Two Years Before the Mast* was published, and you'll never beat Mr. Dana as the champion of the ordinary seaman. You're not going to turn into a radical, are you?"

"No, but I think the workers ought to organise –"

That was as far as they had got by the time of the Centennial, when Jimmy suppressed his radical feelings in favour of patriotism and made the family celebrations memorable. San Francisco prepared for a great Fourth of July, with fire crackers going off through the night before, the ships in port dressed overall and the morning streets crowded with families in their best clothes and on their best behaviour. There were to be fireworks later in the evening, doubtless in more senses than one, and also the first display of electric lighting ever seen in San Francisco, arranged by Father Joseph Neri, SJ, along the façade of St. Ignatius College on Market Street. Every guest at the luncheon for fifty people in the Estrada house on Pine Street, arranged by Jimmy and efficiently catered by his mother, intended to go to see the electric lights after darkness fell, on the way to some evening celebration like a ball or concert.

Jimmy had actually got the Estradas from Sonoma to come to town, and Dr. and Mrs. Scherer from Sacramento would chaperone Maria Estrada at the mayor's ball. Maria, plump and timid at twenty-six, had never been at a ball in her life, and was sure her dress would be unsuitable, but she enjoyed the luncheon immensely, and was ready to stand up and drain her glass when her Uncle Philip proposed the toast of the United States of America. She was surprised, and so was Philip, when her father rose immediately after to propose the health of their hostess.

Luis Estrada, as he told his brother, was only a small farmer now, having been obliged to sell eight hundred of his last thousand acres – not to the Buena Vista winery but to new-comers, Italian vintners called Olivetti. He was still a *hidalgo* when he stood up with his glass in his hand, haggard and handsome in his well-brushed old black suit, and his compli-ments to Content were spoken in graceful English. Then, in his majestic mother tongue, he added a few words which not everybody understood, but which were obviously spoken with feeling.

"In honouring the United States," he said, "which at great cost has fulfilled its manifest destiny, let us also honour the Spanish pioneers who dreamed a dream which has not been fulfilled. In drinking the health of Señora Doña Contenta, who bestowed her hand on a Californio, let us at the same time drink to the Spanish who made the great journey from the City of Mexico in New Spain, and founded the future city of San Francisco."

He sat down to applause, and when the guests rose from the table Jimmy was the first to bow with the respect due to the head of his family and say, "Congratulations, sir! You said it beautifully – and it needed to be said."

★　　★　　★

The Governor of California was unable to join his friends in Pine Street at their celebration of the centenary Fourth of July. He attended a civic luncheon with the mayor and the Board of Supervisors, the commandant of the Presidio, the Engineer-Admiral in command of the Navy Yard and other local celebrities. He had to listen to their long-winded oratory and then, last in the list of speakers (a place chosen by himself in the awareness that the star speaks last) Robert Cord spoke for less than ten minutes on the future of California. He knew that if he kept it short the exhausted reporters would give him the best press of the day, and he had been speaking in public for so long that he could make-them-laugh, make-them-cry, make-them-wait by reflex action. The mayor, not a long-winded speaker himself, said "Thank you, Governor! We'll look forward to hearing you again in October," and they exchanged grim smiles. October 8 had been fixed for the centenary of the Mission Dolores, where there was to be an outdoor pontifical mass and sermon by Bishop Alemany and an address by California's Grand Old Man, Don Mariano Vallejo – each calculated to say nothing of any importance for ninety minutes by the clock.

Robert Cord dined privately with the mayor and went with his party to the municipal ball, where he dragged the mayor's lady, a heavyweight, through one set of lancers and then took leave. He was staying at the St. Francis Hotel, one of the latest of that name, which in a mid-town location was conveniently placed for the governor to receive a visitor, the deputy chief of police. The man brought with him a written police report on the day's doings, which Cord studied carefully when he had gone. It was after midnight, and the day had passed without arson or manslaughter, or undue violence of any sort, except at a demonstration on the sand-lots above Market Street, where an agitator named Sean Kennedy had addressed a rabble on behalf of the Workingmen's Party, and after demanding 'a little judicious hanging of capitalists' in general, had specified the hanging of the governor to a sourapple tree. The police broke up the meeting, and the chief himself had added a note after Kennedy's name: "Drayman. New recruit of Denis Kearney's. Recent immigrant from Ireland, County Wexford."

Governor Cord, with his flair for undercover investigation, had received a number of reports on Denis Kearney, himself a drayman and an Irish immigrant from County Cork. The Workingmen's Party of California, under his leadership, had diverged from its eastern counterpart, which was Marxist in inspiration, and along with its demands for the unionisation of labour and the destruction of land monopoly by taxation, had a virulent undercurrent of racism. Kearney had a real Irish chip on his shoulder. He felt inferior to the Anglo-Saxon Protestants that day celebrating their independence, and the only way to feel superior was to pick on an ethnic group which could be pushed still further down the social scale. A group was ready to Comrade Kearney's hand: the Chinese.

Cord drew the window curtains and looked out. The last Roman candle had flared across the night sky, and the sound of the revellers was beginning to die away. It was a fine July night in San Francisco, where thousands of people had that day celebrated their Americanism. But Cord, who remembered the Indian days, and the Russian days which followed, knew there was not one conglomerate 'America' in the city. There was a powerful group who thought of themselves as Irishmen first and Americans second, there were the dispossessed Hispanics, many of them below the poverty line; there were the Chinese, living by other rules and faiths in their own inner city. He was not strong enough to knit them all together. All he could do was try to keep the peace.

That aspect of his duty as governor came back to Cord again and again during the months which followed. It was clear that Denis Kearney, the Sand-lot Orator as he was called from the wasteland where he plied his trade of rabble-rouser, was going from excess to excess in his pursuit of power. He was agitating for a new constitutional convention, for the eight-hour day, for the regulation of railroads and utilities, for all of which a good case could be made, but he mingled whatever was sensible with incitement to riot and racial hate. There had been one fracas on Nob Hill when Governor Cord thought the Riot Act should have been read. There was a constant harassment of the Chinese population, who were among the quietest and most hardworking members of the community, but who having another language and another colour of skin from the chronically resentful Irish were thought worthy of their contempt. The violence of Kearney's language did not stop at the Chinese. His supposed championship of the underdog won him followers among small farmers and businessmen, as well as ambivalent liberals like Jim Estrada. A fair example of his style lay on Cord's desk one morning, reported in the Sacramento papers:

The Central Pacific men are thieves, and will soon feel the power of the workingmen. When I have thoroughly organised my party we will march through the city and compel the thieves to give up their plunder. I will lead you to the city hall, clear out the police force, hang the prosecuting attorney, burn every book that has a particle of law in it, and then enact new laws for the workingmen.

It was a direct call to anarchy. The Republican governor knew quite well what the Democrats expected him to do, which was to keep clear of San Francisco, sit tight in the Capitol at Sacramento until his term was over, and then pass the buck to his successor. For the younger members of the opposition he was prehistoric, a mastodon from a Rocky Mountain canyon; for their elders he was little better than an amiable dunce with good looks and a seductive voice, the long-term catspaw of the Big Four. "God damn them all!" he swore, "I can't let the rot go on!" He remembered his secret ambition to be President, which Leona and one or two men had divined. Over the years since Lincoln's death he had sometimes thought he would have done as well as Andrew Johnson, who had been impeached before the Senate, or Ulysses S. Grant, whose second Administration had been riddled with bribe-taking and corruption from the Crédit Mobilier scandal to the Whiskey Ring. Now – "What a great President I would have been," he said to himself ironically, "*I*, who can't even handle Denis Kearney!"

But he was still the Governor of California, sitting in his office on the ground floor of the Capitol, with the chambers of the Senate and the Assembly above his head, and the great golden dome surmounted by a lantern and a ball above them all. Recently an unobtrusive little painter had been creeping in and out, working on the governor's portrait commissioned to hang in the Capitol after his term of office ended. He had agreed to give three sittings to an unknown artist, another refugee from Alsace, for whom Ike Scherer had somehow wheedled the commission. Cord believed the Legislature had got the refugee cheap, but Israel Klein had studied in Paris before he fought at Sedan, and seemed to know what he was doing. He painted Governor Cord in the conventional frock coat and white cravat, with his hand on a volume of jurisprudence which he had never read, and a great display of red plush curtain behind him. Mr. Klein had allowed his subject to see the work in progress after every sitting, and it seemed to be a good enough likeness.

That afternoon Jeanie Deans Scherer was taking her father to see the finished painting at the artist's studio on Front Street. He was disturbed enough by the Kearney situation to have broken any other engagement, but he wouldn't disappoint his daughter. They drove in his own carriage down K Street, and he pointed out the old Big Four headquarters, and what had been his office until he went to Washington in 1861.

"Are you sorry you sold your business, papa?"

"I couldn't run it from Washington, and Ivan and Fax have struck out on lines of their own, so it was nothing to them . . . Good heavens, how run down the old waterfront is! That's where the Pony Express office was, and there were theatres, two-bit houses as we used to call them . . . Is this the place?"

The carriage stopped at a shabby red-brick building, where Israel Klein occupied a loft with a north light, and Jeanie Deans took hold of her father's sleeve as they stood on the uneven pavement.

"Papa, let's walk a little way first. I've a confession to make. Ike and Mr. Klein and I played a little trick on you when you were sitting for your portrait. I – don't be angry, please! The picture you're going to see today isn't the one that was painted at the Capitol."

"D'you mean it's a picture of somebody else?"

"No – no, of course not; it's you. It's Mr. Klein's impression of the sketch that man made of you when you and mother were living in your first cabin on the Petaluma. It used to hang in your study in the L Street house –"

"That thing? I haven't seen it for years."

"It's been hanging in my own room since mamma died. I lent it to Mr. Klein, and he thought about it when he was painting you in the Capitol – and it's wonderful, papa!"

Cord allowed himself to be drawn inside the shabby building. Then a thought struck him, and he stopped at the foot of the rickety stair.

"But my dear girl," he protested, "the Legislature commissioned a picture of me as Governor, not when I was felling redwoods on the Petaluma. They'll think this is a joke in poor taste. They'll refuse to pay for it."

"Ike and I have thought of that," said Jeannie Deans quietly. "Wait until they see the picture. Maybe they'll *want* to have the picture of a pioneer in the Capitol, among all the lawyers and storekeepers on the walls. But if they don't, if they insist on having the one you sat for, then Ike and I will buy the other and be proud to have it in our home. Israel Klein is going to be famous when he goes back to Paris, and he's going soon."

Her father gave her an affectionate hug. "Don't be silly, Jeanie Deans," he said. "I won't let Ike and you be out of pocket because of your little joke, though I still don't understand it. Maybe we'd better go right upstairs and see the thing, eh?"

Three floors up, Israel Klein was waiting at his studio door to greet them – a different Klein, Cord noticed at once, from the self-effacing, obsequious little man who had slid in and out of the Capitol on his mission. He was wearing a smock, and baggy corduroy velvet trousers: the big empty studio, into which light was pouring across the farmlands and the wide Sacramento river, looked like a stage-set for *La Bohème*. There were more 'hand-painted pictures' on the walls than the Governor of California had ever seen in his life, and in the middle of the loft, set on an easel from which Klein whisked away a cotton curtain, was the Impressionist's portrait of himself.

It was like no picture he had ever seen. Klein had used the wandering artist's sketch, scrawled in charcoal, as the basis for a study in greens – the grey-green of the river, the grassy banks, the redwoods blotting out the sky – in which the only colour was the red hair and the blue shirt of the woodsman, reflected in the glint of metal from the axe he held. The powerful shoulders and thighs, the muscled arms, were heavy with virility, the face was his and yet not his, a young man's features coming through the governor's official mask presented to Klein in the red plush cage in the Capitol. It was the past and the present melded into one. The canvas had already been framed, in plain wood instead of the usual tortured imitation bronze, and under the space left for the plaque to carry Cord's name and the dates of his two terms as Governor of California, Klein had printed the title:

On the Banks of the Petaluma: 1841.

They were all quiet, Klein smiling slightly, satisfied with his work, and Mrs. Scherer so nervous that she finally broke the silence with "Well, papa? What do you think of it?"

"I like it," Robert Cord said slowly. "I like it very much. It isn't me. But it's the man I used to be."

Next day he told his official staff what he meant to do. The relatively small Chinese community in Sacramento had been tormented through the night by hoodlums shouting the slogan which was terrorising the Chinese in San Francisco, and the time had come to call a halt.

> The Chinese must go!
> Denis Kearney says so!

"By God, gentlemen!" said the governor, "I won't allow the shanty Irish to take over California! Get me a soapbox and I'll beat Denis Kearney on his own ground! Let the Mayor of San Francisco know, and give a statement to the press, that I'll speak on the sand-lot myself at six o'clock tomorrow evening –"

"What are you going to say, Governor?" cried the Attorney-General, hastily summoned to the conference. When he was told he shook his head. "Curtail the right of free speech and free assembly – you daren't do it, sir!"

"*Not I, but the man I used to be.*" The governor's voice was so low that the lawyer doubted if he had heard aright. They all spoke together then, the Lieutenant-Governor protesting that all their lives would be in danger if anything happened to Mr. Cord on the sand-lots of San Francisco: it would be the outbreak of a disastrous civil strife. The private secretary, on his own initiative, sent a telegraphic message to Mr. Faxon Cord at the Central Pacific headquarters, begging for his intervention. Mrs. Scherer was appealed to with no success. Raging and resolute, as on the night he had ridden from Salmon Creek to make the Bear Flaggers set Content Estrada free, Robert Cord travelled to San Francisco, and at six o'clock next evening mounted a makeshift platform on the sandy waste north of Market Street.

A daylight hour had deliberately been chosen, and yet many of the thousand men who had gathered carried lighted torches, which the police, who were thick on the ground, at once ordered them to put out. As fast as one flare was extinguished another was kindled, and it was on a sea of dappled lights that Faxon Cord looked down as he helped his father to the platform and jumped back to join Jim Estrada in the front rank of the pushing, muttering mass.

"Have you seen any sign of Denis Kearney?" asked Jim, and a stranger next him, taking up the query, said Dinnis, God bless him, wouldn't demean himself to come and listen to the owld blaygard, but Sean Kennedy was there to take notes of all the lies that were spoken. Faxon, who heard it all, looked up at his father, standing easily and confidently on the rickety platform, and muttered, "Crazy old fool! Magnificent old fool! I'm with him all the way."

There was not much further to go. The governor spoke above the hoarse murmur of the crowd, in an unusually harsh and penetrating voice. He told them that a bill was in process of being prepared for presentation to the State Legislature, calling for a new Constitutional Convention to supersede the convention held at Monterey in 1847. Every clause of the constitution would be submitted to and debated by the People at duly constituted public meetings before being voted on by their elected representatives. Meantime no outdoor rallies or demonstrations of any sort would be held in California for a period of six months from that night. If any such were held the Riot Act would be read forthwith and the crowd dispersed by the military. Any act of aggression against the Chinese members of the community would be punished by a severe prison sentence. Any – but there Robert Cord's witness to the man he used to be came to an end. He flung up his arms and fell headlong, shot in the back by Sean Kennedy and dying in his son's arms while the illicit torches, flaring up, turned the sand-lot into a scene from hell.

3

At the trial of Sean Kennedy for the murder of Robert Cord the prosecuting counsel, when he rose to address the jury, was shot at point-blank range by yet another resentful Irishman, and the proceedings were summarily halted. A new attorney led for the State, and Kennedy was duly hanged, being followed to the gallows a few weeks later by the court-room murderer.

It was a dual episode of violence remarkable even by San Francisco standards, and coming so soon after the self-congratulations of the Centennial made the more thoughtful citizens wonder how far they had really progressed in thirty years. At the same time the sudden death of Governor Cord was an indication that the first pioneers and leaders of the Conquest would soon be passing from the scene. During the Eighties the gaps in their number began to increase. It was remarkable how many of those who had been rich and power-ful died poor and helpless. Jacob Leese, who had once owned so much land at Yerba Buena and Sonoma, died in penury. Johan Sutter, who had long since been forced to leave Sutter's Fort, died while his claim to a government pension for his great services to California was still under discussion. Don Mariano Vallejo, who took three hundred servants with him when he went to his new villa outside Sonoma, had only one Chinese man-of-all-work, living in a hut opposite the back door, to wait on his wife and himself at the end of their lives. Vallejo lived to a great age and bore witness to a great cycle of material progress, for he, who had heard the coyotes whining as he lay down to bivouac on the ground of Yerba Buena, lived to hang a garland of evergreens on the narrow-gauge engine named 'The General Vallejo' when the Sonoma Railroad was completed. The old rough journey to the city by boat and horse was over; henceforth Sonoma ladies eager for a day's shopping could leave Sonoma at six-thirty in the morning and return at seven-thirty at night.

John C. Fremont, who had owned a fortune in gold in his

Mariposa mine, was another who died broke. In 1885 the Fremonts had given an interview to a young Harvard scholar called Josiah Royce. Born thirty years earlier in Grass Valley, California, about the time when Lola Montez was teaching Lotta Crabtree to dance, the young professor took a revisionist view of history. Refusing to call the Bear Flaggers heroes, he approached the Fremonts to ask for proof about their often repeated claims that Fremont was acting as a secret agent of the United States government in the Bear Flag revolt. The old couple hesitated, blundered, contradicted themselves, and finally could produce no proof of their statements. When Josiah Royce's *California* was published next year he declared that Fremont had lied about his part in the events of 1846, and with the Bear Flag men had wronged the innocent.

This book made Luis Estrada very happy. It was certainly the only English book he ever read from cover to cover, and he discussed Royce on Fremont endlessly with General Vallejo's younger brother, who had come back to Sonoma after a long residence in San Francisco. Luis and Salvador Vallejo had not been close friends as young men, but now they clung together as Californios who had never forgiven Fremont and the Bear Flaggers, nor the imprisonment of the Vallejos and Leese at Sutter's Fort. "Pike County blackguards!" was Vallejo's invariable description of his captors, and Maria de las Mercedes Estrada, pouring wine for the two old gentlemen, wondered if Pike County, Missouri, could really have produced such an army of blackguards as the angry Californios implied. It was a common insult, a retort to the ugly name of 'Greaser' which was still in use, and Maria supposed it did no harm. At least her father and Don Salvador stayed in their own homes for drinking and complaining. The time was past when they could with dignity appear at the old Blue Wing Inn, the El Dorado, the Union Hotel or the new Toscano. Sonoma, once a Mexican pueblo, was fast becoming an Italian town. The Olivettis, who had bought all Luis Estrada's remaining acres except two hundred, had their winery at Santa Rosa, where their Sonoma grapes were taken in carts, and they kept only a small work force in the valley. But a much larger concern, called Sebastiani, had set up in competition to Buena Vista and brought many more Italian workers to Sonoma. On Sundays the inns were full of their large families, eating enormous pasta dinners, and Garibaldi House, a new building on the east side of the plaza, became their social centre.

Out at what Luis Estrada still called the rancho, an Italian immigrant called Federico, or Rico, Gregorio was the foreman of the Olivetti vineyard workers. He lived with his wife and young family in the adobe built on the site of the weaving room where Isabel and Content Estrada were held prisoner by the Bear Flaggers, and Luis was impressed enough by the man's capacity for hard work to give him part-time employment as supervisor of what little arable land he had kept. As Luis became less able to ride through the valley, Gregorio came to the adobe in the plaza for his orders, entering by the garden gate and standing at the foot of the steps with his hat in his hand while Luis talked to him from the verandah above. He was a man in his forties, roughly dressed and in constant need of a shave, but there was something attractive in his large bear-like body and his deep warm voice. He was too shy to address the ladies, if they were present: a deep bow and a murmured "*Signorina!*" was all Maria Estrada ever had from him.

One day the Estradas learned, when milk from their own cows was delivered as usual at the adobe, that Gregorio's wife had died, a few weeks after the birth of a little girl.

"Oh, poor things!" said Maria to her father. "How many other children are there?"

"Three – two – I don't know. I've seen two little boys tumbling about in the yard."

"I wish there was something we could do to help."

"Send them food, Maria. A leg of lamb and cakes, something like that. There'll be a big gathering before the poor woman's buried."

"I meant really help." The pony carriage was a thing of the past. "If you'd lend me your horse, papa, I'd like to ride out and see how they're managing."

"You, querida? That would never do. Gregorio'll have plenty of his own kind to help out. And didn't that boy who brings the milk say some Italian woman was going to take the baby? Well, then! And your mother needs you at home."

In April Isabel Estrada died, at about the same time as John

C. Fremont, after much lobbying in Washington, was restored by Congress to the army with the rank of major-general,
and put on the retired list with pay. Six thousand dollars a year
would have helped the Fremonts out of a poverty so acute that
'General Jessie' could not accompany her husband on his last
campaign, but only three months later he died alone in a
cheerless Manhattan boarding-house. With the death of the
man he hated Luis Estrada seemed to have lost the will to live,
and not long after he was laid beside his wife in Sonoma's little
mountain cemetery. Rico Gregorio was there, pressing an
unsightly derby hat to his chest and crossing himself devoutly,
exactly as if he were still standing at the foot of the verandah
steps to take his orders. He ventured shyly to where Maria
stood swathed in crape between her uncle and her cousin Jim,
and to his stammered words of sympathy she murmured,
"Come and see me soon, Mr. Gregorio. We must have a talk
about the future."

A week later Rico took up his old submissive place at the
bottom of the steps. A woman servant came to tell Maria, who
was in the front parlour, and she at once sent word that he was
to come into the house. They shook hands for the first time,
and Maria was aware of the dry warmth of Gregorio's skin.

The derby was a great encumbrance, but when Maria made
the servant put it on a side table and bring Mr. Gregorio a glass
of wine the guest was more relaxed, and answered, in better
English than she expected, her kind enquiries for his children.
All well, thank God, he said. The *bambina*, little Stella, had
been nursed by the foreman's wife at Santa Rosa, but she was
at home now, and thriving; his poor Lidia had wanted all the
little ones to be together. Then, surprisingly, Gregorio took
the initiative.

"You say, that sad day last week, signorina, that we shall
talk of the future. Signor Olivetti, he ask me to make a
proposal to you, if it is not too soon. He want to go into the
hotel business. He want to make a big resort in the valley, like
Del Monte down at Monterey. He have a partner in San
Francisco, a widow lady, who have much experience with the
hotels, and he would like to put her in charge. He give you a
good price for the two hundred acres Don Luis farmed, if you
will sell for to make a hotel."

"Good gracious, Mr. Gregorio," said Maria, "I don't believe even Del Monte was built on two hundred acres. What does he mean to do – put another big acreage under vines?"

"Maybe so, signorina, he not tell me. But he say, a single lady like Miss Maria Estrada, she not know much about the business. If Don Luis had not been so ill since last May, he would have talked with Don Luis. But he know Estrada and Putnam in San Francisco will advise you right, and help you come to terms with him. Is that fair?"

"Perfectly fair, but I must see for myself exactly what boundaries exist, and where Mr. Olivetti wants to build. Then my cousin, Mr. Jim Estrada, will want to see the whole site too."

"When you come, signorina?"

She could have answered "any time", for Maria Estrada felt that time had stopped for her. She was over forty, fat and frumpish, and no more use, she felt, to anyone in the world. But she knew that she had the respect of her neighbours, as much for her charitable nature as for the name she bore, and that while their visits of condolence continued she must not leave her home. She set a date ten days later for her visit to the vineyard, and assured Gregorio that she had no objection to driving in his carryall. He arrived punctually, with the vehicle washed and polished, and himself freshly shaved and smelling of laundry soap. The front seat of the carryall was high and narrow, and Maria in her crape with Gregorio in his working denims were bounced and jounced together, hip to hip, as they drove out of Sonoma. She did not find the sensation disagreeable.

Since the day nearly fifty years before when Luis Estrada had ridden that same road on his way home after his encounter with the Russians, eucalyptus trees had been planted among the redwoods, and the very hot afternoon brought out their subtle scent. It was the beginning of the vintage, and the smell of the newly picked grapes hung like wine over the green valley protected by the golden hills. It was easy to see where the land which by her father's Will now belonged to Maria began and ended: precisely by the breadth of arable between the vineyards bounded by the road to Santa Rosa and extending on the other side to the foot of Sonoma Mountain. It was also easy to see, even from the carryall, that the land was in good heart.

"I still think two hundred acres is far too big a lot for a resort hotel," said Maria.

"*Sisignorinia!* I tell that to Signor Olivetti, and he say, people they now play the games, like golf, like tennis. They need much space for that."

"Yes, well, my cousin knows more about that than I do. I wrote to my uncle last week, and Mr. Jim Estrada is prepared to meet Mr. Olivetti, either here or in San Francisco. That's the next thing to arrange. Now I want to know exactly where the hotel would be built −"

"Where the old rancho was, he say."

"− and of course I want to see your dear little children."

Gregorio beamed. "Signora Bosetti, who look after them in the day, she say she have them in their best clothes for Miss Estrada. We turn back here, and up the drive, and then perhaps you remember the rancho you used to know."

It would have been a great feat of memory if she had. The rancho built by Santiago Estrada was now no more than a group of tumbledown buildings, some used as dwellings and some for tools and crates, some with little yards in front and two with Castilian roses trained round the doors. One of these was the two-room home of the Gregorio family, the door of which was opened with a flourish by the labourer's wife who looked after the children.

Signora Bosetti had not only dressed the two little boys in their best clothes, she had apparently dressed them in all their clothes. Their chubby legs were encased in knitted stockings, pulled high beneath serge knickers. Spotless flannel under-shirts could be seen beneath stiffly starched sailor blouses, and their serge jackets were wilting in the stifling room. Their faces were crimson and there was sweat in their thick black curls. Only the baby, Stella, wearing a white muslin dress, was cooing and comfortable in her crib.

"What a darling!" Maria Estrada bent over the child and stroked her cheek. "And what nice little lads! Come here, my dears, and tell me your names."

"They no speak English," said their father. "The big one, he

Giuseppe. The other, Giovanni. Six years, and three. Kiss the lady's hand, boys," he added in Italian.

They were very shy at first, but the bag of sweets Maria had brought with her was a great help, and soon they were standing by her knee, munching, while Gregorio had a brief talk with their guardian.

"Signora Bosetti, she wouldn't let them go outside," he explained apologetically. "They want to play in the yard, but she afraid they'd spoil their Sunday clothes –"

Maria nodded understandingly. She couldn't take it upon herself to open the door or the window, though the room was like an oven, and the yard where the children played was a patch of brown grass with a home-made wooden barrow and a store-bought tin train for their only toys. She said, "You know my garden, Mr. Gregorio. I want you to put all three of them in the carryall tomorrow – with Signora Bosetti, of course, to take care of Stella, and bring them to spend the afternoon with me. We'll have a picnic under the trees with ice cream and cake, and the boys can run and jump all they want to. Wouldn't that be nice?"

His beaming smile told her how nice it would be. When they arrived, panting with heat and excitement, the boys found they could take off their heavy boots and stockings and run barefoot on the lawn, or be swung higher and higher on a swing attached to a sturdy bough by a friendly young gardener. On the shady verandah Stella toddled unsteadily from their hostess to Signora Bosetti, taking a very few steps before grasping the security of their hands. She sat on Maria's lap to be kissed and cuddled, and pulled the woman's black hair out of its unbecoming chignon to lie in rich coils on her crape bodice, so that Rico Gregorio, coming to collect his family, saw no longer a mourning woman in middle age, but a flushed and laughing girl. They had two more such picnics in the garden, two more feasts of fresh lemonade and cookies, before Jim Estrada came to discuss Olivetti's offer with his cousin Maria.

★   ★   ★

360

She rather dreaded the interview. Jimmy Estrada had changed so completely from the warm-hearted schoolboy she remembered that she no longer felt able to talk to him frankly, although she knew the change dated from the terrible evening on the sand-lots when he helped Faxon Cord to raise his father's murdered body from the ground. The murder, and the shocking trial which followed, changed Jim Estrada from a youth with a strong sympathy for the underdog into a man not so much opposed to the forces of anarchy as one who refused to become involved with any forces at all. Thenceforth he lived for athletic sports and pleasure, and gave only enough time to the real-estate business to justify the generous salary his father paid him.

The notorious William Chambliss, who wrote the society column in the *Examiner*, and who hated Jews, Negroes and Chinese only a degree less than he hated the millionaires who 'made it from the Leidesdorff Street grogshops to Nob Hill at one stride', once described Jim Estrada as 'one of the tough swells of the Olympic Club', and it was more accurate than most of Mr. Chambliss's descriptions. Jim was a pillar of the Olympic Club in mid-town, which had seawater piped in from the bay to its vast swimming pool, and one of the members who always took part in the club's ritual Christmas Day swim from the beach. In an age of clubmen he belonged only to the Olympic, laughed at the Bohemian with its summertime High Jinks, and belonged to no literary or artistic coterie whatever. San Franciscans were beginning to discover, through the power of innovative writers, that they were living in a marvellous, a romantic city of Mediterranean beauty, with comical, lovable characters at every street corner, and where Mark Twain and Bret Harte led others followed. Jim Estrada refused to enter the literary salons of Russian Hill; if he leafed through the *Argonaut* and the *Overland Monthly* in his father's library that was as far as he would go. He was not interested in the legitimate theatre. As a boy of fifteen he had gone mad, like everybody else, over Lotta Crabtree when she came back from New York to open William C. Ralston's superb new California Theatre on Bush Street. Lotta was then twenty-two, and as big a star in New York as she had been in San Francisco. She had played the dual roles of Little Nell and the Marchioness in a stage adaptation of *The Old Curiosity Shop*, and had created 'Firefly', the heroic little *vivandière* whom Ouida had called 'Cigarette' in *Under Two Flags*. The theme song of that play was 'Bright Champagne', and Lotta had to sing it many times before she left the city where she made her fame, and which a few years later she was to present with a fountain which soon became a landmark. For Lotta went east again, to open in *Heartsease* in Boston, and Jim Estrada was not interested in the dramatic heavies, including Madame Modjeska, who followed her as Ralston's guest stars. He was friendly for a time with David Belasco, a brilliant young playwright and manager of his own age, but Belasco followed Lotta Crabtree to New York when he was still under thirty, to produce plays with such nostalgic California titles as *The Rose of the Rancho*, *A Romance of the Redwoods*, and *A Girl of the Golden West*. Thereafter Jim's theatrical interests were confined to burlesque, and the showgirls he took to supper at Ralston's great new Palace Hotel or the Poodle Dog at its new site on the corner of Eddy and Mason, were the burlesque stars of the Barbary Coast.

The centre of vice in San Francisco had moved away from Dupont Street, which had changed its name and become Grant Avenue, the heartland of the inner city of the Chinese. The so-called Barbary Coast, with its centre on Broadway, provided bigger and better all-night restaurants, with 'pretty waitress girls', brothels, saloons, cabarets and burlesque halls, and it was there, where Faxon Cord maintained a bachelor apartment, that Jim Estrada was most relentless in the pursuit of pleasure. He and Faxon sometimes joined forces with Charlie Fair, the dissolute son of the even more dissolute James G. Fair, one of the Silver Kings, but as a rule they hunted as a couple. They were known to be two of the most vicious womanisers of the Barbary Coast.

There was no objection to young bachelors sowing their wild oats; this was perfectly understood by the girls in the marriage market. What the young ladies who danced with him at the charity balls he attended to please his mother found obnoxious in Jim Estrada was his cynical habit of laughing at all the rules by which their society was governed. He said it was ridiculous that Ned Greenway, a Baltimorean who had come to California as a salesman for Mumm's champagne, should have made himself the social arbiter of San Francisco, deciding who should attend the Bachelors' Cotillions in the Odd Fellows Hall (of all places) the Friday Cotillions and other gatherings which meant social life or death for a debutante. Jim Estrada said the craze for foreign titles was even more ridiculous than Ned Greenway's stranglehold on society. It was the age when rich Californians paid enormous sums to buy titled husbands for their daughters. William Sharon (Comstock Lode and Palace Hotel) was said to have paid $5 million to the English seventh baronet who married his daughter Flora. Mary Ellen Donahue (Gas Works) married a German baron, holder of the Iron Cross. Ben Holladay, a former stage-coach driver, bought two French noblemen for his daughters, while Beth Sperry (flour) walked off with Prince Andrew Poniatowski in the face of all competition. The most pathetic case was that of Eva Bryant Mackay, the crippled stepdaughter of the Silver King John Mackay, who was married at great cost to Prince Ferdinand Colonna and led a life of contempt and maltreatment at his hands.

"But Mr. Estrada," some dainty ballroom partner would protest, "your own sister has a high position in the Grand Duchy of Strelsau!"

"As the wife of the American Minister, yes. But she married an old friend's son, not the Grand Duke. She didn't sell herself for a title."

Jim would reflect, as the dance went on, that given his unconventional tastes the Grand Duke of Strelsau was unlikely to marry any girl, American heiress or otherwise, but his was an urbane little court, enriched by coal mines in Silesia. He was a musical Duke, an artistic Duke and a literary Duke, and Mr. and Mrs. Ivan Cord had found the right niche in his Grand Duchy. Jim had been to visit them, in the course of a three months' vacation in Europe which further enhanced his elegance in the eyes of the soft little geese who had never wandered beyond their own pond, and made his cousin Maria slightly nervous of asking such a 'howling swell' to intervene in her affairs.

He arrived by the evening train to dine and sleep at the Sonoma adobe, and the first thing he did on leaving the station was to hire a rig to take him to the rancho and on to Santa Rosa in the morning. He was charming to his cousin, sympathising with her for being faced with such a decision so soon after her bereavement, and giving her a full account of his talk with Olivetti in San Francisco.

"You put your finger on the weak point right away, Maria," he said. "Two hundred acres is a ridiculous area for a resort hotel. I've a hunch he intends to lay out part of it as a housing estate, just as my father did in the Mission years ago, and if you cared to sell him say fifty acres for his hotel and keep the rest, you might make a killing yourself. What would you think of that?"

"I want to get rid of the whole thing, Cousin Jim."

"It's still a valuable property, and people are beginning to move out of San Francisco. Down the Peninsula at present, I grant you, but if Sonoma got the right publicity it could be made an attractive residential area."

"That's all so much Greek to me, I'm afraid. I've no head for business nor even for farming, and I want to get rid of what's left of the Rancho Estrada. It brought no happiness to my father – nor to yours, did it? I think after nearly sixty years the story should end here."

This was almost exactly what Philip Estrada himself had said when Jim suggested that their firm should buy the land from Maria for a fair price arrived at by independent valuation and redevelop it as a residential area themselves.

"Let it go, Jim," Philip had said. "It's not a sound proposition. Too difficult of access from the city."

"With a train service?"

"It's a train and ferry service, don't forget; all right for an occasional shopping jaunt, but no good for businessmen. I'm not sentimental about the Estrada land, it cost all of us too much, and business hasn't been so good lately that I can afford to finance a redevelopment scheme in Sonoma County."

Philip was secretive about his personal investments, but Jim knew he had had some fairly serious losses in the stock market. He dropped the subject, and told his cousin Maria that he intended to stick Signor Olivetti for twice the price he was offering. "Then," he said, "you can buy yourself a nice little apartment in San Francisco and find a whole lot of new interests in life."

"Thank you, cousin," she said, and blushed. "I have several new interests here."

Next day Jim drove out to the rancho, was impressed by Rico Gregorio, studied the boundaries and drove on to Santa Rosa, where his interview at the Olivetti winery was so successful that Mr. Olivetti sent for his own closed carriage and drove to Sonoma behind Jim's hired rig, so that his wife and he might have the honour of meeting Miss Maria Estrada. The meeting took the form of dinner at the El Dorado Hotel on the north-west corner of the plaza, only a few steps from Maria's own front door. She had never entered the El Dorado in her life, and took Jim's arm to give her confidence as they crossed the lobby. The bar room on the right was noisy and heavy with the smell of smoke and spirits; the restaurant, while pleasant, was hot and noisy too. Olivetti ordered the six course set dinner, which was Italian all the way from the minestrone to the *zuppa al'inglese*, and included lasagne, gnocchi, ravioli and spaghetti with clam sauce, as well as roast veal and guinea fowl. Mr. Olivetti was displeased because only Sebastiani wines were on sale, and sang the praises of the Olivetti cabernet sauvignon to the harassed proprietor. Once Maria got over her shyness and found she was not expected to talk business she enjoyed the evening. She thought the food was too heavy and the service slow, because not enough waiters had been employed to serve the crowd which drifted in at all hours without table reservations, also the tables were set too close together for comfortable talk or ease in serving. She left with the mark of clam sauce on her sleeve, spilt by one of the staff and painfully rubbed off with boiling water by another, and also with the germ of an idea which might add to her new interests in Sonoma.

It was some time before Philip Estrada's solicitors, as well as his son, were satisfied that his niece was getting a fair deal from Olivetti Wineries Inc., and the transaction was not completed until early in 1891. Through the winter Maria Estrada's great interest was the Gregorio children. They came to her three times a week for 'lessons', serious only in the case of Giuseppe, whom she taught to read and write in English, while Giovanni was still learning nursery rhymes. All of them, even Stella as soon as she could talk, were taught to say their prayers in English, and the two boys, as rough and truculent as little animals, went through a gentle civilising process. Their father's gratitude and admiration were boundless. At Christmas he gave *La Signorina*, as he taught the children to call her, a cameo brooch depicting the Virgin and Child which had belonged to his mother 'back in the old country' and a bottle of scent in a pink satin box ordered by mail from Livingston's in San Francisco. Always there were little gifts in the carryall, now driven by Signora Bosetti's husband when the children came to Sonoma. Posies of autumn flowers and berries from the home woods, wild game birds for the table (Rico was a good shot) or little fancy boxes and wooden ornaments which his big competent hands had put together. They were friends.

Olivetti's announcement that the new hotel would be called the River Inn alerted the neighbourhood to the fact that its grounds would cross, not a river, but the Sonoma Creek, and started one of the endless Californian wrangles about water rights. This was not settled until May. The architects and surveyors had been busy in the meantime, and Bosetti, calling for the Gregorio children in the carryall one lovely May evening, said to Miss Estrada: "The breaking men began work today, signorina. Rico, he wonder if you like to see the old place before all is gone."

"Yes, I think I would, Mr. Bosetti."

"I come fetch you, then. Tomorrow morning? Ten o'clock? Good."

The 'breaking men' were working so fast that the demolition of the Rancho Estrada was well advanced. Already the traces of what had been the sala and the family bedrooms had gone. The redwood pillars had been piled up, and the Castilian rose vines were trailing on the ground. The sound of picks and hammers filled the air, and the dust made Maria choke as Rico Gregorio, who had been on the lookout for her arrival, came to help her down from the carryall.

"I hear a lot of noise," she said, "where are the workmen?"

"Not far off," he said, unsmiling. "They taking down the bunk house now."

"But where will the vineyard workers sleep – and eat?"

"Signor Olivetti say the guests at his grand River Inn won't want to see a bunch of Italians working outside the gardens and the tennis. He make a deal with Signor Sebastiani to take our men in along with his while the hotel is built. Then, we see. Will you come into my house, Miss Maria?"

"I'm glad *it's* still standing," she said, trying to joke. "Oh! where are the children?"

"Playing with the Bosetti kids. I want to speak just you and me, signorina."

He had forgotten to ask her to sit down. He stood between her and the window, a not undignified figure in his work-stained overalls, with some grey in his black hair now, and deeply tanned by the early summer sun.

"My little house is not to stand for long," he said. "Signor Olivetti, he think soon the horseless carriages will come, then horseless carts, and this small vineyard he can run from Santa Rosa. Is only twenty-six miles away."

"Yes, I know. But you? What will you do?"

He held out his work-grimed hand in sudden supplication, and Maria laid her own in it.

"The foreman's wife at Santa Rosa, she very sick," said Rico. "She beg her husband take her home to Italia. Signor Olivetti have offered me his job."

The demolition men must have come back to the main buildings, for the sound of the picks was suddenly louder.

"Miss Maria, you must tell me what to do."

"*Don't go!*" It was only a whisper, but it was passionate.

"You mean, don't go to Santa Rosa?"

"Don't go away."

His hand, locked in hers, drew the woman a little closer. "Maria," he said, in a voice no louder than her own, "I must know the truth. Do you want me to stay so you not lose the *bambini*?"

"I love the *bambini*, you know that."

"Yes, I know. And they love you too. When I see you with my Stella in your arms I know how much they mean to you. But is not enough to say 'stay' because of the kids. You must say 'Stay, Rico,' because of me."

"Rico –"

"Is not easy for me to tell this to you, *cara mia*. You have the great name and the high breeding, while I am only what you see – a *paisano*. But I love you, Maria, from the heart. More, I think, than I ever love a woman. Will you be my wife?"

The plain anxious face turned up to his was suddenly buried on his shoulder, and as his arms went round her Maria Estrada whispered, "Stay with me and be my husband. I love you too."

★　　★　　★

Very soon after the remains of the Rancho Estrada were levelled to the ground the last heiress and Rico Gregorio caught the six-thirty train from Sonoma and were married at Old St. Mary's in the city. They had breakfast after the mass was over, and then took a long, slow drive in a hackney carriage to the new Cliff House restaurant at the ocean beach. The driver took them through the Golden Gate Park, which neither had seen before, although it was more than twenty years since work had been started on one thousand acres of the dunes from which sand used to sift through the streets of San Francisco when the trade wind blew. The green sward of the park, the landscaped dells and the basin where the great Victoria Regia lilies grew made the morning enchanting to Rico and his bride. They dismissed the carriage at Point Lobos and strolled down to the Cliff House, admiring from a distance the cypress hedges which, high on the cliffs above the ocean, hid the only residence for miles around. It belonged to Adolph Sutro, the German mining engineer who planned and built the Sutro Tunnel to take silver ore out of the Comstock Lode.

The denizens of the Seal Rocks were barking and the gulls were circling over the Pacific just as they had done thirty years before, when Jerry Lasalle brought Laura Winter to the first little tavern on that spot. The bride and groom approached the Cliff House with caution. They both knew it had a 'fast' reputation as one of the San Francisco restaurants which stayed open all night. Certainly many of the women who had been driven out from town by 'tough swells' from the Olympic Club were frizzed and painted to a degree which frightened Maria, but the service was quiet and polite, and no one other than the waiters paid any attention to the awkward couple seated at a window table. Rico in the black suit he wore to funerals, with a buttonhole carnation as large as a young cauliflower, and Maria in a grey silk dress and a hat with a wreath of white roses, were not like the usual Cliff House customers, but when Rico ordered a bottle of Veuve Clicquot the three-piece orchestra played Lotta Crabtree's old song, 'Bright Champagne', and they laughed and toasted each other and were very happy.

It was a middle-aged, middle-class, humdrum little celebration, but there was nothing prosaic about the consummation of the marriage in the bedroom of the Sonoma adobe where Rosalie drank the love potion and in the very bed where she was first possessed by Carlos Rivera. Instead of youth and guilt and beauty, there was now the simple hunger of a man and a woman: of the male who had never gone with a woman since his Lidia died, and the female who had never even allowed herself to imagine what the act of love might be. They came together in a great explosion of sexual relief and gratitude, and fell exhausted into a deep, sweating, snoring sleep sounder than either of them had ever known.

Next day Maria Gregorio wrote a charming letter to her father's brother to tell him of her marriage and her happiness, and ending 'Federico and I will soon be able to let you know about our future plans.' When this was read at the Pine Street breakfast table Philip Estrada shook his head, Jim smiled like a man whose private hunch had come off, and Content, behind the coffee pot, indulged in a burst of sarcastic laughter.

"They say there's no fool like an old fool," she said. "I say there's no fool like an old maid. Imagine Maria Estrada throwing herself away on an Italian immigrant, an illiterate fortune hunter –"

"You were an immigrant yourself once, ma," said Jimmy. "Before the Conquest, remember?"

"Don't be a fool, Jim. Have you met this man? What do you know about him?"

"Enough to know that he's a very decent sort, and not a fortune hunter, even if Maria had a fortune, which she hasn't. He's always been crazy about her, that was obvious, and she loves his kids –"

"He's got children?"

"Three."

"Oh, good heavens!"

"He's done well by them, certainly," said Philip. "Maria has a substantial house and a modest competence . . . I wonder what she means about their future plans?"

"We'll find out," said Jimmy comfortably. "Be nice to her, ma. Write her a happy letter –"

"I'd have done more than that, if she'd taken us into her confidence before she planned her hole-and-corner wedding. Well," said Content, relenting, "maybe it wasn't such a bad idea to get married quietly at Old St. Mary's, but if she'd brought her husband to us immediately afterwards, I'd have had a nice luncheon for them and a few of our friends, with a bridescake and everything –"

"Maybe they just wanted to be alone," suggested Jimmy. "Some people do, on their wedding day."

"How would *you* know?" said his mother tartly. That her son was still a bachelor at thirty-seven was beginning to be a sore point with her. She was delighted that he chose to live with his parents, and when Philip complained, as he sometimes did, that "the fellow treats this house like a hotel" she always replied stoutly, "It's his home, isn't it?" Jim's mother never commented on his comings and goings. If his bed was not slept in, if he was missing from the breakfast table, she asked no questions. He was still and always her wonderful boy, but now she was beginning to wish for wonderful grandchildren.

"How would *I* know?" Jimmy sighed elaborately. "I guess this is as good a time to tell you as any. I've asked Gertrude Randolph to marry me, and she said Yes."

"Gertrude Randolph!" said his mother, and was speechless.

"My dear boy, congratulations," said his father. "Do we know the young lady? Randolph – I seem to know the name. How long have you known her?"

"I don't believe you've met her father and mother," said Jim. "She's Captain Ransome Randolph's daughter, and we met about three months ago, when Faxon dragged me along to one of Ned Greenway's cotillions."

"Where you used to say you wouldn't be seen dead," said his mother.

"My luck was in that night, ma," said Jim. "She was there."

Content got up and kissed him. "You've taken us by surprise, my dear. But you know we wish you both all the happiness in the world. When will you bring her to see us?"

"Very soon, but would you consider calling on her parents first? Mrs. Randolph's pretty strong on etiquette and all that rot, you see."

"We'll call tomorrow afternoon, if that suits you, Content?" said Philip. "Would five o'clock be a good time? And tell me, Jim . . . you called the father *Captain* Randolph. In what service?"

"Confederate States Army," said Jim shortly. "He was severely wounded at Gettysburg."

"I see."

"Then is Gertrude's mother Elizabeth Warren Randolph?" asked Content.

"She is. Have you heard of her?" said Jim.

"I have, and what I heard I liked," said Content with emphasis. "Don't worry about the Confederate States Army, Jimmy, it's thirty years since the Civil War. Tell Mrs. Randolph I look forward to meeting her."

Whereupon Jim Estrada, thankful to have got over the hurdle of his mother's Northern sympathies, drank another cup of coffee and raved to his parents about the beauty and charm of his Gertrude, her accomplishments and lovely manners, her shyness when she accepted his proposal, until his father looked pointedly at the clock and Jim left for the office. Then Philip said to his wife, "You seem to know something about the Randolphs I don't. Tell me more!"

It was a familiar story. The second migration of Southerners to California had little in common with the first, who arrived soon after the Conquest and became the earliest aristocracy of San Francisco. They had been rich and confident, and soon held many of the reins of power. Those who arrived after the Civil War were, like Ransome Randolph, veterans of the Confederate army, wounded, broken and impoverished. They congregated together, fighting their battles over again, and were quite content to leave the getting of their daily bread to their wives. As Content said, whatever the men were like on the battlefield, it was the women of the South who were indomitable in defeat. In San Francisco gentlewomen who had never had to wash a dish or hem a shirt opened boarding-houses or little dressmaking businesses, or sold the silks and laces they could no longer afford across the counters of the White House or the City of Paris. 'Elizabeth Warren Randolph, Teacher of Elocution, Dancing and Deportment' as a brass plate read on the door of what she called her studio, had chosen another way to support her husband and bring up their only child in a version of the luxury she herself had known in a beautiful plantation house in Georgia, totally destroyed by Sherman's men in their march to the sea. Miss Gertrude Randolph contributed nothing to the family exchequer. She was on the guest lists of all the Southern gentry, and had the entrée to the Presidio balls. The new Presidio set in green lawns, with a ballroom where well-bred girls danced with clean-cut American officers in white mess jackets and gold braid, was very different from the old Presidio of Captain Prado and his ruffianly command.

"Why did you say 'Gertrude Randolph' in such a surprised voice, when Jim told us her name?" asked Philip at the breakfast table.

"Because I *was* surprised, to think that Jim was going to settle down at last."

"There was more to it than that, wasn't there?"

"Well, if you must know, I heard Faxon Cord was paying attentions in that quarter."

"Where did you hear that?"

"At the Mechanics Institute Library committee."

"You bring home a lot of news from the Mechanics, Content. Well, I'm not surprised Miss Gertrude preferred our boy."

She had preferred Faxon Cord at the beginning, but Faxon was too slow with his proposal, and Gertrude Randolph was nearly twenty-three. It was time, her mother said, to marry; she herself had been a war bride at twenty, and after all the suffering of those years she wanted to see her daughter established in a solid home of her own. So Gertrude said Yes to Jim Estrada, who was rich as well as charming, and after a celebration dinner at the Palace Hotel with him and her parents, she prepared to face his father and mother.

The Randolphs lived on the third floor of an apartment house on Bush Street, not far from the California Theatre, and the 'studio' was an attic on the top floor immediately overhead. The classes in dancing and deportment, for which Gertrude sometimes played the accompaniments when a professional pianist was not available, were dismissed early on the day of the Estradas' visit, conducted on such a level of etiquette as to resemble two High Contracting Parties discussing a royal wedding. By accident or design the older persons were merely foils for the lovely girl in white. The two gentlemen wore black frock coats. Mrs. Randolph was in black velvet, while Content, who for some years past had modelled her style on Queen Victoria's, was dumpy and square-shouldered in a black satin mantle and a bonnet tied beneath her chin. Miss Gertrude Randolph was dressed in the height of fashion, in a white lace blouse with leg of mutton sleeves, the high neckband held up by ivory collar supports with coral tips, over a flared skirt of white serge. Her tiny waist was defined by a belt of silver clasps, wide in front and diminishing as they reached the hook at the back. She had light brown hair dressed in a pompadour, which grew naturally into a widow's peak, and eyes of that dark blue poetically called violet. She was lovely. She was also what Tennyson, whom Content had never read, called 'faultily faultless, icily regular, splendidly null'.

Nothing was said on that first formal visit of what Content had already determined must happen: that the couple should make their home in the Pine Street mansion. Gertrude hardly talked at all, but handed teacups and cake with the maximum of deportment, and her mother – who had maintained good looks like her daughter's through years of disappointment and struggle – deferred exquisitely to her husband, who spoke at length of his military campaigns. "I daresay we're going to hear a lot about the Battle of Gettysburg," said Philip on the way home, and Content, who was learning discretion at the age of sixty-seven, clamped her lips on the observation that it was too bad poor Luis was no longer around to hobnob with Captain Randolph. She reflected that where a soldier's pride was concerned there was little to choose between the great Battle of Gettysburg and the skirmish of San Pascual.

It was clear to the Estradas, after they had seen the apart-

ment on Bush Street, that there could be no marriage settlements where on the bride's side there was nothing to bring
into settlement. "I'm not going to buy a house for them," said
Philip. "Jim's thirty-seven, two years older than I was when I
bought the house in South Park. If he'd saved his money
instead of throwing it away on the Barbary Coast he could
have set himself up very comfortably by this time. I like your
idea of having them to live here, Content. See what the
Randolphs say."

Mrs. Randolph was the one to do the talking, and only to
her daughter. She said with truth that newly married couples
were best on their own, and sharing a home with in-laws
almost never worked out well.

"But you went on living with Grandmamma Warren after
you were married," objected Gertrude.

"Until our home was burned about our ears," said Mrs.
Randolph grimly. "But your papa was away at the war. Mrs.
Estrada seems to be a lady who likes her own way; do you
really think you and she will get along together?"

"I don't see why not. She said to me so sweetly that both her
daughters had gone far away from her, and she looked forward to having a girl about the house again. And she's going to
arrange our rooms exactly to my taste."

Gertrude, who had shared a small mid-town apartment
with her parents and a maid of all work, thought there was a
great deal to be said for the handsome house on Pine Street,
with a staff of soft-footed Chinese servants to wait on her, and
the generous dress allowance Philip had decided she should
have. The rooms which Jim and his sisters had occupied in the
old days were being made into a suite of bedroom, sitting
room, dressing room and bath, with a tiny kitchen added.
Chafing-dish cookery was coming into fashion, and Content
said "You may like to prepare a little chafing-dish supper for
Jim when you and he come back late from the theatre. Then
you'll be quite on your own!"

Mrs. Randolph tried once more, with the revolutionary
suggestion that Estrada and Putnam should open a branch
office in Los Angeles, with 'dear James' in charge. The great
land boom in Southern California had begun a few years
earlier, and the opportunity for solid real-estate salesmanship

was very great. It was the rivalry of the railroads which transformed the little dusty Mexican pueblo, too far from its port at San Pedro to have commercial possibilities, into what its publicity called 'The City of Orange Groves and Sunshine'. The monopoly of the Central Pacific, now called the Southern Pacific Railroad, was broken in 1887, when the Santa Fé line broke through the San Bernardino mountains (where the great Yorba ranchos had once been) and established a terminal at Los Angeles. In that year alone the line carried one hundred and twenty thousand new settlers to cultivate the oranges and enjoy the sun.

"You forget, mamma dear," said Gertrude in her engaging way, "Jim and I are native-born San Franciscans. I don't think we'd be happy in Los Angeles, among all those railroad tourists and immigrants. Besides, where would we live?"

Nowhere nearly as comfortably as in the Pine Street house. Gertrude accompanied her future mother-in-law to choose new furniture at W. & J. Sloane (with the Estrada carriage waiting at the kerb) and prettily expressed her views on new carpets and curtains. She sought Content's opinion on every detail of the wedding, and that militant lady was finally moved to say to her husband, "I thought at first Jimmy might have chosen a girl with more spirit. But she's a nice little thing, and seems very much in love."

"Jimmy always was one for the soft option," growled his father. Content only laughed. But two days later she froze when she discovered the hard core of Jimmy, or the dark side of his nature, when she began to make his bedroom ready for the painters and decorators, and found a Colt revolver with a box of ammunition in the drawer of his night table. She took it to her own bedroom, and there charged Jimmy, when he came home for dinner, with the possession of a dangerous weapon.

She saw his face change from its surface amiability to violent anger as he said, "San Francisco's a lawless city, ma. A man has the right of self-defence."

"What lawlessness d'you expect, at the corner of Pine and Jones? You're not on the Barbary Coast here! And a man has no right to endanger the lives of others, with a gun in his table drawer. What if one of the maids had found it?"

"It wasn't loaded."

"I know it wasn't. I checked to see. I loaded it and then unloaded it again."

The anger gave way to laughter. "Well, good for you, ma! That's the latest model Colt, quite a different gun from those two fowling-pieces hanging up in the library, that you bashed the Bear Flaggers with back in '46."

"You can joke, Jim, but I won't agree to your starting out on married life with a gun ready to your hand. There's been too much of that already –" She bit back the words "in this family" just in time.

"That sounds like some old scandal of the Gold Rush days. Gertie's father *carries* a gun; she told me so."

"In memory of Gettysburg, no doubt . . . Look, Jim, this thing's your property. If you want to defend yourself against the drunks and vagrants of Montgomery Street, keep it at the office. In this house, it belongs to me."

"Take it and be – do anything you like with it," said Jim, and flung out of his mother's room. When she was sure of being alone she carried the new model Colt and ammunition to the library, not without a glance at the Rivera duelling pistols on the wall, and locked gun and bullets into an empty drawer of her own escritoire, of which the keys were carried on her personal ring. She wished she could lock away as easily the foreboding that somehow the ugly little weapon meant bad luck for the marriage.

"Pretty Wedding in Grace Episcopal Church," announced the *Chronicle* one May morning in 1892. "Mr. Santiago Putnam Estrada marries Miss Gertrude Emily Randolph in a double ring ceremony." There was a full description of the exquisite bridal gown, the veil of family lace, the six bridesmaids in pink taffeta and the six ushers, all members of the Olympic Club. Mr. Robert Faxon Cord was the best man, red-haired, red-faced and burly in a tight frock coat. He was the least attractive member of the pretty wedding, and in the vestry Content told him he "wasn't half the man his father was", to which Faxon replied with a bow and a scowl and a "Thank you, ma'am."

"The happy couple," enthused the *Chronicle*, "left by train for the Del Monte Hotel." It was the prestige honeymoon of the 1890s, and had been ever since the Southern Pacific opened its branch line through Castroville to Monterey and on a site among trees and gardens above the ocean built what it claimed was the largest resort hotel in the world. The first wooden building was rushed up in one hundred days, and took far less time to burn down a few years later. Jim and Gertrude were guests at the new Del Monte, with its indoor swimming pool, its ballroom and its fifty 'Tallyho!' carriages which made three trips a day along the famous Seventeen-Mile Drive to Carmel and back. They returned to San Francisco the envy of all their friends, except one: Mr. Faxon Cord, who had cut his losses and left for Honolulu.

"This is as good a time as any to make the break," he told his successful rival soon before the wedding. "The Spreckels people have been after me for years to join their organisation. I've everything to learn about sugar, but they've offered me a top job, and I'm dead sick of being one of the heavies of the Southern Pacific. The railroad's blamed for everything in California: land-grabbing, cheating the farmers, nobbling the bay ferries; I've had enough of being one of the tentacles of the Octopus."

Since the days of the Big Four, the railroad they founded had come to be described as 'The Octopus', with its tentacles strangling the whole state, by newspaper cartoonists, by the new breed of muckraking journalists, and by one brilliant young novelist from San Francisco. By the time Jim Estrada was married the power of the Octopus had diminished, but the Workingmen's Party had floated to the surface again, and its current boss, Abe Ruef, was beginning to get a hold on the city government. Jim Estrada, who had abhorred public affairs since the murder of Governor Cord, began to show more interest in what was going on. It was as if his marriage had made him more responsible, or as if the end of the unregenerate Barbary Coast days and the departure of Faxon Cord (from whom no more was heard but greetings cards at Christmas and on their wedding anniversary) had turned Jim Estrada's mind back to the old liberal sympathies of his young manhood. He took to expounding his views to Gertrude in the hour before dressing for dinner, when she was exquisite in one of her trousseau negligees, reclining on a chaise longue. As long as he didn't mind her doing something really useful, like buffing her finger-nails while he talked, she would listen indulgently to extracts from the newspapers or the latest exposé, all commented upon by her husband.

"Darling, don't get yourself so worked up," she said once. "You sound like my papa or one of his friends, raging about the siege of Richmond."

"Darling, with all due respect to your papa," said Jim, "he and his friends haven't moved on since Lee surrendered at Appomattox. But this is here and now, Gertie! Our city and our times! And we're heading towards a new century!"

"I hate to think of growing old," she said, wilfully misunderstanding him as she sometimes did. Well, you couldn't have it both ways. 'The beautiful Mrs. James Estrada', as the papers called her when she appeared at the opera or the Mardi Gras ball, was not, thank God, a New Woman, wanting to wear bloomers and ride a bicycle in the Golden Gate Park. And she was just as 'lovely' (not the same as 'beautiful') when they dined at home with his parents. She made the family dinner into a pleasant occasion, for Gertrude appreciated sitting down to a meal which she had neither prepared or planned. The chafing dish was hardly ever used.

The parents, of course, hoped for the announcement of a happy event as soon as was humanly possible, but two wedding anniversaries went by before Gertrude, blushing modestly, let it be known that she was expecting a child.

"I hope it's a boy," said the delighted Jim. "If it is, we'll call him Philip Ransome or Ransome Philip, after our two fathers. How about that?"

"Wonderful, dearest, but what if *she*'s a girl?"

"Then Violet, for the colour of your eyes."

The future mother, true to her day and age, at once assumed an air of mystery and semi-invalidism which Content, who remembered the women of the frontier, found hard to endure. Gertrude's wishes now became law. She forbade Jim to buy an automobile, which he had hankered to do since his crony Charlie Fair shocked San Francisco by importing the first Panhard a year earlier. Charlie, who was to die in a car crash, had had no serious accident as yet: nothing worse than a number of breakdowns, each accompanied by public laughter and shouts of "Get a horse!" Jim was enthralled to know that the

Del Monte Hotel, one hundred miles away, could be reached in less than eight hours, driving at an even clip of fifteen miles per hour. Gertrude got her doctor to say that she must not go anywhere, even for a drive through the park, in one of the dangerous machines, and she also persuaded the doctor to tell Jim that they must not be what was called 'on terms' for the duration of her pregnancy. Jim sulked and grew restless. He spent more time at the Olympic Club, using the swimming pool and the gymnasium to excess, and once he got Charlie Fair to drive him to Sonoma, returning with amusing stories about the Restaurant Sorrento, which his cousin Maria and her husband had opened in the old adobe on the plaza. Gertrude, weeping, scolded him for risking his life with Charlie, and didn't think running a restaurant was something an Estrada ought to do.

Not long after this episode, when Jim was made to feel a brute for reducing his pregnant wife to hysterics by his late return from Sonoma (the Panhard having inevitably broken down on the way home) he met through a fellow clubman a vigorous individual called John L. Davie. Mr. Davie, like many San Franciscans, had a colourful past, having been an opera singer as well as a miner; he now proposed to enter the coal business. He wanted to build a warehouse on the Oakland waterfront, across the bay from San Francisco, virtually the whole of which was owned by the Southern Pacific Railroad. The Octopus was unwilling to yield even a part of one of its tentacles. The SP discovered reasons to put up new buildings of its own on the very place designated by John Davie in application after application, some of which were turned down flat and others ignored.

Davie then leased two acres of the tidewater land at the bottom of Webster Street in Oakland from the Morgan Oyster Company, and proceeded to build coal bunkers on the property. The SP waited until the fences were up and then sent in their strong-arm men to wreck the fences and bunkers, and as far as possible to scatter the coal. Davie, whose blood was up, supplied arms to a body of young men as dangerous as the SP thugs, known to the police as the oyster pirates of the bay. There was a violent clash on the Oakland waterfront, in which most of the wharfside loafers took the side of Davie's men, and by the time the police got to the scene they had to face a mob of five hundred, fighting them and each other in an orgy of mindless violence. Governor Cord would have had the Riot Act read at once.

'The Waterfront War', as the press called it, captured the imagination of San Francisco. John L. Davie, the man who had dared to challenge the Octopus, was the hero of the hour, and there was immediate financial support for his next move against the SP, which controlled not only the waterfronts on both sides of the bay, but the ferries which plied between San Francisco, Oakland, and the smaller towns where people lived who had to go to work in the city every day.

"Jim, what's this I read in the *Examiner* –" began Philip Estrada one evening a few days later, when Jim arrived in the dining room after his parents had started on a dish of creamed chicken and rice.

"Sorry I'm late, ma," Jimmy interrupted him, and stooped to kiss his mother. "Gertie's feeling poorly, she's having supper on a tray in bed. Never mind soup, Ling" (to the Chinese butler) "some of that chicken will be fine." He shook out his napkin. "What have you been reading in the *Examiner*, sir?"

"That you're one of the subscribers to this man Davie's foolish fund for fighting the Southern Pacific."

"Fighting the *monopoly* of the SP," Jimmy corrected him. "We're buying a fast steamer for the San Francisco–Oakland run, charging a five-cent fare, and those big lumbering railroad ferries won't have a chance against us!"

Philip pushed away his plate. "It's madness!" he said. "They'll crush you in a week. And you – a married man, a man with a child coming – how can you be such a fool as to get yourself mixed up in the Waterfront War?"

"I'm not," grinned Jimmy. "They're calling it the War of the *Rosalie* now."

"The *Rosalie*?" echoed his father, and a grey pallor crept over his face. "Why the *Rosalie*?"

"It's the name of the steamer."

To Philip Estrada and his wife it was a name from the past, a name with unspeakable connotations, and the man, trying to rise, clutched at his left arm and fell back in his chair with a groan. Content hurried to his side and motioned to the butler.

"Ling, help your master to his room and get the amyl from the medicine cabinet. It's all right, Phil, I'm coming! Jimmy, don't detain me now!"

"What the hell's the matter?" said Jim, rising in anger.

"You upset him about the *Rosalie*. He can't bear the name."

"It's only the name of a boat. What's going on around here? Why am I always upsetting somebody? What makes you all think you can treat me like a kid of twenty? Don't buy an automobile. Don't ride in Charlie Fair's new car. Don't sleep with your wife until the doctor says you can. Don't mention the *Rosalie* to your father! I tell you I'm sick of the whole thing! Tell Gertie I've gone to dinner at the club –"

"Tell her yourself," said Content, and fairly ran from the room. As she hurried upstairs, dreading a heart attack for Philip, she heard the front door closed with a crash.

Jim dined and drank at the Olympic Club and went to a burlesque show on Broadway. He picked up a girl there and spent the night with her in a cheap hotel. Next morning he went back to the club and after learning, by telephoning to the butler, that Mr. Estrada had passed a comfortable night without his doctor having to be sent for, he had a shower, a session in the steam room, and a twelve-lap swim in the pool. After breakfast he wrote to his wife, saying that as he seemed to be in everybody's way he would sleep at the club until the Waterfront War was over. He then crossed out 'Waterfront War' and substituted 'War of the *Rosalie*'. If she wanted him for anything in the world she could reach him through the Olympic Club and he would come home at once. Until then he sent his love.

He knew as he walked down to the Embarcadero, as the old wharves were called, that he was acting like a brute and possibly a fool as well, but he couldn't help it, he was genuinely sick of all the mysteries and prohibitions. And the war started by John Davie was the nearest thing to an adventure which had ever come his way. The War of the *Rosalie* was in full swing when he reached the Embarcadero. With a five-cent fare she went out loaded on every trip, and the SP had appealed to Washington to intervene. President Grover Cleveland's Secretary of the Navy was already investigating the

Rosalie's seaworthiness. Davie put more steamers on the transbay run.

The drawback to his 'act of piracy' as his antagonists called it, was that he had no regular docking facilities for his five-cent ferries, and the SP engaged in unarmed combat to prevent the ships from landing. It was great sport for the passengers as the *Rosalie* raced the SP's crack ship, the *Alameda*, for her place in the ferry slips. It was also increasingly dangerous as tempers rose, and engineers piled on the head of steam: some eyewitnesses thought there was great risk of a boiler explosion. The *Alameda* and the *Rosalie* jostled each other like maniacs playing a life or death version of musical chairs at a mad children's party. Jim, like most of John Davie's supporters, made the crossing to Oakland in the *Rosalie* many times. He was on the bridge with the captain on the day when the *Alameda* edged ahead and denied the steamer access to the slip. The signal to stop reached the *Rosalie*'s engine room too late. She crashed fifteen feet into the *Alameda*'s stern and in the collision passengers on both boats were flung into the foul water of the bay. Many were severely injured by machinery or splintering wood. The only one found dead when the rescuers picked him up, with terrible wounds to his head and face, was Jim Estrada.

4

Violet Estrada was only five years old when she first knew the meaning of rejection. She was sitting on a hassock behind one of the window curtains of the Pine Street house, nursing her doll and feeling absolutely secure, when she heard her mother and Uncle Faxon Cord come into the drawing room.

Uncle Faxon was a new and unwanted relative. Violet had already a large family to be loved by and to love. First of all there was mother, the nearest and best, and after her the two dear grannies. Next came Aunt Maria and Uncle Rico at Sonoma, with their two boys and Stella, who was nearer her own age. Uncle Faxon was an old man with thinning red hair and a thick body. Violet, living in a house of women, could not identify the odours of tobacco and whisky, but she thought Uncle Faxon's breath smelled so bad when he kissed her that she had to rub her mouth, which made him laugh. She didn't know how her mother could seem to like that heavy red moustache against her lips. But that morning Violet knew without daring to look round the curtain, knew by the thick hot silence in the room, that Uncle Faxon was kissing mother, and mother was enjoying it.

"My God, Gertie, it's been too long!" she heard the man mutter.

"You don't know what it's been like for me."

"I'll make it all up to you, darling, I swear I will. But I wish you hadn't turned me down when I came back in '96."

"It was all so confused then. Papa dead, and Jim's poor father dying . . ."

"Anyway I've more to offer you now. So it's all settled?"

"*She* seems to think so."

"And she's still the boss. Don't cry, Gertie. I can't stand it when you cry!"

"It was that awful thing she said to you, about stepping into a dead man's shoes."

"Don't forget I've known her longer than you have, and she's always talked like that. Now dry your eyes –"

"But Faxon, are you sure I've done the right thing? Saying I would let her keep Violet? My baby! She's only five –"

"Look, if it means so much to you, let's go back and tell her you've changed your mind. Bring the brat along with you – I don't care."

"No – oh no, I'm sure this is the best way. Violet will go to that fine school . . . and then my own mamma would hate to lose her. And when she's old enough she'll come to visit us, won't she?"

"Sure, honey, any time you say." There was a curious lapping sound, like Violet's kitten drinking milk from its saucer, and then Faxon's blurred voice, saying, "Don't drive me over the edge, Beautiful! Put on a pretty hat and let me show you off at the Palace. I don't feel like lunching with that old witch today."

Violet kept her tears back until she heard the door close behind them. She had been clutching her doll tightly, trying to pretend she hadn't understood. The sinister phrase about 'a dead man's shoes', had only mystified her, but she knew she was 'the brat' meant by Uncle Faxon, because 'bad brat' was what her black nursemaid, Mabel, called her when she misbehaved. And she understood, beyond pretence, that her mother was leaving her. Mother had snivelled a little, but was quick to insist that she was doing the best thing in abandoning her Violet to go off with Uncle Faxon, who had more to offer her now. More than what? More than who? More than a little girl of five years old?

All the guests at the quiet home wedding, when Gertrude Estrada married Robert Faxon Cord a few weeks later, said what an adorable little flower girl her daughter was, holding a bouquet of Parma violets to match her mother's dress of the same colour. She behaved beautifully at the wedding breakfast and kissed her mother goodbye without shedding a tear. She had been coached in her part by Elizabeth Warren Randolph, teacher of deportment, who had been a valuable catalyst in those days of family tension. She explained to Violet that poor mother had been very sad since poor father died before their little girl was born, but Uncle Faxon loved her and would make her happy again. When a lady and gentleman got married, she further said, they liked to be by themselves on what was called a honeymoon; and that was all this was, a rather long honeymoon in a beautiful place called Hawaii, where Violet would visit them some day. She told Content Estrada that if she wanted to keep the child in San Francisco she had better stop baiting Faxon Cord and tilting at Gertrude, because Faxon was quite enough of a bully, like his father before him, to start a suit for custody. She told Gertrude that she was very lucky, as a widow of thirty-two, to be marrying a rich and devoted bachelor of forty-seven, who wouldn't throw his life away in a crackpot adventure like the War of the *Rosalie*. "No strings attached to this one, my dear," she said grimly. "No in-laws for you to live with, no father to boss him at the office! Of course he wants to have you to himself, without a little girl who looks like Jim Estrada watching everything you do. He'll want children of his own, too, and I hope he'll get them. Try to do better with him than you did with poor dear James."

Even before Philip Estrada followed Captain Ransome Randolph, CSA, to his rest in Lone Mountain cemetery, Elizabeth Warren Randolph had a good deal of practice in keeping the peace between Jim Estrada's widow and his mother. Shattered by his death as Content was – and she aged rapidly from that moment – she was only too ready to join battle with Gertrude, each blaming the other for his presence aboard the *Rosalie* on the fatal day.

"What did you say to him that sent him out of the house?" sobbed Gertrude. "He was well, he was laughing and happy, while he was with me."

"If you'd come down to dinner that night like a sensible woman instead of playing the fine lady he might have stayed at home," retorted Content. "Don't forget I saw the letter he wrote you. Just a word to the club to say you – you loved him and needed him, and – oh my God! Jim would be with us now!"

Mrs. Randolph intervened more than once to remind them that violence could harm the coming child. A miscarriage was threatened, which quieted both women, and in due course a little girl was born, sufficiently like her father to make sentimental friends wipe their eyes and say she was his image. It was not true, for though her features were like Jim's, her hair, which grew in a widow's peak like her mother's, was black instead of brown, and her eyes were green, the *ojos verdes* of Castile. By the time she was a little girl rather than a baby Content saw another resemblance, and when she put her arm round Violet for the goodnight kiss it was not her son's child, the last of the Estradas, whom she saw, but a heartbroken girl who had heard the news of her lover's death to the sound of the sea breaking against the harbour wall at Bodega Bay. Sometimes it was even difficult not to say "Goodnight, God bless you, Rosalie!" but the habit of self-command was so strong in Content that the forbidden name never crossed her lips. She watched the child grow strong and happy until her security was threatened by the arrival of Faxon Cord.

Her mother's marriage marked a giant step forward in Violet Estrada's emotional development. She had been wounded and she hid her wound. She had been dependent and she became self-centred. This did not happen overnight, but in the first few months of her life in the most junior class of Miss West's exclusive school for girls on Van Ness Avenue. Soon her nursemaid's escort was unnecessary. Mabel was sent away, and with due warnings about crossing against the traffic and not speaking to strangers, Violet was made free of the streets of San Francisco.

Increasingly crippled by arthritis, Content made retrenchments in her way of life. Philip had left the whole of his estate in trust to her, and it was her own decision to close off the suite of rooms which had been occupied by Jim and Gertrude, put down the carriage, and dismiss five of her seven servants. Stairs were a problem now, and she had the breakfast alcove off the dining room made into a bed- and bathroom for herself, resigned to being the inactive grandmother while Mrs. Randolph, twenty years her junior, took over Violet's little treats and excursions. They went on the 'dummy' cars to see the seals on the Seal Rocks and the riders on the Ocean Beach, to the Japanese Tea Gardens opened during the Midwinter Fair of 1894–95, and the Conservatory in the Golden Gate Park. But what Violet liked best, and both her grandmothers knew it, was to be put in the train for Sonoma and be met at the terminal by Uncle Rico, dancing in front of him down the country road and across the plaza to the old adobe where Zeemaree was waiting.

Zeemaree was the pet name by which Maria de las Mercedes Gregorio was known to her beloved stepchildren. When she and Rico came back from their city wedding the children were waiting at the adobe, having been told by the faithful Signora Bosetti that they had a new mamma. Innocent little Stella at once hailed La Signorina as *"Mamma mia!"* but Maria, catching Giuseppe's scowl, said gently that their own dear mamma was in heaven, and they must call her Aunt Maria – *Zia Maria*. It was too complicated for hungry children, or children in a hurry, and soon became "Zeemaree, kin I have sumicecream?" (Stella) or "Zeemaree, where d'ja put my boots?" (either of the boys).

To be hugged and petted by them all, to share Stella's bed and be called Stella's *piccola sorella*, was a joy to the child from San Francisco. The Gregorio boys called her Cousin Vi, not *la piccola sorella*. Like so many first generation Americans, they disdained what they called Wop talk, and had no interest in stories of the old country. At school in Sonoma they had insisted on being called Joe and Jack, and only some respect for their father had caused them to keep the name of Gregorio. Joe was enrolled in a technical school of hotel management in San Francisco under the name of Joe Gregory, and Jack joined him in the city as a sales clerk in the Olivetti retail store.

Their father was dismayed at their departure. When his bride persuaded him that the old adobe could be converted into a restaurant he had pictured something in the Italian style, in which *la famiglia*, as soon as they were old enough, would all work together for a shared success. Once the Sorrento was a going concern he gave up his job with Olivetti and worked like two men at the adobe, doing half the manual tasks required to convert the long room at the back and the verandah into a restaurant walled in by glass windows which could be opened in hot weather. It held exactly twelve tables. The outdoor kitchen was modernised, and Rico converted the adobe stables and other outbuildings into store rooms, a wine cellar, a laundry, and the walk-in pantry which Violet admired most of all. It had thick adobe walls and a small barred window on the north side, and shelves on which puddings were set to keep cool, alongside other perishable supplies like cheese and sausages.

The Sorrento was a success from the start. It was well organised and above all quiet, offering Spanish California fare instead of heavy pasta twice every evening except Mondays, at six o'clock and eight, by reservation only, and many were the guests at the River Inn who absented themselves from the dinner they had paid for on the American plan to enjoy the Sorrento's *queso ají* soufflé, *chalupas* and *chile rellenos*.

After the boys left home, leaving a bedroom free, Mrs. Randolph was often invited to visit the adobe with Violet. She always had to refuse, for the studio enrolment was booming and she was a very busy woman. It was still the era of home entertainment, when a young lady without musical talent was expected to recite for the pleasure of her family and friends, and Curfew was prevented from Ringing Tonight in many a San Francisco drawing room. The theatre remained the great public entertainment, although there was a new cheap attraction called the penny arcade. This was a rented store equipped with a Kinetoscope, into which the patron dropped a cent to see a peepshow. The penny arcade was superseded by the nickelodeon, admission five cents, where the stores had machines which projected film images on to a white screen. Mrs. Randolph was confident that the nickelodeon craze would soon be over.

In the April when Violet was eleven Mrs. Randolph was tired enough to welcome the idea of a few days at Sonoma with her granddaughter, and on Easter Sunday, the day before they left, she taught the child a poem to be recited to Mrs. Estrada, who expected to hear a hymn or a psalm on Sunday evenings. Her beloved First Presbyterian church, now venerable enough to be called the Old First, had moved to the corner of Van Ness and Sacramento, not far away, but often too far for an old woman with a stiff knee.

The poem that evening was secular, and was meant to have a special appeal for Mrs. Estrada, who like its heroine had gone to sea with her father, and Violet was disconcerted when her grandmother greeted *The Wreck of the Hesperus* with a burst of laughter. Mrs. Randolph, on the other hand, was reassured. She had been worried about leaving a woman of eighty-two alone for four days, even with two devoted maids. Mrs. Estrada had been feebler since the New Year, with more difficulty in walking and occasional lapses of memory. But she seemed to be as alert as ever when she rewarded Violet's curtsy with a crisp, "Very nicely said, my dear. But I don't know why that poem made you think of me. I never had eyes 'blue as the fairy-flax' nor 'cheeks like the dawn of day' and my father needed no advice from me on how to sail his ships. He didn't pile us up when he made Westing round Cape Horn, let alone the 'reef of Norman's Woe'. It's easy to see poor silly Mr. Longfellow was no seaman!"

Thus Content on Sunday evening, but on Monday, after Violet had gone, her mind began to wander, and she moved uneasily from room to room on the ground floor of the house too big for an old woman and a child, looking for her granddaughter. A fleeting glance at the *Chronicle* (she never gave it more than that) told her that Caruso was to sing in the city that night. Another Italian! Like that decent fellow Gre-

gorio who married Maria Estrada! That was where Violet had
gone, of course, off to Sonoma to stay with the Gregorios. In
another flash of lucidity, she remembered the child had said
Uncle Rico was going to drive them to the River Inn to see
where the old rancho stood where her grandpapa had lived
when he was a boy. Then the cloud came down again, and she
was lost in the old dreams: of her young mother, tying on
Content's sunbonnet for her first day at school, of a Russian
wedding at Sitka and the feasting on salmon and vodka . . .
and what else? What year was it, what day was it? The calendar
on Philip's desk in the library said April 17, 1906.

So, she was at home in San Francisco, and here came Ming
with a bowl of beef tea and some crackers to eat with it. She
crunched them avidly. Then she fell heavily asleep, so that
Ming, coming in on tiptoe to take away the tray and finding
her mistress so white and motionless, was frightened, and
went back to the kitchen to tell the cook that they ought to
telephone to Mrs. Randolph in Sonoma and ask her to come
back to the city. The two Chinese women were afraid of their
mistress, but still more afraid of anything happening to her for
which they might be held responsible. The cook finally agreed
to peep into the library and have a look at the old lady. She was
discovered sitting at her escritoire and leafing through some
papers: her "What is it, cook? I don't want to be disturbed,"
was so cutting and so normal that the two women crept away
abashed.

Content had awakened with the rancho on her mind. She
vaguely connected it with the two duelling pistols crossed on
the wall, and the pistols made her think of the Colt she had
made Jim give up to her before he was married. She unlocked
the drawer in which it was hidden, and was immediately
distracted by a bundle of letters of condolence on her son's
death, and a few yellowing newspaper cuttings. She hunted
for her reading spectacles to see what they were all about, and
after limping round the furniture found the glasses on her
nose. The top clipping read:

THE COMTESSE DE MAROLLES
TRAGIC DEATH IN PARIS FIRE

May 16, 1897. Our Correspondent in Paris writes:

Older playgoers in San Francisco who remember the beautiful Miss Laura Winter, one of the stars of the Catt Company, will regret to hear that her body has been identified among the victims of the terrible fire in the rue Jean Goujon at the bazaar of the Société de la Charité Maternelle. One hundred and eighty persons, including the Duchesse d'Alençon, sister of the Empress of Austria, are known to have died in the blaze caused, it is alleged, by the imprudence of the operator in charge of the cinematograph machine at the bazaar. Miss Winter, who was created Comtesse de Marolles by the late Emperor Napoleon III, was fifty-five years of age. She was well known in Paris for her charitable work, especially for women of the unfortunate class. She had donated a pearl necklace, said to be a family heirloom, to be auctioned on behalf of the Société de la Charité Maternelle, which was founded by Queen Marie Antoinette.

Towards the end of the afternoon the maids were startled to smell burning in the house. There were open fireplaces in many of the rooms, in which great logs were burned on andirons, but the heating came from a coal furnace and was spread through open registers: in such a warm April no wood fires had been lit. They paid another cautious visit to the library. They found their mistress on her stiff knees in front of the fireplace, in which she was burning torn-up letters and what appeared to be old newspapers; some of the burning spills had fallen out of the basket grate and were leaving ugly marks on the marble hearth.

"Missie, missie, what are you doing?" cried Ming, and with their hands under her armpits the two Chinese dragged the old woman to her feet. She lost her balance completely, and they lowered her into her armchair, aware that she was glaring at the indignity. They asked if they should bring a basket of wood and light the fire properly. She shook her head, and the cook unobtrusively picked up the matchbox which had fallen on the rug and put it in her apron pocket. Both maids jumped at the sound of the telephone, which was on the table by Content's chair.

She picked it up herself, and the two women heard with relief that she was talking to Mrs. Randolph. Yes, she said, everything was all right in Pine Street, how were they? A good trip, a hearty welcome, and dinner in a grape arbour in the garden? That sounded just right for Sonoma on a fine April evening. Love to Violet and Maria, remembrances to the Gregorios. She would look forward to getting all the news on Friday night.

She hung up and looked at her servants. "I don't remember ringing for you," she said, "but since you're here, I'd like to have a cup of tea. And bring me my Bible from the bookcase."

"She might have burned the house down round our ears," whispered Ming as they went back to the kitchen. "If some of that burning paper had fallen on the rug –"

They were relieved when their mistress asked for supper an hour earlier than usual – "but properly served, mind, not on a tray," and ate steamed sole and a small custard pudding at the head of the dining-room table, under the painting of Captain Putnam. She went to bed ahead of time too, and Ming, putting her mistress's clothes away, purloined another box of matches before she closed the bedroom door. Content was asleep before Enrico Caruso, the world-famous Italian tenor, strode on to the stage of the Opera House to sing in the first act of *Carmen*.

Sleeping the light sleep of old age, she woke several times during the night, but without getting up until in the milky dawn, quite wide awake, she felt on the night table for her spectacles and read the time on Philip's gold watch, which hung in a red plush pouch by the head of her bed. It was exactly five minutes past five.

She rose and shuffled into the bathroom, where it was light enough to see out through the frosted glass. The bathroom was always a problem, for she was unsteady first thing in the morning, and often bruised herself on the appliances. She negotiated them with success, and had put in her dentures when she was thrown violently to the floor. The washbasin was wrenched out of the wall and the mirror above it, like the window, was splintered into a hundred pieces. The room shook, the house moved, and there was a sound as if San Francisco were slipping off its seven hills into the bay.

Content Estrada's first thought was that she had broken her hip. It was her secret dread that this would happen some day, leaving her permanently immobilised, but as the paralysis of shock passed away she found that she could clutch the claw foot of the white porcelain bathtub and then raise herself by the top of the tub, which was firm. She was bruised and shaken, but there were no bones broken. She had taken three steps towards the bathroom door when it was burst open by the combined effort of the two maids, sobbing, and dressed in their night attire.

"Now don't get into a state," she told them, "it's only an earthquake. I've been through the big quakes of '65 and '68 and I survived; we'll survive this one if we keep our heads. Help me into the bedroom and get me my warm dressing gown."

The ceiling was down in the bedroom, but Content had replaced her spectacles in their thick leather case and they were intact. The house had ceased to shake, the rumbling noise had stopped, the earthquake of April 1906 had lasted for twenty-eight seconds.

There was very little damage in the dining room and the library, except that the glass door leading to the side garden was cracked from top to bottom. Content sat down in her big chair.

"I get you a cup of tea, mistress?" suggested the cook.

"No! Don't kindle the fire in the range or the little cooker, don't strike matches anywhere. Go to the top of the cellar stairs and turn the gas off at the main."

"There she sat," Ming told her family before she died, "like the Dowager Empress of China – like the Old Buddha herself, giving her orders to us as calmly as you please. She told us to get our clothes on and then come back and help her to dress properly. 'We may have to go out into the street,' she said. 'I refuse to go out unless I'm suitably dressed.'"

Pine Street, by this time, was full of people far from suitably dressed. Content, having found that her front door was warped and immovable, watched through a window as the Blakeneys from directly across the street and their neighbours the Bakewells, one door down, came out shrieking and crying, clad in dressing gowns, overcoats and Inverness capes, clutching satchels and jewel cases, and went off up Jones Street as if Nob Hill, where the very rich lived, were a fortress. She drank a glass of milk which the maids brought her, and told them – for she knew where their hearts were – that they had better go home to their families in Chinatown and come back when the panic had subsided.

"But you, Lady? What will you do?" asked Ming.

"I'll telephone to Mr. Blake as soon as the office opens, and ask him to escort me to Rosalie at Sonoma." She saw the maids' puzzled faces, realised what she had said, and corrected it to "I'll go to Miss Violet at Sonoma."

They were too much accustomed to obey their mistress, too eager to be among their own people, to waste time in argument. By six o'clock, with their belongings in bags and bundles, they were off the premises, leaving by the delivery entrance on Jones Street, which at that time was quite empty. Content stood looking after them as they ran down the steep street, and then looking upwards, where Jones was steeper still, to the bulk of the Crocker mansion on Nob Hill. "Perhaps I should have gone with the Blakeneys," she thought for the first time, and before the gate was quite closed, while she was still feeling for the heavy bar which could be put across it, she saw the whole cornice of the house on the opposite corner detach itself, and fall with a roar into the gutter. It was almost more frightening than the first shock of the earthquake – that warning that this was only the beginning of the collapse of a whole city.

Back indoors she checked the kitchen range, to make sure the ashes had been well raked out. There was little she could do about the furnace, although testing the sink taps, where no water ran either hot or cold, made her anxious about the boiler. She went back to the library to fetch the binoculars kept in a cupboard under the bookshelves. Then she began the slow crabwise climb to the very top of the house: to the cupola, where she trod on broken glass from the four shattered windows, and through their warped and empty frames looked out on all the quarters of San Francisco.

It was like looking down on a forest of stone trees. Here a chimney stack, there a wall, here again a windmill, stood in a waste of rubble. By far the greatest damage had been done south of Market Street, in the Mission where Philip Estrada had been one of the first builders, for the creeks which he and others had filled in subsided with the earthquake, taking the jerrybuilt houses six or eight feet into the gulf. The landmarks were missing from the financial district, but the wharves and the Ferry Building seemed to be intact. A great crowd of humans, ant-like from the level of the cupola, seemed to be trying to escape from the city by the ferries and the ships in the bay. There were flames behind them now. It was not only from falling brick and stone the citizens were fleeing: it was from fire.

Among the legends which grew up around that day there was one persistent belief that a woman trying to cook breakfast was the cause of sparks escaping through a damaged flue which started the first fire of the morning. It may have been true, but there were so many in the city who had not Content Estrada's foresight that cookers were lighted, hearths were covered with hot ashes from twisted grates, kitchen stoves were overturned and broken gas pipes exposed to the heat of incandescent mantles. Before long more than fifty fires were raging across five square miles of city streets. The underground water pipes and conduits were broken and completely useless. What Content Estrada saw through her binoculars was not a fire but a conflagration.

At eight o'clock, back in the library, she tried to telephone to the Estrada and Putnam office. It was Estrada and Putnam no longer, for after Philip's death the company had been bought by a man called Blake, who had a high regard for the woman who had helped to build it up. "Any little thing Old Lady Estrada wants done we're glad to do it," he instructed his staff. "She was one of the real pioneers." It would not have been a small thing she meant to ask of Mr. Blake that morning, but Mr. Blake was already shepherding his wife and family to the Golden Gate Park for safety. The flames were licking at the office building on Montgomery Street, and the telephone was dead.

The fire won't come as far as Pine Street, was Content's belief as the long day wore on, even although the wind carrying with it a drift of ashes and an ever stronger smell of burning seemed to give her the lie. She saw two men in uniform, mounted and armed with rifles, meet at the street corner and heard one of them shout "They're holding it on Powell!" which gave her cause to hope, as she realised the military had been called out. In fact Mayor Schmitz, a Boss Ruef placeman, was fumbling with the awe-inspiring problem, and the doomed city was now under the effective command of General Funston from the Presidio. It was at daybreak on the second morning, twenty-four hours after the earthquake, that Content heard a man shouting through a bullhorn that federal troops and the police had orders to kill all looters. "Repeat, kill all looters!" the voice from the bullhorn brayed.

The strong uprush of energy which had carried her through the beginning of the ordeal had ebbed away from the old woman. Content had slept at intervals, had foraged for food in the dark kitchen, had suffered lapses when she was living again in the long past, but she was aware that danger was coming ever closer. She could not know that 'they' had not checked the fire on Powell. It had engulfed the city centre, even the City Hall, had utterly destroyed Chinatown where she had sent her maids for refuge, and was now threatening the great houses on Nob Hill. The memorials to the wealth of the Silver Kings and the Big Four were falling one by one, and soon the sparks were floating down on Pine Street.

Content had always been fond of paperwork, and now she made a methodical parcel of the papers in her escritoire. She examined the title deeds of the house, the insurance policy, her Will and copies of her birth certificate and marriage lines and put them in a large manila envelope before she saw the gun taken from her son lying far back in the drawer. "Looters!" she said aloud. "If they come I'll be ready for them!" and she slowly loaded the Colt with her swollen fingers. In her confusion she thought she was back again at the rancho, and the Bear Flagger was threatening Isabel Estrada.

She fetched her mantle from the bedroom, forgetting her bonnet, and put it on intending to set out for Sonoma. The cupola four flights above her head had already caught fire from the conflagration on Nob Hill when the looters came. Unlike the hundreds who had pillaged the downtown liquor stores and were now lying, dead drunk, in the path of the fire, these two men had concentrated on the homes of the rich who had fled in panic to the open spaces, and had a couple of sacks full of jewellery and silver. They flung the sacks over the Jones Street wall before they climbed it, dropping down among the ferns and seeing at once the cracked glass door of the library. A kick dislodged the remaining glass, and the two violent men, their faces black with soot and ash, were inside the house.

They thought it was empty until they saw the frail figure of an old woman, wrapped in what looked like a long black cloak. They were checked for an instant, while the smell of burning and the crackling of the rafters increased above their heads. Then a quavering voice said, "You Pike County black-guards, what are you doing here?"

The leader said, "You shut up, grandma, and you'll come to no harm." Content took a step forward, raised the gun and shot him through the heart. His accomplice clubbed her down, and Content, her trigger finger twitching in a final reflex, shot upwards into his groin. Then the library ceiling collapsed, the walls swayed outwards, and Content and her assailants were buried for ever in the funeral pyre of San Francisco.

Part Two

A Greaser Name

5

In the first twenty years of Violet Estrada's life there were three days which strongly influenced her character and actions. The first two occurred in her childhood, and their effect was imperceptible at the time. The third, in the year she was twenty, was at once seen to be momentous: it marked her first and last meeting with Jack Hastings.

After the day when she felt herself rejected by her mother, when she was only five, Violet's next shock came when she was eleven, when the great earthquake extended so far to the north of San Francisco that Santa Rosa too had its temblor, felt even in Sonoma. With so many people to pet her at the Sorrento, and tell her soothing stories of earlier 'quakes, the child might have come through the day unscathed if Rico Gregorio had not done what so many others in Sonoma were doing: bundled his family into a conveyance and driven them down to the old embarcadero where the creek entered San Pablo Bay to see the flames of San Francisco staining the evening sky. Then Violet knew that her grandmother Estrada was in great danger. When she slept, it was to wake from a screaming nightmare, and for years to come the image of fire in the movies was to start the nightmares all over again. These two shocks, the moral and the physical, worked in Violet Estrada in a way nobody suspected. Beneath the pretty, charming exterior she developed a strong vein of self-pity.

The meeting with Jack Hastings was quite different.

Violet's girlfriends, the 'Crowd' of her schooldays, had been telling her for two years that she ought to be in pictures, and Jack Hastings was the man who was to make their words come true.

More than an hour before their meeting, Violet was standing in an upstairs bedroom of the old Estrada adobe while Zeemaree and her stepdaughter Stella made the final adjustment to her costume for the Sonoma Fiesta. It was a yellow dress which had been part of Isabel Yorba's trousseau, too full in the bosom and too tight in the waist for a girl of 1915, but the needlewomen had done their work well, and sat back on their heels delighted when Violet put a black mantilla over a high Spanish comb.

"Now be quick," said Stella, tying the yellow sash, "the school kids have started already."

"There's six tableaux and two dances before my turn."

It was eighty years since the foundation of Sonoma, and as Spanish fiestas were becoming popular it had been decided to hold a celebration in the former pueblo. San Francisco, risen triumphant from her ashes, had held the Portola Fiesta in 1910, and was now holding the Panama-Pacific Exposition in honour of the opening of the Panama Canal. Violet and Mrs. Randolph had paid an early visit to the Exposition, chiefly to see the portrait of Governor Robert Cord by the great French Impressionist, Israel Klein. It was on loan from Sacramento, and to Cord's name had been added the famous inscription on the Capitol:

Bring me men to match my mountains,
Bring me men to match my plains

Six thousand miles away a great war was raging in Europe, but the United States was neutral and the Exposition quite impartial. There was a French Pavilion, where the sword of Lafayette and the French flags carried at Yorktown were displayed. There was also a German-American Day, when thousands of males from the city's large German community goose-stepped to the Court of Abundance with brass bands playing 'Deutschland Uber Alles', accompanied by pipers representing the Irish Republican Army. Mayor Rolph sent the marchers a message saying San Francisco could not have too much of the spirit of Germany. This was before the Cunard liner *Lusitania* was sunk by a German submarine off the coast of Ireland with the loss of eleven hundred civilians, including one hundred and twenty-eight American citizens.

The sinking of the *Lusitania* only a week earlier caused a certain gloom to fall over the fiesta at Sonoma. The Italian vineyard workers who frequented Garibaldi House were uneasily aware that a Garibaldi Legion, led by one of their hero's sons, was fighting alongside the French, and that it was only a matter of months, perhaps of weeks, before their mother country declared war on the old enemy, Austria-Hungary. They were not in the right mood for a Spanish fiesta. The organisers, knowing this, and feeling that the many descendants of General Vallejo might resent any amateur adult actor taking his part, had wisely confined the tableaux to schoolchildren, and the theme to the coming of Father Altimira, the building of the Mission of San Francisco Solano and the Christianising of the Indians. In the final tableau the tallest boy in the senior class, wearing Mexican uniform, was to play Vallejo, whose young wife, Doña Francisca Benicia, would be played by the prettiest girl.

"There now, you look lovely," said Zeemaree. "If the tableaux have begun it's time Rico and I were in our seats. What are you going to recite, Violet? 'Concepcion de Argüello' I suppose?"

"I'm going to do two short Bret Harte pieces, but not that one, it's too hackneyed. I'm sure everybody's dead sick of poor old Concha."

"Everybody's so thrilled you could come." Zeemaree picked up her straw hat and opened the door. "Stella, I hear your baby crying. Poor Denny'll be out of his mind if you don't go down to them."

"Be right after you!" said Stella. "Violet, do you want to come with us, or wait?"

"Oh, I'll wait here. I don't want to hang around the plaza in fancy dress."

"Right." Stella closed the bedroom door again and lowered her voice. "You were sweet to bring Joe," she said. "It means so much to daddy."

"I didn't bring Joe, Stella, he brought me."

"Yes, but he wouldn't have come without you. Darling, I'm worried about you."

"Why?"

"Because Joe's stuck on you. And, I hate to say it, he's my brother – Joe Gregorio is nothing but a no-good bum."

"Oh, Stella! Ever since you and Denny got married, you think everybody must be stuck on somebody! Granny and I are always pleased to see Joe at the apartment, but he doesn't drop by all that often. He's got his own gang in San Francisco."

"I'll bet!" said Stella significantly . . . "All right, Denny, I'm coming!"

Leaning out of the open window, Violet watched them go: Stella, beginning to put on weight, Denny Smith her dentist husband, and their year-old Freddy in his push-chair. A happy family, lost to sight under the blossoming trees of the plaza. It was a beautiful day at the end of May, and the square was no longer drab or dusty, having been laid with well-kept turf and planted with pines, palms and flowering oleanders. The old landmarks were being restored, chief among them the Mission, which for twenty years had been abused as a hay barn, a winery and a blacksmith's shop. The Mexican barracks was a ruin, but the flag of Mexico floated above it as if defying the Bear Flag monument on the green sward opposite. The tableaux would not include the Bear Flag episode. There were too many of the older inhabitants, like Doña Maria de las Mercedes Gregorio, whose parents had told them the true story of Fremont's rabble, but the heroic bronze figure of an impossibly handsome frontiersman now stood with the flag on a stone plinth in memory of the freebooters and their 'California Republic'.

On high staffs, the Spanish and Mexican flags flew with the Stars and Stripes where Vallejo's Casa Grande had once stood. The platform, reached by wooden steps, had been erected opposite the flags and facing south over rows of wooden benches where every place was filled. There was plenty of room for the young performers in the tableaux and dances to sit on the grass to the east and west. The children looked like an animated flowerbed when Violet in her yellow dress and black mantilla took her place upon the stage.

There was an immediate outburst of applause, and Zeemaree preened herself. She knew it was not the San Francisco elocutionist they were applauding, but the last of the Estradas, and the Estradas had held their land by Spanish grant before the foundation of the pueblo. Then, too, Violet looked ravishingly pretty, as pretty as the narrator of her first poem was meant to be. She chose Bret Harte's 'Her Letter', written by the Gold Rush heiress 'to the best-paying lead in the State' who becomes 'the belle of the season' in New York, but is true to her Californian sweetheart, always thinking

> Of someone who breasted high water,
> And swam the North Fork, and all that,
> Just to dance with old Folinsbee's daughter,
> The Lily of Poverty Flat!

It was exactly the poem, in its blend of humour and nostalgia, to appeal to her audience. As she instinctively curtsied instead of bowing to the applause, she was aware of Zeemaree and Rico, Stella and Denny, all smiling and clapping, of Joe Gregory in his man-about-town finery, and of a youngish man sitting beside Joe who was looking at her with one hand screwed into a funnel and held close to his eye.

She announced her second poem by Bret Harte:

The Angelus
Heard at the Mission Dolores, 1868

Bells of the Past, whose long-forgotten music
  Still fills the wide expanse,
Tingeing the sober twilight of the Present
  With colour of romance!

I hear your call, and see the sun descending
  On rock and wave and sand,
As down the coast the Mission voices blending
  Girdle the heathen land.

> Borne on the swell of your long waves receding,
> I touch the farther Past –
> I see the dying glow of Spanish glory,
> The sunset dream and last!

There was silence in the plaza as Violet recited the four final stanzas. It was not a poem which told a story, like 'Her Letter', but it had a strong emotional appeal for several hundred people come together in honour of the Spanish past. Violet was surrounded when she came off the platform, and the mayor himself requested the honour of offering her a glass of wine. It was time for refreshments, to be followed by dancing to guitar music on a wooden flooring laid in the middle of the plaza. All the Sonoma vintners had contributed barrels of wine, the bakers gave layer cakes of every variety, and there were whole freezers full of ice cream for the children. These good things were set out on trestle tables under the bunting in the Spanish, Mexican and American colours which ran all round the square.

"You were sensational, Cousin Vi!" Joe Gregory, with his straw boater in his hand, pushed his way through the little group of local notabilities. "Better than I ever heard you!"

"Thank you, Joe."

"Here's somebody wants to know you. Can I introduce Mr. Jack Hastings, *the writer*, from Chauvet's Crossing? Miss Violet Estrada."

From Joe's gauche introduction Violet seized on two words, *the writer*, which indicated that the youngish man now bowing gracefully was the person about whom she had heard more than one joke at the Sorrento. Hastings was a newcomer to the district. He had set up house with a male companion (known locally as 'the boyfriend') in an old cabin near the ford in the creek which had once been a short cut round the mountain, with the avowed intention of 'getting away from it all'. It was his bad luck that the name of Jack Hastings was often confused with that of Jack London, the world-famous adventure writer who lived at the Beauty Ranch only five miles from the Crossing, and he had been heard to say pettishly:

"Jack *Hastings*, not Jack *London*! I'm not as well known as he is, neither for books nor for boozing!"

He had published three romances of what he called Old California. Violet had read one called *Russian Roulette*, obviously plagiarised from Gertrude Atherton's *Rezanov*, which made her think he had come to this fiesta in search of local colour for a sequel. She had not read the other two, *Comstock Carnival* and *The Padre's Mistress*. Nor did she know that besides writing for the pulp magazines Hastings had sold five hundred stories to the movies as one-reelers at prices ranging from five to ten dollars a script.

"Congratulations, Miss Estrada," he said. "You gave a beautiful performance. It was worth the whole afternoon, to me. But I didn't realise you were Joe Gregory's cousin until just now."

"He's a cousin only by courtesy, but a very old friend. His stepmother and my father were first cousins."

"You don't live in Sonoma, do you?"

"No, I live in San Francisco. Is that where you met Joe Gregory?"

"Everybody in San Francisco knows Joe. May I ask – have you had any stage experience?"

"None at all. I'm a teacher of elocution at Miss West's school for girls."

Hastings looked at the vivid face under the black mantilla, and smiled. "I should never have taken you for a school-marm," he said, and paused as two acquaintances, both women, came up to flatter Violet. When they moved on he said more urgently, "I don't want to monopolise you, Miss Estrada. But I would like to talk to you, about yourself, for no more than five minutes. Could we sit on that bench under the oleander without attracting too much attention?"

"If you wish."

As soon as they were seated Jack Hastings said, "Has anybody ever told you you ought to be in pictures?"

"Only in fun."

"I'm serious." She saw that it was true. Jack Hastings was not as young as he had appeared to be from the platform, and although his manner was effeminate, his mouth nervous, his voice was steady and assured. He was talking about something he understood. "I think you're a natural for the movies," he said. "You're not only pretty, you're photogenic. And you move beautifully. Where did you learn to do that?"

"My grandmother taught me in her deportment classes."

"Your *grandmother*! That might be a good publicity angle – maybe. Can you ride?"

"I learned to ride in Honolulu, years ago, but I haven't ridden since."

"Honolulu, eh? You've seen a bit of the world, Miss Estrada."

"I spent nearly a year with my mother in Hawaii, after the fire."

"Interesting. Well now, here's the thing. Would you like to take a movie test?"

"*Would I!*" Violet clasped her hands dramatically. "Oh, Mr. Hastings, I've been crazy about the movies, ever since I was a kid and saved my pennies to go to the nickelodeons!"

"What do you enjoy most?"

"Anything Mary Pickford does. *The Perils of Pauline* – I've seen every episode. And now, of course, *The Birth of a Nation.*"

"Yes, you'd be coming in at the right time . . . Tell me: does the name of Willis Jerrold Hastings mean anything to you?"

"I'm afraid it doesn't."

"He's my brother. He used to be an actor, but you wouldn't have heard of him, he never played San Francisco. All his stage appearances were with David Belasco's companies."

"That sounds wonderful."

"He was pretty good. He's a movie director now, with the Essanay Company down at Niles."

"You mean Broncho Billy's Essanay? The ones who signed up Charlie Chaplin?"

"I see you read the trade mags, good for you. Now I happen to know my brother's looking for someone of your type – not for the Broncho Billy one-reelers, you mustn't think that, but for the stock company at Niles. If you're interested, if you'll give me your address, I'll ask him to get in touch with you."

"Oh Mr. Hastings, how can I ever thank you?" She spelled out the address of the modest flat on California Street, three blocks west of Van Ness Avenue, where she and Mrs. Randolph had lived since they came back from Hawaii, and watched eagerly while he copied the telephone number into his pocket diary. Then Hastings said,

"Forgive a personal question, but how old are you?"

"I'm twenty."

"Better make that eighteen."

"Eighteen? But why?"

"Because the camera can be cruel to pretty girls. Most of the kids who've made good in the movies started at fifteen or sixteen, or younger, and even then harsh lighting was too tough for them. But some of Essanay's cameramen are working on that problem – one in particular, my brother says is a lighting genius. You'll be all right if you work with him."

"Then I'd better seem to know *his* name, hadn't I?"

"Timothy Siegrist."

"Violet –" Stella, pale and anxious, was hurrying across the grass towards them.

"Stella! Is anything the matter?"

"I'm so sorry to interrupt," said Stella Smith. "But – could you come home with me? Now? It's Zeemaree. She isn't very well – and she's asking for you." Both Violet and Jack Hastings were on their feet, and the man asked concernedly if there was anything he could do. Violet gave him her hand. "There's nothing," she said, "but I must go. I'm sorry – there was so much more I wanted to hear about Essanay –"

"And I wanted to hear a lot more about you and your family –"

"Joe Gregory can fill you in on that. Goodbye!" She gave him a parting smile across her shoulder, and allowed Stella to hurry her away. All the young woman's Italian excitability had got the better of her, and she was crying.

"For heaven's sake, what happened, Stella?"

"She said she felt faint in all that crowd, and wanted to go home. Daddy and I got her upstairs, and then – she sort of collapsed on the bed and started to say a lot of things that didn't make sense, before she asked for you."

"Have you sent for the doctor?"

"Zeemaree kept saying, 'no doctor, no doctor', just daddy to sit beside her till you came."

"Send Denny for the doctor, Stella – if he's here."

"He took little Freddy out to the yard. Oh, what are we

going to do, Violet, what are we going to do? We're booked out for both the dinners, even had to put in extra tables –"

"I'll help you, and we'll manage somehow." They were at the open door of the adobe, and through the corridor she could see the two waitresses already laying up the tables in the big room above the garden. Violet picked up her long skirt and ran upstairs. At the sound of footsteps Rico came out of the bedroom, with his shaggy grey head and paws for once limp and helpless, looking more like a big bear than ever.

"My Maria's very sick, Violetta," he said.

"Stella said she just – collapsed after she got home –"

"But before, in the plaza, your poem scared her, she said."

"My *poem*? But I saw her laughing and clapping in the audience!"

"I don't know what it was," said poor Rico. "Her head very bad. I put a wet cloth on her brow, was all I could do –"

"Wait here then." She went into the bedroom alone. They had managed to undress Zeemaree, for she was in her white nightdress with a blanket over her, and Rico had indeed laid a wet cloth on her brow, for her grey hair, with the pins removed, lay in a puddle of water. Violet's first act was to take the dry pillow from Rico's side of the bed and gently substitute it for the wet one.

Zeemaree's face was very flushed and her breathing laboured, and inexperienced as Violet was it occurred to her that the poor woman might have suffered a stroke. She laid her cool hand on the damp brow. Zeemaree's eyes opened. She saw the mantilla, the comb, the Spanish dress, and there was no recognition in her look. Then, when Violet whispered her name, she smiled and said feebly, "I thought you were – the sunset dream."

"I'm not a dream, darling. Tell me where it hurts. Tell me what I can do for you."

"My head aches. I wanted you. I wanted to tell you – tell you something." She tried to raise herself, to Violet's alarm. "That poem you said – it frightened me."

"I'll never say it again."

"You looked so like – my father. Not your eyes, but here." She drew her fingers over Violet's forehead, the delicately modelled nose and lips, the firm chin. "And when you said that about the dying Spanish glory – I can't remember the words –"

> I see the dying glow of Spanish glory,
> The sunset dream and last!

Violet was almost afraid to repeat the lines, but Zeemaree nodded, and caught the girl's hand in hers.

"I *lived* with it, dear, for forty years, until they died. My poor father lived on his memories of the Spanish glory; it ruined his life and my mother's. He grew old, he grew poor, sometimes he drank to forget, but he always dreamed the sunset dream. Promise me!" here the blurred voice grew stronger, "promise me, Violet, to live a real life. Not – to dream it all away."

Violet kissed her. Zeemaree's eyes closed again. Asleep, or unconscious? Oh Denny, hurry for the doctor, said Violet's anxious heart. She went silently to the window to see if there were any sign of the doctor on his way. The fiesta was in full swing in the plaza, and the guitar music had begun. The sight of the dancing children reminded Violet Estrada that she was still dressed in the remnants of that Spanish glory which was her inheritance. She took off the mantilla and comb and laid them aside.

The seat beneath the oleanders where she had talked to Jack Hastings was visible in a patch of sunlight, and was empty now, but the dream he had offered her, the fantasy world, had not faded away.

She never saw Jack Hastings again.

Two weeks later she met his brother.

6

My dear madam, [the letter dated June 10, 1915, began]
    I write to ask your permission to invite Miss Violet Estrada to luncheon in the Rose Room of the St. Francis

Hotel on June 17 at 1 p.m. My brother, the writer Jack Hastings, has had the pleasure of meeting Miss Estrada, and admired her performance at the 'Foundation of Sonoma' Fiesta. He feels that our meeting might be profitable both to the talented young actress and the Essanay Company.

Miss Bridget Malloy, our leading lady, will be present at the luncheon, and looks forward, as I do, to making Miss Estrada's acquaintance.

I am, my dear madam,
Very faithfully yours,
Willis Jerrold Hastings

"Well!" said Mrs. Randolph, taking off her spectacles, "this seems a – a very proper letter. But to go to luncheon with a stranger –"

"And his leading lady, don't forget," said Violet. She was wildly excited, and only just able to refrain from snatching the letter from her grandmother's hands and reading it again.

"Wouldn't it be better," said the old lady, snatching at a straw, "if I wrote to Mr. Hastings and suggested he come to meet you here instead?"

"Granny, this is business. I have to do it *his* way, don't you see?"

"I suppose so," Mrs. Randolph sighed. "And you want to go on with this, don't you, Violet?"

"It's my big chance."

Much against her will, she had told Mrs. Randolph about her talk with Jack Hastings. In her self-contained way, she would have preferred to wait until something positive resulted from that talk, but the thought of a telephone call from Essanay intercepted by her unsuspecting grandmother would have meant so much confusion that she told the whole story soon after coming back from Sonoma. Mrs. Randolph made light of it. She had been beaten by the nickelodeons, she had heard that vaudeville shows were now concluded by a film, she accepted finally that movie houses were springing up across the country, but that someone should tell Violet "you ought to be in pictures" was beyond her imagination. Besides, at that time they were both too concerned about Zeemaree's 'seizure', as it appeared to be, to dwell on Jack-Hastings-the-writer.

The doctor's verdict was that Mrs. Gregorio was overtired, over-excited and overheated, that was all: there was nothing the matter that a sedative and a few days' bed rest on a light diet wouldn't cure. Violet left with Joe for San Francisco, both of them reassured, and daily telephone calls from the loyal Stella, now running the Sorrento, continued the reassurance. Zeemaree would soon be herself again. There was no call from Essanay, but now there was the letter, which Mrs. Randolph, with irritating slowness, was reading again.

"Mr. Hastings writes from the Essanay Company, Niles, California," she said. "Where *is* Niles?"

"It's a whistle stop somewhere south of Hayward."

"And Essanay? I know you've told me before, but I can never remember –"

"It means S. and A., granny, for Spoor and Anderson, the two men who founded the company. Mr. Anderson is Broncho Billy in the movies."

Mrs. Randolph groaned. "He calls you the talented young actress. But you're not an actress, Violet!"

"I will be, if I get the right lighting cameraman."

"I don't know what that means."

"Neither do I, but I'm going to learn. Oh granny, what if Mr. Hastings offers me a contract right away?"

"Then you should tell him you'll write and ask your Uncle Faxon's advice."

"What does Uncle Faxon know about the movies?"

Mrs. Randolph sighed. Her son-in-law, the sugar magnate, probably knew as little about the movies as she did herself, but he understood all about business, and Elizabeth Warren Randolph, who had once been the sole support of her family, still believed that business was exclusively a gentleman's province.

★   ★   ★

The seventeenth of June was a warm day for San Francisco and bright with sunshine, so that the splendid white city which had risen on the ashes of the old was sparkling from all its walls when Violet Estrada walked from the California Street cable car down to the St. Francis Hotel. The girl representing

Victory on the tall statue in Union Square, raised after the Spanish-American War, seemed to be pirouetting on her pedestal as if she were wishing Violet good luck. She walked into the foyer of the St. Francis confidently, sure that her plain white dress, and the straw hat on which she had replaced a wreath of yellow poppies with one of blue cornflowers, made her look younger than the doom-laden age of twenty.

"Why are you taking off the poppies, dear?" enquired Mrs. Randolph. "They're new. They're fresher than those old cornflowers."

"I know, but they're the state flower," said Violet. "I don't want Mr. Hastings to think I'm in a tableau as the Spirit of California."

Some of the confidence ebbed as she looked round the crowded foyer, but a tall man who had been standing by the clock came forward quickly with a smile.

"Miss Estrada?"

"Yes."

"I'm Willis Hastings. I recognised you at once from my brother's description."

"How did he describe me?"

"As a Spanish beauty."

"How kind of him. And kind of you to ask me to have lunch with you."

"I hope Miss Malloy doesn't mean to keep us waiting. Ah! Here she comes."

Bridget Malloy came out of a lift, from the interior of the hotel, and greeted her host and Violet very prettily. She was dressed in pale blue. Her matching hat was small enough to show that she wore her blonde hair in ringlets on her neck, like Mary Pickford, and her mouth was rouged into an ingénue's pout. She was the D. W. Griffith heroine incarnate: the fragile, fair-haired girl born to be the victim of a brutal male.

The Rose Room, where Hastings had booked a table, was the fashionable restaurant of San Francisco – famous, for two years, for the music of Art Hickman and his saxophonists. The band did not play at luncheon, but the aura of its fame and the success of six hundred dancing evenings hung round the place. The pretentious cotillion days were over, and for lucky girls like Bridget Malloy and Violet the Jazz Age would soon begin.

"We want to know all about you, Miss Estrada," said Hastings. "My brother said you didn't look like a school-marm, so tell us how a child like you comes to be a teacher of elocution. Too bad the movies are silent, because you have a delightful voice."

"She sure has," said Miss Malloy enviously. Her own accent, to Violet's trained ear, was that brand of San Franciscan known as 'South of the Slot'.

"I hardly know where to begin," said Violet. She was confused and fascinated by the man beside her. Willis Hastings was the handsomest male she had ever seen, like a brilliant enlargement of his brother's sepia, underdeveloped print. He was too old for the movies, being about thirty-five, but she wondered how David Belasco had let him vanish from the New York stage, with that voice, those dark eyes, that mane of copper hair, and the profile. She was not too struck to miss seeing that he had only one good profile, the left, and had arranged the seating to keep that profile towards the room.

"I started teaching almost by accident," she began, hoping this sounded daring and carefree. "My grandmother had a studio on Bush Street where she taught elocution and dancing" (deportment sounded too old fashioned) "but it was completely destroyed in the fire, like her apartment. When we came back to the city after a holiday in Hawaii, where my mother and stepfather live, granny took a job at Miss West's, where I was a pupil, but it got to be too much for her, and I agreed to take it on for a year."

"Which is up when?"

"At the end of this month."

"So you could give up your job then, if you wanted to?"

"I suppose so."

"You don't regard teaching elocution as your life's work?"

"*No!*" It was said so explosively that Bridget laughed, and Violet blushed.

"What do you want to do with your life?" persisted Hastings.

"I want to be a movie actress," she said, and gave him a look from her green eyes of which he coldly assessed the emotional value.

"Well now," he said easily, "as soon as we've all enjoyed

our *saumon en papillote*, Bridget shall tell you what a movie actress's life involves at Essanay."

Miss Malloy enjoyed her salmon to the last bite, patted her rouged lips with her napkin and said judicially:

"If you want to be stuck in a hick town an hour's drive from San Francisco, and work in a glass-roofed shed in the middle of a field, so hot the grease paint runs off your face; or else get up at four o'clock and dodge the snakes in Niles Canyon while Tim Siegrist fiddles with his exposure meters and his camera angles and makes you do ten takes instead of one; and wear costumes out of Wardrobe a scarecrow would turn up his nose at, and eat off a chuck wagon and get back to find there's no water for a shower – then you'll be all right at Essanay Number Two."

Willis Hastings laughed. "Bridget's making the worst of it," he said. "I grant you Niles is short on technical facilities, but our productions get better all the time, and we have a lot of fun among ourselves."

"Just one big happy family," sniffed Bridget.

"But you've made good at Essanay," said Violet shyly. "You're the leading lady."

"Leading lady! O my Gawd!" said the south of Market Street voice, and Hastings intervened.

"I can see I'll have to tell you how our company is organised," he said. "The head office is in Chicago, with Mr. George K. Spoor in charge. Mr. Anderson built the Niles studio in 1908, when he was one of the first movie men to settle in California. His Number One company produces the Broncho Billy one-reelers – you know those, of course – he directs them himself and has his own cameraman. A one-reeler every week, that's his quota. I'm the director, and Bridget's the star, of the Number Two company. We do comedy, westerns, classics, anything that comes along, and mostly two-reelers. Tim Siegrist, our lighting cameraman, is panting for the day when we do a four-reeler, but I don't see that yet awhile."

"And do you direct Charlie Chaplin, sir?" said the fascinated Violet.

"Only Chaplin directs Chaplin," said Hastings with a wry smile. "He works on a closed set, with his Miss Purviance, his

Rollie Totheroh on the camera, and his twelve hundred fifty bucks a week. He made four movies at Niles and then demanded better working conditions, so Mr. Anderson moved him back to L.A., to a little studio Essanay rents at Boyle Heights, to make the eight movies he still owes us by contract. Good riddance and good luck to him, say I."

"So you see what you may be getting into," said Bridget. "It's up to you, kiddo. Or is it?" She looked at Hastings, and Hastings looked at his watch.

"Tim's late," he said. "I wonder where he's got to."

"Prob'ly holding up the bar at Tadich's," said Bridget, powdering her nose.

"I'm talking about our lighting cameraman, Tim Siegrist," Hastings explained to Violet. "Extraordinary fellow! I never can find out how he was discovered. Do you understand what I'm talking about? Everybody in movies has to be discovered if he wants to be a hit. George Spoor discovered me in Chicago when I was in Belasco's production of *A Girl of the Golden West*. My brother gets the credit for discovering you. And Bridget – pay attention, Bridget! – where were you discovered?"

"Selling saltwater taffy at the Cliff House concession," said Miss Malloy.

"As good a place as any. But Tim Siegrist came drifting in from L.A. one day a year ago – I think he'd ridden the Overland with a bunch of hoboes – showed the boss some of his still pix, and he was *in* – like that!"

He came drifting in from the foyer, on cue. Tim Siegrist was a small man, unconventionally dressed in a tweed suit, a blue shirt and a black knitted tie, which made him conspicuous among men wearing high starched collars, cravats with stickpins and white slips to their waistcoats, and he moved between the tables with an odd lop-sided gait. He came up to their table with a breezy "Hi, Bill. Hi, Pidgie, how's the girl?" and bowed formally in response to Hastings's "Miss Estrada, may I present Mr. Siegrist?"

"Glad to know you," he said, and instead of shaking hands moved back a step, almost colliding with a waiter, and screwed his right hand into a little funnel. He looked at Violet through it as Jack Hastings did at Sonoma, but more searchingly, and then on a long breath said "Ye-es. Of course. Jack had the right idea, Bill. Very plastic. Very expressive eyes. Nice!"

"I thought you'd say so," said Hastings. "Sit down and have a drink."

"Thanks," said Siegrist, pulling up a chair and seating himself between Violet and Bridget Malloy. "Bourbon and branch water will be fine." He looked from one girl to the other. "I see what you're getting at, Bill. The blonde and the brunette; perfect. Did you ever play a villainess, Miss Estrada?"

"I never played anybody," said Violet, startled.

"What, no stage experience? No schoolroom theatricals? Not even charades? So much the better, Bill only uses girls who can take direction. What I meant was, would you object to playing bad women?"

"Bad –"

"Fallen women, if you like that better. Fallen angels, murderesses or murderees. We're simple souls at Essanay, you see. The dark-haired girl is always the heavy, the blonde's the heroine, the virginal angel of light. Eh, Pidgie?"

"Don't tease her, Tim," the actress said.

"I won't. Just one more question, Miss Estrada, and it's not impertinent. Out of all the books you've read, out of all the shows you've seen, which of the girls would you like best to play in front of the camera?"

"Cinderella."

Nobody was smoking, but Tim screwed up his eyes as if smoke had got into them before he said slowly, "Ve-ry good. Cinderella, one of the best plots in the world, I've filmed it half a dozen times . . . Well, Bill, I guess that wraps it up. Any chance of hitching a ride back to Niles with you?"

"Sure, if you'll tell them to bring my car round. You all set, Bridget?"

"I'll just go upstairs and get my coat. Nice to've met you, dear," was her farewell to Violet.

"Say au revoir, but not goodbye!" said Tim with a monkey's grin. "Be seeing you, Miss Estrada!"

"Why, the poor man's lame!" said Violet, watching him as he sidled down the room with the young movie star.

"He used to be a rodeo rider," said Hastings, counting out the money to pay the bill the waiter had presented. "Took a bad fall a few years back, before he was a cameraman; he can still direct our stunt men when he's filming westerns."

"I ought to be going too," said Violet. "I've enjoyed meeting you all so much."

"You'll be seeing quite a lot of us from now on in," said Hastings. "That is, if you want to join Essanay Number Two."

"Please, are you offering me a contract?"

"Not a written contract," said Hastings with a laugh which made Violet flush. "That's not company policy, except in the case of Charlie Chaplin, and you'll agree that Chaplin's rather special. I'm only offering you a job."

"But – don't I have to have a movie test?"

"Tim Siegrist was the test. You passed it."

"Oh sir, I don't know what to say –"

"Don't say anything, just shake hands. And don't say 'sir', except to Mr. Anderson the first time you meet him. I'm Bill to my friends." His hand tightened on Violet's. "And we're going to be good friends, aren't we, little girl?"

7

Her 'Crowd' of half a dozen girls, and three young men, were at the depot to wave Violet Estrada away from San Francisco and wish her luck in the movies. They had brought posies from the flower-sellers at Lotta's Fountain and enough candy for a trip to Europe instead of an hour's ride down the eastern side of the bay to a whistle stop called Niles; they also made enough noise for a mob scene in one of Broncho Billy's pictures. The girls were all attractive in their summer dresses, wearing the newly fashionable belted jersey coats; the boys were in white ducks, dark jackets and straw hats. It was a lively departure, very different from the tearful scene of Mrs. Randolph's leavetaking on the day before.

Mrs. Randolph had given her consent to Violet's venture,

but only after she had been given tea and a most sympathetic hearing by Mr. Hastings, who explained that he kept a room at the St. Francis Hotel for his many visits to the city. He had charmed the old lady, an easy task for one who had so often impersonated a Southern gentleman in Belasco plays, and when he promised solemnly that Miss Estrada would only be given refined parts at Essanay, she withdrew all her objections. But she also announced her own decision to leave San Francisco when the school term ended and Violet was free to go to Niles. She wanted to spend six months in Honolulu with her daughter's family. The Cords had visited San Francisco occasionally, but it would be the first time for eight years that Mrs. Randolph had gone to Hawaii.

"What a selfish beast I've been, keeping you away from your grandsons," said Violet remorsefully. She had two half-brothers in Honolulu now, redhaired lads called Robert and Warren Cord, whom their mother idolised.

"I must confess I sometimes hanker for the boys," said Mrs. Randolph, "but you've been my pride and joy, Violet, and I'll be back for Christmas without fail. And you'll have the keys of the flat, and come and go as often as your work will let you – it's not as if you were going to Los Angeles." People were not accustomed to saying 'Hollywood' as yet; it was only two years since Cecil B. de Mille's production of *The Squaw Man* put Hollywood on the map.

Mrs. Randolph was seventy-three, and she broke down when the time came to go on board the ship for Honolulu. Violet was glad that Joe Gregory was there with a supporting arm and a joke, and a keen eye to the porters with the baggage. He had come to see them oftener than usual since Zeemaree's illness, and when he took Violet back to California Street in a taxicab he told her again and again that any little thing she wanted, any little thing he could do, she only had to let him know.

"Except that I never know where to find you, Joe, you move about so much," she reminded him, and Joe, mumbling something about "rooming with two other guys on Columbus", said a note addressed to Coppa's would always be forwarded. It was typical of him to use a restaurant as an accommodation address.

The ferry ploughed its way across the bay, and Violet looked back at the city of her birth, rising in all its hues of white and grey and beige on its seven hills. She had almost forgotten what it looked like on the summer day in 1906 when Uncle Rico took her grandmother and herself through the nightmare cityscape to the same dock as she had visited yesterday. She had been so protected by them all, so cocooned by the safe and beloved landscape of Sonoma, that she had had no idea of the devastation caused by the earthquake and the fire. Even her grandmother Estrada's death had been presented comfortably to her. "She was very old, dear," said Zeemaree, "and died quite peacefully, in her sleep." For all they knew it was the truth. When Rico Gregorio was finally able to enter the devastated city, he found the corner house on Pine Street reduced to smoking ashes and rubble, and its owner listed among the four hundred and seventy-eight officially dead. Of her two assailants nothing was ever known.

Violet was not told until long afterwards, and then by Stella, how Rico searched through streets which had become like the muddy trails of early days, among three hundred thousand homeless people, until he found his two sons helping to organise tent shelters on Lobos Square. They had both done good work as volunteer fire-fighters until the fire was stopped at Van Ness Avenue, but their father had the shock of learning that Joe had dropped out of his course in hotel management and was working for a bookie at Ingleside racetrack, while Jack declared that he was sick of selling booze across a counter and as soon as the trains were running again would try his luck in Chicago. "What I do wrong that both my boys such fools?" mourned Rico, whose only comfort seemed to be the safe conduct of Violet and her grandmother through the city and off to Honolulu, where Faxon Cord was now the master of his own sugar plantation. She had been protected from all the sights of suffering. In the great age of the cover-up, she had never even been told the truth about her father's death. "He died in a drowning accident, three months before you were born," was the official version, and as the train ferry drew into Oakland the girl had no idea that only a few yards from its berth her father had died a horrible death in the disaster of the *Rosalie*.

When the train ride proper began, through the Oakland suburbs and into the rich farming country of the east bay area, Violet was able to gather all her flowers and candy into a large net bag which one girl had thoughtfully brought, and put it on top of her single suitcase. Like all inexperienced travellers she checked out, for the fifth or sixth time, the contents of her handbag: the one-way ticket to Niles, the fountain pen, the comb, pocket-handkerchief and booklet of *papier poudré* leaves. She had the keys of the flat, the key of her suitcase, and a new purse containing one ten-dollar bill, two fives, and some loose change. The sight of the money reminded her of a talk with her grandmother, soon after her going to Essanay was confirmed.

"They're paying you a mere pittance, dear," said Mrs. Randolph uneasily.

"A bigger pittance than Miss West did, and I get board and lodging too, remember."

"If you're sure the lodging will be clean and comfortable."

"It'll be fine."

"If you need anything you must let us know."

"Thank you." And then, out of the blue, Violet asked the question Mrs. Randolph had been dreading for many years:

"Granny, where did all the money go? The Estrada millions? I thought we were meant to be so rich!"

"There were never millions, dear. And your grandfather Estrada had heavy losses before he died."

"I wish you'd tell me about it."

"Your Uncle Faxon is the one who knows all the details."

"How did he come into it?" The girl had never got over her dislike of Faxon Cord, who took her mother away from her.

"He had to look after Gertrude's interests, of course. You see, your poor dear father died intestate, which didn't help when the Cords applied for probate of Mrs. Estrada's estate."

"Uncle Faxon's brother came over from Europe, didn't he?"

"He did indeed." And a tremendous row they had, Mrs. Randolph could have added. In a long life she had known nothing like a disputed inheritance to set families at loggerheads, and in this case the family had been harassed by the firm of solicitors who acted for St. Catherine's Convent and thus for Sister Cecilia, who 'in the world' had been Faith Estrada.

"Granny Estrada always said the house and everything in it would be mine," said Violet.

"I know she did, but in a way she had no right to say it, because the house and its contents were only part of your grandfather's estate, the whole of which he left in trust to her, with the reversion to his daughters and Jim's widow. He didn't know, of course, that Gertrude would marry again."

"But then, wasn't his estate valuable?"

"He had heavy losses in the last years of his life. He made some unwise speculations and sold his railway stock when he shouldn't – or maybe it was the other way round," said Mrs. Randolph helplessly. "And I know he lost a lot in the failure of Mr. Ralston's bank."

"I see."

"But you've been well taken care of, Violet. Faxon and Gertrude bought the flat on California Street for me, and they would have sent you to Mills Seminary if you had cared to go –"

"I know."

"And it isn't as if the Pine Street house were still there. It was insured with one of those wretched companies which repudiated all their claims after the earthquake, and never paid out a cent."

"That corner lot must have been valuable, though," said Violet shrewdly. "I suppose that was put up for sale?"

"It was all arranged when you and I were in Honolulu. And Uncle Faxon put two thousand dollars into the Pioneer Merchants' Bank in your name, remember; it'll be yours absolutely when you're twenty-one."

"I suppose I could ask for an accounting when I'm twenty-one," said Violet dreamily. She smiled, as she jingled the dimes and quarters in her purse, at the recollection of her grandmother's look of horror. It was a shame to have scared the poor darling; but some day it might be fun to throw a scare into Uncle Fax. The sugar plantation, for instance – where had he got the money to buy that?

The train ran into Niles, and two men, who had been eyeing the pretty girl hopefully, jostled each other to hand her bag and suitcase down the high steps to the platform. The town of

Niles, population four hundred, baked in the silence of a July afternoon.

"Hallo, Cinderella!"

She had been looking, rather forlornly, in the wrong direction, after the few passengers who had left the train, while the man who had come to meet her was chatting with the ticket agent. He limped forward to greet her. Unconsciously, she had hoped to see Bill Hastings, as if a director had nothing more important to do than meet the latest recruit to his company: it was an anticlimax to say "How are you, Mr. Siegrist?" and shake hands with the grinning cameraman.

Tim Siegrist was even more casually dressed than in San Francisco, in a blue shirt with a carelessly knotted tie, shabby riding breeches and well-polished boots. He was wearing a soft cloth cap which he did not remove, but tweaked at the brim by way of salutation, as he said,

"I'm standing in for Prince Charming. He's waiting for you at the boss's bungalow, they want to see you right away."

"Do you mean Mr. Anderson?" Violet asked nervously.

"Broncho Billy in person. Don't be scared, he won't eat you. Is this bag all you've got?"

"I've got plenty more clothes at my flat in San Francisco," she assured him, and Tim's face twisted in another smile.

"So you didn't burn all your boats; smart girl," he said, as he carried her bag into the station yard along with the flowers and candy.

"Is this *your* car?" she said in surprise. The French automobile drawn up at the kerb was fire-engine red, with gleaming brasswork, and the hood was down.

"My car's getting an overhaul this week, and this is Prince Charming's glass coach. I'm only the Rat Coachman. He lent it to me as a special favour to bring Cinderella to the palace."

"I wish you wouldn't go on about Cinderella!"

"Sorry, Princess, but you did say it was your favourite rôle, didn't you? You'll have to learn to take a bit of kidding, if you're going to work for Essanay."

He put her belongings in the back of the car and held open the door to the passenger's seat beside him. "Take a good look at Niles," he said, "if you don't you might miss it entirely. Our studio and the bungalows are four miles down the road."

"Who lives in the bungalows?"

"People the boss thinks important. I share one with Jeff Robbins, he's the chief cameraman."

"I thought you were the chief cameraman."

"I'm the lighting cameraman. Rollie Totheroh bunked with us too, but Chaplin took him off to L.A., much to the boss's annoyance . . . This is Second Street, where you'll probably be in one of the company cottages. There's an old girl who arranges the living quarters. And here's the new studio, where the westerns are made. It's a whole city block long, if you can call Niles a city."

It was hardly even a town. It had been built in 1869 on what had been an old Spanish grant to José Vallejo, a brother of the general and Don Salvador, as a service centre for farmers raising cattle, alfalfa and fruit. Niles, perhaps because it remained small, had absorbed the Essanay Film Manufacturing Company far more easily than the Los Angeles suburb of Hollywood, with ten times as many inhabitants, had accepted the eruption of movie-makers from the eastern seaboard. Irate farmers from Iowa, who had hoped to spend a peaceful retirement among the orange groves in the much-advertised sunshine of southern California, found themselves swamped by a constantly increasing mob of 'playactors', noisy, unpredictable and probably as loose in morals as in their use of an incomprehensible technical lingo. The Portuguese fruit ranchers of Niles had adapted to Essanay as far back as 1908, were proud of Broncho Billy, and deeply interested in the brief stay of Charlie Chaplin.

The French car passed the studio with the Essanay trade mark, the Indian head from the copper one-cent piece, and was in the open country before Violet Estrada spoke again.

"Mr. Siegrist –"

"Tim."

"Tim, then – why did you say I was smart not to burn my boats, and keep on our flat in San Francisco?"

He shot her a sidelong glance. "I was only jabbering. But at times it's good to know you've got a place of your own somewhere in the world."

"To hide in if Mr. Anderson says he hasn't got a job for me after all?"

Tim stopped the car. There was no other vehicle within sight. There were men working in the orchards, and there were cattle chewing their cud, but the silence was complete. Even in her nervous anxiety Violet was aware that this countryside, with its odours of lucerne and ripe peaches, of farmyards and orchards, smelled different from the heady tang of Sonoma's dry blend of redwood, eucalyptus and vines. Tim Siegrist took one of her gloved hands in his. "You poor baby," he said, "tell me what's been worrying you."

"What you said, and then his wanting to see me right away –"

"He's going to the city for a week, and it's only natural he should want to see what Bill and I found for him in San Francisco. You've got a job all right, and you've had an easy walk-in compared with some. How long you *stay* in is up to you."

"I understand that."

"Let me tell you about the boss, Vi. In many ways he's a strange man. Some folks laugh at him because he was a flop in his first movie, *The Great Train Robbery*, back in 1903. They kicked him out because he claimed he could ride and kept falling off his horse. But the thing to remember is that he got *back* on a horse and started making cowboy movies on his own. First in Golden, Colorado, and then here in Niles. He made Broncho Billy the top name in westerns, and the men who worked with him into stars. Francis X. Bushman, Buffalo Bill, Wes Ruggles, Ben Turpin, and now Chaplin. He's had them all on his payroll since he and George K. Spoor went into business in Chicago."

Tim started the car and let the engine idle. "Don't be fooled by his manner, or the way he lives here. He has a swell place in Chicago, where his wife and daughter live, but he's thought himself so hard into his cowboy part that in California he wants to live like Broncho Billy. And that's what you must do, Violet. Think yourself into the parts you're given, and show us you're something more than just another pretty face . . . I'm jabbering again," he apologised.

"Does Mr. Anderson make women into stars, or only men?" said Violet innocently.

"Griffith's the woman's star-maker, because he gets the

pick of the young actresses, but Essanay has a girl called Gloria Swanson who's got star quality, even if Charlie Chaplin claimed he couldn't work with her."

"And Bridget Malloy?"

"Pidge? You may be playing opposite her tomorrow, so I'll let you judge Pidgie's talent for yourself. And now we'd better hit the trail, or they'll be thinking we've eloped."

Gilbert Anderson's was the largest of the group of bungalows built round the glass-roofed studio which had succeeded the barn where the first Essanay movies were made, but there was nothing about the interior to suggest that the man had made a fortune out of being the father of all the western movies that ever would be screened. Tim ushered Violet into a room furnished with a roll-top desk, two or three chairs, and a table ringed with the marks of wet glasses, which held a brass ashtray overflowing with cigar and cigarette butts. Through an open door there was a glimpse of a bedroom even more spartan, with a single light bulb, unshaded, hanging above an iron bedstead, and a grocery box, also with an overflowing ashtray, as a bedside table. The owner of the seedy place was sprawled in one of the uncomfortable chairs, from which he heaved his bottom up about six inches in acknowledgment of Tim's perfunctory "This is Violet Estrada." The other occupant of the room, who was Willis Jerrold Hastings, was on his feet immediately, with a handshake and a white-toothed smile which warmed Violet's young heart.

Hastings was wearing what seemed to be the moviemaker's uniform of a white shirt open at the neck, whipcord riding breeches and knee-high boots, but unlike Tim Siegrist's hard-worn gear his impeccable outfit somehow gave the impression (quite wrong, as it happened) that the wearer had never ridden horseback in his life. Gilbert Anderson, to one who knew his screen image as well as Violet did, seemed naked without the Stetson hat and the two six shooters on their leather belt. He was half in and half out of his Broncho Billy costume, in the familiar plaid shirt worn with blue jeans for comfort, and carpet slippers. His face was set in the Billy mask of the roughneck cowboy with the heart of gold, capable of besting horse thieves and city slickers alike: it slipped not at all as he said to Violet:

"Take your hat off, miss."

She removed the straw hat with the faded cornflowers, which she now regarded as her lucky hat, and stood before them in a girlish blouse and skirt of blue chambray – disconcerted by the next order, which was to turn slowly round.

Mr. Anderson lit a cigarette, and blew smoke rings in her direction. "Very nice," he said. "She'll make a good foil for Whatsername – little Malloy. Blonde and brunette; the folks like that, don't they, Bill?"

"They sure do."

"Give her a bit in the serial, and see how she shapes up. She could play a Spick or a Mex with those looks, or even an Indio, with the right make-up."

"Not with those eyes," said Tim, speaking for the first time.

"Her eyes are beautiful," said Hastings softly, and the green Castilian eyes flashed Violet's gratitude. She was half sick with shame and embarrassment. To these men she was an object in a flesh market, not even worth being addressed directly: she shut her lips on angry words.

"Take her over to the studio, Tim," commanded the boss of Essanay. "Jeff's there, he'll want to see her too. And shoot about a dozen stills of her, I'd like to look 'em over before I go to Frisco. You trot along with Tim, miss – what's your name again?"

"Violet Estrada – sir."

"Won't do." Broncho Billy shook his head. "Can't have a Greaser name, the folks don't like it. Audiences only go for one hundred per cent American monikers. You got any ideas?"

Bill Hastings came quickly to the rescue. "What about your grandmother's name, Randolph? It was your mother's maiden name, so in a sense it's yours as well. Violet Randolph – I like that."

"Too high and mighty," said the oracle. "Make it Letty Randolph, that's cute and classy too. Letty Randolph – fine. Now that's settled, miss, off you go."

"Take it easy, kiddo," advised Tim Siegrist as soon as they were out of the bungalow. He had closed the door, but the windows were wide open, and he dreaded an outburst which could be heard inside. He took Violet's arm and hurried her down the short path, so that they were half way to the studio before she exclaimed,

"How dared he! Oh, how dared he! Calling Estrada a Greaser name, as if my family were cholos or riff-raff from Sonora! The Estradas were Spanish aristocrats, and my great-grandfather was one of the first rancheros on the northern frontier! His wife was a de la Guerra, and their eldest son married a Yorba! Our family has its roots in the history of Spanish California –"

"I wouldn't doubt it for a moment," said Tim, "but it's ancient history now, and Letty Randolph's a swell name for a movie actress."

"My great-grandfather raised cattle on twelve thousand acres in Sonoma while *that man*'s was nothing but a Pike County blackguard –"

"I don't believe they came from Missouri," said Tim with one of his crooked smiles. "Now calm down, and be nice to Jeff Robbins – he's one of the real good guys."

The good guy, who had finished shooting early, was loading his cameras for the next morning's work in one of the side rooms of the studio which was used for such meagre technical facilities as Essanay provided. The glass-roofed studio was insufferably hot, and furnished with a nondescript indoor set, which a half-grown boy, who was promptly told to get the hell out, was dusting and sweeping. Tim introduced the new actress to Robbins as Letty Randolph.

"Well now," said the chief cameraman cheerfully, "I see we got ourselves a genuine beauty at last. Glad to know you, Miss Letty. What's Tim going to do – shoot a few stills? That's a mighty important start, because while we know what the human eye sees in you, we have to know what the camera eye sees too. Where do you want her, Tim? Standing, with a back light, or on the sofa?"

"Oh please!" said the new Letty, "isn't there some place where I could wash and brush my hair? I feel so hot and grubby from the train."

"That's just the way I want you," said Tim, "hot and bad tempered; you'll get a chance to pretty up later. No, don't put your hat back on, just sit on the sofa and have a chat with Jeff."

He limped off to another side room and came back with a camera not much larger than the Kodaks of which the girls at Miss West's school were so proud. There was none of the apparatus which a cabinet photographer used. No tripod, no clamp to hold her head in place, no black cloth enveloping the photographer's head; Tim strolled around while she listened to Jeff Robbins's soothing tale of the serial they were making, and now and again she heard the camera click. Then Tim said abruptly, "All right, that's enough of that. Go to the washroom, through the door on the left, and take off your shirtwaist and your camisole, or whatever you wear underneath."

"*Mr. Siegrist!*"

"Come on, come on!" he said impatiently. "I'm not going to sculpt you in the nude. I told the wardrobe girl to leave out a couple yards of tulle for you to wrap up in; if it's not hanging on a peg give me a yell and I'll find something else. I want to be able to shoot your bare neck and shoulders. Oh, and let your hair down too."

There was no need for a yell, because the length of pale-blue tulle was on the bar which held a roller towel. It was not particularly fresh, being stained with wet-white in several places, but after Violet had a wash and brushed her hair she thought the tulle covered her breasts well enough, and made a frame for her shoulders and slender upper arms. Jeff Robbins smiled encouragingly when she went back to the men. Tim said nothing, but posed her sitting, leaning back, bending forward, with one arm raised above her head, and finally half turned away and looking back at him over her shoulder.

"Let's make this a good one, Cinderella," he said, and when her nervous disappointment found expression in a retort of "Don't call me Cinderella!" he took his last photograph, and said elliptically to the watching Robbins, "See what I mean?"

"My God, yes," said Robbins. "You've got something there all right."

"Wait till you see the proofs," said Tim, and to the girl, "Go get your togs on and I'll drive you back to town. You did fine, Letty – all the way through. And don't worry about what the boss said about a Greaser name. His own name isn't Gilbert Anderson. It's Max Aronson."

8

"We sure threw you in at the deep end, darling!" Willis Jerrold Hastings was to say to Letty a few weeks after she arrived at Niles. She had learned by then not to take 'darling' seriously, since it was used indiscriminately by members of the company, but it was a thrill to hear him say it in his deep stage voice, and to know the director felt she had survived her first plunge into the strange waters. She had also learned how lucky she was in her timing, starting out when Broncho Billy, after six weeks of intensive filming, had driven in his green Mercedes to San Francisco to have a look at a musical comedy in which he had an interest, taking Jeff Robbins with him and leaving Hastings and Siegrist to wind up a serial in which nobody believed and nobody acted well. Letty made her first appearance in the last instalment, made up and dressed as an Indian maiden with her black hair in two plaits, having nothing to do but hiss "White squaw, I hate you!" at the blonde and beautiful Bridget Malloy.

She had the consolation of knowing that in Mary Pickford's early days in movies Griffith had often cast her as an Indian, notably in *A Pueblo Legend*, back in 1912. "Mary was a real trouper," said Mrs. Brice, the housekeeper of the company, who had been a wardrobe woman with Griffith in those days. "She'd play any part she was given, good or bad, and see where she is today!"

Letty Randolph saw. She saw that being in pictures was not the glamorous adventure she and her Crowd had imagined, but that there could be great rewards for a willing learner, and she was ready to learn. After a good night's sleep she was ready for anything. Mrs. Brice was a comfort, for after showing Letty to a tidy bedsitting room in her own cottage she brought the girl a bowl of broth and a plate of hot buttered toast and advised bed after the early supper was eaten. "If you've a four o'clock call you're going to need all the sleep you can get," she said. "They say Mr. Siegrist's a stickler for punctuality on the set. By the way, it was a Miss Violet Estrada he told me to expect; what happened? Mr. Anderson make you change your name?"

"Yes, he did."

Mrs. Brice chuckled. "Lord bless you, he does that to all of 'em. Poor little Kitty O'Rourke came to me in tears after he told her she was to call herself Marcella Meade. Can't have two Irish names in my Number Two company, says Mister High and Mighty, and of course Bridget Malloy was first on the scene. Have you met her yet?"

"I met her in San Francisco, with Mr. Hastings."

"Oh sure, with Mr. Hastings. Her poor old drunk of a father came down here last month and started a row with that same Hastings – and him with a good kind daughter like Bridget, who's been his sole support since he got fired from the St. Francis Hotel . . . There now, I mustn't stand here gossiping," said Mrs. Brice, picking up the supper tray. "If you'd like to take a nice hot bath, it's down the hall."

The serial which to everyone's relief was coming to an end was called *The Trials of Terry*, and was Essanay's mistaken attempt to cash in on the popular serial form. Originally begun as a tie-in with newspaper serial stories, the movie version had long outstripped the format, and audiences who had never heard of the *Chicago Tribune* avidly followed *The Adventures of Kathlyn*. Pathé and the Hearst newspapers had cashed in on *The Perils of Pauline*. One hundred and nineteen episodes of *The Hazards of Helen*, begun in 1914, would run for two years, and in a glutted market there was hardly room for *The Trials of Terry*. Bridget Malloy exulted profanely, as she stripped off her make-up that evening, that her own trials as Terry had come to an end.

So began Letty's bonding with the company, which grew stronger every day. If they were shooting on location, which usually meant the rugged scenery of Niles Canyon, where many a badman fled from the sheriff's posse, she actually enjoyed the trip at daybreak, before even the Portuguese fruit pickers were astir, and the rich soil of Alameda County exuded the very smell of fertility. If they were working on the studio floor there were other odours to endure from the Cooper-Hewitt mercury vapour lamps hanging from the ceiling, a form of lighting preferred by Tim Siegrist to the newer Kliegs. He was always the first on the scene, indoors or out, with his cameras and magazine loaded, and his boy assistant (the same who swept the studio) ready with his check list of the ground glass pressure pad, the aperture plate, the hand magnifier and the white sheet ready for instant use as a hand reflector. He was a thorough professional, a big advance on the old style camera-man who swore that all he needed was 'one box lunch, one two-dollar bill and one roll of film'. It was Tim, cranking his heavy Bell and Howell camera, with the inevitable cap twisted back to front on his head, and his mouth twisted in some sarcastic comment, who brought life to the mediocre stories they were putting on film.

Willis Jerrold Hastings, as a director, was hampered by the conventions of the stage. He thought of films as stage plays, divided into acts, each act beginning with a fade-in and ending with a fade-out. He had advanced as far in technique as the sequence of long shot, medium shot and close-up, but he was unable to follow Tim when the cameraman talked of 'floating composition' and 'creative editing'. All Hastings knew about editing was that the finished film had to be cut from the negatives, a laborious process, and he forbade Tim to waste time on out-of-focus shots and fluid camera movements. With only three days at his disposal to make a one-reeler, he was always urging speed, and one old style cameraman's expression often on Tim's lips was "D'you want it fast or d'you want it good?"

On the first day they worked in the glass-roofed studio Tim asked Letty to stay behind when the shooting schedule ended, and produced a set of the still pictures taken when she came to Niles. She gasped when she saw them. They were completely unlike the sepia-tinted cabinet photographs which her mother insisted should be taken every year, so that the Cord family in Honolulu might have a record of dear Violet's progress from one party dress and one hair style to another. Tim's pictures had not been retouched, nor were they glossy. They were rough and grainy and highly emotional, showing a woman with a sullen, sensual Spanish beauty, a greedy mouth and brilliant eyes. The last in the series, Letty's reaction to the Cinderella taunt, could only be called vicious.

"What do you think of them?" said Tim.

"They're not very flattering."

"I didn't mean them to be flattering. I meant them as a frame of reference."

"For what?"

"For the kind of parts I'd like to see you play some day."

"They make me look much older than eighteen."

"Yes, well, you *are* older than eighteen, so quit fooling. Next time I want to shoot some action stills with a high-speed Graflex, and the lens covered with silk net, and see how those come out. Sorry you don't like this lot."

Letty was fairly certain that she didn't like Tim, but she was annoyed when she heard some of the promoted horse-wranglers who played in the Broncho Billy films calling him Gimpy Tim, and betting him he couldn't do a Brodie or a bulldog now, or any of the stunts which had been the beginning of his work in movies. The poor man couldn't help being lame! But he could help being sarcastic, and it was his sarcasm Letty hated, when he used it at her expense. Bill Hastings was the only one who could protect her from it, but when they broke for lunch and rested under the trees of Niles Canyon, it was Pidgie Malloy who had the director's company, while Tim Siegrist, as often as not, picked up his platter of food and mug of coffee and sat down by Letty Randolph. One day he actually praised her riding. "You're the best horsewoman in the company," he said. "It must be your proud Spanish blood."

"Thank you," she said, refusing to be drawn. "I hadn't ridden for years, but I suppose one doesn't forget how."

"No," he said, "one doesn't." And Letty, unexpectedly, felt pity, wondering if the lame man with the thin, downcast face missed the rodeo riding which had been his life for so long.

"When did it happen?" she said, and Tim, understanding, touched his right hip and said "This? Three years ago, at the Calgary Stampede. I was trying a bump, what we call a one-oh-eight – that's a comic fall backwards – and I came a cropper and was ridden over. That's all there was to it."

"But how did you get started in the rodeos? You're a Canadian, aren't you?"

"No, whatever made you think that? I'm a Californian pioneer, just like your noble self. Not that humble Switzers like the Siegrists can match up to the great Estradas, but my great-grandad was one of Sutter's men at Sutter's Fort in the Bear Flag days. Too bad he hadn't the wits to cash in on the discovery of gold in Sutter's mill race."

"A Swiss!" she said. "So your family defended the northern frontier, like my own!"

"The Swiss are strictly neutral," said Tim with his mocking smile. "But they usually do better financially than the Siegrists. My old man died broke, and I didn't even finish high school, but I got taken on as a stable hand at the Miller Ranch, where cowboys like Tom Mix and Buck Jones learned how to stunt for the movies. Pretty soon I got to work with the stunt men, and didn't do too badly in two or three races, so then I was picked for the rodeo team. Four of them were Indians – and say, their half-breeds make the best stunt men in the game – and we went the rounds of the rodeos until I blew that one-oh-eight at Calgary."

"It must have been awful for you." The man wondered if Letty Randolph knew how beautiful she was then, even in one of the frayed and mended dresses from Wardrobe, with her green eyes soft with sympathy and her black hair gleaming in the sunlight falling through the leaves. He knew it would be out of keeping with the character he had created for himself to kiss her hand.

"Maybe it was a blessing in disguise," he said jauntily. "A. D. Kean was filming the Calgary Stampede – you've heard of him, the guy they call the Cowboy Cameraman – and Colonel Zack Miller hired him to do some filming at the 101 Ranch on the old Spanish grant at Santa Monica. When I got out of hospital I went back there, to work in the offices they said, but A. D. Kean taught me how to use a camera instead, and he got me my first job with Mack Sennet . . . What gives, Bert?"

Bert, his young assistant, came to say Mr. Hastings was

ready to start. He wanted to wrap this one up today. 'This one' was an effort by Jack Hastings, *the writer*, on a theme dear to Broncho Billy. An all-American family, oozing goodwill and rustic humour, is beset by a city slicker's attempts to seduce the blonde daughter, and a crooked lawyer's threat to foreclose the mortgage on the farm. Letty as the blonde girl's brunette sister had one good scene where she stood up to the crook and revealed his villainy. They took it very fast, and Bill Hastings had his movie in the can before the sun went down.

There was seldom time for a rehearsal or even a walkthrough of the two-reelers. Whether the subject was a great classic novel or a piece of trash from the pulp magazines, it had to be condensed into two thousand feet of film and rushed to the distributors. It was as if the world beyond the Niles orchards was stalked by a new monster called the Movie Audience, multi-national, polyglot and insatiable, with all of its many heads demanding a daily ration of movie fare. Essanay's girl scenarist in Chicago, Louella Parsons, was turning out the stuff like hamburger meat. Playhouses like palaces were being built to house the monster. Stars rose and fell at its whim. Cameramen like Gimpy Tim worked round the clock to create the dream images which the monster took for reality. And the actors, for whom early publicists were inventing glamorous lives, were too exhausted by the end of each day to desire anything more glamorous than a good night's sleep.

But before they could sleep they had to unwind, and that could only be done in each other's society. Most of the cowboys in the Billy saga liked to do some evening drinking in one of the town's three hotels, but the members of the Number Two company usually gathered in one of the bungalows for an hour or so of beer and sandwiches, cards and 'stunts', meaning charades, or solo performances. The children of the camera were always 'on camera', doing imitations of Douglas Fairbanks or Lillian Gish, or even of each other. Living as they did in an enclosed community they thought they knew one another inside out, and the company gossip flowed like an endless river. 'Everybody' predicted that Hastings's affair with Pidgie Malloy would soon be on the skids, even if he still drove her to San Francisco for supper twice a week and for the whole day on Sunday. Pidgie had grown irritable and unreliable. The charitable said it was because of her wretched father, dismissed from his job as a baggage man at the St. Francis Hotel for persistent drunkenness. The more sophisticated, with pursed lips and knowing nods, hinted at another reason for Pidge's alternating moods of excitability and depression, and thought someone should have a word with Mr. Anderson. Nobody was willing to be the one.

Letty Randolph was perfectly happy in this tense environment. She had found the acceptance she craved, and her vanity was fed by increasing praise. Tim had taken a flattering series of action stills, all shot in the woods and orchards, of a happy, smiling Letty, and Broncho Billy himself had approved them, going so far as to say that some of these pix might be hanging in a 'theayter' lobby one day soon. Letty wrote excitedly to Sonoma and Honolulu, and even to Joe Gregory care of Coppa's Restaurant about her brilliant prospects, receiving affectionate letters and from Joe a comic postcard in reply.

Mrs. Randolph alone struck a plaintive note.

It worries me, dear child [she wrote] that you have never found time to go up to San Francisco and visit our little home. I know the superintendent is looking after the utilities, but I should like to hear from yourself that all is well. I think they must be working you too hard, and you ought to have a day off now and then. Don't you have Sundays free?

It was the end of September, and although it was still very hot in the fruit country, cooler weather would be coming in, and Letty decided to go to the city, set her grandmother's mind at rest about the flat, and bring back some warmer clothing. She took care to enquire about the Sunday train schedules during a lunch break on Friday, two days after reading her letter. She was told in a chorus that the Sunday trains were hopeless, that the city was jammed with visitors to the Panama-Pacific Exposition and most uncomfortable, but said with a heroic sigh that there was no help for it, she must take the ten-thirty train on Sunday morning, and fight her way to California Street on the cable car. She tried to hide her elation when at ten-ten, as she was nearing Niles station, Bill Hastings stopped the French tourer by her side and said, "Jump in. I'll get you to San Francisco faster than the train."

"What about Pidgie? I thought you took her to town on Sundays."

"Not this Sunday."

★   ★   ★

"Well!" he said an hour later, as he parked his car outside her apartment building, "are you going to invite me in and show me where you live?"

"It may take me half an hour to pack. Don't you want to drive to the St. Francis and come back? You said you had some business telephone calls to make."

"They can wait till after lunch," he said, and walked round the car to help her out. The building superintendent, who had been peeping through a side window, was holding open the door.

"Nice to see you back, Miss Estrada," he said. "You going to stay a while?"

"Not this time, Mr. Rooney," said Letty. "Are you and your wife quite well?"

"Sure we are, and you'll find everything in good order in your apartment. You might tell your grandma I put new washers on the kitchen taps."

"Mrs. Randolph will be glad to know that; she was worried about the drips," said Letty distantly. "Thank you very much."

"You're welcome, Miss Estrada." All the time Rooney was speaking his eyes were on Bill Hastings, summing him up: a dude, dressed to kill, shooting a line with the Estrada doll – all the clichés went through the limited brain of the 'super', a small balding man in a decent blue serge suit, with slits cut in his shoes to accommodate his bunions. He watched the couple as they climbed the two flights of stairs which led to Mrs. Randolph's apartment.

"What a charming room," said Bill conventionally.

"But my heavens, it's hot!"

"Let me do that." The man opened the window wide.

"I think Mister Rooney, as he likes to be called, might have

434

aired it out from time to time," said Letty. "He's a horrid little man. Bill, do sit down – I shan't be long."

Hastings remained standing, looking round the room. It was not charming at all, but so impersonal with its newish rug and its newish, modern furniture that he had to remind himself that it belonged to a lady who twice in her life had had her home burned down – the first time by the Union army, the second time in the San Francisco earthquake and fire. There were no family portraits, no memorabilia: only several well-filled bookshelves gave any clue to the owner's background.

"Would you like a drink, Bill? I'm afraid there's only brandy."

Letty had come back quickly, carrying a papier-maché tray with a bottle, a carafe of water and one glass. Southern hospitality – of course!

"Brandy will be great, darling, thank you."

"I'll pack as quickly as I can."

"Take your time." The brandy was of the vintage kept for medicinal purposes, and as the iceman's visits had been discontinued the tap water was too warm; Bill Hastings drank a little of the mixture, feeling that things were getting out of hand. He could have sworn that little Letty was giving him the come-on when she went into that routine about catching the ten-thirty train, and he had planned accordingly: first the trip to California Street, then an early lunch at the hotel, then an invitation to his room while he put through his 'business calls' – his brother, *the writer*, at Chauvet's Crossing could co-operate in any code – and then the promise of a great part in a great movie 'if you'll be nice to me, baby . . .' The industry was still in its infancy, but a director's favour already had its price.

There was something in this room, so plain, so dignified, so unlike that pigsty of Pidgie's south of Market, which made Bill Hastings falter in his conquering stride. He looked at the upright piano, the glass-fronted china cabinet, the bookcase, for inspiration. The books! That might do the trick.

It was twenty minutes before Letty returned, with a leather portmanteau in one hand and a cloth coat over her arm. "Please forgive me for being so long," she began, and gasped when he took her belongings from her and held her in his arms. "Darling," he said, "I didn't mean to tell you yet, but I can't resist you . . . you're so sweet, and so clever . . . Anderson's going to give you a leading part."

"Me – playing a lead? Oh Bill, what in?"

"One of the Bret Harte stories. Put the book in your bag –"

"What book?"

She had gone over the edge, he realised, as he pressed her body to his own and felt her passionate response. He could have her now, without any bargain struck, here in this silent, private place where the blinds would be drawn in an unaired bedroom with no sheets on the stripped bed. He kissed her deeply and felt rather than heard her moan. With a mighty effort he subdued his rising lust. This thing was running out of control, like a film when the cameraman had used a technical trick to speed up the action. I'm in trouble enough already, he thought, furious with himself. Pidgie could wreck me if she wanted to, and that rat-faced little Mick in the lobby might be a younger version of Pidgie's stinking father. Very gently Bill Hastings began to withdraw from Letty's passionate embrace.

"Darling, how can I think about books or anything else while you're so lovable?" he whispered. "You are so young that you make me young again." He couldn't remember which play that line was from, possibly an Italian melodrama called *Malatesta*, but it worked on his bewildered audience of one as it had once worked in Belasco's theatre. "You've got to help me keep my head for both our sakes. Help me to be sane and sensible and take you away from here, back to where the crowds are, and talk about the new play and your future. So that we can both tell Tim exactly what we want him to do for you . . ."

"What's Tim Siegrist got to do with it?" asked Letty in a drugged voice. She was standing away from Hastings now, and, shivering, crossed her arms upon her breast.

"He'll be your director."

* * *

When she was back in her room at Niles, and it was midnight, Letty as she watched the waning moon through her window had almost succeeded in forgetting that scene in her grandmother's apartment. She remembered running cold water over her wrists in the narrow bathroom, and powdering her flushed face before they left to drive to the St. Francis, where they drank wine with their soft-shell crabs and petrale from the bay. She remembered very little about what Hastings said about the new movie and her part in it. But she did recollect, and always would, how when they left the hotel he pointed to the statue of Victory in Union Square, the bronze figure of a slender girl poised on one foot with a laurel wreath in her hand.

"She reminds me of you," Bill Hastings said.

Letty went to work on Monday morning in a high-strung mood which appeared to be shared by no one else. Bridget Malloy had reported sick, which upset the shooting schedule. Tim Siegrist had left for Oakland on Sunday afternoon in his battered Winton and had not returned. "Off on one of his drinkin' jags," Mrs. Brice told Letty. "He's been real good lately, but something" (she looked slyly at the girl) "seems to have upset'm yesterday." Willis Jerrold Hastings was in conference with Jeff Robbins, discussing how the two gaps were to be filled, and how Robbins was to 'shoot around' Broncho Billy, who had gone to Los Angeles for a business talk with Charlie Chaplin. An unsatisfactory day's work was done.

Letty spent the evening alone in her comfortable room, which had a gas ring for making soup or coffee. It was a dark night, with a hint of wind and rain blowing down from San Francisco. The off-hand "Keep your fingers crossed" could stories by Bret Harte which she had brought from the living room in California Street. She had never read any of them but *The Luck of Roaring Camp*, and there was no woman's part worth mentioning in that.

"The scenarist did an adaptation of *Tennessee's Partner* for Mr. Anderson," Hastings had said. "It worked pretty well, but there again there wasn't a woman's part. Tim thinks the right stories are sure-fire box office, and he was saying only the other night *In the Carquinez Woods* was tailor-made for you as Teresa. But Douglas Fairbanks is filming it for Triangle right now, so that's out. *The Half-Breed*, they're calling it. I hear Beth Fairbanks disapproved of her husband being cast as what she called a dirty Indian."

"Charming lady. And what about Teresa? Was she a dirty Indian too?"

"No, she was a Mexican. Wonderful part for the right girl."

So now, in her basket chair beneath the flaring gas, Letty was absorbing the part which Tim Siegrist had thought to be tailor-made for her. She wouldn't have been cast as Nellie Wynne, the preacher's pretty and virtuous daughter, oh no! Teresa had 'come from a circus troupe' and 'used to dance at the Alhambra'; she 'stabbed Dick Carson, her lover' before she fled from the officers of the law to seek shelter with the half-breed (in reality a distinguished botanist) in the Carquinez Woods. Just the right part for a girl with a Greaser name! The insult offered her by Max Aronson, alias G. M. Anderson, boiled up again in Letty's passionate young heart. She read no further, although Hastings had hinted that *Mliss* was the story they might choose for her. *Mliss* could wait.

Tim Siegrist was back at work next morning, haggard and uncommunicative except for the curses he heaped on his assistant, Bert. He had a bruise along his right jaw which suggested that the drinkin' jag had ended in a free-for-all. Tim kept out of everyone's way until Broncho Billy came back from Los Angeles, looking as battered as if he had been in a verbal free-for-all with Charlie Chaplin. Tim had supper in the boss's bungalow, where they talked for hours, and at the end of the next day's shooting Bill Hastings walked off the set with Letty and murmured that Gimpy Tim had made a great pitch for *Mliss* and had as good as gotten Broncho Billy's say-so.

"Keep your fingers crossed, little girl!" was his farewell, and Letty, removing her make-up, could hardly equate the banality with his passionate words of that hot Sunday in San Francisco. The off-hand "Keep your fingers crossed" could have been said to anybody. He had called her lovable; was he really determined to 'keep his head for both their sakes'? The old feeling of rejection, first experienced when her mother left her for Faxon Cord, came back in strength as she again sat alone in her room, to be dispelled when Mrs. Brice's cheerful voice sang out:

"Gentleman visitor for you, Miss Letty!"

She sprang up eagerly, letting the volume of Bret Harte

stories fall to the ground. But it was not Bill Hastings who had come to see her. It was Tim Siegrist, who said, hesitatingly for him, "Hallo, Letty. You don't mind – I mean, is it all right for me to call on you here?"

"Yes, why not? Sit down, Tim, if you don't object to the rocking-chair, and tell me what's on your mind."

He adjusted himself to the creaking chair, and said "I hear you've been reading *Mliss*."

"I've just finished it, as a matter of fact. It doesn't take long to read."

"Not unless you read between the lines, and that's what we have to work on."

"Who's we?"

"The actors and myself, as soon as we can get the cast together. And that can't be done in a day."

"I thought at Essanay most things could be done in a day."

"Well, this isn't one of them. *Mliss* can't be rushed, as I explained to Mr. Anderson," said Tim, "and finally I got him to see it my way. But he refused to let me make a four-reeler. Says he can't afford it, not after all this trouble with Chaplin."

"So is it to be a one-reeler or a two?"

"A two, thank God. Now tell me what you thought of Melissa Smith, the orphan of Red Mountain."

"Of Mliss herself? I thought she was very sweet, much nicer than that Teresa creature Bill said you wanted me to play in *The Half-Breed*."

"Bill told you that, did he?" Tim frowned. "Well, the question doesn't arise, it's *Mliss* we're filming, and unfortunately not until the last week in October. Can't fit it into the shooting schedule any sooner. Now this is what I came to ask you: are you willing to spend time on evening rehearsals and walk-throughs, say three times a week before the shooting starts? Just one hour at a time would make all the difference to the production."

"I'll do anything I'm told to do, you know that," she said indifferently.

"But be enthusiastic, Letty, please!" said Tim. "Please believe in me! With the right casting *Mliss*'ll be great box-office, *and* a star-maker!"

439

"What d'you mean by the right casting?"

"I'll try to persuade Anderson to hire an established juvenile to play opposite you, like Arthur Johnson or James Morrison. If he won't meet their price I've got my eye on one of the cowboys. And then I need a youngster to play the schoolgirl, Clytie –"

"Not Bridget Malloy?"

"She wouldn't go for second billing. And something's the matter with poor old Pidgie these days. Too many ups and downs, always over the moon or down in the dumps. I need a kid easier to direct."

"What will Bill say to all this juggling about with his actors? Cutting out Pidgie, and bringing in one of the cow-pokes?"

"It's got nothing to do with Bill Hastings," said Tim quietly. "I'm directing this one. Letty, listen to me!" (as she stooped to pick the Bret Harte volume from the floor) "Is Bill's opinion so important to you? Do you really think that old hambone of Belasco's is a top authority on movie-making?"

"He said he and I would work together on *Mliss*."

"When did he say that?"

"Last Sunday in San Francisco."

"When you were silly enough to invite him to your home?"

"What the hell do you mean?" said Letty, and she too was on her feet. "What business is it of yours where I choose to go with Bill Hastings?"

"A man twice your age, who's been through two New York divorces, and enjoys seeing you make a fool of yourself as Pidgie Malloy did before you –"

Letty drew her hand back, with the leather-bound book in it, but before she could throw it at his face Tim Siegrist caught her wrist in his strong fingers and forced her to drop it. "Well done!" he said admiringly. "That's the look I caught before, the day you came to Niles. That's the look I want for Mliss. Now cry, you little spitfire!"

She was crying in spite of herself, angry tearing sobs through which she gasped, "You have no right to interfere!"

"No right, perhaps, but a pretty good reason," said Tim sadly. "You see – I happen to be in love with you."

She stared at him incredulously. "Is this another of your jokes, Tim?"

"It *is* funny, isn't it? Gimpy Tim daring to raise his eyes to Señorita Doña Violetta Estrada, La Favorita of Niles, California?"

"But you aren't even *nice* to me!"

"I know I got off on the wrong foot with you at the start. All that kidding and joshing . . . But it was only a cover-up, Letty. I fell for you the first day I saw you, and I believe I can make you care for me. Will you give me a chance? Can we go back to the beginning and start over?"

"You'd only make yourself unhappy, Tim."

"That means there's no hope for me? All right, it can't be helped. But if you ever need me, you know I'll be right there, and meanwhile you're going to work at bringing in a real good movie, aren't you?"

"I'm going to try."

She did her best, but like most of the rest of the cast Letty Randolph had difficulty in coping with Tim's ideas on how to film an old standby of the stage like *Mliss*. The actor and actress chosen to play the hypocritical pastor and Clytie's mother, known to the miners as the Per-airie Rose, were seasoned troupers who had actually played in the dramatised version of the early 1870s. They seemed quite unable to grasp what Tim was telling them at the rehearsals on which the fledgling director insisted. It was a sweetly pretty story, they declared. Mliss, otherwise Melissa Smith of Smith's Pocket, the orphan daughter of a miner who died broke on Red Mountain, wants to get an education. She is jealous of Clytie, her pretty schoolfellow, who seems to be favoured by the schoolmaster. She finds comfort in the forest and the creatures of the woods. She threatens to run away with a company of strolling players, and the schoolmaster, returning her love, takes her away with him instead.

"And that's all there is to it, Tim!" insisted old Burton, who played the pastor. "Mliss is a lovely child of nature, and you're trying to turn her into Lady Macbeth!"

"Mliss is a bully and an emotional blackmailer," said Tim. "When she threatens to commit suicide or run off with the actor guy, she only wants to bring the schoolmaster to heel.

Do you notice Harte didn't even bother to give the poor chap a name? Mliss is a shrew and their life together will be hell, and that's the way I'm going to film it, see?"

Even Broncho Billy, who took only a lukewarm interest in the production, thought Tim was on the wrong track. "You're gettin' too big for your britches, boy," he said when Tim asked him to hire a 'name' actor to play the schoolmaster. "Me go outside my own company for one of the matinée idols – not a chance! Arthur Johnson's been a star for seven years, he'd cost a fortune, and I know for a fact that James Morrison's getting seventy a week right now –"

"He's the exact type for the part, though."

"Well, look about you and pick the same type from my own payroll. Haven't I upped you to thirty a week to do the donkey work on this fancy project? Get Bill to help you if you can't handle it alone."

Eventually Tim picked a James Morrison type from the Broncho Billy company. It was the young stunt rider he had mentioned to Letty, a boy of eighteen, thin-faced and charming, passive enough to take direction well and active enough to be convincing in his muted love scenes with the turbulent Mliss. He was the only one who seemed to understand what Tim meant when he talked about creating emotion out of motion, or about using deep focus shots to develop action spatially. The fifteen-year-old girl who played Clytie, and who chewed gum all through Tim's talks, was obviously out of her depth but paid attention because the promoted stunt rider told her to, and Letty had a jealous feeling that Tim was an innovator and a creative artist far above a girl like herself who knew little more than how to recite 'Bingen on the Rhine' to an uncritical audience. The stunt rider's awareness annoyed her, and she thought his name ridiculous: it was Willie Bleer.

In 1941, when Willie Bleer had been world-famous for years as Wayne Blackwood, he won the Oscar award for Best Actor in a Hollywood war movie. He played the part of a heroic American yachtsman who organises, single-handed, the evacuation of the British Expeditionary Force from Dunkirk. In his acceptance speech Blackwood generously stated, to applause, that the first person who really taught him about acting was 'that veteran genius of the camera, Timothy Siegrist'. Wayne Blackwood was then a handsome man of forty-four; it was an eighteen-year-old whom Tim put through his paces, and as soon as shooting began Letty knew that she must act better than she had ever done if she were to outmatch Willie Bleer. It was a gruelling week, for the leaves were off the orchard trees, and they had to go deeper and deeper among the evergreens of Niles Canyon for the woodland scenes, while the studio sets, in which lighting was a key factor, were used for exercises in pictorial composition. The old troupers shook their heads at the final fade, which showed Mliss and her schoolmaster walking off, not into the conventional sunset, but under dark and ominous clouds, but the movie was in the can, and that was enough for most of them. By way of celebration, Tim got out his car and drove 'my two stars', as he called them, up to Oakland and gave them dinner at the Hotel Metropole.

It was a pleasant, impersonal evening, as the whole of Tim's conduct had been since his surprising declaration of love for Letty. It was also a much needed escape from the atmosphere of frustration which had hung over the Essanay studio since G. M. Anderson returned from his Los Angeles meeting with Charlie Chaplin. Somehow the reason for the trip leaked out. Chaplin had been offered $25,000 for two weeks' personal appearances in New York, which of course would mean the interruption of filming at the Boyle Heights studio. After an acrimonious discussion, Anderson had agreed to pay Chaplin the same sum, $25,000, to forgo the trip to New York. He could afford to do so, for every Chaplin film – so the comedian estimated – was now earning $50,000 for Essanay, and these astronomical sums caused heartburnings at Niles, where salaries were low and production costs cut to a minimum. The actors were not business people, but they were all smart enough to know that 1915 was the year when, with *The Birth of a Nation*, Hollywood had emerged as the movie capital while they had sidetracked themselves into Alameda County, 'working for a penny-pinching bastard like Anderson'.

The Birth of a Nation had been sold to exhibitors on a franchise basis, the purchasers having the right to show the picture in defined territories. The New England rights went to a junk dealer called Louis B. Mayer. He had done well out of the deal; so had they all, and D. W. Griffith, in spite of the furore created by the National Association for the Advancement of the Coloured People, who called his picture racist and sought to ban it, was casting for an even more spectacular movie to be called *Intolerance*. There was a growing feeling among the Essanay actors that they might be smart to cut their losses and head for Hollywood and bit parts in *Intolerance*.

Broncho Billy was quite aware of the disaffection in his company. Though the principal concern was Chaplin, who in spite of all the bonuses was threatening to leave Essanay when his contract expired and go to Mutual, he hoped to mend his fences at Niles by giving his actors an unusual treat. The Panama-Pacific Exposition was due to close in December, by which time over eighteen million people would have passed through its gates. One great attraction was still in reserve: the sixth of November was designated Lotta Crabtree Day, when San Francisco's most beloved actress would once again appear before the public.

Lotta Crabtree never married. She had made her home in the east since retiring from the stage in 1891 after a career which had lasted for thirty-six triumphant years. Only the oldest generation of San Franciscans remembered Lotta singing 'Bright Champagne' at the opening of the California Theatre in 1869, but to the youngest, buying flowers and meeting their sweethearts at Lotta's Fountain, her name was evergreen. She was to be the guest of the city at the St. Francis Hotel, and although her appearance at the Exposition would be a celebration of the Gold Rush era, when a tiny Lotta first danced on a blacksmith's anvil at Rough and Ready, it would also be a celebration of the city's long devotion to the performing arts. Broncho Billy organised transportation to the city for all his company, and places in the special area round the platform where a choir would serenade the uncrowned Queen of the Rocky Mountains.

Those favoured with seats in the roped-off area were already in their places when Miss Crabtree left her hotel, escorted by the millionaire banker William Crocker and his wife. They drove in a stage coach drawn by four white horses, with outriders dressed as placer miners, first to Lotta's Fountain where a cheering crowd had gathered, and then out to the

Marina, as the Exposition district had come to be called.

The eleven great exhibit palaces and the pavilions of foreign nations were showing the effects of ten months' exposure to San Francisco weather, but the Festival Hall was brightened by a mass display of yellow chrysanthemums on the platform, where the Exposition Chorus of three hundred and fifty singers, themselves dressed in yellow, had assembled to serenade the heroine of the day. In the audience the Essanay players formed a solid block, with Broncho Billy in full cowboy array on the platform. Letty found herself seated between Willis Jerrold Hastings and Tim Siegrist. One had called her lovable, the other had said he loved her; neither was paying her more attention than if she had been the elderly actress who played the Per-airie Rose. Only Bill admonished her to watch Lotta Crabtree's every movement. "You're going to see a living legend, darling," he said. "She's as graceful as she was thirty years ago, when I saw her in a revival of *Firefly*, not long before she retired. Of course I was just a kid then."

"D'you mean you've seen her since she came to San Francisco?"

"I met her with her party last night in the hotel."

"How old is she?"

"Going on for seventy, I should think."

"Sixty-eight," said Tim curtly. He was more silent than usual, as if his thoughts were far away. Letty knew that he had been working hard on the cutting and editing of *Mliss*, which was to be shown to the cast and any others interested next Sunday afternoon.

"Here she comes!" All the voices in the Festival Hall became one voice as the platform party appeared: the civic notabilities, the Native Sons of the Golden West and the California Society of Pioneers fully represented, the furred and feathered ladies, and in their midst one small figure, slender and erect, her hair more silver than red now: Lotta Crabtree in a shimmering golden gown.

"Lotta! Lotta!"

It was the acclamation she had heard since childhood, in the young and lusty San Francisco of sixty years ago, and there were tears in the star's eyes as she bowed with her own grace to right and left of the crowd. As soon as she was seated the choir began to sing the 'Hallelujah Chorus'.

It was a splendid ovation, and as she watched and listened and applauded Letty Randolph felt the same pang of jealousy as so many of her competitors, including Laura Winter, had felt when Lotta Crabtree held the stage. Why should she be jealous of an old woman? A woman who had never been a beauty, never married, lived a lonely life? But who had something that still drew the crowd, that made men like Bill Hastings and Tim Siegrist sit forward in their seats and watch every smile, every fleeting expression which crossed the little lady's face. Star quality was what they called it. I'll be a legend too, vowed Letty Randolph. *Mliss* is only the beginning. And on Sunday they'll all see what I can do.

"What a trouper!" said Bill Hastings, rising and stretching when the ceremony was over, "she never batted an eyelid through all that hogwash they called speeches. Well, we've made our bow to the legend, kids; why don't you come back to the St. Francis and have a drink in my room? I'll round up some of the others, and we can eat in comfort, the dining room'll be jammed today. Letty, what do you say?"

"I can't, Bill, I'm afraid," she said coolly. "I've promised to go to tea at the Fairmont with two of my girlfriends; I haven't seen them for ages."

"Just as you like," said the man, helping Letty on with her coat. "But if you care to come on later, you'll find us all in room 306. You all set, Tim?"

"Thanks, but I'm going back to Niles and have another look at my rough cut before you and Anderson see it on Sunday."

"Sure, Sunday's the big day," smiled Hastings. "I'm looking forward to that."

He genuinely sympathised with the first-time director's anxiety. He thought Tim had made far too much fuss over *Mliss*, and was not sure that the Sunday screening was a good idea, for Hastings was too completely a man of the stage to adapt to movie innovations. Very few of his actors ever saw themselves on screen, unless they happened to get to Oakland or San Francisco when an Essanay picture was showing, and the projection of daily 'rushes', later to become standard practice in the industry, had never been the custom at Niles.

Occasionally Broncho Billy ran through some of his own one-reelers, and there was a screen, a projector and a qualified operator at the studio. They were all pressed into service on Sunday afternoon, when not only the small cast of *Mliss*, but nearly all the members of the Number Two company, and even some of the cowboy friends of Willie Bleer, assembled to watch the new two-reeler.

Tim and G. M. Anderson sat alone in the front row, so their expressions were invisible to the actors behind them, perched on chairs and stools and even crates. The picture began with the scene in the schoolhouse where Mliss, in rags and tatters, comes seeking an education. Letty's beauty shone through the grime on her cheeks and her unkempt hair, and Bleer, his thin grave face illuminated by a single spot ("Hit him with the baby!" Tim had directed) was seen to have a photogenic quality never revealed in his cowboy parts. Their first scene together was conventional, with a strong element of pathos, and there was a murmur of approval from the audience. But when the action shifted to the 'forest' Tim's camera angles and use of lighting gave another aspect to the story. He shot Letty from below and upwards, increasing her height and authority, and the nameless schoolmaster from above and down, putting him in a position of inferiority. He cross-cut the forest with the schoolroom, so that autumn leaves blew against the cabin walls when Mliss defied the pastor, and lit her face with flames from the wood fire when her animosity to Clytie flared up. In the show-down between the master and the strolling player, when Mliss is ready to hand a knife to the weaker man whom she loves, "Bet you she'd use it too!" one of Bleer's mates was heard to mutter. The threat of suicide which preceded the master's surrender to one who was less a child of nature than a force of nature was a signpost to the unhappy ending under Tim's stormy sky.

There was an awkward silence when the lights went up. It was powerful, Tim's first film, but was it box office? How would John Q. Public react, after the sweet heroines of Gish and Pickford, to a tough baby like Melissa Smith of Red Mountain? They waited for a lead from Anderson. Who stood up, sighed, scratched his left armpit and took out his cigars.

447

"Better come up to the bungalow, Tim boy," he said heavily. "We gotta talk."

The two men left the studio, and the chatter broke out at once.

"You were lovely, Letty," said the blonde teenager who had played Clytie. She could afford to be generous, for she had come out well in a thankless supporting part. And "Terrific, Letty!" said Willie Bleer, who was happy too. He didn't know yet that he was Wayne Blackwood, but he had a hunch that with this one movie his feet had been set on a long and lucrative path.

"I hated myself," said Letty abruptly. "I was awful. Let's not hang about here. Can anybody give me a lift in to Niles?"

"My car's right outside," said old Burton. He understood better than any of them how the girl was feeling. Tim's newfangled movie had turned out much as he had expected. He thought the boss was probably telling Gimpy Tim to junk the whole thing.

"Don't be downhearted, Miss Letty," he said as they drove away. Even at his preferred speed of twenty miles an hour it would not take long to reach Niles. "You did well. If *Mliss* doesn't turn out to be the hit we hoped, it's Tim Siegrist's fault, not ours."

"Mr. Anderson didn't even speak to us at the end. Not a single word of praise for anyone!"

"It's natural he'd want to talk to the director first."

"And Bill Hastings, where was he? He promised to be there!" Letty's real grievance burst out now. She had watched for Hastings as they assembled, listened for his step when the studio was in darkness, while he hadn't cared enough for Letty Randolph to keep his promise, his *assurance* to her –

"Bill drove Bridget Malloy to the city this morning," Burton said. "I thought you knew why."

"Knew what?"

"Miss Bridget was taken ill last night, it seems. She wanted to go home and see her doctor."

"There's a doctor in Niles." Letty said no more, but the old trouper saw that her hands were clenched in her lap, and he didn't like the feverish colour rising in her pale face.

"Why don't you lie down and rest awhile?" he said when

they reached her door. "You've gone and gotten yourself all excited over just one show that didn't work the way you thought it would, but it's all in the day's work, dearie! When you've got the bird as often as I have, you'll know how to take a flop in your stride. Not that this one's a flop, or anywhere near it –"

"Thank you, Mr. Burton, you've been very kind." She let herself into the silent house. She changed her knitted tam o' shanter for a felt hat, her jersey jacket for her winter coat, and put the keys of the California Street flat, with all her ready money, into her bag. She was not going to collapse into bed. She was going to the city to confront Bill Hastings.

9

There would have been time enough, on the train ride north to Oakland and the ferry crossing to San Francisco, for a normally balanced girl to regret her impulsive flight from Niles and to realise that she was about to make a fool of herself. But Letty Randolph had been thrown off her normal balance by disappointment, hurt pride and jealousy, and by the Spanish vanity and passionate self-will which had been characteristics of Rosalie Estrada and Laura Winter. Old Burton's attempts at comfort had had the reverse effect, implying that *Mliss* was a flop and that she, Letty, would 'get the bird' when it was shown, and she intended to use those words to Hastings and tell him that as the official director of the company he "shouldn't have let Tim Siegrist get away with it". He should have come to the showing as he promised to see Tim's nightmare vision for himself, instead of going on his usual Sunday jaunt to San Francisco with his mistress from South of the Slot. Letty nursed her wrath and kept it warm during the hour in the train when noisy children careered up and down the aisle of the overheated coach, and the news-butcher seemed to come round every five minutes shouting his wares of magazines, candy and soda-pop.

It was dark by the time of the ferry crossing, and a heavy fog had fallen on the city. The horn of every ferry-boat using the bay was in action, and the lights along the wharves were dim and misty. Out on the deck, cold enough to wrap her red coat tightly round her, but longing for fresh air, Letty could scarcely see the outlines of her native city. The tall buildings which had survived or succeeded to the fire were in darkness, the offices being shut for Sunday, and the passengers hurried out of the depot into obscurity.

Letty found a cab on Market Street and was driven to the St. Francis. By the time she reached the hotel she had formed a plan of sorts. She would go straight to Hasting's room – she remembered the number from Lotta Crabtree Day – and tell him he had let her and all the actors down. If he tried to coax her by caresses, begged her to stay, she would redeem her pride by a contemptuous departure. If Pidgie Malloy were there to see and hear, so much the better.

The fog was less thick round Union Square than on the waterfront, and the lights were bright enough to reveal the graceful girl figure on the tall plinth, commemorating Admiral Dewey's victory in Manila Bay. The Victory! "She reminds me of you!" Bill Hastings had said, and the memory of the empty flattering words sent Letty into the big warm lobby of the St. Francis as resolute as when she ran out of her lodgings at Niles. "I hate him! I love him! I must see him!" she said to herself, and walking through the crowd to the lift was borne with a group of chattering people to the third floor.

No one appeared to notice her, the only person to leave the lift there, and no one, as she looked right and left, was in the wide red-carpeted corridor. She looked at the numbers and arrows. Room 306 was some distance away, round a bend in the passage. As Letty reached it she passed a man in a porter's green baize apron, with a suitcase on his shoulder, obscuring his face. No doors opened, no hotel guests appeared, until she came to 306. She knocked twice and received no answer. Then she tried the knob, found it open, and went in.

Room 306 was not a suite, but it had a little lobby with a jardinière, a carved Oriental chest on which a familiar overcoat and hat of Bill's had been flung down, and a velvet sofa large enough for two. Letty hesitated. There was no sound of voices from the room beyond, and when she said "Bill?" tentatively there was no reply. She pushed the bedroom door open and saw that the room was brightly lit.

Bill Hastings was lying on the floor between the bed and a low table where beside a vase of flowers, capsized and with water dripping on the carpet, was a salver holding a half-empty glass. He was flat on his back with his knees drawn up in pain, and one hand was making helpless gestures towards his chest. A heavy knife had been driven into his flesh. As Letty stood in frozen horror he succeeded in touching it, his hand fell away, and he mouthed the one word "Help!"

"Bill!"

With no thought of herself, but only of removing the source of his pain, Letty flung herself down by the wounded man's side and tugged at the knife. It had been driven in with great force, and she succeeded only in moving it a little way, but the movement was followed by a gush of blood which stained her hands and Bill's jacket, already ominously red. She looked round for a telephone, saw one on a writing desk piled with letters and scripts, and with one wild look at Bill's contorted face got to her feet and seized the instrument.

"Can I help you?" asked the operator.

"Yes, oh yes, send someone quickly, Mr. Hastings has had a terrible accident. Send a doctor –" She had been watching Bill's face all the time. Now, like his whole body, it collapsed. His knees straightened in a final convulsion, his head fell on one side, and as Letty again shrieked his name, he died. She could hear the operator's voice from the telephone receiver, which she had allowed to fall to the end of its cord.

That was how the men found them five minutes later, like a tableau in one of Willis Jerrold Hasting's favourite fade-outs. The dead man, fully dressed, was on the floor, with a capsized chair behind him and the upset vase the only signs of a scuffle apart from the blood now staining the carpet. The untouched bed was spread with its daytime satin cover and the wood fire had not been lit. The girl, with her hat awry and her red coat stained like her hands with blood, was pressed against the writing desk, rigid with horror and fear.

The first men who came were the hotel manager, the doctor who was always on call, and the chief of the house detectives.

They had just succeeded in getting Letty's name and the statement that 'she found him on the floor' when the next detachment arrived, and they, summoned by telephone, were the city police. Two of them were assigned to guard Letty in the little lobby, where she had to wait while more and more police experts crowded into the bedroom, and after a while Bill Hastings's sheeted body was carried out on a stretcher. After that Letty had no need of the customary caution about any statement she might make. She was beyond speech when she was placed under arrest. In a catatonic condition, able to move only because the policemen had her by the arms, she was taken down in the freight elevator to the Black Maria waiting at the service entrance of the hotel.

The old Hall of Justice had been destroyed in the earthquake and fire of 1906, and for some years all the city offices had been dispersed throughout San Francisco. The police wagon, with its siren blaring, raced along Market Street to the temporary City Hall building which was soon to be replaced by a more grandiose structure. The police doctor, who travelled with the prisoner and was sure that she was shamming, took her hat off to hold a cold compress to her forehead and kept a bottle of smelling salts under her nose. The fog still lay heavy over Market Street as Letty was helped to get out, but the bright lights in the corridors along which she was led partly aroused her from her stupor, and she was able to stand unaided before a high desk at which sat a man in uniform and tell him her name was Violet Estrada.

"You said it was Letty Randolph," said the detective who made the arrest.

"That's my professional name."

"And what profession might that be?" said the desk sergeant with a grin.

"I'm a movie actress."

"Your address?"

"The Essanay studio at Niles." She was more aware now, she saw that a uniformed stenographer was taking her answers down, and even that two young men at the back of the room were writing quickly in reporters' notebooks.

"Was that where you first met the victim?" the detective said.

"Yes – no – it was at the St. Francis Hotel – but you don't understand! Mr. Hastings is our director! I came to see him tonight about a new movie, that was all. And I found him – dying!" She buried her face in her hands.

"Save it for the court," said the desk sergeant. "You'll get your chance to tell the tale tomorrow morning. Right now you get to put in one telephone call. I guess you'll want to talk to your attorney."

"I haven't got an attorney."

"Okay then, anyone at all, any time you like, that's your right. Matron, you'd better get her cleaned up a bit before they take the mug shots and fingerprint her."

A stout woman in uniform appeared at the prisoner's side and said "Come on now, Violet. My! You're in a real mess, aren't you? Just look at your hands!"

They were still stained with a dead man's blood.

"What has happened to me?" said Violet Estrada, and the matron answered literally, "You're in custody till ten o'clock tomorrow morning, that's what. Now come and use the facilities."

The way to the facilities lay down a stone corridor between barred cells filled with others on remand. It had been a busy Sunday night on Market Street and in the Mission, and the drunks, whores and vagrants were snoring, singing and vomiting as the police matron hurried her charge along. In the lavatory Violet asked for a glass of water. With the cold taste in her burning throat, and the cold clean sting of water and disinfectant soap on her face and hands she revived sufficiently to know that she was in grave danger. Those men thought she had killed Bill Hastings. Who could prove that she had not? An attorney? She knew only one attorney, the elderly, prosy lawyer who had acted for her grandmother in a vain attempt to make good her insurance claim for the destruction of her property on Bush Street after the earthquake. Even if he were still alive he wouldn't be much good.

The police photographer was taking his mug shots, frontal and in profile, and making more fuss with his camera than Gimpy Tim ever did, when she thought, by association, of the man who had said "If you ever need me, you know I'll be right there." She said to the matron:

453

"Am I to spend the night in a cell, with some of those – other women?"

"We don't have private accommodations, lady."

"Please, I'd like to use my right to make a telephone call."

"You girls!" said the woman. "Don't know your minds from one minute to another. Officer Daniels" (to the photographer) "if you've *quite* finished, I'll thank you for your escort back to the charge room. Violet's decided to call her attorney after all."

"Smart gal," said Officer Daniels. But Violet's request to the police operator was not for legal aid. "Please connect me with the Essanay studio at Niles," she said. "I want Mr. Timothy Siegrist's bungalow." And waited, praying that he would be there and not enjoying a Sunday supper party somewhere else, while the policeman talked and the circuits opened, and at last a jerk of the head told her she might pick up the phone.

"Tim, it's Letty."

"Hallo, darling, I've been looking for you all over. Where're you speaking from?"

She looked round at the strangers in uniform and asked "Where am I?"

"1231 Market Street," said the matron, "San Francisco."

"Tim, I'm in prison."

★   ★   ★

Tim Siegrist hung up the receiver. It was not ten minutes since the phone had rung. The cigarette he had lit a few seconds before was still smouldering in the ashtray, the ice in his untouched highball had scarcely begun to melt. He swallowed a mouthful which might have been tap water for all the taste it had. He checked the time: nine-thirty. Just over twelve hours before Letty, who was Violet again, was to be arraigned on a charge of murder.

Appalled as he was by the story, Tim already saw it through a camera's eye. He, and he alone, knew how to direct Violet, how to film Violet as she stood at the bar of justice; the mischief was that he would have no opportunity to rehearse Violet and prompt her through her lines. And she was going to be a terrible witness, he knew that already from the incoherent, hysterical way she had told her story. The one positive thing he had got out of her was the time of the train she had caught at Niles, which roughly established the time of her arrival at the St. Francis to find Hastings dying and commit the utter folly of touching the knife.

"Were you wearing gloves?" he interrupted her to ask.

"I forgot my gloves."

The crazy little fool! Old Burton had driven her in to town; that much Tim learned when he went back to the studio after two hours of argument with Broncho Billy, and Burton said she seemed upset about the movie. Tim drove to Niles himself to tell Letty it was all right, Mr. Anderson would release the movie on condition that Tim substituted a happy ending for the ambiguous one, with Mliss and the schoolmaster fading out in a romantic clinch. There was no one at the cottage, and Tim, after looking in at one or two of the bungalow parties, gave it up. That must have been about the time of her arrest in San Francisco.

"They'll grant you a public defender," he said when he could make her listen. "Tell him to ask for your release on bail. In the court room say 'not guilty' and not a word more. Leave it all to me, darling. I'm on my way to you."

He was not quite on his way, for there was something to be done first, and Tim blessed the circumstance that Jeff Robbins was having supper with G. M. Anderson in the latter's bungalow. He could break the news of the Hastings murder to both of them together. And Jeff would help him to make Broncho Billy understand that this was a real-life occasion when the noblehearted cowboy must outwit the sheriff's posse and cut off the badmen at the pass.

It was nearly midnight when Tim took the wheel of the Winton and started the drive to San Francisco. G. M. Anderson, and Jeff Robbins too, had been deeply shocked by the news of Bill Hastings's violent end. Both had liked the man personally and overrated him as a director. Both were horrified to hear of Violet Estrada's arrest. But Anderson at first refused point-blank to go bail for her, if bail were granted when she appeared before the judge.

"After this, how can I trust that Greaser kid?" he asked. "She'd skip to Mexico and leave me holdin' the baby."

"No she won't, I'll keep an eye on her," said Tim. "And it'll be great publicity for you, sir."

"Seems like we'll get more publicity than we can handle, with a director in the morgue and an actress in the cooler," said Broncho Billy. "And say, hasn't the girl got a rich stepfather, Cord the Sugar King? Why don't he stand surety for her?"

"He's in Honolulu, and she comes up for arraignment tomorrow morning." Tim watched the multimillionaire's face intently. He dared not say, "You gave Chaplin $25,000 to cancel a trip to New York, which he wouldn't have got anyway, because the company which made the offer went bust within a month. Can't you put up as much to bail a girl out of prison and give her a chance to prove her innocence?" Anderson mused in silence, looking from one man to the other.

"The case looks very bad against her, if all she told you on the phone was true. The police caught her red-handed, as you might say. Do you really believe she isn't guilty?" he asked.

"I'll take my oath she's innocent, sir. She's a proud impulsive little fool, but she's not a killer – the thing's absurd."

"I agree with Tim," said Jeff Robbins, and Broncho Billy sighed.

"All right then, I'll go bail for her," he said. "But it'll be me myself personally, not a company matter. George Spoor would think I'd got brain softenin' if I let Essanay in for this."

"Thanks a million," said Tim, and Anderson, a better judge of character than he was an actor, said "She's got a champion in you, son. Better hit the trail for San Francisco and start lookin' for the proof to clear her, if there is such a thing."

He was her champion, riding to the rescue, but more than once during the long dark drive to San Francisco Tim's misgivings fought with his vaguely formulated plan of action. He remembered the fierce promptitude of her attack on himself with the volume of Bret Harte stories, and he remembered the scene from *Mliss* in which he had rehearsed Letty Randolph until she was word perfect. Although it was a silent movie he had insisted that the author's words be spoken, and Letty had achieved a terrible realism when she told the schoolmaster:

"I gave you the knife. I was there under the bar. Saw you hit him; saw you both fall. He dropped his old knife. I gave it to you. Why didn't you stick him?"

Through his fitful sleep in a downtown hotel in the city Tim Siegrist heard those words repeated, saw again the expression on the girl's face. *Why didn't you stick him?* He might have been able to forget them, might have slept better, if he had known that in the small hours the detectives in the Hastings case received a lab report with an unexpected twist. The Estrada woman's fingerprints had been on the doorknob of the murder room, the telephone, the edge of the desk and very clearly on the weapon. On the knife handle, too, there was a smudge made by the dying man. But there was also, on the underside of the handle, something like the print of a workman's glove. It was, the report concluded, the sort of glove a garbage man might wear.

★ ★ ★

FAMOUS MOVIE DIRECTOR STABBED
ACTRESS HELD ON MURDER RAP

It was the lead story in the *Chronicle*. Tim read about the death of Willis Jerrold Hastings and the arrest of Violet Estrada as he drank coffee, which to him tasted bitter, at the drugstore counter nearest to his hotel, jostled by early morning workers who were devouring the headlines with their breakfast. He threw the paper into a trashcan as he walked back to his car, parked not far away, and drove off to the address filed at Essanay for Bridget Malloy.

The street where she lived, south of the Slot, had been rebuilt since the disaster of 1906, but although the tenement buildings and warehouses were only six or seven years old they looked shabby enough to be much older. One or two derelicts were sleeping in the lee of an unoccupied shed, and the surly men starting out to work were illclad and unshaven. Tim was not disturbed by this environment. He knew that girls with the flower-like beauty which had been Bridget Malloy's often blossomed from such a compost heap. Her flat was on the top floor of a four-storey, eight-tenant building, in which none of the windows had remotely clean curtains, and there was no answer to his repeated knocking at the door. The electric bell appeared to be broken.

"Who are youse to come banging and bashing and rousing a decent man from his sleep?" The door on the other side of the landing was flung open, and a woman with a shawl over a grubby nightdress, her arms akimbo, came snarling out at Tim.

"I'm sorry," he said, "I didn't mean to disturb anyone. I only want to speak to the Malloys."

The woman took in his blue nap overcoat and his grey fedora, the formal attire Tim Siegrist seldom wore, and said in a more conciliatory tone, "Are youse a doctor, mister?"

"No, ma'am, I work for the same film company as Miss Malloy. The boss wants to get in touch with her because she's needed on the set today –"

"So the boss don't know what happened?"

"That's what I'm here to find out."

"*Kathleen!*" came a roar from inside the flat. "Who're ye talkin' to?"

"The milk." The slattern wound her shawl more tightly round her lean shoulders and closed the door as far as she dared. "That's me man, he's just off the night shift and needin' his rest. Well, me fine Miss Bridgie come home yesterday with a gent in a red automobile, that I've seen here afore; and after a while there was a great cryin' and shoutin' among them, as if ould Paddy Malloy was on the drink again, and next an ambulance came and took the gerr'l away and her da with her, and the toff went off in his charry-ot, and that's all I know, mister –"

"*Kathleen!*"

"Just a minute," Tim begged. "What hospital did they take her to? Was the name on the ambulance?"

"Sure it was: San Francisco General." The door banged in his face.

A patrolman, swinging his nightstick as he made the rounds, told Tim the 'General' was "uptown a ways, at Twenty-second and Potrero," and there the officials were less responsive than the voluble Kathleen. Yes, Bridget Malloy had been admitted at half past three on Sunday afternoon. They were not permitted to give any information regarding her condition, but she was not on the danger list, though visitors were not allowed. Yes, her father had been with her when she was brought in, and remained in the waiting room – no one knew for how long. Mr. Siegrist could enquire again tomorrow.

Mr. Siegrist had better luck at the temporary City Hall, where he found a policeman willing to point out a young lawyer called Fiske, the public defender who had been picked out of a list to represent the prisoner, Violet Estrada, when she appeared in court for arraignment at ten o'clock that morning. Mr. Fiske was a junior member of the highly respectable firm of Wyatt, Baxter and Wyatt of Sansome Street, and he had already been accosted by a man in a plaid suit and a derby hat, who identified himself to Tim as Joe Gregory, Violet's cousin, come to see what he could do to help.

"You must be one of the Sonoma family I've heard so much about. Are you Stella's brother?"

"That's me. Vi's been like a little sister to Stella all her life. Isn't this the hell of a note?"

"It is!" said Tim, and turning to Mr. Fiske told him he had brought an important message from the studio at Niles. "Mr. Gilbert Anderson of Essanay will go bail for Miss Estrada," he said.

"That *is* good news," said Dwight Fiske. "She was worrying about bail."

"You've seen her?"

"I was here at half past eight and talked to her for half an hour."

"How is she?"

"Very agitated, but I got her to calm down and promise to say nothing in court but 'not guilty'. I explained that the application would be made by me."

"Better make it stick," said Tim gruffly. "She mustn't be left in this hell hole for another night."

Fiske grimaced. "I'll do my best, but I warn you the police have a strong case. The hotel doctor said Hastings had been dead only a few minutes when he arrived, and she was right there in the room with him."

"That's not to say she killed him," said Joe Gregory.

"Quite so," said the young counsel. "It does mean that if the judge grants bail he's liable to set it pretty high. I take it this is a personal bond by Mr. Anderson? Good. One piece of luck, we're going before Judge Weatherby. He's known to be lenient to beauty in distress. And Miss Estrada's a very lovely girl."

"She is," said Tim. "Come on, Gregory, we'd better make sure of finding seats." He was impatient to get on with it, to see the lovely girl and smile his reassurance.

"That kid gives me the willies," said Joe in the corridor. "Fresh out of law school and still wet behind the ears. If this damned case goes to trial Vi ought to have a better man. 'Dutch' Kramer might take it on. He's done real well for pals of mine."

Tim Siegrist had steered clear of the lawmen, but he knew that 'Dutch' Kramer was a mobsters' mouthpiece, whose appearance on behalf of a girl charged with murder might seriously prejudice her case. He said, "Let's discuss it later," as he removed his overcoat. The court room was packed, and it was warm.

When they had found places at the side which would give them a clear view of the empty chairs directly in front of the judge Joe surprised Tim Siegrist by murmuring, "Say, didn't you use to be a jockey? Didn't I see you ride a winner for Zack Miller out at Ingleside, just before they closed the track?"

"I had a few wins that holiday season before the fire."

"Christmas '05. They called you 'Kid' Siegrist then."

"I was fifteen."

"Given it up, hey?"

"It gave me up." His right hip, broken in the stampede, badly set, broken again and reset, was giving Tim hell that morning. He got to his feet with difficulty when a deputy shouted "Silence for Hizonner!" and Judge Weatherby in his black robe came into the court.

And there she was, in one of the empty front seats, with the police matron on one side of her and young Fiske on the other. Violet Estrada, accused of the murder of Willis Jerrold Hastings, saying "Not guilty, your honour" in the rich contralto which Tim thought would make her fortune if talking pictures ever became a reality. She was dressed exactly as he had seen her at the showing of *Mliss*, less than twenty-four hours earlier,

460

in a plain grey wool dress from which the belt had been removed in prison. Her black hair, coiled and pinned in the studio, now fell loosely round her ears, and was tied back with the narrow ribbon Violet had worn at her throat. For all his distress and anxiety, Tim's camera eye approved the clever touch. She caught his eager glance, and gave him a little trembling smile.

The formality of an arraignment was something quite new to Tim, so that he was almost glad of the running commentary provided by the knowledgeable Joe. He had expected something dramatic, like the appearance of the State Attorney-General, or at least a bullying DA, instead of which there was only the monotonous voice of Detective-Inspector Finnegan who had arrested Violet, giving his version of events. The police had been called to the St. Francis Hotel by the manager, he said (at which point Fiske managed to get on the record the fact that Miss Estrada had called the management in the first instance), the medical examiner had given his verdict, the prints on the murder weapon tallied with the prisoner's, and so on and on, until the judge said something barely audible which brought three men up to his rostrum, arguing in tones hardly less audible, as if the public administration of justice had become a private conversation.

"What the hell are they doing now?" whispered Tim, and Joe said they were arguing about the date of the trial. At least the fat one from the DA's office was; the District Attorney wanted it postponed until after the Christmas recess. Fiske, as instructed, was demanding release on bail for his client, while the police wanted Violet Estrada remanded in custody. The noise from the public benches grew louder, until the judge rapped his gavel for order and the three men returned to their seats, two of them with disgruntled faces. Tim caught Fiske's look of satisfaction, and his spirits rose.

"The case of the People against Violet Estrada," said Judge Weatherby, "will be heard in Superior Court at a date as near as possible to the last day of November. The prisoner will be released on bail, which I hereby set at ten thousand dollars."

In the babble which broke out it was not immediately seen that the prisoner had fainted.

★   ★   ★

Tim Siegrist's limp was more pronounced than usual when he came back to the main lobby of City Hall after a conference with Violet's young counsel. Joe Gregory was waiting for him in a quiet corner, and after one look at Tim's face Joe burst out, "What's the trouble? Anderson hasn't reneged on the bail, has he?"

"Not on the bail, no. Fiske talked to him, and he's arranging for a certified cheque to be sent to Wyatt, Baxter and Wyatt before the banks close today. But hell is up and flaming down at Niles, Joe. The place is overrun with reporters, looking for scandal and getting it too, and things are beginning to come out that Anderson never dreamed of. He's going to hold me personally responsible for Violet's surrendering to her bail when the time comes. He doesn't want her to come back to Niles until her innocence is proved, and perhaps not even then. He doesn't want to hear the sound of what he has the nerve to call her Greaser name."

Joe grunted. "Where's Fiske now?"

"He went back to Sansome Street after the phone call to Anderson. He'll meet us here as soon as the cheque comes through. There'll be some more legal hocus-pocus before she's released."

"Then what, if she can't go back to Niles?"

"Exactly; where do we go from here?"

"There's the flat on California Street that she shares with her grandmother."

"But the grandmother's in Honolulu," said Tim, "I don't think Violet should be alone tonight."

"The best thing would be for me to take her to Sonoma," said Joe. "They love to have her there."

"Great!" said Tim. "And it's not too far from the city. After she's gotten over the first shock, she'll have to come back here to consult a trial lawyer, and I don't mean some kid picked off the public list."

"I'll go telephone my sister right away."

"And while you're phoning I'm going to make a quick trip uptown."

Tim drove back to the San Francisco General Hospital. This time he got past the main reception area and as far as the desk on the floor where Bridget Malloy was a patient, but the ward sister who allowed him five minutes of her time was a martinet who would give no information about a patient's state to anybody not a relative. Miss Malloy was not in danger, her condition was stationary, and she was not allowed to have visitors. "Not even her father?" hazarded Tim. Sister had not seen Miss Malloy's father since she came on duty. Now, if you'll excuse me, please . . .

He went back to City Hall, or rather to the coffee shop next door where he was to meet Joe Gregory, and this time it was Joe's turn to greet him with a face of storm. Joe had anglicised his Italian name but not his Italian temper, and it was in the oaths of his mother tongue that he damned Jack Hastings *the writer*, his own father and his sister Stella. Out of the wild incoherence Tim gathered that the author, having been informed by the police, as the next of kin, that his brother had been murdered and Violet Estrada arrested, had driven late at night to the Sorrento, after the restaurant was closed, roused the family and made a violent scene.

"Of course, he was hopped up to the eyes," said Joe, "but they're too dumb to know that, and Zeemaree got sick, like she did once before, and my father threw Jack out and drove to Santa Rosa for the new doctor. Now *he's* sick, and furious with me for bringing riff-raff like Jack about the place, and my sanctimonious sister Stella says Violet has disgraced the family. 'You used to call her *mia piccola sorella*' says I, and she says, '*Puttana! Vergogna!* Violetta is no sister of mine! Take her to your low companions, Giuseppe, but don't bring her here again!'"

The waitress came over to take their order.

"Look here," said Tim, when she had gone, "what exactly do you mean when you say Jack Hastings was hopped up to the eyes? Was he on dope?"

"Oh, Jack's a real hophead, cocaine's his poison. I don't think *Bill* Hastings was a user."

"Was he a trafficker?"

Something wary flickered in Joe Gregory's eyes, and he seemed to be glad of the interruption when the waitress put coffee and doughnuts before them. Tim reflected how little Violet had really told him about this man who claimed to be her cousin. He had been in a succession of jobs, bookmaker's clerk, bartender, billiard marker, carney barker, and was what old-fashioned people called a ne'er do well: could he also have criminal connections?

"Why do you ask that about Bill?" said Joe.

"Because people at Niles were beginning to hint that his girlfriend, Bridget Malloy, had got started on drugs, and I wondered if Bill was her supplier."

"Where was Bridget Malloy yesterday evening?"

"Exactly my own thought," said Tim with a glimmer of a smile. "She's got a watertight alibi. She was admitted to the San Francisco General at half past three, and she's there still – *incommunicado.*"

They sat silent, making a pretence of eating and drinking, until they heard the factory whistles blowing and the shouts of the newsboys as the noon edition of the *Call* hit the streets.

"Getcha *Call*!" shrilled the lads. "Latest on the Hastings murder! Accused actress collapses in court!"

Tim flung fifty cents on the table and they hurried into Market Street to buy a paper each.

Except for one brief paragraph on the war in Europe and a huge grocery-store advertisement, the *Call* had devoted its entire front page to the murder of Willis Jerrold Hastings. Centred was a copy of the photograph Tim took of Letty on her first day at Niles, when the unwelcome Cinderella joke had made her glare at him like an angry cat. The tulle round her shoulders had been brushed out, so that she appeared to have posed in the nude, and the caption read, 'Violet Estrada: Naked Passion.'

"How the hell did they get hold of that?" said Joe.

"It was in the studio files," groaned Tim. "My guess is a little bastard called Bert stole it and sold it to the snoopers for twenty bucks."

The full-page spread contained interviews with Mr. Burton, the last person to see the girl at Niles ('She was distraught'), with Mr. Rooney, superintendent of the apartment building on California Street ('She was alone with Mr. Hastings in her flat'), and of course with the bereaved next of kin, Mr. Jack Hastings ('the well-known writer, who made a dramatic dash to the city at midnight, to get at the truth about his brother's death'). In an early morning press conference at the Palace Hotel, Mr. Hastings said emotionally, "I feel responsible for this tragedy. It was I who made Miss Estrada known to my brother after a concert in Sonoma."

"My God!" said Joe when he had read it all, "the papers are out to do a hatchet job on that poor kid!"

"I'll get Bert fired tomorrow, if Anderson hasn't fired him today," said Tim, "and I sure would like to wring that Rooney's neck. But first off I'm going to call Fiske."

Joe had time to smoke two cigarettes before Tim came back.

"Fiske had seen the paper," he announced, "and he says of course Violet mustn't go back to her flat. He's going to book her in to the Bayview Hotel, a quiet place in the North Beach area, under the name of Mary Brown, and he thinks it'll be possible to get her there without a press escort. Then I called Niles, and arranged for a nice woman, a Mrs. Brice, to come up and spend the night with Vi at the Bayview. After that we just have to live it a day at a time."

"Good work," said Joe, "but when are they actually going to spring her?"

"About two o'clock, Fiske thinks."

Joe stubbed out his final cigarette and got up. In the busy lobby he had to raise his voice when he said, "Give her my love when you see her and tell her I'll be around."

"You're not leaving now?"

"There's no point in staying. If she see's me she'll think I've come to take her to Sonoma, and we needn't get started on all that yet. Where I might do some good is at the Palace, having a straight talk with Brother Jack."

"You might try leaning on him a little."

"Why not? That whining faggot's bent already. Will you call me at six o'clock and tell me how you all made out?"

"Where can I reach you?"

"I'll be at Coppa's Restaurant. Say, before I forget, did Fiske say anything about the defence?"

"He says the best trial lawyer in the city is Albert Duval."

"That'll cost a packet. Well, I'll donate all I've got to Violet."

"Me too." They shook hands, and as Tim watched his ally make his way out to Market Street he saw a crowd beginning to gather round the great doors in expectation of the release of the prisoner on bail. Would she be smuggled out of a back door, or would she have to push her way through the hostile crowd, hearing jeers and catcalls instead of the applause she craved? He didn't think she would faint again, as in that moment of reprieve in court. Tim Siegrist, who loved her, believed that in her last appearance as Letty Randolph the fallen star would give the best performance of her brief career.

10

Albert Duval, the celebrated trial lawyer, was a third generation San Franciscan. His grandfather was a French immigrant in the days of the Gold Rush, who having duly 'seen the elephant', opened a small bakery on Bush Street in the days when lower Bush Street, where the church of Notre Dame des Victoires later stood, was still called French Hill. His son turned the small bakery into a chain of bakeries, featuring Duval's French Sourdough Bread, *brioches* and *croissants*, and branching into *pâtisseries* and Weddings Catered For. Albert Duval, at sixty, was famous, prosperous and a widower, the father of two fashionable married daughters living down the Peninsula. He was one of the few men who in 1915 still wore a Prince Albert coat and a tall silk hat on weekdays in the streets of San Francisco; they were part of the persona he had invented for himself, and thus arrayed he walked the short distance from his office on Montgomery Street round the corner to Sansome and the office of Messrs Wyatt, Baxter and Wyatt.

"This is extremely kind of you, Mr. Duval," said the senior Mr. Wyatt. They were old friends and members of the Pacific Union and Bohemian Clubs, where they were 'Albert' and 'Conrad' to each other; in business they never failed to use the formal address. "Very good of a busy man like you to leave your office and come to mine. But the circumstances are rather unusual. The young lady –"

"Is taking quite a mauling from the press," said Duval. "Where have you hidden her?"

"She's with my confidential secretary, Miss Wiggins, having a cup of tea."

"And who is this gentleman?"

"Mr. Timothy Siegrist, from the Essanay studio at Niles."

Tim, who had been standing by the window, limped forward to take Mr. Duval's proffered hand. The lawyer, accustomed to size up a witness at a glance, thought this young man with the drawn face and steady grey eyes would not be liable to crack under pressure.

"What is your interest in the case, Mr. Siegrist?" he said, as Mr. Wyatt motioned to them to be seated.

"I'm only a messenger boy," said Tim. "Mr. Anderson sent me here with the actual cablegram he received from Honolulu on Tuesday, I mean yesterday night."

"Of which Mr. Wyatt gave me the gist on the telephone this morning," said Duval. "May I see it?" He put on his pince-nez to study the flimsy sheet and then read it aloud.

"'I guarantee that I will pay all expenses incurred in the defence of Violet Estrada on one condition stop she must not approach her heartbroken mother and grandmother in any way stop confirmatory letter follows signed Robert Faxon Cord.'"

"Yes," he said, taking his glasses off, "that's the same old Faxon Cord I used to know."

"I'd forgotten you were boyhood friends," said Mr. Wyatt.

"Not so much when we were boys, for he and poor Jim Estrada were Dr. Durant's students and I attended St. Ignatius College. When we were young men we saw a good deal of each other."

"I knew his older brother better," said Mr. Wyatt. "Ivanhoe Cord. He made his home in England and died there, after he retired from the Foreign Service."

"Having vowed never to live in California after his father's – murder."

The word was spoken. The reason for their meeting was out in the open. And Tim, watching and listening intently, knew that Faxon Cord's brutal cable, which had given satisfaction to Broncho Billy, still uneasy about his bail cheque, was the talisman which had made Conrad Wyatt, attorney-at-law, willing to undertake the defence of Violet Estrada, and the great trial lawyer ready to accept his brief. He and Joe Gregory could only give devotion; now hard cash had come to Violet's aid.

"Jim Estrada was a great charmer, but as wild and impulsive as they're made," Duval continued. "He threw away his life for nothing in the wreck of the *Rosalie* before his daughter was born. It appears that she too is a reckless young creature?"

Nobody answered, and he went on in the same tone of genial reminiscence. "However, I don't think her case is absolutely hopeless. After your call this morning, Mr. Wyatt, I had a word with the lieutenant in charge of the case and asked him if any fresh evidence had come to light in the past forty-eight hours. He was most unco-operative. However, after I called Mayor Rolph and Police Chief White and they got back to him, he changed his tune, and told me one fact that I consider promising. Obviously they don't want the San Francisco Police Department to look foolish."

Mr. Wyatt smiled for the first time. He knew how often, in open court, Duval had made the SFPD look like a bunch of Keystone Cops, and he also knew his friend's fondness for a defence which seemed no better than a forlorn hope. Then he could give free rein to his flamboyant rhetoric, his sentimentality, his ruthless bullying of the prosecution and his running enmity with the District Attorney and his aides. "It's the Frenchman in him," said his detractors, but his admirers, who were far more numerous, knew that 'Albert Duval for the defence' was one of the slogans of legal power in San Francisco.

"Are you going to tell us about your discovery?" said Mr. Wyatt.

"I'd prefer to tell Miss Estrada first, but it'll go on the stenographic record, of course. Mr. Wyatt, I hate to take over your premises and your secretary, but I would like to see Miss Estrada now – and alone. All I want to do today is hear her own story, ask her a few questions, and try to establish some confidence between us. Does she know about her stepfather's guarantee?"

"Yes, but not about the proviso. And the newspapers have been kept from her, of course."

"The papers have been vile," said Tim.

"Scandal sells papers, my dear Mr. Siegrist," said Duval. "They'll calm down in a day or two."

"May I see Miss Estrada, sir, before she goes back to the hotel?" Tim appealed to Mr. Wyatt. "I haven't seen her since Monday afternoon – and nothing seemed to be making any sense then."

"Of course you may see my client, and in private," said Mr. Wyatt kindly. That was the clincher, of course. Young Mr. Fiske was out of the picture, waiting for his next experience as a public defender, and the combined wisdom of Wyatt, Baxter and Wyatt was at the disposal of *their client*, the stepdaughter of Faxon Cord, who if she passed her examination would have the support of Albert Duval for the defence.

Mr. Duval met her in a room which, apart from two filing cabinets flanking a stenographer's table with a typewriter and two telephones, was quite unlike an office. It was furnished with comfortable chairs and sofas, in front of one of which stood a tea table, and the curtains were made of English chintz. Miss Wiggins, an attractive woman in her forties, was talking pleasantly to Violet Estrada, who stood up with a schoolgirl's politeness when Mr. Duval was introduced. She was dressed like a schoolgirl, in a navy-blue tailored coat and skirt with a white silk blouse, and a navy hat to match. They had been brought from the California Street flat by Mrs. Brice, who armed with Violet's keys had given the cringing Rooney what she called a tongue-lashing, before coming away laden with fresh clothing for the girl. Violet's pallor and shadowed eyes still showed the effects of extreme shock, but she knew she must be calm, and listened attentively to Mr. Duval.

"I'm sometimes called a frustrated actor," he began in his genial way, "and you of course are a professional actress, so I'm sure we shall get on famously. In fact what I want us to do today is rehearse a little play, just to give you an idea of what to expect in Superior Court. To make it more realistic I'm going to ask Miss Wiggins to take the part of the court stenographer – you don't mind, do you, Miss Wiggins?"

"Of course not, Mr. Duval," said the confidential secretary, taking the cover off her typewriter.

"I'm going to call it 'Motive and Opportunity'," said Duval, "and in it I'll play the counsel for the prosecution, not for the defence, while you'll play yourself, Miss Estrada. But before the curtain rises I want you to tell me exactly what happened on Sunday afternoon, before you left Niles, and through the early evening up to the time of your arrest."

He led her through the details gently. Her disappointment with the showing of *Mliss*, her anger with Bill Hastings, her hurried trip to San Francisco and then the – the dreadful discovery. Violet had to feel for her handkerchief then, to dry her tears.

"We know what time your train arrived in San Francisco," said Albert Duval. "Then, you say, you took a taxi. Have you any idea what time you arrived at the hotel?"

"I suppose it was about seven o'clock."

"It was a little later. I must tell you that a responsible citizen, an engineer from Fresno, has told the police he saw you enter by the front door and go straight to the elevators. He was standing by the clock, where his fiancée had agreed to meet him at seven, and she was ten minutes late when he saw you cross the lobby at seven-ten."

"How did he know it was me?"

"He saw your picture in the papers," said Mr. Duval drily. "Now, the switchboard operator logged your call for help at seven-eighteen. That would give you exactly eight minutes to reach Mr. Hastings's room and drive a heavy weapon into his chest, which is too narrow a margin of time for a quarrel to develop."

"Was it only eight minutes? It seemed much longer. Mr. Duval –"

"Yes?"

"Did the gentleman from Fresno say what I was wearing? What I was carrying?"

"A red coat and hat, and a small red leather handbag."

"This bag." Violet lifted it from the sofa. "Just large enough for my purse and keys. Not nearly big enough to hold a – a big knife."

Duval nodded. She was using her head, instead of sitting there in that stunned apathy. He said, "So we have some useful details from one observant person who noticed you. Did *you* see anybody after you left the elevator on the third floor?"

"Only a man carrying a suitcase."

"A hotel guest?"

"No, I think he must have come from the baggage room. He was wearing a green baize apron."

"Would you recognise him again?"

"Oh no. The suitcase was on his shoulder, and his face was hidden."

"Was it indeed?" said Albert Duval. He took off his pince-nez and put them into their case with a resounding snap. It was a mannerism known to every court reporter, who recognised it as a signal that the fireworks were about to start.

"Now our play begins," he said. "Remember, I'm the prosecutor, not your defender."

It was as if an invisible director had shouted "Camera! Lights!" Albert Duval seemed to change in appearance before Violet's eyes. His cheeks swelled, his lips grew heavy, and a shake of the head brought his white locks about his ears. Crossing the room like a bull entering the arena, he caught the skirts of his Prince Albert back with one hand, and extended the other towards an imaginary jury box.

"Gentlemen of the jury!" he began. "Motive and opportunity are what you must always look for in your deliberations on a capital charge of murder. The prosecution will now hear from Violet Estrada's own lips that she had both motive and opportunity to bring about the death of Willis Jerrold Hastings."

He crossed back to Violet's sofa and loomed above her.

"Was Willis Hastings your lover, madam?" he barked out.

"He was not!"

"Let me put the question in another way, so that the jury may be quite sure you understand it. Were you Willis Hastings's mistress?"

"Certainly not!"

"But your relationship was warmer than what is usual between a film director and one of the ladies of the company?"

"Mr. Hastings had many warm relationships."

"And you were jealous of them? You permitted yourself to indulge in romantic passages with him when the opportunity offered, as when you were alone with him in your San Francisco flat? Come now, Miss Estrada; remember you are on oath. Were there endearments, kisses, caresses on that occasion?"

"A few."

"And when you were in his room at the St. Francis, was the lovemaking resumed?"

"I was never in Mr. Hastings's room until – that night."

"The jury will not take that statement seriously. On the fatal night you neither asked for Mr. Hastings at the reception desk, nor used the house telephone to call his room, for the good reason that you knew exactly where to go. It was not your first visit to room 306."

"I knew where to go because Mr. Hastings told me the number on Lotta Crabtree Day, when he asked several members of the company to a party in his room."

"Which you attended?"

"I did not. I went to tea at the Fairmont with two women friends instead. Do you want to know their names?"

"I am asking the questions, madam. I suggest to you that you were aware that Mr. Hastings's interest in you had cooled, and that he had rejected you in favour of another woman. That was the *motive* for your frenzied dash to San Francisco, was it not?"

"I went to the city to discuss a new movie with him, in which some of us had been disappointed."

"Armed with a knife? With the knife" (he gestured at the tea table) "which has been produced in court as Exhibit A?"

"I could never have carried such a big knife in my little bag."

"But you had a belt on your dress, did you not? You could have strapped the knife to your body underneath your coat."

"Then I might have been the one to be stabbed, mightn't I?"

"You are in no position to indulge in levity, madam." And so on, and on, hectoring and bullying, pacing the room, ranting at the imaginary jury, until Albert Duval mopped his brow and said to the petrified girl:

"Not bad. Not bad at all. Now you have some idea of what to expect. And you've given me some ideas too, Miss Estrada, something to work upon. You shall hear from me very soon."

In Mr. Wyatt's room, in answer to Mr. Wyatt's anxious query, Duval said briefly, "All right, I'll take the case. Mind you, it'll be touch and go, for the DA will argue that she was caught red-handed, which is literally true. Also, once the first shock has worn off, I think she might be awkward on the stand. I'll be in touch. Mr. Siegrist, I believe she's expecting you now."

★   ★   ★

"My darling!" It was all Tim Siegrist could find to say when they were alone together, when Violet flung herself into his arms. He had never expected such a complete surrender; her arms round his neck, her wet cheek pressed to his, her mouth opening under his first kisses. "Darling, darling, it's going to be all right," he repeated between the kisses, and she, no more coherent, was murmuring, "Thank you, thank you, Tim . . . you've been so wonderful . . . you took such care of me on Monday afternoon . . ."

"Monday was a living nightmare," he said.

"Those awful crowds on Market Street, yelling and screaming at me! But you got me away −"

"In all fairness," said Tim, "the bright idea came from Mr. Fiske. Up in a taxi to the Fairmont, with all the press cars shrieking behind us, and when they thought you were safely in a room where they could get at you, down to the Powell Street level and a getaway car. There's been no problem at the Bayview, has there?"

"None, and Mrs. Brice has been terrific. But Tim, she won't let me see the papers."

"Oh well, they're playing it rough, as usual. I'm sorry I've got to take Mrs. Brice down to Niles tonight, but she'll be back with you again at the weekend."

"Tim − what's going on down there?"

"Everybody's very sorry, and worried about you. A lot of the boys sent their love." But not all the boys, he could have added, for Bill Hastings had been popular, and sorrow for his death far exceeded the sympathy for the girl known as Letty Randolph.

"I did ask you on Monday, didn't I, to take my best thanks to Mr. Anderson? Paying all that money, just for me!"

"He'll get it back," said Tim, "and yes, you did remember to say thank you, in the middle of all that shouting, and I passed your message on."

473

He was going to say something about Albert Duval for the defence, which meant that she had nothing to fear in Superior Court, but Violet seemed unable to concentrate, for the next thing she said was, "Joe was with you for a long time on Monday, wasn't he? Where is he now?"

He decided that half a truth was better than the whole truth, and said, "Joe's in Sonoma, darling. Mr. and Mrs. Gregorio are both on the sick list, and Joe went down on Tuesday to give Stella a hand in the restaurant."

"Joe working with Stella? I can't believe it! And how do you mean they're on the sick list? Zeemaree! I can't bear it if anything happens to Zeemaree!"

"Hush, darling, nothing's going to happen to her. She just had a bad turn, Joe was told. Nothing serious."

"The same sort of bad turn as she had the day of the sunset dream?"

"The sunset – ?"

"The poem I recited that upset her so. 'I see the dying glow of Spanish glory, the sunset dream and last.' She had a bad turn then, and I think it was much worse than the local doctor knew. Oh Tim! That was the day I met Jack Hastings, and he said I ought to be in pictures. And now Bill's dead, and whatever happens to me I'll never forget – that awful knife –"

Tim tightened his grasp on her slim trembling body. "Vi, there's one thing I've *got* to know. Were you ever really in love with Bill Hastings?"

"I thought I was," she answered honestly. "I suppose it was just a sort of schoolgirl crush. Oh, hold me, darling, don't let those men get me . . . even though I've been such an awful fool."

★　★　★

While the *Chronicle*, the *Examiner* and the *Call* ranted on about the girl accused of murder and released on bail ('Broncho Billy to the Rescue!' made a good horsy cartoon) enjoying all the luxuries of 'the swank Fairmont Hotel', Violet was at the Bayview, which had started in 1907 as a modest boarding-house for some of the many homeless of the earthquake and the fire. In 1915 the two sisters who ran the place extended and redecorated it for visitors to the Panama-Pacific Exposition and made a satisfactory profit, working so hard that they seldom had time to read the daily papers. In the middle of November their guests were out-of-towners, retired people able to take an autumn holiday and enjoy the fading glories of the Exposition; neither the hoteliers nor the visitors were interested in anything but clean sheets, good food, transportation to the Exposition on the Marina or the never failing charm of riding the cable cars into the city centre. If they knew that a girl registered as Mary Brown was living at the Bayview Hotel it did not occur to any of them to associate her with the headlines in newpapers they seldom read, and Violet's cover was not broken during her entire stay at North Beach.

The entrance to the hotel was on Hyde Street, but most of the rooms had a fine view across the greensward where aging Italian fishermen mended their nets to the commercial harbour of the dwindling fishing fleet. Between the hotel and the bay was the turntable of the Hyde Street cable car, and Violet at her window could see the holidaymakers not as yet called tourists, watching with deep interest as the grips turned the cars around, using the power of their arms, for the trip back to town. She grew to like the clang of the cable bells, which in that quiet season was echoed only by the clamour of the seagulls. She liked even better, on the Thursday morning after Mrs. Brice had gone back with Tim to her work for Essanay, to be free to go out unescorted about ten in the morning, when the staff were cleaning the rooms and the guests had gone off to the Exposition, and explore the waterfront unescorted. Free.

It was a busier community down there on the shore than it appeared when seen from the demurely curtained bay windows of the hotel. There was a cannery and a factory, both operational, there were ship's chandlers' stores and some selling fishing tackle, and there were two or three eating shops offering *ciaoppino* and sand dabs to customers braving the November fogs. There was also a newsstand, where Violet bought the papers, and learned for the first time to what extent she was front page news.

'Albert Duval for the Defence!' topped 'Faxon Cord supports his Stepdaughter!' as the banner head, but their ignorance of Violet's real whereabouts had driven the editorial staff into writing fiction about her luxurious life at the Fairmont, and hardly less fictionalised accounts of the Estrada and Cord families. One cub reporter, ordered to dig into the morgue biographies, had come up with reminiscences of the accused woman's grandfather, Felipe or Philip Estrada, and his position as a 'pioneer', a 'buccaneer', a 'tycoon' and even a 'land shark' in the early days of San Francisco. The vow to 'put the Estrada brand on this city', which Philip had indiscreetly repeated to more than one person, was revived that day seventy years later in the *Chronicle*. The cartoonist had drawn Violet's face, copied from Tim's unlucky photograph, on the centre page. Superimposed upon it was the ox yoke in the shape of a primitive E used at the Rancho Estrada, now distorted to resemble a hangman's noose. The caption read 'The Estrada Brand: 1915 Style.'

Some of the intellectual coterie of San Francisco, the reviewers for the little magazines and the authors of slim volumes of free verse, professed to find deep social significance in the newspaper's sustained polemic in the Estrada case. It came from a hatred of the Spanish, who had colonised the land and oppressed the Indians, said one group. It came from a hatred of 'robber barons' like Philip Estrada, the target of the currently fashionable muckraking journalists, said another. Few had the honesty to admit that much of the sustained personal attack on Violet Estrada sprang from the underdog's envy of youth and beauty and a measure of talent, and no one in 1915 saw, in the blowing-up of the Hastings murder into a scandal of immense proportions, the closing of the middle-class ranks against the adolescent film industry, already an apparent threat to bourgeois morality. Albert Duval did not indulge in any pseudo-intellectual speculations. He merely remarked to a few cronies, over luncheon at Tadich's Grill, that there was a great deal to be said for the British law that while a case was *sub judice* it might not be publicly commented upon. "The newspapers have found my client guilty of murder and condemned her to death well in advance of her jury trial," he said. "We still have a good deal to learn from the British."

Duval returned to his chambers in an evil mood, and strode

through the outer offices without looking to left or right. They were crowded, as always, with would-be litigants, bellicose claimants, underworld informers and the junior assistants to the great man. One of these followed him into his private room and told him a Mr. Gregory was in one of the waiting rooms with information about the Hastings murder.

Joe Gregory. From the files of his astonishing memory Mr. Duval drew the name, that of a small-time con man who had so far managed to evade the law, and who while not dealing in women and drugs was known to consort with those who did. "Show him in," he said curtly, and was mildly surprised when his visitor turned out to be a well-dressed, darkly handsome man in his early thirties, whose Italianate good looks were spoiled by a bruised cheek and a blackened left eye.

Joe's story was soon told. During his condolence call at the Palace Hotel on Monday afternoon he had 'persuaded' Jack Hastings to admit that Bridget Malloy had been hooked on cocaine, a habit which his virtuous brother Bill was helping her to kick. He had taken her to San Francisco on the fatal Sunday to get her admitted to a hospital for treatment. He had obviously been relaxing with a drink in his room at the St. Francis when Violet Estrada, a monster of jealousy, made her murderous attack.

"You must have been very persuasive, Mr. Gregory," said Duval. "Was that when you got the shiner?"

"No, that was later. Tuesday morning I took the train down to Sonoma. My folks are sick, and I hung around for a bit at home until I heard what the doctor had to say, and then I borrowed my dad's car and drove down the creekside to Glen Ellen. You know it's a wide-open sporting village, just a string of saloons one after the other. Luckily it wasn't one of their big days, when Jack London comes down the hill from his Beauty Ranch and buys drinks for all the moochers, so things were pretty quiet. I played some pool and sank a few beers and kept my ears open and spent the night at the hotel. On Wednesday I drove back to Chauvet's Crossing and talked to this guy Glidden, who's shacked up with Jack Hastings at what they call their ranch."

"Where was Jack?"

"Back in the city arranging the funeral. I had to rough up

Glidden a bit, and he's a lot tougher than Jack" (he touched his cheek) "but he sang at the end, and confessed the place was a coke drop and his job was to cut the stuff with powdered sugar before it was sold on the street. Bill Hastings was a supplier and had half a dozen customers at Niles alone, only he went too far with Pidgie Malloy. After the roughhouse I called the Sonoma police and they jailed him about six o'clock last night."

"So now he's under the jurisdiction of Sonoma County. Why the hell didn't you telephone Wyatt, Baxter and Wyatt right away? You knew they were representing Miss Estrada. Jack Hastings may be a fugitive from justice by now."

"He was still at the Palace Hotel an hour ago."

Mr. Duval stood up, the skirts of his Prince Albert billowing out behind him like the wings of victory. "So there's no time to lose," he said. "Thank you, Mr. Gregory. You may have given us just the break we needed. The expenses of your trip will be included in the bill sent to Mr. Cord in Honolulu. Give my clerk a note of your city address as you go out."

It was an abrupt dismissal, but justifiable given the need for haste, and Albert Duval paused only to take out the slim file marked 'The People v. Violet Estrada' and verify one page in it before he called Conrad Wyatt at his office.

"Mr. Wyatt? Duval here. I have before me a copy of the statement Timothy Siegrist made to you about his visit to the Malloy apartment south of Market and a neighbour's testimony about a quarrel between Bill Hastings and Miss Malloy's father last Sunday afternoon. Will you contact Mr. Siegrist at Essanay and ask him to come up to the city, please? He'll be required to repeat his statement on oath at police headquarters . . . What's that? No, they don't know about it, I'm going to call David A. White now . . . Yes, I'm on to something, I think . . . I'll call you back."

He hung up and immediately called the Police Chief of San Francisco.

"Mr. White? Albert Duval here, representing Violet Estrada. I want you to pull in Jack Hastings for questioning, he was at the Palace Hotel an hour ago. Along with him I need a man called Glidden, presently in custody at Sonoma for operating a coke-cutting factory at Chauvet's Crossing . . .

Yes, I agree, Narcotics will be interested. I need a statement from Bridget Malloy, now in San Francisco General Hospital, and a statement from the doctor in charge of her case . . . Damn their medical ethics, you can issue a subpoena if it's necessary. Then have your men check the baggage-duty roster at the St. Francis Hotel last Sunday evening, I want to check out all the names of the men on duty . . . Eh? Of course I'm not trying to run the show, I'm trying to help you. I want to prevent a grave miscarriage of justice, and the possibility of a suit against the police for false arrest . . . Who's going to sue? Faxon Cord on behalf of his minor stepdaughter, that's who . . . Now don't fly off the handle, I haven't finished yet. I want you to find, and detain for questioning, at his home or elsewhere, the key witness to our plea of not guilty. The father of Bridget Malloy.''

Now wouldn't it be interesting, Duval thought, as he began to write a précis of his two telephone calls, if those two amateur sleuths had blown the police charge to shreds? Siegrist, who was obviously mad about the girl, and Gregory, who reminded him of his grandfather's French proverb about old poachers making the best gamekeepers? And what about his own search for Motive and Opportunity? Malloy, whose daughter had been turned on to drugs by Bill Hastings, and who though dismissed for drunkenness knew the St. Francis Hotel like the back of his hand, had them both.

Duval sent for his young men and told them the situation. "We've got to get a line on Malloy as fast as we can," he said. "Having arrested and charged Miss Estrada, the SFPD may drag its feet a little in looking for an alternative criminal. Try all the usual sources to find out if Malloy skipped town, or if he's still in the city, and where. Remember any tip may be important."

One tip, from one of the winos who used Malloy's street as a shelter, paid off in the small hours, when a tri-state alarm was issued. At noon next day Malloy was arrested by a country constable, on a charge of vagrancy, in a hobo jungle just across the Nevada state line. He was fighting drunk, and the cop sobered him up with the hose from the railroad water tank, but he was maudlin enough, when taken to the village jail, to sob out his confession.

Bill Hastings had 'ruined' his lovely Bridgie, bringing her home drugged and as weak as a sick cat, so that the doctor himself had said she must be treated in the hospital, and while they were waiting for the ambulance he had cursed and sworn at Hastings until the rat drove away as bold as brass in his swank automobile. And then out at the hospital it had come over him that he should kill Hastings for the dog he was, and he went home for his work gloves and a knife and went back to the hotel by the back door. He knew the baggage staff would be at supper, so he took an apron and a valise and put them back where he got them after he stuck the knife in Hastings. Then he got drunk, and slept rough for a couple of nights. He hadn't seen the papers because he didn't read so good. He tried riding the rods, but he was too old and stiff to buck the brakemen, and he got thrown off the freight cars twice before he made it as far as Nevada. That was the truth, so help him God, and he would like to see a priest.

★   ★   ★

"How are you going to handle it, Albert?" asked Mr. Wyatt. It was after business hours on Friday, and they were sitting in a secluded corner of the Pacific Union Club on Nob Hill, which had once been the mansion of the Silver King, James Flood. "Are you going to have your client surrender to her bail on the appointed day, and then make a grand fireworks display of her innocence in Superior Court?"

"Is that how you would handle it if you were me?" said Albert Duval.

"Well – knowing how much you enjoy a big day in court . . ."

"Not this time, Conrad." Duval poured two fingers of rye from a bottle on the silver tray between them and filled his glass with water. "I want to get that girl off the hook as fast as possible. In fact, I don't like to think of her sweating it out down there at North Beach. But I need the weekend for the paperwork, and there's nothing to be done until Monday morning anyway. Then I would like you to come with me to the Law and Motion judge at Superior Court and enter a plea to dismiss the charge against Violet Estrada."

"The DA will oppose us."

"Of course he will, but when he sees our case is watertight he'll prefer to look a fool in the judge's chambers instead of in open court. Especially as next year is election year. And he'll get his conviction against Patrick Malloy, unless *his* defender pleads unsound mind, or extenuating circumstances – I know which I would choose. Now there's a chance for your boy Fiske!"

"Knowing you, I suspect you've already made an appointment with the judge for Monday morning."

"Nine-thirty too early for you?"

"Not at all. What about Miss Estrada?"

"It isn't necessary for her to put in an appearance. And Conrad, the less she says the better."

"Is that why you're ready to pass up the grand finale in Superior Court?"

"I told you already, I'd be afraid of her on the witness stand. She's too pretty and too bold to make a good impression on the jury. That was a dirty cartoon they ran in the *Chronicle* about the Estrada brand, but my God! there was a grain of truth in it after all. The Estradas are a marked family, Conrad. There were some queer rumours, my grandfather used to tell me, about a daughter who went wrong years ago, in the Russian time, but that was all hushed up before the Gold Rush days. Then Don Luis, you remember him, he was what the Yankees would call an unreconstructed rebel, never got over the Conquest, and his brother Felipe, in his quiet way, was just as much a robber baron as the Big Four or the Silver Kings. This girl's father went wild over the *Rosalie* adventure, and last Sunday she herself acted like a crazy fool. Perhaps it's a good thing she's the last of the line."

"The last of the Estrada *name*, certainly," said Mr. Wyatt with gentle emphasis. "I don't think Timothy Siegrist will worry too much about the Estrada brand."

★　　★　　★

Tim Siegrist went to find her on Monday afternoon, clanking down Hyde Street in a cable car to the Bayview Hotel. He had followed Mr. Wyatt's advice to keep away from Violet, raising no false hopes until her freedom was assured, and Mrs.

Brice, who had again come up from Niles to be with her, had no idea of what was going on. It was Mrs. Brice who told Tim that the poor lamb was restless, and had gone out for a walk to see the sunset.

The wintry sun was setting like a red ball of fire beyond the Golden Gate, and the massed clouds above the strait were shot through and through with a lurid light. But already the peak of Mount Tamalpais was shrouded in fog, and the fog was stretching long fingers down and down over the Marin slopes to mask the steel-blue waters of the bay. It was growing cold, and there were not many people about, the little eating shops were putting up their shutters. Tim saw Violet far along the waterfront, not walking but standing still with her hands in the pockets of her old black coat. She might have gone out to admire the sunset, but she was looking at Alcatraz Island, the 'Rock' of the pioneers, now Army property and housing a United States Disciplinary Barracks. Behind those barred windows, stained with sunset, men were in prison. The lighthouse threw its revolving beam upon Violet, making a barred pattern of darkness and light. Tim wondered, as he quickened his limping pace, if she was thinking that before long the doors of another prison might close upon herself.

"Violet!"

She turned and saw him, and came running to his arms with the wonderful abandon of their last meeting, ready to be kissed. But before he kissed her Tim told her it was all right, she was free, they had found the guilty man and the case against her was dismissed. It was some time before she fully understood, or could do more than lay her head against his shoulder, breathing long choking sighs of relief. How could a judge – and she had never heard of a Law and Motion judge – dismiss her case without a trial, without even hearing her plead not guilty? She thought all cases went to trial by jury. Would Patrick Malloy be tried instead of her, and what about poor Bridget, would she be tried too? Would Mr. Anderson get his money back, even if she hadn't surrendered to her bail? Tim stopped the incoherent questions with his lips.

"It's growing cold, darling. Let's go home before you catch a chill."

"But where's home?" she said.

"Well – back to the hotel. You'll have to stay there tonight, because Mr. Duval and Mr. Wyatt want to see you in the morning, to complete the legal formalities. Then you'll be free to go home whenever you like."

"The reporters will be waiting for me at the flat."

"Waiting to congratulate you this time." He put his arm round her and they walked away under the last windblown banners of the sunset.

"I can't go to Sonoma, Tim, I know that. I telephoned to Joe at Coppa's, I simply had to know about Zeemaree. He told me the truth, she's had a stroke. I can't be a bother to them now."

"Was that all Joe told you?"

"Wasn't it enough?"

"When we get back to the Bayview I'll tell you how much we owe to Joe. Have you thought of getting away from all this? Going to your mother in Honolulu for a bit?"

"My mother deserted me for Faxon Cord years ago. I'm glad he's paying the lawyers' expenses, he owes it me, but I know I'm not wanted in his house."

The old animosity, the old sense of rejection, gave a biting edge to her words. Tim stopped near the green slope where the Italians spread their nets.

"Did Mrs. Brice give you any news from Niles?" he asked.

"Just kind messages. From Willie Bleer and the other people who were in *Mliss*."

Well, good for the woman, she had been discreet. Niles had been a hotbed of gossip since Bill Hastings' activities as a supplier of cocaine came to light. And besides –

"Is there some *special* news, Tim?" She was sharp all right, she knew there was something.

"I suppose I'm not wanted back at Essanay."

"Violet, it isn't that!" Tim said desperately. "It's – the Niles studio is closing down for good."

In the grip of her self-absorption she asked if she was to be blamed for that too.

"It's got nothing to do with you. Billy – Mr. Anderson is pulling out, I guess because he's had about enough. All that rowing with Charlie Chaplin took a lot out of him. He's sold his share in the concern to his partner, George Spoor, and

Spoor will go on working out of Chicago or move to Hollywood – we don't know yet."

"And you? What will *you* do?"

"I'm one of the lucky ones, Violet. I was offered a swell job right away. Lighting cameraman on the movie de Mille's going to make with Dustin Farnum."

It was almost too dark to see Violet's face, but Tim heard her pitiful whisper. "So you're going to leave me too!"

He seized her in his arms. "I'll never leave you, my darling girl, as long as you need me. You know I love you: come away with me. Come with me to Hollywood – and marry me."

BOOK FOUR

Sunset and Sunrise

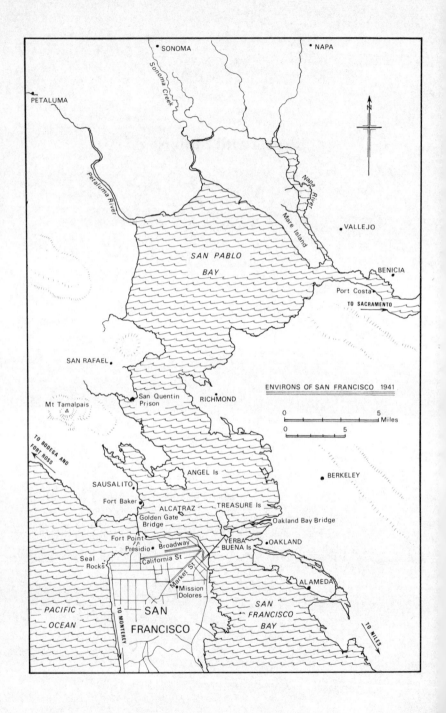

San Francisco was an uneasy city in 1916. A disturbed city in a restless nation. 1916 was an election year, which meant that because of an electoral system devised to suit the conditions of the eighteenth century there would be an upheaval of the body politic lasting for longer than twelve months. In 1916, while the petty placemen contended in the usual way for their offices and their cut from the pork barrel, the election of the Chief Executive was a matter of unusual anxiety. President Woodrow Wilson, seeking the Democratic nomination for a second term in the White House, had kept the United States out of the war in Europe for two years, surely long enough for the Central Powers to beat the Triple Entente, or the other way round. But the war dragged on, nation after nation entered the fray, and how long (said the war party in Congress) after the sinking of the *Lusitania*, could America stand aside? How sincere (said the pacifists) was President Wilson in his repeated declarations of neutrality?

'Preparedness' was now the watchword of the Administration. It had been led up to by programmes to develop the army and the navy, never really extended since the Civil War. In December 1915 Mr. Wilson made his Preparedness speech to Congress. Preparedness for what, cried his opponents. Preparedness to sacrifice American boys to the bloody war in Europe? Woodrow Wilson persevered. Demonstrations were held. Preparedness Day parades, with fife and drum, took place in the major cities. On June 14, 1916, the President electrified the nation by joining in the Preparedness Day in the capital, marching through the streets of Washington dressed in a dark jacket, white trousers and a straw boater, and carrying the banner of the Stars and Stripes over his shoulder.

Elsewhere the parades had been less successful. In California there was a strong radical movement of protest against 'the militarism forced on us and our children', and the protesters, notably one Tom Mooney, urged direct action against the Preparedness Days. Bombs were thrown in Los Angeles, either by the International Workers of the World, nicknamed the Wobblies, or by pro-German saboteurs, and in San Francisco there was open antagonism between the Chamber of Commerce and the labour unions. On July 10 a Committee of Law and Order (which brought back memories of the Vigilantes of the Gold Rush era) was set up to ensure that the Preparedness Day Parade fixed for July 22 should be a peaceful demonstration. The Governor, the Honourable Hiram Johnson, who had finally broken the stranglehold of the Southern Pacific Railroad on Californian politics, was coming from Sacramento to lead the procession along with Mayor James Rolph, who had stopped making laudatory speeches to the German community.

San Francisco, which seventy years earlier had been a pueblo of one thousand inhabitants, was now a city of half a million, and in that half million there were strongly marked national groups. Of the European belligerents the Italians, who had entered the war against Austria, were the largest group, but the Germans were not far behind, and clashes between them might be expected at the Preparedness Day parade. Tim Siegrist, waiting beside his camera truck at the foot of Market Street, was hoping for one or two such clashes. They would make for excellent cinema.

Behind him the procession was forming between the bottom of Market Street and the Ferry Building which had survived the earthquake and the fire of 1906. The marchers would proceed, to martial music, on to City Hall – not, Tim was glad to think, to the temporary building where Violet had spent a night in jail, but to the great domed City Hall dedicated by Mayor Rolph in the previous December. He wondered if Violet would be interested in watching the parade. She had been restless and edgy since they came back to San Francisco.

Certainly she hadn't sounded interested in Preparedness Day when he left their downtown hotel after breakfast. She was intent on finding a place for them to live, and had three addresses to visit that morning. It wasn't going to be as easy as it was in Hollywood, where everything was extemporised, and even on a lighting cameraman's salary of thirty-five dollars a week (five dollars better than he was getting at Essanay) it was possible to rent a garden apartment, so-called because it was one of eight shacks built round a little orange grove. The other tenants were young married couples, the husbands technicians like Tim without an actor among them, and yet as the actors who had left the Niles companies arrived in Hollywood the news began to filter down that pretty young Mrs. Siegrist was Violet Estrada, the girl in the Hastings case.

It was a damned shame, her husband thought. His previous Hollywood experience had been too brief and too specialised for Tim to understand the thinking of the new movie moguls. The ex-furriers and ex-junkmen now running a growth industry were terrified of moral turpitude in any form which affected actors about whose private lives the cash customers were clamouring to know more. The Hastings case was turpitude plus. It had murder, 'dope fiends' and homosexuality. A scapegoat was needed to protect the industry, and that was the girl who had been charged with murder, Violet Estrada.

The real girl in the case, Bridget Malloy, was being cured of her addiction in a state hospital, where she received over a hundred proposals of marriage, many of them from inmates of lunatic asylums. The real villain of the case was her father, Patrick Malloy, who thanks to an emotional plea of extenuating circumstances and the vote of a sentimental jury escaped with ten years in San Quentin instead of the death penalty demanded by the District Attorney. The appearance of Jack Hastings and Glidden on narcotics charges kept interest in the Hastings case alive, and Violet Estrada, bearing the Estrada brand, knew the full weight of society's disapproval.

It sometimes crossed the mind of Conrad Wyatt, as he watched the continuing smear campaign in the press, that his brilliant friend Albert Duval had outsmarted himself when he got the charge of murder against Violet Estrada dismissed by the Law and Motion judge. It might have been better to face the music in open court, produce the evidence of Malloy's guilt, and permit the judge, with the whole press corps taking down his words, to announce that the prisoner, Miss Violet Estrada, left the court without a stain on her character. Then there would have been cheering from the fickle crowd on Market Street, instead of the innuendoes that her discharge had been fixed, that wealth and privilege had prevailed over justice, and that the Cord fortune had influenced the judge's decision. That these statements were libellous troubled no one, least of all the judge, for as Albert Duval consoled his friend, "San Franciscans would rather hear evil spoken of themselves than not be spoken of at all."

Tim Siegrist did not lose his job with deMille/Lasky because he was married to a girl who had got mixed up with 'dope fiends' and been caught in a man's bedroom by a hotel detective. He was too good at his work for that. He was pleased to be lighting four-reelers at last, and as most of the new Farnum movie was shot on location he ate his box lunch, which cost the management thirty-five cents, with a camera crew and a director who enjoyed discussing innovative ideas with him. It was a satisfying time for Tim Siegrist, with Essanay behind him, the strain of Violet's arrest behind him, and the future before him with the beautiful girl he loved.

He wasn't fool enough to think she was in love with him, Gimpy Tim, a guy who didn't come within shouting distance of the handsome hunks of men crowding into Hollywood. She had married him out of gratitude and the need for protection, on a wet day in Salinas on their way south, in a Presbyterian minister's study with the pastor's wife and son as witnesses. They spent their wedding night in a raw new commercial hotel in the artichoke country, and Tim was almost too nervous to take her to bed. Tim's considerable sexual experience, gained with the girls who followed the rodeos or hung about the taverns where he occasionally drank to excess, had not prepared him for marriage with a highly-strung virgin bride. To his incredulous joy she came more than half way to meet him. Violet was ripe for love, and in Tim's embrace her humiliation was forgotten.

But the images of a murdered man, a night in jail, a lawyer's hectoring and an exile to North Beach came back to torment her in the long hours she spent alone when Tim was on location, and this he never fully understood. His imagination was entirely visual: the Alcatraz light wheeling across a girl wandering on the desolate wharf made him think at once of prison bars, but he could picture no bars over the spirit of the lovely girl who came across the scented orange grove to welcome his return. He thought she was happy in Hollywood, and almost hesitated when the time came to propose a change.

The year 1916 ushered in the golden age of the movies. The coming of sound and colour might bring bigger spectacles and more glittering names to the cinema, but the excitement of the silent years was the the constant thrill that sped around the world. Huge fortunes were in the making. At Essanay George K. Spoor took over the wooing of Charlie Chaplin, offering him $350,000 for twelve two-reelers, but withdrew his offer when Chaplin asked for a $150,000 bonus on signing of the contract. Chaplin got that exact sum as a bonus from Mutual when he signed for a much better deal, eight two-reelers for $670,000. Suddenly everybody was talking money, and in astronomical terms. De Mille/Lasky amalgamated with Adolph Zukor in the summer, and Tim Siegrist thought it was time for him to be moving on. He was offered a job with a newsreel company called Movie Gazette, operating in and around San Francisco. The pay was forty dollars a week. It was not on the Chaplin scale, but it was the best money he had ever earned.

When he put the new proposition to Violet, as carefully as he could, her reaction was unexpected. He thought she might object to going back to San Francisco for her own sake, but her concern was all for him.

"Leave Hollywood? Tim Siegrist, are you crazy? How often have I heard you say this is where everything's happening, where all the new ideas begin?"

"A newsreel's a new idea, Vi. And it's the kind of filming I really want to do."

"How's that?"

"Making movies of things happening. Of reality. And the company's based on Hollywood; this is only a temporary assignment to San Francisco, probably about six months."

"And then what? Will your newsreel company go bust and leave you looking for another job?"

"That's the risk we all run in this game, Violet." Tim had been drinking a mint julep, which she had concocted for him from a Southern recipe of her grandmother's and a few sprigs of the wild mint, *yerba buena*, which grew at the side of the garden apartment. Tim took a sip and set the glass on the living-room floor before he answered her impatient sigh and shake of the head.

"D'you know the Hollywood job I'd really like to have? Second cameraman to Billy Bitzer, who works for Griffith. He's the best man in town, but unluckily he's got a swell second cameraman already, fellow called Karl Brown. I meet them around. I've told you about them both."

"I'm sure you have," she pouted. "*Second* cameraman, with your experience! You haven't much ambition, Tim."

"I could learn from Billy Bitzer, you see."

"Why don't you try for a job as assistant director?"

"On the strength of *Mliss*?"

He meant it for a joke, but Tim was lighting a cigarette and didn't see her face. He was quite reconciled to the fact that *Mliss*, the film into which he had put his fresh ideas and his best camera work, would never be shown. It was not only 'in the can' but on the shelf, and it could never be offered to the distributors because of the scandal hanging round the neck of the girl who had played the leading part. Tim Siegrist's career as a director was over before it had begun.

Only Violet's sob told him that his attempt at humour had caused her pain.

"Why do you bring *Mliss* up now?" she said. "You know it makes me think of that awful day –"

"Now Violet –"

She flung herself down beside his chair and laid her head on his knee.

"Oh Tim, why was I such an unspeakable fool! Why didn't I go back to Mrs. Brice's and wait for you? Why did I go racing up to San Francisco and get us all into that hideous mess?"

Tim stroked the silky black hair gently. It was the first time Violet had ever admitted that her own impulsive folly, and nothing else, had brought about her trouble, the first time she had said 'us' instead of 'me'. It was not much, but it was a beginning. He said,

"When you lit out for the city you were playing a tragedy queen, dear, that was all."

"And now I'll never get a chance to act again."

He thought that was true enough. But he said, "Everything's going so fast in the industry, there may be another part

for you some day. Right now, I'm afraid you have to live
with –"

"Notoriety?"

"There's something worse to live with than notoriety."

"What?"

"A lame leg."

She gave a little remorseful cry and let Tim pull her up into
his arms. He took her to bed, and as far as a man could tell she
returned his passion with all the force of her being, but, as
always, in a silence broken only by incoherent murmurs. To
Tim's erotic words she reacted with her body but never with
her voice. He began to wish ungratefully that her climax
might be celebrated by a gasped "I love you!" the words he
had never heard her say.

He was thinking of her, wondering if after all she would be
somewhere in the dense crowd which now filled Market Street
almost as far as the eye could reach. Four miles away rose the
Twin Peaks, now tunnelled for traffic and built over with
dwellings; between the Peaks and the Ferry Building the silent
throng seemed to be waiting for the war to start. Tim Siegrist
climbed aboard the Movie Gazette truck. He was going to
work three cameras, his two assistants filming the people on
the pavements, and himself on a platform in the rear shooting
the procession as it followed the truck and the mounted police
up Market Street. He twisted his cap round, peak to the back
of his head, and began to turn the handle of his camera. A few
establishing shots showed the milling crowd in front of the
Ferry Building being marshalled into some semblance of
order. A band out of camera range struck up 'The Star-
spangled Banner'.

"Can't march to that!" said one of Tim's assistants, over the
rising noise of the crowd. "Hey, Tim! Whaddya bet the
mayor'll start 'em off with 'Smiles'?"

"No takers!" Tim shouted over his shoulder. "He'll save it
up for City Hall!" The mayor, James Rolph, known for his
affability as 'Sunny Jim', had taken 'Smiles' for his signature
tune, and his every appearance was heralded by "There are
smiles that make you happy – " Some of the children pushed
to the front of the pavement were singing it already.

But the bandmaster had already had second thoughts about

the national anthem. When the drums, brasses and wood-winds came in sight, followed by the outriders, followed by the limousine in which the governor and the mayor were riding, followed by the military, the civic dignitaries and all who could get or wanted a place in the Preparedness procession, they had changed their tune to 'America the Beautiful'.

> America! America!
> God shed his grace on thee!
> And crown thy good with brotherhood
> From sea to shining sea!

They were only a little way up Market, not far from the corner of Steuart Street, when the bombs exploded. Bomb or bombs, limpet device attached to a wall, grenades flung from a high window, mine on the roadway – the machinery of terrorism was not determined in the first moments of panic. Nine people lay dead, forty were groaning and bleeding in the street, children were crushed on the pavements, and the driver of the newsreel truck, struck by a metal shard, lost control of the wheel and drove his vehicle straight into the crowd. The assistant cameramen jumped off in time, and one was uninjured. His mate was knocked out by the iron-shod hoof of a terrified police horse. Tim Siegrist lay on the splintered platform underneath his camera, with blood pouring from the multiple wounds of Preparedness Day 1916.

. . . He had never seen snow, except on the distant peaks of the Sierra Nevada, but he came back to semi-consciousness in a world of snow. His motionless body was wrapped in snow, covered with snow, and icy white were the bodies, vaguely seen, which bent over him, corpse-like the lips which mouth-ed words like the dripping of icicles. He strained to listen. He made out one word, *amputation*, at which he thought he shouted "No!" – the doctors and nurses round his bed saw nothing but the faintest movement of his bloodless lips. But then he heard another voice, wild, even hysterical, as Violet, with her warm hand over his, cried out, "You're not to do it! You're not to hurt him more! . . . Oh darling, speak to me! I love you, Tim! I love you!"

2

"Keep that Chicana girl out of here unless her husband's actually dying," said an angry young intern to the night sister on duty (and 'Chicana' meant to him what 'Greaser' meant to Broncho Billy). "I can't have the whole ward upset with her yelling and screaming." But two days later, when Tim Siegrist's tenacious hold on life was confirmed, a senior surgeon pointed out to the intern that the Chicana had yelled and screamed to some purpose. She had made them all think twice about an amputation, so that her husband's left leg was saved – a matter of especial importance to a man already lame from an injury to his right hip. "Congratulations, Mrs. Siegrist," he said on her next permitted visit. "It'll be a long haul, but we'll get him on his feet for you – eventually."

None of the doctors or nurses recognised in the pale woman, huddled into a black coat, the dangerous and insolent beauty whose picture had appeared in so many papers so few months ago. The Hastings murder was old news. All that now mattered was the Preparedness Day massacre, and the capture of the criminals responsible. There was a wide choice of the guilty. Were they the 'Wobblies' who believed the murder of the innocent was the right way to preserve neutrality? Were they German saboteurs, the secret espionage agents already responsible for explosions in American munitions factories? Or were they the home-grown revolutionaries whom the committee of Law and Order had been formed to defeat? Before long arrests were made. Tom Mooney, the labour leader, a man of thirty-one, and his twenty-two-year-old accomplice, Warren Billings, were brought to trial and found guilty. Billings began a term of life imprisonment: Mooney was condemned to death which, given the procrastination of American justice, merely meant the beginning of a long sojourn on Death Row.

The shocking event, the trial and the sentences, followed at once by petitions for mercy, denials of guilt and demands for investigations which should reveal the probity and innocence of Mooney and Billings, shook the self-confidence of San Francisco. Not even the oldest inhabitant could recall the violence of the Gold Rush days, the banditry, the clashes between the Hounds and the Vigilantes, for these had passed into legend and romance. But at least the old violence had meant confrontations between men with names and faces, known to their fellow citizens, while the Preparedness Day massacre was a faceless, nameless crime, and there was nothing romantic about the spilt blood of civilians struck down in the heart of the city on a warm July afternoon. The earthquake of 1906 was a natural disaster, seen by some as the apocalyptic beginning of the new century. But there was nothing natural about the bombing in Market Street, and 1916, not 1906, was when the twentieth century began for San Franciscans in the deadly birth of terrorism.

Tim Siegrist spent two months in hospital, but he could walk on crutches by the time he was discharged, and unlike some of his fellow victims he was able to spend his convalescence in the country. That was a surprise arranged for him by Violet, who was always smiling and hopeful when she came to see him, always 'managing splendidly' and 'all right for money'. One of his few consolations was that he had taken out a life-insurance policy on his marriage, and remembering the Calgary Stampede a general and accident policy as well. So payments would be made on that, and there might be some compensation from the city as well – the lawyers were arguing about it. Then Violet had money of her own since her twenty-first birthday, left in the same interest-bearing account in her bank. Weak from shock and loss of blood, worn down by pain, Tim was content to leave all their financial affairs in Violet's unexpectedly capable hands.

Orphaned at twelve, and earning his own living since he was thirteen, Tim had never thought much about his wife's curious relationship with her mother and stepfather. They didn't get on, so who cared? He knew that a cautious correspondence with Faxon Cord had been resumed when his trusteeship ended on Violet's twenty-first birthday, and that her grandmother had written to her affectionately, but when Tim was in hospital and proposed that Violet should go back to the California Street flat, which was standing empty, rather than occupy a hall bedroom in their downtown hotel, he was not surprised to hear her say,

"The flat's Faxon Cord's property. I don't think granny will ever be strong enough to come back to San Francisco, so it's his to rent or sell as he pleases. I won't be beholden to him for another dollar. When you're well again we'll find a nice place of our own."

If Zeemaree had still been alive she would have remembered the days when as little Maria de las Mercedes Estrada she had known her father's obstinacy, which his brother's grandchild had inherited. For Faxon Cord read John C. Fremont, she might have said. But Zeemaree had suffered a third and final stroke when the Siegrists were in Hollywood, and Violet had wept alone in the garden apartment to think that Zeemaree had died thinking ill of her, and that on the day of the first 'bad turn' which the local doctor had not diagnosed for what it was, her kind old kinswoman had been so perturbed by the verses:

I see the dying glow of Spanish glory,
The sunset dream and last!

It was Joe Gregory who put an end to the painful situation: Joe who was outside the hospital ward one day when Tim was on the mend, and took her to a little room where a woman in deep mourning was waiting, and Violet was once again in Stella's arms.

"Violetta, *carissima*, can you ever forgive me?"

"There's nothing to forgive," said Violet. I was innocent, and you believed me guilty; acquitted, because Joe found proof; rejected, when only Tim was faithful; Stella, there is nothing to forgive.

"Thank you for bringing her, Joe," she said. "Could Uncle Rico really spare her?"

"He's better today. He sent you his love, Vi."

"He wants to see you," said Stella with a sob. "He and Zeemaree always believed in you, darling. It was I who was harsh and unkind. Only I was so upset, when that awful Jack Hastings made such a scene at the Sorrento, and the whole town was talking –"

"Hush, Stella, it's all over now."

497

"No it isn't!" cried Stella. "There's your poor husband, maimed by those anarchists, or Bolsheviks or whatever they call themselves! We read about it in the paper, and what's he going to do when he gets well? Will he be lamed for life?"

"The doctors haven't said so, and I'm sure he'll find something to do –"

"You bet," said Joe heartily. "Stella, why don't you stop snivelling, and tell Vi about your plans?"

Stella explained, more or less clearly, that the Sorrento restaurant had been sold. With Zeemaree gone, and daddy in failing health, she wasn't able to carry on single-handed. Just then, just when Denny had got a marvellous chance to go into partnership with a fine dental surgeon in Stockton, a San Francisco bank had offered to buy the restaurant, intending to tear the old adobe down and put a Sonoma branch of their bank on the site. The Sorrento would serve its last Californio dinners on Labour Day, the first Monday in September, and by Thanksgiving she and Denny and little Freddy, taking Rico with them, would be settled in Stockton.

"Couldn't you and your husband come to us for a few weeks, after the dining room closes?" Stella begged. "We'd feed him up with cream and chickens and good wine, and he'd soon get back his strength."

"Oh, Stella, I just don't know . . ."

"Zeemaree would have wanted it," said Stella, and at that reminder of Zeemaree's unfailing kindness Violet weakened, and whispered, "If only I could have seen her, just once, before she died!"

In tears their bitterness melted, but Violet waited for the doctor's final verdict before she told Tim about the invitation to Sonoma. That came on the day when he walked up and down the ward on crutches, saying airily that he was an old crutch hand, he'd learned to use them in Calgary. The doctor watched him and said "That's enough! Just keep away from the movie stunts and the cattle stampedes, and your legs'll carry you for a long time yet!" Back in bed, Tim was still excited. He wanted to tell Violet about a talk he'd had the day before with Jeff Robbins, now in a good job with Triangle, who had made the long trip from Los Angeles over Sunday to visit his old colleague in hospital and tell him all the Hollywood gossip. "And what d'you think?" said Robbins, "I met a rich guy called Zinnia who's starting a collection of early movies. Says it'll be called an archive some day. He's got a lot of French film already. Seems he bought some Essanay stuff before it was chucked into the incinerator. He's got some episodes of *Terry*, and my *Cattle Rustlers* and *Tennessee's Partner*, starring Billy, and I be damned if he didn't buy the rough cut *and* the print of *Mliss!*"

"I hear Mary Pickford's going to do a remake of it with Marshall Neilan. Bet you she'll be as sweet as sugar candy," was Tim's only comment on the last item. But he talked about it so much during the evening hour for visitors that Violet had hardly time to tell him about Sonoma before the departure bell was rung. His first reaction was the same as hers; he 'just didn't know'.

"I wonder if it's the right thing to do," he said doubtfully.

"Why not?"

"Because you and I have a talent for being in the wrong places at the wrong time."

"I don't think we'll come to much harm in Sonoma. And I'd like to see the old place before the wreckers move in."

"The cradle of the race?"

"I suppose the River Inn is the real cradle of the race, but somehow I've never been able to picture the Rancho Estrada there. You could, perhaps."

Violet knew that Tim's pictorial imagination was twenty times stronger than her own. He was impatient to get away to Sonoma, but the time went by and Violet had found a flat for them before he was discharged from hospital. The season which the Indians called the Time of Woodland Fruits was nearly past, and the lilac dusk of late September lay over Sonoma when their train stopped at the little clapboard station. Uncle Rico was there to greet them, thin and bent but beaming as of old, and Denny Smith helped Tim into the wheelchair which Zeemaree had used when she was still able to go out of doors. The golden hills were umbered, and a chilly breeze blew across the plaza, but enough of the childish feeling of holiday and freedom remained for Violet to clutch Tim's hand in happiness as they made their way to Stella's welcome at the old adobe.

To spare Tim the stairs, Stella had rearranged the ground-floor room at the left of the front door. Divided from the room to the right by a passage since Luis Estrada enlarged the adobe, it had long been used as a little parlour, but Stella had turned it back into a bedroom by installing two narrow divans, low enough for Tim to get in and out of comfortably. An old wooden stool stood between them. It was the stool on which Rosalie had sat to drink the love potion on her wedding night, while Carlos Rivera's vaquero brought his valise and double-barrelled pistol to the other room.

No intimations from the unknown past troubled Violet as she helped her husband to bed and brought him the hot milk which was all he wanted for supper. His only request was for a candle, because the electric light from the ceiling fixture hurt his eyes, and in the soft golden glow the shuttered room with the thick adobe walls seemed to float back through the shadows of seventy years. Violet's features were dislimned in the gold, a mirage of green eyes and shining hair, and Tim watched it with her hand in his until he fell asleep.

That was the gentle beginning of the time they called their second honeymoon. Their first, on the drive from San Francisco to Los Angeles with the Winton threatening to collapse at every pothole on the road, had been divided between long silences by day and torrid sex at night. At Sonoma they talked to one another round the clock, through Tim's sleepless hours into the warm mornings when they sat on the verandah after Violet prepared breakfast for Tim, Rico and herself. Then the old man puttered contentedly round the garden which had been his pride, and which within a short time would be the new parking lot for the Pioneer Merchants' Bank of San Francisco. As soon as the noon whistles blew over Sonoma the whole Smith family appeared, with Freddy on his tricycle, and Denny and Stella carrying well-filled lunch baskets. During an enchanted week of Indian summer they were able to eat among the flowers in the garden. "Like old days," said Rico, "when you were a bambina, Stella, and my Maria, she have you here with the little boys to swing and make the picnic. Was the happy time!" He had to wipe away the tears when he spoke of his *povera Maria*, although he sometimes confused her with his *povera Lidia*, the mother of his children, and Stella, too, dabbed her eyes at Zeemaree's name. But Violet saw that it meant nothing to Stella to be leaving the only home she could remember. Stockton was Denny's home town, and it was there that Freddy and the new baby expected in April would go to school and grow up in a thriving, bustling city "with a future", as she often said. She gave Violet some trinkets belonging to Zeemaree: an old-fashioned coral with silver bells ("for your own baby, some day, *cara*") a garnet brooch and earrings, and better still, some old photographs of Violet's father and his sisters, taken when Jim Estrada was about sixteen. "Take these too," said Stella, handing over two daguerreotypes in faded morocco cases, "they're Zeemaree's father and mother. We think Don Luis looked like *your* father, don't we, Denny?"

"And Vi looks like both of them," said Denny Smith.

"Thanks, Stella," said Violet. "I'm glad to have them, especially the picture of my father. You know everything my grandmothers had was destroyed in the fire ten years ago." Her voice was so strained that Tim knew the similarity of feature, repeated in the handsome older man, the attractive youth, and herself, had reminded her of that fatal phrase, *the Estrada brand*. He said easily, "Fine looking family! But how about the Smiths? Now you've got a photographer handy, don't you want me to record your handsome faces for posterity?"

"Great!" "Oh Tim, could you really? We've got nothing but our wedding pictures and some rotten snaps!" "What's Uncle Tim goin' to do to us, mommy?" That was Freddy, who was circling the group on his tricycle.

"Sure I could do it," said Tim. "Violet packed my Graflex, didn't you, sweetie? Soon as I get more mobile, I'll try some action shots, and I also want to shoot the house from the plaza, before the Pioneer Merchants' Bank starts the demolition job."

"I'll push you round the plaza in the wheelchair," said Violet.

"You will not."

"I do that," said Rico eagerly. He could never accept that the great strength of former days was his no longer, and was proud of helping Tim up and down the steps which led to the verandah.

No more was said about the Estrada portraits, but at bedtime Tim saw that the two daguerreotypes had been set up on the stool which served as a bedside table, with the boy picture of Jimmy between them. He was wakeful that night, and was not surprised, when Sonoma town was silent, to hear Violet moan in her sleep, and then cry out as she raised herself in bed.

"Are you all right, darling?" he said softly.

"I was dreaming, Tim."

"Was it a bad dream, love? Can you light the candle?"

In the golden light he saw her face was pale.

"I was dreaming about horses," she said. "I thought I heard horses galloping across the plaza."

It might have been that she was dreaming true. There had been horses galloping towards the old adobe times without number: Luis Estrada with his vaqueros behind him, Rosalie's bridal cavalcade, Robert Cord riding in to town to save Content from the mock justice of the Bear Flaggers. Who could tell what atavistic memories had stirred in Violet's sleep while the old pictures lay on the older stool? But Tim's comfort did not echo the historic past. He moved the candle so that his face was in shadow, and said, "I understand, darling. I often dream of horses myself. But I don't hear them galloping. I'm riding them."

"Oh Tim!" In her new closeness to him she understood how, much more than the injuries from the bomb, the accident which ended his riding days had affected Tim. Suddenly the weight of all their troubles, the uncertainty of their future, were too much for Violet, and she said with a sob, "I'm afraid, Tim! How are we going to manage? What are we going to do?"

"Right now you're coming to bed with me." He had turned, not without difficulty, on his left side, and was holding open the blanket and the sheet.

"You know what the doctor said –"

"Damn the doctor."

She was in his arms and he was a whole man again. It was

not the old wild perfection, but it was ease, it was satisfaction, it was comfort to the bodies of them both. The divan was narrow, but Violet never thought to leave it for her own. She slept with her hot face in Tim's neck, and a caponera of palominos from the Rancho Estrada could have galloped across the plaza without waking her from a sleep as deep as the sea.

From that night Tim shed the invalidism enforced upon him by hospital routine and his own weakness. When Stella appeared at ten next morning (she was constantly slipping over from her own bungalow on the next cross-street to bring Tim hot beef broth in a Thermos or creamy egg-nog in a chilled jug) she found he had laid aside his crutches and taken to walking sticks. With two stout sticks he walked up and down the level floor of the now empty restaurant with a much more even gait than when the crutches hurt his armpits and made him hunch his shoulders. The garden paths were more difficult, but when they all gathered for their midday meal in the grape arbour he was more optimistic than before about his progress and his plans for the future. It was swell of Movie Gazette to keep his job open for him. Well (seeing Denny's raised eyebrows) not exactly his old job, because he could hardly handle a Bell and Howell leaning on two sticks, but editing film in their Market Street studio would be work he enjoyed, and then he could use their facilities for processing his own pix once he was more mobile. Violet had found them a swell flat – no, he hadn't seen it yet, but he took her word for it – near enough to Movie Gazette for him to get there on foot, without hobbling on and off the street cars. It was on Ellis near Mason, which meant nothing to three of his hearers, for whom the new flat might have been adjacent to Nob Hill. Actually it was in the heart of the Tenderloin, about which the politest thing to say was that it was convenient for San Francisco's theatre-land. Violet had rented it because the flat was cheap.

Meantime Tim, in his new well-being, was eager to start work again. Violet fetched his precious Graflex to the garden, and he took a series of candid shots of the family which Violet guessed would be a big surprise to his subjects when they saw the prints. He wanted to use his sticks and walk right out to the plaza, but this was vetoed, and Tim had to admit, next day, that the wheelchair was still needed to get him round the centre of the town. It was a light contraption, quite easy for his wife to push, but Rico walked beside her with a possessive hand on the crossbar and with the pride of a man who was doing all the work.

It was the right moment for professional photographs of the old pueblo to appear. Conservation was in the air, and the adobes of the northern frontier were becoming recognised as part of California's heritage. Tim turned up his nose at the pretentious and disproportionate City Hall, which misguided civic pride had erected ten years earlier, and merely sniffed at the bronze Bear Flagger on his pedestal, but the Mission, the Mexican barracks (in dreadful disrepair), the servants' quarters which were all that remained of Vallejo's Casa Grande, and the adobes on the side streets as well as those in the plaza, delighted him. So did the people. The citizens of Sonoma had no idea how many of them were photographed that day, even when they were coming up to give their friendly greetings to 'dear old Mr. Gregorio' and his young friends.

Violet had dreaded her first appearance in the plaza, but she had nothing to fear. She was not cold-shouldered. She might be that silly Estrada girl who got into bad company in the city, but after all she was one of their own, and my! she surely was devoted to that poor crippled fellow, the anarchists' victim. Maybe now when President Wilson saw what tragedies happened at his Preparedness Day parades, he would stop trying to work the country up to war. War was a very sore subject in the Italian community of Sonoma, which followed with despair the Italian defeats in the many battles raging along the line of the Isonzo in 1916. Nice to've met you again, Mrs. Siegrist, and you get well quick, sir, you hear?

"You're my passport to respectability, Tim," said Violet when they were alone in their room, and he was lying, obviously tired, on the divan.

"You're my passport to life, darling," he said as he pulled her down and kissed her. "It's thanks to you that I *can* walk on two legs, and not on one and a half. You'll see, I'll soon be back on location for Movie Gazette."

"I hope they know how lucky they are," said Violet grimly.

Her husband was taking a cut in salary to go back to an indoor job.

He knew what she meant. "At least I can use their dark room," he said. "Wait till you see the prints of the pix I shot today." His confidence was justified: the 'Sonoma Sequence', as he called it, was the first and most popular of the series called 'Siegrist's People and Places' which twenty years later, when art books came into fashion, appeared on coffee tables across the nation.

Violet felt less confident when she spent a day alone in San Francisco. Their tenancy of the Ellis Street flat began on October 1, and on the fifteenth she took the train to the city to accept delivery of household goods already ordered from the Emporium, a department store which stood where St. Ignatius College had given the first exhibition of electric lighting on the centenary Fourth of July. The apartment building did not boast a superintendent, or even a janitor. Garbage was thrown down internal chutes by the eight resident families, and removed twice a week by a refuse collector; of other amenities, including telephones, there were none. Lighting, cooking and heating depended on gas. The Siegrists' front door, on the ground floor of the common entry, opened on a narrow passage with the living room and bedroom on one side, each with a window on Ellis Street. A row of spikes on the outer windowsills were intended to discourage loungers from sitting down. On the other side of the passage were a kitchen and bathroom and a second bedroom, each with a small window on a yard with clothes lines, and the iron containers connected with the garbage chutes. It was a long way down the San Franciscan ladder from the great house on Pine Street where Violet was born.

But at least the place was clean, and the Emporium delivery van having arrived punctually at nine-thirty, was cleaner still after Violet set to work with her new bucket and scrubbing brush. The bedroom and living room faced north, but the wallpaper in both rooms was a cheerful yellow, and the cheap furniture was light both in weight and colour. When they arrived together from Sonoma ten days later Tim was delighted with what Violet had accomplished on the very small sum of money he had given her. After the bunkhouses and stables of his early riding days it seemed to him like a luxurious home.

"But my God, Vi!" he said. "The Tenderloin! It's worse than I remembered. It's not a right place for you to be living!" They had arrived in the early evening. School was out, and children were playing hopscotch and skipping rope on the pavement, yelling and jostling the shabby women running out to the corner grocery for bread or milk. The streetwalkers were on the beat already, under the flaring lamps. It was the Barbary Coast without the entertainment, the concert halls and clubs: the Tenderloin was sullen, vicious and cold.

"We're not going to stay in the Tenderloin for ever," she said confidently. "A ground-floor flat, no stairs for you, and only a few blocks from the studio – I think we're in luck, that's what!"

"You're a great little sport, darling."

"Are you going to be a good sport too?"

"What d'you mean?"

"Are you going to smile and look pleasant when I tell you I want to take a part-time job?"

"Like hell I am!"

"Dear, we really need the money."

"Go on," said the man, and his shoulders slumped as he lay back in his chair. "Rub it in, if you feel you have to. Sure, we're nearly broke, and it's all my fault for leaving Hollywood, and getting myself to the corner of Steuart Street on the twenty-second of July. But I won't let you go out to work, Vi. To begin with, what could you do?"

"More than I did in Hollywood, where I spent hours just waiting for you to come home."

"You learned to drive the car."

"Well, now we haven't *got* a car, and we never *will* have a car unless we earn more money. The *Examiner*'s full of Situations Vacant –"

"Cut it out!"

She turned away, and Tim was instantly remorseful. "I'm sorry, honey. I didn't mean to chew you out. It's just that I was thinking of that little back room you haven't furnished yet . . . Wouldn't it be great if we had a kid sleeping there, Violet? A cute little guy like Freddy at Sonoma, or a lovely baby girl just like her mother?"

"You're my baby, Tim."

"No by God I'm not!" he said angrily. "I'm your husband. And I'm going to take care of you properly, so you can forget about the vacant situations. I'm going back to work tomorrow."

★   ★   ★

It took Tim Siegrist less than three months to come off his high horse and agree to Violet's looking for part-time employment. His insurance money had paid his hospital bills, his compensation for the furnishing of the flat, and now his reduced salary at Movie Gazette (less than he had been earning as a bachelor) had to take care of all their expenses. He knew that if his health failed, and one bad cold caught in the rainy San Francisco winter would do it, they would run into debt immediately, unless they dipped into Violet's two thousand dollars, which he was absolutely determined not to do.

He still required two walking sticks to get him to the studio and back, although on the return trip there was always some decent guy on the staff ready to lend an arm at the kerbs if he needed it. Then the guy would be invited into the Ellis Street flat, made brighter by the curtains sewed by Violet, and offered a glass of beer. Violet put out the sign for the iceman every day, but there were storage problems in the tiny kitchen, and she quickly got into the slipshod Ellis Street way of giving some urchin a nickel to 'rush the growler' for steam beer from the nearest saloon. She began to enjoy a sip of beer herself.

Twice in that dark November Violet had the pain of being cut dead in the street by former schoolfellows, walking demurely with their equally dismissive mammas, and it was clear that for the Crowd of old days Violet Estrada was still the Scarlet Woman of the newspaper cartoons. It was no wonder she preferred the company of Tim's new associates. To those very young men, working without guidelines in a very new medium, the only news that mattered was today's, or even tomorrow's, and the Hastings murder, if they remembered it at all, seemed as far away as the assassination of President Lincoln. If they had been told that pretty Vi Siegrist was the Violet Estrada vilified in the newspapers twelve months before, they would have shrugged and said, "So what?" In newsgathering Movie Gazette was a jump ahead of the news-papers, the great problem was getting the newsreels on to the screen fast enough – although the number of cinemas in San Francisco was increasing every month. The Gazette got Charles Evans Hughes on film when the Republican candidate for the Presidency visited California. Until the time of his visit he had been the front runner, for the Irish-Americans in the eastern states deserted Wilson in droves for his failure to protest against the execution of Irish rebels by the British following the Dublin rising. But Hughes made enough mis-takes in California to lose his expected majority, and the forty-four electoral votes of the Golden State won Wilson the Presidency in the closest contest for forty years. Now it remained to be seen if he could still keep America out of war.

Here was a topic to discuss over a steam beer at the Siegrists, which soon developed from one schooner of beer into beer and sandwiches, as in the get-togethers of Niles, and from get-togethers of four or five people in the little living room with the yellow walls and the gay curtains to suppers at one of the many cheap restaurants of the Tenderloin. There they talked, often far into the night, about President Wilson's peace drive, his claim to speak for 'the silent mass of mankind everywhere' and the German declaration of unrestricted submarine war-fare – *spurlos versenkt*, or sink at sight, any American or neutral ship entering the European war zone.

The date of the German declaration was January 31, 1917, two weeks after Violet began her part-time job as cashier at the Poppy Playhouse, on Jessie Street at the back of the Empor-ium. There she sat in a kind of rabbit hutch, selling tickets to the movies from one to five in the afternoon, when she was relieved by an older woman who took charge from five to ten. Four hours a day, six days a week, for the princely wage of ten dollars, while Tim was getting twenty-five for skilled work – it made no sense. But "You can buy a lot of food and fun for ten dollars," said Violet to Tim, "and maybe you'll sell more freelance stuff soon." He had got a good price from the *National Geographic Magazine* for his pictures of the ruined Mexican barracks and the doomed Estrada adobe at Sonoma, captioned 'Last Outposts of the Northern Frontier'.

"It must be a real flea-pit if it's on Jessie," grumbled Tim.

"The Poppy Playhouse! Why'd they call it after the state flower?"

"It's not the flower, it's the opium," said Violet, glad enough to shock him. "Some of the customers bring their pipes along."

"Good God, you'll be raided one of these days! They *smoke* in the cinema? The manager must be crazy!"

"Oh, the hopheads are quiet, it's the winos that bother him because they're noisy. When they take the bottles in the brown bags out of their jacket pockets, Oscar bounces them fast enough. If they fall asleep, that's fine, but he throws them out before the evening show. That's after I've started on my way home, of course."

"So I should hope. You oughtn't to be there at all –"

"I'm enjoying it. I told you I'd get back into the movies, didn't I?"

Back to a wired hutch, issuing flimsy pink tickets in exchange for quarters. It wasn't exactly having her name in lights outside an uptown playhouse, but in its crazy way the Poppy was entertaining. Once Violet slipped in, with her cashbox under her arm, to watch ten minutes of *The Trials of Terry*, with herself in black plaits and brown pancake make-up hissing "White squaw, I hate you!" at Bridget Malloy. None of the dazed patrons of the Poppy's matinées, not even the eagle-eyed Oscar the bouncer, recognised the girl on the screen as the young woman in the pay-box, who turned over the cashbox to her relief and ran out to breathe the fresher air of Jessie Street. Tim wanted to come to meet her every night, but though he was walking with one stick now he still tired easily, and it was her pride to get home before him, hurrying unmolested through the teeming streets. After President Wilson broke off diplomatic relations with Germany on February 3 San Francisco was effervescent, divided like the whole nation on the issue of peace or war: turning the other cheek to Germany or joining the Allies who had fought to a stalemate for two and a half long years. Through those spring weeks of argument and vacillation, when across the bay the slopes of Mount Tamalpais began to turn green again, quarrels broke out freely in and around the corner saloons, which Violet side-stepped as she hurried across Market Street past Eddy to

Ellis, hearing at a little distance the clang of the cable cars on Powell Street mingling with the newsboys' shouts of a revolution in Russia and the abdication of the Czar. Her immediate concern was with the purchase of soup meat, free vegetables included, a mess of sand dabs at the fishmonger's, and a loaf of sourdough bread.

After the Senate and the House had voted to fight, President Wilson signed the United States declaration of war on the German Empire on the afternoon of Good Friday, April 6.

★   ★   ★

The action speeded up, in San Francisco as elsewhere, in Hollywood in particular. Americans, who had read their President's declaration on April 2 that they had no quarrel with the German people, had to be taught to hate all Germans before the regular army's 'race to France' began. A committee on Public Information was set up under George Creel to spread anti-German propaganda, and a Photographic Section of the Signal Corps founded at the beginning of the Civil War was created to accompany the American Expeditionary Force to France. Two of Tim's friends at Movie Gazette volunteered to join the Photographic Section, but most of the men were draftees from Hollywood, who bitterly resented the army discipline and low pay. Few of them looked well in their slovenly-worn breeches, puttees and campaign hats.

"Those bastards don't know how lucky they are," complained Tim Siegrist. "Why the hell do I have to be stuck with a lame leg now, when I'd do anything to get to France?"

"You'd do anything for an adventure, wouldn't you, Tim?" said Violet, not unkindly.

"W. R. Hearst's had his own cameramen with the German army for I don't know how long," said Tim. "I'd like to give the Hearst boys a good scooping."

"But you wouldn't do everything the High Command tells you, and that's what those guys are going to have to do, now they're enlisted men."

"Maybe you're right," said Tim with a grin. "I hear all the negs are going to be censored by the War College Division. Government censorship'll mean bad box office, and even George Creel hasn't latched on to the idea that box office appeal's what's needed from the front. They ought to send D. W. Griffith over, with Billy Bitzer on the camera. Or me."

"Oh Tim, I'm sorry you're disappointed," said Violet, and stooped to kiss him in his easy chair. "But how could I get on without you?"

Tim stroked her hand abstractedly. "Maybe, with the boys away, I'll get a chance to go on location again. I'll try walking without my stick tomorrow."

The Selective Military Conscription Bill was passed in May, calling all men between the ages of twenty-one and thirty inclusive to register for service. Training camps were built, soldiers were clothed and armed, and the huge transportation problems involved were tackled by the organising genius of Newton D. Baker, Secretary of War. On August 1 sixteen new National Army Divisions were created, part of the twenty-nine which eventually saw active service in France. One of the new divisions included the 363rd Infantry, which with its original intake of recruits from Central and Northern California counties earned the title of San Francisco's Own. To the great surprise of Tim and Violet, one of the volunteers in the 363rd was Joe Gregory.

They had seen very little of Joe since they went to live in Ellis Street. He had got a new job, for once outside the city, and for once more explicitly described than Joe's usual range of temporary jobs. He had been – he said – assistant manager at a small hotel in San Diego when the spirit moved him to enlist, he being, at thirty-three, older than the conscription limit. The manager had cordially approved his patriotism. The Siegrists knew that they would never get at the truth of the San Diego story, but there was Joe in uniform, on his way back to camp outside San Francisco after forty-eight hours' leave in Stockton, to say goodbye to his father.

"Poor old pop, he's in a bad way," he said. "He kept thinking I was my brother and calling me Giovanni; and the Smiths were a bore, but I'm glad I went."

"Do you never hear of Jack?" asked Violet.

"He's still in Chicago, as far as I know. If I come through this scrap in France I'm going to look the old boy up."

"What made you enlist, Joe?" said Tim. "You didn't have to."

"You wait! They'll push the age limit up to forty-five, and I'd rather go of my own accord than be drafted."

"You look great in uniform," said Violet. "Will you be in the City Hall parade on Thursday?"

"For the mayor's farewell to San Francisco's Own? We'll all be there, Vi," said Joe with the condescension of a military man to a woman's ignorance.

"So will Tim."

"Not filming?"

"Bet your life I am," said Tim. "I've been filming a couple weeks now, but this is the big deal, buddy – I'm going to do you proud."

"I'm scared stiff," said Violet. "Scared of another bomb."

"You don't scare easy, Vi," said Joe. He thought she looked cool and relaxed in a white summer dress as she poured him another glass of beer. It was a pleasant September evening, marred only by the row the people upstairs were having. The sound of their yells, and of breaking furniture, came clearly down the garbage chute, while outside Ellis Street was tuning up its usual evening orchestra.

"Bombs don't strike twice in the same place," said Tim, lighting a cigarette. "Say, did you see where Mooney got another stay of execution?"

"Sure did," said Joe. "But Mooney's in the slammer, out of harm's way, and it's been a long hot summer this year, just like last."

"And there's more to come, they say."

Even without their leader, Tom Mooney, the strike promoters of San Francisco had been active. The 'Wobblies' had been urged not to turn out fir and spruce for the wooden planes required for the air force, and special persuasion had been needed to make them get on with the job. In San Francisco, in August, the United Railroad Workers struck against the open shop, and paralysed troop transportation. In September a strike of 30,000 workers was planned in the shipyards, foundries and machine shops. His signature song of 'Smiles' would hardly be appropriate to Mayor Rolph when, on behalf of the city, he bade farewell to San Francisco's Own.

Tim Siegrist was going to film the scene for Movie Gazette single-handed. He needed a driver for the camera truck and someone to help him up the steps and then he was on the camera platform and in his element. His second unit would be free-ranging, shooting the background at high angle: the dome of the City Hall, the Federal Building, the Public Library which stood on the very spot where Robert Cord was murdered, and he instructed them to take pictures of some dramatic faces in the crowd. There were almost as many citizens present as had lined Market Street for the Preparedness Day Parade.

Tim, with his passion for camera gadgetry, was going to shoot a triptych. It wasn't original, for Phillips Smalley had done it in *Suspense* and Turner in *Sheridan's Ride* even before *The Birth of a Nation*, and Turner had hired five hundred extras for the battle scenes. Now Uncle Sam had provided the extras free of charge, and as the troops stood to attention Tim slowly began to film.

With the camera masking everything but a central triangle, Tim concentrated on the solo appearance of Mayor 'Sunny Jim' Rolph, bidding Godspeed to "Our boys of the Glorious West", the 363rd Infantry, San Francisco's Own. That would be the central image of the triptych. Then, still slowly, he shot the figure of the commanding officer, who would appear in the left-hand corner of the triptych, above the mayor. Tim swung his camera to the face of a woman he had picked out in the front row of spectators, the archetypal face of a mother who hadn't raised her boy to be a soldier and was weeping bitterly to see him go. With her the three-sided picture was complete, and with all the masking off, the scrim removed from the lens, Tim silently and profanely told the mayor to get on with it, and ordered his driver to get ready for the travelling shots. The truck moved back as the ranks closed, wheeled, stepped out to the cheering of the crowd. What would be seen in the cinemas of America was the slow dissolve from one identifiable image to another – the mayor, the officer, the mother, and then as the triptych burst open the wave of trained and eager young men, speeded up by the camera to show them in one irresistible rush to save the world for democracy –

For the Yanks are coming, the Yanks are coming
And they won't come back till it's over, Over There!

3

The send-off of San Francisco's Own was memorable, and even more so was the jubilant return of the American troops from Europe after the war to end wars was won. Both celebrations were tame compared with the New Year's Eve of 1919, when every hotel, restaurant, tavern and bar in San Francisco was crowded with revellers making the most of the last big celebration before Prohibition. The Eighteenth Amendment to the Constitution, prohibiting the manufacture, sale and transport of intoxicating liquor, meant that 'Bright Champagne', the favourite party drink since the Gold Rush, would disappear from San Francisco's tables along with the produce of the valley vineyards and all the other drinks enjoyed by a city of gourmets for eighty years. Nineteen-nineteen went out on a river of booze and an orgy of dancing, bagpipe playing and whistle blowing in the seething streets, while the Roaring Twenties came in on an alcoholic howl of despair.

At eight minutes past midnight the first baby of the decade to be born in one of the city hospitals added her little cry to the clamour, and before long a nurse was telling a man with a rubber-tipped walking stick, who nearly overbalanced when he stood up at her entrance, "You have a daughter, Mr. Siegrist. A splendid little girl."

"And my wife?"

"She's in great shape."

"That's marvellous, nurse, I mean Sister, sorry. Can I see them?"

"You can see the baby. Mrs. Siegrist needs a good night's sleep. Come to the nursery, please."

He followed the starched back on tiptoe, holding his breath at what he was going to see. Someone who had never lived before, lived now, already card-indexed as 'Baby Siegrist', a new human being with all her life before her. In the dimly lit nursery he saw a young nurse coming towards him with a shawled bundle in her arms. By chance the girl was a Hispanic, with a creamy olive skin like Violet's, and black hair visible beneath her cap. When she held the baby up with its cheek against her own, and he saw the pink yawn, and the milky-blue eyes like a kitten's, he said "Oh poor little devil, she's going to look like me!" and instinctively held his hands out to his child.

The nurse giggled. You could always trust a new father to make a fool of himself. The sister in charge said quickly, "Don't touch her, Mr. Siegrist, please. Come back at nine tomorrow morning and you can make as big a fuss of both of them as you want to."

"Thank you, ma'am." He got himself home to Ellis Street, a kennel of staggering drunks and vomit, and he got himself back to the hospital armed with a bunch of roses from the stand at Lotta's Fountain. Then, what a touching sight was Violet, in bed in the tiny private room he had insisted on, and what a plain little baby she was holding on her arm!

"Isn't she beautiful, Tim? Isn't she perfectly lovely?" was her greeting, and Tim, kissing her lips and the baby's tiny hand, lied like a trooper and said their daughter was a little beauty, the prettiest baby he ever did see. He laid the roses at the foot of the bed. "First bouquet for my two girls," he said unsteadily, and Violet laughed through tears, and they were very happy.

"But what are we going to call her, Tim?" she said presently. "I was so sure we'd have a boy, I never thought of any other name but James Timothy, for my father and you."

"Tim and Jim – I thought we'd sound good together," her husband agreed. "But since that's out – I was wondering – would you mind if we called her after my great-grandmother?"

"Your *great-grandmother*?" she repeated. "I didn't know you even knew her name!"

"Oh yes, I do. Her name was Adelheid Basler, and she married Hans Siegrist in Zürich, exactly one hundred years ago. I guess it took just as much guts, in those days, to travel from Switzerland to Sutter's Fort as it did to travel from Mexico City to Alta California."

"More, I should think; they had to cross the ocean. But – Adelheid Basler, it's a bit of a mouthful isn't it? . . . Tim! I know! We can call her Heidi!"

"I was hoping you'd say that, darling!"

"*Heidi*! I loved the book when I was a kid. My little Swiss girl!" She hugged the baby, which squeaked a protest loudly enough to make the day nurse come in and shoo Tim off to the corridor. He felt so great that he hardly used his stick at all as he went downstairs. He wanted to tell the world he was the father of a girl called Heidi.

San Francisco was felled by a monumental hangover on that last New Year's Day before Prohibition, so Tim had to wait until the second of January before passing out the cigars at Movie Gazette. Straightaway from a public telephone box in the St. Francis lobby he called Stella Smith in Stockton, who bubbled over with congratulations and love to her *piccola sorella* and baby 'Adela'. Later, he sent a Western Union cable to Honolulu, although before the birth Violet had said she doubted if her mother would take kindly to the name of granny. Then he went home and looked at the little back room, once used for storage and now as clean as white enamel paint and white muslin curtains could make it, with a white rattan crib standing clear of the wall. The yard beyond was as dismal as ever. He wondered if the garbage containers outside the window would be unhealthy for the baby. Probably they ought to find a better place to bring up a kid. The trouble was, they had both got accustomed to the Tenderloin.

How accustomed, they realised when mother and child came home, and Ellis Street, to the last streetwalker, expressed its interest in little gifts for the baby. Bootees and bibs, soft toys and celluloid ducks, suitable and unsuitable, the offerings piled up in the yellow living room, and when Violet, slim and lovely again, pushed the secondhand perambulator as far as the shops, everyone peered under the hood and, lying as manfully as Tim, said the baby was beautiful. It was the last season of friendliness in a poor area of San Francisco before the Eighteenth Amendment and the Volstead Act, working with suspicion and betrayal on their side, created a new class of criminal: the bootlegger, the rumrunner and the speakeasy hood.

Tim's cable to Honolulu had an unexpected result, happier and more positive than Mrs. Cord's tepid message of welcome to her first grandchild. On a February afternoon, when Adelheid Basler was nearly six weeks old and her christening had been fixed for St. Valentine's day, Violet was sitting in the warm living room, with the baby in a rush basket by her side. She was looking through a parcel which had just arrived from Stockton with Stella's gifts to the bambina. It contained a beautifully smocked white silk dress and matinée jacket, made by Stella herself, and a white lace mantilla to be worn in church instead of a christening robe. "It was one of Zeemaree's treasures," Stella wrote, "and was yellow with age, but I have bleached it on green grass, and the pattern is beautiful. I don't know the story, but I think it probably belonged to her mother, like the black one you used to wear." It was the white mantilla which Rosalie Estrada wore on her wedding day.

Violet was holding the fine lace up to the dying light when the door bell rang. She turned up the gas and pulled the yellow curtains close before she fastened the safety chain on the front door and opened it a crack. "Who's there?" The light in the hall showed her the shape of a tall man in uniform, who said uncertainly, "This is Lieutenant Cord."

"Lieutenant Cord!" She slipped the chain and opened the door as wide as it would go. "Why, Bobby! Don't you know me? How did you find me here?"

"Violet, is it really you?"

"Of course it's me! Come in and get warm! What a giant you've grown!"

"I was only six when you saw me last."

They hardly knew what to say to each other, this half-brother and sister, or how to tread delicately over the past they might have shared. Robert Cord III was a tall young man of nineteen whose war experience made him look older. He had red hair in a military trim, well-cut features and a general air of being equal to anything. "Mother told me where to find you," he said as they sat down. "She wrote to me in Washington about the baby – gosh! Is *this* the baby?" He eyed the rush basket doubtfully.

"It certainly is! That's our little Heidi."

"Cute name. Cute little kid!" Heidi's grey eyes, which had lost their milky blue, stared unwinkingly at the strange face.

"She's not very like you, Violet."

"She's more like her father. He'll be so pleased to see you. He'll be home any minute."

"How is he really?"

"Very much better, he hardly needs a stick at all now."

"You've had a rough time, you two."

"Yes," she agreed. "Which would you rather hear about, the murder charge or the anarchists' bombs? I suppose you know the governor commuted Tom Mooney's death sentence to life imprisonment?"

His look made Violet ashamed of her sarcasm. "I only want to hear you say you're happy," said Bobby Cord.

"Very happy now."

"I'm glad. There's just one thing I want to ask you, while we're alone together. Why didn't you stay on with us in Honolulu, that time after the fire? Warren and I missed you when you went away."

"Because I used to play catch with you for hours on end?" She smiled. "Granny Randolph was a very independent lady. She wanted to get back to San Francisco."

"I don't think that's the whole story, is it?"

"No, it's not. But it's an old story, Bobby, and you and I are too young to dwell on the past. Tell me about yourself. You're still in the army?"

"Until the day after tomorrow, when I get my discharge at L.A., where I enlisted."

"At seventeen, and said you were eighteen, you wild boy! How did you get away with it?"

"I guess I was big enough to pass for eighteen, and they didn't ask any questions."

"Just like your Uncle Ivanhoe, when he ran away to join the Federal navy in the Civil War."

"Well, not quite." He grinned. "Uncle Ivan bolted, and my father and mother approved of what I meant to do. Or said they did."

"Granny Randolph was so proud of you and so afraid for you. I wish she'd lived to see you come home."

"I do too. But I got a sort of office-boy's job at our embassy in Paris and stayed on there for a bit."

"The Paris Embassy!" she said. "Uncle Ivan again! And

518

now you've been to Washington. Does that mean you're going to enter the Foreign Service, Bobby?"

"Quick thinking," he confessed. "Yes, I could have joined the service if I'd wanted to. But it didn't appeal. Hawaian sugar's more in my line."

"Mother will be so glad."

"I wish you'd write to her oftener. She worries about you –" Before Bobby had time to finish his sentence, or notice the hardening of Violet's mouth, Tim Siegrist had come in, surprised and pleased, when Violet introduced "my brother, Robert Cord."

"Say, Lieutenant, good to see you," he said heartily, and the tall boy, who had hardly let his eyes move round the meagre room, noticed that Tim was thin and not well dressed, but obviously proud of his beautiful wife and the staring, silent baby. There was a flurry about drinks, Tim declaring that he was 'one jump ahead of the Eighteenth Amendment', and when Violet brought in a bottle of bourbon and a carafe of water she said Heidi must have her bottle too, and carried the baby off to the warm little room with the white crib. The walls were so thin that she could hear the men talking about the fighting in the Argonne, where Lieutenant Cord had won the ribbon he wore on his blouse, and prayed that the brawlers upstairs might not choose this evening to start throwing the furniture around. When Heidi was settled her mother had worked out how to make supper for two stretch into supper for three, and was disappointed, when she went back to the living room, to find Bobby on his feet.

"But you can't be leaving yet! We've hardly talked at all!"

"Sorry, Violet, I've got a date. Taking a girl to dinner and the theatre."

"Oh, in that case –"

"But we'll keep in touch after this, won't we?"

"I'd like to. Must you really be in L.A. the day after tomorrow."

"That's what my movement orders say."

"It seems a shame you can't be with us on the fourteenth for Heidi's christening."

"I wish I could, but the army wouldn't see it that way. I'll be thinking of you all and wishing you luck. Is Heidi her full name, by the way?"

"It's Adelheid Basler Siegrist," said her father. "A-d-e-l-h-e-i-d."

"Bobby," said Violet as he stooped to kiss her cheek, "if you're leaving so soon, I suppose you won't have time to go to Sacramento?"

"No, what for? I don't know a living soul in Sacramento."

"I thought you might like to see your grandfather's portrait in the Capitol."

" 'On the Banks of the Petaluma: 1841'? Dad's got a photograph of it on his office desk. He must have been quite a boy, my grandfather."

"But a photograph's not the same thing at all! It's the colours that matter in the painting! Israel Klein was one of the greatest of the French Impressionists –" She stopped, and kissed him. "Don't worry, Bobby. If you want to know what the Robert Cord in the portrait was like, just take a good look in a long mirror when you go back to your hotel tonight."

Lieutenant Cord was as good as his word to remember them on St. Valentine's Day. When he was aboard the *Lurline* en route for Honolulu, and Violet was laying out Stella's dress and jacket to take her baby to church, wrapped in the priceless white mantilla, a special messenger arrived from Shreve's with a white box fastened with ribbon and red sealing wax and addressed to Miss Adelheid Basler Siegrist. Inside was a sterling silver christening mug with the initials ABS. Beneath it was an envelope inscribed 'Long life and happiness to my Little Niece from Uncle Bobby' and a cheque for five hundred dollars.

Heidi's parents were speechless. To them it was a fortune.

"Do you know what I'd like to do with this?" said Violet at last.

"Just don't get on your high horse and say you're going to send it back to that nice kid."

"That *would* be a rotten way to treat his generosity. I'd like you and me to open a bank account for Heidi, to start a fund for her education. I want her to have the very best. I want her to have all the things I never had –"

"You had a damned sight better education than I did," said

Tim. "You didn't do too badly at Miss West's School. *And* you could have gone to college if you'd wanted."

"I'll tell you one thing Heidi's going to have that I didn't."

"What's that?"

"A mother's love."

If he had been directing her then Tim would have told her she was over-acting. But he knew she was also over-excited, so he kissed her instead and promised Heidi should have the best of schooling. "Because," said the infatuated father, "I think she's going to be very bright."

★ ★ ★

Heidi Siegrist *was* very bright, as her parents discovered long before she started school in the building round which the Ellis Street kids played tag with the truant officer. "She sure wasn't around when they was handin' out good looks," as the noisy woman in the flat above jocosely said, but she was quick to walk and quick to talk, and showed manual dexterity with beads and building bricks. She disliked dolls, and was quickly bored by picture books and nursery rhymes. What she liked best was to be read to 'out of real books' while with one fat finger she followed the mysterious symbols on the page. Her father read *Heidi* aloud until they both knew their favourite passages by heart, and the American Heidi identified completely with the little mountain girl in her passionately loved Swiss home. Tim read well: he could make the child see the hut with its sheltering pine trees, and the 'red flower' blossoming on the snowy peaks at sunset. "Wish I could film her in it," he said once to Violet. "Should be some good locations in the Sierra Nevada."

Daddy was for daylight or gaslight, when he read the marvellous tales of the little boy who asked for more, and another little girl called Nell who tramped through the countryside with her grandfather. Mother was for night time, when all she had seen and done during the day left Heidi so excited that she couldn't sleep, and hearing the voices next door called out for help, to be lulled asleep by her mother's soft voice saying what she called the magic poem, 'Concepcion de Argüello'. As soon as she heard the opening verse the child closed her eyes.

Looking seaward, o'er the sandhills stands the fortress, old and quaint,
By the San Francisco friars lifted to their patron saint,
All its trophies long since scattered, all its blazon brushed away,
And the flag that flies above it but a triumph of today

She was asleep before the end of the immortal story of Concha and her Russian lover, but Heidi forced herself to keep awake long enough to hear the swinging rhythms of

Count von Rezanov, the Russian, envoy of the mighty Czar,
Stood beside the deep embrasures where the brazen cannon are

"More, please, mommy!"

Till beside the brazen cannon the betrothed bade adieu
And, from sallyport and gateway, north the Russian eagles flew

Then the brazen cannon were engulfed in a tide of sleep, and Violet went on tiptoe from the room.

Daddy and mother adored their lively daughter, and they were the twin pillars of her happy world. She never realised how, as the early Twenties brought ever-increasing prosperity to California, they began to feel left behind in the race for fame and riches. The great directors were bringing out the great movies, from *Hearts of the World*, the war propaganda movie Tim had wanted to make himself, through *Way Down East* and *Orphans of the Storm*, while Tim Siegrist was turning a newsreel camera in the streets of San Francisco. Chaplin, now a millionaire, had joined forces with D. W. Griffith, Mary Pickford and Douglas Fairbanks, and Mary, who had made *Poor Little Rich Girl* and *Stella Maris* after *Mliss*, was called America's Sweetheart. Fairbanks began his costume dramas with *The Mark of Zorro* (Tim said enviously, "My God, just see how Fred Niblo works his cameras!"), and went on to *The Three Musketeers* and *Robin Hood*. It was all a long way from Movie Gazette.

Violet's frustrations took another form. In her late twenties she began to ask herself "Is this all there is?" as she cleaned the little flat, did the frugal shopping, and pushed Heidi's pram to the nearest space of air and greenery, which happened to be Union Square. There on Monday afternoons she could see beautifully dressed young women of her own age, who had organised their lives better, getting into their cars outside the St. Francis after attending the luncheons combined with fashion shows which were the highlight of society's week. A lady's social standing depended on where she was seated in the Mural Room (once the Rose Room, where Violet and Bill Hastings met) by the favour of the head waiter, repulsively known to the patrons as the 'maiter dee'. It was all as silly as the society Chambliss had excoriated when Violet's mother was a girl, but it was humiliating to sit there on a park bench in the shadow of the Victory, and not be a part of it.

With an infant to take care of, Violet saw none of the new movies. Radio was her home entertainment, provided by a crystal set with earphones with which she could hear musical broadcasts from the Fairmont Hotel and the Palace, and learn what a good time everybody else was having: to this she much preferred the fan magazines now flooding the market. Everyone wanted to read about the new films and the movie stars. *Photoplay* was the first and best of them, but Violet was not interested in what the editor, James Quirk, had to say about the Industry. She read greedily, spitefully and endlessly about the movie scandals, of which in the Roaring Twenties there were many.

The unlucky St. Francis, the scene of the Hastings murder, was also the scene of the great scandal of 1921, when a comedian called Roscoe ('Fatty') Arbuckle, who only a month earlier had been chosen to promote the idea of 'wholesome Hollywood', was accused of the murder, in his hotel room and in a singularly depraved manner, of a girl called Virginia Rappe. He was eventually acquitted, but his career was ruined, and so, next year, were the careers of two popular women stars, Mary Miles Minter and Mabel Normand, accused of involvement in the murder of a man called Taylor. Mabel Normand was revealed as a drug addict: drugs, in 1923, caused the death of a handsome leading man named Wallace Reid. Hollywood went on a morals crusade, and Violet Siegrist, gloating over the details served up hot in the fan mags, said "*Now* some of them will find out what it's like to be persecuted!"

She had arguments with Tim about this, and their friends joined in, inflamed and inspired by hard liquor. The few bottles which Tim laid in before Prohibition were soon empty, and those who had been quite content to drink a glass of beer or wine before the Eighteenth Amendment became law were now only satisfied with gin or whisky. The law was easy to break, for the rugged Californian coast was made for smugglers, or bootleggers as the suppliers were called, running in illicit liquor from ships outside the three-mile limit, and the bootlegger who took the stuff to the Movie Gazette office was a reliable man in his way. None of them was ever poisoned by a mixture of bathtub gin and methylated spirit, or blinded by wood alcohol, but in the spirit of American rebels defying the law they all drank three times as much and three times harder than they used to. The arguments in the Siegrist's flat became quarrelsome, noisy, tearful and then frankly drunken. They were soon as rowdy as the folks upstairs, but at least they never broke the furniture and somebody was sure to say sooner or later, "Hush! The kid's asleep!"

Heidi was not asleep, but listening to it all, sometimes reverting to babyhood and whispering the magic lullaby to herself:

Long beside the deep embrasures where the brazen cannon are
Did they wait the promised bridegroom and the answer of the Czar!

Sometimes it worked, sometimes it didn't, and sleep only came when the last reveller had departed and her parents stumbled off to bed. Those night scenes left no mark on a naturally courageous child. Heidi, especially after she went to school, was always ready to greet the new day with a cheer.

Heavy drinking was only an occasional problem for the Siegrists in the prosperous middle Twenties. Physiotherapy, developed in the war, had come too late to help Tim, but his dogged daily exercise in walking to and from the studio had paid off in keeping his injured limbs from permanent stiffness, and he was now able to drive a car. He made a down payment on a Ford Model T, the 'tin Lizzie', the 'flivver', which was the most popular car in the nation, and took his two girls out for Sunday spins to the ocean beach and the park. He used it for doing freelance photography at the weekends, and sometimes, when she was too small to carry any of his equipment, he took Heidi alone 'to help him to take pictures'. One such occasion stayed in her mind long after school experiences had blotted out most of Heidi's childhood memories.

It was spring, after she turned six, and San Francisco was celebrating something difficult for a little girl to pronounce: the Sesquicentennial. It was one hundred and fifty years since the arrival of the Spanish, and the *National Geographic Magazine*, which bought much of Tim Siegrist's work, had commissioned him to do a set of photographs of the Mission Dolores, the oldest building in the city. It was no longer used as a place of worship, having become as dilapidated over the years as the Mission at Sonoma, and being damaged in the earthquake and fire of 1906. It had been completely restored for the Sesquicentennial and was now one of the city's treasures. Tim and Heidi started out in the Ford very early one Sunday morning, so as to reach the Mission Dolores before the visitors, but the handsome boulevard which Dolores Street had become was already full of worshippers at the early masses in the Catholic church next door. Built for the Centennial, this church too had suffered in 1906, and was rebuilt in the pseudo-Spanish style now popular, with two ugly embossed towers. Tim did not acknowledge it by a glance as he parked the car further down the boulevard, took Heidi's hand and walked back to the Mission Dolores.

Only the Mission and the little garden cemetery, now neat and bright with flowers, remained of the wilderness through which Rosalie Estrada had stumbled looking for her baby's grave, and nothing at all was left of the derelict buildings in which Carlos Rivera had handed over that baby to the Indian band. The taverns, the shacks, the race tracks and duelling grounds had disappeared long ago, and the Mission Dolores now stood in a prosperous, bourgeois district of paved streets and handsome houses. The Mission was the same, with new magenta bougainvillaea flowering along the newly whitewashed adobe walls, four feet thick, with the steps where the ragged Indians once sat before the portal, the Mexican bells on the open balcony, the single Cross above the clay-tiled redwood roof. There was nobody there at that hour but the guardian with whom Tim had already made arrangements, and who brought Heidi a little stool to sit on and told her she must be quiet in church.

She had no idea of being noisy. She was fascinated by the tiny chapel, and she already knew that she must be still while daddy was busy with his camera. He was having problems with the lighting, for the place was very dark under the ceiling which the Indians had painted with soft vegetable colours. Tim moved about looking for angles, opening the west door and shutting it, shooting the primitive whittled statues and the eighteenth-century altars carved in Mexico. Heidi sat on her stool and watched. She knew it was a church, but a very different church from the Old First Presbyterian where she had been christened, and where her mother occasionally took her to the children's service. And she could feel, without telling, that it was very old. It belonged to the past, which for Heidi meant yesterday: she felt, as a new experience, the unimaginable touch of time.

Tim took her out of the dark church into the spring sun. He shot more pictures of the memorials raised to those early San Franciscans who died by the rope and the bullet, and the modern imitation of the Grotto of Lourdes raised 'to the neglected and forgotten'. Birds were chirping among the yews and poplar trees, and there were fuchsias growing between the tombstones. One or two passersby stopped and leaned on the wall to watch Tim work. Heidi began to play among the flowers.

"Had enough, baby?" said Tim fondly. "Just one more to do, and then we'll drive out to the beach."

He consulted the notes the magazine had sent him. The last pic they wanted to see was the tomb of the only Californio-born governor of California, Don Luis Argüello, the brother of Doña Concepcion, Rezanov's lover. It was a concrete tomb topped with a monument, and Heidi came to stare up at it by her father's side.

"Can you read that name, Heidi?" She had been able to read long before she went to school, much to her teacher's annoyance, but these were difficult words and she repeated them with care, "Luis An-ton-i Argü-ello. Who was he, daddy?"

"You'll learn about him in school," said Tim diplomatically. "Or ask mommy. She knows a lot of history."

"Here's a tiny stone beside the big one. I can read that too, daddy. It says 'Rosalie'. Do you know if she was his little girl?"

" 'Fraid I don't," said Tim, putting his equipment together. It was the memorial which Luis Estrada, with the consent of Don Luis Argüello's widow, had set beside that of the man who had been Rosalie's godfather. Rosalie, murderess and suicide, had been buried in an unmarked grave, one of the neglected and forgotten of the Mission Dolores, but her brother had set her name beneath the Cross and among the flowers.

★   ★   ★

The other memorable occasion came a year later, when Heidi was seven and better able to recall it. Tim was doing so well with his photography that he had begun to play the stock market in a modest way, and they planned to rent a cottage at Inverness for two weeks' holiday by the sea. That was to be in June, but Tim, exhilarated by a windfall, said they must have a celebration long before midsummer. He would take his two girls for an Easter Sunday luncheon at the new Mark Hopkins Hotel.

From the first days of Vioget's tavern hotels had been immensely important in the social life of San Francisco. In the Twenties the Palace, rebuilt since the fire and modernised, had somehow become the dowager of the hotel world, and the Fairmont, named by the daughter of James G. Fair, one of the Silver Kings, was the Jazz Age girl who had her own radio station and was running the first scheduled flights between San Francisco and Los Angeles. Both of them were in competition with the St. Francis, which had the most exciting events

(Hastings, Arbuckle), the most exotic guests, and possibly the best chef in town. Beginning in 1926, all three of the famous hotels had to compete with a Nob Hill newcomer called the Mark Hopkins.

It took its name from one of the Big Four of the Railroad, the man who had panned for gold at Hangtown with Robert Cord when they were young men, and who had built a mansion on Nob Hill which he never occupied. Now a nineteen-storey hotel stood on the site, with spacious lobbies and restaurants so fashionable and so crowded that Tim Siegrist was advised to book a week in advance for Easter Sunday luncheon in the Room of the Dons. He chose it rather than the Spanish Restaurant or the Peacock Court, but all the hotel's restaurants were so busy that the Siegrists, like everybody else, had to stand in line for over twenty minutes before the 'maiter dee' showed them to a table. None of them minded the delay. For Heidi, who had never been in such a palace in her life, the sight of a marble patio containing a tiled fountain and pool with floating flowers was a feast in itself. She was very conscious of her white socks and gloves, with the white pocket-book her father had given her as an Easter gift, eying the other little girls waiting to be seated with a competitive eye. They were nearly all prettier than she was, but not one of them had such a pretty mother.

Violet at thirty-two had kept her slender figure, and the knee-length skirts of the day revealed her lovely legs. She had bobbed her black hair, and though Tim had protested he admired the new style now, when the 'Easter bonnet' he asked Violet to buy sat so smoothly on her short hair. She had chosen a black felt hat cut to the shape of her head, with little feather wings of an unusual rosy pink outlining her black earlocks, and Tim told her there wasn't a woman in the room to touch her as they touched their tea glasses with Heidi's lemonade tumbler and wished each other a happy Easter. Violet was happy; she thought she was back at last in the world of luxury that was hers by the right of birth.

"Daddy, what does it mean, the Room of the Dons?" asked Heidi when dessert was served.

"Better ask your mother that, she's the expert," said Tim, and smiled at his wife.

"The Dons were the Spanish, darling, who founded California. Don't they teach you that in school?" said Violet.

"No, we're only at the Assyrians yet," said the child, and both parents laughed. "Even I got bogged down in the Assyrians," said Tim, and Violet said they'd been old favourites at Miss West's.

"All those men in the paintings round the walls, murals they're called, were Spanish Dons," Tim explained, and Heidi asked if she might get down from her chair and walk round the room and look at them.

"Certainly not, you must wait at table until we're finished," said Violet, who had just ordered coffee.

"Some of the other kids are running around."

"That has nothing to do with you. Finish your ice cream and sit still."

Heidi disobeyed so far as to twist on her chair to see the pictures behind her, and while the orchestra was playing 'Always' her father and mother heard her say, "Don Luis Estrada, the Hero of San Pascual".

"What's that?" said Violet.

"Don Luis Estrada, mother, the man in the picture behind you. He has the same name you had before you married daddy, and I think he looks like you."

Her parents looked at the mural. It showed a handsome Californio, superbly mounted, with his lance in rest. The casque he wore was shaped like Violet's new felt cloche and pointed up the resemblance between them.

"Did you know him, mother?"

"Why no, dear, he lived a long time ago. He was my grandfather's brother, and I've a picture of him when he was a much older man. I'll show it to you when we get home." She added to Tim, "How extraordinary they should have his likeness here – and a good likeness, too!"

"What does it mean, the hero of San Pascual?" persisted the child.

"Well, it looks like he means to fight," said Tim, "so I guess it was a battle."

"Was he fighting Injuns?"

"Probably."

"So Don Luis was a soldier really?"

"Maybe. For a while."

"He was a soldier all his life," said Violet. The child, glancing uneasily from one to the other, felt instinctively – as at the Mission Dolores – that a corner of the past had been lifted: the past which made her and of which she must make the future. She forgot it before they walked down the Mason Street hill to Ellis, Heidi carrying the woven basket of tiny Easter eggs which was a gift from the Mark Hopkins. She had no more to do with metaphysical speculations, but remained a child of the present, happy in her games and lessons, until her father was arrested and sent to prison.

4

When bad times came again Violet said Joe Gregory brought them with him. In this she was less than fair to Joe (but Violet was past being fair by then) because although Joe Gregory was responsible for great misfortune he was not in San Francisco when Tim lost his job.

He had been worried about the job for some time. Tim Siegrist had been with Movie Gazette for thirteen years when a new young managing editor arrived from the Hollywood office, and almost at once objected to Tim's use of his Sundays (other spare time he had none) for highly lucrative freelance photography. "What if a big news story breaks while you're out takin' pix of the Coit Tower or the Japanese Tea Garden?" said Mr. Bronson. "From now on every man who wants to work for Movie Gazette's goin' to be on the job seven days a week! When sound comes in we may have to work round the clock, eight-hour shifts, and there's no room here for freeloaders, understand?"

"We've had the earthquake, we've had the war and now we've got Bronson," said Tim at home, in the usual ill-natured tones of a favoured employee at loggerheads with a new boss. "And sound, yet! I've never worked a sound camera in my life."

"You'll learn," Violet comforted him. "And I thought you were all for sound movies."

"A voice like yours on the sound track would be great," said Tim, "but every actor's not so lucky. You can see what's happening already, since Vitaphone came in. Stars out of work, directors out of work, musicians fired – the industry's turned topsy-turvy since *The Jazz Singer* was released. Oh well, I guess I better cut out the freelance racket till Bronson's settled down." He sighed dispiritedly.

"Come on, cheer up, Tim, this isn't like you," said Violet. "You used to be interested in every new thing that came out. Remember how you used to tell me about working for Kinemacolor?"

"Before I went to Sennett? Sure, but I was a greenhorn in those days, I didn't realise there was just one theatre in the whole of California that had a projector to show Kinemacolor. No wonder the poor old Sunset Boulevard studio folded after I'd been there a year. D. W. Griffith took it over . . . Say, Vi, d'you realise that's sixteen years ago? Maybe filming's a young man's game. I'm pushing forty and Bronson's twenty-five, and now he's got some damn fool idea about using the Moviola. Wonder what joker he'll have up his sleeve tomorrow?"

It was only a week after that when Tim scared his wife by marching into the flat at ten o'clock in the morning, flinging a tripod and a heavy bag of equipment on the sofa and shouting, "Hi there! I've got my walking papers!"

Violet came out of the kitchen in a hurry. "Tim! You don't mean you're fired?"

"One month's severance pay and get your stuff out of here, that's how it went. That bastard Bronson! He started on me again about using the treadle Moviola for the film I was cutting in my hand. 'Listen, Bronson,' I said, 'I've been hand-cutting all my working life, and it's the only way to catch the rhythm, that's the whole basis of editing,' and he said 'Listen, old timer, that sort of malarkey went out with *The Great Train Robbery*', and after that it was only a question of walking out or being fired. I let him fire me after I told him what he could do with his Moviola, because I figured I needn't lose the severance pay, and – I hate like hell to have to tell you, Vi – here I am."

"Wait a minute," she said. "There's a pot of fresh coffee on the stove."

Tim lit a cigarette and waited until she brought in two cups of steaming coffee. "Thanks, that hits the spot," he said . . . "I thought you'd be mad."

"Why? This'll turn out to be a blessing in disguise. You were getting into a rut at the Gazette. Now, with all the agency and magazine contacts you've got, why should you worry? You'll be earning more than Bronson paid you, in no time flat."

"A guy sure hates to be canned, though. You won't tell Heidi?"

"We'll tell her you're starting business on your own – which is true, and I bet you she'll be thrilled."

"But what'm I going to do about a dark room? That was what Bronson meant about freeloading."

"He had his nerve!" she said indignantly. "You've always had the use of the dark room, right from the start!"

"Maybe I could do a deal with the Cala Agency, I've kind of got the inside track there."

"There, you see, it'll all work out."

"You don't think we should cancel the booking at Inverness? Seems like a funny time to be taking a vacation."

"Nonsense, it'll do you good. And what about Heidi and me? Don't we rate a holiday? It's not as if we couldn't afford it. Look how well you're doing on the stock market!"

Of course he was doing well, like everybody else in America who had joined in the great orgy of speculation which lasted through three boom years. It was drawing to a close in that summer of 1929, but only a handful of economists recognised it: President Coolidge's last message to the nation told it to 'anticipate the future with optimism'. The Siegrists enjoyed Inverness to the full, and made trips along the north coast in the Ford. One day they drove as far as Bodega Bay for lunch in a fish restaurant at the harbour, and then went on across the Russian River, through Jenner-by-the-Sea and along the switchback road to Fort Ross. Tim took some pictures of the tumbledown stockade and the little Orthodox church, which was in ruins. "So this is where the Russians were," he said. "No wonder they threw their hands in and went home."

"It smells good," said Heidi. The old scent of sunwarmed thyme was rising from the cliffs.

"Now don't you go too near the edge."

July, August, September went by, with plenty of work for Tim from Cala and two other agencies, and stock prices, according to a Yale professor, on 'a permanently high plateau'. Seven days from this prediction, on October 23, and during the last hour of trading, the stock market dropped like a plummet. Next day, called 'Black Thursday', thirteen million shares changed hands, and by the end of the month not only the leviathans of the New York Stock Exchange were engulfed in the wave of failure, but the little fish, the myriad of smalltime speculators like Tim Siegrist, were sunk without a trace.

It was hard, then, not to give way to panic when all that stood between millions of little families and poverty was some modest savings in banks in which the depositors had lost confidence. Tim Siegrist had been wiped out completely. Violet still had her $2,000 intact, and the fund for Heidi's education now stood at $1,400, Bobby Cord having sent $100 every year on the child's birthday. Tim's earnings for November and December were enough to feed them, and no more. The streets of San Francisco were filling with panhandlers, soon to be dependent on soup kitchens and breadlines in a country where there was neither social security nor unemployment insurance.

"I should have made a down payment on a house instead of a car," said Tim. "Then we'd have had some sort of equity –"

"You needed the car for work, like the telephone. And we couldn't pay a lower rent than we do now. Thank God we stayed on Ellis Street."

"I'd planned on moving somewhere better before Heidi started growing up."

"She's only ten this New Year's Day."

"She'll get a swell birthday present – the Great Depression."

In the New Year, however, there were three changes of fortune. While Movie Gazette folded, the Cala Picture Agency 'reorganised', and having let three younger men go took Tim on the permanent staff at a salary of twenty dollars a week. Heidi won a prize for arithmetic, and Joe Gregory reappeared in San Francisco.

It was almost, Tim said later, like someone coming back from the dead, except that Joe was very much alive. Thirteen years had passed since Joe marched off to war with San Francisco's Own, and in all that time his family and friends had had nothing from him, but a few uninformative cards. He had a good war record and decoration: that was published in the *Chronicle*. He had gone to Chicago and joined forces with his brother Giovanni, a.k.a. Jack Gregg, in what he called the catering business. What they now learned, when he appeared in Ellis Street, was that he had been married and divorced, no children. Gina Marinello, her name was, he said. "I was a goddamn fool to marry a Wop," he said. "She was a no-good bitch."

"Take it easy, Joe," said Tim. "Little pitchers." Heidi was sitting close to her mother, with a frown which reminded Violet of somebody from days long past.

"Bet she hears worse than that on Ellis Street," said Joe with a wink. "Fancy you still in this dump after all this time! Well, let's have a drink to good times coming." He felt in the pocket of his handsome overcoat and produced a heavy silver flask. "Nothing wrong with this Scotch. Straight off the boat. One for the road, and we'll all go and have a good feed at the Palace."

"You must have struck it rich, Joe." He gave another wink and said with another oath that he had. "Maybe I can cut you in on the deal, Tim," said Joe. "We'll see."

He was the same old Joe, with his deals and his boasting, but the rough language was something new, and in spite of the expensive tailoring there was a coarseness about the heavy, swarthy man of forty-six which had not been there before. Violet disliked the way he spoke of his sister. Now that dear old pop had gone Joe didn't plan to go to Stockton. What, and get another sermon from the saintly Stella? Be called a lost soul because he was a divorced man? Have to listen to her squalling brats – four of them, weren't there, now? He bet the four of them put together weren't as bright as little Heidi here. "Haven't you got a smile for your Uncle Joe, Cutesy?" he coaxed. Heidi's face grew red, but she answered politely "Yes, sir," and waited until her mother was helping her into her best coat and hat before she whispered fiercely, "He's not my uncle! I don't like that man!"

She liked the Palace Hotel, though, and the splendid dinner ordered by Joe, and Violet was glad they had bought enough clothes in the days of their prosperity to see them through the Depression, however long it lasted. They were as well dressed as any of the Palace guests, but possibly hungrier, and food on top of Scotch made Violet bland enough to raise no objection when Joe said he and Tim would drive the ladies home and then have a nightcap at a most respectable speakeasy on Broadway, which had a working arrangement with the police. She was heavily asleep when Tim came home and the dirty dawn was putting out the lights of Ellis Street when she became aware that he was standing naked by the bed and shredding newspaper. Then he fell into bed beside her and took her into a drunken, flailing embrace which ended miserably for them both, and fell asleep. When Violet opened her eyes again she saw that what she had taken for newspaper was a scattering of crumpled dollar bills – ten fives and three singles, as she found when she gathered them up.

"What the hell was that about?" she challenged him when Heidi had been hustled off to school. "Where did you get that money? And how dared you throw it at me as if I were a Broadway whore?"

"I won it at roulette," said Tim sulkily. "There was a wheel in a back room at the speak. And I didn't throw it at you, I was giving it to you. We can use it, can't we?"

"We can use it all right." She was sure she felt as bad as he did, and looked it too. A real Tenderloin slut, slopping about in a dressing gown and rundown bedroom slippers. "Well," she said impatiently, "you gambled and you got yourself a katzenjammer; did you happen to find out what Joe's new project is?"

"He's going to manage the Valkyrie restaurant in Sausalito."

"Sausalito! That's a new one. I didn't know the mob had extended its operations to Marin County."

"Joe's not a mobster."

"Next thing to it, then? What sort of a joint is this Val-kyrie?"

"It used to be an old German *Rathskeller*, a beer garden, something like that. Not selling beer now, of course."

"Only spirits?"

"Good God, Vi, just because you've got a hangover, don't take it out on me! I never heard of the Valkyrie in my life till last night."

"I never heard of it at all, but I drank Joe's Scotch, the stuff he said was straight off the boat. Which boat do you think that was?"

"One of the Oriental steamers, probably, San Francisco's an international port. And now, if you don't mind, I'm going to shave."

"Good idea," said his wife. "And if you're planning to play roulette again in the near future, just think how silly you're going to look when the cops raid that joint."

There was no more roulette and no more Joe until a week had elapsed, when he reappeared with a bottle of brandy, straight off the boat, and a complicated jigsaw puzzle for Heidi, whose measure he had taken as not being a dolly girl. When Violet told him that she knew Sausalito quite well but had never heard of the Valkyrie, he was most forthcoming.

"You've gone there on picnics with the kiddy? Ah well, you wouldn't know the place, it's a bit too far for her to walk. Out at the far end of Bridgeway, along a boardwalk: romantic sort of place, with the sea coming up under the planks."

"Sounds exciting," said Violet. "The end of Bridgeway, I'm sure that's not too far for Heidi. Have you gone to live in Sausalito, Joe?"

"More or less."

"Then some day Heidi and I will take the ferry over and ask you to give us lunch."

"Great, but we're not open for business yet. The place needs a lot of fixing up before we're ready for the summer trade."

Sausalito was a favourite spot for summer picnickers and walkers, being only five miles from San Francisco on the north side of the strait. Until the Golden Gate was bridged, a project now under study, it was accessible from the city only by ferry across the bay. It had once been the huge Spanish grant given

to William Richardson, the English sailor who raised the first
tent dwelling at Yerba Buena Cove and taught Don Santiago
Estrada how to vaccinate the Indians. He had only one neighbour, an Irishman called Read, who liked to call his cattle
home in the evening by playing 'Robin Adair' on his bugle.

Since those pastoral days Sausalito had developed from a
fishing cove to a suburb of San Francisco, whose residents
lived in picturesque cottages and cabins clinging to the slope of
a wooded hill in the shadow of Mount Tamalpais. This setting
caused Californians who had never been to Europe to compare
Sausalito to a Mediterranean village.

When on a fine Saturday in March Violet Siegrist told her
daughter that they were going on a ferry ride to Sausalito, the
little girl was delighted.

"But aren't we taking a picnic, mother?"

"Not today, dear. We're going to see Uncle Joe's new
restaurant, and if he can't give us lunch we'll get something in
the village. Now don't make that ugly face! Uncle Joe's very
fond of you."

"I only hope he doesn't kiss me."

A ride on a ferry-boat was worth a kiss from Uncle Joe to
Heidi. It was one of her great treats to be out on the bay,
throwing crusts to the seagulls which followed the ferries, as
the great boats plied to and fro across the water. Her favourite
run was to Sausalito, sailing past the rock of Alcatraz, looking
at Goat Island, which the Spanish had called Yerba Buena, and
Angel Island, where the first foreign sailors had gone ashore
for wood. Then there was a glimpse of the Golden Gate and
the Pacific before the ferry veered to port under wooded bluffs
to Sausalito Point and Whalers' Bay, once Whalers' Harbour,
where that unknown figure in Heidi's story, Skipper Putnam,
had berthed his vessel before the Argonauts came. As it was a
Saturday, and sunny, there were many light craft on the bay,
and white-sailed yachts heading for Sausalito; Heidi ran from
side to side of the deck in the excitement of seeing them all.

On previous excursions she and her mother had always
turned right at the landing stage and walked along Bridgeway,
past the harbours used by the yachts and the fishing fleet, to eat
their picnic lunch in a park where there were other children for
Heidi to play with. Today mother started out in the opposite

direction, walking left past the small two-storey buildings of the 1890s, with shops below and living quarters above, and so down a short flight of steps to a pathway by the water's edge. It was fun for Heidi, who ran on ahead and made circles between the water and the rocks, until they reached Joe's boardwalk, where the sea did indeed come under the planking, and the few houses were built on piles. Violet reflected that a child of six could have walked the distance in the time.

"Is this Uncle Joe's restaurant?" asked the ten-year-old by her side.

"Looks like it." The word VALKYRIE appeared in large rusted metal capitals on top of a clapboard, barnlike building with dirty windows, through which vague shapes could be seen at tables; the clapboard had not been painted for many a day. The Valkyrie had been a Sausalito institution since the 1890s – some said the 1870s – and appeared to have fallen upon evil days.

"It's sort of dismal, isn't it, mother?" The sun was shining, there was no wind, and the sea was pulling and tugging, not disagreeably, beneath the little plank bridge on which they stood, leading from the end of the boardwalk to a street with rough paving on which the door of the Valkyrie opened. And yet the child was right, it *was* dismal, even sinister, perhaps because of the wooded bluff which made one wall of a little natural cove in which dark objects were bobbing. "What are those things?" said Heidi fearfully.

"Crab pots, darling, there's a lot of crab fishing here, but I never saw so many pots so close in shore before."

"Uncle Joe should be able to serve nice fresh crabmeat, shouldn't he? I mean, the fishermen could sit in the windows and haul up the pots without troubling to go to sea, couldn't they?"

"Let's go in and find out."

The street door led directly into a long room with a bar at one end, virtuously empty of bottles, and about twenty tables with soiled check tablecloths, nearly half of which were filled. The customers might have been the crab fishermen of Heidi's fantasy. They wore sailors' caps, roll-necked jerseys and sea boots, and while most of them were playing cards they all had glasses in their hands, which contained what the charitably minded might have supposed to be root beer. There was a bank of slot machines at one side of the room. The customers turned a concerted stare on the woman and the child.

"Yes ma'am?" A redhaired waiter with a long grimy apron came forward as Violet stopped uncertainly.

"Is Mr. Gregory here, please?"

"Who wants him?"

"Mrs. Siegrist and her daughter."

"He ain't here."

"Oh – I see. Are you serving lunch, please?"

"Only beverages, ma'am." There was a laugh from the back of the room and Violet flushed.

"No thank you," she said.

"You're welcome."

"I don't think that was a nice place," said Heidi gravely when they emerged on the narrow street.

"I don't either. Let's see –" Violet looked around. "I suppose this is where the beer garden was. It mightn't be too bad in summer." There was a fenced-in space behind the Valkyrie, the fences edged with tarweed, empty except for a pile of metal chairs and tables in one corner.

"I wish we'd brought a picnic, mother."

"Never mind. We'll go back to that nice bakery we saw on Bridgeway and get something good to eat, and then we'll go down to our little park by the boat basin so you can play on the swings for a bit before we take the ferry back to the city. Isn't it a lovely day?"

It was like any other of their Sausalito afternoons, with the great treat still ahead of boarding the ferry for the return journey and watching San Francisco appear, like a conch shell full of coloured fondants, through the trailing veils of spring-time mist. This time Heidi noticed that her mother, who usually went directly to the big cabin with the benches and armchairs, stayed on deck with her and watched intently as the ferry-boat backed out of its slip and made a wide turn about past the Bridgeway and the boardwalk. There were no lights in the Valkyrie, but the crab pots were still bobbing in the little cove.

It was seven o'clock when Joe Gregory appeared in Ellis

Street, armed with a big box of chocolates and many apologies for having missed them in Sausalito.

"If I'd known you were coming!" he said. "Why didn't you call me, Vi?"

"We left in a hurry, didn't we, Heidi? It was too fine a day to miss."

"Sure, but I'd have taken you to lunch at the Casa Madrone. Fact is, I was lunching there myself with a business friend . . . I sure hated missing out on my two best girls!"

"Thank you," said Violet, "but I was very interested in what I saw of the Valkyrie Restaurant."

He said slowly, "Like that, is it?"

"Like that."

"Tim not back yet?"

"He's on a job down the Peninsula, at some society bash they want to get in the rotogravure sections. He said he'd be back before eight o'clock."

"Oh, fine. Now I'll tell you what we'll do to make up for this noon (I didn't like to think of you two among those roughnecks), we'll all go out and have dinner, somewhere with real class. The Mark, maybe, or the Fairmont –"

"No thank you, Joe," said Violet. "Not tonight. I have a bad headache and I'd rather not."

"Listen, honey, I think you've got me all wrong –"

"Wait a minute," said Violet. "Heidi, why don't you get a saucer from the kitchen and pick out four of those lovely chocolates, and then go in your room and finish your homework. Try to get it all done before daddy gets home."

The homework had been methodically finished on Friday evening, but Heidi knew better than to argue. Between the kitchen and her little bedroom, now comfortably furnished with a basket chair and a student's desk under the green-shaded gas lamp, she heard her mother say "Why the hell didn't you stay in Chicago? You could have run all the hooch you wanted across the lake without messing up our lives." She shut her door very firmly. Then the voices were lowered, and Heidi forgot them in the pages of *Kidnapped*, until she heard her mother say,

"Is the roulette wheel fixed too, to let him win?"

An angry-sounding mutter, and then Violet again:

"You said when you came back, you wanted to cut Tim in on your next deal. Well, you can cut it *out*! Tim Siegrist's a genius, not a small-time hood, and if you do anything to get Tim into trouble, I swear to God I'll kill you!"

★   ★   ★

"All he wants me to do is be night watchman at the Valkyrie," said Tim. "As soon as the truck moves off, I scram."

"Why you?"

"Because he trusts me."

"And he doesn't trust the others?"

"Not much."

"When's this to be?"

"I won't know until the night."

"Oh my God, Tim, are you crazy?"

It was a week and a day after the visit to Sausalito, and Heidi was safely out of the house at Sunday School. Violet knew her husband had seen Joe twice in the interval; now he was telling her about the deal they had finalised.

"Just two things," he said. "One: he's paying me a thousand dollars for the job, and I made him pay me five hundred in advance. I've got it on me now."

"That's a lot of money for a night watchman. What sort of a load's going into the truck?"

"That's the second thing. I said to Joe, running in booze is fine with me. Prohibition's a damn stupid law, it makes criminals of us all –"

"Even you."

"Even me. But drugs I will not handle. And he vowed he wasn't running drugs. Swore it on his mother's memory."

"He can scarcely remember his mother, so he says."

Tim said reluctantly, "Joe says the crab pots gave you a clue."

"A clue! Everybody in the city knows the crab-pot story. An honest fisherman *accidentally* finds a keg of Canadian whisky in his pot and peddles it to a speakeasy or whatever. Straight off the boat, three miles outside the Gate, and the whole Coast Guard can't catch all the rumrunners in the business. But using a truck means a bigger haul. How many kegs of whisky to a truck? Twenty? Thirty?"

"Depends on the size of the truck, and anyway I'd rather you didn't know."

"So I can't squeal when the cops come asking."

"They won't come asking."

"Don't be too sure. Oh Tim, what's got into you? What's five hundred dollars, or even a grand, compared with your safety? We'll get by without a bootlegger's money! Tell Joe you're pulling out, and say you'll have nothing more to do with him."

"How ungrateful can you get?" said Tim quietly. "Have you forgotten all Joe Gregory did for you when you were in trouble fifteen years ago? Before Mr. Cord was heard from, he told me, 'I'll donate all I've got to Violet!' and when you were released on bail he hunted down Jack Hastings and Glidden, and helped to lead the police to Pat Malloy. He's not a guy I'd want to let down, even if you do."

"Oh, I see," said Violet, her voice as quiet as Tim's. "That's the big come-on, is it?" (I'm talking like a gangster's moll in the movies, she thought). "In that case, there's nothing I can say. I'll have that old trouble round my neck for the rest of my life. So go ahead, pay our debt to Joe Gregory, and don't blame me if you both land in prison. Have you set a night for the great adventure yet? In the dark of the moon, I imagine?"

He took his wife in his arms. "You were my great adventure once," he said. "Don't be so bitter. It'll be all over in a few hours, you'll see. But I don't know when until the night. If I don't come home some evening, you'll understand." He kissed her and stroked her hair.

"Oh damn the Depression," she said furiously. "It's turning men into swine . . . My poor darling! All you ever wanted to do was tell stories on film, and look at you!"

He said, with the shadow of his old twisted smile, "Maybe I'll get some new plots in San Quentin."

"Don't talk like that!" She let her head fall on his shoulder . . . "I wish I'd never seen that horrible Valkyrie. I knew it meant bad luck."

★　　★　　★

When the night came, Tim understood what his wife had meant about the Valkyrie. It was an ominous place, even to a man's eyes, and after sitting for an hour in the dingy room barely lit by one ten-watt electric lamp and closed by heavy shutters, he had had enough of his company. With any authority he would have told them to stop drinking, but the redhaired fellow who scared Violet away was pouring the drinks and scowling from time to time at Tim as an interloper. The four others, burly Italians, paid no attention to him at all.

He rose and went out through a complication of passages and pantries into the former beer garden. A part of the fencing had been removed and a milk truck backed into the space, with the rear doors open on the side street. On the other side, close to the piled chairs and tables, was the Ford Model A which he himself was to drive behind the loaded truck to Petaluma, where the cargo of whisky shipped from Canada was to be off-loaded into one of the old warehouses used for storing potatoes when Petaluma was the bread-basket of the young township by the bay. That was the interpretation which Joe had put on his duties as a night watchman, to continue far outside the Valkyrie's yard. A rival gang of rumrunners was in the area and might hi-jack the milk truck's cargo if – and this was the big *if* – some of Joe's own mob were prepared to sell out to Toselli. From what he had seen of them inside the restaurant Tim thought they would sell out to the devil for a modest profit.

It was a dark midnight. A faint glow in the sky reflected the street lamps of San Francisco; over sleeping Sausalito there was no reflection in the sky at all. There were no houses near the Valkyrie except the few built on piles along the boardwalk, and these, he had been told, were only occupied in the summer. The rough road to his left marked the slope down which the casks of fresh water had been rolled when San Francisco depended on the springs of Sausalito for its water supply, and up that slope would come the bootleg whisky now.

The plan was for the rumrunners to bring their cargo to Whalers' Bay by motor launch and transfer it to two old longboats, like those used in the Spanish days, to bring the kegs of liquor right up to the little planking bridge which led to the Valkyrie. Tim let himself out of the beer garden by the side gate and walked catfooted to the bridge. The air smelt heavily

of salt and the refuse of the tides, mingled with the grass and
tarweed crushed when the fence was taken down. It seemed to
Tim that he could hear the plash of muffled oars.

He went back into the restaurant by the way he came. "Here
they are!" he said briefly, and the five men jumped to their feet,
saw the light extinguished and followed him out of doors. The
Italians, he saw, were buckling on their holsters.

"I won't carry a gat," he had said to Joe, "we're not in a
shooting war."

"For your own safety, Tim –"

"Safety be damned, this isn't a Broncho Billy Western. If it
comes to a shoot-out, I'll surrender. I don't want to be killed
for a gallon of whisky and a thousand bucks."

What he wanted at that moment was his stick. He had
brought it along as a crutch, not an offensive weapon, and he
had flung it on the passenger's seat of the Ford Model A. But
the soft damp night air had started up the pain in the leg injured
at Calgary, and he was moving to the car when he heard the
shots.

They seemed to come from some distance away. But Tim,
like the other men, was galvanised into starting forward at
once towards the cove, where the shape of the leading longboat could now be dimly seen.

"The Coast Guard – ?"

"Toselli's gunsels – ?"

Tim heard the grunts as the burly men ran past him. He
heard no answer as the longboat came up, a rope was thrown
and the first keg of bootleg whisky was lifted on to the plank
bridge. He did seize on one of the men from the boat, who had
climbed ashore behind the keg, and said in what seemed to
himself like a shout but was only a hoarse whisper, "Where's
Joe Gregory?"

"There's trouble – back at Whalers' Bay – for God's sake,
hurry!" The word was echoed by the redhaired fellow from
the restaurant, who seemed to have taken charge. "Hurry!
Unload the second boat! Let's go!"

Fast, well organised, and sensing danger, the men loaded
the kegs into the milk truck, all working together before the
longboat's crews ran back to the cove. The redhaired man
took the wheel of the truck, the four Italians piled inside and

the doors were shut. The truck pulled as quietly as possible out of the gap in the fence. Tim turned the ignition key of the Model A and followed. Both vehicles were heading for the highway which led upstate to Petaluma.

They got no further than the first intersection. There, four flares lit up the crossroads and a detachment of motorcycle policemen surrounded the truck. Tim saw the rear doors open and heard a fusillade of shots. He put the Ford in reverse and started to back down the road. There was nowhere to go except into the one-time beer garden or into the sea, but he wasn't going anywhere. Four of the motorised patrol were forcing him off the road, into the tarweed and the broken fence. The passenger door was pulled open and a powerful torch played over his face and hands. A powerful voice told him to get out.

"Officer, you're making a big mistake –" he began.

"*Out!*"

There was the familiar twinge in his right hip as he pushed himself out from behind the wheel. He seized his stick and hit the ground, striking the patrolman as he fell. There was a swinging blow to his head, and Tim Siegrist was dead to the world.

5

"If you do anything to get Tim into trouble I swear to God I'll kill you." Heidi was not alarmed by the passionate words she overheard her mother say to Joe Gregory, because 'Drop dead!' was too popular an expletive in the Tenderloin for killing to have any significance. Hers was not a nature to brood over unpleasant words, as Violet had brooded for years over Faxon Cord's careless "Bring the brat along with you – I don't care." But when she learned a few days later that Uncle Joe *was* dead, had been shot on a lonely sea-shore by a bad man called Toselli, the child knew fear for the first time, and cried in her fright when she found that daddy had done something wrong too and might be punished for it. Violet spared her little daughter nothing in her own abandonment to grief, liberally mixed with anger because Tim had ignored her warnings. From the newspapers, which nobody kept from her, Heidi got a garbled idea of what had happened.

The police had had an eye on the Valkyrie, and after rushing to the affray at Whalers' Bay when Joe Gregory was killed by the leader of the hi-jackers, they had moved in on the restaurant. In the shoot-out at the crossroads the redhaired man, wounded himself, had killed a policeman, and he, like Toselli, was later executed. In the course of the trial the DA seized an opportunity to tell the jury that Giuseppe Gregorio, as Joe was once more called, was the brother of the notorious Giovanni Gregorio, alias Jack Gregg, one of the lieutenants of the Chicago gangster, 'Bugsy' Moran, to whose mob Toselli had once belonged. Whereupon a publicity-hungry judge, with an eye on the press benches, said he was determined to rid San Francisco of Italian criminals and their Chicago affiliates, and made dark references to the Mafia, the Sicilian Union, and Cosa Nostra. He congratulated the jury on their comprehensive verdict of guilty, and said exemplary sentences would be passed.

'John Siegrist, unemployed, of no fixed address' was cleared of attacking a policeman with an offensive weapon, but having been in the convoy of bootleg liquor he was sentenced to one year in San Quentin.

"But why's daddy calling himself John?" asked Heidi in distress.

"It's his middle name, dear, you know that."

"But why 'no fixed address'? We know his address. He lives here!"

"He did it to protect us," said Violet with a sob. "He didn't even want me to go to court during the trial –"

"I would have gone," was on the tip of Heidi's tongue, but with a wisdom beyond her years she was silent. She saw that her mother was beside herself. 'Sick to my soul' and 'ready to die of shame!' were words often on her lips. She refused to go out, sent Heidi to the shops, and cut off for ever her contacts with the family in Hawaii and 'poor Stella, how humiliated she must be' in Stockton.

Heidi felt no shame, only longing for her father. Among the Ellis Street kids, whom she had dominated since she was first allowed to play with them, she was something of a heroine. "Say-y-y, I hear ya pop's inside?" from one of the kids was almost an accolade, when a pop was 'inside' for reasons as spectacular as Tim's. Tackling a cop was well thought of in the Tenderloin. There, and elsewhere in San Francisco, the judge's admonitions had misfired. Rumrunning appeared to be no crime, but a gay adventure, appealing to the rebel in every red-blooded American, and bootleggers were rapidly becoming the new folk heroes.

Mother had had to give a lot of her own money, she told Heidi, to a Mr. Fiske, a 'counsellor', who spoke for dad in court, although the mean old judge wouldn't let him out on something called 'bail', and yet mother was never short of money. Even before she had leave to visit John Siegrist, unemployed, across the bay in San Quentin, a strange man came to see her and told her she would be well looked after. "We take care of our own, signora," was what Heidi heard him say.

The strangers – never the same man – came again and again during the year that Tim was in prison. No man stayed longer than ten or fifteen minutes in the Ellis Street flat, but each time mother had folding money in her purse next day, and a bottle of French brandy or Armagnac in the cupboard. She always had a glass, or two, out of the bottle when she came back pale and chilled from the ferry ride across the bay to the huge, white, almost medieval looking prison called San Quentin.

"Daddy sent you lots of love, Heidi."

"Why didn't he ask to see me?"

"He doesn't want you to see him in that place, darling."

"But he's quite well?"

"He's fine."

So worn, so pitifully apologetic, there behind the barrier they put up between the prisoners and their visitors, "I'm fine," he said. They'd given him a job in the library, putting new oilcloth covers on the battered books. How about her? How about Heidi? The conversations always followed a pattern. Before the year of Tim's detention was over, Violet felt that a glass barrier had grown up between them, stronger than anything the jailers of San Quentin could erect. She was glad, in a guilty way, to get back to the comforts – even in summer – of the gas fire, the old dressing gown, the cigarettes and the drop of spirits which helped her to go to sleep.

"Mommy, you're asleep already. Please go to bed. It's so hot in here!"

The child was on her knees, picking spent matches from the rug. Her mother caught her by the chin, turned her face up, and said with dignified pauses between each word:

"Sometimes – you – remind – me – of my grandmother – Estrada. Same cen – censorious face. Same – scolding . . ."

"Daddy thinks I look like him."

"Daddy's wrong as usual. Content Putnam lives again! At least you're not marked with the Estrada brand."

"Oh mother, you're not making any sense."

The barrier rose between Heidi and her mother, as between Tim and his wife. Violet turned into a lazy, frowzy woman with cigarette ash down the front of her dress and a pile of fan magazines to help her live the life of a movie star at second hand. She made herself presentable for Tim's return, but it was spoiled by the arrival of one of the swarthy strangers, which provoked an argument.

"I appreciate all you and the boys have done, Emilio," said Tim, "but now I'm back I don't need your help. I've a good job to go to."

"Say, I guess you don' know, mister, but the Cala Agency folded two months ago. We been doin' you a favour because you was a paisano of Giuseppe's –"

"I'm no paisano, and it wasn't a favour. How much did these guys bring you, Violet?"

"Five hundred dollars, all told."

"Exactly right, the other half of what poor Gregory agreed to pay me. So now we're quits, Emilio; better be on your way. I'm through."

When the man had gone he turned on Violet. "Why the hell didn't you tell me Cala had folded?"

"What the hell could you do about it, across the bay?"

"Oh God, what am I going to do now?"

"Maybe you cut loose from your gangster friends too soon."

The scene was all the uglier because they were both sober. But that didn't last long, and the reunited pair were maudlin when they went to bed. One problem was solved a few days later, when a man from the police department's Welfare and Rehabilitation Service found Tim a job in the Emporium department store, selling camera film across the counter.

★   ★   ★

When Heidi was thirteen she dreamed of restoring the family fortunes. Nineteen thirty-three was a lucky year for America, for the people had elected a new President, Franklin Delano Roosevelt, who told them they had nothing to fear but fear itself, and who brought them a New Deal. The Depression was nearly over and so, after having damaged the morals of the nation, was Prohibition, which was repealed on December 5. It was a merry Christmas in San Francisco.

The girl knew her mother's family had been rich once, for Violet, when she was in a good mood, would go to the Old First Church with Heidi and then take the cable car up California Street to Jones. Walking down Jones, catty-corner to Grace Cathedral which mother had sometimes attended with Granny Randolph, she would show Heidi the site at the corner of Jones and Pine where she herself had been born and Granny Estrada died. It was now occupied by a handsome apartment building; that section of Pine was tree-shaded and very attractive.

"The Estradas were rich people, weren't they, mother?"

"Very rich, I believe."

"Then why aren't we rich now?"

"The money was lost somehow – I don't know."

We wuz robbed, said Heidi to herself without any intention of disrespect. She had grown accustomed to her mother's lugubrious tones. But she was sure that the important thing was not to mourn over lost wealth but to begin at the beginning and start getting rich again. At thirteen this is not easy. At fifteen everything is possible – if you are young in San Francisco, that phoenix among American cities, born in conflict and rising again and again from its own ashes.

At fifteen, Heidi was in Pomodoro High School, at the head of her class. She had dissuaded her new teachers from calling

549

her Adelaide, and threatened violence to any classmate who called her Addie. There was always some gawky boy or another who wanted to carry her books home from school, and "I think she talks them into it," said her mother, "goodness knows it's not her looks." Heidi's childish pigtails had been replaced by a page-boy bob of light brown hair held in place by an imitation tortoiseshell barrette, and she had what her father called a curly smile. Her looks had turned out well in an understated way, but nobody was ever going to tell Heidi Siegrist that she ought to be in pictures.

She knew nothing of her mother's brief career in pictures until she was sixteen. At that age she liked to compare her life to a rat-race, because outside of school hours she was holding down two paying jobs. On week nights she worked in the packing room at the Emporium, making up parcels for despatch by train, and on Saturday evenings she was an usherette at a cinema on Bush Street, not far from where Mrs. Randolph had held her classes in deportment. The deportment of the movie customers was far from perfect, and Heidi quickly learned how to swing her torch effectively on a groping hand; she also saw, in bits and pieces, some first-rate movies. She had a savings account of her own in the Crocker Bank.

One wet afternoon, coming home from school, she stopped at a newsstand to buy *Modern Screen* and *Motion Picture* for her mother. Violet had a cold, or a toothache, or some other of the minor ailments which constantly beset her, and which she treated with whisky toddy and aspirin; the new fan mags would be a help. There was one on the newsstand which Heidi had never seen before, called *Tinsel Town*. She spent another dime on that and boarded a street car.

Tinsel Town seemed like all the others, a mish-mash of gossip paragraphs and movie stills with a spread of Garbo and Boyer in *Conquest*. And what was obviously meant to be the start of a series called 'Whatever Became of . . .

The name beneath the boldhead was LETTY RANDOLPH. And the picture beneath the name was of Heidi's mother.

A fat man sitting next to her got up and sent a shower of raindrops from his coat across the page as he shuffled out. The text was still quite legible and reasonably accurate. The story of the Hastings murder was rehashed, with the emphasis on

the dope angle and the confession and trial of Patrick Malloy.
"Letty Randolph never appeared on the screen again," the
writer concluded. "She was briefly seen as a Hollywood
housewife, married to a cameraman, and then disappeared
from view."

Heidi thrust *Tinsel Town* to the botton of her school satchel
and walked up Fifth Street in the rain. That Letty Randolph
('real name Violet Estrada' said the story) had been accused of
murder and found innocent was a stunning fact, if true, and it
explained so much in her mother's personality. She kissed
Violet with unusual tenderness when she got home. When she
reached the Emporium next afternoon, it being late closing
day, when the sales force and the packers left the building at
the same time, she went to the Photographic Supplies counter
and seized an opportunity to whisper to her father, "Buy me a
coffee after work, dad?"

"Sure thing, baby!" Tim always enjoyed a coffee break with
his girl, even if it only lasted fifteen minutes.

"Meet you on the corner of Jessie, then!"

The Poppy Playhouse had long since disappeared from
Jessie Street, but a clean, bright coffee shop had appeared
opposite the Emporium on Market Street, specialising in
doughnuts (chocolate, raspberry, coconut and plain) and behind its plate glass windows, through which a steady stream of
people could be seen hurrying past, Heidi laid the copy of
Tinsel Town before her father. He put on his spectacles, read
'Whatever Became of Letty Randolph?' and sighed.

"Is it true, dad?"

"Quite true. Remember I told you that your mother and I
met when I took her photograph?"

"Yes."

"That was the photograph." From the blistered page the
lovely face looked confidently out, and Heidi said, "How
beautiful she was!"

"And how unlucky."

"Not when she married you, dad. Tell me, was this why
you gave a – more or less a false name, and no address, to the
police, that Sausalito time?"

"You remember that, do you?"

"How could I forget? Mother said you did it to protect us."

"Heidi, the newspapers ran a smear campaign against your mother before she had a chance to prove her innocence that I don't believe she ever really recovered from. If I'd said anything that led the press to Violet Estrada I don't think she would've got over it. I was going to be sent up anyway, so what did it matter about my name?"

Heidi nodded. "I see that. And I bet you were the one who helped her beat the rap."

"Some, and Joe Gregory helped too."

"Was *that* why –"

"Why I got involved in that crazy caper? Yes."

"Now I'm beginning to understand. Can you tell me more?"

He told her everything, taking the blame on himself for most of it. "Remember, if I'd stayed on in Hollywood and tried to get ahead there none of the rest would have happened," he said honestly. "No bombs, no Joe, no San Quentin. And for the last part, as she reminds me every day, I should have listened to your mother." He added anxiously, "You're not going to show her that fool mag, are you?"

"Good heavens, *no*! Father" (she never called him 'daddy' again) "I think you're wonderful. Somehow or other, we've got to get you back into pictures."

★   ★   ★

Of course he laughed at her, as she sat there eating her neglected doughnut. Tim Siegrist, nearer fifty than forty, hard-up and lame, getting back into the glittering, frenetic world of Hollywood! But that heart-to-heart with his daughter was a turning-point in Tim's drab life. Unemployment was no longer the great bogey of the past. Roosevelt's New Deal had been effective, and in spite of the disastrous longshoremen's strike of 1934 there were no more breadlines and apple-sellers in San Francisco. He could just afford to take a chance. True, Violet kept telling him (when she remembered) that he was a genius, but as long as he brought home a safe wage from the Emporium she was perfectly happy to have genius spend its days making out slips for the developing and printing of amateur film, usually under- or over-exposed. It was time for a change. Since business had picked up there were

552

new demands in the fields of commercial photography, beginning with the reproduction of invoices and receipts. There were new cameras for the new Kodak 8 mm film, giving four exposures in the area of one 16 mm frame, and before he handed in his notice at the Emporium Tim bought a supply of the new equipment at employee's rates. He also made sure of being able to process his film by entering into an arrangement with a little old man in a *yarmulka* called Nathan Wildstein to share the dark room attached to his photographic studio at Second and Mission. Part of the cost would be paid by Tim in kind, or rather in services, by retouching the cabinet photographs of wedding groups or departed loved ones, for which in spite of the Depression there had been a continuing demand in the Mission.

Heidi, anxious to help in any way, tried her hand in the dark room, and was a failure from the start. "You can't seem to get the hang of it somehow," said her perplexed father. "Better leave it all to me, and you keep the books. What do you say, Nathan? Heidi's a real whizz-kid at math, but she's no darn good at developing!"

The commercial photography was soon successful, and so were Tim's off-beat photographs of San Francisco scenes. The time was ripe for an original photographer such as Arnold Genthe had been in an earlier generation. The great dream of bridging San Francisco Bay, under study for fifteen years, was about to be realised, not in one place but in two. In January of the lucky year 1933 construction work had begun across the Golden Gate, which the Indians called Yulupa, the Sunset Strait, as the steam shovels broke ground in the anchorage on the northern, or Marin County side. Six months later work started on what would be called the Oakland Bay Bridge between San Francisco and Oakland. The first would be seven miles wide, the second eight, and their commencement in 1933, with the Depression barely over, was San Francisco's supreme act of self-confidence. The double engineering feat, as it developed month by month, was eagerly followed by citizens whose imagination was touched by the soaring spans and openwork pylons. San Franciscans were looking up and skywards in those days, not back at the gutter of the Depression. The Argonauts in their sailing ships had conquered the ocean. The railroad had spanned a continent. Now was the time for the mastery of the air.

Already in 1917, before Heidi Siegrist was born, a woman had set a non-stop distance flight record from San Diego to San Francisco. Katherine Stinson had covered the distance of six hundred and ten miles in nine hours and ten minutes, and she was an inspiration to the other solo flyers of her day. But commercial flying had developed quickly – as witness the Fairmont Hotel's initiative – and by 1927 a municipal airport had been opened at Mills Field. Now, simultaneously with the bridging of the bay, Pan American Airways began regular flights from San Francisco to the Orient. The Golden Gate was swinging wide on its hinges and California was ready to send out its argosies to China and Japan.

Anticipating, of course, some traffic in the opposite direction.

The Pan Am publicity people were delighted to let Tim Siegrist take pictures round their hangars. They were flying Boeing B-314 Clippers, which meant that the manufacturers of the flying boats were interested in his work, and Tim got commissions in Seattle which brought in more hard cash. Heidi's seventeenth birthday was celebrated in champagne, and there was another celebration on the twenty-seventh of May, when the Golden Gate Bridge was opened with a Pedestrian Day. Heidi helped her father with his apparatus, for he used a movie camera to shoot the thousands who crossed and recrossed the bridge on foot, and the aircraft which took part in a fly-over before the bridge was opened to the motorised traffic expected to chase the old ferry-boats off the bay. That evening, judging her parents to be sufficiently mellowed, she told them about her future plans.

Heidi had begun planning her career before school started after Labour Day. She had given up her job at the Emporium, having learned all there was to learn about tying up parcels and pasting on Emporium labels, and devoted her evenings to school work. Pomodoro High had a large intake of Hispanic students and gave courses in Spanish, but not in French or German, so Heidi attended an external class in French and joined a German Club, formed by some classmates from San Francisco's large German community. She led her class in mathematics, but not in the natural sciences, and her English compositions were too matter-of-fact to satisfy her teacher, a lady who modelled her own style on the *Idylls of the King*. Passable at games and gym, Heidi ran for class president and was defeated by a tall boy who was the school's basketball star, but she led Pomodoro High to victory in an inter-school debating contest. She had a fair idea of her limitations and abilities, and like Content Putnam before her, she knew what she wanted.

"Father, mother, I've been thinking over what I ought to do when I graduate from high this summer."

"You're going to college," said her father promptly.

"Well no, not exactly." Going to Mills or Berkeley meant working her way through college, waiting on table and baby-sitting, and Heidi hadn't time for that. College might have been in her programme if Uncle Bobby Cord had continued his contributions to the education fund, but mother (trust her) had put paid to his generosity by her melodramatic decision at the time of Tim's imprisonment to sever all connections with her relatives rather than bring shame upon them. Poor old sweeties, thought seventeen-year-old Heidi, they haven't got an ounce of money sense between them.

"I don't think I'd get much out of college," she said. "I'm not the academic type. I'd rather go to business school. Not just classes in shorthand and typing, but a real training school for a business career. I'd like to learn commercial French and German, not the kitchen German the girls chatter at the club. And bookkeeping, and how to make out bills of lading, and international law, and – oh, everything!"

"Why, that's a tall order, Heidi," said Tim. "Where would you go to learn all that?"

"I got prospectuses from several places," she said eagerly. "I'll show them to you if you like. The best one seems to be the Tauchnitz School on Post, opposite the Mechanics' Library. Nettie Holz is going there."

"I never liked that Holz girl," put in Violet helpfully.

"Tauchnitz guarantees a good job after a year's course."

"What sort of a job?" asked Tim. "You've kind of surprised us, baby. With your grades we thought you were all set for three years at college, and then you'd be a teacher. Maybe even a university instructor."

"Doesn't appeal," said Heidi. "I want to get all sorts of experience in business houses here, and then abroad."

"Not *abroad!*" cried Violet, who had never been out of California in her life.

"Take it easy, mommy," said Tim, "she isn't going abroad tomorrow, or even next year. One thing I like about this plan is that we'll keep her at home for a long while yet . . . Can I see the Tauchnitz School prospectus, dear?"

In the interest of discussing the prospectus, and going back over the events of Pedestrian Day, none of them thought of opening the newspaper, which was left lying on the kitchen table. The *Examiner* was thrown out with the garbage in the morning. Thus Tim Siegrist failed to see a filler at the foot of a column which might have interested him:

> Millionaire connoisseur Adolph Zinnia has gifted the Cinémathèque Française of Paris, France, with his collection of early movie prints from Kalem, Triangle and Essanay. The latter group includes Willis Jerrold Hastings' *The Trials of Terry* and Timothy Siegrist's *Mliss*.

6

The Oakland Bay Bridge was opened six months before the bridge over the Golden Gate, but it was the mighty span between the bay and the Pacific Ocean which captured the imagination of San Franciscans and became the symbol of the city to the world. The Bay Bridge, however, had one distinctive feature. It had an anchorage on an island in the middle of the bay, the same which the Spanish had called Yerba Buena and their successors by the ugly name of Goat. Traffic had hardly started to flow across the two bridges before studies were begun to see if Goat Island could be turned to some profitable use.

Research into the Yerba Buena shoals (for the island had been rechristened with its Spanish name) revealed a seven hundred and thirty-five acre reef under the surface of the bay which could support a second island, man-made as the Marina had been made for the Panama-Pacific Exposition of 1915. The thought of a new Exposition was tempting to the Mayor, Angelo Rossi, and the Governor of California, Frank Merriam. It was a long time since San Francisco had had a regular fiesta, a real celebration, something to show the world that she was the Paris of the Pacific: what better reason than the bridging of the Golden Gate, that triumph over the doldrums of the Depression? Architects were consulted, whose vision saw a grand imperial city rising from the waves, and housing the treasures of the world. Army engineers were set to work, and in eighteen months had built it on the new Treasure Island.

While the work was only half completed, Heidi Siegrist finished her year at the Tauchnitz School and went on to her guaranteed job. It was in the correspondence department of the San Francisco branch of the Crédit Lyonnais, and she worked under the supervision of a cantankerous old Frenchman who was merciless to the slightest error in her work. For colleagues she had four young Frenchmen who took her to frugal lunches in Chinatown, danced with her at the Roseland ballroom and inevitably propositioned her. Heidi laughed at them and with them. The French boys were easy to handle, and she missed them when, following her own plan, she left to work in another language for the leading German import-export company of the city, Thomas Lang and Son.

Mr. Lang was a stout, benevolent man of sixty, born in San Francisco of German parents who had left the Fatherland after the Year of Revolutions, 1848. His father had a grocery stall in the old California Street Market, from which a thriving wholesale grocery business was gradually built up: Mr. Thomas Lang now directing it from offices in Drumm Street, while Son ran the Tokyo office. They imported spices from the Orient as well as specialities from Japan and China, with European delicacies like *Zürcher Leckerli* and *Pfeffernüsse*. Heidi was Mr. Thomas Lang's secretary, and had to take a fair amount of German dictation, afterwards typing the letters in the old Gothic script which the German Führer had brought back into use.

She owed her job to a recommendation from the father of her school friend, Nettie Holz. Like Mr. Lang, he was an office-bearer in the San Francisco chapter of the German-American *Bund*, the *Turnverein*, the *Sangverein* and all the other *Vereine* of a sociable and closely-knit community. Both were American born, over-age to join the army in the war to end all wars, when neither had the slightest ambition to go back to Europe and be killed for the Kaiser.

Mr. Lang never mentioned politics in the office, although German political ambitions were occupying more and more space in the *Chronicle*, but he did confide in Heidi about his domestic problems. Frau Lang – "Mrs. Lang I should say" – was tired of the mansion on Van Ness Avenue where they had lived all their married life. Nothing but automobile concessions there now, on both sides and in front of them! Heidi had to type letters (in English) to real-estate agents about orders to view properties on Russian Hill.

The wholesale grocery trade in 1939 was as wholesome and stodgy as rice pudding, and like all the other working girls in the city Heidi was delighted to read the posters put up in February:

ON SAN FRANCISCO BAY
1939
WORLD'S FAIR
GOLDEN GATE INTERNATIONAL EXPOSITION

Sometimes the readers smiled, because there was a World's Fair in New York that year, and the promoters were not happy with San Francisco's gentle reminder that the Far West, too, had attractions for the international exhibitor. Those who saw both Fairs said the Golden Gate show had by far the more beautiful setting, on Treasure Island, attached to Yerba Buena Island by a nine-hundred-foot causeway. Then the buildings were so beautiful, axed on the Court of Pacifica and built in what was called 'Pacific Basin style', unkindly compared by some to the current Fascist architecture, but at least protected by heavy windbreaks. As soon as the Exposition opened in February various 'Days' were designated as special attractions. There was a Scout Day, a Twin Day, a Freckles Day and even a Public Wedding Day in the Court of Flowers. There was also, on March 15 – the day when Hitler's troops entered Prague – a San Francisco Architectural Club Day. It was not revealed what the average architect thought of the 'great imperial city' but the average family was delighted with the Tower of the Sun, the Court of the Moon, the Promenade and Court of the Seven Seas, and with the Arch of Triumph, tinted coral pink.

The foreign nations which had undertaken to exhibit at the fair did so under difficulties. Looking steadily east to the Orient and stressing the importance of the Pacific could not disguise the fact that the Western countries meant to continue the Thirty Years' War which had not really ended in 1918. Germany invaded Poland on the first of September, and on October 29 the Golden Gate Exposition closed six weeks early and $4 million in debt.

The promoters of the Fair had encountered sheer bad luck in the outbreak of a European war which had not been anticipated when Treasure Island opened in February. Sheer bad taste made them try it again next year, when the war in Europe was raging. Denmark and Norway had been invaded and occupied by Germany in April, Holland and Belgium in May, when 'The Fair in Forty' opened its doors again. The British and French Allies were about to sustain a crushing defeat, ending in the evacuation of Dunkirk. It cast a gloom over the reopening of the Fair. Treasure Island, slightly shabbier from the winter weather, began to seem a place of fantasy. Yet the crowds gathered, not because San Franciscans were callous – they had too many ties with Europe for that – but because the city was extremely self-contained. For the last time, within six years of the centenary of the hoisting of the Stars and Stripes in the old plaza, San Francisco was a small, compact city of very little more than the half-million population of twenty years before. A city of groups where everybody knew everybody else, and where although there was pride in a cosmopolitan culture there was also determination to be let alone.

Those were the theories expounded to Heidi Siegrist by Andrew Kirk, a cub reporter on the San Francisco *Clarion*, after he met her one Saturday night on Treasure Island when there was moonlight and dancing.

"Care to dance?" was how he introduced himself. It was all quite informal round the open-air dance floor, and Heidi was with so many boys and girls that she looked round to make sure she was the one spoken to before she got up and said to the stranger, "Yes, I'd like to." Her friends were looking on critically and she was glad to find that her new partner danced well.

"D'you come here often?" he asked when they had gone round the floor in silence. She answered coolly, "When I've nothing better to do."

"Not a Fair fan, are you?"

"It's not as good this year as last."

"Nothing's as good this year as last," he said . . . "Why, particularly?"

"Too much honky tonk. The Aquacade and Sally Rand's Nude Ranch are hardly classical treasures of the world, are they?"

"Do you object to nudity? What do you do?"

"I'm a secretary at Thomas Lang and Son."

"I'm a reporter on the *Clarion*. Look, let's stop dancing and have a drink and talk." There was an imitation French café not far from the dance floor.

"Just coffee will be fine," said Heidi, taking the white painted chair he pulled out for her. "Are you here on a special assignment tonight?"

"You must be kidding," he said, "it's Saturday and we don't publish on Sundays. But let me ask you one question. What's a nice girl like you doing working for a Nazi out-fit?"

She looked at him in amazement as a waitress in a *soubrette*'s white frilly cap and apron put their coffees on the table. She thought he was a good-looking kid, too lanky for his height, with intense brown eyes and tumbled brown hair, very well dressed in a grey flannel suit thin enough for one of the few hot nights of June 1940.

"Now *you*'ve got to be kidding," she said, "if you're not plumb crazy. Lang and Son a Nazi outfit! Mr. Lang is a most respectable, old-fashioned German, with a signed photograph of Chancellor von Hindenburg on his desk. Nothing pro-Hitler about *him*."

"He's very close to the German Consul-General, Wiede-mann, and *he*'s Hitler's man, all right."

"I know nothing about that," said Heidi. "Are you what's called a muckraking reporter, Mr. –"

"Kirk. Andrew Kirk, forgive me, I should have said. No, I'm not a muckraker. I'm not much better than a copyboy yet, I've only been with the *Clarion* since the beginning of April."

"Before that what did you do?"

"I was graduated from Stanford last year. My father staked me to a winter in Europe for a graduation present. I got to London the week before Hitler invaded Poland."

"That was quite a present."

"It was a big thing for pops to do, because he wanted me to go into his insurance company."

"The company he works for?"

"He's the president."

"In San Francisco?"

"No, in Hartford, Connecticut."

"Why did you come west to go to college?"

"To see more of the country. Like last year I wanted to see Europe. Some day I want to be a foreign correspondent, like Ernest Hemingway, or Ed Murrow, or – famous guys like that."

"You chose an interesting time to go to Europe. I plan on working there one day, if I get a chance."

"You'll get a chance all right – as an army nurse."

"You think we'll get into the European war? That's ridiculous!"

Andrew Kirk launched into a speech which lasted for more than five minutes, about complacency, and isolationism, and small-town ignorance. He said war was inevitable from the moment Adolf Hitler became Chancellor of Germany in 1933, only all the ostriches had their heads in the sand and refused to see it. He said a company of the National Guard could have stopped Hitler when he invaded the Rhineland in '36, only neither the British nor the French had the guts to do it: his winter in Europe had left Andrew Kirk highly critical of the British and the French. "The British appeasers were perfectly happy with their phony war, and the French were sitting pretty behind their rotten Maginot Line," he said, "and look what happened!"

"The moment you turned your back," said Heidi mockingly. "And I imagine you'd left this country before Congress passed the Neutrality Act!"

Heidi was not politically minded. All she remembered about the passage of the Neutrality Act of September 1939 was Mr. Lang rubbing his ample waistcoat with satisfaction and saying "Good old FDR! He knows how to keep the country out of the mess in Europe!" though in fact Congress passed the act against Roosevelt's will. The chief topic in Heidi's home about that time had been the governor's pardon to Mooney and Billings, who after twenty-three years in prison for the bombs of Preparedness Day had walked out free men at last.

"A pardon doesn't mean they're innocent," said Violet when she heard the news.

"Innocent! They're as guilty as the devil," said Tim disgustedly. "Nine dead and forty injured, and it didn't stop the war – any more than the damned Neutrality Act will keep us out of this one."

Heidi brought her mind back to Andrew Kirk, who was waving his arms and saying "Just look at the rubes! Off to see a glorified carney show like the Cavalcade of History and gape at the dioramas of Valley Forge and Gettysburg, without ever thinking that bigger and bloodier battles than we ever fought before will be in our new chapter of history! Never thinking, as they oh! and ah! at the Treasure Island fireworks, that tonight Paris is under German occupation –" He looked so wretched that Heidi said,

"You poor man! There must be someone over there you care for very much –"

Andrew Kirk glared at her. "My God, that's exactly like a girl – turn everything into personalities. Women never think you can suffer for an abstract cause or a country. There's always got to be some sweetheart, or some dear old mom at the back of it all –"

"Except in combat," said Heidi.

"You're right," he said, deflated. 'I'm sorry. I talk too much. Please will you tell me your name?"

"Heidi Siegrist."

"That's an unusual name. Any relation to the great Timothy Siegrist?"

"He's my father."

"You don't say! That was a wonderful spread he did for *Life* on Treasure Island – you wouldn't think it was this same place where we're sitting. I've always wanted to be an ace photographer, like Robert Capa or Margaret Bourke-White . . . photojournalism, you know, that's the medium of the future! Gee, I'd like to meet your father some time!"

"Right now," said Heidi, getting up, "it's late, and I can't keep my friends hanging about. I'll tell my father you're a fan; he'll be delighted."

"I suppose you wouldn't let me drive you home?" said Andrew Kirk. "I've got a car."

"So have we," said Heidi. "Goodbye now, it was nice talking to you."

"But we've just begun," said the boy, catching at her hand. "Can't we meet again? Here, very soon? Or for dinner, some place? Or shall I call you at Thomas Lang and Son?"

"No, don't do that, they don't approve of private calls in business hours. That's the Nazi discipline." She was sorry for her feeble joke when he said "Don't kid about the Nazis!" and eventually she agreed to meet him on Treasure Island next Saturday night at eight o'clock.

"But where on Treasure Island?"

"Billy Rose's Aquacade!" she said gaily, and was off. Andrew Kirk followed her with his eyes as she joined her friends in the crowds making for the nearest exit. It *was* late, but compared to his earlier mood he felt as if his evening at the Fair had just begun.

"I met a fan of yours last night, father," said Heidi next day. "A cub reporter from the *Clarion*, name of Andrew Kirk."

"Never heard of him," said Tim, buttering toast.

"I shouldn't think he gets a by-line yet. But he's very ambitious. He wants to be a foreign correspondent like Hemingway – personally I think Richard Harding Davis is more his style – *and* a photographer like Robert Capa, and he wants to meet the great Siegrist."

"Why not?" said Tim. "He sounds as green as I was, at his age. You going to see him again?"

"We're having another frolic at the Fair next Saturday."

"I don't like you going out with newspapermen," worried Violet.

"He's a nice kid, mother," said Heidi soothingly. She knew her mother didn't really want her going out with anybody, for a new element of jealousy had entered into their relationship. Not the jealousy of an aging beauty for an attractive girl, nor even of a woman past her time for appealing to young men, but a possessive jealousy aroused whenever Heidi expressed a liking for any other person, be it man or woman. An evening at the movies with Nettie Holz was a grievance to Violet, whose daughter would find her sulking when she got home. "I should think you'd like to spend an evening with your own mother," she would say. "Do you think I can enjoy listening to Amos 'n' Andy on the radio, while you're running about heaven knows where?"

"I told you we were going to see Barbara Stanwyck in *Union Pacific*, mother."

"Was she any good? Tell me the plot."

Heidi told her the plot, and followed it with a poor imitation of the star, whereupon Violet did a much better one, and was all smiles again.

It never failed.

★   ★   ★

Heidi and Andrew Kirk had more than one date at the Golden Gate Exposition. The first began at Billy Rose's Aquacade, where they applauded the swimming of Esther Williams. They went on to the equivocally named Gayway, where they ate sea food out of paper cups and nibbled pink clouds of candy floss. Andrew had not a word to say about the state of affairs in Europe. But the seed of doubt which he had sowed in Heidi's mind began to put down roots and flourish. Was it possible Thomas Lang and Son was a Nazi-front organisation? Heidi, as Mr. Thomas Lang's personal secretary, could see no evidence in his office diary that he had any transactions with the German Consul-General, Herr Fritz Wiedemann. They could certainly meet at the gatherings of the *Turnverein* and the

Sangverein, or most controversial of all the rallies of the German-American *Bund*. And in September, when the Battle of Britain began, Herr Wiedemann came to the grocery offices twice. Heidi herself ushered him into Mr. Lang's room – a handsome, sturdy, middle-aged man who gave her a searching look as he passed her. Heidi decided to ask Andrew about the German's background next time they met. But before then Tim had received the letter which changed their lives.

It had a foreign look about it, though the stamp was American and the postmark Los Angeles, and Tim turned the thin envelope with the spidery handwriting in green ink round and round suspiciously before he opened it. The sender's name was written European style on the back of the envelope. "Turbin!" said Tim. "What the devil can he want with me? I didn't even know he was in America."

"Who's Turbin?" asked Violet.

"Alexis Turbin, the big French director," said Tim. "Russian by birth, but filming in Paris for the past ten years –"

"*Nana!*" said Heidi. "Remember, mother, we saw it last Christmas holidays."

"Perhaps he wants your father to make a movie with him," said Violet sarcastically.

"He might do worse," said Tim.

Alexis Isaievich Turbin, the latest recruit to a Hollywood filling with foreigners since the disasters of 1940, was four years old when his parents took him out of Russia to escape from the pogroms of 1906. In Berlin he had gone up the ladder of German cinema from clapperboy to director in the experimental days of Pabst and Ufa, and became one of the chief exponents of the *Strassenfilm*. He was one of the few Jews with the wits to leave Germany when Hitler's National Socialist party scored its first big success in the elections of September 1930. He realised all his assets and left for France. At the Neuilly studios he was a counterweight to the romanticism of René Clair and Julien Duvivier, and one of the first to practise *ciné vérité* or use a hand-held camera. In 1939 he had a smash hit with an implicitly sexual version of *Nana* which barely passed the American censors, and on the strength of *Nana* his application for an American visa was sponsored by Metro-Goldwyn-

Mayer when France was overrun with uniformed Jew-baiters in the summer of 1940.

One of the last things he did before leaving Paris was to pay a farewell visit to his friend Henri Langlois, the founder of the Cinémathèque Française, and to take their minds off the approaching disaster Langlois screened one or two items from his collection, including a two-reeler called *Mliss*. Turbin asked him to run it again, and freeze on the director's name in the credits.

"Timothy Siegrist," he said respectfully when the screen went dark. "Have you anything more of his, Langlois?"

"Nothing. So far as I know, *Mliss* was his only movie."

"It is *the* most remarkable forerunner of my own work I've ever seen," said Turbin. "*Ciné vérité*, 1915 style, with all the sex repressed but blazing. I could work with that man, Langlois! If he's still alive and in Hollywood, I'll find him!"

Alexis Turbin was a professional survivor. On the congested French highways, while the Luftwaffe was bombarding the refugees from Paris and the north, he was cool enough to film some of the atrocious scenes, and carried on shooting in the chaos of Bordeaux. There he managed to board a Portuguese coasting vessel bound for Oporto, and once in Portugal his cash and his American connections got him a seat on a Clipper flight from Lisbon to New York. He arrived in Hollywood with an enormous reputation, an idea for a movie, some film footage and action stills for background, but of course without the print of *Mliss*, which remained in Paris.

"We'd have to see it, Alex, before we can figure out exactly what you have in mind," he was told over lunch in the commissary at Metro-Goldwyn-Mayer. "Any idea where we could rustle up another print?"

"A man called Zinnia gave the print I saw to the Cinémathèque Française."

"Adolph Zinnia, sure, we know about him. Lives in Beverly Hills, we'll get in touch with him."

Mr. Zinnia, it was soon discovered, had a rough cut of *Mliss* in his possession. "I couldn't part with it," he confessed, "it's a real curiosity." Alexis Turbin nodded understandingly. "But I'll lend it to you with pleasure if you'll take good care of it. In fact I'll bring it to the studio myself."

It was a very small audience which saw a showing of *Mliss* for the first time since 1915 – Turbin, Mr. Zinnia, three studio executives and two technicians, and the cut they saw was very rough indeed. The technicians thought a new print could be made; the executives were dubious. "You're right, Alex," said their spokesman, "it's got something, and the girl's good. So's Wayne Blackwood. Imagine that skinny little kid Willie Whosis being the great Blackwood. But even with his name, is it box office?"

"Try it and see," said Turbin coolly. "Make a new print and release it! But I don't want to sell it on Wayne Blackwood's name, fine actor though he is. He stays on the credits as Willie Bleer."

"You can't release a two-reeler, Alex, unless it's in a retrospective."

"Try that then."

After much debate, and the circulation of endless inter-office memoranda, it was decided to put together a 'Bret Harte Celebration' and release it at a sneak preview in San Bernardino before the latest Ronald Reagan and Ann Sheridan vehicle. Gilbert M. Anderson (Broncho Billy) in *Tennessee's Partner* and Douglas Fairbanks in *The Half-Breed* would precede Letty Randolph and Willie Bleer in *Mliss*, and the cinema audience was given cards to mark their preferences. There was the usual groan when the sneak was announced, few of the audience having heard of Bret Harte, but the three two-reelers were a novelty and applauded at the end. The cards showed the choice of Douglas Fairbanks as best actor and *Mliss*, on ninety-five per cent of the cards, as the best film.

"Well, gentlemen?" challenged Alexis Turbin when the cards were counted, "what do you say now?"

"I say we do a double check and show the 'Celebration' in San Francisco, Harte's a cult figure there."

"With Reagan and Sheridan?"

"I'd like to see it on its own," said one of the MGM cameramen. "We could beef it up with newsreels and cartoons for one of the art houses."

"You understand, Alex, we're not in the revival business. We don't care a hill of beans for *Mliss*, but we're rooting for the movie you're going to do for us, and we've got to see if

Siegrist can work as well now as he did twenty-five years ago.
He's clean, by the way, we checked him out. No political
background at all. He was a bomb victim in '16 and did a year
in San Quentin for bootlegging in '29, but otherwise there's
nothing against him."

Then they wondered why Alexis Turbin laughed.

The substance of the letter from Turbin which Tim read
aloud to his wife and Heidi was that he had seen *Mliss* at the
Cinémathèque and admired it, that a new print had been
shown to the public and applauded, and that he and the
executives of MGM would like to discuss with Mr. Siegrist a
projected contemporary film, with Alexis Turbin as director
and Timothy Siegrist as chief cameraman. He hoped Mr.
Siegrist would make it convenient to visit the studio in the
very near future. A railway voucher was enclosed for a
sleeping compartment on the night train to Los Angeles and
a reservation had been provisionally made for him at the
Beverly Hills Hotel. Meanwhile, he might like to know that
Mliss would be shown, beginning Wednesday, at the Griffith
Theatre in San Francisco.

"My God!" was all Tim found to say, and "I can't believe
it!" said Violet in a whisper.

"You've hit the jackpot, father!" said Heidi briskly.
"They're certainly going to give you the red-carpet treatment!"

"Yes but – I made *Mliss* in 1915, long before sound. What
makes them think I could work on a modern story, contemporary as they call it? Turbin's good, but he'll be swamped at
MGM, they'll probably want him to make a musical with Judy
Garland, and where'll I be then –"

"Don't make so many difficulties, sweetie," Heidi said.
"You haven't lost your touch, whatever they want you to do.
And I'm going to call the Griffith tomorrow and find out what
time *Mliss* is showing. All right if I ask Andrew Kirk to join
us?" She thought it would be as good a time as any to
introduce her new friend to her parents, who would be too
busy talking about the movie to pester him with questions
about himself. The relationship with Andrew was so new, so
tenuous that Heidi wanted to impose no strain on it. But
Andrew, invited by telephone, had to decline. He had the late

turn on Wednesday and wouldn't be off the desk until midnight. But he would catch the show on Thursday without fail.

It took some persuasion to get Violet to the Griffith, which was a small art house on Mason, between Post and Geary. She dreaded seeing the movie for more reasons than one. First, there was the contrast between the Letty Randolph of twenty-five years ago and what that girl had become – flabby, grey-haired, with petulant lines etched from nose to mouth. She shied away from the reminders of the past. Would it all be raked up again to breach their hard-won quiet? A preview in the *Chronicle*, praising the Bret Harte Celebration as a whole, commended Miss Letty Randolph as Mliss, and mentioned that Miss Randolph had later married the director, Mr. Siegrist, the couple being now resident in San Francisco. Nothing offensive there! No mention of the Estrada brand! Violet plucked up her courage and went to the eight o'clock showing at the Griffith, sitting between her husband and Heidi.

MGM showed all three movies exactly as they were made, with no added sound-track of words or music. There were no interpolations to the sub-titles nor alterations in the credits, and a tinny piano, with an elderly lady at the keyboard, provided the music for the show. The cinema was well-filled, and *Tennessee's Partner*, in which Broncho Billy played with unexpected pathos, was well received. Its second frame, announcing the director as Willis Jerrold Hastings, made Violet gasp. It was made before her arrival at Niles, and she had forgotten it was a Hastings film. Tim took her hand firmly in his, and they sat thus through the Fairbanks movie until *Mliss* began.

Heidi knew at once what Alexis Turbin had seen in it. The story was old but the theme – the domination of a weak man by a dynamic woman – was popular in the Thirties: Bette Davis was the leading exponent of the part. Letty Randolph was more beautiful than Bette Davis, but undisciplined – her performance owed a good deal to Willie Bleer, as in life she had owed so much to the man who couldn't make her a star. The camera work was as modern as tomorrow and had been carried out by one hand alone. No second unit had been used; the film was obviously signed Tim Siegrist.

There was an intermission after the Bret Harte Celebration,

and under cover of a clamorous demand for popcorn the Siegrists left the Griffith Theatre. "I couldn't sit through the rest of the programme after *Mliss*," said Heidi. "Father, it was wonderful. Mother, you looked perfectly lovely."

"Thank you, darling," said Violet, and Tim said "Let's get a taxi and go straight home. Unless you girls want to go to the Palace or somewhere and celebrate?"

"We'll celebrate when you bring your *new* movie in, Tim," said Violet. "I'm tired. I'd like to go home now." And Heidi said, "I want to go home too, but I'd rather walk. I've been cooped up all day and I need some air."

She thought, as she followed the taxi up Post Street, that they were better off alone. It was a big thing for them, poor pets, a red-letter day, and it looked as if poor father had got his break at last. It was also the day, September sixteenth, when the Selective Training and Service Act came into force, when all men between the ages of twenty-one and thirty-six would have to register for the draft. Another step towards war, a giant step away from Melissa Smith of Red Mountain's pictured loves and hates! But back in the familiar living room in Ellis Street the woman who had played Melissa Smith was in her husband's arms, and saying through tears:

"Do you remember how you said to me, one night at Niles, 'Please believe in me! My movie'll be great box office *and* a star-maker!'"

"I remember," he said, and kissed her.

"You were right, Tim. It *was* a star-maker. Only the star wasn't me. It was you!"

★   ★   ★

Heidi had half expected that young enthusiast, Andrew Kirk, who wanted to be a famous foreign correspondent and an ace photographer at one and the same time, to be bitten with the movie bug after seeing *Mliss*. He hadn't very much to say about the film, however, after they met on Saturday afternoon at what had become 'their' French café, except a few complimentary things about the wonderful camera work and her mother's beauty and dramatic power. Then he went on to his latest enthusiasm, which was for the Navy Day display about to be held on another part of the island, and he dragged Heidi through the crowds to the brave music of a distant drum.

She had forgotten it was Navy Day. There had been so many Days in the two years of the Golden Gate Exposition that the public was all but sated. They had got as far as Apple Day ("scraping the bottom of the barrel," said Heidi) honouring the apple capital of California, Sebastopol, which had grown up not far from the rancho where Felipe Estrada had tried his hand at fruit farming. There had even been Plum Day, with a film called *The Plums of Plenty* shown thrice daily as a counterblast to *The Grapes of Wrath*. The people of San Francisco, in the concluding weeks of The Fair in Forty, were more interested, according to their individual means, in the hot-dog concessions, the dance floors, or the smart restaurants like the Persian Room. There was only a fairly large turn-out for the sailors.

Nor was there much space for naval manoeuvres between the Courts and the Towers and the Arches of Treasure Island. The Navy men drilled, marched and counter-marched while a critical crowd looked on. The civilians were seeing something that scared them – a demonstration of armed power, a token of America's defensive strength.

"They're not liking it much, are they?" asked Heidi, looking up at Andrew Kirk. That he was liking it there was no doubt. He was looking from the marching men to the flag above their heads, and had to drag his attention away to answer her.

"They like it all right, Heidi, but they're scared to show it. The draft has got them all riled up. They hate Hitler, but they don't want to go to war to stop him."

"Do you?"

"I want to join the Navy."

"When?"

"Well, not tonight! But before my draft number comes up, that's for sure."

The blue-clad ranks marched off, and Heidi sighed. "The war in Europe's six thousand miles away."

"Oh, Heidi!" The Navy Day audience had dispersed and the two of them were almost alone, sitting on a stone bench, with pigeons pecking round their feet. "I wish I could explain how I feel, but you can run rings round me in an argument, and anyway patriotism's gone out of fashion. I'd feel a fool sitting here reciting 'My Country, 'tis of thee', and you'd only laugh at me. Here's what I want you to do. I've actually got an assignment at Treasure Island on Friday. I've been marked to report Evelyn Anderson's speech at the Temple of Religion. She's asked for the right of reply to Camellia Otis Grunt, who made a talk there last week on behalf of the Committee for the Defence of America First. I'd like you to come and hear her with me."

"Camellia – oh, the lady novelist, my mother loves her books. I've often wondered why she hasn't changed her name. But Evelyn Anderson – haven't I seen her byline in the *Chronicle*?"

"Sure you have. She's a local girl, and her stuff's syndicated in the *Chronicle*, as well as God knows how many other papers. She's been a war correspondent for the Chicago *Clarion* in every war for the past twenty years."

"I don't know if I want to listen to an old battleaxe talking about war."

"She's not an old battleaxe, she's not much more than forty. If you'll come with me, the meeting's at seven, I'll take you out to dinner after."

"I don't need a bribe to listen to a speech. And won't you have to hang around and interview *her* afterwards?"

"I'm going to do an interview *before* the speech, at her brother's house. That's why she's here, for a rest with her family. She was with the French army up to the surrender, and she had a bad time getting out of France."

"You'll get a byline for this one, won't you?"

"I hope so."

Heidi knew how much the first byline meant to him. She said, "Okay, you've sold me. I'll be there. But now you've got to do something nice for me. Walk me over to the Pan Am landing ramp and let's watch the China Clipper coming in from Manila."

"It's a deal. I'll treat you to a twenty-minute ride over the bay in the Sikorsky amphibian, if we can get places this late."

"Oh, Andrew!"

★   ★   ★

Evelyn Anderson sat on the platform of the Temple of Religion and listened to the chairman, a local clergyman, hacking through his introduction. She had a well-founded conviction that every chairman was every public speaker's natural enemy, who would spoil the pitch if he could, and this one was doing it royally. After a fulsome reference to her late father, 'Mr. John Anderson, the popular president of the Pioneer Merchants' Bank of San Francisco', he had embarked on a résumé of her own career, read off a crumpled sheet of paper, and wrong in most of the details. True, she had been in Anatolia with Kemal Pasha when he defeated the Greeks in 1922, but she had not borne arms at Dumlupinar, or anywhere else. She had been in the Gran Chaco in 1932, but the chairman got the names of the belligerents wrong, and she had been in Shanghai, not Hong Kong, when the Japanese invaded China in 1937. She expected trouble when he reached the Spanish Civil War, and she got it, for the reverend gentleman, who had obviously never heard of the Geneva Convention, mildly rebuked her for 'fighting' with the godless Republicans against the Christian troops of General Franco. He concluded with the oily hope that her 'message' would be one of peace.

Evelyn Anderson, who had won more battle honours and citations than many a field officer, noted as she rose to speak that the Temple of Religion was almost full. That was a tribute to the local celebrity, the banker's daughter, not to the war correspondent who represented danger. It had been standing room only for Camellia Grunt, whose message had been appease, submit, surrender, don't send more American boys to die in foreign wars. The Grunt was a charter member of America First, of which Colonel Charles Lindbergh, once the national hero, was the pro-German figurehead. The Committee's incoherent aims included keeping America out of the war in Europe and continuing to do business with Nazi Germany, and it was Miss Grunt's emotional statement of these aims which had brought Evelyn Anderson, who disliked speaking in public, out of her brother's charming home to Treasure Island.

She began by giving a first hand account of the German *Blitzkrieg* across France and the plight of the refugees, and Heidi Siegrist, sitting beside Andrew Kirk, felt his emotional response to the words 'the fall of France', which never failed to stir him. She also noted that his shorthand was much slower than her own.

He had just time to tell her, as they took their seats, that the interview had gone well, and that *she* was 'merely great'. Heidi admitted that she looked great, and certainly not a battleaxe. Evelyn Anderson at forty-three was tall and slim, and if there was any grey in her ash-blonde hair it was not noticeable. Her head, like her hands, was bare, which seemed to scandalise the conventional matrons in her audience, who normally wore white gloves to second a vote of thanks at the Garden Club. The war correspondent was entirely feminine. She wore a tailored suit of soft black material, with a white silk blouse tied in a bow at the neck. Her stockings were sheer silk, her black pumps had four-inch heels, and her lipstick and nail varnish were a matching shade of red. For her only ornament she wore a diamond crescent brooch in her lapel. When Heidi, looking at the ringless hands, whispered, "She's not married?" Andrew replied "Divorced for years. S-sh!"

Evelyn Anderson was talking about Japan. "In 1936," she said, "Germany, Italy and Japan made a pact against communism, which a few months ago was joined by the Christian General's Spain. That was an ideological pact, a consensus of ideas. What if these partners – and I discount Spain – should before long appear as military allies, sworn to aid each other against the only power which now defies the Axis? How long can Britain, alone, prevail against them? How long will America stand aside from the struggle on which her own life depends?"

There was no applause, but there was silence in the Temple of Religion. Heidi, once the prize debater of Pomodoro High, knew what that silence meant. She's holding them, but only just. She's telling them things they don't want to hear, and she's getting away with it. She's got a lot of guts.

"Ladies and gentlemen," said Evelyn Anderson, "after Italy invaded Abyssinia, and the British imposed sanctions on Italy which did nothing to stop the war, I was in the press gallery of the League of Nations Assembly in Geneva when the Emperor Haile Selassie made his eloquent appeal for military assistance. I shall never forget his words. '*If my tardy allies never come,*' he

574

said, '*the West will perish.*' Those words were true then, they are truer still today. If Britain's tardy allies never come – and we are her only allies now – the *world* will perish."

Within days of that speech, which the America Firsters denounced as warmongering, Germany, Italy and Japan concluded a three-Power pact at Berlin, pledging total aid to each other for a period of ten years, and San Franciscans were left wondering on what a vista the Golden Gate might open. Forty-eight hours later the lights went out and the doors closed for ever on The Fair in Forty, the last fiesta before the darkness fell. Soon demolition of the gaudy buildings was begun, and quickly ended, for after all they were only made of wood covered with paint and stucco. The fantasy city was destroyed, and San Francisco exchanged its sunset dream for grim reality. Treasure Island was taken over by the Navy.

7

Evelyn Anderson left no message of peace with her Treasure Island audience. But she made a deep impression on Heidi Siegrist. After Andrew had telephoned in his story to the *Clarion* they went to dinner, and while Heidi listened to the boy's ravings about the brilliant, marvellous woman she felt such acute jealousy that she had to question her own feelings for the young reporter. Why should I care what he thinks of her? He doesn't mean anything to me. Just a nice kid, fun to be with when he's not steamed up about liberty-equality-fraternity, and anyway she's old enough to be his mother.

. . . She may be the kind of woman he admires. Tall and blonde, and rich enough to afford those marvellous clothes, not like my shirt-waisters from the Emporium. So I can't compete, and who cares?

. . . Funny how she looked like father right at the end. When she bowed to the people with that little twisted smile that meant she knew she hadn't really got across to them. That's the way he smiles when mother nags him and he has to hide his feelings. But things are going to go right for my father from now on in.

Tim returned jubilant from Hollywood. He had got the job with MGM to shoot Turbin's new movie, to which the Russian had given the working title of *Resistance*. It was a new word in October 1940, as applied to a France still in chaos since the surrender, but out of his own experiences Turbin had devised a very simple story. A young Frenchman of the middle class, a survivor of the fighting in Norway, goes to work as a *passeur*, taking stray British Tommies out of the Occupied Zone and across the mountains into Spain. He is helped by a young American girl whom he meets in the confusion of Bordeaux. Turbin's own *ciné vérité* shots would be cut in as film fax with newsreel clips of the German advance.

MGM wanted a happy ending. Instead the girl dies, killed by a Spanish sentry's bullets in the forests of the Pyrenees. Tim filmed that sequence in the Santa Cruz mountains, investing the last scene between the girl and her lover with all the tragic significance of the woodland scenes in *Mliss*, which was exactly what Turbin wanted. The two men worked in the perfect harmony a director and a cameraman can only achieve when they are right for each other, also they worked fast. His early training with Sennett and Essanay had given Tim a speed he never lost, and Turbin was fast too, because he knew he had to prove himself to MGM in their own idiom. His foreign reputation was high, but let him flop once in America and he'd be out on the dust-heap. Besides, his story had to be filmed while it was still hot. Within six months the war movies would be pouring out, and the world would be sick of French squabbles: the sad end of 1940 was the moment for a simple tale of love and sacrifice.

Resistance was made in a month, and that month Violet spent with her husband at the Hollywood Hotel. She worried about leaving Heidi alone in Ellis Street, to which the girl replied "I'm an Ellis Street brat, and I'll be twenty-one in January!" She saw by the beaming faces of her parents as they hung out of the window of the train leaving the SB terminal at Townsend and Third that they were not really anxious about her. Their own future was beckoning again.

While they were gone America was convulsed by a presidential election, and Mr. Roosevelt made history by getting himself elected for a third term. Andrew's paper, the *Clarion*, always beaten in the circulation war by the Hearst giants, gave some quavering support to Wendell Willkie, the Republican candidate, and at the last minute slid off the fence on the winning side. Andrew was very busy. His interview with Evelyn Anderson had pleased the editor, especially when her prediction of an Axis alliance with Japan came true, and he was marked for so many election meetings that he had no time to badger Heidi about working for a Nazi firm.

The warehouse of Thomas Lang and Son smelled of spices, not of Hitlerism, and even Andrew had to admit that the presence of 'Son' – Mr. Henry to the staff – in the Tokyo office was not necessarily a pointer to Fascist intrigue. The German Consul-General paid no more calls in Drumm Street, but Heidi had not lost interest in Herr Fritz Wiedemann. The inadequate library of the *Clarion* yielded up only a few innocuous facts about him. He had taken up his post in San Francisco in March 1939, and lived with his wife and daughter down the Peninsula in a big house on Floribunda Drive in Hillsborough. He drove his Mercedes to and from the city daily, enjoyed giving and attending parties, and from the outbreak of war in Europe had had to push his way through daily pickets outside his office door. One out-of-town clipping in the library said he had been 'a wartime comrade of the German Führer'.

Wiedemann had been a good deal more than that. As a young army captain in the First World War he had been Corporal Hitler's company commander, and in a reversal of fortune years later he became the Führer's aide-de-camp. In 1938 he was employed on a secret mission to Lord Halifax, the British Foreign Secretary, to assure him of Hitler's goodwill and suggest a peaceful solution of the Sudeten question. It was a fruitless errand, because the Sudeten, or Czech, question was solved by Chamberlain's act of appeasement at Munich, and it earned Wiedemann the dislike of Ribbentrop, the German Ambassador to Britain: the posting to San Francisco meant that Hitler's ADC had been kicked upstairs. What further secret diplomacy he had in mind he hid under a playboy image, which did not sit well on a big, burly man of fifty, known in Hitler's entourage as a stolid regimental type.

"Young lady wanted, 20–25, good shorthand and typing skills, to act as assistant to personal secretary to the German Consul-General. Knowledge of German essential. Apply in writing to Frau Hilde Hess, 26 O'Farrell Street."

Heidi could hardly believe her luck. She wrote her application, enclosed her brief curriculum vitae, and gave Thomas Lang and Son, wholesale grocers, as her reference. Two days later she was summoned to an interview, not with Frau Hess, but with Mr. Thomas Lang himself, who said he was surprised to learn that she wanted to leave them.

"I thought you were happy with us, Miss Siegrist," he said.

"I've been very happy here, Mr. Lang, but I want to get a different kind of experience."

"You young people are all so restless. Tired of wholesale groceries, are you?"

"Not exactly, but –"

"You think working at a Consulate-General will be more glamorous, eh? You ought to know what you're letting yourself in for if you're hired – and Mr. Wiedemann will certainly hire you on my recommendation. Frau Hess is the lady you'll be working for, and she's a slave-driver. You'll get her job if she's promoted to Washington, but that's by no means certain. You'll have to work longer hours for less pay than you get here – and talking of pay, would a raise help to make you change your mind?"

Heidi thanked him for his generosity and said No. A few days after that she took the cable car up California from Drumm and walked over to O'Farrell, where the German Consulate was on the ninth floor of a building almost at the triangle where O'Farrell Street met Grant Avenue and Market, one block from Lotta's Fountain, where the *Clarion* office faced the bastion of the Hearst empire. It was a gloomy suite of rooms with four windows on O'Farrell Street and six on a side alley; Frau Hilde Hess (Frau by courtesy, since she was a spinster) had a small office next door to Herr Wiedemann's large, imposing room. She greeted Heidi with the Nazi salute and the words "Heil Hitler!"

Heidi took dictation in German, typed the result, and in

German answered the woman's questions on her schooling and previous experience.

"Quite satisfactory," was the grudging compliment. "Herr Lang writes warmly of your work for him. How long a warning must you give his firm?"

Heidi said respectfully that she must give a fortnight's notice.

"So! I am overwhelmed with work, but if it must be thus, we shall expect you here two weeks from Monday."

Heidi was curtly dismissed. She took the lift to the ground floor, found a public telephone and told Andrew Kirk her news.

"For heaven's sake, Heidi, are you crackers? First a Nazi grocer, then the Nazi consul: why?"

"That's why," said Heidi. "I wasn't sure about the grocer – no proof; I *am* sure about the consul. Like you once said, he's Hitler's man, and if he's up to any mischief *I'll find out.* See you later." She hung up well satisfied. Maybe she wasn't a famous war correspondent in a black suit and a diamond crescent, but she had got herself inside the lion's den as neatly as any mouse, and she wouldn't bite through the lion's net, she would bind it around him.

She had been in her new job for a week when Violet and Tim came back in triumph to San Francisco. They had stayed on in Hollywood until the sneak previews of *Resistance* proved that it was a hit, perhaps even a smash hit, not to be confined to the art houses but distributed to the big box-office theatres across the nation. The timing of its release had been perfect, and movie fans had taken two unknown young actors to their hearts. MGM had wanted Charles Boyer for the Frenchman and Jean Arthur as the spirited American girl, but "they're both too old" said Turbin, and the parts went to "a couple of kids", just as Willie Bleer and Letty Randolph had been kids in *Mliss*. Turbin and Siegrist were now under contract to MGM for another movie, and were already blocking out a vehicle for Wayne Blackwood.

All this good news came to Heidi by telephone. Sometimes it was her father, speaking from the studio, and assuring her that *Resistance* wasn't a one-off, that he wasn't being taken for a ride, and that a man knew how to handle himself when he was a hit at fifty. Sometimes it was her mother babbling from their Hollywood Hotel room about the new house they were going to have . . . she was looking at houses every day and Heidi must come on down and help her. She had to tell them, when they came back to Ellis Street to collect their daughter and their furniture, that she wasn't going with them. She had a job at the German Consulate and a rented flat on Fillmore Street, and "don't *cry*, mommy!" the time had come when she wanted to be on her own.

"You're too young to be on your own," wept Violet.

"I'm the same age you were when you married daddy."

"That was different! That was marriage! Heidi, you haven't got mixed up with some boy? That Andrew Kirk you talked about?"

"Don't *worry*, mother!" It was not long before the Ellis Street flat, the home of so many years, was broken up. A few pieces of furniture were shipped to the ranch-style house in Westwood Village which the Siegrists were buying, and the battered old pots and pans went to the studio apartment on the top floor of a two-storey building in that lively stretch of Fillmore Street between Clay and Sacramento. Heidi was on her own at last.

"I don't seem able to get away from the movies," she told Andrew Kirk when they met at Lotta's Fountain in the foggy winter evenings when toyon berries had taken the place of roses on the flower stand. Frau Hess might have been over-whelmed with work, and she alone was permitted to answer the consul's bell, but the letters dictated to Heidi were of the most banal nature. Fraternal greetings to Consul Baron Edgar von Spiegel in New Orleans and Consul Dr. Herbert Scholz of Boston covered enquiries about the whereabouts of this or that German immigrant to the United States or the problems of certain 'tourists' whose visitors' visas had expired. There was nothing the most determined spy-hunter could find suspicious, and the movie letters, as Heidi called them, were as open as the day.

Alexander Korda was making a movie called *That Hamilton Woman* (*Lady Hamilton* in England) with Laurence Olivier as Nelson and Vivien Leigh as Nelson's mistress. It was charged with sex on one level, supercharged with British patriotism on another, while as glorifying the British victories over Napoleon it enraged Senator Gerald Nye of the America First Committee. The Committee had already attacked the movie industry for producing pro-British films, and the delighted German Ambassador to Washington supported the attack, declaring that the industry was infiltrated by Jewish money and British agents. The Consul-General in Los Angeles, in whose territory Hollywood was included, backed up his ambassador. Captain Wiedemann backed *him* up, and while Senator Nye requested the Senate Committee on Foreign Relations to examine the influence of British agents on the movies, the whole band of German officials and America Firsters turned their guns on *That Hamilton Woman*. The love of Admiral Nelson and Lady Hamilton was irrelevant. The real cause of the pro-German fury was speeches like "You cannot make peace with dictators, you have to destroy them," lines said to have been written into the script by the arch-fiend Churchill himself.

The letters and the accusations flew backwards and forwards from coast to coast, and Heidi typed industriously, wondering when her country would go to war with Germany. Wiedemann, whom she very seldom saw, came into the secretaries' office once or twice while she was typing his 'Hamilton' letters, and picked up the sheets from the wing of her desk to read them over. She always stood up respectfully, like a good Hitler *Mädchen*, and spoke only when she was spoken to.

The consul was a ladies' man, and not above a mild flirtation with the young American secretary, although the fish-like eye of Frau Hess was a check on enterprise. He had already a standing joke with Heidi about her name, which of course appeared on her working papers as Adelheid Basler Siegrist. "A good German name," he told her, and when she said stiffly that her father's ancestors came from Switzerland with Captain Sutter, he retorted, "Sutter's parentage was Swiss, but he was born at Baden in Germany. Perhaps your ancestors were born there too, Fräulein Adelheid!" It was best to acquiesce and laugh, and resign herself to being Fräulein Adelheid – even Frau Hess took up the name as a mark of favour.

To Heidi, Wiedemann, seen on those rare occasions,

seemed like a fish out of water. He was so entirely the regimental officer, of a type more common in the Kaiser's day than Hitler's, with his short burly figure, his dark hair cut very short and his military bearing. He was always going off to lunch at the St. Francis, or to cocktails at the Top of the Mark, and he always looked as if instead he should be putting in an appearance at the sergeants' smoking concert. He was the enemy, but he seemed to be a sensible man: it could only have been the streak of mania in the German temperament which made him behave as foolishly as he did on the eighteenth of January, 1941.

It was a Saturday, and such was the pressure of business among the resident or visiting German nationals that the Consulate was open all day on Saturdays. Heidi, who now travelled from Fillmore Street on the downtown bus, saw an unusually large crowd round the door of 26 O'Farrell Street, as if the pickets had been doubled and had broken their usual defiant silence to push and shout at everybody passing into the building. From the opposite side of the street she saw why. From each of the four windows of the consulate which looked out on O'Farrell Street, as from the six on the side alley, a swastika banner was hanging limply in the winter air.

Dreading to hear of a German victory in Britain, where the Luftwaffe raids on London had lasted for over ninety days, she pushed her way through the pickets, not without being pushed and pulled herself. On the ninth floor the secretaries' room was empty, though she could hear Frau Hess talking to the Consul in his room next door, and there was a good deal of angry shouting coming from the main office. Before she could take the cover off her typewriter the telephone rang. It was a call from an angry man in the business offices immediately below.

"I want to speak to Wiedemann!" said the voice passionately. "He's got no right to block the entrance to this building!"

"I'm afraid the Consul-General is engaged at present," said Heidi. "This is a member of the staff speaking. Shall I ask Mr. Wiedemann to call you back?"

"Just you tell him to read his lease, miss! Remind him tenants are not allowed to hang out flags or bunting – or balloons – or dirty linen – on the O'Farrell street side of this building! Tell him to get the swastika down and clear the pickets away, or else I'll send for the police!"

The telephone was laid down with a bang. Heidi glanced out of the window. The pickets immediately below had spread over the pavement, and on the opposite side of the street another staring crowd was gathering. She heard a man shout, "Pull down the swastika!"

Frau Hess ran into the room, and with a nod to Heidi began rummaging in a filing cabinet.

"Frau Hess, the people downstairs are complaining –"

"Yes, I know, I know, they all are," said the woman. "My God, where did I put our copy of the lease?"

"Isn't that it in your hand?"

"My head is spinning –" Frau Hess turned the stiff pages of a legal document. "Yes, here it is. Flags and bunting may only be hung from the windows of the above designated premises overlooking the side alley – I *told* the Consul-General so!" She was at the door on her way out when Heidi stopped her. "Please, Frau Hess," she begged, "tell me what it's all about. Why are we flying the Nazi flag from every window in this office? Has Germany declared war on the United States?"

"Heaven forbid!" cried Frau Hess. "No, Fräulein Adelheid, it is a celebration. Mr. Wiedemann decided the flags should be flown in commemoration of the foundation of the German Empire. That took place on the eighteenth of January, seventy years ago today. Now don't detain me, please."

"But the German Empire collapsed in 1918!" Heidi was speaking to an empty room. "And after the German Empire came the Weimar Republic, and now it's the Third Reich, Hitler's thousand-year-Reich, and the swastika banner has nothing to do with the old Empire!" She looked out again. The crowd had bellied out into the middle of the street, and a mounted policeman was trying to clear a way for motor traffic.

"Pull down the swastika! Pull – down – the – swastika!" The slogan had caught on, a man with a bull-horn was directing the crowd.

"They're going to storm the consulate!" Frau Hess was back again, wringing her hands. She had left the door open, and they could see Wiedemann, shouldering aside a protesting knot of men. Tenants from several of the lower floors had gathered on the landing, and were hammering on the locked door of the consulate.

PULL DOWN THE SWASTIKA!

"We're not in any danger, Frau Hess," Heidi soothed her. "But it mightn't be a bad idea to take in those flags."

"That would betray the honour of Germany," said Frau Hess. "I, for one, am prepared to give my life-blood for my Führer! Look out, Fräulein Adelheid. Tell me if there are more of those Bolsheviks outside the building?"

"About a thousand, at a rough guess," said Heidi. "But a whole lot of cops have turned up too, so we may see some fun."

San Francisco's Finest, however, had their orders. They cordoned off the area, and then stood back in formation, doing nothing to stop the shouts of "Pull Down the Swastika". The Chief of Police was on the telephone, telling Herr Wiedemann that he could not plead diplomatic immunity for a flagrant breach of the terms of his lease, while the company which managed the building was on another line, saying the same thing. The crowd increased steadily while inside the consulate there was a flurry of telephoning. The Consul-General in Los Angeles advocated hauling down the flags, while Wiedemann swore he would never give in to the rabble of paid agitators in O'Farrell Street. The Chief of the city fire brigade called up to say he would send a hook-and-ladder squad up to the ninth floor of 26 O'Farrell Street if those goddamned flags weren't down in half an hour. Finally the German Ambassador in Washington found a solution. "It's Saturday," he said. "Declare a half-holiday, close the office at one o'clock, and withdraw the flags with the proper honours before you draw the blinds. Then leave the building by the service exit, else you may have a street brawl on your hands. You will hear more of this, Mr. Consul-General."

Heidi longed to know what the proper honours might be. Would they sound a bugle, beat a drum, or sing the Horst Wessel Song? The cheers from the triumphant crowd were demonstration enough. The consular staff was dressed and ready for the street before the clock struck one, and Heidi, with a mocking "*Auf Wiedersehen!*" made for the elevator. "I've got a date, Frau Hess," she explained. "I've got to get straight out to O'Farrell."

There was a row of policemen with their substantial backs braced against the street door, and Heidi was asking to be let through when she was plucked from their midst by the hand of Andrew Kirk. He was so thankful to see her that he gave her a hearty shaking before pulling her away from the building which housed the German consulate, and hurrying her round the corner into Stockton Street. "What's been going on?" he said. "Are you all right?"

She told him quickly what had happened, and he groaned. "That's what the sergeant told me," he said. "I couldn't believe it. *Flaunting* the swastika – no wonder they were yelling to pull it down. And wouldn't you know it would happen on a Saturday, just at the right time for the Hearst early editions? We won't get a word into the *Clarion* till Monday morning, when the story's as dead as mutton!"

"That's the right way to look at it," approved Heidi. "You might write a think-piece on the foundation of the German Empire, January eighteenth, eighteen seventy-one."

"The guy must be mad."

"That's what I think, but at least he's tipped his hand to San Francisco. Showing the swastika was a typical piece of German arrogance, and he didn't get away with it."

"And you've got a half-holiday, so we can have a decent lunch. Where would you like to go?"

"Have you got the car?"

"It's parked a couple of blocks away."

"Then could we go out to Ocean Beach?"

"Anywhere you like." He thought it would be cold and foggy at the beach, but comfortable inside the Cliff House, which had been renovated not too long before. When they got there the sun was shining cold and pale on the ocean, in one of the freak changes in San Francisco weather, and after he parked the Buick convertible alongside the few other cars which had come out from the city on this January day, Heidi wanted to walk along the sands before they went inside the restaurant. "I need some fresh air," she said, "that place reeked of fear."

"But you weren't afraid?"

"What was there to be afraid of? I was safe in my native city."

"That's what they thought in London, before the *Blitz*."

Heidi looked around her. It was the very scene Laura Winter saw when she watched Lotta Crabtree riding with the girl from the Long Tom melodeon. Behind her was not the same Cliff House where Rico and Maria Gregorio ate their wedding breakfast, for two restaurants of that name had been destroyed by fire, but the sea-lions were barking on the Seal Rocks and the seagulls raising their eternal clamour. On the broad sweep of land above the sands, where El Camino Real ran, the roller-coasters, gondola swings and fun fair attractions of Playland-at-the-Beach were dismantled and covered up against the winter weather. The signs forbidding bathing because of the undertow had been taken down and laid beside the flights of stairs which at regular intervals ran down from the upper level to the ocean. Andrew Kirk had no idea what made Heidi cry without warning "Race you to the next steps!" and start running over the hard grey sand.

Was it a challenge to the male, or the sheer vitality of a young animal escaping from a trap? Andrew let her run for twenty yards while he stood still, the chemistry of his body changing as he watched the little figure racing across the beach. He had been strongly attracted to Heidi Siegrist when they first met on Treasure Island, but the attraction had remained static, held at the level of their Saturday dates, and Heidi's instinct had been sound when she felt jealousy of his admiration for Evelyn Anderson. There was nothing physical in that candidly expressed admiration, but Evelyn the mature woman was the same type as the girls Andrew had enjoyed taking out when he was at Stanford and taking to bed in Paris. His taste ran to tall athletic blondes, stereotypes of the Californian tennis champions – the kind of girls his grandfather's generation had called 'long-stemmed American beauties', the very opposite of the bossy, opinionated minx now much too near her goal. He started to run in long loping strides, overtook Heidi within a yard of the steps, seized her in his arms and covered her face with kisses.

Her winter coat was an unusual shade of orange-tawny wool, which by some trick of refracted sunshine gave a glow to her pale face and light-brown hair. He pulled off her matching cap and dragged her hair into his left hand, forcing her to arch back against his taut body, and cursed her for her bravado.

"So brave little Heidi wasn't scared, eh?" he said furiously. "How about me? I don't mind telling you I was scared stiff. What if those trigger-happy Germans had loosed off a few rounds while all that racket was going on? One wild shot and you might've been killed. Darling, darling Heidi, don't you realise that? Promise me you won't go back on Monday –"

"Not a chance."

"What are you trying to prove, taking wages from the Nazis? You ought to chuck the rotten job now –"

"Never, until we declare war on Germany or Wiedemann's kicked out of San Francisco. Whichever comes first."

*   *   *

By Monday morning, when the anxious German staff had to run the gauntlet of a picket of ordinary proportions, Herr Wiedemann, in public, was taking a debonair view of what he called *der Flaggenzwischenfall* – the flags incident. He said his demonstration of loyalty to a German ideal had been misunderstood by American hooligans who had never heard of the Franco-Prussian War and its imperial outcome. Unspecified 'authorities' had apologised for the harassment, and on behalf of the *Deutsches Reich* he had been equally courteous: the matter was closed. In private he said some personnel changes might be made, and that the consulate would have to move to a better part of town than the Market Street area, where a hostile crowd could collect at a moment's notice.

Some of the more intelligent press and radio commentators said it was not nostalgia for the triumphs of 1871 which lay behind the flaunting of the swastika, but defiance of the Lend-Lease Bill which President Roosevelt had announced in one of his radio 'fireside chats' just before the end of the year. When it became law it would give the President power to provide defence articles to any country whose defence was vital to the defence of the United States. This, translated, meant arms, ammunition and shipyard facilities to Britain, the only country in Europe besides Switzerland still capable of defending itself.

The first staff change concerned Frau Hess, who returned from a brief interview with Herr Wiedemann to tell Heidi that she had been posted to the German Embassy in Washington.

"It's what you wanted, isn't it, Frau Hess?" Heidi ventured. The woman's long, dismal face looked drearier than ever.

"Yes indeed, and after that terrible experience on Saturday I'll be thankful to leave San Francisco. Only I could wish that Dr. Walter –" she broke off.

"Who's Dr. Walter?" asked Heidi. "The new secretary?"

"Certainly not, Dr. Walter is a lawyer. He has come to give the Consul-General the benefit of his legal advice."

Nothing was seen of Dr. Walter in the secretaries' room, and the Consul-General appeared there only once on Monday, when he looked in to say kindly *"Wie geht's*, Fräulein Adelheid? None the worse of that nasty experience on Saturday?"

"Not at all, sir."

Frau Hess gathered up her personal belongings on Friday morning, when she caught the noon train to Washington, and on Friday afternoon Heidi was summoned to Herr Wiedemann's office, where a tall man with a lean dark face was lounging near his desk.

"This is Dr. Anton Walter, Fräulein Adelheid," said Wiedemann. "He wants you to type a legal memorandum for him. You may sit down and take his dictation."

Dr. Walter's dictation was very fast and highly technical. It dealt with the double conveyancing of an unspecified property to an anonymous purchaser, with details in Spanish varas and German metres of the external and internal measurements of the property. Heidi's pencil flew over the symbols and she typed at top speed, for she believed this was some sort of test. There were no comments on her work, but on Monday morning Wiedemann offered her the position as his secretary, with an increase in salary, "though it's only temporary, you understand," he said, "the post should go to an experienced consular officer like Frau Hess. But it will be helpful to have an American young lady, how do you say, 'on the job' while we have so much real-estate business to transact. I want the move away from O'Farrell Street to be as fast and smooth as possible."

"I'll try to give you satisfaction, sir," said Heidi, and Dr. Anton Walter, in his old lounging position by the big desk, smiled a saturnine smile.

For some weeks Heidi's work consisted in corresponding with the leading real-estate agents of San Francisco, going herself to inspect the houses on their lists which were thought suitable, and translating into German the preliminary correspondence and her own reports on the available mansions. A mansion was needed. There were to be no more arguments over the common rights of other tenants, or the use of the elevator, or with sulky American janitors. The German Consulate-General was now to be a self-contained establishment, with a German couple in the basement to act as caretakers, and the only Americans, apart from Fräulein Adelheid, would be the staff of a cleaning contractor, coming in from five to eight o'clock every weekday morning.

"So you're the only American citizen on the executive staff!" said Andrew to Heidi. "You'll be there to take the rap when anything goes wrong!"

Nothing went wrong with the purchase of a very grand house, almost too grand for the purpose, in what the agents called the 'exclusive' residential district of Pacific Heights. It was at 2090 Jackson, built on a corner lot over the period 1894 to 1896 by one of the commercial pioneers who in the 1850s had followed the Argonauts of the Gold Rush. Mr. Whittier had made a fortune in wholesale paints and oils, and had spent lavishly on a house which having survived the earthquake and fire of 1906 was regarded as historical by the San Franciscans.

Jackson Street, at the corner of Laguna, commanded from its rear windows a magnificent view of the bay and the Contra Costa. The houses had delightful front gardens, and there were pleasant little parks in the vicinity, but as far as the neighbours were concerned the Germans might as well have stayed on O'Farrell Street. As soon as the Whittier mansion was conveyed by Whittier's daughter through two nominees to *Das Deutsches Reich* on April 29 the angry protests began. The district was restricted to non-commercial buildings, it was declared. Wiedemann, who representing the Reich had paid $44,000 for the mansion, pointed out that the Soviet Consulate had been in the same neighbourhood since 1934. He might have added that the Swedish Consulate was lodged in a small palace only a few blocks away. But neither the Soviets nor the Swedes had outraged public opinion by flaunting the swastika which, even in a resolutely neutral country, was now a hated symbol.

The Jackson Street house was not one of the many viewed and described by Heidi Siegrist and afterwards vetted by Dr. Anton Walter, presumably from the legal point of view. Her first sight of it was a surprise and a mystery. If a suite on the ninth floor of a downtown office building had been considered adequate for the German Consul-General, what increased volume of business did they expect to fill the thirty rooms of 2090 Jackson? It was a family residence, requiring a retinue of servants to maintain it, and quite unsuitable for office space. Heidi had a good look through it on removal day, when the place was full of men carrying the files and furniture from O'Farrell Street up the main staircase to the right of the vast entrance hall. She had her own inventory, dictated by Dr. Walter, without which she could never have named the precious woods and stones in each room. The Mexican mahogany and Florentine mosaic in the living room, the smoking room behind it in oriental style, the *rose carnagione* marble mantel in the communicating dining room, all suggested a background for lavish entertaining rather than consular routine. Even the reception room just inside the front door, where persons requiring help and advice were expected to wait, was octagonal and finished with gold-spangled *vernis martin* and looked like a lady's boudoir.

It was possible that Herr Wiedemann, that eager party-goer, had intended the heavily handsome rooms (furnished as they had been in Mr. Whittier's time) to be the scene of reciprocal entertaining, including consular receptions. But Heidi was never asked to send out invitations, and there seemed to be no private visitors, although once or twice in the late afternoons when her day's work was done she heard the hum of male and female voices from the smoking room, which was like a Victorian 'cosy corner' with red Turkish lamps round the walls. There were one or two luncheon parties in the dining room, catered by a restaurant, when the guests exclaimed at the superb view. The ground dropped sharply beneath the house under the dining-room windows, which faced north, and on the slope there was a patch of dried-up grass and plants, not well looked after by the caretaker. He and his wife, and the cleaners, came and went by a gate in the garden wall.

Since the swastika incident, fewer and fewer invitations arrived for the luncheon and cocktail parties Wiedemann enjoyed. He spent most of his day in the two-room office suite upstairs, sometimes with the vice-consul in attendance, more often with Dr. Walter, who had found a small apartment not far away on Sacramento Street. Nobody except the caretakers slept in the consulate. And yet Heidi had the impression that the huge house was full of people. The main staircase leading to the next floor was ostentatiously roped off, because the rooms above were not in use, but there was a rear staircase on which at quiet moments cautious footsteps could be heard, and there was a service elevator from the basement to the attic which sometimes gave a betraying creak. A door in the entrance hall led to the basement, but it was locked on the inside, as Heidi discovered when Wiedemann told her to take half a dozen box cartons 'all the way downstairs'. She was shaking the door when her wrist was seized by Dr. Walter, who had come up behind her on rubber soles.

"Where do you think you're going, Fräulein Adelheid?"

She told him what the Consul-General had said, and his grasp relaxed.

"Herr Wiedemann meant you to use these cupboards," he said, pointing to a recess beneath the stairs. "You really must familiarise yourself with the new system, young lady."

"I'll do my best, Herr Doktor."

"Mind you do."

He walked close behind her up the broad shallow staircase and went into Wiedemann's room. The door communicating with her own small office was not quite closed, and she could hear Dr. Walter say,

"Do you allow that girl complete access to the files?"

"Only the back files, Anton. The new stuff is under lock and key."

Dr. Walter lowered his voice, and the only words Heidi could distinguish were *die Stute*, 'the mare'. Probably a sarcastic reference to her attack on the locked basement door. Mare indeed! Heidi returned to her typing. There was nothing to alarm her in that brief exchange. But as the afternoon wore on she became more and more unnerved by the creak of the hidden lift and the stealthy tread of footsteps on the hidden stair. There were more people in the house than the consular staff, and why? She decided to confide her fears to Andrew Kirk.

One of the advantages of the move to Jackson Street was that Heidi could now walk to and from the Consulate-General. At half past five she set off down Jackson Street to Fillmore and by a quarter to six was opening her own front door, painted a peeling terracotta. Inside, up a steep stair, a second door with a Yale lock led into the studio, with the landlord's furnishings in Early Salvation Army, and cheerful red and white striped curtains.

As soon as she took off her hat and coat she called the *Clarion* office.

"Andrew, what time shall you be free tonight?"

"About nine with any luck. I'm marked for the Planning Commission meeting at seven, and you know how long-winded they can be."

"Yes. Could you stop by the flat on your way home?"

"You bet! Are you throwing a party, by any chance?"

"No party, just you and me. I've got a problem, Andrew. I'd like to discuss it with you."

"Be right there."

Throwing a party! Andrew had only been invited to the studio twice, each time for a party with other guests with whom there had been more arguments than harmony. Perhaps it was a mistake to invite Heidi's high-school friend, Nettie Holz, to the housewarming party in January. A Stanford classmate of Andrew's had questioned her sharply about her father's membership of the German-American Bund. Nettie retorted angrily, and everybody's temper frayed. In April Heidi had invited seven guests, not including Nettie, to partake of white wine and cold platters of sea food, unfortunately on the day when, Lend-Lease now being law, the

United States seized all Axis shipping in American ports. This caused another row, started by an older *Clarion* reporter who turned out to be a supporter of America First. Heidi was dismayed, but much more accomplished hostesses were having the same experience with awkward guests in Nob Hill dining rooms and famous restaurants. San Francisco had paraded its courage in the aftermath of the Depression; it lost its good humour under the advancing shadow of war.

Andrew had never been alone with Heidi in the little studio flat, which was not much more than a bedsitting room with the additions of a tiny bathroom with a shower fitting and an equally tiny kitchen. There was a sofa which after strenuous dragging open turned into a single bed at night, and there were two chairs with arms and one without – some of the guests at the unsuccessful parties had to sit on cushions on the floor. There were new photographs of Tim and Violet on a shelf above the electric fire, some books, a portable typewriter, and inside a locked cupboard some of Tim's leftover camera equipment. It was not a décor which incited to passion, and yet Heidi felt that alone with Andrew, yielding to his embrace, she might experience that onslaught of passion felt for the first time on the sands at Ocean Beach. She knew she was on the verge of falling in love, and unlike the Estrada girls who had gone before her Heidi rebelled at the idea of throwing herself headlong into a man's arms. Her telephone call to him that evening had not been an invitation to lovemaking, but an SOS.

She took a shower, put on a fresh silk art dress, blue with a pattern of black leaves and a tightly swathed waist, and sat down by the open window to eat a sandwich by way of supper. After a lifetime in the Tenderloin, in the ground-floor room with spikes on the outer windowsill, it was still a pleasure to be living on this particular block of Fillmore, one flight of stairs above the passersby, and able to watch the goings-on in the little restaurants, Italian, Chinese, Jap, and hear people moving about in the bookstore above which she lived. There was a neighbourhood cinema, showing Ray Milland and Claudette Colbert in *Arise my Love*, of which, Tim had told her, Paramount had made two versions, one pro-British, one, in the dialogue at least, inoffensive to . . .

other belligerents. Typical! The street population of Fillmore between Sacramento and Clay was beginning to thin out, the May twilight to fall. Heidi switched on her little radio set. The sinking of an American freighter by a German U-boat was announced, presumably in the Atlantic: no details would be given until the next of kin had been informed. Those U-boats were everywhere. The Vichy naval commander at Martinique, Admiral Robert, had a gentleman's agreement with FDR to help keep a look-out in the Caribbean for German submarines. That wouldn't do much good in the Pacific, where the U-boats could be passing the Golden Gate even now, like the rumrunners of her father's adventurous days. Heidi was beginning to shake with cold and nerves. She closed the window and moved restlessly up and down the little room.

It was nearer eleven than ten when Andrew's Buick drew up at the narrow door beside the bookstore. He hadn't taken time out for a drink in a Market Street bar, and was tempted to stop at the liquor store on the corner of Sacramento, which kept late hours, and buy a bottle of whisky. He doubted if Heidi would have any liquor in her kitchen, but somehow he couldn't turn up at her funny little place like a guy visiting some floozy with free booze in his pocket. He rang the bell, and kissed her as soon as she opened the front door.

"I'm sorry to be so late," he said as he followed her into the studio. "All hell was let loose in the office after the story broke. I nearly called you to check, but the city editor reached Wiedemann at home, and after we got his denial there was no need to bother you. It was good timing, too: we hit the first edition without having to replate."

"What are you talking about?" said Heidi.

"The telescope story, of course, what else?"

"Wait a minute. I've got some Scotch, do you want soda or plain water?"

"Water and a lot of ice, please. Gee, I'm thirsty!"

When the drink was in his hand she said, "Begin again. What telescope story?"

"You really don't know? I thought it might be the problem you wanted to discuss. Okay, I'll tell you. Soon as the Planning Commission meeting started, one of the commissioners upped and said he lived near the German Consulate-

General on Jackson Street. He charged your Herr Wiedemann with having installed a six-inch telescope 'to keep an eye on everything that goes on in the Golden Gate. It is so powerful that the gun batteries at Fort Baker appear to be just across the street.' That's a direct quote, Heidi, and when we read it aloud to Wiedemann, down in Hillsborough, he said it was a piece of nonsense. Then the commissioner said he was lying, and they had to adjourn the meeting. It's a swell front-page story, you know everybody's spy-crazy, and I get the by-line!"

"Fort Baker's on the Marin side of the bridge," said Heidi. "It must be *some* telescope."

"Have you ever seen it?"

"Me? I don't even get to go down to the basement." She told Andrew about the incident with Dr. Walter at the basement door, and the snatch of conversation she overheard.

Andrew took his second gulp of Scotch. "Sounds as if Walter was the Gestapo man in that outfit, and Wiedemann just the stooge. Is that what was worrying you, darling?"

She told him she was sure that there were others in the consulate besides the regular staff. "There's a whole bedroom floor above the offices, and attics above that, and the description of the house says there's a huge room in the basement which the Whittiers used for supper parties and dancing. Wiedemann could have fifty men hidden in the Consulate without anybody knowing!"

"Pretty difficult to keep fifty men hidden in Jackson Street for any length of time. Besides, what's he going to do with them? Charge City Hall at the head of his private army? Overthrow the government of the United States? It doesn't make sense to me –"

"As much sense as this crazy story about a telescope."

"Heidi, you're letting your nerves get the better of you. Why didn't you fix yourself a drink? Here, have a sip of mine." Andrew knelt down beside her chair and held the glass to her lips. "Look, the swastika and the telescope and the mysterious creaking elevator are beginning to get you down. I do ask you again to chuck the whole thing. Give the bastards a week's notice before a real big row blows up."

"I want to be there when it does," she said obstinately.

Andrew took back his glass and drained it before standing up and lifting Heidi into his arms.

"I'm going to scram now and let you get a good sleep," he said. "I fancy you'll have a busy day tomorrow, when Wiedemann gets into his stride about the commissioner's accusation."

"You think that's all there is to it – the great telescope row?"

"I'm sure of it." Andrew kissed her. "Oh Heidi, I do love you. I love your hair the colour of butterscotch, and that cute curly smile. And I adore you when you're out to fight the Germans single-handed. Goodnight, my sweet."

8

Herr Wiedemann's telescope was front-page news, and a hilarious subject for the cartoonists, for just one day. On Wednesday the story was dead. The papers were full of the sinking of the giant German battleship *Bismarck* in a British naval and air attack on May 27, and – more important to Americans – President Roosevelt's broadcast declaring a state of Unlimited National Emergency. This was the result of the sinking of the American freighter announced on the radio. "The war is coming very close to home," said the President. The Axis raiders and submarines were attacking merchant vessels "Actually within the waters of the western hemisphere . . . it would be suicide to wait until they are in our front yard."

These ominous words drew a blast of protest from the America Firsters, who had developed the theory that there was a British-Jewish-capitalist conspiracy to drag America into the war. They now numbered sixty thousand members, enlisted within one year, and included such notabilities as Joseph Kennedy (recently removed from his post as Ambassador to Britain), Alice Roosevelt Longworth and John Foster Dulles. Herr Wiedemann was in close touch with the San Francisco chapter of the organisation during the day when Heidi clipped and marked innumerable copies of the local papers, preparing cuttings books of the telescope incident for circulation to Washington and the other German consulates. It was mechanical work with scissors and paste and she was glad of it. Her mind was free to range over the problem which Andrew Kirk had dismissed as 'nerves' and a girl's exaggeration. She was generous enough to own that Andrew at twenty-four was no longer the excitable boy newly back from Europe and agonising over the fall of France. He had been licked into shape in San Francisco. Yet it was he who had begun the whole thing at their first meeting on Treasure Island, when he denounced – she remembered the exact words – the 'complacency, isolationism and small-town ignorance' of those who refused to admit that danger lay ahead. She had done her best to match his fervour in her own small way, and now she was advised to chuck it and get a good night's sleep!

. . . Supposing the farcical telescope story were true, and the Germans could enjoy a close-up view of the gun batteries at Fort Baker on the Marin side of the bridge. Were those batteries any more lethal than the Civil War cannon at Fort Point on the city side, near the Presidio? Even if they were the most sophisticated known to modern weaponry, what would the Germans gain by putting them out of action? Possibly no more than John C. Fremont had gained in 1846. Nothing within the scope of the most powerful telescope installed in the rear window of a house on Jackson Street was a sufficiently important target to warrant keeping a clandestine company of men in the basement or the attics of that house. The men, whether they were trained to attack by land or sea, must have a far more important objective in view.

It was not until the second night from Andrew's visit, after two days of gruelling work in Jackson Street, that Heidi found the solution. She had been thinking too much about the basement and Dr. Walter's refusal to let her enter it, and not enough about that half-heard conversation between him and Wiedemann on the subject of the files, the 'new stuff' which was safely under lock and key. Then came that muffled allusion to *die Stute*, the mare, which she thought was meant for her. Supposing it meant something else? Supposing Dr. Walter was talking about Mare Island?

Heidi was at home when the shattering thought occurred to her. It was still daylight, and she went out and walked as far as Steiner Street and round the block; the little studio was not big enough to contain her and her dread. Mare Island, not too far from Sonoma Creek, had once been the property of General Mariano Vallejo. It was now a vast Navy Yard complex including a radio station, a Marine barracks and a naval hospital, and the chief naval construction centre on the Pacific coast. Heidi Siegrist had been there, though not since she was thirteen years old. She had been with her father when he went to Mare Island to take pictures of a heavy cruiser, the USS *San Francisco*, when it was launched as the first warship commissioned during the Roosevelt Administration. She had no idea how many capital ships might be lying at Mare Island now; she did know that an act of sabotage committed there would be a major disaster which would more than compensate Hitler for the American seizure of Axis shipping.

She believed that if she went to the police or the FBI with her suspicions she would be shown the door; the first thing was to get some concrete evidence. Heidi felt alone and – helpless? No, not helpless, for the mouse was in the lion's den and could, with luck, secure the needed proof. Wiedemann had said the 'new stuff' was under lock and key, which was not necessarily true. The communications file which held the correspondence with other consulates and signals to and from Berlin, was unlocked by him every morning and locked when he went home at night with a key kept on his own chain, but it was sometimes left unlocked when he went to lunch. First of all she had to find out if there was anything about Mare Island in that file.

Herr Wiedemann was out and about in the city, and Dr. Walter sat on guard in his room, but on Thursday he was back at his desk and discussing the Emergency with the vice-consul when Heidi summoned up her courage and went in. She had considered whether Mare Island material would be filed under S for *Stute*, or I for *Insel*, and decided on the first.

"Yes, what is it, Fräulein Adelheid?" Herr Wiedemann looked round in irritation.

"Excuse me for disturbing you, sir," said Heidi. "I need the back correspondence with Dr. Scholz in Boston."

"Get it out quickly, then." He went on with whatever he was saying to the vice-consul, and Heidi saw that the filing cabinet was open. She stooped to open the drawer marked S and riffled quickly through the folders. It was there! So thin it could only contain one page, but it was there! She pulled the thick Scholz folder and slipped quietly from the room.

She considered the next step that evening. It was too dangerous to steal the Mare Island material, for it might be missed at any time, and she would be the first person to be suspected. It would have to be photographed, and she had hardly the skill or the equipment for that, but at least she knew how it was done. She had watched her father at work in Nathan Wildstein's studio when he had commissions to make photocopies of valuable manuscripts, including some of the diseños of the old Spanish grants. The fragile material required special pins: long blunt-headed pins to hold the paper or parchment in place without leaving a mark, and drawing pins to fix the long pins to a drawing board. Tim had his camera on a tripod and used four lamps, each throwing its light diagonally across the opposite corner. She would have to proceed without so many refinements; but she had his camera with the process lens. On her way to work next morning, with the camera in a shopping bag, she bought a roll of film – Agfa 1FF, which Tim had explained was slow. She loaded the camera in the ladies' room next to her office in the consulate, never used by anybody but herself. She also carried away a frivolous boudoir lamp with a pink silk shade, standing on the dressing table beneath a mirror.

It was a Friday, and Wiedemann's diary contained an engagement to lunch at the Italian Consulate. He was on the telephone to the Washington Embassy for twenty minutes before he left in a great hurry, accompanied by Dr. Walter and driving his own Mercedes. Heidi watched them go from her office window and then went into Wiedemann's room. As she had hoped, the haste of his departure had kept him from locking the communications file.

She pulled the Mare Island folder and carried it to her own desk, locking the doors to the landing and the room she had just left. As she expected, the folder contained one page only. It was a letter from Heinrich Himmler, head of the Gestapo, ordering Operation Mare Island to be carried out on the sixth of June, and addressed to Dr. Anton Walter.

Heidi laid the single sheet on her empty desk, took off the pink shade of the boudoir lamp and set it with her own reading lamp at diagonally opposite corners of the letter. The lighting was the problem, and she took four pictures with the window curtains drawn and four with daylight added to the lamplight, the camera held steady in her hands. She put it back in her shopping bag, unlocked the doors and carried the Mare Island folder back to the files. When she had rearranged the lamps she sat down and tried to drink some coffee from the Thermos she brought with her on days when the Consul-General was lunching out. He liked his office to be constantly supervised.

It was after three when Wiedemann came back, all the mellower for libations of Chianti and Strega, and dictated a long message to Washington on his talks with the Italians about the Emergency. It was to be sent *en clair* by Western Union, with a coded copy to Berlin, and it was nearly six before Heidi was free to find a taxi and be driven to Nathan Wildstein's photographic studio on Mission Street.

"Miss Heidi, what a nice surprise!"

"I've come to beg for a great favour, Mr. Wildstein."

"You have only to ask, my dear. Have you good news of your papa?"

"Oh yes, the best – if he were here I wouldn't be bothering you. I want you please to develop and print the roll of film inside this camera." She saw his look of surprise and said humbly, "I couldn't trust myself to take it out."

"Is it so important?"

"Very – and top secret."

Wildstein said slowly, "Are you still working for the Germans, miss?"

"Not for them. *Against* them! Oh please help me, Mr. Wildstein!"

"So what is in this camera is against them?" Heidi nodded, speechless. "My brother's two sons died in Dachau, Miss Heidi. I will help you gladly. But first I make you a glass of lemon tea."

When she had drunk the lemon tea, and Mr. Wildstein had disappeared into his dark room, Heidi sat still in the studio and smoked a cigarette. The 'Closed' sign was on the outer door now, and she might have sat on the shabby sofa as long as she pleased, but the strain of three days of waiting had left her at once aching with fatigue and restless enough to walk to Ocean Beach. She had let herself out into the street before she remembered that she must call Andrew.

She walked slowly up Second Street to Market. Ninety years before, if she had known it, her great-grandmother Content had bustled along Second, ordering food and merchandise to be sent to her fine new house in South Park. Now South Park had gone, and Rincon Hill, levelled to make way for the anchorage of the Oakland Bay Bridge, and soon this day so dramatic for Heidi Siegrist, so far-reaching in the effects of what she had done, would be one with all the other dramatic days of an earlier San Francisco. In the present, it was a fine May evening, and Market Street was crowded with sightseers, drunks, panhandlers, late office workers and people hurrying to the theatres. She came to the corner of Kearny, and her usual trysting-place with Andrew at Lotta's Fountain. Presently, when she felt less tired, she would cross to the other side of Market and call him from the lobby of the *Clarion* building. She could see the lights in the newspaper offices four floors above the street.

Her thoughts since she handed the camera to Nathan Wildstein were very disjointed. Lotta's Fountain – she had been only four years old when Lotta Crabtree died, leaving four million dollars to charity and a tangle of lawsuits arising from her contested Will. The flower sellers had packed up for the night except for one old woman with a tray of gardenias, made up in corsages for the theatre trade. Andrew would buy her one as soon as he joined her. And Heidi knew exactly what she was going to say to him:

"It wasn't nerves or imagination. I've got the evidence. I've got a letter from Himmler himself. I'd like you to take a copy to the FBI."

★   ★   ★

"Congratulations, Miss Siegrist. You did a fine job."

He said his name was Mr. Smith, the nondescript individual who came with Andrew to Heidi's apartment on Saturday evening and briefly showed her an identification from the FBI. He was so inconspicuous that the only way to describe him would have been 'Male, Caucasian, 5 foot 9' and after that there would be a hesitation. Were his eyes grey or blue, his hair grey or blond, had he no distinguishing marks except – was that a mole or a tiny birthmark on his left cheek? Would it necessarily be there after he had shaved? Andrew, sitting beside him on the sofa bed, looked so definite by contrast with his strong features and expressive dark eyes. Mr. Smith looked as if he might melt into the fog hanging over the Golden Gate and be seen no more.

"I wish you'd tell me what's been going on," said Heidi. "I've been cooped up indoors all day, and there's been nothing on the radio."

She had been told to go home and stay home, when the new sequence of events began as Mr. Wildstein brought them the prints of Himmler's letter and said proudly, "Not up to your father's work, Miss Heidi, but two of them are very clear. Clear enough to stand this man Walter up in front of a firing squad!"

It was Andrew, stunned and horrified, who had put her in a taxi and sent her home before he went with the letter to the FBI, who as soon as they knew they were dealing with a newspaperman forbade him to give the story to his editor under pain of imprisonment. The G-men had been on familiar ground with Andrew Kirk, they had not been so smooth with Anton Walter. Their previous experience with rumrunners and other domestic villains had not trained them to handle the suicide squad, and Dr. Walter, arrested at his flat, had only been under interrogation for ten minutes when he succeeded in conveying a cyanide capsule from his signet ring to his mouth. Mr. Smith and his colleagues had to admit a failure.

"What's been going on," said Mr. Smith – and his voice was as indeterminate as the rest of him, classless, unaccented but monotonous – "is that Dr. Walter is dead."

"*Dead?*"

"Of a heart attack, in the early hours of this morning. At the same time fifteen men were found on the premises of the German Consulate-General and transferred to other accommodations downtown."

"Transferred? You mean they weren't arrested?"

"They hadn't committed any offence, Miss Siegrist. Mr. Wiedemann explained when he came up from Hillsborough to assist us in our enquiries that they were distressed German citizens, unable to find employment, for whom he was arranging transportation to Germany."

Heidi looked in amazement at Andrew, who shrugged his shoulders.

"What will happen to them?" she asked.

"I'm not at liberty to say, ma'am. You're my concern now, and I want to ask you just one question. How do you feel about going to work as usual at the Consulate on Monday?"

"I don't feel anything at all."

"You mean you don't feel up to it?"

"I mean I haven't even thought about Monday."

"I think Miss Siegrist rates a holiday," said Andrew. "A few weeks with her parents would do her a world of good."

"Well, Miss Siegrist, how d'you feel about that?"

"You want me to go back, don't you?"

"The Bureau would like you to go back," said Mr. Smith. "It may only be for a few days, because I don't think Consul Wiedemann will last much longer in San Francisco. But every day he carries on as usual gives us a better chance of finding out the truth about this Mare Island plot – who was in it, what they planned to do, and what help they've been getting from inside."

"That's a horrible thought!" said Heidi.

"There's another thing," said Mr. Smith. "If you quit now, without a day's notice, it might look as if you'd had something to do with all the commotion, and there could be reprisals. That's why we asked you to stay at home today."

"It makes sense," said Andrew reluctantly.

"I hate the very idea of going into that house again," said Heidi. "I'll do it if you think it's right."

Behind the pillared portico the massive doors of the German Consulate-General, usually open on the marble and mosaic vestibule during business hours, were shut at a quarter to nine on Monday morning. Heidi, never given a front-door key, rang several times before she was admitted by one of the clerks, who gave her no more than a brief good morning. The vice-consul, who heard her coming upstairs, was waiting on the landing.

"Sad news this morning, Fräulein," he greeted her. "Dr. Walter is dead."

"*Dead?*"

"Apparently he suffered a heart attack. The daily maid found him dead in bed on Saturday morning."

"How awful." Heidi hoped she sounded convincing. "He was quite a young man, wasn't he?"

"Forty-three, according to Herr Wiedemann. The police sent for him at once, of course, after the maid telephoned. It's very sad, but none of us knew Dr. Walter well. He was a very reserved man, wasn't he?"

"Very."

"Seconded to us from Washington, I understood. But Herr Wiedemann sent a signal to Berlin about his death. He took charge of all the arrangements, naturally."

"The funeral arrangements, do you mean?"

"There's to be a private cremation service this afternoon, Fräulein. I shall be representing the Consul-General."

"Why, isn't he here?"

"He went to Los Angeles on the 'Lark' last night for a conference with his colleague. So! We shall work together, you and I, till he returns."

The problem was to find enough work to do. The daily business of the offices had almost come to a standstill. Some of the younger men, dreading a return to Germany and service in the armed forces, swore the telescope story had scared away German-Americans from approaching the Consulate-General for any reason whatever. The great house was eerily silent. The hall door to the basement stood ajar, and there were no sounds from the rear staircase or the service elevator. Heidi made work for herself to do until invention failed and she sat reading German magazines and out-of-date newspapers through the nervous hours.

Andrew's work schedule must have been seriously upset at that time, for he never failed to be waiting in the Buick when Heidi came out of the consulate. He never parked in the same block, but at one of the corners where, in that unusually flat stretch of San Francisco, Heidi could see the convertible at once, and then he drove her somewhere on Fillmore for a quick drink or a hasty coffee before hurrying back to the *Clarion*. He was not especially tender during those brief meetings, but his "I had to see you – I had to know that you're all right!" and his snatched kiss were comfort enough for Heidi.

Herr Wiedemann was in his room on Thursday morning, abstracted and distant with his secretary, domineering with the clerks, two of whom were detailed to carry papers to the incinerator in the basement. It looked like the beginning of the end. But Wiedemann was in and out continually, keeping up what social contacts were left to him, and in constant touch with the representatives of Italy and Japan. They returned his calls, they all went out to lunch together, they sent Western Union telegrams to their Washington embassies. Among these foreign visitors an early caller was Mr. Smith of the FBI, who passed Heidi on the staircase without a flicker of recognition. That day Wiedemann dictated and Heidi typed a long memorandum to Washington about the complaint he had registered of the plight of fifteen German nationals, male, of military age, held incommunicado in the Mariposa Hotel, Folsom Street, and threatened with deportation.

On Friday, just before the end of the business day, he sent for 'Fräulein Adelheid' and told her he had a very painful duty to perform.

"In view of the aggressive attitude of the United States government," he began pompously, "the German consular representatives have decided to terminate the contracts of all American citizens in their employment . . . In your particular case there is nothing personal in this decision, Fräulein, because your work for me has been very satisfactory."

"Thank you, sir."

"I'm sure you'll have no difficulty in finding another post suited to your ability," Wiedemann went on. "I would gladly provide you with a warm recommendation, only" (with an unusual flash of humour) "I doubt if any American company would appreciate a recommendation from me. I have something more substantial for you instead."

He took a sealed envelope from his desk drawer.

"I am required to pay you two weeks' salary in lieu of

notice," said Captain Fritz Wiedemann, ex-company commander, ex-Hitler's ADC, "and I am pleased to add an extra week's wage, although you haven't been with us very long."

"You're very good, sir," Heidi managed to say.

"Just a token," said Wiedemann kindly, "of my appreciation of your loyalty at a most trying time."

9

Los Angeles was only five hundred miles from San Francisco, but it was another world. Heidi sat beside her father as he drove her home from the SP station, amazed at the urban sprawl, the chain of mismatched communities in search of an identity, and compared what she saw with the concentrated force and beauty of her native city. But Westwood, when they reached it, was a pleasant 'village', and the Siegrists' ranch house had a garden front and back. It was like no ranch house Heidi had ever seen, being built in the new split-level style, and it had three bedrooms and four baths. Violet Siegrist was proud of this luxury, and almost equally proud of the one avocado and two lemon trees in the back yard, because "you only needed a drop of oil to make your own avocados *vinaigrette!*"

This was a sample of the incoherent chatter which accompanied their breakfast in the patio, after Heidi had a shower in one of the four bathrooms and told her parents how splendid they were looking. "Hollywood agrees with you, father," she said, "and mommy, you look twenty years younger!"

"She joined a health club and took up tennis," said Tim, beaming, "and I think she did something to her hair."

Violet had lost weight, and her greying hair was raven black again, with an artful streak of pure silver running back from her widow's peak.

"Thank you, Heidi," said Violet, "pay no attention to your father. It's *you* who need to be looked after now. Why didn't you come straight to us after that wretched job with the Germans folded?"

"I had to stay in San Francisco and look for another job, mother."

"I'm sure there are plenty of openings in Hollywood for a girl with your qualifications."

"Yes, have you thought about that, darling?" said Tim eagerly.

"Enough to know I want to stay in San Francisco, even if they don't grow avocados on Fillmore Street. I had three jobs offered me in one week, so I could pick and choose."

"What were they?"

"One was to be secretary to the editor of the *Clarion*. Andrew Kirk got me an interview for that, but I turned it down."

"That might have been interesting."

"I didn't want to work in the same office as Andrew."

"Why not?"

"I thought it might take the gilt off the gingerbread," said Heidi, and Violet looked perplexed.

"The other two I don't believe you'd call interesting at all. One was with an insurance broker and the other with an investment trust company on Montgomery Street. I'm going to the investment trust."

"American?"

"As American as apple pie."

"No more Germans, eh?" said Tim tentatively.

"Figures this time, not politics. And I don't have to start until the first of July."

"Oh, great, you can have a nice long holiday," said Violet. "I want you to relax this morning in the garden – perhaps you'll catch a nap after your train trip – and I'll make an afternoon appointment at the beauty parlour. You've *got to do* something about that hair!"

Life in the split-level ranch house was indeed relaxing. A Mexican girl called Ramona came in every day except Sundays to do the housework, and Violet and Heidi were free to take tennis lessons together and go swimming in their new friends' pools. Violet was very popular in Westwood, where women whose husbands could talk of nothing but the Industry found her a mine of information culled from twenty years' perusal of *Photoplay*, *Modern Screen*, *Motion Picture* and all the rest of the fan mags. She could name the five wives of Wayne Blackwood, which he sometimes said was more than he could do himself; she knew how much alimony one male star was paying, and who was the real father of another starlet's child. She went to all but the very grandest studio parties with her husband, and in the warm June evenings hung Chinese lanterns in their own patio and had people in for cocktails. These gatherings did not last long, for Hollywood was an early town, but there was always some star attraction present. One night it was Wayne Blackwood. He had his Oscar now, and after his big success in *Dunkirk* was looking forward to another hit in the new Turbin movie.

"I can't seem to get away from the goddamned Channel!" he complained humorously, for in *The Victoria Cross* he was playing a heroic Canadian flyer in the Battle of Britain, who prefers death in the Channel waters to crash-landing in a little fishing village nestling beneath the white cliffs of Dover. In Blackwood's case the English Channel was the body of water between the California mainland and Catalina Island, and there were boats out of camera range where hot drinks and dry garments were ready for him after every take, because even if the stunt man did the flying bit the hero had to drown in person.

"Is it going to work, father?" Heidi asked anxiously, after hearing the star's comical account of his sufferings. "Seems to me he's pretty flip about it."

"That's because he *is* the flight-lieutenant, on or off camera," Tim chuckled. "All nonchalance and stiff upper lip. Wayne believes in living his parts, that's why he's an Oscar winner. Anyway it was a nice party, wasn't it?"

"It certainly was. Didn't mother look lovely – and so young!"

"Yes, she did," said Tim . . . "I've made it up to her, I think."

"Made up for what?"

"Oh, the rotten time she had when we lived here before," said Tim, hedging. Twenty-five years back the notorious Violet Estrada had been the girl in the Hastings case. There had been so many Hollywood scandals since then, sensational divorces, lethal abortions, drug suicides and homosexual blackmail that the Hastings murder had been forgotten. "Did those characters leave us any cigarettes?" he asked.

Heidi investigated. "There's a few in the silver box . . . Father, doesn't all this cost rather a lot?"

"What, drinks and cigarettes for a few friends?"

"I mean the whole set-up. The house and the car and Ramona, and all the frills."

"Whoa back, Heidi, you're not an investment counsellor yet," said Tim drily. "I've bought an annuity for your mother, so she'll be all right whatever happens, and my Sonoma book comes out in a couple of weeks. If it's a hit then *People and Places* will take care of a whole lot of frills. I'm on a winning streak, baby, so don't you fret! Enjoy yourself!"

After so many lean years in Ellis Street, Heidi was happy that her father and mother were enjoying life at last, and she enjoyed herself too, all the more for having spent six months inside the enemy camp. She saw that the Industry was more important than the War in Hollywood, although there was admiration and sympathy for Britain under air attack. There was also criticism of the unsuccessful British campaign in North Africa, and of British actors of military age who chose to remain in the safety of California. David Niven, who had gone home to fight, was called the best of the bunch. Then, on June 16, came the government order for all German consulates in the United States to be closed.

Some people thought the Italian and Japanese consulates should be closed too. Others, when the Axis retaliated against American consulates abroad, saw the closures as another step on the road to war. It was insignificant compared with the giant step taken by Adolf Hitler six days later. On June 22 his troops invaded Russia.

On that same Sunday the arch anti-Communist, Winston Churchill, broadcast a statement which was received in America:

"The Russian danger is our danger, and the danger of the United States, just as the cause of any Russian fighting for his hearth and home is the cause of free men and free peoples in every quarter of the globe."

Two days later President Roosevelt extended Lend-Lease aid to Russia.

As Tim Siegrist said, it was a whole other ball game. In Hollywood the heads of studios who had leaned over backward not to give offence to Germany trembled at the prospect of scenarios glorifying Stalin, presented by writers long suspected of being crypto-Communists. In Westwood Violet was amused by a phone call from Wayne Blackwood, who jocularly proposed that Willie Bleer and Letty Randolph should get together again as the last Czar of Russia and his Czarina.

"They weren't Reds, Wayne."

"What the hell, they were Russians, weren't they?"

Alexis Turbin arrived in person, demanding Tim's help in the Russian epic which he of all men in Hollywood was best fitted to direct.

"Don't stick your neck out, Alex," Tim advised. "MGM won't be ready for a Russian movie yet awhile."

"Why not?"

"Because Russia was Germany's ally less than a week ago. That non-aggression pact they made in 1939 sparked off the war; who can tell what pact they'll make when Hitler adds Russia to his conquests?"

"I didn't know you were a politician, Tim."

"I'm not, but I've sized up MGM better than you have. *The Mortal Storm* was a controversial film, and it wasn't good box office here; now Louis B.'s got his guts in an uproar about making something as pro-British as *Mrs. Miniver*. *Mrs. Miniver*, of all lumps of sugar candy! What makes you think he'll go for a blood and guts epic of Bolshevism?"

Turbin sulked.

"Tell you what we might do," Tim went on maliciously, "after *The Victoria Cross* is in the can. We could suggest a costume drama about the Russians in California, and how well they got on with the Spanish, and what good guys they were, and then put in a message for today. They might buy that at the studio."

"I know nothing of the Russians in California," said Turbin.

"They were here all right, a hundred years ago. Vi! 'Mem-

ber that trip we took to Fort Ross when Heidi was a kid? That
was their garrison. I used some pix of Fort Ross and Bodega
Bay in my Sonoma book; they'd make swell establishing shots
for a movie."

"Don't mind Tim, Mr. Turbin, he's teasing you," said
Violet. "Have another glass of vodka and one of these smoked
salmon rolls you like so much."

"Yes, do mind Tim!" said her husband. "I'm not going out
on a limb for the Russkies, Alex, and you're not either. My
hunch is that the next batch of Hollywood movies will be
real patriotic; comical, folksy service stuff. Like *Buck
Privates*."

Luckily for Timothy Siegrist some of the excitement about
the invasion of Russia had died down before his book was
published. The subscription had been good, and *People and
Places: Sonoma*, with a fine review in the *Los Angeles Times* on
the morning of publication day, was launched at a booksellers'
buffet luncheon at the Brown Derby. The author was relaxing
with his family in the patio that evening, and had just opened a
bottle of champagne, when Heidi went indoors to answer the
telephone.

"Heidi darling, is that you?"

"Andrew! Where are you? Your voice sounds so close!"

"I am so close. I'm at the Beverly Hills Hotel."

"For heaven's sake! How – how did you get here?"

"Hitched a ride with a guy I know. Heidi, can I come to see
you? I won't be butting in on anything?"

"Of course you won't. Come on and drink success to my
father's book, it came out today –"

"Oh Lord! Are you having a party?"

"No, just us."

"Be with you in ten minutes."

Before she went back to the patio, she put on fresh powder
and lipstick, and brushed out the page-boy bob which Andrew
called the colour of butterscotch, and which now had gilt
highlights put in by a Hollywood hairdresser who gave his
customers actress styles, and did his best to make Heidi look
like Margaret Sullavan. Then she went to tell her parents,
rather too nonchalantly, that Andrew Kirk was on his way.

"Good heavens, have I time to change my dress?" cried Violet.

"Not if he got a cab right away," said Heidi, and then Andrew was ringing the front-door bell, being led through the house, and respectfully greeting Mr. and Mrs. Siegrist. That he had had time to change was obvious. For a man who shared the driving for five hundred miles in an open MG he was remarkably well groomed, having thrown away an old sports shirt at the Beverly Hills and put on a new white one after a shave and a shower. Heidi saw that her mother was impressed by his good looks. Andrew's dark blue suit was very formal next to Tim's white Mexican shirt and pants, bought in the Olvera Street market.

"I'm glad to meet you at last, Mr. Kirk," Violet was saying graciously, as Heidi gave him a glass of champagne. "We'd hoped to meet you in San Francisco before we left, but there was such a rush at the end –"

"Of course," said Andrew with his eyes on Heidi. Then, recollecting himself, he raised his glass to Tim and said, "Congratulations on the book, sir. And on *Resistance*, it was a great movie."

"You're interested in movies?"

"Yes, but more in photography. Is this the new book? May I look at it?"

Heidi had stood a copy of *Sonoma* on the white patio table, with a little vase of flowers beside it. Tim put it into Andrew's hands, and watched as the young man turned the pages. "It's beautifully produced," he said.

"They did a fine job," said Tim. "Do you recognise any of the places?"

"I've never been to Sonoma," said Andrew, "I don't know why, it's less than fifty miles from San Francisco."

"That's my old family home in Sonoma," said Violet, leaning forward to indicate a page. "The Estrada adobe, they used to call it. Tim took that picture just before the demolition squad moved in. It's a bank now, alas."

"I dedicated the book to my wife," said Tim, and Andrew turned to the flyleaf. The simple inscription read TO VIOLET ESTRADA.

"It would take me hours to study all this properly," said

Andrew helplessly, and Tim took pity on him. "I'll send you a copy for yourself," he promised. "Have some more champagne."

"It'll be wonderful to have the book," said Andrew, as Heidi silently refilled his glass. She had hardly said a word since he arrived. "I'm – awfully sorry to crash your family celebration," he went on, "but I was hoping to take Heidi out for dinner and dancing tonight. I know it's very short notice, but –"

"But you must have dinner with us," said Violet. "It's all ready to put on the table. Perhaps you and Heidi could go dancing tomorrow night instead."

"I'm afraid I've got to go back to San Francisco on the midnight train, Mrs. Siegrist."

"Tonight?"

"Yes, tonight."

"Heidi said you drove down," said Tim, breaking the awkward silence. "What time did you get in?"

"About half past six, I think it was."

"You must try to stay longer next time," said Tim with his crooked smile.

"I'd love to go dancing," said Heidi.

"Sure," said her father. "This is your holiday, right?"

"Only I must change first. I shan't be long, Andrew."

"I'll call a cab for you," said Tim, and while they were both gone Violet talked charmingly to the visitor, finding out more about his family in Connecticut, father, mother who did charity work for the Community Chest and the March of Dimes, and kid brother Pete who was at Andrew's old school, Lawrenceville, than he had told Heidi in a year. When the girl came back he jumped to his feet with a look which said much more than words. Heidi was wearing a chiffon dress the colour of eau de nil, with a long scarf of the same material round her bare shoulders, and the light from the living room shone on her glinting hair.

"You look very nice, dear," said Violet. "You won't be late?"

"I'll bring her right back," Andrew said, "and then I can take the cab on to the railroad station. Thank you very much for letting me share your celebration. Goodnight, Mrs. Siegrist. Goodnight, sir." They heard him telling the waiting taxi driver to go to the Cocoanut Grove.

"Well!" said Violet, "there's a young man in a hurry! What did you think of him, Tim?"

"Nice kid," said Tim laconically. "He sure came a long way to spend the evening with his sweetheart, considering she'll be back in San Francisco inside a week."

"But are they sweethearts? They hadn't a word to say to one another."

"You ask me, they're both head over heels in love, only they haven't settled down to each other yet."

"When did you and I settle down to each other, I wonder?"

"Oh – south of Salinas, somewhere in the artichoke country." He shared the last of the second bottle of champagne between their glasses as Violet laughed.

"Do you realise that boy's making a round trip of one thousand miles, half of them driving, 'just to dance with old Folinsbee's daughter, The Lily of Poverty Flat'?"

"What are you talking about, Vi?"

"Quoting one of my old recitations. Or maybe I'm talking about what it is to be young and pretty . . . And she *was* pretty tonight in her green dress, wasn't she?"

"Lovely." Tim's grip tightened on her shoulder. "Look, old Folinsbee would like some dinner. And then let's make an early night of it. I've a hunch Heidi won't want to chatter to you or me, when she comes back from the Cocoanut Grove."

★　★　★

"You look absolutely ravishing, darling; what have you been doing to yourself?" whispered Andrew. Acutely conscious of the driver and his rear-view mirror, he had only kissed her hand when they got into the taxi and kept it in his own.

"I've been going to mother's beauty parlour."

"It's more than that. You were so damned tired when you left San Francisco, and now – you glow."

"I want to hear about everything that happened after I left. All you couldn't tell me on the telephone."

"There's plenty to tell, and not much time to tell it –"

"But darling, why the rush? Must you get back tonight?"

"It was like pulling teeth to get old Corbett to give me a day off in the middle of the week –"

"Old brute, you've hardly had a day off since Christmas."

"But when I met this guy – a guy I was at Stanford with – going south to join his ship at San Diego, and he offered me a hitch to L. A., I had to take him up on it. I had to see you, darling, and meet your folks. There's something I want to tell you, and after that there's something I want to ask you, and – here we are at the Cocoanut Grove."

It was rather early for the Cocoanut Grove, but the place was filling up with well-groomed young men and girls in pretty dance dresses, and the room was full of the big band sound. They were shown to a table in a not too crowded part of the ballroom, and Andrew said they'd better stick to champagne.

"What would you like to eat, Heidi?"

"Nothing right now. We had an enormous lunch at the Brown Derby."

"Bring a bottle of Dom Perignon '37, please," Andrew told the waiter, "and we'll order in about half an hour."

"Now tell about Wiedemann, do," she begged when the man had gone.

Herr Wiedemann, Andrew said with relish, had made an almighty fool of himself after he was kicked out. He made an attempt to return to *der Vaterland* via Japan, and was brought ignominiously back to make the long journey home across the Atlantic, with the risk of being torpedoed by the British en route. As for the men concealed in the Consulate, "and thanks for tipping me off about Folsom Street, Heidi," said Andrew, "I kept a death-watch on the Mariposa Hotel and was right there when they were marched out and deported as undesirable aliens. Pity we haven't any concentration camps like Dachau to shove them into."

"But where were they deported *to*?"

"They were shipped out to Vancouver."

"Where they'll be interned as soon as they go ashore."

"That was the idea." He grinned at her. "I have to hand it to you, Heidi, you sure cleaned that rat's nest out!"

"Nonsense, it was a federal decision to close the consulates."

"Let's say you gave the Feds a good push in the right direction."

"Were they pushed as far as Mare Island? Was any traitor unearthed there?"

"I tried to quiz our friend Smith about that, but of course I got nowhere. Ah! Here comes our champagne." It was in an ice-bucket on a stand. "Let's have a sip, darling, and then let's dance. That's a swell tune they're playing."

It was 'When You Wish Upon a Star', which had just won the Oscar for Best Song, and a girl in a strapless dress was at the mike in front of the orchestra, singing along with the big band sound. Heidi, held close to her tall partner, kept her head low and her eyes on the green slippers dyed to match her dress. There were coloured lights playing across the ballroom, and all round them the dancers were pressed closer to each other, moving in a more languorous rhythm. "Heidi," whispered Andrew, "look up, darling! Have you ever wished on a star? I have, often!"

The smoky grey eyes looked up at him reflectively.

"What star, Andrew?"

"*You!*"

When they were back at the table she asked him, as if they were still talking about the sentimental melody, if that was what he had come to tell her.

"About wishing on a star? It was and it wasn't. Facts first, Heidi, and I'll give it to you straight. I'm going to join the Navy, a few weeks from now."

Heidi took it very coolly. With only a slight contraction of her brows she said, "It's what you always wanted, isn't it?"

"You mean I've been talking about it for long enough?"

"You haven't talked about it for ages. I thought you were going to wait for the draft."

"I'm sick and tired of waiting for the draft! I want to volunteer and get a commission, and be all set before we get into the war. It won't be long now."

She said, "Is this a snap decision, because Hitler's invaded Russia?"

"It's got nothing to do with Russia. I've talked to Corbett about it several times. He always tries to sell me a bill of goods about the national importance of moulding public opinion. As if the *Clarion* could mould pastry, let alone public opinion! As if anything I write couldn't be written just as well by some other hack!"

"That's not so, and you know it," said Heidi.

"But now I guess Corbett's as fed up with the whole issue as I am. He's asked me to stay on till the middle of July, and then it's me for the Navy."

"But why the Navy? Have you a Navy tradition in your family?"

"No such thing. I like messing about in boats, that's all."

Heidi thought a destroyer might be more difficult to mess about in than a sailboat. She said, rather desperately searching for every loophole, "Look here! I thought the law said you *had* to wait for your draft number to come up. Can you really volunteer, since Selective Service? Can you just walk in off the street and say 'I want to join the Navy?'"

"Sure! I only have to go to the nearest Enlistment Office in San Francisco and tell them I want to volunteer for the Navy. I'm a college graduate. If I pass my physical, I'll be eligible for a naval officer's training course, and if I pass that I'll be commissioned."

"Where would you do this course? At Mare Island?"

"New York."

For the first time he saw her flinch. "Andrew, that *is* a long way away."

"And that's only the beginning. When I'm passed out I'll be a ninety-day wonder, liable to be posted anywhere and ready for sea duty – and that's what it's all about, Heidi; I want to serve my country."

As Andrew had said a year ago, patriotism was not in fashion, and he spoke the last words as if he were almost ashamed of them. Heidi laid her hand on his and Andrew took it in a tight clasp.

"So that's it, darling, I've tried to lay it on the line. When I'm commissioned I'll only be drawing an ensign's pay, and I haven't any money of my own. I can't make a down payment on a house or a new car or a washing machine, and I've nothing to offer a girl except a handout from the government. It takes a lot of nerve to ask you what I'm going to ask you now, Heidi. Will you marry me before I go to sea?"

If he had stopped short at "will you marry me?" she might have hesitated. She might have asked for time to think, time (silly as it sounded in 1941) to talk it over with her parents – any excuse would have done to postpone the ultimate decision. Because Heidi, much as she loved him, had felt one slight impediment between them since she insisted on remaining at the German Consulate until the end. A tiny disparagement of what she tried to do, the faintest resentment of her success amounted to a microscopic fragment of grit in the well-oiled machinery of natural selection. But Andrew had chosen the right moment and the right words for his proposal. Instead of a romantic solitude, the Cocoanut Grove put them in the setting of their own generation, young, thoughtless and brave, dancing towards the edge of the gulf which had opened already for their counterparts on the other side of the world. In that setting it was right to snatch at happiness, however fleeting, to make promises, however reckless, which affirmed the future.

Will you marry me *before I go to sea*, Andrew had asked, and at once she saw the vast surges of the Pacific beyond the Golden Gate, out beyond the Farallones, with a ship in distress on the ocean. Torpedoed – dive-bombed – there were no survivors . . . the words which the past two years had made sickeningly familiar danced before Heidi's vision. *I want to serve my country* still rang in her ears. She was aware of Andrew's anxious brown eyes, and a pulse beating in his cheek. She put her other hand into his and whispered under the drum-beat of the band:

"Yes I will, Andrew. Yes, I'll marry you whenever you like."

*   *   *

The United States Naval Reserve Midshipmans' School New York, as it was formally called, was located in an old vessel, the USS *Prairie State*, moored in the Hudson river in uptown New York, in the vicinity of 130th Street in Harlem. The training courses for naval officers held every quarter in the *Prairie State* were part of the vast defence plan for the United States, including a two-ocean navy, for which President Roosevelt signed the bill in July 1940, just after the fall of

France. Andrew Kirk was one of the first intake, his quarter beginning on August 1, 1941. From one hundred to one hundred and twenty officer candidates were processed every quarter, crowded into three- or four-tiered bunks and kept on the run from 6 a.m. reveille onwards; they silently groaned their way through morning PT for the first week or so, and then the Navy discipline took hold and they all pulled together. Hartford was near enough to New York for Andrew's parents to visit with his young brother Peter, on holiday from Lawrenceville. Now that Andrew had taken the big step of volunteering, his parents took the news of his engagement in their stride, although both they and the Siegrists, in an exchange of cordial letters, thought the young people were being too hasty in their marriage plans and ought to wait for half a year at least 'until we see how things turn out'.

There was no longer any doubt about how things would turn out, for the German armies were driving across Russia, and the United States was neutral only in name. In July US Task Force 19 sailed from Newfoundland for Reykjavik to support the British in their occupation of Iceland, begun over a year before. In September the USS *Greer*, a destroyer en route for Iceland, escaped from the torpedo attack launched by a German submarine, and President Roosevelt ordered all naval vessels to shoot at sight and all merchant vessels to be armed. He had already met Winston Churchill in Argentia Bay and signed with him the Atlantic Charter proclaiming the Four Freedoms and the common principles on which they based their hopes for a better world. The officer candidates aboard the *Prairie State* discussed these new developments seriously, and light-heartedly enjoyed, in their off-duty hours, the lavish hospitality offered them in the city of New York.

Andrew danced with pretty young women, visited welcoming homes and dodged out of seeing the sights he had seen often enough before, without for a moment forgetting the girl he left behind him. Heidi was wearing his engagement ring now, chosen by herself and highly original. She had passed up all the diamond eternity rings in Shreve's in favour of a rough ring made out of some Argonaut's nugget and set at random with chips of mountain gemstones. "It's too heavy for your little paw," Andrew objected, but it suited Heidi better than the ruby dinner ring his mother sent her. She could wear her nugget to the investment trust company's offices where she had found her true niche in business. Before Andrew had passed out of the *Prairie State* she was promoted from her secretarial job to a junior executive's post in the mutual funds department, and followed in her great-grandmother Content's footsteps along the Wall Street of the West.

Heidi had his ring and he had her photograph, taken specially by her father. "Shoot me through linoleum if you must," Heidi had implored Tim, "but do please make me look nice!" Tim made her wear her soft chiffon dance dress, and shot her through scrim, properly lighted, and the result was much admired by Andrew's parents and his shipmates. Andrew liked the photograph too, but it wasn't the Heidi he loved best. He thought of her most tenderly as the exhausted girl he met on a summer evening at Lotta's Fountain, while Nathan was making prints of Himmler's letter. That girl had had the dogged courage to go back to the Germans for five working days after that night. He would never know if Heidi had been inspired by patriotism or the need to take up his unspoken challenge.

The officer candidates completed their ninety days in training school towards the end of October, and Andrew read his orders from the Navy Department, Bureau of Navigation, Washington, DC.

'On the execution of the Acceptance and Oath of Office under your commission as an Ensign, D/V (G) USNR, you will regard yourself as detached from all duties at your present station.' He was to delay for ten days in reporting for active duty, such delay to count as leave, and then report to the commandant of the Twelfth Naval District, San Francisco.

He was elated beyond words. He had hardly dared to hope for a San Francisco assignment. He and Heidi had discussed alternative plans for their wedding so thoroughly that all he had to do was telephone her to put Plan A into action and listen to her gasp of joy three thousand miles away. He had to stand in line for half an hour to use the telephone and then keep it short, because the next man was tapping on the glass of the telephone box. He put a call in to Hartford later, and his parents came in to say goodbye at the railroad station. His mother cried, and his father slapped his shoulder and gave him a handsome cheque for a wedding present. "I wish we could see you and Heidi married, son," said Mr. Kirk, "but your mother isn't up to such a long train trip."

If so, she was the exception, for the whole of the United States seemed to be on a wild travel binge. All the trains were crowded. Ensign Kirk had to sit up in a day coach as far as Chicago before he got an upper berth in a Pullman where the male passengers wandered up and down the aisle all night, smoking and drinking and generally raising hell. The washrooms and the club car were packed, and there were endless lines for the diner. But the train pulled in to Oakland at last, and San Francisco rose out of the bay like an urban Venus, nacreous in the twilight hour.

Andrew forgot the train, the ferry and the noisy terminal when he had Heidi in his arms, and they were in a taxi on California Street before he asked her where they were going.

"I've got you a room at the Mark, and one for father and mother when they come up from L.A.," she said capably, and then collapsed against his shoulder when Andrew said, "Darling, is it true? Are we really going to be married in City Hall on Friday?" He didn't seem to be sure of anything until they were in the cocktail bar at the Top of the Mark, with the whole panorama of the lighted city at their feet. The Top of the Mark was crowded too, and so many of the men were in uniform that the draft boards and the Enlistment Offices must have been working overtime. There was a ceaseless promenade, round and round, of people trying to see the fabulous view through all the picture windows. Conversation was difficult. Heidi wanted to hear about life aboard the *Prairie State*, but security reasons kept Andrew from discussing naval matters in a public place where waiters constantly passed their table with trays of cocktails or empty glasses. Besides, he only wanted to look at Heidi. He was obsessed by the shortness of their time together. He wanted to take her to his room and make love to her. There was plenty of lovemaking going on in the Mark tonight, he was sure, for the lift had stopped many times on its way up to the cocktail bar, and on every floor there were open bedroom doors and guys in uniform stumbling along the

corridor with their arms round consenting girls. And he and
Heidi were to be married on Friday.

During the few weeks he remained in San Francisco after she
promised to marry him Andrew had controlled his acute
desire to possess her, although he hardly dared be alone with
her in the Fillmore Street studio in case he turned into a rapist
and wrecked their happiness. Plenty of engaged couples were
jumping the gun, it was part of the growing war fever, but
Andrew felt that he and Heidi should not be one of them. Now
it was different. They might have no more than ten days
together – two weeks at most, depending on his orders, so
why waste hours of happiness? He only had to say, "It's
impossible to talk up here. Why don't we go down to my
room, order another drink from room service, and then I'll tell
you all about the *Prairie State*." No, he wouldn't bring the USS
Prairie State into it. That might be too like the classic invitation
to see his etchings. But to suggest getting out of this jabbering
crowd – well, why not? Heidi wasn't a teaser, but she was
sexy and terribly desirable. Why not try his luck? But what if
she turned him down? Andrew gave up. It was better to leave
that down-East coolness inviolate – until Friday night.

Next day at noon, when she was to meet him for an early
lunch in the coffee-shop and go for their blood tests and
application for a marriage licence, all thoughts of sex had been
knocked out of Ensign Kirk's head. Although he was on leave
and need not report until after the wedding, he was so eager to
hear about his assignment that he had gone in the morning to
the office of the commandant Twelfth District . . . and now
he knew. He had to set his jaw when he saw Heidi come in
smiling, wearing her old orange-tawny coat and cap.

"Darling!" she said, with her face lifted to be kissed, and he
said "Darling – I sail on Sunday."

"Oh no!"

"'Fraid so. I went to the Twelfth District Office this morning and that's what I was told. Here, sit down for a minute –"

They both sat down on one of the sofas in the foyer, next to
a white marble and gilt table holding a jar of bronze chrysanthemums.

"Is it the *San Francisco*?"

"I hope you're only guessing."

"Oh, don't be angry, Andrew, it's not a breach of naval security. Everyone and his brother knows the *San Francisco*'s in port and puts to sea on Sunday. She's in harbour for everybody to see, and she's the city's own ship. Everybody's interested in the *San Francisco*." Heidi could have told him that in a city which had followed ship movements since the *California* arrived with the first Argonauts in 1849, everybody knew not only the day and the hour of the USS *San Francisco*'s sailing, but her destination as well.

"When do you report for duty?" she asked.

"Saturday afternoon at seventeen hundred hours."

"It doesn't give us very long together."

"No." Andrew took Heidi's hands. She was wearing gloves, but the chill came through. "Why, you poor little thing, you're shivering! Come and have a drink and something to eat, and then we'd better get on with our programme."

★   ★   ★

As the time was so short they had already decided against a church wedding and a reception, and the only guests at their civil marriage would also be their witnesses, Heidi's father and mother. Violet had hoped for "at least a service of blessing in the Old First. You and I hadn't a grand wedding, Tim, but we *were* married by a minister."

"Let them manage it their own way," said Tim. "They'll be each other's blessing."

Violet sighed. She was unpacking in the room Heidi had reserved for them at the Mark Hopkins. "To think they won't even be able to have their friends for the little party they were planning next week. It really is too bad!"

"That can't be helped," said Tim. "They can throw a party when Andrew comes ashore. Cheer up, Vi! The boy's only going to sea, he's not going into combat! We've got to look on the bright side, for Heidi's sake."

"I wonder what Heidi'll say when she hears you're going to direct your next movie?"

Tim's hunch had been right, and service movies were to be the fashion in 1942, not inspirational movies like *The Victoria Cross*, successful though that had been, but like the new one

623

Tim was going to direct, which dealt comically with a bunch of rodeo riders who volunteered for the US Cavalry. Some of the top brass still thought of war in terms of horse soldiers, and with sixteen million men registered for Selective Service every arm of defence was worth a movie. Tim owed his promotion to director to his knowledge of rodeo riders, while Turbin, who had called the shots wrong, was on a Culver City back lot with a second string cameraman, shooting a movie which presented Peter the Great as a forward-looking, Western-thinking Russian.

"I shan't give Heidi a chance to say anything. I'm not going to hog the wedding limelight," said Tim. "So don't you say a word about it." He limped across the room and took up the phone. "Now I've got to check on those two cars. Do you realise I'm doubling in brass as the bride's father *and* the best man?"

Violet took the phone from his hand. "You are the best man, darling," she said, and kissed him.

"Hey, what's all that about?" said Tim with his arms around her. "You didn't say that to me on *our* wedding day!"

"I didn't know it then. I do now."

★   ★   ★

Andrew Ferguson Kirk and Adelheid Basler Siegrist were married in City Hall at half past eleven on Friday morning, which meant that in the limousine hired by Tim they were back at the Mark Hopkins shortly after noon. In the Room of the Dons the luncheon guests, who at that early hour were mostly elderly people, were all smiles at the arrival of what was obviously a bridal party. The handsome ensign in Navy blue and the glowing girl seemed to typify the romantic face of war. Heidi wore a white wool dress and a white hat with a little veil, and Andrew's white gardenias, which he had not bought at Lotta's Fountain, were pinned to the silver fox cape which was her father's wedding present. She had her nugget ring on her right hand and the new wedding band on her left, and her mother envious of her youth saw that she was radiantly happy.

Tim, in his quiet way, was pleased with his new son-in-law. He had never known the helter-skelter Andrew with the facile enthusiasms of a year ago: his first sight of the young man was when he came to Westwood with the fixed intention of asking Heidi to marry him. Now he saw a still more purposeful Andrew, ready to make war as well as love, and while he kept reminding himself that the nation was not at war, Timothy Siegrist marvelled that though the boy was no Annapolis graduate but a ninety-day wonder from the USS *Prairie State*, he was already convincing as a naval officer. He ordered martinis, and drank long life and happiness to the bride and groom.

The head waiter, smiling professionally, brought them a pile of telegrams which had arrived while they were at City Hall. There were loving messages from Andrew's parents, congratulations from his shipmates, would-be comic efforts from his brother and the editorial staff of the *Clarion*, and there were good-luck telegrams from Heidi's new colleagues and her old friend Nettie Holz. "The only one missing is Herr Wiedemann," whispered Andrew. "Wonder where *he* is today?" "Being bombed by the RAF, I hope," Heidi whispered back. Since Andrew got his orders she had been able to put the affair of Herr Wiedemann into the right perspective. What she had done required nerve and daring on one day and self-command on five more, and then it was all over. What lay ahead of Andrew was weeks, perhaps months, of sea duty: he was the one who was in for the long haul.

Handing the telegrams round and discussing them took so long that the dessert stage was reached before Tim said to the bride:

"Do you remember the first time you saw that picture, on an Easter Sunday long ago?" He indicated the mural of Don Luis Estrada, eternally young and gallant, with his lance in rest before the battle of San Pascual.

"Oh, do I ever! I was so thrilled to think he was my ancestor I got a book from the school library about the Spanish pioneers, and was peeved because it didn't say much about Don Luis Estrada."

"Is that the man who had the rancho at Sonoma?" asked Andrew with a sidelong smile at Heidi. "There should have been a picture of it in your great book, sir."

"There wasn't any picture of the rancho because it didn't

exist by 1916," said Tim. "There's still a hotel on the site, isn't there, Violet?"

"I suppose so, but I haven't been out there since I was a little girl. It was the old adobe the Estradas called the town house, that I knew so well when I was growing up."

"I thought the hotel was called the River Inn," persisted Andrew, and Heidi giggled. Tim looked shrewdly from one to the other. "Now then," he said, "they promised to have your car at the door by two o'clock. Vi, do you want to take Heidi up to the room and get her overnight bag?"

He signed the restaurant bill, added a generous tip, and turned to Andrew.

"I don't know a damn thing about the Navy," he said. "I don't know if you're going on manoeuvres, or on patrol, or keeping station, or whatever you call it. I just want you to come back safe to that girl of mine, because I think she loves you as much as you love her."

"Thank you for today," said Andrew. "Thank you for Heidi."

At ten past two the rented car wheeled in front of the Mark Hopkins, and there was a last wave of the hand from the bridal couple. Violet, on the steps with Tim, saw Heidi pull off her wedding hat and throw it on to the back seat beside her bag and Andrew's Valpak before she settled down into the passenger's seat. The car turned left on California and disappeared.

"Well, there they go," said Violet, shivering. "It's all before them now. If only he didn't have to go away so soon!"

"His ship may be back in port in a few weeks," said Tim, determinedly cheerful.

"I wonder where they're going to spend the night. It can't be very far away."

"Come on, honey, get wise to yourself! Surely you could guess from what they *didn't* say in the Room of the Dons?"

"Where then?"

"To Don Luis's old home, of course. The River Inn at Sonoma. Otherwise the Rancho Estrada."

"My father guessed where we were going," said Heidi as the car turned into Van Ness.

"We might as well have told them. They weren't going to

tie a 'Just Married' sign to the back of the car."

"Or throw confetti."

"Are you going to feel gypped in the years to come because we didn't have confetti?" He put his hand on her knee and felt the wool slide over the satin slip and the silk stockings below. "Oh, darling, can you realise we're married?"

"Even without confetti – yes."

The car crossed the Golden Gate bridge and climbed the brown hills of Marin under a tranquil sky with a few cirrus clouds above the Pacific which would turn purple at the sunset hour. They passed the ancient landmarks of Heidi's heritage, with Mount Tamalpais brooding above them all: Vallejo's Petaluma rancho half-fallen into ruin, the Sonoma Creek where Luis Estrada met the Russians, the tule reeds where he hunted wildfowl with Peter Gagarin. Forty miles from San Francisco, at the beginning of a long avenue of eucalyptus, they came upon a sign saying 'To the Valley of the Moon. Sonoma 6 Miles'.

It was a new name for the valley, conferred on it by Jack London, who believed Sonoma to be an Indian word meaning 'the valley of the moon', and used it as the title of one of his best books. A college professor said it was certainly an Indian word, meaning 'the chief's nose' in the Wintun dialect, but the local boosters brushed off the professor and adopted the spurious romantic name. All along the avenue there were billboards advertising the Valley of the Moon Winery, Valley of the Moon Dairies, Valley of the Moon Ice Cream Parlour, Valley of the Moon Drugs. Andrew began to wonder about the River Inn.

The plaza of Sonoma had kept its dignity. When Andrew stopped the car by the grass verge of the wide lawns the square was quiet in the golden light of afternoon and scented with late autumn flowers and burning leaves. Heidi got out of the car and they stood hand in hand, looking for the images of the past.

"That must be where the Estrada adobe stood," said Andrew.

"Yes, on West Napa Street, catty-cornered to the Jacob Leese house. How well *that's* been preserved! While Don Luis's home has become the Pioneer Merchants' Bank of San

627

Francisco. Andrew! Isn't that your friend Evelyn Anderson's bank?"

"Her father's bank. No wonder your mother never wanted to come back and see a place she loved turned into a place like that."

"But it hasn't all been redeveloped," said Heidi, "and there aren't any ads for the Valley of the Moon. Let's walk round the plaza and have a look."

He did it to please her. Andrew was not interested in the past, and only too aware of fleeting time in the present, but as they walked on he felt the quiet charm of a little country town in which the old buildings had been lovingly restored but which had not been turned into a museum piece in the process. The Russian bell stood at the door of the Mission of San Francisco Solano, and the chapel looked much as it did when Rosalie and Carlos knelt at the altar rail with the golden scarf of wedlock round their necks. The Blue Wing Inn and the El Dorado were open for custom, as they had been when Luis Estrada and Salvador Vallejo drowned the sorrows of the Resistance, and the golden hills were eternal.

Heidi shared in his feeling of contentment. Of the Estrada story she knew only the little her mother had told her, and she had neither a historical imagination nor the power of visualising the past, but she knew, as they sauntered past the open space where a white oleander tree stood in the place of General Vallejo's Casa Grande, that here men and women had lived complete lives of love and pain. Again, as once or twice in her childhood, she saw through a gap in the curtain of the past. When they returned to the car she looked across the street and said, "I wish the Estrada adobe were still standing like the others. But it's an old story, and my mother would say it ended with her."

"Oh no, it didn't," said Andrew. "It began again today with us."

Heidi sighed contentedly. "I wonder if any of those old Estradas were ever as happy as you and me!"

They got back in the car and drove along the road Don Luis Estrada had ridden so often – not as the soldier of San Pascual with lance in rest, but as the weary disappointed man stripped of his acres and his inheritance – to the place where as a youth he had helped to build his father's house. The first River Inn, built of wood and burnt down five years after its opening, had vanished as completely as the Rancho Estrada; the second, built of lime and rough-cast, aped the Mission-Revival style of the turn of the century, and had pseudo-Spanish grilles over the downstairs windows. It was a summer resort, and the fashions were changing: holidaymakers no longer spent a summer, or even a month in the same place, and the River Inn had not adapted to the transient trade. It was somewhat run down, and if the owners were presumably waiting until spring to repaint the façade and resurface the two dilapidated tennis courts, they could at least have cleaned the dried green slime from the basin of a fountain in front of the entrance, which had ceased to play. If Andrew and Heidi had gone on down the gravel path which led to the creek and the cottonwoods where the Bear Flagger met his fate at Content's hands, they would have seen that the jungle was closing in. Jim Estrada's prediction of fifty years back had come true. Part of the hotel's grounds had been sold for the development of a row of mean tract houses, hidden from the guests' eyes by a row of evergreens, among the roots of which blackberry vines were twining, with the tendrils of a Castilian rose.

Instead they went into a vast dark hall, lighted only by the flames of a big log fire, and repeated ringings of a bell marked Reception finally produced an elderly desk clerk and a boy to carry their bags upstairs and park their car. The suite Andrew had reserved was warm and comfortable, and there was no need to close the shutters, because a thick screen of tall bushes growing close against the window gave them complete privacy. When Andrew switched off the lamps the room was filled with a green subaqueous twilight in which Heidi's body, when he drew off her white satin slip, gleamed like marble.

He had told her in the car, varying the words of love, what a pretty bride she was, with her butterscotch hair and her lovely curly smile, and how elegant in the silver foxes which he proposed one day to supplement by mink. Now the only words he could find were simple and true.

"Oh my love, I knew you would be beautiful!"

Andrew was glad he had waited to take her as a bride, for first there was the fumbling innocence, the shock, and then the tremulous response which turned into a throbbing and a mounting rage. She learned about love quickly because there were so few hours for the lesson; even if they lost count of time they were aware of time, as if the hammer strokes of Andrew's passion were in rhythm with the hands of a gigantic clock. They slept, and when Andrew awoke to a sated luxurious idleness the room was in total darkness. He felt Heidi's moist cheek against his own and her damp silky hair spread across his naked shoulder.

What's the time?

He had no idea what he'd done with his watch, and for all he knew it was the middle of the night. He lay there half asleep and half awake, until he heard the ringing of a dinner gong and the shuffle of feet in the corridor as other guests started for the stairs. It was enough to arouse Heidi. He could feel her stirring in his arms, a blind instinct urging her back to the source of life. He could just see her face now, for a faint luminous brightness was beginning to creep through the screen of trees. As he slipped his arm from beneath Heidi's head and rose to possess her again, Andrew Kirk knew they had both reached the valley of the moon.

★ ★ ★

Early on Sunday morning, after time ran out and Andrew joined his ship, Heidi left the rented car in a parking lot and walked half-way across the great bridge. It spanned what the Indians called Yulupa, the Sunset Strait, and was now the Golden Gate, by any name leading sailors to the Orient. Like all the other girls and women at the terracotta painted railings, Heidi was looking back to the city in the early convulsions of another change. It was the custom for sweethearts and wives to watch a warship going through the Gate, and although Andrew at their parting had warned her, "Navy wives don't cry!" there were as many tears as there were jokes and laughter in the crowd. Heidi said 'Hi!' and 'Hi!' again to strangers, answered questions, smiled, although her body and mind ached with longing and an unnamed fear. The sun was rising, but the city was covered by a light November haze which hung over the surface of the bay, and the waiting women never saw the Stars and Stripes until the USS *San Francisco* took grey shape below them.

"Here she comes!"

She was almost at the Gate, and the cheering rose from the officers and men, looking up, laughing and waving their caps to the shrieking girls. Heidi waved a bright scarf and called her husband's name. She hoped he saw her. She only thought she saw him, for there were so many tanned smiling faces, so many boys in uniform lining the rails of the USS *San Francisco*, the strong men and pride of a generation. The cruiser passed under the bridge quickly, and headed for the open sea.

Most of the women ran across the bridge, dodging the traffic to see the last of their men. Heidi stayed where she was, holding tightly to the railing while an incoherent prayer formed in her mind. She looked dazedly around her, left to Mount Tamalpais and Fort Baker, which the Germans were accused of watching through a telescope, and right to the casemates of Fort Point, where the antique cannon had once been mounted in defence of San Francisco. It made her think of the magic poem of her childhood, with the insidious rhythms which came sliding through the gates of sleep:

Long beside the deep embrasures where the brazen cannon are
Did they wait the promised bridegroom

There would not be long to wait. Heidi would soon have news of her bridegroom. He was not bound for the Iceland convoys or the danger zone of the Atlantic. The USS *San Francisco* was a unit of the Pacific Squadron, and her destination was Pearl Harbor.